SELECT EDITIONS

Selected and Edited by Reader's Digest

THE READER'S DIGEST ASSOCIATION, INC.
PLEASANTVILLE, NEW YORK • MONTREAL

SELECT EDITIONS

Some of our staff's favorite mysteries

EDITORIAL

Global Editor-in-Chief: Laura E. Kelly

Deputy Editor: James J. Menick

Managing Editors: Paula Marchese, Joseph P. McGrath

Senior Editors: Barbara K. Clark, Thomas S. Clemmons, Amy M. Reilly

Editorial Administrator: Ann Marie Belluscio

A Great Deliverance
BY ELIZABETH GEORGE

The Maltese Falcon
BY DASHIELL HAMMETT

EDITORIAL OPERATIONS

Senior Production Manager: Dianne Robinson

Art Director: Robin Arzt
Assistant Art Director: Gretchen Schuler-Dandridge

Production Editor: Lorraine Burton
Production Assistant: Lisa A. Crockett

RIGHTS AND PERMISSIONS

Director: Lisa Garrett Smith
Manager: Carol Weiss Staudter
Administrative Assistant: Arlene Pasciolla

The Killing Floor
BY LEE CHILD

INTERNATIONAL EDITIONS

Executive Editor: Gary Q. Arpin
Senior Editor: Bonnie Grande

Inside

The deadliest place

for a killer to strike

is the place called home.

MARY HIGGINS CLARK

A NOVEL

No Place Like Home

Prologue

TEN-YEAR-OLD Liza was dreaming her favorite dream, the one about the day when she was six years old, and she and Daddy were at the beach, in New Jersey, at Spring Lake. They'd been in the water, holding hands and jumping together whenever a wave broke near them. Then a much bigger wave suddenly rushed in and began to break right over them, and Daddy grabbed her. "Hang on, Liza," he yelled, and the next minute they were tumbling under water and being thrown around by the wave. Liza had been so scared.

She could still feel her forehead slamming into the sand when the wave crashed them onto the shore. She had swallowed water and was coughing and her eyes were stinging and she was crying, but then Daddy pulled her onto his lap. "Now *that* was a wave!" he said as he brushed the sand from her face, "but we rode it out together, didn't we, Liza?"

That was the best part of the dream—having Daddy's arms around her and feeling so safe.

Before the next summer came around, Daddy had died. After that she'd never really felt safe again. Now she was always afraid, because Mom had made Ted, her stepfather, move out of the house. Ted didn't want a divorce, and he kept pestering her to let him come back. Liza knew Mom was afraid, too.

Liza wanted to go back into the dream of being in Daddy's arms, but the voices kept waking her up.

Someone was crying and yelling. Did she hear Mom calling? What was she saying? Liza sat up and slid out of bed. She could see the light in the hall. It was Ted's voice she heard now. He was yelling at Mom, and Mom was screaming, "Let go of me!"

Liza knew that Mom was so afraid of Ted that she even kept Daddy's gun in her night table. Liza rushed down the hall, her feet moving noiselessly along the carpet. The door of Mom's sitting room was open, and inside she could see that Ted had Mom pinned against the wall and was shaking her. Liza ran past the sitting room into her mother's bedroom and yanked open the night-table drawer. Trembling, she grabbed the gun and ran back to the sitting room.

She pointed the gun at Ted and screamed, "Let go of my mother!"

Ted spun around, holding on to Mom, his eyes wide and angry. The veins in his forehead were sticking out. Liza could see the tears streaming down her mother's cheeks.

"Sure," he yelled. With a violent thrust, he shoved Liza's mother at her. When she crashed into Liza, the gun went off. Then Liza heard a funny little gurgle, and Mom crumpled to the floor. Liza looked down at her mother, then up at Ted. He began to lunge toward her, and Liza pointed the gun at him and pulled the trigger. She pulled it again and again, until he fell down and began crawling and tried to grab the gun from her. When it wouldn't fire anymore, she dropped it and got down on the floor and put her arms around her mother. There was no sound, and she knew her mother was dead.

After that Liza had only a hazy memory of what happened. She remembered Ted's voice on the phone, the police coming, someone pulling her arms from her mother.

She was taken away, and she never saw her mother again.

Twenty-four Years Later

I CANNOT believe I am standing in the exact spot where I was standing when I killed my mother. I ask myself if this is a nightmare, or if it is really happening. After that terrible night I had nightmares all the time. I spent a good part of my childhood drawing pictures of them for Dr. Moran, a psychologist in California, where I went to live after the trial. This room figured in many of those drawings.

The mirror over the fireplace is the same one my father chose when he restored the house. In it I see my reflection. My face is deadly pale. My eyes no longer seem dark blue, but black, reflecting all the terrible visions that are leaping through my mind. The color of my eyes is a heritage from my father. My mother's eyes were a sapphire blue, picture perfect with her golden hair. My hair would be dark blond if I left it natural. I have darkened it, though, ever since I came back east sixteen years ago to attend the Fashion Institute of Technology in Manhattan. I am also taller than my mother was by five inches. Yet, as I grow older, I believe I am beginning to resemble her, and I have always lived in dread of someone saying, "You look familiar . . ." My mother's image still turns up periodically in stories that rehash the circumstances of her death. I, Celia Foster Nolan, formerly Liza Barton, the child the tabloids dubbed "Little Lizzie Borden," am far less likely to be recognized as that chubby-faced girl with golden curls who was acquitted—not exonerated—of killing her mother and trying to kill her stepfather.

My second husband, Alex Nolan, and I have been married for six months. Today I thought we were going to take my four-year-old son, Jack, to see a horse show in Peapack, a town in northern New Jersey, when suddenly Alex detoured to Mendham, a neighboring town. It was only then that he told me he had a wonderful surprise for my birthday and drove to this house. Alex parked the car, and we went inside.

Jack is tugging at my hand, but I remain frozen to the spot. Energetic, as most four-year-olds are, he wants to explore. I let him go, and in a flash he is running down the hall.

Alex is standing a little behind me. I can feel his anxiety. He believes he has found a beautiful home for us to live in, and his generosity is such that the deed is solely in my name, his birthday gift to me. "I'll catch up with Jack, honey," he reassures me. "You look around and start figuring how you'll decorate."

"Your husband tells me you're an interior designer," Henry Paley, the real estate agent, is saying. "This house has been well kept up, but every woman, especially one in your profession, wants to put her own signature on her home."

Not trusting myself to speak, I look at him. Paley is a small man of about sixty, with thinning gray hair, neatly dressed in a dark suit. I realize he is waiting for me to show enthusiasm for my gift.

"My boss, Georgette Grove, was showing your husband properties nearby when he spotted the FOR SALE sign on the lawn," Paley says. "The house is quite simply an architectural treasure, situated on ten acres in the premier location in a premier town."

I know it is a treasure. My father was the architect who restored a crumbling eighteenth-century mansion into this charming and spacious home. Mother and Daddy found the fireplace mantel in France, in a château about to be demolished. Daddy told me the meanings of its sculptured work, the cherubs and pineapples . . .

Ted pinning Mother against the wall . . .

I am pointing the gun at him. Daddy's gun . . .

Ted spinning Mother around and shoving her at me . . .

The gun going off . . .

Lizzie Borden took an axe . . .

"Are you all right, Mrs. Nolan?" Henry Paley is asking me.

"Yes, of course," I manage, with some effort. My mind is racing with the thought that I should not have let Larry, my first husband, make me swear that I wouldn't tell the truth about myself to anyone, not even to someone I married. In this moment I am fiercely angry at Larry for wringing that promise from me. He was ashamed of my past, afraid of its impact on our son's future. That fear has brought us here now.

Already the lie is a wedge driven between Alex and me. He talks about wanting to have children soon, and I wonder how he would feel if he knew that Little Lizzie Borden would be their mother.

It's been twenty-four years, but such memories die hard. Though I agreed to live in this area, I did not agree to live in this town or in this house. I can't live here. I simply can't.

To avoid the curiosity in Paley's eyes, I walk over to the mantel and pretend to study it.

"Beautiful, isn't it?" Paley asks. "The master bedroom is very large and has two separate, wonderfully appointed baths." He opens the door to the bedroom, and reluctantly I follow him.

Memories flood my mind. Weekend mornings in this room. I used to get in bed with Mother and Daddy. Daddy would bring up coffee for Mother and hot chocolate for me. Looking out the back windows I see the Japanese maple Daddy planted so long ago.

Tears are pressing against my eyelids. I want to run out of here. If necessary I will have to break my promise to Larry and tell Alex the truth. I am not Celia Foster, née Kellogg, the daughter of Kathleen and Martin Kellogg of Santa Barbara, California. I am Liza Barton, reluctantly acquitted by a judge of murder and attempted murder.

"Mom, Mom!" My son's footsteps clatter on the floorboards. He hurries into the room, energy encapsulated, small and sturdy, a handsome little boy, the center of my heart.

I bend down and catch him in my arms. Jack has Larry's light brown hair and high forehead. His beautiful blue eyes are my mother's, but Larry had blue eyes, too. I taste again the bitterness of knowing that his father was ashamed of me.

Ted Cartwright swears estranged wife begged for reconciliation . . .

State psychiatrist testifies ten-year-old Liza mentally competent to form the intent to commit murder. . . .

Was Larry right to swear me to silence? At this moment I can't be sure of anything. I kiss the top of Jack's head.

"I really, really, really like it here," he tells me excitedly.

Alex is coming into the bedroom. He planned this surprise for me with so much care. When we came up the driveway, it had been festooned with balloons, swaying on this breezy August day—all painted with my name. But the exuberant joy with which he handed me the key and the deed is gone. He can read me too well.

"When I told the women at the office what I'd done, they said no matter how beautiful the house, they'd want the chance to decide about it," he says, his voice forlorn.

They were right, I think as I look at him, at his reddish-brown hair and brown eyes. Tall and wide-shouldered, Alex has a strength about him that makes him enormously attractive. Jack adores him. Now Jack slides from my arms and puts his arm around Alex's leg.

My husband and my son.

And my house.

THE Grove Real Estate Agency was on East Main Street in the New Jersey town of Mendham. Georgette Grove parked in front of it and got out of the car. The August day was unusually cool, and her short-sleeved linen suit was not warm enough for the weather. She moved with a quick step up the path to the door of her office.

Sixty-two years old, Georgette was a handsome, whippet-thin woman with short wavy hair the color of steel, hazel eyes, and a firm chin. She was pleased at how smoothly the closing had just gone on one of the smaller houses in town. Even though she had split the commission with another broker, it would give her a few months' reserve until she landed another sale.

So far it had been a disastrous year, saved only by her sale of the house on Old Mill Lane to Alex Nolan. She had very much wanted to be present this morning when Nolan presented it to his wife. I hope she likes surprises, Georgette thought. She had tried to warn him about its history. He put it in his wife's name, so if she doesn't like it, she—Georgette—might be open to a nondisclosure suit.

It was part of the real estate code of New Jersey that a prospective buyer had to be notified if a house was a stigmatized property, meaning one impacted by a factor that could cause apprehension or fears. Since some people would not want to live in a house in which a crime or a suicide had been committed, the real estate agent was obliged to reveal any such history.

I tried to tell Alex Nolan that there had been a tragedy in the house, Georgette thought defensively as she opened the office door and stepped into the reception room. But he cut me off, saying that his family used to rent a two-hundred-year-old house on Cape Cod, and its history would curl your hair. But this is different, Georgette thought. I should have told him that around here the house he bought is known as Little Lizzie's Place.

She wondered if Nolan had become nervous about his surprise. At his request the driveway had been decorated with festive balloons and the porch had been draped with papier-mâché. He had asked that champagne and a birthday cake be waiting at the expensive glass patio table and chairs he had ordered from a nearby furniture store. He had also asked Georgette to be sure there were a dozen roses in every room. "Roses are Ceil's favorite flowers," he explained. "I promised her that she'd never be without them."

He's rich. He's handsome. He's charming. And he's clearly devoted to his wife, Georgette thought. But how will she react when she starts hearing the stories?

Georgette tried to push the thought away. She glanced around her reception room, which was a matter of special pride to her. Robin Carpenter, her secretary-receptionist, was at a mahogany desk to the right. On the left, a brightly upholstered sectional couch and chairs were grouped around a coffee table where clients sipped coffee while she or Henry ran tapes showing available properties.

"How did the closing go?" Robin asked Georgette.

"Smoothly, thank God. Is Henry back?"

"No. I guess he's still drinking champagne with the Nolans. I still can't believe it. A gorgeous guy buys a gorgeous house for his wife for her thirty-fourth birthday. That's exactly my age. She's so lucky.

Did you ever find out if Alex Nolan has a brother?" Robin sighed.

"Let's all hope that after she hears the story of that house, Celia Nolan still considers herself lucky," Georgette snapped nervously.

Robin knew exactly what she meant. Small, slender, and very pretty, with a heart-shaped face and a penchant for frilly clothes, she gave the initial impression of an airheaded blonde. Or so Georgette had believed when she applied for the job a year ago. Five minutes of conversation, however, had led her to reversing that opinion and hiring Robin on the spot. Now Robin was about to get her own real estate license, and Georgette welcomed the prospect. Henry simply wasn't pulling his weight anymore.

"You *did* try to warn the husband about the history of the house. I can back you up on that, Georgette."

"That's something," Georgette said as she headed down the hall to her private office at the rear of the building. But then she turned abruptly and faced the younger woman. "I tried to speak to Alex Nolan about the background of the house one time only, Robin," she said emphatically. "And that was when I was alone in the car with him. You couldn't have heard me discussing it."

"I'm sure I heard you bring it up one of the times Alex Nolan was in here," Robin insisted.

"I mentioned it to him once in the car. Robin, you're not doing me or yourself any favors by lying to a client," Georgette snapped.

The outside door opened. They both turned as Henry Paley came into the reception room. "How did it go?" Georgette asked.

"I would say that Mrs. Nolan put up a very good act of seeming delighted by her husband's birthday surprise," Paley answered. "However, she did not convince me."

"Why not?" Robin asked.

"I wish I could tell you," Henry said. He looked at Georgette, obviously afraid that he had somehow let her down. "I swear," he said apologetically, "when I was showing her the master suite, all I could visualize was that kid shooting her mother and stepfather in the sitting room years ago. Maybe it's all those flowers the husband ordered. It's the same scent that hits you in funeral homes. I got it full force in the master suite of Little Lizzie's Place today. And I have a feeling that Celia Nolan had a reaction like that, too."

Henry realized that unwittingly he had used the forbidden words in describing the house on Old Mill Lane. "Sorry, Georgette," he mumbled as he brushed past her.

"You should be," Georgette said bitterly. "I can just imagine the kind of vibes you were sending out to Mrs. Nolan."

"Maybe you'll take me up on my offer to back you up on what you told Alex Nolan, Georgette," Robin suggested, a touch of sarcasm in her voice.

"BUT, Ceil, it's what we were *planning* to do. We're just doing it a little faster. It makes sense for Jack to start pre-K in Mendham. We've been cramped for these six months in your apartment, and you didn't want to move downtown to mine."

It was the day after my birthday, the day following the big surprise. We were having breakfast in my apartment, the one that six years ago I had been hired to decorate for Larry, who became my first husband. Jack was getting dressed for day camp.

I don't think I had closed my eyes all night. Instead I lay in bed, my shoulder brushing against Alex, staring into the dark, remembering, always remembering. Now I was trying to appear calm as I sipped my coffee. Across the table, impeccably dressed as always in a dark blue suit, Alex was rushing through the slice of toast and mug of coffee that was his everyday breakfast.

My suggestion that, while the house was beautiful, I would want to completely redecorate it before we moved in had been met with resistance from Alex. "Ceil, I know it was probably insanity to buy the house without consulting you, but it was exactly the kind of place we both had in mind. Besides the fact the firm is moving me to New Jersey, the added plus is that I can get in some early morning rides. Central Park just doesn't do it for me. And I want to teach you how to ride. You said you'd enjoy taking lessons."

I studied my husband. His expression was both contrite and pleading. He was right. This apartment really was too small for the three of us. Alex had given up so much when we married. His apartment in SoHo had included a large study, with room for his splendid sound system and even a grand piano. The piano was now in storage. Alex has a natural gift for music and thoroughly enjoys playing. I know he misses that pleasure. He's worked hard to accomplish all he has. Though a distant cousin of my late husband, who himself had come from wealth, Alex is decidedly a "poor relation." I knew how proud he was to be able to buy this new house.

"You've been saying you want to get back to decorating," Alex reminded me. "Once you're settled, there'll be plenty of opportunity for that, especially in Mendham. There's a lot of money there."

I hadn't heard Jack come into the dining room. "I like the house, too, Mom," he piped up. "Alex is going to buy me my own pony when we move there."

I looked at my husband and son. "It looks as though we have a new home," I said, trying to smile. Eventually I'll find a house in one of the other towns, I thought. Alex did admit that it was a mistake to buy without consulting me, after all.

A month later moving vans were pulling away from 895 Fifth Avenue and heading for One Old Mill Lane, Mendham, New Jersey.

HER eyes ablaze with curiosity, fifty-four-year-old Marcella Williams stood at her living-room window watching the moving van chug past her home. Twenty minutes ago she had seen Georgette Grove's BMW go up the hill. Marcella was sure the Mercedes that arrived shortly after that belonged to her new neighbors. She had heard that they were rushing to move in because the four-year-old was starting prekindergarten. She wondered what they'd be like.

People didn't tend to stay in that house long, she reflected, and it wasn't surprising. Nobody likes to have their home known as Little Lizzie's Place. Jane Salzman was the first buyer after Liza Barton went on her shooting spree. She always claimed the house had a creepy feeling. Last year's Halloween prank was the finish for the last owners, Mark and Louise Harriman. Louise flipped out when she saw the life-sized doll with a pistol on her porch. She and Mark had been planning to relocate to Florida anyhow, so they moved in February, and the house had been empty since then.

Marcella had been living there when the tragedy occurred, and she could still picture Liza at age ten, with her blond, curly hair and quiet, mature manner. I went out of my way to be nice to Liza after Will Barton died and Audrey married Ted Cartwright, Marcella thought. I said that she must be thrilled to have a new father, and I'll never forget the way that little snip looked at me when she said, "My mother has a new husband. I don't have a new father."

I told them that at the trial, Marcella reminded herself with some satisfaction. And I told them that I was in the house when Ted collected all Will Barton's personal stuff in boxes to store in the garage. Liza was screaming at him and kept dragging the boxes into her room. She wouldn't give Ted an inch. She made it so hard for her mother. And Audrey was crazy about Ted.

Who knows what happened there? Marcella thought as she watched a second van follow the first one. That restraining order Audrey got was absolutely unnecessary. I believed Ted when he swore that she had asked him to come over that night.

Ted was always so grateful for my support, Marcella remembered. My testimony helped him in the civil case he filed against Liza. Well, the poor fellow *should* have been compensated. It's nasty to go through life with a shattered knee. He still has a limp. It's a miracle he wasn't killed that night.

When Ted got out of the hospital, he had moved a few towns away, to Bernardsville. Now a major developer, his latest venture had been building town houses in Madison. Over the years Marcella had bumped into him at various functions. He'd had a string of girlfriends, but he always claimed that Audrey was the love of his life. Marcella admitted to herself that she'd been casting around for a reason to call him. Maybe I'll let him know that the house has changed hands again, she thought, and headed for the phone.

As she crossed the spacious living room, she gave a brief smile of approval to her reflection in the mirror. Her shapely body showed the benefits of daily exercise. Her frosted blond hair framed a smooth face tightened by Botox. She was confident that the new liner and mascara she was using enhanced her hazel eyes.

Marcella called information and got the number for Ted Cartwright's office. After instructions to "dial one for this, dial two for that," she reached his voice mail.

Her voice distinctly coquettish, she said, "Ted, this is Marcella Williams. I thought you'd be interested to hear that your former home has changed hands again, and the new owners are in the process of moving in."

The sound of a police siren interrupted her message. An instant later a police car hurtled past her window. "Ted, I'll call you back," she said breathlessly. "The cops are on the way to your old house. I'll let you know what develops."

"I AM so sorry, Mrs. Nolan," Georgette stammered. "I just got here myself. I've called the police."

I looked at her. She was dragging a hose across the bluestone walk, hoping, I suppose, to wash away some of the destruction.

The house was set back one hundred feet from the road. In thick billboard-sized letters the words LITTLE LIZZIE'S PLACE. BEWARE! were painted in red on the lawn.

Splashes of red paint stained the shingles and limestone on the front of the house. A skull and crossbones were carved in the mahogany door. A straw doll with a toy gun in its hand was propped against the door. I guessed it was supposed to represent me.

"What's this supposed to be about?" Alex snapped.

"Some kids, I guess. I'm so sorry," Georgette Grove explained nervously. "I'll get a cleanup crew here right away, and I'll call my landscaper. He'll resod the lawn today. I can't believe . . ."

Her voice trailed off as she looked at us. Thank God I was wearing dark glasses. I was standing beside the Mercedes, my hand on the door. Next to me, Alex was clearly angry and upset.

Hang on, I told myself desperately. I knew that if I let go of the car door, I would fall.

"Celia, are you okay?" Alex had his hand on my arm. "Honey,

I'm so sorry. I can't imagine what would make anyone do this."

Jack had scrambled out of the car. "Mommy, are you okay?"

Jack, who had only a dim memory of his own father, was instinctively frightened that he would lose me, too. I forced myself to try to focus on him, on his need for reassurance. Then I looked at the distress on Alex's face. A terrible possibility rushed through my mind. Does he know? Is this some terrible, cruel joke? As quickly as the thought came, I dismissed it. Of course Alex had no idea that I had ever lived here. It was one of those horrible coincidences that just happen. But my God, what shall I do?

"I'll be all right," I told Jack, managing to force the words out through lips that felt numb and spongy.

Jack ran onto the lawn. "I can read that," he said proudly. "L-i-t-t-l-e L-i-z-z-i-e . . ."

"That's enough, Jack," Alex said firmly. He looked at Georgette. "Is there any explanation for this?"

"I tried to explain something to you when we first viewed the house," Georgette said, "but you weren't interested. A tragedy took place here nearly twenty-five years ago. A ten-year-old child, Liza Barton, accidentally killed her mother and shot her stepfather. The tabloids called her Little Lizzie Borden. There have been incidents here since then, but never anything like this." Georgette was on the verge of tears. "I should have made you listen."

The first moving van was pulling into the driveway. Two men jumped out and ran behind it to open the door.

"Alex, tell them to stop," I demanded, then was frightened to hear my voice rising to a near shriek. "Tell them to turn around right now. I can't live under this roof."

Alex and the real estate agent were staring at me, their expressions shocked. "Mrs. Nolan, don't think like that," Georgette Grove protested. "I am so sorry this has happened. I can't apologize enough. I assure you that some kids did this as a joke."

"Honey, you're overreacting," Alex said. "This is a beautiful home. I'm sorry I didn't listen to Georgette about what happened here, but I promise, before the day is over, this mess will be gone."

He put his hands on my face. "Look at me. Come on around the back. I want to show Jack the surprise I have for him."

One of the moving men was heading for the house, Jack scampering behind him. "No, Jack, we're going around to the barn," Alex called. "Come on, Ceil," he urged. "Please."

I wanted to protest, but then I saw the blinking lights of a patrol car rushing up the road.

When they pulled my arms away from my mother, they made me sit in the patrol car. Someone got a blanket and tucked it around me. And then the ambulance came.

"Come on, honey," Alex coaxed. "Let's show Jack his surprise."

"Mrs. Nolan, I'll take care of talking to the police," Georgette Grove volunteered.

I walked quickly along the path with Alex to the spacious grounds behind the house and was startled to see that in the month since I had been here, a riding enclosure had been built. Alex had promised Jack a pony. Was it here already? The same thought must have occurred to Jack because he began running toward the barn. He pulled open the door, and then I heard a whoop of joy.

"It's a pony, Mom," he shouted. "Alex bought me a pony!"

Five minutes later, his eyes shining with delight, his feet secure in the stirrups of his new saddle, and Alex at his side, Jack was walking the pony around the enclosure. I stood at the split-rail fence, taking in the expression of pure bliss on his face.

"This is another reason why I knew this place would be perfect," Alex said as he passed me. "Now Jack can ride every single day."

There was somebody clearing his throat behind me. "Mrs. Nolan, I'm Sergeant Earley. I very much regret this incident. This is no way to welcome you to Mendham."

I hadn't heard the police officer and Georgette Grove approaching me. Startled, I turned around.

He was a man who appeared to be in his late fifties, with an outdoorsman's complexion and thinning sandy hair. "I know just which kids to question," he said grimly. "Trust me. Their parents will pay for whatever has to be done."

Earley, I thought. I know that name. When I packed my files last week, I read the hidden one again, the file that began with the night I killed my mother. There had been a cop named Earley mentioned in the article.

Alex had left Jack on the pony to join us. Georgette Grove introduced him to Sergeant Earley.

"Sergeant, I know I speak for my wife when I say that we don't want to start our life in this town by signing complaints against neighborhood kids," Alex said. "But I hope you make them understand they're lucky we're being this generous."

Earley, I thought. In my mind I was rereading the tabloid articles about me, the ones that had made me heartsick when I looked at them again only a week ago. There had been a picture of a cop tucking a blanket around me in the back of the police car. Earley had been his name. Afterward he had commented to the press that he'd never seen a kid as composed as I had been. "She said, 'Thank you very much, officer.' You'd think I had given her an ice-cream cone." And now I was facing this same man again.

"Mom, I love my pony," Jack called. "I want to name her Lizzie, after the name on the grass. Isn't that a good idea?"

Lizzie!

Before I could respond, I heard Georgette Grove murmur in dismay, "Oh, Lord, here comes the busybody."

A moment later I was being introduced to Marcella Williams, who, as she grabbed and shook my hand, told me, "I've been living next door for twenty-eight years, and I'm delighted to welcome my new neighbor."

Marcella Williams. She still lives here! She testified against me. She verified everything Ted told the court.

"Mom, is it all right if I name her Lizzie?" Jack called.

I *have* to protect him, I thought. I have to get rid of all the memories. I have to act the part of a newcomer annoyed by vandalism.

I forced a smile, turned, and leaned on the fence. "You call your pony any name you want, Jack," I called.

I've got to get inside, I thought. Sergeant Earley, Marcella

Williams—how soon will they see something familiar about me?

One of the moving men was hurrying across the lawn. "Mr. Nolan," he said, "the media is out front taking pictures of the vandalism. A reporter from a television station wants you and Mrs. Nolan to make a statement on camera."

"No!" I looked at Alex imploringly. "Absolutely not."

"I have a key to the back door," Georgette Grove said quickly.

But it was too late. As I tried to escape, the reporters came hurrying around the corner of the house. I felt light bulbs flashing, and as I raised my hands to cover my face, I felt my knees crumble and a rush of darkness envelop me.

Dru Perry had been on Route 24 on her way to the Morris County courthouse when she got the call on her car phone from the *Star-Ledger*. Sixty-three years old, a veteran reporter, Dru was a big-boned woman with iron-gray shoulder-length hair. Wide glasses exaggerated her penetrating brown eyes.

"Dru, keep going to Mendham," her editor ordered. "There's been more vandalism at Little Lizzie's Place."

Little Lizzie's Place, Dru thought as she drove through Morristown. When she had covered the story last Halloween, the cops had been tough on the kids; they had ended up in juvenile court. What would make kids try it again in August?

The answer became obvious when she drove up Old Mill Lane and saw the moving vans. Whoever did this wanted to rattle the new owners, she thought. Then she caught her breath as the full impact of the vandalism registered. This was serious damage.

She parked on the road, behind the truck from the local television station. As she opened the door of her car, she saw two reporters and a cameraman start to run around the side of the house. Running herself, Dru caught up with them. She got her digital camera out just in time to snap Celia toppling over in a faint.

Then, with the gathering media, she waited until an ambulance pulled up, and Marcella Williams came out of the house. The reporters peppered her with questions.

She's in her glory, Dru thought, as Mrs. Williams explained that Mrs. Nolan seemed shaken but otherwise fine. Then, as she posed for pictures, she went into the history of the house in great detail.

"I knew the Bartons," she explained. "It was all such a tragedy."

When Mrs. Williams went back inside, Dru walked up to the front door to study the skull and crossbones. Whoever did this is really creepy, Dru thought. This wasn't slapped together. On a hunch she waited around to see if anyone representing the new owners came out to make a statement.

Ten minutes later Alex Nolan appeared before the cameras. "As you can understand, this is a most regrettable incident. My wife will be fine. She's exhausted from the packing, and the shock of the vandalism simply overwhelmed her. She is resting now."

"Is it true you bought the house as a birthday present for her?" Dru asked.

"Yes, that's true, and Celia is delighted about it. Now if you'll excuse me." Alex turned, went into the house, and closed the door.

Dru took a long sip from the bottle of water she kept in her shoulder bag. Marcella Williams had explained that she lived just down the road. I'll go wait for her there. Then, after I talk to her, Dru decided, I'll look up every detail I can find about the Little Lizzie case. I'd like to do a feature article about it. Wouldn't it be interesting if I could find out where Liza Barton is now? If she did deliberately kill her mother and try to kill her stepfather, chances are she's gotten into trouble again somewhere along the way.

WHEN I opened my eyes, I was lying on a couch the moving men had placed in the living room. The first thing I saw was the terrified look in Jack's eyes. He was bending over me.

I pulled him down beside me. "I'm okay, pal," I whispered.

"You scared me," he whispered back. "You really scared me."

Alex was on the cell phone, demanding to know why the ambulance was taking so long to arrive.

Still holding Jack, I pushed myself up on one elbow. "I don't need an ambulance," I said. "I'm all right, really I am."

Georgette Grove was standing at the foot of the couch. "Mrs. Nolan—Celia—I really think it would be better if—"

"You really must be checked," Marcella Williams said.

"Jack, Mommy's fine. We're getting up." I swung my legs around and, ignoring the wave of dizziness, pulled myself to my feet. I could see the look of protest on Alex's face. "Alex, you know how busy this week has been," I said. "I simply need to get the movers to put your big chair and a hassock in one of the bedrooms and let me take it easy." I looked directly at Georgette Grove and Marcella Williams. "I know you'll understand if I just want to rest quietly."

"Of course," Georgette agreed. "I'll take care of things outside."

"Maybe you'd like a cup of tea," Marcella Williams offered, clearly unwilling to leave.

Alex put his hand under my arm. "We don't want to keep you, Mrs. Williams. If you'll excuse us, please."

The wail of a siren told us that the ambulance had arrived.

The EMT examined me in the second-floor room that had once been my playroom. "You got kind of a nasty shock, I would say," he observed. "Take it easy for the rest of the day, if that's possible."

The sounds of furniture being hauled around seemed to be coming from every direction. I remembered how after my trial, the Kelloggs, my distant cousins from California, came to take me back with them. I asked them to drive past the house. An auction was going on, and they were carrying out furniture and rugs and paintings. Remembering that moment, I felt tears streaming from my eyes.

Alex was brushing the tears from my cheeks. "Celia, I have to go outside to those reporters. I'll be right back."

"Where did Jack go?" I whispered.

"The moving guy in the kitchen asked Jack to help him unpack the groceries. He's fine."

Not trusting myself to speak, I nodded and felt Alex slip a hand-kerchief into my hand. As desperately as I tried, I could not stem the river of tears that poured from my eyes.

I can't hide anymore, I thought. I can't live in horror that some-one will find out about me. I have to tell Alex. I have to be honest. Better Jack learns about me when he's young than have the story hit him in twenty years.

When Alex came back, he slid down beside me on the chair and lifted me onto his lap. "Ceil, what is it? It can't be just the condition of the house. What else is upsetting you?"

I felt the tears finally stop, and an icy calm come over me. Maybe this was the moment to tell him.

"That story Georgette Grove told about the child who acciden-tally killed her mother—"

"According to Marcella Williams, that kid must have been a lit-tle monster. After she killed her mother, she kept on shooting the stepfather until the pistol was empty. Marcella says it took a lot of strength to pull that trigger."

I struggled from his embrace. With his preconceived notion, how could I possibly tell Alex the truth now? "Are all those people gone?" I asked.

"Everyone's gone except the movers."

"Then I'd better tell them where I want the furniture placed."

"Ceil, tell me what's wrong."

I will tell you, I thought, but only after I can somehow prove that Ted Cartwright lied about that night and that when I held that gun, I was trying to defend my mother, not kill her. I need to know why Mother was so afraid of Ted. She did not let him in willingly. I know that. There must be a trial transcript, an autopsy report.

"Ceil, what is wrong?"

I put my arms around him. "Nothing and everything, Alex," I said. "But that doesn't mean that things can't change."

He leaned back and put his hands on my shoulders. "Ceil, there's something not working between us. I know that. Frankly, living in the apartment that was yours and Larry's made me feel like a visitor.

That's why when I thought this house was the perfect place for us, I couldn't resist. I know I shouldn't have bought it without you. I should have let Georgette Grove tell me the background, although, from what I know now, she would have glossed over it."

There were tears in Alex's eyes. I brushed them dry. "It's going to be all right," I said. "I promise."

JEFFREY MacKingsley, prosecutor of Morris County, had a particular interest in seeing that the mischief that had once again flared up at the Barton home be squelched once and for all. He had been fourteen and in his first year in high school when the shooting happened. Even then he'd been avidly interested in crime and criminal law, so he'd read everything he could about the case.

Over the years he had remained intrigued with the question of whether ten-year-old Liza Barton had accidentally killed her mother and shot her stepfather or was one of those kids who are born without a conscience. And they do exist, Jeff thought with a sigh.

Sandy-haired, with dark brown eyes, six feet tall, and quick to smile, Jeff was the kind of person law-abiding people instinctively liked and trusted. He'd been prosecutor of Morris County for four years now and had quickly become a star.

On both sides of the courthouse he was known as a straight arrow, tough on crime but with the ability to understand that many offenders, with the right combination of supervision and punishment, could be rehabilitated.

Jeff had his next goal in mind—to run for governor, after the incumbent's second term ended. In the meantime, he intended to exercise his authority as prosecutor to make sure that Morris County was a safe place to live.

That was why the repeated vandalisms at the Barton home infuriated him. "Those kids, privileged as they are, have nothing better to do than to rake up that old tragedy and turn that beautiful home into the local haunted house," Jeff fumed to Anna Malloy, his secretary, when the incident was reported to him. "Put me through to police headquarters in Mendham."

Sergeant Earley brought him up to date. "I answered the phone call from the real estate agent. A couple named Nolan bought the house. She was really upset, actually fainted."

"I understand that this time whoever did it wasn't satisfied with wrecking the lawn."

"This goes beyond anything that's been pulled before. I went straight over to the school to talk to the kids who pulled the Halloween trick last year. Michael Buckley was the ringleader. He's twelve and a smart aleck. He swears he had nothing to do with it."

"Do you believe he wasn't involved?"

"His father backs him up, says they were both home last night." Earley hesitated. "Jeff, I believe Mike, not because he isn't capable of pulling the wool over his father's eyes, but because this just wasn't a kid's trick."

"How do you know?"

"This time they used real paint, not that stuff that washes off. This time they did a job on the front of the house, and from the height of the carving it's clear that someone a lot taller than Michael did it. Something else—the skull and crossbones were done by someone artistic. Finally, the doll wasn't a beat-up rag doll like the other one was. This one cost money."

"That should make it easier to trace."

"I hope so. We're working on it."

THE next morning when I awoke, I looked at the clock and was startled to realize that it was already quarter past eight. In a reflex gesture I turned my head. The pillow beside me was still indented from where Alex's head had rested on it. Then I saw a note propped against the lamp on his bedside table.

Darling Ceil,

Woke at 6 a.m. So glad to see that you were sleeping after all that you went through yesterday. Took off for an hour's ride at the club. Will make it a short day. Hope Jack takes well to his first day at school. Love you both, A.

I got up, pulled on a robe, and walked down the hall to Jack's room. His bed was empty. I walked back into the hall and called his name, but he did not answer. Suddenly frightened, I began to call louder, "Jack . . . Jack . . . Jack"—and realized there was a note of panic in my voice. I forced my lips shut, scolding myself for being ridiculous. He probably just went to the kitchen and fixed himself some cereal. But the house had a disconcerting silence about it as I raced down the stairs and from one room to the other. I couldn't find a trace of him.

And then, in a moment of breathtaking release, I knew where he was. Of course. He would have hurried out to visit his new pony. I yanked open the door that led from the kitchen to the patio, then sighed with relief. The barn door was open, and I could see Jack's small pajama-clad figure inside.

The relief was quickly followed by anger. Last night we had set the security alarm, but Alex had not reset it when he left this morning. If he had, I would have known that Jack was on the loose.

Alex was trying so hard, but he still was not used to being a parent, I reminded myself as I walked across the backyard. Trying to calm down, I forced myself to concentrate on the fact that it was a beautiful September morning, with just a hint of early fall. I don't know why, but autumn has always been my favorite time of the year. Even after my father died and it was just Mother and me, I remember evenings with her in the library off the living room, both of us deep in our books. I'd be propped up with my head on the arm of the couch, close enough to her to touch her side with my toes.

As I made my way across the backyard, a thought flashed into my mind. On that last night, Mother and I had been in the study together. Before we went upstairs, she had turned on the alarm. Even as a child I was a light sleeper, so it surely would have awakened me if that piercing sound had gone off. But it had not gone off, so Mother had no warning that Ted was in the house. Had that ever come up in the police investigation? Ted was an engineer, and it probably wouldn't have been difficult for him to disarm the system.

I walked into the barn and tousled Jack's head. "Hey, you scared me," I said. "I don't want you to ever go out before I'm up. Okay?"

Jack nodded sheepishly. "I just wanted to talk to Lizzie," he said earnestly. "Who are those people, Mom?"

I turned and looked at the newspaper photo that had been taped to the post of the stall. It was a snapshot of my mother and father and me on the beach in Spring Lake. My father was holding me in one arm. His other arm was around my mother. I had a copy of the picture and the article that accompanied it in my secret file.

"Do you know that man and woman and that little girl?"

Of course, I had to lie. "No, Jack, I don't."

"Then why did someone leave their picture here?"

Why indeed? Was this another example of malicious mischief, or had somebody already recognized me? I tried to keep calm. "Jack, we won't tell Alex about the picture. He'd be very mad if he thinks anyone came here and put it up."

Jack looked at me with the penetrating wisdom of a child who senses something is very wrong. "Did whoever put the picture near Lizzie come while we were asleep?" Jack asked.

"I don't know." My mouth went dry. Suppose whoever taped it on the post had been in the barn when Jack walked in alone. What might he have done to my son?

Jack was standing on tiptoe, stroking the pony's muzzle. "Lizzie's pretty, isn't she, Mom?" he asked, his attention completely diverted from the picture that was now in the pocket of my robe.

The pony was rust-colored, with a small white marking on the bridge of its nose. "Yes, she is, Jack," I said, trying not to show the fear that was making me want to snatch him in my arms and run away. "But I think she's too pretty to be called Lizzie. Let's think up another name for her."

Jack looked at me. "I like to call her Lizzie," he said. "Yesterday you said I could call her any name I wanted."

He was right, but maybe there was a way I could change his mind. I pointed to the white marking. "I think any pony with a star on its face should be called Star," I said. "That will be my name for Lizzie. Now we'd better get you ready for school."

BY PLEADING, CAJOLING, AND offering a handsome bonus, Georgette Grove managed to find a landscaper who would cut out the damaged grass and lay sod that same afternoon. She also secured a painter to cover the red paint on the shingles. She had not yet been able to hire a mason to repair the stone, nor a woodwork expert to remove the skull and crossbones carved in the front door.

The events of the day had resulted in an almost sleepless night. At six o'clock, when Georgette heard the sound of the newspaper delivery service in her driveway, she leaped out of bed and hurried to the side door to retrieve the papers. The Morris County *Daily Record* gave the picture of the house its entire front page. On the third page of the Newark *Star-Ledger* there was a picture of Celia Nolan, caught at the exact moment she began to faint. The *New York Post* and the *Star-Ledger* rehashed the sensational case. "Unhappily, Little Lizzie's Place has acquired a sinister mythology over the years," the reporter for the *Daily Record* wrote.

That reporter had interviewed Ted Cartwright about the vandalism. He had posed for the picture in his home in nearby Bernardsville, his walking stick in his hand. "I have never recovered from the death of my wife, both physically and emotionally. I don't need a reminder," he was quoted as saying. "I still have nightmares about the expression on that child's face when she went on her shooting spree. She looked like the devil incarnate."

It's the same story he's been telling for nearly a quarter of a century, Georgette thought. But behind that bereaved-husband façade, he's ruthless. I've seen Ted Cartwright conduct business. If he had his way, we'd have strip malls instead of riding trails in Mendham and Peapack. He may fool a lot of people, but I've been on the zoning board and I've seen him in action.

Georgette read the *Star-Ledger*. "Alex Nolan, a partner in Ackerman and Nolan, a New York law firm, belongs to the Peapack Riding Club. His wife, Celia Foster Nolan, is the widow of Laurence Foster, former president of Bradford and Foster investment firm."

Even though I did try to tell Alex Nolan about the stigma on the house, Georgette thought for the hundredth time, it's in his wife's name, and she knew nothing about it. If she finds out about the stigma law, she could demand that the sale be voided. Tears of frustration in her eyes, Georgette studied the picture of Celia Nolan caught in the process of fainting. I could probably let her take me to court, but that picture would have a big impact on a judge.

Georgette went into her bedroom and began to untie the knot of her robe. Is it time to close the agency? she wondered. I can't keep on losing money. But what would I do? I can't afford to retire, and I don't want to work for anyone else.

Then her mouth tightened. This is my livelihood, she thought, and a faint hope occurred to her. Alex Nolan is a member of the riding club. He told me his law firm asked him to head up their new Summit office, so there are reasons he wants to be in this area. There are a few other listings that might interest him and his wife. If I offer to show Celia Nolan other houses, and even forgo my commission, maybe she'll go along with me.

She showered and dressed. One Old Mill Lane started out as a very happy home, she thought, when Audrey and Will Barton bought it. I remember driving by to watch the progress of the renovation and seeing Will and Audrey working together, planting flowers, with Liza standing in her playpen on the lawn.

I never believed for a minute that Liza intended to kill her mother or tried to kill Ted Cartwright that night. She was a child, for heaven's sake. If that ex-girlfriend of Ted's hadn't testified that he roughed her up, Liza probably would have been raised in a juvenile detention home. I never could understand what Audrey saw in Ted in the first place. He wasn't fit to carry Will Barton's hat. If only I hadn't encouraged Will to take riding lessons . . .

Half an hour later, reinforced with juice, toast, and coffee, Georgette got into her car. As she backed out of the driveway, she gave an appreciative glance at the pale yellow clapboard house that had been her home for thirty years. Despite her business worries, she never failed to feel cheered by its cozy appeal.

I want to spend the rest of my life here, she thought, then tried to brush off the sudden chill that washed over her.

ST. JOSEPH'S CHURCH WAS BUILT on West Main Street in 1860. A school wing was added in 1962. Behind the church there is a cemetery, where some of the early settlers of Mendham are buried. Among them are my ancestors.

My mother's maiden name was Sutton, a name that goes back to the late eighteenth century, when gristmills and sawmills and forges dotted the rolling farmland. My mother grew up on Mountainside Road, the child of older parents who fortunately for them did not live to suffer her death at age thirty-six. Their home, like so many others, has been gracefully restored and expanded. I have the vaguest of childhood memories of being in that house. One firm memory I do have is that of my grandmother's friends telling my mother that my grandmother never approved of Ted Cartwright.

When I was enrolled at St. Joseph's School, there were mostly nuns on the staff. But this morning, as I walked down the hall to the pre-K class, Jack's hand in mine, I could see that the teachers were almost all members of the laity.

Jack had already been to nursery school in New York, and he loves to be with other children. Even so, he clung to my hand as the teacher, Miss Durkin, came over to greet him. "You will come back for me, won't you, Mom?" he asked.

His father has been dead two years. Surely whatever memory he has of Larry has faded, replaced probably by a vague anxiety about losing me. I know, because after the day a priest from St. Joseph's, accompanied by the owner of the Washington Valley stables, came to our home to tell us that my father's horse had bolted and that he had died instantly in a fall, I was always afraid that something would happen to my mother.

And it did. By my hand.

My mother blamed herself for my father's accident. A born rider, she had often said she wished he could ride with her. Looking back, I believe he had a secret fear of horses, and, of course, horses sense that. For my mother it was as necessary to ride as it was to breathe.

I felt a tug on my hand. Jack was waiting for me to reassure him. "What time is class over?" I asked Miss Durkin.

She knew what I was doing. "Twelve o'clock," she said.

Jack can tell time. I knelt down so that our faces would be even. Jack is quick to smile, but his eyes sometimes hold a hint of worry, even of fear. I held up my watch. "What time is it?"

"Ten o'clock, Mom."

"What time do you think I'm going to be back?"

He smiled. "Twelve o'clock on the dot."

I kissed his forehead. "Agreed."

I got up quickly, as Miss Durkin took his hand. When Jack turned, I slipped out and made my way back down the hall.

In the month since my birthday, I had avoided coming to Mendham. But now I got in the car and drove a few minutes down Main Street. Reaching a shopping center, I bought the newspapers and went into a coffee shop, where I ordered black coffee. I forced myself to read every word of the stories about the house, and cringed at the picture of me, my knees buckling. If there was any morsel of comfort, it was that the only personal information was the brief mention that I was the widow of the philanthropist Laurence Foster and that Alex was a member of the riding club and about to open a branch of his law firm in Summit.

Alex. What was I doing to him? Yesterday, typical of his thoughtfulness, he had hired enough help so that by six o'clock the house was in as good shape as it could possibly be on move-in day. How hurt he had been by my refusal to allow the movers to unpack the good china and silver and crystal. Instead I had them placed in one of the guest bedrooms. I could see his disappointment as I sent more boxes to be stacked. He knew that it meant our stay in the house would probably be measured in weeks, not months or years.

Alex wanted to live in this area, and I knew that when I married him. I sipped my coffee and reflected on that simple fact. Summit is only half an hour from here, and he was already a member of the Peapack Club when I met him. Is it possible that subconsciously I have always wanted to come back here to the familiar scenes that are embedded in my memory? Certainly I could not in my wildest dreams have imagined that Alex would happen to buy my childhood home, but the events of yesterday and the newspaper pictures have proved to me that I'm tired of running.

I sipped the coffee slowly. I wanted to learn the reason that my mother became deathly afraid of Ted Cartwright. After what happened yesterday, it would not seem inappropriate for me to make inquiries at the courthouse, saying that I would like to learn the truth of that tragedy. I might even find a way to clear my own name.

"Excuse me, but aren't you Celia Nolan?"

I judged the woman who was standing at the table to be in her early forties. I nodded.

"I'm Cynthia Granger. I just wanted to tell you how terrible the townspeople feel about the vandalism to your house. We want to welcome you here. Do you ride?"

I skirted the answer. "I'm thinking of starting."

"Wonderful. I'll give you a chance to get settled, and then I'll drop you a note. I hope you and your husband will join us for dinner sometime."

I thanked her, and she left. I paid for my coffee, did some quick food shopping, and got back to St. Joe's well before twelve. Then we went home. After Jack had gulped down a peanut butter sandwich, he begged for a ride on Lizzie. Even though I refused to ride after my father died, the knowledge of how to saddle the pony seemed second nature as my hands moved to tighten the girth.

"Where did you ever learn that?"

I whirled around. Alex was smiling at me.

"Oh," I stammered, "my friend Gina loved to ride when we were kids. I used to watch her take lessons."

Lies. Lie following lie.

"I don't remember you mentioning that," Alex said. "But who cares?" He picked up Jack and hugged me. "The client I was supposed to spend the afternoon with canceled. She wanted to change her will again, but she wrenched her back. I beat it out fast."

Alex had opened the top button of his shirt and pulled down his tie. I kissed the nape of his neck, and his arm tightened around me. "Tell me about your first day at school," he demanded of Jack.

"First, can I have a ride on Lizzie?"

"Sure. And then tell me about your day."

"They asked us to talk about our most exciting day this summer, and I talked about the cops coming and how today I went out to see Lizzie and there was a picture—"

"Why don't you tell Alex after your ride, Jack?" I interrupted.

"Good idea," Alex said.

"Jack had a sandwich, but I'll start lunch for us," I said.

"How about having it on the patio?"

"That would be fun," I said hurriedly, and headed into the house. I rushed upstairs.

My father had redesigned the second floor to have two large corner rooms that could be used for any purpose. When I was little, one was his office, the other a playroom for me. I had the movers put my desk in Daddy's office. The desk is a nondescript antique I purchased for one primary reason. One of the file drawers has a concealed panel that is secured by a combination lock that looks like a decoration. The panel can only be opened if you know the combination.

I yanked the files out of the drawer, tapped out the code, and the panel opened. I pulled out a thick file, opened it, and grabbed the newspaper photo that had been taped in the barn.

If Jack ended up telling Alex about it, Alex, of course, would ask to see it. If Jack then realized he had promised me not to talk about it to Alex, he'd probably blurt that out, too.

And I would have to cover with yet more lies.

Putting the picture in the pocket of my slacks, I went downstairs. Knowing Alex loved it, I had bought smoked salmon at the supermarket. I fixed it on salad plates with capers and onions and slices of hard-boiled eggs. I set out place mats and silver on the wrought-iron patio set Alex had bought, then the salads and iced tea, along with heated French bread.

When I called out that everything was ready, Alex and Jack came to the patio. I could have cut with a knife the change in the emotional atmosphere. Alex looked serious, and Jack was on the verge of tears. There was a moment of silence; then in a level tone Alex asked, "Was there any reason you weren't planning to tell me about the picture you found in the barn, Ceil?"

"I didn't want to upset you," I said.

"You don't think the police should know that someone was trespassing here during the night?"

There was only one answer that might be plausible: "Have you seen today's papers?" I asked quietly. "Do you think I want any follow-up? For God's sake, give me a break."

"Jack tells me he went out before you woke up. Suppose he had come across someone in the barn? I'm beginning to wonder if there isn't some kind of nut around here."

Exactly the worry I had but could not share. "Jack wouldn't have been able to get out if you had reset the alarm," I said sharply.

"Mommy, why are you mad at Alex?" Jack asked.

"Why indeed, Jack?" Alex pushed back his chair and went into the house.

MARCELLA Williams was enjoying a second cup of coffee and devouring the newspapers when her phone rang. She picked it up and murmured, "Hello?"

"By any chance, would a beautiful lady be free for lunch?"

Ted Cartwright! Marcella felt her pulse begin to race.

"No beautiful ladies around here," she said coyly, "but I do know a lady who'd very much enjoy lunch with Mr. Cartwright."

Three hours later, having carefully dressed in tan slacks and a vivid silk shirt, Marcella was sitting opposite Ted Cartwright in the Black Horse Tavern on West Main Street. In breathless detail she told him all about her new neighbors. "When she saw the vandalism, Celia Nolan was really upset. I mean she fainted, for heaven's sake. Probably she was worn out from the move."

"It still seems a strong reaction," Cartwright observed skeptically.

"I agree, but it was a shocking sight. Ted, I tell you, that skull and crossbones was just plain chilling."

Smiling wryly, Cartwright reached for his glass and took a long sip of pinot noir. "Tell me more about your new neighbors."

"Very attractive," Marcella said. "She could be anywhere from twenty-eight to early thirties. I'd guess he's in his late thirties. The little boy is really cute." She took a bite of her salad. "I dropped over to Georgette Grove's office yesterday afternoon. She was upset about the vandalism, and I was concerned about her."

Seeing Ted's raised eyebrows, she decided to acknowledge that she knew what he was thinking. "You know me too well." She laughed. "I wanted to see what was going on. Georgette wasn't there, so I chatted with Robin, her receptionist or whatever she is."

"What did you find out?"

"That the Nolans have been married six months and that Alex bought the house as a surprise for Celia's birthday."

Cartwright again raised his eyebrows. "The only surprise a man gives a woman should be measured in carats."

Marcella smiled across the table at Ted. He was studying her, too. I know I look darn good, Marcella thought, and if I can judge a man's expression, he thinks so, too.

"Want to know what I'm thinking?" she challenged him.

"Of course."

"I'm thinking that a lot of men pushing sixty are starting to lose their looks. But you're even more attractive now than when we were neighbors. I love it that your hair has turned white. With those blue eyes of yours, it makes a great combination."

"You flatter me, and I don't mind a bit. Now, how about a cup of coffee? After I drop you off, I've got to get to the office."

Ted had suggested that she meet him at the Black Horse, but she had asked him to pick her up. "I know I'll have a glass of wine, and I don't want to drive afterward," she had explained. The fact was that she wanted the intimacy of being in a car with him.

Half an hour later Ted pulled into her driveway. He got out of the car and walked around to open the door. As she stood up, a car passed along the road. They both recognized the driver—the Morris County prosecutor, Jeff MacKingsley.

"What's that all about?" Cartwright asked sharply. "The prosecutor doesn't usually get involved with simple vandalism."

"I can't imagine. Yesterday Sergeant Earley acted as if he was running the show. I wonder if anything else happened. I was planning to make some cinnamon rolls tomorrow morning and take them up to the Nolans," Marcella told him. "I'll give you a call if I hear anything."

I TRIED to calm myself after Alex left and to calm Jack as well. I could see that the past few days' events were overwhelming him, and I suggested that he curl up on the couch and I would read to him. He willingly selected one of his favorite books. Within minutes he was in the deep sleep that tired four-year-olds achieve so easily. The telephone rang, and I ran to the kitchen. Let it be Alex, I prayed.

But it was Georgette Grove. Her voice hesitant, she said that if I decided I did not want to live in this house, she had others in the area she wanted to show me. "If you saw one you liked, I would forgo my sales commission," she offered. "And make every effort to sell your house also without commission."

It was a generous offer. Of course it did assume that we could afford to buy a second house without first having the money that Alex had put in this one, but then I am sure Georgette realized that, as Laurence Foster's widow, I had my own resources. I told her I'd be very interested and was surprised at the relief in her voice.

When I hung up the phone, I felt more hopeful. When Alex came back, I would tell him that if Georgette found a house, I would lay out the money to purchase it myself.

I was restless, so I just wandered through the first-floor rooms. Yesterday the movers had arranged the furniture, and the placement was all wrong. I am not into feng shui, but I am, after all, an interior designer. Before I was even aware of what I was doing, I was shoving the couch across the room and rearranging chairs and tables and carpets so that the room no longer looked like a furniture store.

The doorbell rang. Suppose it was a reporter? But then I remembered that Georgette Grove had told me that a mason was on his way to repair the limestone, so I opened the door.

Standing in front of me was a man in his late thirties with an air of authority about him. He introduced himself as Jeffrey MacKingsley, the prosecutor of Morris County, and I invited him in.

"I was in the vicinity and decided to express my personal regrets at the unfortunate incident yesterday," he said, following me into the living room.

As I mumbled, "Thank you, Mr. MacKingsley," his eyes were darting around the room, and I was glad that I had rearranged the furniture. Despite the fact that there were no window treatments or paintings, the room still suggested that I was a normal owner with good taste settling into a new home.

That realization calmed me, and I was able to smile when Jeffrey MacKingsley said, "This is a lovely room, and I only hope that you will be able to get past what happened and enjoy this home. I assure you my office and the police will work together to find the culprits. There won't be any more incidents, Mrs. Nolan, if we can help it."

"I hope not." Then I hesitated. Suppose Alex walked in now and brought up the photo in the barn. "Actually . . ."

The prosecutor's expression changed. "Has there been another incident, Mrs. Nolan?"

I reached in my pocket. "This was taped to a post in the barn. My little boy found it." Choking at the deception, I asked, "Do you know who these people are?"

MacKingsley took the picture from me, carefully holding it by its edge. He looked at me. "Yes, I do. This is a picture of the family who restored this house."

"The Barton family!" I hated myself for managing to sound genuinely surprised.

"Yes," he said. "Mrs. Nolan, we might be able to lift some fingerprints from this. Who else has handled it?"

"No one else. My husband had already left this morning when I found it. It was taped to the post too high up for Jack to reach it."

"I see. I want to take it and have it examined for fingerprints. Were you or your husband planning to let the police know that you'd had another trespasser on your property?"

"This seemed so trivial," I hedged.

"I agree that it doesn't compare with what happened yesterday. However, fingerprints we get off this picture may prove helpful in finding who is responsible for all this. We'll need your fingerprints for comparison. I'll arrange for a police officer to come over in a few minutes. He can take them right here."

A frightening possibility occurred to me. Would they just use my fingerprints to distinguish them from any others on the picture, or would they also run them through the system? Suppose the police decided to check the juvenile files. Mine might be on record there.

"Mrs. Nolan, if you find any evidence of someone being on this property, *please* give us a call. I'm also going to ask the police to ride past the house regularly."

"I think that's a very good idea," Alex said from the doorway.

I had not heard him come in, and I guess MacKingsley hadn't either, because we both turned abruptly. I introduced the two men, and MacKingsley repeated to him that he would check the picture for fingerprints.

To my relief, Alex did not ask to see it. MacKingsley left after that; then Alex and I looked at each other. He put his arms around me. "Peace, Ceil," he said. "I'm sorry I blew up. It's just that you've got to let me in on things. I am your husband, remember?"

He took up my offer to get out the salmon that he had left on the lunch table. We ate together on the patio, and I told him about the offer Georgette Grove had made. "Certainly, start looking," he agreed. "And if we end up with two houses for a while, so be it."

The doorbell rang. I opened the door, and the Mendham police officer with the fingerprint kit stepped inside. As I rolled the tips of my fingers in the ink, I thought of having done this before—the night I killed my mother.

WHEN SHE ARRIVED AT THE office, Georgette Grove sensed the tension in the air between Henry and Robin. Henry's habitual timid Caspar Milquetoast expression was now one of petulance, and Robin's eyes were sending angry darts at him.

"What's up?" Georgette was not in a mood for hissy fits.

"It's very simple," Robin snapped. "Henry is in one of his doom-and-gloom moods, and I told him you had enough on your plate without him hanging out the crepe."

"If you call the potential of a lawsuit 'doom and gloom,' you ought not to come into the real estate business," Henry snapped back. "Georgette, I assume you've read the newspapers? I ask you to remember I have a stake in this agency, too."

"A twenty percent stake," Georgette said levelly, "which, if my arithmetic hasn't failed me, means I own eighty percent."

"I also own twenty percent of the Route 24 property, and I want my money from it. Either sell it or buy me out."

"Henry, you know perfectly well that the people who want to buy that property are fronting for Ted Cartwright. If he gets his hands on it, he'll have enough land to press for commercial zoning. Long ago we agreed we'd eventually deed that property to the state."

"Or that you would buy me out," Henry insisted stubbornly. "Georgette, let me tell you something. That house on Old Mill Lane is cursed. You're the only real estate agent in town who would accept the exclusive listing on it. You've wasted this firm's money advertising it. When Alex Nolan asked to see it, you should have told him the truth about it right then. I saw the picture in the newspaper of that poor girl collapsing, and you are responsible for it."

Robin looked at Georgette. "I was hoping to spare you from getting hit with this the minute you walked in."

Henry doesn't care anymore whether he makes a sale or not, Georgette thought. He wants to retire so much that he can taste it. "Look, Henry," she said, "there is a potential solution. I'm going to go line up some houses to show Celia Nolan. If I find something she likes, I'll waive the commission. I have a feeling she'll be amenable to settling this matter quietly."

Henry Paley shrugged and, without answering, turned and walked down the hall to his office.

It was an unexpectedly busy morning. A young couple who seemed seriously interested in buying a home in the Mendham area dropped in. Georgette spent several hours driving them to view places in their price range. She had a quick sandwich and coffee at her desk, and for the next two hours went through the multiple-broker listing and studied it carefully in the hope that one house would jump out as an attractive prospect for Celia Nolan. She finally culled the list down to four possibilities. Her fingers crossed, she called the Nolans' number and was relieved and delighted that Celia seemed totally amenable. Next she made phone calls to the owners and asked to see the houses immediately.

At four o'clock she was on her way. "I'll be back," she told Robin. "Wish me luck."

Three of the houses she eliminated from consideration. All were charming in their own way, but not, she was sure, what Celia Nolan would be interested in. The one she had saved for last seemed, from the description, to be a real possibility. It was a farmhouse that had been restored and was vacant now because the owner had been transferred on short notice. It was near the town line of Peapack, in the same area in which Jackie Kennedy once had a home.

A beautiful piece of property, she thought as she drove up the long driveway. It has twelve acres, so there's room for the pony. She parked at the house's front door, opened the lockbox, let herself in, and walked through the rooms. The house was immaculate. Every room had been repainted recently. The kitchen was state-of-the-art, while retaining the look of an old-fashioned country kitchen.

With growing hope, she inspected the finished basement. A storage closet was locked, and the key for it was missing. I know Henry showed this house the other day, Georgette thought with growing irritation. I wonder if he absentmindedly pocketed the key. There was a splotch of red on the floor outside the closet. Georgette knelt down to examine it. It was paint—she was sure of that. This was probably the storage closet for leftover cans of paint.

She went back upstairs, locked the door, and returned the house key to the lockbox. As soon as she reached the office, she called Celia Nolan and raved about the farmhouse.

"It does sound worth taking a look at."

"If ten tomorrow morning is all right, I'll pick you up."

"No, that's all right. I like to have my own car. That way I can be sure I'll be on time to pick up Jack at school."

"I understand. Well, let me give you the address," Georgette said. She listened as Celia repeated it after her, then was about to give directions, but Celia interrupted.

"There's another call coming in. I'll meet you at ten sharp."

Georgette snapped shut her cell phone and shrugged. That house isn't the easiest place to find. Celia probably has a navigation system in her car, she decided.

"Georgette, I want to apologize." Henry Paley was standing at the door to her office.

Georgette looked up.

Before she could answer, Paley continued, "That is not to say I didn't mean every word, but I apologize for the way I said it."

"Accepted," Georgette told him, then added, "Henry, I'm taking Celia Nolan to see the farmhouse on Holland Road. I know you were there last week. Do you remember if the key to the storage closet in the basement was there?"

"I believe it was."

"Did you look in the closet?"

"No. The couple I took out were obviously not interested in the house. It was too pricey for them. We stayed only a few minutes. Well, I'll be on my way. Good night, Georgette."

Georgette sat for long minutes after he left. I always said I could smell a liar, she thought, but what in the name of God has Henry got to lie about? And why, after he viewed it, didn't he tip me off to the fact the house is sure to move fast?

AFTER she wrote up the vandalism on Old Mill Lane, Dru Perry went straight to Ken Sharkey, her editor, and told him she wanted to do a feature story on the Barton case. "It's absolutely perfect for my Story Behind the Story series," she said.

"Any idea where Liza Barton is now?" Sharkey asked.

"No, not a clue."

"What will make it a real story is if you can track her down and get her version of what happened that night."

"I intend to try."

"Go ahead. Knowing you, you'll find something juicy."

Ken Sharkey's quick smile was a dismissal.

"By the way, Ken, I'm going to work at home tomorrow."

"Okay with me."

Early the next morning Dru settled at her desk in the office she had created in what would have been a second bedroom in her house. The wall in front of her desk was covered with a corkboard. When she was writing a feature story, she tacked all the information she downloaded from the Internet on it. The wall was a jumble of pictures, clippings, and scrawled notes that made sense only to her.

She had downloaded everything available about the Liza Barton case. Twenty-four years ago it had stayed in the news for weeks. When the verdict was released, psychiatrists, psychologists, and pseudo–mental health experts had been invited to comment.

"Rent-a-Psychiatrist," Dru mumbled aloud as she read the quotes attributed to several medical professionals who believed that Liza Barton was one of those children capable of murder. One psychiatrist had said, "I wouldn't be surprised if she was able to fake that so-called trauma when she didn't say a word for months."

Dru always listed on the board any name she came across connected with the story. A name that jumped out as being of special interest was that of Diane Wesley. Described in the papers as "a model and former girlfriend of Cartwright," she told the court that Ted had been physically abusive to her during their relationship.

Benjamin Fletcher, the lawyer appointed to defend Liza, was another one who set Dru's antenna quivering. When she looked him up, she found that he had worked as a public defender for only two years, then quit to open a one-man office. He was still in practice in Chester, a town not far from Mendham. Dru calculated his age now to be seventy-five. He'd be a good starting point, she decided.

She leaned back in her swivel chair and began twirling her glasses, a gesture her friends compared to a fox picking up a scent.

MARCELLA hasn't changed a bit, Ted Cartwright thought bitterly as he sipped a Scotch in his office in Morristown. Still the same nosy gossip and still potentially dangerous. And what was Jeff Mac-Kingsley doing on Old Mill Lane today? The question had been in his mind ever since he saw MacKingsley drive past Marcella's house. Prosecutors don't personally investigate vandalism.

The phone rang, his direct line. His sharp bark of "Ted Cartwright" was greeted by a familiar voice.

"Ted, I saw the newspapers. You take a good picture and tell a good story. I can vouch for how brokenhearted a husband you were. I can prove it, too. And, as you've probably guessed, I'm calling because I'm a little short of cash."

WHEN Georgette phoned to suggest seeing other houses, I was quick to respond. Once we are out of this house and living in a different one, we will have regained our anonymity. That thought kept me going all through the afternoon.

Alex had asked the movers to put his desk, his computer, and boxes of books in the library, a large room he took as his home office, pointing out that it would also accommodate his grand piano. After our late lunch he began unpacking his books.

When Jack woke up, I brought him upstairs. Luckily, he's a child who can amuse himself. While he played with blocks, I busied myself with files I had meant to clean out before we moved.

By five o'clock Jack had tired of the blocks, so we went downstairs. Alex had papers scattered over his desk. He looked up and smiled. "Hey, you two, I was getting lonesome down here. Jack, we didn't get very far with your pony ride. How about we try it now?"

That was all Jack needed. He rushed for the back door. Alex got up, came to me, and cradled my face in his hands.

"Ceil, I read those newspapers. I think I'm beginning to understand how you feel about living here. Maybe this house is cursed. Personally, I don't believe in that stuff, but my first goal is your happiness. Do you believe that?"

"Yes, I do," I said over the lump in my throat.

The phone in the kitchen rang. I hurried to answer it. It was Georgette Grove telling me about a wonderful farmhouse that she wanted me to see. I agreed to meet her, then heard the call-waiting click. I switched to the other call as Alex started out the back door. He must have heard me gasp, because he turned quickly, but then I hung up the phone. "The beginning of a sales pitch," I lied.

What I had heard was a husky voice, obviously disguised, whispering, "May I speak to Little Lizzie, please?"

THE three of us went out for dinner that evening, but all I could think of was the call. I did my best to act festive with Alex and Jack, but I knew I wasn't fooling Alex. When we got home, I pleaded a headache and went to bed early.

The next morning, after I dropped Jack off at pre-K, I headed out to keep my appointment with Georgette Grove. I knew exactly where Holland Road is located. My grandmother lived near that road. It's in a beautiful section. On one side of the road, you look down into the valley; on the other, the properties are built along the hill. The moment I saw the house where I was meeting Georgette, I thought this could be the answer.

Georgette's silver BMW sedan was in front of the house. I glanced at my watch. It was only quarter to ten. I parked behind the BMW and went up on the porch and rang the bell. I waited, then rang it again. Perhaps she can't hear me, I thought. Not quite sure what to do, I turned the doorknob and found it unlocked. I went in and called her name as I walked from room to room.

The house was bigger than the one on Old Mill Lane. In addition to the family room and library, it has a second dining room and a study. I checked all the rooms, even the three powder rooms. Georgette was nowhere on the downstairs floor. I stood at the bottom of the staircase and called her name, but there was only silence.

I began to feel uneasy, but then I remembered that in the kitchen I had noticed the door to the lower level was open a few inches, so I pulled it wide and switched on the light. I called Georgette's name again and started down the stairs. My instinct now told me something was terribly wrong. Had Georgette had an accident? I wondered.

I turned on the switch at the foot of the stairs, and the oak-paneled recreation room blazed with lights. There was a faint but pungent odor in the room, a smell I recognized as turpentine.

It became stronger as I crossed the room and went down a hall. As I turned a corner, I stumbled over a foot.

Georgette was lying on the floor, her eyes open, drying blood caked on her forehead. A can of turpentine was at her side. She was still holding a rag in her hand. The gun that had killed her was lying precisely in the center of a splotch of red paint.

I remember screaming.

I remember running out of the house and into my car.

I remember driving home.

I remember dialing 911, but I could not get a word out when the operator answered.

The next thing I remember is waking up in the hospital.

JARRETT Alberti, a locksmith, was the second person to find Georgette Grove. He had an appointment to meet her at the farmhouse at eleven thirty. When he got there, he saw that the front door was open and went inside looking for her. He duplicated Celia's grim search, found Georgette's body, then dialed 911.

An hour later the coroner was with the body and the forensic team was searching the house. Yellow tape kept the media away. Prosecutor Jeff MacKingsley and Lola Spaulding, a detective from the police department, were questioning Jarrett on the porch.

"What time did Georgette call you?" MacKingsley asked.

"About nine o'clock. She said that the key was missing for a storage closet in this house. She wanted me to get over here by nine in the morning to replace the lock. I told her I couldn't get here until ten, and she said in that case to make it eleven thirty."

"Why was that?" Jeff asked.

"She said that she didn't want me working on the lock while her client was here and that she surely would be gone by eleven thirty."

"Georgette referred to the client as 'she'?"

"Yes," Jarrett confirmed.

"Do you know where she was when she called you?"

"Yes. She told me she was still in her office."

"Okay, you can open the closet."

Jarrett removed the lock and pushed open the door. The light went on automatically over shelves with neatly labeled paint cans.

Jeff MacKingsley looked at the cans on the bottom shelf, the only ones that were not sealed. Three were empty. The fourth was half full. The lid was missing. The splotch Georgette had been trying to clean up probably came from this one, Jeff thought. All were labeled DINING ROOM. All had contained red paint. It doesn't take a genius to figure out where the vandals got the paint for the Nolans' house, he thought. Is that why Georgette was murdered?

"Thanks for all your help, Jarrett. We will need a formal statement from you, but that can be done later."

As Jarrett walked down the hall, Clyde Earley crossed the room, his expression grim.

"I just came from the hospital," Earley said. "We took Celia Nolan there in an ambulance. At ten after ten she dialed 911, then just gasped into the phone. They alerted us, so we went to her house. She was in shock. No response to our questions. We took her to the hospital. In the emergency room she started to come out of it. She was here this morning. She says she found the body and drove home."

"She found the body and drove home! How is she now?"

"Sedated, but okay. The husband is on his way, and she insists she's going home with him. There was a scene at the school when she didn't pick up her son. One of the teachers brought the kid to the hospital. He's with her now."

"We have to talk to her," Jeff said. "She must have been the client Georgette Grove was expecting to meet."

"Well, I don't think she'll buy this place. Looks like she has her hands full living in one crime scene."

"Jeff, we found something in the victim's shoulder bag." With gloved hands Detective Spaulding brought over a newspaper clipping. It was the picture of Celia Nolan fainting. "It looks as if it was put in Georgette's bag after she was killed," Spaulding said. "We've checked, and there aren't any fingerprints."

I THINK what really calmed me down was the panic I saw in Jack's face. When he came into the emergency-room cubicle, he was still sobbing. He usually goes willingly into Alex's arms, but after I wasn't there to pick him up at school, he would only cling to me.

We rode home in the backseat of the car, Jack's hand in mine. Alex was heartsick for both of us. "God, Ceil," he said. "I can't even imagine what a horrible experience that was for you. What's going on in this town?"

What indeed? I thought.

It was nearly quarter to two, and we were all hungry. Alex opened a can of soup for us and made Jack his favorite, a peanut butter and jelly sandwich. We had barely finished eating when reporters started ringing the doorbell.

Alex went outside. For the second time in forty-eight hours he made a statement to the press.

When he came back inside, I said, "What did they ask you?"

"I guess what you'd expect: Why didn't you call the police immediately? Weren't you carrying a cell phone? I pointed out that the killer might still have been in the house, and you did the smartest thing possible—you got out of there."

A few minutes later Jeff MacKingsley called. Alex wanted to put him off, but I immediately agreed to see him. Every instinct told me I should give the appearance of being a cooperative witness.

MacKingsley arrived with a man I guessed to be in his early fifties. Chubby-faced, with a serious demeanor, he was introduced as Paul Walsh, the detective in charge of the investigation into Georgette Grove's death.

With Alex sitting beside me, I responded to their questions. I explained that we wanted to stay in the area, but the history of this house and the vandalism was too upsetting.

"You were not aware of the background of this house before you saw it last month?" Detective Walsh asked.

I felt my palms begin to sweat. "I was not aware of the reputation of this house before I saw it last month."

"Mrs. Nolan, do you know about the law in New Jersey that mandates that a real estate broker must inform a prospective buyer if a house has a stigma on it?"

I did not have to feign my astonishment. "I absolutely did not."

"She did try to tell me that the house had a history, but I cut her off," Alex explained.

"Nevertheless, from what I read in yesterday's papers, you bought this house as a gift for your wife. It's in her name, so Ms. Grove had a responsibility to disclose the history to her."

"No wonder she was so upset about the vandalism," I said. I felt a flash of anger. Then I thought of Georgette as I had seen her in that split second before I ran, the blood on her forehead, the rag in her hand. She'd been trying to get rid of that red paint on the floor.

"Mrs. Nolan, did you ever meet Georgette Grove before you moved into this house?"

"No," I said.

"Then you only saw her the day you moved in?"

"That's right," Alex said, and I caught the edge in his voice. "Georgette didn't stay long on Tuesday. She wanted to get back to her office and arrange for the house and the lawn to be restored."

Walsh was taking notes. "Mrs. Nolan, let's go through this step by step. You had an appointment to meet Ms. Grove this morning."

"I dropped Jack off at school about quarter of nine, went to the coffee shop in the shopping center, then drove to meet Georgette."

"She gave you directions to Holland Road?" Walsh asked.

"No. I mean YES, of course she did!"

I caught a flicker of surprise on both their faces.

"Did you have any trouble finding the house?" Walsh asked. "Holland Road isn't that clearly marked."

"I drove slowly," I said. Then I described walking through the entry, going downstairs, smelling the turpentine, finding the body.

"Did you touch anything, Mrs. Nolan?" This time the question came from MacKingsley.

In my mind I retraced my steps. "I turned the handle on the front door," I said. "I pushed open the door to the lower level."

"Do you own a pistol, Mrs. Nolan?" Walsh asked.

The question came out of the blue. "No, of course not."

"Have you ever fired a pistol?"

I looked at my inquisitor. Behind his round glasses, his eyes were a muddy shade of brown. Once again I lied. "No, I have not."

Walsh pulled out a clipping in a plastic bag. It was the photograph of me in the process of fainting. "Have you any idea why this would be in Ms. Grove's shoulder bag?"

Alex stood up. "Why would my wife know what Georgette Grove was carrying in her shoulder bag? I am sure you can understand that this has been another stressful day for our family."

Both men got up immediately. "We may need to talk to you again, Mrs. Nolan," the prosecutor said. "You're not planning any trips, are you?"

Only to the ends of the earth, I wanted to say. "No, Mr. Mac-Kingsley. I'll be right here, at home."

ZACH Willet's leathery face and callused hands gave testimony to the fact that he was a lifelong outdoorsman. Now sixty-two, Zach had worked at the Washington Valley Riding Club from the time he was twelve years old. He started by mucking out the stables on weekends. At sixteen, he quit school to work at the club full time.

He liked grooming and exercising horses. He could skillfully repair tack. On the side he ran a tidy business reselling the artifacts of the horsey set. And when the regular instructors were booked, Zach would sometimes give riding lessons.

Thirty years ago Ted Cartwright had kept his horses at Washington Valley. A couple of years later he had moved them to the nearby but more prestigious Peapack stables.

Early Thursday afternoon the word of Georgette Grove's death spread through the club. Zach had known and liked Georgette. She had recommended him to people looking to board a horse.

"Why would anybody want to kill a nice lady like Georgette Grove?" was the question everyone was asking.

Zach did his best thinking when he was out riding. Frowning thoughtfully, he saddled one of the horses he was paid to exercise and took off on the trail up the hills. Near the top, he veered onto a trail on which few riders ventured. The descent was too steep.

If you can do that to one human being who's in your way, you can do it to another, he reasoned as he kept the horse to a walk. No question, I heard enough around town to know Georgette was in his way. He needs that land on Route 24. If he did it, wonder if he'd be stupid enough to use the same gun?

Zach thought of the bent cartridge he had hidden in his apartment on the upstairs floor of a two-family house in Chester. Last night, when Ted slipped him the envelope in Sammy's Bar, there was no mistaking the threat Ted had whispered: "Be careful, Zach. Don't push your luck."

Ted's the one pushing his luck, Zach thought as he stared down into the valley. At the precise spot where the trail turned sharply, he tightened his fingers on the reins, and the horse stopped. Zach fished in his vest pocket for his cell phone, pointed it, and clicked. A picture is worth a thousand words, he thought.

BECAUSE she had been covering a trial in the Morris County courthouse, Dru Perry did not learn immediately about Georgette Grove's death. When the judge declared a lunch break, she checked messages on her cell phone and called Ken Sharkey, her editor. Five minutes later she was on her way to the crime scene on Holland Road.

She was there when Jeff MacKingsley held a brief press conference. The bombshell was that Celia Nolan had been the one to find the body, and it raised a barrage of questions. Dru next headed to the Nolan home. She arrived only a few minutes before Alex Nolan made his statement.

Her next stop was the Grove Real Estate Agency on East Main Street. She half-expected to find it closed, but to her astonishment, Marcella Williams opened the door, invited her in, and introduced her to Georgette Grove's associates.

Both the man and the woman looked annoyed and were obviously about to refuse her request for an interview. Marcella intervened on her behalf. "You really should talk to Dru," she told Robin Carpenter and Henry Paley. "In the *Star Ledger* yesterday, she wrote very sympathetically about how distressed Georgette was at the vandalism."

"Georgette Grove was important to Mendham," Dru said. "She deserves to be remembered for all her community activities."

As she spoke, she was studying both Carpenter and Paley.

Despite the fact that Carpenter's blue eyes were swollen and her face blotched from tears, there was no mistaking the fact that she was beautiful, Dru decided. She's a natural blonde, but those highlights came from the hairdresser. Lovely face. Big, wide-set eyes. Come-hither lips. She also knows how to dress, Dru thought, noting Robin's well-tailored, cream-colored pantsuit and low-cut pink-and-cream blouse.

If she's trying to be sexy, though, she's wasting her efforts here, Dru decided as she concentrated on Henry Paley. The thin, nervous-looking sixtyish real estate agent appeared to be more worried than grieved, a thought she tucked away for later consideration.

They told her they were just about to have coffee and invited her to join them. Cup in hand, Dru followed Robin to the couch.

"What do you think happened to Georgette?" Dru asked.

"I think somebody found a way to get into that house and was surprised when she showed up, or else somebody deliberately followed her in with the idea of robbing her, then panicked."

"Did she come into the office this morning?"

"No, and we didn't expect her," Robin said. "When Henry and I were leaving yesterday, she told us she was planning to go directly to the farmhouse on Holland Road."

"Did Georgette stay after you left?"

"This was Georgette's second home. She often stayed late."

Dru could tell that Henry Paley was about to object to her questions. "Let's talk about the kind of person Georgette was. I know she's been a leader in community affairs."

"She kept a scrapbook," Robin said. "Why don't I get it for you?"

Fifteen minutes later, her notebook filled with jottings, Dru was ready to leave. Marcella Williams got up to go with her. Outside the office, when Dru started to say good-bye, Marcella said, "I'll walk you to your car."

"It's terrible, isn't it?" she began. "I still can't believe Georgette is dead. The prosecutor and a detective were just leaving when I got to the office. They'd been questioning Robin and Henry. I came over because I wanted to see if there was anything I could do."

"That was nice of you," Dru said drily.

"Robin told me that Henry cried like a baby when he heard about Georgette, and I believe it," Marcella continued. "From what I understand, ever since his wife died a few years back, he's had a thing for Georgette, but she wasn't interested. I also heard that his attitude has really changed. He's told people he'd like to close the agency and sell the office. In addition to that, Henry bought property on Route 24 with Georgette as an investment years ago. He's been wanting to sell it, but she wanted to deed it to the state."

"What will happen to it now?" Dru asked.

"Your guess is as good as mine. Georgette has a couple of cousins in Pennsylvania she was close to, so I bet she remembered them in her will." Marcella's laugh was sardonic. "One thing I'm sure of. If she left that land to her cousins, the state can whistle for that property. They'll sell it in a heartbeat."

When they reached the car, Dru said good-bye to Marcella and agreed to keep in touch. As she drove away, she reflected on the fact that Marcella Williams had gone out of her way to tell her that Henry Paley would profit by Georgette Grove's death. *Does she have a personal grudge against Henry,* Dru wondered, *or is she trying to protect someone else?*

CHARLEY Hatch lived in one of the smallest houses in Mendham, a four-room cottage. He had bought it after his divorce. The attraction of the property was that it had a barn that housed all his landscaping and snowplowing equipment. Forty-four years old and mildly attractive, with dark blond hair and an olive complexion, Charley had a deep-seated resentment toward his wealthy clients. He cut their lawns from spring until fall, then plowed their driveways in the winter, and always he wondered why he hadn't been the one to be born into money and privilege.

A handful of his oldest customers trusted him with a key and paid him to check their homes when they were away. If he was in the mood, he sometimes spent the night watching television in their family rooms and helping himself to their liquor cabinets. This gave him a satisfying feeling of one-upmanship—the same feeling he had when he agreed to vandalize Old Mill Lane.

On Thursday evening, after the news of Georgette Grove's death had broken, Charley was settled in his imitation leather recliner when his cell phone rang. He took his phone from his pocket, recognized the number of his caller, and mumbled a greeting.

"Charley, you were a fool to leave those empty paint cans in the closet. Why didn't you get rid of them?"

"Are you crazy?" he answered heatedly. "With all that publicity, don't you think cans of red paint might be noticed in the trash? You got what you wanted. I did a great job."

"Nobody asked you to carve the skull and crossbones. I warned you to hide those carvings of yours."

"I don't think—" he began.

"That's right. You don't think! You're bound to be questioned by the police. They'll find out you do the landscaping there."

Without answering, Charley snapped shut his cell phone, breaking the connection, and stood up. With growing anxiety he looked around the cluttered room and counted six carved figures. Cursing quietly, he wrapped them in a roll of plastic and carefully stacked them in a garbage bag. He carried the bag out to the barn, hiding it behind fifty-pound bags of rock salt.

Sullenly he went back into the house, opened his cell phone, and dialed. "What did you get me into anyhow?" he asked. "Why would the police talk to me? I hardly knew that real estate woman."

This time it was the other person who broke the connection.

"THE hour of death is nigh. 'Tis time to drop the mask. . . ."
I don't know why that quote kept running through my head the rest of the day, but it did. Alex had to cancel appointments when he rushed home, so after the prosecutor and detective left, he went into his office to make phone calls. I took Jack outside and let him have a long ride on the pony. I didn't go through the farce of asking Alex to help me with the saddle. He had seen that I was perfectly capable of tacking up the pony myself.

After a few times of walking around the enclosure next to him, I gave in to Jack's pleadings and let him hold the reins. "Just sit on the fence and watch, Mom," he begged. "I'm big."

Hadn't I asked my mother something like that when I was Jack's age? She started me on a pony when I was only three. It's funny how a memory like that will come over me. I always tried not to think about my early life, even the happy times, because it hurt too much to remember. But now the memories are crashing around me.

Dr. Moran, my psychologist in California, told me that suppressed memories never stay suppressed. But there's still something that I've tried to remember about that night, and it always seems I can't dig deep to find it. When I woke up, I thought the television was on, but it wasn't. It was my mother's voice I heard first, and I am sure she called my father's name or spoke of him. *What did she say to Ted?*

Then, as though I'd changed channels, Georgette Grove's face loomed in my mind. Did that appointment cost Georgette her life? She couldn't have suspected anything. She must have been on her knees working on the stain when she was shot.

That moment, as Jack rode by, I made the connection. Was that red paint the same paint someone had used on this house?

It was. I was sure of it. I was sure also that the police would be able to prove it. Then they would not only be questioning me because I found Georgette's body, but because her death may have been tied to the vandalism.

Whoever killed Georgette had carefully placed the pistol on that splotch of paint. The paint was supposed to be tied to her death. And tied to me, I thought.

The hour of death is nigh. 'Tis time to drop the mask.

The hour of death has come, I thought—Georgette's death. But unfortunately I can't drop the mask. I can't inquire about getting a transcript of my trial. I can't get a copy of Mother's autopsy report. How can I possibly be seen walking around the Morris County courthouse looking for that information?

If they find out who I am, will they think that when I got to that house and saw Georgette cleaning up the paint, I connected her with the vandalism and shot her?

Beware! Little Lizzie's Place . . .

Lizzie Borden had an axe . . .

"Mom, isn't Lizzie a great pony?" Jack called.

"Don't call her Lizzie," I screamed. "You can't call her Lizzie! I won't have it!"

Frightened, Jack began to cry. I rushed over to him, encircled his waist with my arms, and tried to comfort him. Then Jack pulled away. I helped him down from the pony. "You scared me, Mom," he said, and ran into the house.

ON FRIDAY morning, the day after Georgette Grove was murdered, Jeff MacKingsley called a meeting in his office for the detectives assigned to her homicide. Joining Paul Walsh were two veteran investigators, Mort Shelley and Angelo Ortiz.

After the barest of greetings, Jeff went straight to the point.

"The red paint used to vandalize the Nolan home came from Tannon Hardware in Mendham and was custom mixed for the Holland Road house. It shouldn't have taken a call from me to the owners in San Diego to find that out."

Ortiz responded, his tone defensive. "I looked into that. Rick Kling, with the Mendham police, was assigned to check out the paint stores. Kling realizes he dropped the ball. If we had known the red paint was part of the overage on that redecoration, we would have been on Holland Road on Wednesday, confiscating the remaining paint."

The weight of what he was saying hung in the air. "That doesn't mean we could have saved Georgette's life," Jeff acknowledged. "She may have been the victim of a random robbery attempt."

"Jeff, in my opinion the importance of the paint is not *when* we found it, but that it was used on Little Lizzie's Place. The murder weapon was centered on the splash of paint to emphasize that fact, which brings us to Celia Nolan, a lady I think needs a lot of investigating." Paul Walsh's dry tone bordered on insolence.

"That gun was deliberately placed, that was obvious," Jeff said. "But I do not agree with your theory that Mrs. Nolan is concealing something. I think the woman has had one shock after another, and naturally she is distressed. Clyde Earley said that she couldn't have faked the state of shock she was in. She couldn't even speak until she got to the hospital."

"We have her fingerprints on that picture she found in the barn. I want to run them through the database file," Walsh said stubbornly. "I wouldn't be surprised if that lady has a past she might not want us to find out about."

"Go ahead," Jeff snapped. "But I want you concentrating on finding a killer, not wasting your time on Celia Nolan."

"Jeff, don't you think she was lying when she said Georgette Grove gave her directions to Holland Road? She contradicted herself when I asked her that question. Incidentally, I checked the time she called 911. It was ten after ten."

"Your point is?"

"My point is that according to her testimony, she went into the house on Holland Road at quarter of ten and walked around calling Georgette's name. That's a big house, Jeff. I went back last night and clocked the trip between Holland and Old Mill Road. Normal driving, by which I mean about ten over the speed limit, it took me nineteen minutes. So let's do the arithmetic. If Nolan left that house by nine minutes of ten, she was in it only four to six minutes."

"Which is possible," Jeff said. "Fast, but possible."

"That would also assume she drove straight as an arrow and knew exactly when to turn on unfamiliar and confusing roads while she was in a state of severe shock."

"Paul, I suggest you make your point," Jeff said grimly.

"My point is that she either got there much earlier and was waiting for Georgette or that she has been at that house before and was sure of the roads back and forth."

"Again, your point?"

"Nolan's husband bought the house for her, and she wanted no part of it but didn't dare tell him. She got someone to mess up the house, arrives and pulls the fainting act, and she has her way out. Somehow Georgette caught on to her act. She was carrying a picture of Celia Nolan doing her swan dive in her purse. I say she was going to show it to Nolan and tell her she wasn't going to get away with it."

"Then why weren't there any fingerprints on the picture, including Georgette's?" Ortiz asked.

"Nolan wiped it clean. She may have handled it but been afraid to take it in case people had seen Georgette with it."

"You've missed your calling, Paul," Jeff snapped. "You should have been a trial attorney. You sound persuasive on the surface, but it's full of holes. Celia Nolan is a wealthy woman. She could have bought another house with a snap of her fingers. Go ahead and check her prints in the database, and then let's move on. What's happening, Mort?"

Mort Shelley pulled a notebook from his pocket. "We're putting together a list of the people who had access to that house and interviewing them. People like other real estate agents who have keys to the lockbox, and people who do housecleaning or landscaping. We're investigating to see if Georgette Grove had any enemies, if she owed any money, if there's a boyfriend in the picture."

"All right. Keep me posted." Jeff stood up, signifying the meeting was over. As they were leaving, he called out to Anna, his secretary, to hold any calls for an hour.

Ten minutes later she buzzed him on the intercom. "Jeff, there's a woman on the phone who claims she was in the Black Horse Tavern last night and heard Ted Cartwright threatening Georgette Grove. I knew you'd want to talk to her."

"Put her on," Jeff said.

AFTER she left Marcella Williams, Dru Perry went directly to the *Star-Ledger* offices to write her story about the homicide on Holland Road. She then cleared it with her editor, Ken Sharkey, that she would work at home in the morning to put together a weekend feature on Georgette.

That was why, with a mug of coffee in her hand and still dressed in her pajamas and robe, she was watching local Channel 12 on Friday morning. The news anchor was interviewing Grove's cousin, Thomas Madison, who had come from Pennsylvania when he received the news of Georgette's death. Madison, a soft-spoken man in his early fifties, expressed his family's grief and outrage at her coldblooded murder. He announced that a memorial service would be held at 10 a.m. on Monday at Hilltop Presbyterian, the church Georgette had attended all her life. As Dru pressed the remote button and snapped off the television, she decided to attend the service.

Dru turned on her computer and began to search the Internet for references to Georgette Grove. "Pay dirt," she said aloud an hour later as she came across a school picture of Georgette Grove and Henry Paley when they were seniors in Mendham High. Henry's skinny arm was around Georgette, and while she smiled directly into the camera, his fatuous smile was only for her.

Boy, he looks lovesick, Dru thought—he must have been sweet on Georgette even then. She leaned back in her creaking desk chair and looked up at the ceiling. When they had talked yesterday, did Henry Paley talk about his whereabouts when Georgette was killed? Dru pulled out her notebook and jotted down the questions and facts that were jumping into her mind.

Where was Henry Paley the morning of the murder? Did he go to the office at the usual time? Lockboxes have a computerized record. It should show how often Henry visited Holland Road. Was he aware of the paint cans in that storage closet? He wanted the agency to close. Would he deliberately sabotage the Old Mill property to embarrass Georgette?

Dru closed her notebook and went back to the Internet. In the next two hours she was able to form a clear picture of Georgette Grove, an independent woman who, judging from her many awards, was not only community minded but a dynamic force in preserving the quality of life, as she saw it, in Mendham.

Lots of people must have wanted to strangle her, Dru thought as she came upon reference after reference to Georgette Grove successfully arguing against bending the existing zoning guidelines.

She picked up the phone and dialed the agency. Henry Paley answered her call.

"Henry, I'm so glad to reach you. I'm working on the article about Georgette, and I was thinking how nice it would be to include some of those wonderful pictures from her scrapbook. I'd like to borrow it or at least copy some of the pictures."

After some encouragement Paley reluctantly agreed. "I don't want anything taken out of it," he said.

"Henry, thank you very much. I'll see you around noon. I won't take too much of your time."

MARTIN and Kathleen Kellogg of Santa Barbara, California, were the distant cousins who adopted me. At the time of Mother's death, they had been living in Saudi Arabia. They did not learn anything about what had happened until Martin's engineering firm relocated them back to Santa Barbara. By then the trial was over and I was living in the juvenile shelter here in New Jersey while the Division of Youth and Family Services decided where to place me.

In a way, it was good that the Kelloggs hadn't had any contact with me until that time. Childless themselves, they came to Morris County quietly and, without publicity, petitioned to adopt me. The court readily approved them as my guardians and adoptive parents.

At that time the Kelloggs were in their fifties, not too old to parent an eleven-year-old. More important, though, they were genuinely compassionate. The first time I met Kathleen, she said, "I always wanted a little girl. Now I want to give you back the rest of your childhood."

I lived with them for seven years. During all that time I saw Dr. Moran once a week. When I could not speak, he had me draw pictures. Over and over I drew the same ones. A ferocious apelike figure holding a woman against the wall. A gun poised in midair. A child holding the dead figure of her mother.

I had lost a year of grammar school but made it up quickly and went to a local high school. In both places I was known as "quiet but nice." I had friends but never let anyone get close to me. I was constantly having to guard my tongue and conceal my emotions.

The same year I moved to New York to attend the Fashion Institute, Martin reached compulsory retirement and they moved to Naples, Florida. Now past eighty, he has become what Kathleen calls "forgetful," but which I fear is the beginning stages of Alzheimer's.

When we married, Alex and I had a quiet wedding in the Lady Chapel of St. Patrick's Cathedral. Shortly after that, Alex and Jack and I flew down to visit Martin and Kathleen. One day when we were lingering over lunch on the patio, Martin called me Liza. Fortunately, Alex and Jack had headed to the beach for a swim.

AFTER my outburst over the pony's name, I followed Jack into the house. He had run to Alex and was sitting on his lap, tearfully telling him that Mommy scared him. "She scares me too, sometimes, Jack," Alex said. It might as well have been stamped on Alex's forehead: He thought I was having some sort of breakdown.

He tried to explain to Jack about the pony: "You know, a long time ago a little girl named Lizzie lived in this house, and she did some very bad things. Nobody liked her, and they made her go away. What's something you hate more than anything else?"

"When the doctor gives me a booster shot."

"Well, think about it this way. Would you want to call your pony Booster Shot?"

"Noooooooooo."

"So now you know how Mommy feels hearing the name Lizzie. Let's think about another name for that pretty pony."

"Mommy said we should call her Star because she has a star on her forehead."

"That's a great name, and we should make it official. Mommy, don't we have some birthday wrapping paper?"

"I think so." I was so grateful to Alex for calming Jack down, but oh, the explanation he gave!

"Why don't you make a big star, and we'll put it on the barn door so everyone will know Star lives there?"

Jack loved the idea. We made a ceremony of pasting the glittery star on the door of the barn.

That night, when Alex tried to draw me close to him, he sensed my resistance and immediately released me. "Ceil, why don't you take a sleeping pill?" he suggested. "You need to relax. I'm not sleepy. I'll go downstairs and read for a while."

When I take a sleeping pill, I usually break it in half, but that night I swallowed a whole one and for the next eight hours slept soundly. When I awakened, it was almost eight o'clock, and I pulled on a robe and rushed downstairs. Jack was up and dressed, having breakfast with Alex.

Alex came over and kissed me. "I've got to be off. You okay?"

"I'm good." And I was. As the remnants of sleep left me, I knew what I was going to do. After I dropped Jack at school, I would go to one of the other real estate agents and try to find a house we could rent or buy immediately.

Later that morning I went to the Mark Grannon Agency. Mark Grannon himself took me around. "Georgette was the one who got the exclusive listing on your house," he told me. "None of the rest of us wanted to touch it. But Georgette always had a guilty feeling about the place. She and Audrey Barton had been good friends at one time. They went to Mendham High at the same time."

I listened, hoping Grannon could not sense the tension rushing through my body.

"Audrey was a great horsewoman, you know. Her husband, Will, was deathly afraid of them and embarrassed about it. He wanted to be able to ride with her. It was Georgette who suggested that he ask Zach at Washington Valley Riding Club to give him lessons, something they agreed to keep secret from Audrey. She knew nothing about it until the police came to tell her Will was dead. She and Georgette never spoke again."

Zach!

The name hit me like a thunderbolt. It was one of the words my mother had screamed at Ted the night I killed her.

Zach. It was part of the puzzle!

ON FRIDAY afternoon Ted Cartwright's secretary informed him that a Detective Paul Walsh from the prosecutor's office was in the waiting room and needed to ask a few questions.

In a way Ted had been expecting the visit, but now that it actually had happened, he felt perspiration form on the palms of his hands. He wiped them dry on his jacket. "I wasn't aware that Mr. Walsh had made an appointment to see me," he spat into the intercom. "However, send him in."

Paul Walsh's suit-off-the-rack, slightly rumpled look immediately triggered Cartwright's contempt. The round frame of Walsh's glasses reminded him of the color of his tan riding boots.

"I really don't like unexpected drop-ins," he said. "I'm going to be on a conference call in ten minutes, so we'd better get to the point, Mr. Walsh. It is Mr. Walsh, isn't it?"

"That's right," Walsh replied, his steely tone out of sync with his mild-mannered appearance. He handed Cartwright his card and sat down in the chair facing Cartwright's desk.

"What can I do for you?"

"I am investigating the murder yesterday morning of Georgette Grove. You knew Ms. Grove. Were you friends?"

"We had been friendly enough. In recent years Georgette became very confrontational. On the zoning board, she was an obstructionist. For that reason I, along with a number of other people, ended any semblance of friendship with her."

"When was the last time you saw her?"

"On Wednesday night, at the Black Horse Tavern."

"What time was that, Mr. Cartwright?"

"Between nine fifteen and nine thirty. She was having dinner."

"Did you approach her?"

"She beckoned to me, and I went to greet her and was astonished when she all but accused me of being responsible for the vandalism of the house on Old Mill Lane."

"What did you tell her?"

"I demanded to know why she would think that. She said that I was working with Henry Paley to put her out of business so that she'd have to sell the property on Route 24."

"What was your response?"

"I told her I was not working with Paley. I told her that while I would certainly like to develop that property, I had plenty of other projects. And that was the end of it."

"I see. Where were you yesterday morning between eight and ten o'clock, Mr. Cartwright?"

"At eight o'clock I was riding my horse on a trail at the Peapack Riding Club. I rode until nine o'clock, showered at the club, and drove here, arriving at about nine thirty."

"The house on Holland Road in which Ms. Grove was shot has wooded property behind it. Isn't there a riding path on that property that connects to a Peapack trail?"

Cartwright stood up. "Get out," he ordered angrily. "And don't come back. If I have to talk further with anyone from your office, I'll do it in the presence of my lawyer."

Paul Walsh stood and walked to the door. "You will be seeing me again, Mr. Cartwright. And if you speak to your friend Mr. Paley, tell him he'll be seeing me as well."

At four o'clock on Friday afternoon Charley Hatch pulled his van into the driveway behind his barn, then unhitched the trailer he'd used to haul his riding mower. Some nights he didn't bother to do that, but tonight he was going out again, meeting some pals at a bar to watch the Yankee game. He was looking forward to it.

It had been a long day. The sprinkler system at one of the places he serviced had broken down, and the owner was due home from vacation soon. It was one of Charley's easier jobs, and he didn't want to lose it, so he had spent time getting the sprinkler guy to fix the system, then hung around until the grass was properly soaked.

Still upset by his phone conversation the previous night, he'd used the time while he was waiting to examine his clothes. He was wearing the same jeans he had worn on Monday night, and he found three drops of red paint on the right knee. The jeans were old but comfortable. He'd have to get the paint off with turpentine.

Charley put away the trailer and went into the house, heading to the refrigerator. He pulled out a beer, flipped off the top, and began to drink. A glance out the front window made him withdraw the bottle from his lips. A squad car was turning into his driveway.

Charley glanced down. The three drops of paint suddenly looked as if they were billboard size. He rushed into his bedroom, pulled off his sneakers, and was dismayed to see that the sole of his left one was smeared with paint. He put on a pair of corduroy pants, shoved his feet into loafers, and answered the door after the second ring.

Sergeant Clyde Earley was standing there. "Mind if I come in, Charley?" he asked. "Just want to ask a few questions."

"Sure, sure, come on in, Sergeant." Charley watched as Earley's eyes swept the room. "Sit down. How about a beer?"

"Thanks, but I'm on duty, Charley." Earley selected a straight chair, one of two at the butcher-block table. Charley sat on the edge of the worn club chair that had been part of the living room décor he shared with his wife before their divorce.

"Terrible thing, what happened on Holland Road yesterday," Earley began.

"I should say so. It gives you the creeps, doesn't it?"

Earley had removed his uniform hat, and his sandy hair was damp. "You just get home from work, Charley?"

"That's right."

"Any reason you changed into corduroy pants and leather shoes? You didn't work in them, did you?"

"Trouble with a sprinkler system. My jeans and sneakers were soaked. I was heading for the shower when I saw your car, so I pulled these on."

"I see. Well, I just need a few facts. You do the landscaping for Ten Holland Road, right?"

"Yeah. When Mr. Carroll got transferred, they asked me to keep up the place until it's sold."

"Have you got a key to the house?"

"Yes. I go in every couple days to mop. Sometimes the real estate agents bring people in when it's raining, and they track in mud."

"When was the last time you were in the house?"

"Monday. I always go in after the weekend."

"Did you know there was red paint in the storage room?"

"Sure. There are a lot of paint cans there. I guess the decorator ordered more colors than they needed."

"You didn't know that red paint was used to vandalize the house on Old Mill Lane?"

"I read about Little Lizzie's Place being messed up, but I didn't know that the paint came from the Holland Road house. Who would do such a thing, Sarge?"

"I was hoping you'd have some suggestions, Charley. The key to the storage room is missing. Did you know that?"

"I know it was there last week."

Earley smiled. "The way I look at it, maybe the person who did that job on Little Lizzie's Place got scared because Ms. Grove was onto him. That's the real shame. The most time somebody would get for vandalizing would be a year or so, but if that person killed Grove to keep her quiet, he could get the death penalty. Well, I'll see you, Charley." Earley got up, then let himself out.

Charley held his breath until the squad car drove away, then pulled out his cell phone and dialed, in a panic. A computerized voice announced that the number he was calling was out of service.

AT FIVE o'clock Thomas Madison entered the Grove Real Estate office. Henry and Robin were just about to lock up.

"I'm glad I caught you," Madison said. "I thought I'd stay for the weekend, but there really isn't any point, so I'll come back Sunday night. We'll all be here for the service—I mean my wife, my sisters, and their husbands."

"We'll be open tomorrow," Henry told him. "As fate would have it, we seem to be about to close several sales. Have you been to Georgette's house yet?"

"No. The police haven't finished going through it. I don't know what they're looking for."

"I would imagine any personal correspondence that might give them a lead to her killer," Robin said. "They went through her desk here as well."

"It's a lousy business. It's just . . ." Madison's shrug conveyed his dismay at the circumstances. "I've got to get home," he said. "I'm the coach of my kid's soccer team, and we have a game tomorrow."

Henry smiled politely. He had absolutely no interest in Georgette's cousin's soccer team. What he did care about was immediately nailing down business details with Georgette's heir. "Tom," he said, "from what I understand, you and your two sisters will share in Georgette's estate."

"That's right. Her lawyer has a copy of the will. He's submitting it for probate, but that's the way it reads." Madison shrugged again. "Henry, I know that you own twenty percent of both this place and some property on Route 24. I'll tell you this—we have absolutely no interest in continuing the business. My suggestion is that we get three appraisals, then you buy us out, or if you're not interested in keeping the business going, we close the office and sell everything."

"You do know that Georgette intended to deed the property on Route 24 to the state," Robin said.

"I know about that. Frankly, we'd all like to kiss Henry's feet for not letting her play Lady Bountiful to the state of New Jersey. I've got three kids, my sisters each have two, and whatever we get from the sale of Georgette's real estate will go a long way."

"I'll start getting appraisals immediately," Henry promised.

Madison turned to leave, then stopped. "The family will be having lunch after the church service. We'd like to have you join us. I mean, you two were Georgette's other family."

Henry waited until the door closed behind Madison. "*Are* we her other family?" he asked dryly.

"I was very fond of Georgette," Robin said quietly.

"Were you so fond of her that you don't mind the fact that Wednesday night she went through your desk?" Henry asked.

"I wasn't going to say anything about it. You mean she went through your desk as well?"

"She not only went through my desk, she removed a file. Did she take anything from yours?"

"Not that I've noticed. There's nothing of any interest to her."

"You're *sure* of that, Robin?"

They were still standing in the reception room. Henry was not a tall man, and Robin's three-inch heels put her at eye level with him. For a long moment they looked directly at each other. "Want to play *I've Got a Secret?*" he asked.

THE weekend went unexpectedly well. Both days were very warm. Alex went for an early morning ride on Saturday, and when he returned, I suggested we go to Spring Lake. A client of mine had been married there in July. We had attended her wedding and stayed at the Breakers Hotel. Because we'd been there together, it was one place that I didn't have to worry too much about letting slip the fact that I was familiar with it.

Alex liked the idea. Jack loved it. Alex called over to the club and was able to hire one of the kids who worked weekends at the stable to come over to take care of Star.

It worked out just as I had hoped. We got two connecting ocean-front rooms at the Breakers. We stayed on the beach all afternoon. After dinner we took a stroll on the boardwalk, and the breeze carried the salty scent of the ocean. Oh, how the ocean calms my soul. I was even able to think about being here before, when I was a child, my hand in my mother's, as Jack's was now in mine.

In the morning we went to early Mass at St. Catherine's, the beautiful church that never fails to comfort me. We spent the rest of the day on the beach, went to Rod's Olde Irish Tavern in Sea Girt for an early dinner, then, happily tired, started back to Mendham. On the way, I told Alex that I was signing up for lessons at the Washington Valley Riding Club.

"Why not at Peapack?" he asked.

"Because there's a guy at Washington Valley who is supposed to be a wonderful teacher. I called Friday afternoon, and he agreed to take me on. I told him that I didn't want to start out at a place where my husband's friends could see how inexperienced I was."

My throat choked on the lie. The truth, of course, was that taking lessons from Zach would be the most natural way for me to be around a man whose name had been on my mother's lips seconds before she died.

DETECTIVE PAUL WALSH WAS one of the first to arrive at Hilltop Presbyterian Church for Georgette Grove's memorial service on Monday morning. To be sure that he didn't miss seeing anyone who showed up, he chose a seat in the last pew.

The weekend search of Georgette's house had proven fruitful. One of the Mendham cops had found a file hidden in the closet of her bedroom that contained an exchange of e-mails between Henry Paley and Ted Cartwright. Cartwright promised Paley a bonus if he could force Georgette to sell the property on Route 24. Paley had written that the agency was in a shaky financial situation and that he was doing everything possible to keep it that way.

Nice guy, Walsh thought; he was actively trying to put his partner out of business. MacKingsley's mind-set is that Paley was the killer, having panicked because Georgette got her hands on his Cartwright file, but Walsh wasn't so sure.

It was common knowledge that Jeff MacKingsley intended to make a run for the governor's office in two years, and a lot of people thought he would make it. This kind of high-profile case was just what he wanted. Well, Paul Walsh thought, solving this case would also be a nice feather in my cap, too.

At ten minutes of ten the organ began to play, and suddenly the church began to fill with people. Walsh recognized some members of the local media who, like him, stayed in the back pews. Dru Perry was easy to pick out with her mane of gray hair. Marcella Williams sat in the fourth pew. Thomas Madison and his two sisters went down the aisle and took seats in the front. Henry Paley, looking suitably mournful, and Robin Carpenter were the next to come down the aisle. Just as the minister stepped before the altar, Celia and Alex Nolan took seats a few rows ahead of Walsh.

Dark glasses shielded Celia's eyes. Her long, dark hair was twisted into a knot. When she turned to whisper something to her husband, Walsh had a full view of her profile. Classy-looking, he admitted to himself—a killer with the face of an angel.

A soloist began to sing "The Lord Is My Shepherd," and the congregation rose. The pastor, in his eulogy, spoke of a woman who gave selflessly for the good of others: "Time after time, over the years, people have told me of Georgette's selfless efforts to preserve the tranquil beauty of our community. . . ."

At the end of the ceremony, Walsh left the church. He found Robin Carpenter waiting for him just outside. "Detective Walsh," she said hesitantly, "when we were sitting inside at the service, I kept thinking about Georgette, of course, and then of something she happened to say to me on Wednesday evening. It was about six o'clock, and I went in to say good night to her. She had her scrapbook on her desk, and she was looking at it intently. She never even heard me push open the door. It wasn't fully closed, you see, and I heard her say something that maybe I should share with you."

Walsh waited.

"Georgette was talking to herself, but she said something like, 'Dear God, I'll never tell anyone I recognized her.' "

"Where is that scrapbook?" Walsh demanded.

"Henry lent it to Dru Perry for the story about Georgette that ran in the *Star-Ledger*. He wasn't planning to, but she persuaded him. She's returning it this afternoon."

"I'll be over to get it. Thank you, Ms. Carpenter."

SUE Wortman was the young woman who had taken care of the pony while we were in Spring Lake. She was in the barn with Star when we got home Sunday evening.

Sue has a way with children, and Jack took to her immediately. He explained to her why his pony used to be called Lizzie, but now she was Star. Sue told Jack that she would bet he was going to become a champion rider on a pony named Star.

On the way home from Spring Lake, Alex had suggested that we ought to attend Georgette's service. That was why, when Sue told me she was available for babysitting, I hired her on the spot. I had planned to go to the Washington Valley Riding Club while Jack was in school, but with Sue to take care of Jack, I was able to change my riding lesson with Zach to 2:00 p.m. on Monday.

I had assumed we would drive to the memorial service in separate cars because Alex was going to work afterward, but he said he'd drop me back home when it was over. Sitting there in that church, all I could think of was Georgette as I saw her for the first time, the distress on her face, her frantic apologies. Then my mind jumped to that moment on Holland Road when I almost tripped over her body.

Of course, Alex sensed my distress. "This was a lousy idea, Ceil," he whispered. "I'm sorry."

We walked back to the car. I knew by now that Alex was concerned about the time. I said I was sorry that he was running late. Unfortunately, Marcella Williams had walked up behind us in the parking lot and overheard our conversation. "Why waste time dropping off Celia?" she insisted. "I'm going straight home, and it will give us a chance to visit."

Alex and I exchanged glances. Mine reflected dismay, I know, but I climbed into Marcella's car. She was wearing a Chanel suit, and it occurred to me that she had come to the service dressed to be seen and admired.

"I'm so glad to have the chance to be with you, Celia," she said warmly as she steered her BMW convertible along Main Street. "That was a nice turnout, wasn't it? It was so good of you to come. Georgette sold that house to your husband without telling him the background. Then you had the horror of being the one to find her body. Even with all that, you came to pay your respects."

"Georgette gave Alex a great deal of time when he was house hunting. He felt we should be there."

"I understand that you were already looking for a different house and that was why you went to Holland Road. I'd love to keep you for a neighbor, but I can certainly understand. I'm very good friends with Ted Cartwright. He's the stepfather Liza Barton shot after she killed her mother. I guess you know the story?"

"Yes, I do."

"You wonder where that kid is now. Ted said he hopes she fell off the earth."

Was she toying with me? "I can understand that he wants to put everything behind him," I said.

"In all these years he never remarried. Oh, he's had girlfriends, but he sure was crazy about Audrey. When she dropped him for Will Barton, it just about broke his heart."

My mother dropped Ted for my father! I'd never known that. I tried to sound casual when I asked, "You mean Audrey was serious about Cartwright before she married Barton?"

"Oh, my dear, was she ever. Big engagement ring, plans for a wedding. But then she was maid of honor at a friend's wedding. Will Barton was the best man, and as they say, the rest is history."

Why didn't I ever know that? I wondered. And why was Mother suddenly afraid of Ted? Why had he thrown her at me?

We were turning down Old Mill Lane. "How about stopping at my house for a cup of coffee?" Marcella asked.

I managed to get out of that by saying I had phone calls to make before I picked up Jack. Uttering the vaguest of promises to get together soon, I got out of her car and let myself in the kitchen door.

The message light was blinking on the phone. I picked up the receiver, pushed the PLAY button, and listened.

It was that same shadowy voice I had heard the other day. This time it whispered, "More about Little Lizzie . . .

"And when the dreadful deed was done,

"She gave her father forty-one.

"Thursday got another gun,

"Shot Georgette and began to run."

JEFF MacKingsley called a two-o'clock meeting of the detectives assigned to the Grove investigation. Paul Walsh, Mort Shelley, and Angelo Ortiz were present and ready to give their reports.

Shelley went first. "The personal codes of eight brokers were programmed into the lockbox on Holland Road. Two of those eight were Georgette Grove and Henry Paley. There's a record of which broker's code was punched in and the time it was punched. Paley told us he'd been out there once. The fact is, he was there three times. The last time was Sunday afternoon, a week ago. The paint in that storage room was used on the Nolan house sometime Monday night."

He glanced down at his notes. "The other brokers who showed the house last week all swear they did not leave the kitchen or patio doors unlocked. But the alarm system is programmed for fire and carbon monoxide, not for entry or exit, since the house is empty and Charley Hatch keeps an eye on things."

"Do any of the brokers you spoke to remember seeing the key in the door of the storage closet?" Jeff asked.

"One of them, from the Grannon Agency, showed the house on Sunday morning. He said the key was there. He remembers because he opened the door. The cans of paint were all unopened."

"Let's go step-by-step," Jeff suggested. "We know the key was there on Sunday morning. Paley showed the house on Sunday afternoon and claims he didn't notice if the key was there. Wednesday, in the Black Horse Tavern, Georgette publicly accused Ted Cartwright of conniving with Henry to force her to sell her property on Route 24. Now that we found Henry's file in her closet, we know she had proof. I don't see Paley painting that lawn or carving that skull and crossbones, but I can see that either he or Cartwright might pay someone to do it. I can also understand why Henry might panic if Georgette had proof that he was connected to the vandalism."

Jeff linked his fingers together and leaned back in his chair. "Henry knew the paint was there. He wanted to get his money out of the office property. He also wanted his money out of the Route 24 parcel. Cartwright had promised him a hefty bonus if he forced the sale. If Georgette Grove knew all that, from what I hear of her, she would have hung on to that property even if she was starving. I say that Paley and Cartwright are our primary suspects, so let's keep the heat on them."

"Jeff, respectfully, you're barking up the wrong tree," Paul Walsh said. "Georgette's death has everything to do with the pretty lady on Old Mill Lane."

"You were going to run Celia Nolan's fingerprints through the database," Jeff said. Even though his voice was quiet, there was no mistaking the anger that was building in him. "What did you find?"

"Oh, she's clean," Walsh admitted. "She never committed a crime for which she's been caught. But there's something fishy there. Celia Nolan is hiding something. When I was leaving the service for Georgette, Robin Carpenter stopped me outside the church. She told me that on Wednesday evening she went to say good night to Georgette. Georgette's door was ajar. She was looking at her scrapbook and, not realizing she was being overheard, said, 'Dear God, I'll never tell anyone I recognized her.' "

"Who was she talking about?" Jeff asked.

"My guess is that a picture of Celia Nolan may be in that book."

"Have you got the scrapbook?"

"No. Henry lent it to Dru Perry from the *Star-Ledger,* who promised to return it this afternoon. I'm going to pick it up later."

"Once again, Paul, I think it's necessary to keep an open mind, or else you're going to miss the obvious," Jeff snapped. "We had this conversation on Friday. Let's move on. What about fingerprints?"

"They're all in the usual spots in the Holland Road house," Mort Shelley reported. "Doorknobs, light switches, kitchen drawers—we've run them all through the database, and we came up with zip."

"How about the gun?"

"Saturday night special, impossible to trace."

Angelo Ortiz was next. "Clyde Earley talked to the landscaper, Charley Hatch, Friday afternoon. He felt that Hatch was nervous, like he's got something to hide."

"Is Earley checking Hatch out?" Jeff asked.

"Yes. I talked to him this morning. He hadn't uncovered any reason for Hatch to have a grudge against Georgette Grove. But Earley's got one of his hunches. He's still sniffing around Hatch."

"Well, tell him not to pull any of his tricks," Jeff said. "The trouble with Clyde is that ever since he got publicity on the Barton case twenty-four years ago, he's been trying to find a way back into the spotlight again." He stood up. "Okay, that's it."

TEN miles away, Sergeant Clyde Earley was standing outside Charley Hatch's barn. He'd already established that Charley wasn't home, having seen his landscaping van at one of the houses on Kah-dena Road. I'm just paying a little visit to go over Charley's Holland Road schedule, Earley told himself. Sorry he's not here.

The trash barrels by the barn were full. Wouldn't hurt to take a look, would it? Clyde thought. The lid's practically off this one any-how. I know I can't get a search warrant at this point, because I don't have probable cause, so I'll have to make do without one. I like it the way it used to be, when the courts considered garbage abandoned property, and no warrant was needed.

The first barrel was stuffed with two black trash bags, securely tied and knotted. With a strong yank Clyde opened the top one. It contained the unappetizing remains of Charley Hatch's most recent meals. With a muttered expletive Clyde threw it back in the barrel and opened the other bag. This one was stuffed with clothes that suggested Charley had cleaned out his closet.

Clyde shook the contents onto the ground. The last items to fall out were sneakers, jeans, and a bag of carved figurines. With a sat-isfied smile he examined the items closely and found what he was looking for: drops of red paint on the jeans, a smear of red paint on the sole of the left-foot sneaker. Charley must have jumped into those corduroy pants when he saw me coming, Clyde thought.

The figurines were a half-dozen statuettes of animals and birds, all intricately carved, all about six inches tall. These are good, Clyde thought. Why would he get rid of these? Doesn't take a genius to figure that one out, he decided. He doesn't want them around, be-cause he carved the skull and crossbones on the door at Lizzie's place. Somebody has to know about his little hobby.

Thoroughly satisfied with his detective work, Sergeant Clyde Ear-ley carefully placed the figurines, the sneakers, and the jeans in the squad car. He stuffed the rest of the clothing Hatch had discarded back in the trash bag, retied it, but deliberately left it on the ground. Let him sweat blood when he sees someone's been here, he thought.

Earley got back in the squad car. I don't think I have to worry about Charley Hatch reporting a theft, he told himself. That ludi-crous possibility made him snicker out loud as he drove away.

MY FIRST instinct was to erase that horrible message, but I didn't do it. Instead I took the answering tape out of the machine and brought it up to my office. I tapped in the combination that opened the hidden panel. As if my fingers were burning, I dropped the tape in the file. When the panel was safely secured again, I sat at my desk, holding my hands on my knees to keep them from trembling.

I simply could not believe what I had heard. Someone who knew I was Liza Barton was accusing me of murdering Georgette Grove. I've spent twenty-four years wondering when someone would point at me and shout my real name, but how could anyone think I would kill a woman I've met once in my life and for less than an hour?

Detective Walsh. His name sprang into my mind. *"Have you ever fired a gun?"* It was the kind of question you ask a person you view as a suspect. Was it possible that Walsh had left that phone message and was playing a cat-and-mouse game with me?

But even if he knows I'm Liza Barton—and *how* would he know?—why would he think I would kill Georgette Grove? Did Walsh imagine that I was angry enough at Georgette to kill her? That possibility made me sick with fear.

Even if Walsh is not the one who knows I am Liza Barton, he's suspicious of me. I've already lied to him. I can't answer any more questions. I've got to hire a criminal lawyer.

But how would I explain that to my lawyer husband?

It was time to pick up Jack. As always, his need for me is the focus of my life. I got up, went into my bathroom, and washed my face with cold water, trying to shock myself into reality. I changed into jeans and a cotton sweater. As I got in the car, I reminded myself that I had to buy a new tape for the answering machine.

I collected Jack at St. Joe's and suggested we have lunch at the coffee shop. I managed to persuade him to eat a grilled-cheese sandwich instead of peanut butter and jelly. He was filled with stories about pre-K, including the fact that a girl had tried to kiss him

"Did you let her kiss you?" I asked.

"Oh, sure. I'm going to marry her someday."

His fourth day in class, and his future is already settled.

It's funny how my love for Jack was the root cause of my marrying Alex. I had met Alex for the first time at Larry's funeral two years ago. Even standing at my husband's casket, I couldn't help being aware that Alex Nolan was a very attractive man. I didn't see him again until he came up to me at a charity dinner a year later. We had lunch the next week and went to dinner and the theater a few nights later. It was obvious that he was interested in me, but I had genuinely loved Larry, and the realization of how disturbed he had been about my past had unsettled me terribly.

Larry was the man who had told me that the happiest part of his life began the day he met me. Larry was the man who shouted with joy the day I told him I was pregnant, and who did not leave me for one single minute of my long and difficult delivery. Larry was the man who, in his will, left me one third of his wealth and made me residual heir of Jack's estate.

Larry was also the man who on his deathbed, his hand clutching mine, begged me not to disgrace his son by revealing my past.

Alex and I began to date with the understanding that this was going nowhere, that this was all platonic. "But don't for a minute believe I *think* platonic," he would joke. Then he'd turn to Jack. "Hey, guy, how can I make your mother like me?"

We'd been in that mode for four months when one night everything changed. Jack's babysitter was late. By the time she got to the apartment, I was expected at a dinner party on the West Side. The doorman was getting a cab for someone else. I rushed out to hail another cab. I didn't see the limo pulling out from the curb.

I woke up in the hospital two hours later, battered and bruised, and with a concussion. Alex was sitting by my bedside. He answered my question before I asked: "Jack's fine. Your babysitter called me when the police couldn't reach your parents in Florida."

He ran his hand across my cheek. "Ceil, you could have been killed! I'll stay at your place with Jack tonight. You know he'll be comfortable with me."

Alex and I were married two months later. While we were seeing each other without commitment, I owed him nothing. Now that I am his wife, I owe him the truth.

All these thoughts were leaping through my mind as I watched Jack finish the last crumb of his sandwich. We started to drive home, but then I remembered I hadn't bought the answering machine tape. We backtracked, and as a result, it was twenty of two by the time we got to the house. Sue was there, ready to babysit, and I rushed upstairs to trade my sneakers for boots that would work for my first riding lesson.

It's funny that it didn't occur to me to cancel the lesson. I was distraught at the dual threat that somebody knew I was Liza Barton and that Detective Walsh was suspicious of me. But every instinct in my being said that by getting to know Zach, I might learn why my mother had screamed his name that night she and Ted fought.

I parked at the Washington Valley Riding Club, went inside, and told the receptionist I had an appointment with Zach Willet.

Zach came to fetch me. I judged him to be about sixty. His lined face suggested long exposure to the elements, and the broken capillaries in his cheeks made me suspect he liked his liquor. His eyes were an odd shade of hazel, almost faded in color.

Introductions over, he said, "I tacked up a horse that's used to beginners." As we walked back to the stables, he asked, "Ever ridden before?"

"My friend had a pony. She'd let me have rides on it."

"Uh-huh." Clearly he was unimpressed.

There were two horses saddled and tied to the hitching post. The large mare was obviously his. A docile-looking gelding was there for me. I listened attentively to Zach's first instructions about riding. "Here, I'll boost you up," he said. "His name is Biscuit."

It had been a long time since I had sat on a horse, but I immediately felt at home. We walked the horses around the ring. I was with Zach for an hour, and while he was far from gregarious, I did get him to talk. He told me how being around horses was a lot more satisfying than being around most of the people he knew. He told me that horses were herd animals and liked each other's company. I remembered to make the mistakes new riders do, like letting the reins slide, letting out a squeal when Biscuit picked up the pace.

Of course when Zach realized I lived on Old Mill Lane, he connected me with Little Lizzie's Place. "You're the one who found Georgette's body!"

"Yes, I am."

"Lousy experience for you. Georgette was a nice lady. I read that your husband bought that house as a birthday present. Some present! Ted Cartwright, the stepfather the kid shot that night, used to keep his horses here. We're old friends."

I tried to sound casual. "Didn't I hear that Liza's father died as a result of a riding accident somewhere around here?"

"That's right. Next time you come, I'll show you the spot. Well, not the exact spot. That's on a trail only the real experts take. Nobody can understand why Will Barton went on it. He knew better. I was supposed to be with him that day."

"Were you? What happened?"

"He'd had about ten lessons and could tack up his own horse. My horse had picked up a stone in its hoof, and I was trying to get it out. Will said he'd start ahead. Anyhow, I was about five minutes behind him, and I started to worry that I wasn't catching up. Never occurred to me to look for him on that trail. But I couldn't find him anywhere, and by the time I got back to the stable, the word was all over the place. He and the horse had gone over the cliff."

"Why do you think he went on the trail?"

"Got confused."

"Weren't there signs to warn him?"

"Sure there were, but I bet the horse got frisky, and Will was so nervous he didn't notice them. Then when he saw what he was up against, my bet is that he yanked on the reins and the horse reared. In a way I've blamed myself all these years. I should have made Will Barton wait for me."

Mother might have blamed Zach for that, I thought. But why would she have screamed his name at Ted?

"We'll turn back to the stable," Willet told me. "You're okay. Stick to it, and you'll make a good rider."

DRU Perry wrote a brief story about Georgette Grove's memorial service, turned it in to her boss at the *Star-Ledger*, and then went back to work on the Story Behind the Story feature. It was her favorite kind of reporting, and she was intrigued with the prospect of taking a fresh look at the Liza Barton/Little Lizzie Borden case.

She had left a message on the answering machine of Benjamin Fletcher, the lawyer who had defended Liza at her trial. He finally called her back on her cell phone, and they had arranged that she would come to his office in Chester at four o'clock. Now Dru sat in his cubbyhole office, staring at him across a jumble of files and family pictures. She didn't know what she had expected, but it wasn't that he'd be a giant of a man, six feet three or four and at least a hundred pounds overweight. His few remaining strands of hair were damp with perspiration.

"Do you have any idea how many times over the years some reporter has called me about the Barton case?" he asked. "Don't know what you people think you're going to find to write about that hasn't been written before."

"I guess we all know the basic facts of the case," Dru agreed. "But I'd like to talk about Liza. You were appointed by the court to defend her. Is it true that she never spoke to anyone?"

"From the time she thanked that cop for putting a blanket around her in the squad car, she didn't say a word for two months. Even after that, the psychiatrists couldn't get much out of her. They asked her about her stepfather, and she said, 'I hate him.'"

"Isn't that understandable, since she blamed him for her mother's death?"

Fletcher pulled a wrinkled handkerchief out of his pocket and rubbed his face with it. "Ms. Perry, that little girl never intended to kill her mother, that's a given. But Ted Cartwright, the stepfather, is something else. I was always surprised that the press didn't dig a little more into Audrey Barton's relationship with him. She'd been engaged to Ted, then broke it off when she married Will Barton, and the old flame got rekindled after she was widowed. The kid resented him from the get-go."

"Then why was Audrey so afraid of him?"

"We'll never know for sure, but my guess is that life with the three of them under the same roof was unbearable, and obviously Audrey couldn't dump her child. But don't forget one more point." Benjamin Fletcher looked sharply at Dru. "The alarm system. One of the things we managed to get out of Liza was that her mother set the alarm that night before the two of them went upstairs. But when the cops came, the alarm was turned off. Cartwright didn't break in. If he'd disconnected the alarm from the outside, there'd be a record of a malfunction. I believed him when he said Audrey had called him and invited him over to discuss a reconciliation."

"I read an interview with Diane Wesley in one of those trashy tabloids about two years after the trial. She testified that Cartwright physically abused her."

Fletcher chuckled. "She sure did, but the abuse she got from Cartwright was that he dropped her for another woman."

"You mean she was lying?"

"Now I didn't say that, did I? I think the real truth is that they'd had an argument. In sympathy for Liza, Diane dressed up her story a little. She's got a good heart. That's off the record, of course." The lawyer's face became stern. "Ms. Perry, trust me, if it wasn't for Diane, Liza Barton would have been confined in a juvenile detention center until she was twenty-one."

"Have you any idea where Liza is now?"

"No. I wonder about her from time to time. I just hope she got the psychiatric help she needed. If she didn't, I wouldn't put it past her to sneak back around here someday and blow Ted's brains out."

LATE MONDAY AFTERNOON Charley Hatch sat in his living room, drinking a beer and waiting nervously for the call he'd been told to expect. He was going over in his mind how he would explain that there was a problem.

It's not my fault, he thought. After that cop, Earley, left on Friday afternoon, I tried to call the usual number. Then my phone rings. I'm told to go out and buy one of those cell phones with minutes on it so nobody can trace it.

Then, in an effort to show that I was being careful, I mentioned that I'd noticed some spots of paint on my jeans and sneakers, and managed to change them before I let the cop in. I thought that would show I'm on the ball, but instead I'm told to get rid of the jeans and sneakers and to make sure there's no paint spots on the van. Then I have to listen to how dumb I was to do the carving in that door.

So over the weekend I left the jeans and sneakers with my carvings in the garage, and then I decided I'd better get rid of them. My garbage is picked up every Tuesday and Friday. I thought putting it in the bin Sunday night would be okay. I'll bet that nosy cop rummaged through and found them. Anyway, they're gone.

Charley's regular cell phone rang. His throat suddenly tight, he took a deep breath, then answered. "Hello?"

"Give me the number of the other phone. I'll call you on it."

When his new phone rang, he picked it up. Instead of giving his carefully rehearsed explanation, he blurted out, "I threw my sneakers, jeans, and my carved figures in the garbage. Someone fished them out. I think it was that cop who came to see me Friday."

The long silence that followed was worse than the angry tirade he'd been subjected to because of the skull and crossbones.

When his caller spoke, the voice was calm and even. "Why did you put that stuff in the garbage?"

"It was supposed to be picked up tomorrow."

"I didn't ask for the garbage schedule. You should have just thrown it in a Dumpster behind some store. Listen and try to keep straight what I'm telling you. I don't know who shot Georgette

Grove, but if the cops have evidence you did the job on the Nolan house, they'll blame you for it."

"Blame us for it," Charley corrected.

"Don't threaten me, Charley. That cop had no right to go through your garbage without a search warrant, so even if they found something, they can't use it. They can, however, wear you down. So get a lawyer and refuse to answer questions."

"A lawyer! Who's going to pay for a lawyer?"

"You know I'll pay for it." There was a pause. "Charley, you'll never have to worry about money again if you can get through this without messing it up."

ON MONDAY night Zach had a hamburger and a couple of drinks at Marty's Bar and debated in his mind about calling Ted Cartwright. The picture he had mailed him must have arrived at his office by now.

The cops had to be questioning Ted about Georgette Grove, he figured. Everyone in town knew how furious he was that she was always blocking his building plans. The case against him would be a lot stronger if a certain Zach Willet decided to share a certain memory with the police.

I'm the minnow who can lead them to the shark, Zach thought.

He decided against having a third Scotch and got into his car to drive home. Home! He used to really like his place. Three rooms and a back porch, where on nice days, when he wasn't working, he could settle down with the papers and his portable TV. But last year Old Lady Potters died, and her daughter moved into the downstairs apartment. She had four kids, and one of them had a set of drums. The racket was driving Zach nuts.

Ted's building town houses in Madison, Zach thought. They're about finished, and they look real nice. I wouldn't mind having a little more room. And a place to park, he added to himself as he drove down his street and found every spot taken. It was clear the landlady's kids were having a gang of friends over.

Zach finally parked a block and a half away and sullenly walked back to the house. He unlocked the door that led to the second-floor apartment and climbed the stairs with a deliberately heavy foot. He had looked forward to sitting outside on his back porch and settling down with a cigar, but there were kids in the backyard, all shouting at each other.

He got out his cell phone and put it on the table, trying to decide whether or not to make the call. He'd hit Ted up only a week or so ago. But that was before Georgette took a bullet in the head. Ted must be real nervous now, Zach told himself.

The sudden beat of the drums from downstairs made him jump. Muttering a curse, he dialed Ted's cell phone.

"The customer you are trying to reach is unavailable. . . ."

Zach waited impatiently until the computerized voice had finished, then said, "Sorry to miss you, Ted. Know how upset you must be about Georgette's death. I bet you're taking it real hard. Hope you can hear me. The racket downstairs is driving me nuts. I really need another place to live, like one of those town houses you're building. I hope you got that nice picture I sent you."

ALL Monday evening I struggled to tell Alex that I wanted to hire a criminal defense lawyer, but the words kept dying in my throat. The pleasant weekend at Spring Lake had relaxed the tension between us, and I was coward enough to want that good feeling to last a little while longer.

After dinner, when Alex said he had to go to Chicago tomorrow afternoon to take a deposition and would be there for at least one night, possibly two, I almost was relieved. If any more of those terrible calls came in, he wouldn't be around to hear them. And I wanted to call Dr. Moran, who had treated me when I was young. He's retired now, but I have his number. I needed his advice.

All this I was thinking while I was getting Jack ready for bed. I read him a story, then left him to read one himself before it was time to turn off the light.

I went into the kitchen. Alex had volunteered to clear the table and to put the dishes in the dishwasher. "Just in time," he said with a smile. "Espresso's ready. Let's have it in the living room." We sat opposite each other in the fireside chairs. By then I had a feeling he was picking the right moment to bring up something. "What time did you tell Jack he has to turn out the light?" he asked.

"Eight thirty. But you know he'll be asleep before that."

"I'm still getting used to the way a kid begs for more time, then falls asleep the minute his head hits the pillow." Alex looked at me. "Ceil, my piano is being delivered on Saturday."

He raised a hand before I could protest. "I miss having the piano. It's been six months since I put it in storage. You may find a different house tomorrow, or it could be a year from tomorrow."

"You want to stay here in this house, don't you?" I asked.

"Yes, I do, Ceil. I know that with your talent, if you decorated it, this would be a showplace. We can put up a security fence to be sure we never have a vandalism episode again."

"But it will still be Little Lizzie's Place in people's minds," I protested.

"Ceil, I know a way to put a stop to that. This house was originally called Knollcrest. Let's call it that again and have a sign made to put at the gate. Then we could have a cocktail party, have a picture of the house on the invitation, and welcome people to Knollcrest. I believe the name would begin to stick. How about it?"

The look on my face must have conveyed my answer. "Well, never mind," Alex said. "It was a lousy idea." As he stood up, he added, "But I *am* going to have the piano delivered on Saturday."

THE next morning Alex gave me a hurried kiss on his way out. "I'm going for a ride. I'll shower and dress at the club. I'll call you tonight from Chicago."

I don't know if he suspected that I had been awake most of the night. He came to bed about an hour after me, moving quietly, assuming that I was asleep, and settling on his side of the bed without even the perfunctory kiss that was becoming our nightly routine.

After I dropped Jack at school, I went to the coffee shop again. Cynthia Granger, the woman who had chatted with me last week, was seated nearby with another lady. When she saw me, she asked me to join them. After expressing concern for the shock I had experienced on Holland Road, she told me the feeling in the community was that Ted Cartwright was involved in Georgette's death.

"Ted's always been considered a Mafia type," Cynthia explained to me. "With all his charm, you sense that underneath you're dealing with one very tough cookie. I understand that somebody from the prosecutor's office was in his office Friday afternoon."

For what turned out to be a short interval, I felt as if everything might be all right. If the prosecutor thought Ted Cartwright was connected to Georgette's death, I might have been wrong about Detective Walsh zeroing in on me. Maybe, in their eyes, I was only the lady who had the bad luck to buy a stigmatized house.

Lee Woods, the woman seated with Cynthia, had moved to Mendham last year from Manhattan. It turned out that she had a friend whose apartment I had decorated before I married Larry, and she was effusive in her praise of it. "Then you're Celia Kellogg," she said. "Talk about coincidence. I was redoing our apartment and I called your number, but your assistant said you had a baby and wouldn't be taking on clients. Is that still true?"

"It won't be much longer," I said. "Sooner or later I do plan to hang out my shingle around here."

It felt so good to be Celia Kellogg, the interior designer, again. Cynthia and Lee even had a suggestion for a housekeeper. Gratefully, I took her name. But as we got up to leave, I had a sudden sense of being watched. I turned around and saw the man who was sitting at a nearby table.

It was Detective Paul Walsh.

AT THREE o'clock on Tuesday afternoon, feeling irritable and unsettled, Jeff MacKingsley told his secretary, Anna, to hold his calls. Paul Walsh had come back to the office at noon and reported that he had followed Celia Nolan all morning. "I really jolted her when she saw me in the coffee shop," he said. "And then I followed her over to Bedminster, where she went into that place where they sell riding clothes. When she came out with a bunch of boxes, I thought she'd have a heart attack on seeing me parked behind her. I knew she was picking up the kid, so I let it go for today."

He looked at me as if he's defying me to take him off the case, Jeff thought, and I won't do that, at least not yet. As far as I'm concerned, the investigations into Georgette Grove's death and the vandalism on Old Mill Lane are going nowhere fast.

Who had a motive in killing Georgette? Two people. Ted Cartwright was one. Henry Paley was the other. Cartwright had been riding Thursday morning and could have turned onto the trail that went behind the house on Holland Road. He could have been waiting for Georgette and followed her into the house.

The problem with that scenario, as Jeff saw it, was that Cartwright would have to know that Georgette was showing the house that morning. Of course, Henry Paley could have tipped him off, but how could Cartwright be sure that Celia Nolan wouldn't have driven over with Georgette? If Nolan and Grove had shown up together, would Ted Cartwright have killed both of them?

Henry Paley is the one who makes the most sense for both crimes, Jeff thought. He admitted that he knew Georgette was scheduled to meet Nolan at the Holland Road house. He could have been waiting for Georgette to show up, then followed her in, killed her, and made his escape before Celia Nolan arrived. Money was his motive, and another motive surely would be fear of disclosure. If she was able to tie him to the vandalism, he was facing a jail term, and he knew it.

Henry Paley admits to being in the vicinity of Holland Road on Thursday morning, he reflected. He was at a nine-o'clock open house. The other brokers Angelo talked to remember seeing him there at about nine fifteen. Celia Nolan arrived at the Holland Road house at quarter of ten. That means Henry had somewhere between fifteen and twenty minutes to leave the open house, cut through those woods, shoot Georgette, go back to his car, and take off.

But if Henry is the killer, then who did he hire to vandalize the Nolan house? I don't think he did it all by himself, Jeff thought. Those paint cans were heavy. Also, there was nothing amateurish about the carving in the door.

The telephone rang. He had told Anna to hold calls unless they were urgent. He picked up the phone. "Yes, Anna."

"Sergeant Earley is on the phone. He says it's very important."

"Put him through." Jeff heard a click and said, "Hello, Clyde."

"Jeff, I got to thinking about who would be likely to do that job on Little Lizzie's Place, and how that landscaper, Charley Hatch, who had round-the-clock access to the Holland Road house, would have known about the paint cans in the storage closet. Anyhow, I had a little talk with him Friday afternoon."

"Go on," Jeff said.

"I got the feeling that Charley was real nervous. Remember how hot it was Friday afternoon? First thing I noticed was that he was wearing heavy corduroy pants and loafers. Frankly, I got real curious about where his regular work pants and shoes might be. So this morning I waited by Charley's place until the guy who picks up the garbage showed up and followed him till he was off Charley's property. I think, as of then, we can consider the bags to be legally abandoned. I asked the waste engineer, as he calls himself, to open Charley's trash, and lo and behold, we found a pair of jeans with red spots, sneakers with red paint, and nice little carved figures with the initials CH on the bottom. Apparently, Charley Hatch loves to do wood carvings. I've got all these items in my office."

At the other end of the call, Clyde Earley smiled to himself. He did not think it necessary to inform the prosecutor that, at 4:00 a.m. today, while it was still pitch-dark outside, he had returned to Charley's property and had put these items back into their original bag, with all the old clothes that still sat in the bin awaiting today's pickup. The plan had worked perfectly when he had retrieved the evidence in full view of a reliable witness—Mr. Waste Engineer.

"The garbageman witnessed you opening the bag, and he knew it came from Charley's?"

"Absolutely. He had carried the bags to the truck on the street, right in front of Charley's place."

"Clyde, this is a real breakthrough," Jeff said. "That's great police work. Where is Charley now?"

"Out landscaping somewhere."

"We'll send the clothes to the state lab, and I'm sure they'll match the paint, but that could take a day or two. I think that we have enough probable cause to file a complaint for criminal mischief and pick him up. Clyde, I can't thank you enough."

Jeff hung up the phone and went on the intercom. "Come in please, Anna. I've got a complaint to dictate."

She had barely settled in the chair across from his desk when the phone rang again. The call was from Earley.

"We just heard from the 911 dispatcher. A hysterical woman on Sheep Hill Drive reported that she found her landscaper lying on the ground at the north end of her property. Charley Hatch was shot in the face, and she thinks he's dead."

AT TWELVE thirty on Tuesday afternoon Henry Paley walked from his office to the Black Horse Tavern to meet Ted Cartwright, who had insisted they have lunch together. When he arrived, he glanced around the dining room, half-expecting to see either Detective Shelley or Ortiz. Over the weekend both of them had separately stopped by the office to ask again what Georgette had said to him that last evening—and what Georgette meant when Robin overheard her say, "I'll never tell anyone that I recognized her."

I told them both I have no idea who she recognized, Henry thought, and both acted as if they didn't believe me.

As usual, most of the tables were occupied. Ted Cartwright was already at a corner one. He's probably halfway through his first Scotch, Henry thought as he made his way across the room.

"Do you think this meeting is a good idea, Ted?" he asked as he pulled out a chair and sat down.

"Hello, Henry. Yes, I think it's an excellent idea. As the owner of twenty percent of the Route 24 property, you had every right to be in contact with someone interested in buying it. I could wish that you hadn't put our bonus arrangement on paper, but nothing can be done about that now."

"You sound a lot less upset about those notes than you did the other day," Henry commented, then realized the waiter was at his side. "A glass of Merlot, please," he said.

"Bring another one of these while you're at it," Cartwright told the waiter.

He's drinking fast even for him, Henry thought.

Cartwright looked across the table at Henry. "I do feel somewhat better, and I'll tell you why. I've hired a lawyer, and the reason for this lunch is not only to let people see we have nothing to hide, but to tell you you'd better hire a lawyer, too. The prosecutor is going to try to prove that we agreed to get rid of Georgette and that one of us actually shot her, or hired someone else to do it."

Henry stared at Cartwright but said nothing until the waiter returned with the drinks. Then he took a sip of the Merlot and said reflectively, "I had not even considered that the prosecutor would be looking at me as a possible suspect. It simply isn't in my nature to hurt anyone. I have never even held a gun in my hand."

"Are you practicing for your defense?" Cartwright asked. "If so, you're wasting it on me. I know your type, Henry. You're a sneak. Were you behind what happened on Old Mill Lane? It's just the sort of trick I'd expect of you."

"Shall we order?" Henry suggested. "I have an appointment to take some people house hunting this afternoon. It's quite interesting that Georgette's death gave our agency a shot in the arm. We've suddenly had quite a few drop-ins."

The two men did not speak again until the steak sandwiches they both ordered were served. Then Henry said, "Ted, now that I've persuaded Georgette's cousin to sell the Route 24 property, I'd appreciate the one hundred thousand dollars you offered me."

Cartwright stopped the fork he was holding in midair. "You have got to be kidding," he said.

"No, I am not kidding."

"The deal was that you would persuade Georgette to sell that property instead of deeding it to the state."

"The deal was, and is, that the property is for sale. Somehow I anticipated that you might not wish to pay the bonus you owe me. Over the weekend I got in touch with Thomas Madison. I pointed out that while your offer was reasonable, other offers for that property have also been made. I suggested that I contact the people who made them and see if they would like to begin negotiations."

"You're bluffing," Cartwright said, anger rising in his face.

"I really am not bluffing, Ted. But you are. You're scared you'll be arrested for Georgette's murder. You were horseback riding near the house on Holland Road. You had a quarrel with Georgette in this very room the night before her death. Now, shall I pursue those other interested parties, or shall I expect your check within forty-eight hours?" Henry stood up. "Thanks for lunch. Oh, by the way, are you still seeing Robin? Or was she only last year's diversion?"

LORRAINE Smith was the woman whose hysterical 911 call about Charley Hatch had brought not only the police, but an ambulance, the medical examiner, the media, and the team from the Morris County prosecutor's office, including the prosecutor himself.

Lorraine gradually regained her composure sufficiently to join the investigative team in the breakfast room of her Federal-style home. "Charley got here about one o'clock," she told Jeff, Paul Walsh, Angelo Ortiz, and Mort Shelley. "He comes every Tuesday."

"Did you talk to him at all?" Jeff asked.

"Today I did. Normally when he's just doing the lawn, I don't talk to him, but today I was annoyed." Lorraine took a sip of coffee. "Charley's supposed to come at nine o'clock, and I had friends over for lunch. We were on the patio and had to listen to the roar of his power mower. I finally told him to finish tomorrow."

"What did he say?"

Lorraine Smith paused. "His cell phone rang. Or I should say, one of his cell phones rang. He took one out of his breast pocket, then the other out of his back pocket. He told the person to wait, then said, 'I'll load my stuff and get out of here now, Mrs. Smith.' "

"Did you happen to hear the name of the person?"

"No. He obviously did not want to talk in front of me. I went back inside, my friends and I finished lunch, and they left at about two fifteen. I didn't realize that Charley's van was still in the back. When I saw it, I went looking to see where he was."

"How long was that after your friends left?" Angelo Ortiz asked.

"Only a few minutes. I could see he wasn't in the backyard, so I walked around the pool and tennis court. Just past them is that row of boxwoods at Valley Road. Charley was lying on his back in the little space between two of them." Lorraine Smith rubbed her hand over her forehead as if to erase the memory.

Jeff stood up. "Mrs. Smith, we'll ask you to sign a statement later, but thank you for being so helpful. It makes our job easier."

The four men walked to the front door. Detective Lola Spaulding from the forensic unit met them as they came out of the house.

"Jeff, his wallet is in the van. Doesn't look touched. No sign of a cell phone. But we did find something in his vest pocket." She offered him a plastic bag containing a photograph.

The photograph, like the one that had been in Georgette Grove's shoulder bag, had been cut out of a newspaper. It showed a stunningly attractive blond woman in her early thirties. She was wearing riding breeches and a hunt coat and holding a silver trophy.

"This hasn't been tested for fingerprints," Lola said. "Any idea who it is?"

"Yes," Jeff said. "This is Liza Barton's mother, Audrey, and this is one of the pictures the newspapers used last week when they carried the story of the vandalism."

He gave the picture back to Spaulding and walked to the yellow crime scene tape that had been strung up to hold back the media. Audrey Barton lived on Old Mill Lane, he thought. The psycho who killed two people is leaving those pictures and is either playing a game with us or begging to be stopped.

What are you telling us? Jeff mentally asked the killer as lightbulbs began to flash. How can we stop you before you kill again?

ON THE way home from shopping in Bedminster, I kept looking to see if Detective Walsh was still following me. I decided he wasn't, because I couldn't see any trace of that black Chevrolet sedan. I picked up Jack at school, brought him home, washed his face and hands, and drove him around the corner for a playdate. After promising to be back at four o'clock, I went home.

Jack's friend's mother had invited me to have a cup of coffee with her while she gave the boys lunch, but I begged off, saying that I had phone calls to make. Unlike yesterday, when I'd given Marcella Williams that excuse, this time I was being honest. I had to talk to Dr. Moran. It was about ten o'clock in California, a good time to reach him. And I wanted to call Kathleen. She was the only one other than Dr. Moran in whom I could confide.

As soon as I got home, I ran to the answering machine. When Jack and I stopped at the house, I'd noticed the light was blinking, but I was afraid to play the message for fear it was one of the Lizzie Borden calls.

It was Detective Walsh. He thought that possibly I had been wrong about the time I found Georgette's body, saying it was impossible that someone who didn't know the route from Holland Road to my house could have made the trip so quickly. "I understand how traumatized you were, Mrs. Nolan," he said, his voice smooth but sarcastic, "but by now I imagine you could sort out the time element."

I pushed the DELETE button, but erasing Walsh's voice from my answering machine could not erase the implication of what he was saying. Now I was even more anxious to talk to Dr. Moran.

He answered on the second ring. "Celia," he said, his voice as warm and reassuring as always, "you've been on my mind a lot lately. How is everything going?"

"Not that great, Doctor." I told him about Alex buying this house, about the vandalism, about Georgette's death, the phone calls, and the threatening way Detective Walsh was treating me.

His voice became increasingly grave as he asked questions. "Celia, you should tell Alex the truth," he said.

"I can't, not now, not yet, not until I can show him that what they say about me isn't true."

"Celia, there's a chance that detective will dig into your past and find out who you are. I think you should protect yourself. Is the lawyer still practicing who defended you when you were a child?"

"Benjamin Fletcher. I don't know. I didn't like him."

"But he got you acquitted. Get a directory and look him up."

The telephone books were in the cabinet under the phone. I pulled out the yellow pages. "He's listed here," I told Dr. Moran. "He practices in Chester. That's only twenty minutes away."

"Ceil, anything you tell him will be protected by attorney-client privilege. At the very least, he could recommend a suitable lawyer. Call him, and keep in touch."

"Yes, I will."

I called Kathleen next. When she answered, I could hear Martin in the background. "It's Celia," she called to him. I heard his response, and it chilled my blood.

"Her name is Liza," he said. "She made up the other name."

"Kathleen, does he tell that to people?"

"He's gotten so much worse. I never know what he's going to say. I'm at the end of my rope. I took him to a wonderful nursing home a mile away, but he cried like a baby. For a little while he was perfectly lucid and begged me to keep him home."

I could hear the despair in her voice. "Oh, Kathleen," I said. Then I insisted that she find a live-in aide and that I would gladly take care of the expense. Of course, I didn't talk to her about what was going on in my life. It was clear she had enough on her plate. But suppose Martin blurted out my story to someone, and that person talked to friends or wrote about it on an Internet chat room?

I took the only action open to me. I dialed Benjamin Fletcher and

made an appointment. Then I called Zach and asked if he was free
for another lesson at two o'clock. He agreed, and I rushed upstairs
to change into the breeches and riding jacket that I'd just bought.

I drove to the club, arriving there at ten of two. We went out on
the trail, and the riding expertise I had gained as a child became
second nature to me again. Zach was much quieter today, but obviously was in a good mood. On the way back to the stable, as we hit
the open field, he said, "Let's go," and began to canter. Biscuit immediately followed him, and we raced across the grass until we
pulled up at the barn.

We slid off the horses, and Zach's eyes were wary when he faced
me. "You've done a lot of riding," he said flatly.

"I told you my friend had a pony."

"Well, unless you want to waste your money, why don't we figure out how good you are and start your lessons from there."

"That would be fine, Zach," I said quickly.

"Ted, you admitted that Zach . . ."

Suddenly I was hearing my mother's voice screaming words I had
heard when I woke up that night.

What had Ted admitted to her? Trying not to let my face give me
away, I mumbled to Zach that I would call him, and then I went
straight to the car.

As I drove down Sheep Hill Road, I could see that something
must have happened at the corner house. There were squad cars
and media trucks parked in the driveway. I tried to take a right turn
onto Valley Road. It was closed to traffic, and I could see a mortu-
ary van at a break in the hedge. I kept going straight, not caring
where the road took me, because all I wanted to do was to get away
from the trappings of death.

It was quarter of four when I got home. Still dressed in my riding
outfit, I walked over to pick up Jack from his playdate, then strolled
home with him hand in hand.

We were barely inside and having a soda together in the kitchen
when the bell rang. Even before I opened the door, I knew that I
would be looking at Detective Paul Walsh.

This time he was accompanied not only by the prosecutor, but by two men introduced to me as Detectives Ortiz and Shelley.

There was something about the way they all stared at me as I stood there in my riding clothes that made me know that my appearance had startled them. As I would later learn, all four of them were mentally comparing me with the newspaper picture of my mother that they had found in Charley Hatch's breast pocket.

DRU Perry went to the courthouse late Tuesday morning to search through old records. At first she thought she was wasting her time. Liza Barton's adoption records were sealed. The record of Liza's trial was sealed. She'd wanted to see if there was any point in the *Star-Ledger* testing the public's "right to know" law.

"Forget it," she was told matter-of-factly by a clerk. "Juvenile and adoption cases don't come under that law."

Then, as she was leaving the courthouse, a grandmotherly woman who introduced herself as Ellen O'Brien caught her at the door. "I love your Story Behind the Story series in the *Star-Ledger*. Are you going to do one of them again soon?"

"I'd like to do one on the Liza Barton case," Dru admitted. "I thought I'd do some research here, but I'm hitting a stone wall."

"I've been at this courthouse thirty years, and I've seen a lot of cases, but nothing like that one," Ellen enthused.

Thirty years, Dru thought. That means she worked here when that case was going on. She noticed it was twelve o'clock. "By any chance, are you on your way to lunch?"

"Yes, I am. I'm just popping into the cafeteria."

"Then is it all right if I join you?"

Fifteen minutes later, over a Cobb salad, Ellen O'Brien was willingly sharing her recollections about what happened from the time Liza Barton was taken into custody. "They photographed and fingerprinted her. She was cool as a cucumber. Never once asked about her mother or stepfather. Then she was taken to the juvenile detention center and examined by a state psychiatrist."

Dru broke off a piece of roll. "I understand that Liza didn't say a word for the first several months she was in custody."

"That's right, except my friend who was an aide in the detention center said that Liza used to say the name 'Zach' sometimes, then start shaking her head and moving her body. Do you know what 'keening' is?"

"Yes. It's a lament for the dead, a kind of wailing," Dru said. "It's a word you see particularly in Irish history."

"That's exactly right. I'm Irish, and it's a word I remember my grandmother using. Anyhow, my friend says she overheard the psychiatrist describe Liza's emotions that way whenever she said that name."

Important, Dru thought. Very important. She made a single notation in her book: "Zach."

"It leaked out that she was profoundly depressed and on a suicide watch," Ellen continued. "When she was acquitted, the Division of Youth and Family Services tried to find her a home. Then some relatives showed up and adopted her. It was very hush-hush. They felt Liza's chance for a normal life meant burying the past."

"Has anybody any idea who they were?"

"From what I understand, there weren't any close relatives. Audrey and Will Barton were both only children. It's almost ironic. Audrey's ancestors settled here before the Revolutionary War. Liza's mother's maiden name was Sutton. But the family died out. So God knows how distant the cousin might have been who took her in."

Ellen took a final sip of iced tea. "The State of New Jersey calls," she announced. "I can't tell you what a pleasure it has been talking to you, Dru."

"I can't thank you enough, Ellen. Now, if you'll point me to where the marriage records are kept, I'll get back to work."

I'll trace Liza's ancestry back at least three generations, Dru thought. I'll collect the names of the people the Sutton family members married and trace their descendants to see if one of them has a thirty-four-year-old daughter. It's worth a shot.

I KNEW THAT I HAD TO TAKE a stand. I could not have these men come into my house and question me about the death of a woman I had met only once. These people from the prosecutor's office did not know I was Liza Barton. They were trying to tie me to Georgette's death only because I had not dialed 911 from Holland Road and because I had driven home so quickly.

Jack had followed me to the door, and now he slipped his hand in mine. My anger at what all this might be doing to him gave me the backbone to go on the attack.

"Mr. MacKingsley, will you please explain to me why Detective Walsh was following me around this morning?"

"Mrs. Nolan, I apologize for any inconvenience," MacKingsley said. "But the other day you showed me a photograph of the Barton family that was taped to the post in the barn. There were no fingerprints on it except yours, which, as you can understand, is unusual. You took it off the post, but someone had to have handled it first. We have not released this information publicly, but in Georgette Grove's shoulder bag we found a newspaper picture of you taken just as you fainted. That also had no fingerprints on it. Today we found a picture of Audrey Barton at another crime scene."

I almost blurted out, "A picture of my mother!" My nerves were just that raw. Instead I asked, "What has that got to do with me?"

"Mrs. Nolan, the landscaper for the house on Holland Road was shot to death a few hours ago. We have proof that he vandalized this property. He had a picture of Audrey Barton in his pocket. What I am trying to say is that Georgette Grove's murder and this homicide are somehow connected to this house."

"Did you know Charley Hatch, Mrs. Nolan?" Walsh asked.

"No, I did not. Why did you follow me to Bedminster?"

"Mrs. Nolan," Walsh said, "I believe you either left the Holland Road house, where you discovered the body of Georgette Grove, much earlier than you have admitted, or that you are so familiar with these roads you could make a number of confusing turns and still make that phone call to 911 at the time it was received."

Before I could respond, MacKingsley said, "Mrs. Nolan,

Georgette Grove sold this house to your husband. Charley Hatch vandalized it. You live in it. There's an obvious connection, and we are trying to solve two homicides. That is why we are here."

"Are you *sure* you never met Charley Hatch?" Walsh asked.

Anger put steel in my voice. "I never even *heard* of the man." I looked straight at Jeff MacKingsley. "I arrived here last week to find this house vandalized. I had an appointment to meet Georgette Grove and found her dead. I do not know what is going on, but I suggest that you try to find whoever is guilty of these crimes and leave me and my family alone."

I began to close the door. Walsh put his foot forward to block it. "One more question, Mrs. Nolan. Where were you between one thirty and two o'clock this afternoon?"

That one seemed easy to answer. "I had a two-o'clock riding lesson at the Washington Valley Riding Club. Why don't you clock the distance from here to there, Mr. Walsh? That way you can figure out all by yourself what time I left this house."

I slammed the door against his shoe, and as I turned the lock, a horrible possibility occurred to me. The police activity on Sheep Hill—could that have anything to do with the death of the landscaper? If so, I had placed myself directly in the area where he died.

ON TUESDAY afternoon at four o'clock Henry Paley returned to the realty office. "How did it go?" Robin asked.

"I think we have a sale. This is the third time the Muellers have looked at the house." Henry smiled and walked over to her desk. "Robin, did I tell you that you're looking quite provocative today? I don't think Georgette would have approved of that sweater, but then she wouldn't have approved of your boyfriend, would she?"

"Henry, I'm not very comfortable with this subject," Robin said.

"I'm sure you're not. I wonder if at the end, Georgette wasn't on to you, but maybe not. She certainly never got wind of the fact that you and Cartwright were seeing each other last year. If she had, you'd have been out on your ear."

"I knew Ted Cartwright before I started work here. I do not have a personal relationship with him. The fact that I knew him never undermined my loyalty to Georgette."

"Robin, you're the one who fielded phone inquiries about available properties. You're the one who handled the drop-ins. I admit that I haven't worked hard for a while, but you're something else."

The door opened. Startled, they looked up to see a grim-faced Sergeant Earley come into the office.

"I'm glad to catch you," he said. "You know Charley Hatch, the landscaper who took care of the Holland Road property?"

"I've seen him around," Paley answered.

"This afternoon, sometime between one thirty and two o'clock, he was shot to death while he was working."

Robin jumped up, her face pale. "Charley! That can't be!"

Both men stared at her. "Charley was my half brother," she wailed. "He *can't* be dead."

AT FIVE o'clock on Tuesday afternoon Zach Willet drove to the neighboring town of Madison and parked in front of the sales office of the Cartwright Town Houses Corporation. Inside, he found a sales clerk, a woman in her thirties, tidying up for the day. He noted the nameplate on her desk.

"Hi, Amy," Zach said. "I can see you're ready to skedaddle, so I won't take two minutes of your time."

On the walls were sketches of different models of the town houses. Zach walked from one to the other. Brochures on the table listed prices and sizes and particular features. He picked up one and read aloud. "Four-story town house, four bedrooms, master bedroom suite, state-of-the-art kitchen, three fireplaces, four baths, double garage, private patio and yard, all services." Zach smiled appreciatively. "Looks as though you just can't go wrong with that one." He pointed to the biggest picture. "Now, Amy, I know you're probably rushing out, but how about showing me that homestead?"

"I'll be glad to take you over, Mr. . . . ." Amy hesitated. "I don't think you introduced yourself."

"That's right. I didn't. I'm Zach Willet."

Amy opened her desk drawer and fished for her key ring. "That's Eight Pawnee Avenue. I have to warn you that is our top-of-the-line town house. It's fully loaded with every conceivable extra, and naturally that is reflected in the cost. It's also the furnished model."

"Sounds better and better. Let's take a look at it."

On the way through the development, Amy pointed out that the landscaping was scheduled to be featured in a national gardening magazine and that the driveways were heated to prevent ice in the winter. "Mr. Cartwright has thought of everything," she said.

"Ted's a good friend of mine," Zach said expansively. "Has been since we were kids riding bareback at the stable."

"Here we are at number eight," Amy said. "As you can see, it's a corner unit, and it really is the crown jewel of the development."

Zach's smile broadened as Amy opened the door and led him into the family room on the entry level. "Raised-hearth fireplace, wet bar—what's not to like?" he asked rhetorically.

"Some people use the room on the other side for a gym, and, of course, there's a full bath with a hot tub right beside it."

Zach insisted on riding the elevator to each of the floors. Like a child opening presents, he took pleasure in every detail. "Plate-warmer drawer! My, oh my, Amy. Two guest bedrooms!"

They rode back down in the elevator and went outside, and Zach said, "I'll take it. As is. Furnished."

"That's wonderful." Amy locked the front door. "Are you prepared to make a deposit now?"

"Didn't Ted Cartwright tell you he's giving me this unit?" Zach asked, his tone astonished. "I saved his life once, and Ted never forgets a favor. You must be proud to be in his employ."

ALEX called shortly after the prosecutor and his entourage left. He was at the airport in Chicago. "I'm going to have to go back tomorrow for a couple of days more," he said. "But I miss you guys and just want to get back for the night. Why don't you see if Sue is available to babysit, so you and I can go out for a late dinner in Morristown at the Grand Café?"

"Sounds great," I told him. "I'll call Sue right away."

I phoned Sue. She was free to come over. I gave Jack a ride on Star, then settled him in front of the television with a Muppet tape and went upstairs. In the bathroom that my father had designed for my mother, I luxuriated in her deep English tub, trying to wash away the bewildering events of the day.

How much should I tell Alex? Or should I just say nothing and try to have a stress-free evening with him? He has to go back to Chicago tomorrow morning. Maybe in the next few days they would solve these two crimes and the prosecutor's office would lose interest in me. I tried hard to believe that, because it was the only thing I could believe and stay sane.

When I got out of the tub, I put on a robe, fed Jack, bathed him, and put him to bed. Then I went to get changed.

I have a dark green silk shantung pantsuit that's dressy without being fussy. I decided to wear it tonight. While living in New York, Alex and I had gotten in the habit of going out a couple of times a week for a late dinner. Sometimes we'd go with friends, but more often it would be just the two of us.

The feeling of being a newlywed certainly has been erased since we moved in here last week, I thought. I decided to let my hair hang loose, knowing that Alex likes it that way. I clipped on my favorite emerald-and-gold earrings.

I hadn't heard Alex come in and didn't know he was there until I felt his arms around me. He laughed at my startled gasp, then turned me to him. His lips found mine, and I responded, eager for his embrace.

"I've missed you," he said. "Those stupid depositions are turning out to be endless. I simply had to get home overnight."

I smoothed his hair back. "I'm so glad you did."

Jack came running in. "You didn't say hello to me."

"I thought you were asleep." Alex scooped him up, so that now his strong arms were hugging both of us. It felt so good. It felt so right, and for a few hours I was able to pretend that it was.

Several people stopped by our table at the Grand Café. They

turned out to be friends of Alex's from the Peapack Riding Club. All of them offered their regrets about the vandalism. Alex's response was that we were thinking of giving the house its old name again, Knollcrest, and he promised each visitor, "When Ceil does her magic, we'll have the mother of all cocktail parties."

When we were alone at our table, he smiled and said, "You can't blame me for hoping."

That was when I told him about the prosecutor coming to the house and about Detective Walsh following me and telling me that there was something suspicious about the fact I made it home so quickly from Holland Road.

I watched as the muscles in Alex's face tightened. "Do you mean those people have nothing better to do than worry about the fact that you managed to get home quickly in a catatonic state?"

"It gets worse," I said, and told him about the murder of the landscaper. "Alex, I don't know what to do. I swear they're looking at me as though I was responsible for Georgette's death."

"Oh, Ceil, that's ridiculous," Alex protested, but then he saw that once again I was on the verge of breaking down. "Honey," he said, "I'm going to talk to that prosecutor tomorrow. He has some nerve to let his detectives follow you around. I'll be on his doorstep at nine o'clock. I'll go straight to the airport from there, but I'll call and tell you how it went."

On the one hand, I felt gratitude. My husband wants to fight my battles. On the other hand, what will Alex think when the next time Walsh or Jeff MacKingsley shows up, I refuse to answer their questions on the grounds that I might incriminate myself?

"Ceil, you have nothing to be concerned about. This is ridiculous." Alex reached across the table, but I pulled my hand away, fishing in my purse for my handkerchief.

"Maybe this isn't the best time for me to stop by, Celia. You seem to be upset."

I looked up at Marcella Williams. Her voice was kindly and soothing, but her eyes were alive with curiosity.

The man standing at her side was Ted Cartwright.

AT FOUR THIRTY ON TUESDAY afternoon Jeff MacKingsley had barely returned to his office when Sergeant Earley phoned to tell him that Robin Carpenter was Charley Hatch's half sister. "I've called a press conference for five o'clock," Jeff told him. "Ask her to come to my office at six. Or better yet, drive her over."

As he had expected, the press conference was confrontational. "The man who collected Charley Hatch's garbage claims that Sergeant Earley confiscated a bag from Hatch's trash and took out jeans and sneakers and figurines. Was Hatch a suspect in Georgette Grove's death?" the *New York Post* reporter asked.

Jeff cleared his throat. "Charley Hatch was shot sometime between one forty and two ten this afternoon. We believe his assailant was known to him and possibly had arranged to meet him. We believe the deaths of Charley Hatch and Georgette Grove were connected and may be linked to the Old Mill Lane vandalism. We are pursuing several leads and will keep you informed."

He made his way back to his office, aware that his frustration and irritation were landing squarely on Clyde Earley. I'll bet anything that he didn't wait to go through Charley Hatch's garbage until it was off the premises, he fumed. I'll bet Charley knew it had been disturbed and panicked.

And where does that sexy receptionist who claims to be Charley Hatch's half sister fit in the picture?

At six o'clock Robin Carpenter arrived at Jeff's office. Walsh, Ortiz, and Shelley sat in on the meeting.

"Ms. Carpenter, I'd like to extend my sympathy," Jeff said. "I'm sure your brother's death has been a shock."

"Thank you, Mr. MacKingsley, but I don't want to give the wrong impression. I am very sorry about Charley, but I never even knew he existed until a year ago."

Robin explained that at age seventeen her mother had given birth to a baby. In a private adoption, she had signed him over to a childless couple. "My mother's been dead for ten years. Then one day last year, Charley showed up on my father's doorstep. He had his birth certificate and pictures of himself in my mother's arms.

"In all honesty, Charley may be my half brother, but I didn't care for him. He was always whining. He complained that he had to pay too much to his wife when they were divorced. He said he hated landscaping and couldn't stand the people he worked for."

"Did you have much contact with him?" Jeff asked.

He'd call and ask me to have a cup of coffee with him. The divorce was fairly recent, and he was at loose ends."

"Ms. Carpenter, we have reason to believe Charley vandalized the house on Old Mill Lane."

"That's absolutely impossible," Robin protested. "Why would Charley do that?"

"That's exactly what we want to know," Jeff replied. "Did Charley ever come into your office to see you?"

"No, never."

"Would Georgette or Henry have had contact with him?"

"Possibly. I mean if Georgette had an exclusive listing on a property, she'd make sure it was kept up. But his name never came up."

"Then Henry Paley might have known Charley."

"Of course."

"When was the last time you spoke to your half brother?"

"It was at least three months ago."

"Where were you today between one forty and two ten?"

"In the office. You see, Henry was having lunch with Ted Cartwright. When he came back a little after one, I ran across the street to get a sandwich and bring it back in. Henry had an appointment at one thirty to take a client out."

"Did he keep that appointment?"

Robin hesitated, then said, "Yes, he did, but Mr. Mueller, the buyer, phoned to say he was delayed until two thirty."

"Then Henry was in the office with you until that time?"

Robin Carpenter's eyes moistened, and she bit her lip. "I can't believe that Charley is dead. Is that why . . . ?"

Jeff waited. "Ms. Carpenter, if you have any information that would assist this investigation, it is your obligation to reveal it."

Robin's composure broke. "Henry has been trying to blackmail me," she burst out. "Before I went to work for Georgette, I dated Ted Cartwright a few times. When I realized how much she despised him, I didn't mention it. Henry's been trying to twist everything to make it sound as if I was undermining Georgette. That wasn't true, but what is true is that Henry was not in the office from the time he left at one fifteen today until nearly four o'clock."

AT QUARTER of three Dru Perry received a call from Ken Sharkey telling her that Charley Hatch, the landscaper of the Holland Road house where Georgette Grove had been murdered, had been shot to death. Ken wanted Dru to attend the press conference Mac-Kingsley was sure to call.

Dru assured Ken she would wait around for the press conference, but she did not share the stunning information she had just uncovered. She had traced back three generations of Liza Barton's maternal ancestors. Liza's mother and grandmother had been only children. Her great-grandmother had three sisters. One never married. Another married and died without issue. The third married a man named William Kellogg.

Celia Foster Nolan's maiden name is Kellogg, Dru remembered. I think it was the guy from the *Post* who gave the background about her—that she had her own design business, Celia Kellogg Interiors.

Maybe the fact that her name is Kellogg is merely the wildest of coincidences, Dru thought. But Celia Nolan is exactly the right age to be the grown-up Liza Barton. Is it really a coincidence that Alex Nolan just happened to buy that house as a surprise? If he did, it has to mean that Celia never told him about her true background. My God, how shocked she must have been. Was she in such a frenzy about all that publicity that she would kill Georgette?

At the press conference, Dru was uncharacteristically silent. Later she went back to the office. On the Internet she found an article in *Architectural Digest* calling Celia Kellogg one of the most innovative new designers. It gave her background as the daughter of Martin and Kathleen Kellogg of Naples, Florida.

It's not time to call them yet, Dru decided. They're sure to deny that their adopted daughter is Liza Barton. The next thing to do is to get Liza's picture computer-aged; then I have to decide if I should share my suspicions with Jeff MacKingsley. Because if I'm right, Little Lizzie Borden is not only back, she's very possibly unhinged and on a killing spree. Her own lawyer said he wouldn't be surprised if someday she blew Ted Cartwright's brains out.

And I've got to find out who Zach is. If his name sent her into spasms of grief, maybe she has a grudge against him, too.

EVEN as Ted Cartwright was being introduced to me I was sure that seeing me was triggering something inside him. He could not take his eyes off my face, and I am certain that in looking at it, he was seeing my mother.

"It's very nice to meet you, Mrs. Nolan," he said.

His voice was jarring—hearty, resonant, commanding, confident, the same voice that rose to a jeer as he shoved my mother at me.

I looked up at him. I did not touch his extended hand, but neither did I want to raise questions by being overtly rude. I murmured, "How are you?" and turned back to Alex. Unaware of what was going on, Alex covered the awkward silence with polite conversation, telling me that Ted was a member of the Peapack Club and that they'd run into each other occasionally.

Of course, Marcella Williams could not leave without trying to find out why I had been dabbing at my eyes. "Celia, is there anything at all I can do to help you?" she asked.

"Perhaps minding your own business would be a start," I said.

Marcella's smile froze on her face. Before she could say anything, Ted took her arm and pulled her away.

I saw distress in Alex's face. "Ceil, what was *that* all about? There was no reason to be so rude."

"I think there was," I said. "We were having a private conversation. That woman couldn't wait to find out what is upsetting me."

"Ceil, I think Marcella was genuinely trying to be helpful. My God, she drove you home yesterday when she learned I had a time problem."

"You told me Zach saw you!"

My mother's voice was shouting in my mind. Hearing Ted's voice again had verified the flash of memory I had this past week. Now I had a few words more: *"You told me Zach saw you!"*

What did Zach see Ted do?

The day my father died, he had ridden ahead of Zach and then taken the wrong trail. At least that was the story Zach told me. But Zach also bragged that he was Ted's friend. Had Ted been riding that day? Did he have anything to do with my father's accident?

"Ceil, what is it?" Alex said. "You look as pale as a ghost."

I had literally felt the blood drain from my face. At least I could tell a half-truth. "Before Marcella barged over, I was about to tell you that I had been talking to my mother. She tells me my dad's Alzheimer's is worse."

"Oh, Ceil, I'm so sorry. Is there anything we can do?"

The "we" was so comforting to hear. "I've told Kathleen to hire a full-time aide. I told her I'd take care of it."

"Let me do that."

I shook my head as I thanked him. "That's not necessary, but I love you for wanting to help."

"Ceil, you have to know that I'd give you the world on a platter if you'd take it."

"I just want a tiny piece of the world," I said. "A nice, normal piece of it, with you and Jack."

Our check came, and we went home. Alex suggested that I take a sleeping pill, and I did.

It was nearly eight o'clock when I woke up. My first awareness was that sometime during my dreams I had heard the first part of what my mother screamed at Ted.

"You admitted it when you were drunk."

JEFF MACKINGSLEY WAS AT HIS desk at eight thirty on Wednesday morning. He had a sense that it was going to be a long day and not a good one. That was why, when Anna came in to tell him a Mr. Alex Nolan was at her desk, Jeff's instinct was to welcome the opportunity to talk with Celia Nolan's husband. On the other hand, he did not want to have a meeting after which he might be misquoted.

"Is Mort Shelley in his office?" he asked.

"He just went by with a container of coffee."

"Tell him to put it down and come in here at once; then send Mr. Nolan in. And if Paul Walsh stops at your desk, I don't want him to know Alex Nolan is here."

Barely a minute later Mort Shelley came in.

"Celia Nolan's husband is here, and I need a witness to the conversation," Jeff told him. "Don't take notes in front of him. I get the feeling that this is not going to be a friendly chat."

It was clear from the moment Alex Nolan entered the room that he was both angry and spoiling for a fight. He barely acknowledged the introduction to Shelley, then demanded, "Why is one of your detectives following my wife?"

Jeff admitted to himself that if he had been Celia Nolan's husband, he would have reacted exactly the same way.

"Mr. Nolan, please sit down and let me explain something," Jeff said. "Your new home was vandalized. The agent who sold it to you was murdered. We have evidence that a man who was shot yesterday committed the vandalism. I'm going to lay my cards on the table. You know, of course, that Liza Barton fatally shot her mother and wounded her stepfather in your house. There was a picture of the Barton family in your barn the day after you moved in."

"The one of them on the beach?" Alex asked.

"Yes. There were no fingerprints on it except those of your wife, who took it down and gave it to me."

"That's impossible," Alex Nolan protested. "Whoever put it up must have left fingerprints."

"That's exactly the point. That picture had been wiped clean of fingerprints. Georgette Grove had a picture in her shoulder bag of your wife fainting. It had been cut out of the *Star-Ledger.* It also had no fingerprints on it. Finally, Charley Hatch, the landscaper who was shot yesterday, had a picture of Audrey Barton in the pocket of his vest. Like the others, it had no fingerprints on it."

"I still fail to see what that has to do with my wife."

"It may not have anything to do with your wife, but it has everything to do with your house, and we have to find the connection. We know Mrs. Nolan had to have driven past the house on Sheep Hill Road where Charley Hatch was shot within the time frame of his death. We have checked at the Washington Valley Riding Club, where she arrived for a riding lesson at approximately eight minutes of two. She may have seen another car when she came down that road. She may have seen someone walking on it. Don't you think it's reasonable that we question her?"

"I am sure that Celia would want to cooperate in any way with your investigation," Alex Nolan said. "But I insist that you call off this Detective Walsh. I will not have her harassed and distressed. Celia has gone through a lot in the last several years."

Jeff noticed that Nolan's eyes softened when he spoke of his wife.

"Ceil told me about a beautiful house she had visited years ago, and it sounded just like this one. Should I have let her see it before I bought it? Of course. But I'm not here to second-guess myself. I'm here to make sure my wife is not bullied by people on your staff."

He got up and extended his hand. "Mr. MacKingsley, do I have your word that Detective Walsh will stay away from my wife?"

Jeff got up. "Yes, you do," he said. "I need to ask her about driving past the house where Charley Hatch died, but I'll do it myself."

"Do you consider my wife a suspect in these homicides?"

"Based upon the evidence we have now, I do not."

"In that case, I will advise my wife to talk with you."

"Thank you. That will be very helpful. I'll try to arrange a meeting for later today. Will you be around, Mr. Nolan?"

"Not for the next few days. I've been taking depositions in Chicago, and I'm going straight back there now."

After the door closed behind Nolan, Jeff looked at Mort Shelley. "What do you think?"

"I agree, I don't consider Celia Nolan a suspect. But I think there's something she hasn't told us yet. I swear, when she opened the door yesterday in those riding clothes, I thought for a minute she had posed for the picture we found in Charley Hatch's pocket."

"I had the same reaction," Jeff said. There was something about Celia Nolan that reminded him of Audrey Barton. And it was more than the fact that they were both beautiful women in riding clothes.

ON WEDNESDAY morning Ted Cartwright made a stop at the Cartwright Town Houses Corporation in Madison. Amy greeted him, smiling. "How are things at the North Pole, Santa Claus?"

"I don't know what that's supposed to mean," Cartwright said irritably, and I'm not interested in finding out. I've got a busy day."

"I'm sorry, Mr. Cartwright," Amy said apologetically. "It's just that I can't help thinking how few people would be so generous, even to someone who saved their life."

Cartwright had been about to go into his office but stopped suddenly. "What are you talking about?"

Amy swallowed nervously. "I'm so sorry," she said. "Mr. Willet didn't tell me that it was a secret you were giving him the model town house because he saved your life years ago."

"He saved my life, and I am giving him the model town house! Is that what Zach Willet told you?"

"Yes, and if it isn't true, we may have lost a sale. The couple from Basking Ridge called, and I told them it was sold."

Cartwright stared at Amy, his normally ruddy complexion draining of color, his eyes boring into her face.

"Mr. Willet phoned a little while ago. He intends to move in over the weekend," she went on. "I told him that since that unit is our furnished model, maybe he could wait until we're sold out, but he said that wouldn't be possible."

"I'll talk to Mr. Willet," Ted Cartwright said quietly. Then, unexpectedly, he smiled. "Amy, I have to tell you that for a minute I was just as taken in as you were. All this is Zach's idea of a joke. A lousy joke, I admit. We have been friends for many years. Last week we made a bet on the Yankees–Red Sox game. Our bet was a hundred bucks, but Zach threw in that if the difference in the score was over ten runs, I owed him a town house." Cartwright chuckled. "I guess Zach decided to test the waters. I'm sorry he wasted your time."

I DROPPED Jack off at school at eight fifteen. There was no way I was going to go into the coffee shop this morning, what with the possibility that Detective Walsh would be waiting there for me. Instead I drove directly to Chester. My appointment with Benjamin Fletcher was for nine o'clock.

There was the tang of fall in the clear, crisp air. At one minute of nine I climbed the steps to Fletcher's second-floor office. I walked into a small anteroom that held two vinyl armchairs. The table between them held a haphazard pile of dog-eared magazines.

"That's got to be Celia Nolan," a voice from the office yelled.

Just hearing that voice made me want to turn and run down the stairs. But I was too late. That giant of a man was filling the doorway, his hand extended, his smile as mirthless as I remembered it. "Always glad to help a pretty lady in trouble. Come on in."

There was nothing I could do except follow him into his cluttered private office. He settled himself behind his desk, beads of perspiration on his face even though the window was open. I believe his shirt was fresh, but with the sleeves rolled up and the top buttons opened, he looked like what I suspected he was, a retired lawyer who kept his shingle out because it gave him a place to go.

But he was not stupid. I could tell that the minute I reluctantly took the seat he offered me. "Celia Nolan of One Old Mill Lane in Mendham," he said. "That's a very exciting address."

"Yes, it is," I agreed.

"I read all about you. That's a lot going on in your life. Now, how did you hear about me and why are you here?"

Before I could attempt to answer, he raised his hand. "I charge three fifty an hour plus expenses and require a ten-thousand-dollar retainer before you get to say, 'Help me, counselor, for I have sinned.' "

I pulled out my checkbook and wrote the check. "I'm glad you looked me up," I said. "Then you'll understand how it feels to have the prosecutor's office practically accuse me of murdering Georgette Grove."

"Why would they even begin to think that?"

I told him about the three pictures without fingerprints, about how I had managed to drive home quickly after I found Georgette, and that I might have driven past the house on Sheep Hill Road around the time the landscaper was killed. "They think I'm involved in some way, and it's all because of that house my husband bought."

"Surely you must know the history of it by now."

"Of course. My point is that because of those three pictures, the prosecutor's office feels all this has to do with the Barton family." I don't know how I managed to say my surname so matter-of-factly.

And then he said something that chilled me to the bone. "I always thought that kid, Liza, would come back here someday and shoot her stepfather. But it's crazy that those birds in the prosecutor's office are bothering a stranger who had the hard luck to get that house as a birthday present. Celia, I promise you, we'll take care of them, because you know what will happen? You start answering their questions, and they'll confuse you so much that *you'll* believe you killed those people because you didn't like the house."

"Do you mean I shouldn't answer questions?" I asked.

"That's exactly what I mean. I know that Paul Walsh. He's out to make a name for himself. Now, if he or Jeff MacKingsley or anyone else in that crowd tries to question you, send them to me. I'll take good care of you."

LENA Santini, the divorced wife of the late Charley Hatch, agreed to speak to Angelo Ortiz at eleven o'clock in Charley's home in Mendham. A small, thin woman with flaming red hair, she seemed genuinely sorry about his death. "I can't believe anyone would shoot him. Doesn't make sense. He never hurt anybody."

They were sitting in the living room. Lena took a puff of her cigarette. "Look at this place," she said with a dismissive wave of her hand. "It's so messy it makes my skin crawl. That's the way it was when I was living with Charley. And he'd complain. Let me tell you, he was a prizewinner in the complaint department. I finally couldn't take it anymore, and we split a year ago."

Lena's face softened. "But you know, those figures he carved were really beautiful. I used to tell him he should start selling them, but of course he wouldn't listen. He only felt like carving them once in a while. Oh well, God rest him." A brief smile appeared and then disappeared on her lips.

Ortiz, perched on the edge of Charley's lounge chair, had been listening sympathetically. Now he moved into the questioning. "Did you see much of Charley since you've been divorced?"

"Not much. Every once in a while he'd give me a call."

"Was he close to his half sister, Robin Carpenter?"

"That one!" Lena raised her eyes to the ceiling. "That was another thing. The people who adopted Charley were real nice folks. When the mother was dying, she told Charley his real name. I guess he hoped his birth family would turn out to be worth a lot of money. Boy, was he disappointed. But he met his half sister, Robin, and ever since then, she's been playing him like a fiddle."

Ortiz tensed. "Then they saw each other regularly?"

"Did they ever! 'Charley, can you drive me into the city? Charley, would you mind taking my car to be serviced?' "

"Did she pay him?"

"No, but she made him feel important. You've met her, I guess. She's the kind that guys look at. Anyhow, she used to take Charley out for dinner in New York sometimes. She didn't want to be seen with him around here, because she's got a rich boyfriend. Oh, and get this. Charley had the keys to the houses of people who were away, so Robin had the nerve to ask him to let her use those houses when she was with her boyfriend. Can you imagine?"

"Ms. Santini, we have reason to believe that Charley committed the vandalism on Old Mill Lane."

"You've got to be kidding. Charley would never do that."

"Would he do it if he was paid to do it?"

"Who would ask him to do a crazy thing like that?" Lena Santini crushed the butt of her cigarette in the ashtray. "Come to think of it, the only person I know who could get Charley to do a stupid trick like that is Robin."

"Robin Carpenter told us that she has not been in touch with Charley for three months."

"Then why did she have dinner with him in New York recently at Patsy's Restaurant on West Fifty-sixth Street?"

"Do you happen to remember the exact date?"

"It was Saturday of Labor Day weekend. I remember because it was Charley's birthday, and I called and offered to buy him dinner. He told me Robin was taking him out to Patsy's."

Lena's eyes suddenly glistened. "If that's all you want to ask me, I have to go. This morning I asked you to meet me here because I wanted to get a couple of Charley's carvings to put in the casket, but they're all gone."

"We have them," Ortiz told her. "Unfortunately, since these items are evidence, we have to keep them."

DETECTIVE Mort Shelley walked into the Grove Real Estate Agency with the late Georgette Grove's scrapbook under his arm. Everyone on the investigative team had gone through the book and found not one newspaper clipping that might be tied to Georgette having suddenly recognized someone. But, Shelley thought, returning it gives me good reason to have another chat with Robin and Henry.

Robin was at her desk and looked up on hearing the door open. Her professional smile vanished.

"Thanks for lending the scrapbook," Mort said mildly.

"I hope it was useful," Robin said. She dropped her eyes to the papers on her desk.

With the air of a man who has nothing to do, Mort sat down on the sectional sofa that faced Robin's desk.

Clearly annoyed, she looked up. "If you have a question, I'll be glad to answer it, Mr. . . . I'm sorry, but I've forgotten your name."

"Shelley. Like the poet. Mort Shelley."

"Mr. Shelley, I went to the prosecutor's office yesterday. I can't add a single word to what I said, and while this agency is still functioning, I have a job to do."

"And so do I, Ms. Carpenter. Have you had lunch yet?"

"No. I'll wait till Henry returns. He's out with a client."

"Now, suppose he didn't come back till, let's say, four o'clock. Would you have something sent in?"

"No. I'd put the sign with the clock on the door and run across the street and grab something."

"Isn't that what you did yesterday, Ms. Carpenter?"

"I already told you that I brought my lunch in yesterday."

"Yes, but you *didn't* tell us that you put that sign on the door sometime before two o'clock, did you? That elderly lady in the curtain shop down the street noticed that sign at two oh five."

"Oh, I see what you're getting at. I had a headache. I ran to the drugstore to get aspirin. I was in and out in a few minutes."

"Uh-huh. On another subject, my partner was talking to your exhalf-sister-in-law a little while ago."

"Lena?"

"That's right. Now, you told us you hadn't talked to Charley in three months. Lena says you had dinner with him in New York less than two weeks ago. Who's right?"

"I am. About three months ago he happened to phone when my car wouldn't start. I was meeting a friend in New York at Patsy's, and he drove me in. That night he said he wanted me to take him there for his birthday, and I jokingly said, 'It's a date.' Then I left a message on his phone saying it wouldn't work out. The poor guy thought I was serious about going."

"Are you involved with any particular man at this time?"

"No, I am not. As I told all of you yesterday, Ted Cartwright is just a friend. We dated a few times. Period."

"Ms. Carpenter, your half brother's former wife tells us that you asked Charley to allow you and your rich boyfriend to stay overnight in houses he was looking after. Is that true?"

Robin Carpenter stood up. "That does it, Mr. Shelley. Tell Mr. MacKingsley that if he or any of his lackeys want to ask more questions, they can contact my lawyer."

DRU Perry had a friend, Kit Logan, whose son Bob was a New Jersey state trooper, working in the computer lab. On Wednesday morning she called Kit, exchanged pleasantries, then asked for Bob's phone number. She caught Bob on his way to work.

"Sure, I can use the computer to age a picture for you, Dru," he promised. "If you drop it in my mailbox today, I'll have it for you tomorrow night. Get the clearest picture you can find."

Dru mulled that over as she spread marmalade on whole wheat toast and sipped coffee. The news photographs reprinted after the vandalism had been mostly of Liza with her mother and father. None of them, however, had been particularly clear. She considered how to go about getting access to other photos, then got an idea.

At nine o'clock she phoned Marcella Williams. "Mrs. Williams, this is Dru Perry of the *Star-Ledger.* I write a feature called The Story Behind the Story for the Sunday edition—"

"I know that feature. I always look forward to reading it," Marcella interrupted.

"I'm preparing one on Liza Barton. You knew the family intimately, and I wonder if I could come interview you."

"I'd be delighted to be interviewed by a fine writer like you."

"Do you happen to have any pictures of the Bartons?"

"Yes, of course I do. When Audrey married Ted, I took a slew of pictures, but I have to warn you, there isn't a single one where you'll see Liza smiling."

This is my lucky day, Dru thought. "Would eleven o'clock be convenient for you, Mrs. Williams?"

"Perfect. And please, call me Marcella, Dru."

"How nice. Marcella, will you just think and try to remember if Audrey or Will Barton had a friend named Zach?"

"Oh, I know who Zach is. He's the riding instructor Will had at Washington Valley stables. The day he died, Will rode out ahead of

Zach and got on the wrong trail. That's why he had that accident."

That fatal accident, Dru thought. Was it Zach's fault that Will Barton died? Had he been careless to let Barton ride off without him? And if Barton's death was not an accident, when·did Liza learn the truth about it?

AT ONE o'clock Ted Cartwright rounded the corner of the Washington Valley Club House and headed to the stable. "Is Zach around?" he asked Manny Pagan.

Manny, one of the grooms, was brushing a skittish mare. "Easy, easy, girl," he was muttering soothingly.

"Is Zach around?" Cartwright shouted. "Are you deaf?"

An annoyed Manny was about to snap, "Find him yourself," but when he looked up, he realized that Cartwright, whom he knew by sight, was trembling with fury. "He's eating his lunch at the picnic table." He pointed to a grove of trees about a hundred yards away.

Ted Cartwright covered the ground with rapid strides. Zach was eating a baloney sandwich. Ted sat down opposite him. "Who do you think you are?" he asked, his voice now a menacing whisper.

Zach took another bite of the sandwich and a swig of soda. "Now that's no way for a friend to talk to a friend," he said mildly.

"What makes you think you can go over to my town houses and tell my sales rep I'm giving you the model unit?"

"Did she tell you that I'm planning to move in over the weekend?" Zach asked. "I tell you, Ted, that place where I'm living has turned out to be sheer hell. The landlady's kids are having parties every night, playing the drums till I think my ears are gonna bust, and here you have that nice place, and I know you want me to have it."

"I'll call the police if you try to set one *foot* inside it."

"Now, why do I think that won't happen?" Zach asked.

"Zach, you've been bleeding me for twenty-seven years. You've got to stop, or you won't be around to bleed me anymore."

"Ted, that constitutes a threat, and I'm sure you don't mean it. Maybe I should be going to the police. The way I look at it, I've been keeping you out of prison all these years."

"There is also a penalty for blackmail," Cartwright spat out.

"Ted, that town house is a drop in the bucket to you, but it would be a comfort to me. And then there's the matter of my conscience. Suppose I were to wander down to the Mendham police station and say that I knew about an accident that wasn't an accident at all and that I have proof? I'd have guaranteed immunity."

Ted stood up. The veins in his temples were bulging. His hands gripped the table. "Be careful, Zach. Be very careful." His words were clipped and sharp as a dagger.

"I am being careful," Zach assured him cheerfully. "That's why, if anything happens to me, the proof of what I'm saying will be found immediately. Well, gotta get back. I have a lady coming in for a riding lesson. She lives in your old house—the one where you were shot. She's real interested in that accident you and I know about."

"Have you been talking to her about it?"

"Oh, sure. Everything but the good stuff. Think it over, Ted. Maybe you'll want your sales rep to have the refrigerator stocked when I move in on Saturday. That would be a nice welcoming gesture, don't you think?"

AT TWO o'clock on Wednesday afternoon Paul Walsh, Angelo Ortiz, and Mort Shelley gathered in Jeff MacKingsley's office to review their findings in what the media was now calling the "Little Lizzie Homicides." Ortiz started with his report. He gave them a quick rundown of his interview with Lena Santini.

"You mean Carpenter's story yesterday was a bold-faced lie?" Jeff asked. "How stupid does she think we are?"

"I saw Carpenter this morning," Shelley said. "She explained away the so-called birthday date by saying it was his idea, and she left a message for him that it wouldn't happen. She absolutely denies being in Patsy's that night."

"Let's get pictures of Carpenter and Hatch and show them to the maitre d', the bartender, and all the waiters at Patsy's," Jeff said. "We'll subpoena her credit cards and E-ZPass as well. Either Carpenter or the ex-wife is lying. Let's find out which it is."

"Jeff, I understand that you're planning to see Celia Nolan to-day," Paul Walsh said.

"I'm not seeing her," Jeff said shortly. "When I called, she referred me to her lawyer, Benjamin Fletcher."

"Benjamin Fletcher!" Shelley exclaimed. "He was Little Lizzie's lawyer! Why on earth would Celia Nolan go to him?"

"He got her off before, didn't he?" Walsh asked quietly.

"Got who off?"

"Liza Barton, who else?" Walsh asked.

Jeff, Mort, and Angelo stared at him. Enjoying the astonishment on their faces, Walsh smiled. "I lay odds with you that the deranged ten-year-old who shot her mother and stepfather has now resurfaced as Celia Nolan, a woman who flipped when she found herself back in home sweet home."

"You're crazy," Jeff snapped. "And you're the reason she got a lawyer. She'd have cooperated if you hadn't been in her face."

"I have taken the time to look up Celia Nolan's background. She is adopted. She is thirty-four years old, exactly Liza Barton's present age. We all felt the impact of seeing her in those riding clothes yesterday, and I'll tell you why: Audrey Barton was her mother."

Jeff sat silently, not wanting to believe what he was beginning to believe—that perhaps Walsh was onto something.

"After I saw Celia Nolan in riding clothes, I made a few inquiries. She's taking lessons at the Washington Valley Riding Club. Her teacher, Zach Willet, was giving Will Barton riding lessons at the time of his death from a fall with his horse," Walsh continued, barely able to conceal his satisfaction at the impact he was making.

"If Celia Nolan is Liza Barton, do you think she holds Zach Willet responsible?" Mort asked quietly.

"Let me put it this way: If I were Zach Willet, I wouldn't want to be alone with that lady for long," Walsh answered.

"Your theory, Paul, completely overlooks the fact that Charley Hatch vandalized the house," Jeff told him. "Are you suggesting that Celia Nolan knew Hatch?"

"No, I am not, and I accept the fact that she never met Georgette before she moved into the house. I do say that she became unbalanced when she saw the writing on the lawn and the splattered paint. She wanted revenge on the people who put her in that position. She found Georgette's body. If she is Liza Barton, there's an explanation for why she knew her way home. Her grandmother lived only a few streets away from Holland Road. She admits that she was driving past in the time frame when Hatch was killed."

"How would she have found out he vandalized the house?" Ortiz asked.

"The garbageman was talking about Clyde Earley taking Hatch's sneakers and jeans and carvings out of the trash."

"Are you suggesting," Jeff said, "that Celia Nolan, even if she is Liza Barton, happened to hear the gossip of a garbageman, figured out where Charley Hatch was working, got him standing at the hedge, shot him, and then went off to have a riding lesson?"

"She put herself on that road at the right time," Walsh insisted stubbornly.

"Paul, you want to pin everything on Celia Nolan, and I agree that it will make a great story. But someone else hired Charley Hatch. I don't for a minute believe Earley's story. I bet Clyde went through that garbage when it was on Hatch's property. I wouldn't be surprised if he took it and Hatch knew it was gone. Then Earley could put it back in the trash and wait to have a witness see him open it after it's been abandoned. If Hatch panicked, whoever hired him may have panicked. And my guess is that Georgette Grove learned who ordered the vandalism and paid for it with her life."

"Jeff, you'd have made a great defense lawyer. Celia Nolan is very attractive, isn't she? I've noticed the way you look at her." When he saw the prosecutor's icy stare, Walsh realized he had gone too far. "Sorry," he mumbled. "But I stand by my theory."

"When this case is over, I am sure you'll be happier reassigned to another division in the office," Jeff said. "You're a smart man, Paul, and you could be a good detective, except for one thing—you don't keep an open mind, and frankly, I'm sick and tired of it. Here is what we're going to do now.

"We should be getting Charley Hatch's phone records later today. Mort, prepare an affidavit for the judge to get the phone records of Carpenter, Paley, and Cartwright—I think we have sufficient grounds. I also want Carpenter's and Hatch's credit card bills and E-ZPass statements. And I am going to petition the Family Court to allow us to unseal the adoption records of Liza Barton." Jeff looked at Walsh. "I will lay you odds that even if Celia Nolan is Liza Barton, someone is trying to trap her into being accused of committing these murders."

WHEN I left Benjamin Fletcher's office, I drove around aimlessly for a while, trying to decide if I should have gone to him at all. I told myself that I now reasonably could say to Alex that since everything that happened seems connected to the Liza Barton case, I went to Liza Barton's lawyer for help.

I knew that eventually I would have to tell Alex the truth about myself—and risk losing him—but I didn't want to do it yet. If only I could remember what my mother shouted at Ted that night, I would have the key to why he threw her at me.

Zach was the key. All these years I had never considered my father's death anything but an accident. But now, as I try to piece together my mother's final words, I can't find the missing ones:

"You admitted it when you were drunk. . . . Zach saw you . . ."

What did Ted tell my mother? And what did Zach see?

It was only ten o'clock. I called the Morris County *Daily Record* and was told that all back issues were on microfilm in the county library on Randolph Street. At ten thirty I was in the reference room, requesting the microfilm that included May 9, the day my father died, twenty-seven years ago.

Of course, the minute I read the May 9 edition, I realized that any account of my father's death would be printed the next day. I glanced through it anyhow and noticed that twenty collectors were competing in an antique-gun marksmanship contest scheduled at noon, including Ted Cartwright. I looked at the picture of Ted, in his late thirties then, his hair still dark, a devil-may-care look about him. He was holding in his hand the gun he planned to use.

I moved the microfilm to the next day. On the front page I found the story about my father. His picture was exactly as I remember him—the thoughtful eyes that always held a hint of a smile, the aristocratic nose and mouth, the dark blond hair. The account of his accident was what Zach Willet had told me. The consensus of opinion was that something may have frightened the horse and that "Barton, an inexperienced rider, was unable to control him."

Then I read the sentence that seemed to explode before my eyes: "A groom, Herbert West, who was exercising a horse on a nearby trail, reported hearing a loud noise that sounded like a gunshot at the time Mr. Barton would have been near the fork that led to the treacherous slope."

I moved the microfilm to the sports pages of that day's edition. Ted Cartwright was holding a trophy in one hand and an old Colt .22 target pistol in the other. He had won the contest, and the article said he was going to celebrate by having lunch at the Peapack Club with friends and then going for a long horseback ride.

My father died at three o'clock—plenty of time for Ted to have had lunch and gone out for a ride along the trail to the Washington Valley trails. Was it possible he came upon my father, the man who had taken my mother from him?

The only way I could learn the truth was from Zach.

I printed out the articles. It was time to pick up Jack. I left the library and drove to St. Joe's.

I could tell by Jack's woebegone face that the morning hadn't gone well. He didn't want to talk about it, but by the time we got home and were having lunch, he opened up.

"One of the kids in my class said that I live in a house where a kid shot her mother. Is that right, Mom?" he asked.

I took a deep breath. "From what I understand, one night someone tried to hurt that girl's mother, and so she tried to save her."

"If someone tried to hurt you, I'd save you," Jack promised.

"I know you would, sweetheart. So if your friend talks about that little girl again, say she was very brave. She couldn't save her mother, but that was what she was trying so hard to do."

"Mommy, don't cry."

"I don't want to, Jack. I just feel sorry for that little girl."

"I'm sorry for her, too," Jack decided.

I told him that if it was okay with him, Sue was going to come over, and I'd go for another riding lesson. I saw a shadow of doubt across his face. "Sue is teaching you to ride, and I'm taking lessons so I can keep up with you."

That helped, but then Jack came around and lifted his arms to me. "Can I sit on your lap for a little while?" he asked.

"You bet." I picked him up and hugged him. "Who thinks you're a perfect little boy?" I asked him.

This was a game we played. I saw a hint of a smile. "You do."

"Who loves you to pieces?"

"You do, Mommy."

"You're so smart. I can't believe how smart you are."

Now he was laughing. "I love you, Mommy."

My little boy fell asleep in my arms, just a nap for about twenty minutes. I wondered if I gave him the same sense of security my father had given me that day the wave crashed us to shore. I prayed to learn the truth about my father's death. I thought of my mother at my father's funeral, wailing, "I want my husband!"

You admitted it when you were drunk. You killed my husband. You told me Zach saw you do it.

That was what my mother had screamed that night! I was as certain of it as I was that my little boy was in my arms. For a long time I sat quietly, absorbing the import of those words.

When Sue arrived, I left for my riding lesson with Zach Willet.

MARCELLA Williams had a stack of pictures that she thought might interest Dru Perry. "After Liza went on her shooting spree," she explained, "I got them together and gave some to the media."

I'll just bet you did, Dru thought. But as she went through them, she could barely hide her emotions from Marcella's inquisitive eyes.

I'll do computer-aging, she thought, but I think I know the result. Celia Nolan is Liza Barton. She looks like both her parents.

"Marcella, did you ever meet this Zach guy, the one who gave Will Barton riding lessons?"

"No. Audrey was furious when she heard that Will had been taking lessons from him without her knowledge, but Will wanted to learn to ride so that he could keep his wife company."

"Do you know if Audrey blamed Zach for the accident?"

"She really couldn't. Everyone at the stable told her that Will insisted on starting out alone, despite Zach's asking him to wait."

Marcella's phone rang just as Dru got up to go. Marcella rushed to answer it, and it was clear that it was disappointing news.

"That's the way it goes," she told Dru. "My lunch date was with Ted Cartwright, but now he has to see someone on an urgent matter. Maybe it's just as well. Ted is in one of his ugly moods, and that is not the time to be around him."

After Dru left, she drove to the county library. She submitted her request for *Daily Record* microfilm, including the day after Will Barton's death. The reference librarian smiled. "That day is mighty popular this morning. I released that same segment an hour ago."

Celia Nolan, Dru thought. If she's been talking to Zach Willet, she may suspect something about the accident. "I wonder if that could have been my friend Celia Nolan," she asked. "We're both working on the same project."

"Why, yes it is. She did several printouts."

Several, Dru thought. I wonder why several.

Five minutes later she was printing out the account of Will Barton's death. Then she kept going until she found the sports section, and, like Celia Nolan, reasoned that Ted Cartwright might very well have been in the vicinity at the time of Will Barton's accident.

Desperately troubled by what Celia's state of mind might be, Dru made one more stop, this one at the police station in Mendham.

Sergeant Clyde Earley was on duty and was delighted to be interviewed by her about the Little Lizzie case.

"I bet that night is still clear in your mind," she mused.

"You bet it is, Dru. I can still see that kid sitting in my squad car, thanking me for the blanket I wrapped around her."

"You drove off with her, didn't you? Where did you take her?"

"Right here. I fingerprinted her and took her picture."

"Do you still have her fingerprints?"

"Once a juvenile is cleared of any wrongdoing, we're supposed to destroy them."

"Did you destroy Liza's fingerprints, Clyde?"

He winked. "Off the record, no. I kept them in the file, sort of like souvenirs."

Dru thought of the way Celia Nolan had tried to run from the photographers that first day she'd met her. She felt sorry for her but knew she had to finish her investigation.

"Clyde, there's something you have to do," she said. "Get Liza's fingerprints to Jeff MacKingsley right away. I think Liza has come back and may be taking revenge on the people who hurt her."

I SENSED that there was something different about Zach Willet when I met him at the stable. He seemed somewhat tense, guarded. I knew he was trying to figure me out, but I didn't want him to become wary. I had to get him to talk.

He helped me tack the horse up; then we walked the horses to the spot where the trails begin to snake through the woods. "Let's take the trail to the fork where Will Barton had his accident," I said.

"You sure are interested in that accident," he commented.

"I've been reading up on it. It was interesting that a groom heard a shot. Is Herbert West still around?"

"He's a starter at Monmouth Park Racetrack now."

"Zach, how far were you behind Will Barton that day? Three minutes? Five minutes?"

Zach and I were traveling side by side. A strong breeze had blown the clouds away, and now it was sunny and cool, a perfect afternoon for a ride. The trees were showing the first sign of fall under a vivid blue sky.

"I'd say I was about five minutes behind him," Zach answered, "And, young lady, I think we better have a showdown. Why all the questions about that accident?"

"Let's discuss it at the fork," I suggested. Making no further effort to conceal my ease on horseback, I pressed my legs against my horse's sides, and he broke into a canter. Six minutes later we drew rein at the fork.

"You see, Zach," I said, "we left the stable at ten after two. It's two nineteen now, and part of the time we've been going at a pretty good pace. So you really couldn't have been only five minutes behind Will Barton, could you?"

I saw the way his mouth tightened.

"Zach, I'm going to level with you," I began.

Of course, I was only going to level with him up to a point. "My grandmother's sister was Will Barton's mother. She went to her grave sure that there was more to his death than was reported. That gunshot would have scared a horse, wouldn't it? I mean, I wonder if you might have seen Will Barton galloping down that trail on a horse you knew you couldn't stop. And maybe you saw the man who fired the gun. And maybe that man was Ted Cartwright."

"I don't know what you're talking about," Zach said.

"Zach, you told me you're a good friend of Cartwright. I can understand you'd be reluctant to get him in trouble. But Will Barton should not have died. Our family is comfortable. I've been authorized to pay you one million dollars if you will go to the police. The only thing that you did wrong was to lie to them about what happened, and I really doubt they could charge you after so many years. You'd be a hero, a man with a conscience, trying to right a wrong."

"Did you say one million dollars?"

"Cash. Wired to your bank."

Zach's thin lips narrowed. "Is there a bonus if I tell the cops that I saw Cartwright charge his horse at Barton's, forcing it up that trail, and then fire the shot?"

I felt my heart begin to pound. "There'll be a ten percent bonus, an extra hundred thousand dollars. Is that the way it happened?"

"That's the way it happened, all right. Cartwright had his old Colt pistol. That takes a special bullet. The second he fired it, he turned and went back on the trail that connects to Peapack."

"What did you do?"

"I heard Barton yell when he went over the edge. I knew he didn't have a chance. I guess I was pretty shocked. I just rode around as if I was looking for him. Eventually somebody spotted the body in the ravine. In the meantime, I had gotten a camera and gone back to the fork in the trail. I wanted to protect myself. I'd grabbed a copy of the newspaper that contained a picture of Ted holding the Colt he was planning to use in a marksmanship contest. I photographed that picture next to the bullet he'd fired, then pried it out of the tree trunk with my hoof pick. I found the casing, too. Then I walked onto the trail and took a picture of the scene below."

"Will you show me those pictures? Do you still have the casing and the bullet?"

"I'll show you the photos. But I keep them until I get the money. And yes, I also have the bullet and the casing."

I don't know why I asked this next question, but I did. "Zach, is money the only reason you're telling me this?"

"Mostly," he said, "I'm kind of sick of Ted Cartwright getting away with murder and then threatening me."

"When can I get this proof you're talking about?"

"Tonight, when I go home."

"If my babysitter is free, can I get it about nine o'clock?"

"That's okay with me. I'll give you my address."

We rode to the stable in silence. Zach's cell phone rang as we were dismounting. He answered, then winked at me. "Hello," he said. "Oh, the town house is worth seven hundred thousand, so you'll give me the money? You're too late. I've had a better offer. Good-bye."

Zach scrawled his address on the back of an envelope. "See you around nine. The house number is kind of hard to read from the street, but you can tell it by the drums banging."

"I'll find it," I said.

I left knowing that if Ted Cartwright ever went to trial, his lawyer would argue that Zach's testimony had been paid for. But how could they refute physical evidence that Zach had kept all these years? And how different was this from what the police do all the time—post rewards for evidence?

I was just offering a lot more than they do.

AT FOUR o'clock Sergeant Clyde Earley and Dru Perry were waiting outside Jeff MacKingsley's office. "I don't know if he's going to like the fact that you're with me," Clyde groused.

"Listen, Clyde, I'm a newspaperwoman. This is my story. I'm going to protect my exclusive."

Anna was at her desk. "Hope you're bringing good news," she told Clyde in a friendly tone. "He's in one horrible mood today."

As she watched Clyde's shoulders slump, her intercom went on. "Send them in," Jeff said.

"Let me talk first," Dru murmured to Clyde as he held the door to Jeff's office open for her.

"Dru, Clyde," Jeff greeted them. "What can I do for you?"

"Jeff," Dru said, "what I have to tell you is very important, and I need to have your word that there'll be no leak to the press. I am the press in this story, and I'm bringing it to you because I'm worried that another life may be in danger."

Jeff leaned forward, his arms crossed on his desk. "Go on."

"I think Celia Nolan is Liza Barton, and thanks to Clyde, you may be able to prove it."

Seeing the grave look on Jeff's face, Dru realized two things: Jeff had been aware of the possibility, and he would not be happy to have it verified. She took out the pictures of Liza that she had taken from Marcella Williams. "I was going to have these computer-aged," she said. "But I don't think it's necessary. Look at them and then think of Celia Nolan. She's a combination of her mother and father."

Jeff laid the pictures out on his desk and turned to Clyde. "Why are you here?"

"Well, you see—"

"Jeff," Dru interrupted, "Clyde is here because Celia Nolan already may have killed two people, and she may be gunning for the man responsible for her father's accident. Clyde booked Liza the night she killed her mother."

"I kept her fingerprints," Clyde Earley said bluntly. "I have them with me now. You can find out fast if Celia Nolan is Liza Barton."

"Jeff," Dru said, "if Celia is Liza, she may be out for revenge. I interviewed the lawyer who defended her twenty-four years ago, and he told me he wouldn't be surprised if someday she blew Ted Cartwright's head off. And a court clerk told me that she had heard that when Liza was in the juvenile detention center, still in shock, she would say the name Zach and then go into spasms of grief. Take a look at these articles from the library. Maybe they show why that happened. I phoned Washington Valley this afternoon to speak to Zach. They told me he was giving Celia Nolan a riding lesson."

"All right. Thank you," Jeff said. "Clyde, you know what I think of your habit of ignoring the law to suit your purposes, but Dru, it's your story. You have my word."

When they were gone, Jeff sat for long minutes at his desk, studying the pictures of Liza Barton. She's Celia, he thought. We can make sure by checking her fingerprints against the ones on the picture in the barn. I can never use the old ones in court, but at least I'll know who I'm dealing with.

The picture in the barn.

Deep in thought, Jeff was now gazing blankly at the photos that were on his desk. Was this what he had been missing?

In Criminology 101 they tell us that the motive for most homicides is either love or money, he thought.

He turned on the intercom. "Send Mort Shelley in."

When Shelley came in, Jeff said, "Drop whatever you're doing. There's someone I want checked out from top to bottom." He showed Mort a name he had written on his notepad.

Shelley's eyes widened. "You think?"

"I don't know what I think yet, but put as many of our people on it as you need. I want to know when this guy cut his first tooth and which one it was."

As Mort Shelley got up, Jeff handed him the copies of the newspaper stories. "Give these to Anna, please." He turned on the intercom. "Anna, there was a death at the Washington Valley Riding Club twenty-seven years ago. I want the complete file on the investigation. You'll get the details from the papers Mort is giving you. Also call that club and see if you can get Zach Willet on the phone."

WHEN I got home from the stable, the barn was empty, and Jack and Sue were gone. She was evidently taking him for a walk around the neighborhood on Star, and that was fine with me. I called my accountant to be sure that I had at least one million one hundred thousand dollars at the ready in my account at the brokerage house.

"It's your money, Celia," Larry's investment counselor said. "But I must warn you, wealthy as you are, that's a very tidy sum."

"I would pay ten times that to accomplish what I am hoping to with that money," I said.

And it was true. If Zach Willet had the proof he claimed to have and if Ted went on trial, I would happily take the witness stand and testify to those final words my mother screamed at Ted. And for the first time the world would hear *my* version of what happened.

Alex phoned at dinnertime. He was staying at the Ritz-Carlton in Chicago, his favorite hotel there. "Ceil, I'm definitely going to be stuck here till Friday afternoon, but I was thinking, do you want to go into New York this weekend? We could see a couple of plays? Maybe your babysitter would mind Jack on Saturday night."

It sounded wonderful. "I'll make a reservation at the Carlyle," I told him. Then I took a deep breath. "Alex, there's something I have to tell you that may change the way you feel about me, and if it does, I will respect your decision."

"Ceil, nothing would ever change the way I feel about you."

"We'll see, but I have to take the chance. I love you."

When I replaced the receiver, my hand was trembling. I knew, though, I had made the right decision.

ZACH LIVED IN CHESTER. I HAD looked up his street on the map. He lived in a neighborhood of small two-family homes. I found his house—the number was 358—but I had to drive to the next block before I could find a parking space. There were streetlights, but they were hidden by the heavy trees that lined the sidewalk.

Zach had been right—you could identify his house by the sound of drums being played somewhere inside. I went up the stairs onto the porch. There were two doors, a center one and one to the side with a name over the doorbell, and by squinting, I was able to make out the letter Z. I rang the bell and waited, but there was no answer. With the drums beating, I could not be sure if the bell was working.

I was uncertain what to do. It was just nine o'clock. I decided that maybe he had gone out for dinner and wasn't home yet. I went down and stood on the sidewalk looking up. The windows on the second floor were dark. I didn't want to stand there any longer, but I didn't want to give up hope that Zach would be along any minute. I decided to get my car and double-park in front of his house.

I don't know what made me turn and look at the car parked directly in front of the house. I could see Zach sitting in it. The driver's window was open, and he seemed to be asleep. "Hi, Zach," I said as I walked over. "I was afraid you were standing me up."

When he didn't respond, I touched his shoulder, and he fell forward against the steering wheel. My hand felt sticky. I looked down. It was covered with blood. I grabbed the door of his car to steady myself, then frantically wiped it with my handkerchief. Then I rushed back to my own car and drove home, trying to wipe the blood away on my slacks. I don't know what I was thinking. I just knew I had to escape.

When I walked in the house, Sue had put Jack to bed and was watching television in the family room. Her back was to me. "Sue," I called. "I'm late phoning my mother. I'll be down in a minute."

Upstairs, I rushed into the bathroom, stripped, and turned on the shower. I felt as though my whole body had been washed with Zach's blood. I threw my slacks into the shower and watched the water turn red at my feet. I dressed hurriedly and went back downstairs.

"The person I was supposed to see wasn't home," I said.

After Sue left, I poured a stiff Scotch and sat in the kitchen sipping it, wondering what I was going to do. Zach was dead, and I had no way of knowing if the evidence he had for me was gone.

I finished the Scotch, went upstairs, undressed, got into bed, and realized I was facing a sleepless night of worry, even of despair. Knowing it was the wrong thing to do, I took a sleeping pill. Somewhere around eleven, I was aware that the phone was ringing. It was Alex. "Ceil, you must be in a dead sleep. I'm sorry I woke you up. I had to let you know that no matter what you say you have to tell me, it won't change one iota of the way I feel about you."

I was glad to hear his voice. "I believe that's true," I whispered.

Then, with a smile in his tone, Alex said, "I wouldn't even care if you told me you were Little Lizzie Borden. Good night, sweetheart."

THE body of Zachary Eugene Willet was found by a sixteen-year-old drummer, Tony "Rap" Corrigan, at 6:00 a.m., as he was leaving on his bicycle to do his morning paper route.

"I thought Zach had tied one on," he explained to Jeff MacKingsley and Angelo Ortiz, who had rushed to the scene after the Chester police notified them of the 911 call. "But when I saw all that dried blood, I thought I'd throw up."

No one in the Corrigan family remembered seeing Zach park the car. "It had to be after dark," said Rap's mother, Sandy. "I know because there was an SUV parked there when I got home from work. Zach was planning to move over the weekend," she volunteered.

"Did he tell you where he was moving?"

"Yes. He was taking the model unit at Cartwright Town Houses in Madison."

"Cartwright?" Jeff said casually. "I would think that one of those town houses would be quite expensive."

"Especially if it comes furnished," Sandy Corrigan agreed. "Zach claimed Mr. Cartwright was going to give it to him because he saved his life once."

"Two moving men came by to pack for Zach yesterday, Mr. Mac-

Kingsley," Rap said. "I told them one of them could have done the whole job in an hour. Zach didn't have much stuff. They only took out a couple of boxes that didn't weigh much."

Jeff and Angelo looked at each other. "Can you describe these men?" Jeff asked.

"One of them was a big guy. He had dark glasses and funny looking blond hair. I think it was dyed. He was kind of old—more than fifty. The other guy was short and maybe about thirty or so."

"I see." Jeff turned to Sandy. "Have you got a key to Zach's apartment, Mrs. Corrigan?"

"Of course."

The forensic unit was dusting the doorbell to Zach's apartment. "Oh, we've got a nice clean one here," Dennis from the lab commented. "We got a partial off the door of the car, too. That one someone tried to wipe off."

"I haven't had a chance to tell you," Jeff told Angelo as he turned the key and pushed the door open. "I spoke to Zach Willet by phone at five o'clock last night."

They started upstairs. "What kind of guy did he seem?"

"Cocky. Sure of himself. When I asked if I could talk with him, he told me he was thinking of arranging a meeting with me. He said he might have some interesting things to tell me, that between the three of us, he was sure we could come to an understanding."

"The *three* of us?" Angelo asked.

"Yes, the three of us—Celia Nolan, Zach, and me."

There was a narrow hallway at the top of the stairs. They walked a few steps and looked into what was meant to be a living room.

"What a mess," Angelo said.

The couch and chairs had been slit in every direction. Stuffing oozed out from the faded upholstery. The rug had been rolled up. Silently they walked into the kitchen and the bedroom. Everywhere it was the same—contents of drawers had been tossed. The mattress on the bed had been sliced open.

"The self-proclaimed moving men," Jeff said quietly. "I wonder if they found what they were looking for."

"Time to talk to Mrs. Nolan?" Angelo asked.

"Maybe she'll answer some questions with her lawyer present."

They went back into the living room. "The kid downstairs said the moving men took out some boxes," Jeff said. "Maybe they were looking for safe-deposit-box or storage-room receipts."

"How's this for artwork?" Ortiz asked dryly, lifting a broken picture frame. "Looks as though this was the mirror over the couch, and Zach took the mirror out and made this monstrosity." A large caricature of Zach Willet was surrounded by dozens of taped pictures and notes. Ortiz read the inscription. "'To Zach, on the occasion of your twenty-fifth anniversary at Washington Valley.' "

"Let's take that with us," Jeff said. "We might find something interesting in it. And now it's past eight o'clock, not too early to pay a visit to Mrs. Nolan."

Or a visit to Liza Barton, he corrected himself silently.

"MOMMY, can I stay home with you today?" Jack asked.

The request was unexpected, but I soon had an explanation.

"You were crying. I can tell," he said matter-of-factly.

"No, Jack," I protested. "I just didn't sleep very well last night, and my eyes are tired."

"You were crying," he said simply.

"Want to bet?"

"What kind of bet?" Jack asked.

"I'll tell you what. After I drop you off at school, I'll take a nap, and if my eyes are nice and bright when I pick you up, you owe me a hundred trillion dollars."

"And if they're not nice and bright, you owe me a hundred trillion dollars." Jack began to laugh. We usually settled those bets with an ice-cream cone or a trip to the movies.

The wager decided upon, Jack willingly let me drop him off at school. I managed to get home before I started to break down again. I felt so trapped and helpless. For all I knew, Zach had told other people I was meeting him. How could I explain he had proof Ted Cartwright killed my father? And where was that proof now?

I was dead tired and decided I should do what I'd told Jack I would do—take a nap. I was halfway up the stairs when the bell rang. My hand froze on the banister. I was sure it was someone from the prosecutor's office. All I have to say, I reminded myself, is that I will not answer questions unless my attorney is present.

When I opened the door, Jeff MacKingsley was standing on the porch with the young detective.

I could only imagine what they were thinking when they saw me with my red-rimmed eyes. For a moment I don't think I cared.

"Mrs. Nolan, I know you are represented by an attorney," Jeff MacKingsley said. "But I believe you may have some information that could help us regarding a crime that was just committed. Zach Willet was found shot to death early this morning."

I did not say anything. Let them think that my silence indicated shock and distress.

MacKingsley said, "We know that you took a riding lesson from Zach yesterday afternoon. Did Zach indicate to you that he had plans to meet anyone?"

"Was he planning to meet anyone?" I repeated, my voice rising. "I have an attorney." I managed to lower my pitch. "I won't speak to you without him being present."

"I understand. Mrs. Nolan, this is a simple question. The picture of the Barton family that you found taped to your barn. Did you ever show it to your husband?"

At least the question was one I could answer without fear. "My husband had already gone to work when I found it. He came home as I was giving it to you. No, Mr. MacKingsley, he did not see it."

The prosecutor nodded and thanked me, then said in a tone that sounded strangely sympathetic, "Celia, I really think everything is falling into place. I think that you are going to be all right."

JEFF MacKingsley was quiet on the drive back to the office, and Angelo Ortiz knew better than to intrude. It was clear his boss was troubled, and he was sure he knew why. Celia Nolan seemed to be on the verge of a total breakdown.

The forensic group was waiting for them when they arrived. "We've got nice prints for you, Jeff," Dennis, the fingerprint expert from the lab, announced with great satisfaction. "A nice index finger from the doorbell, and a thumbprint from the car."

"Were there any in Zach's apartment?" Jeff asked.

"Lots and lots and lots of Zach's. Nobody else."

"Dennis," Jeff said, "I have two sets of fingerprints I want you to check against the ones you just got."

Dennis got back to him in half an hour. "You've got yourself a match, Prosecutor. The three sets belong to the same person."

"Thanks, Dennis." Jeff sat quietly for almost twenty minutes. Then he reached for his phone and dialed information to get the number of Benjamin Fletcher, attorney-at-law.

JIMMY Franklin was a newly appointed detective unofficially under the guidance of his good friend Angelo Ortiz. On Thursday morning, following Angelo's instructions, he stopped with his cell phone camera at the Grove Real Estate office, ostensibly to inquire about the availability of a small starter house in Mendham.

Jimmy was twenty-six but, like Angelo, had a boyish look that was very appealing. Robin explained pleasantly that there were very few starter houses available in Mendham but that she did have some in neighboring towns.

While she marked listings for him to study, Jimmy pretended to be on the phone. What he was doing was taking close-up pictures of Robin. The night before, he had managed to get a picture of Charley Hatch from Charley's former wife, a picture she assured him did not do poor Charley justice.

Jimmy took the pictures of Robin and Charley with him when he drove into Manhattan, to Patsy's Restaurant. It was quarter of twelve when he arrived. The restaurant had not yet begun to fill with the luncheon crowd, and Jimmy laid the pictures on the bar. He flashed his badge. "Recognize these people?" he asked the bartender.

The bartender studied the pictures. "They look familiar, especially the woman, but I can't be sure."

Jimmy had better luck with the maître d'. "She comes in some-times, but that's not who she's with. Let me ask the waiters."

When he returned, the maitre d' had a waiter in tow. "Dominick will fill you in. He never forgets a face."

Dominick was holding the pictures. "She comes in once in a while. Good-looking. A little sexy. That guy was with her once a couple of weeks ago. Reason I remember, it was the guy's birthday. She had us put a candle on a slice of cake, then gave him an envelope. I could see she'd laid some nice change on him. Twenty hundred-dollar bills."

"That's a nice birthday present," Jimmy agreed. "You say she comes in here with some other guy. Can you describe him?"

"Sure."

Jimmy got out his notebook and jotted down the description.

THE news of Zach's death had spread through the Washington Valley Riding Club. The idea that someone had shot him seemed unthinkable to the people who worked in the stables. "He wouldn't harm a fly," a scrawny old-timer named Alonzo said when Paul Walsh asked if Zach Willet had any enemies. "Zach kept to him-self. Never got in an argument in the fifty years I've known him."

"Do you know if anybody had it in for him for any reason?"

No one could think of anything until Alonzo remembered that Manny Pagan had made some comment about Ted Cartwright get-ting into an argument with Zach yesterday. "Manny's exercising a horse in the ring. I'll get him," Alonzo offered.

Manny Pagan came over to the stable. "Mr. Cartwright practi-cally shouted at me. I never saw a guy so mad. I pointed out where Zach was eating at the picnic table and saw Cartwright go charging over to him. I swear there was steam coming out of his ears."

"That was yesterday at lunchtime?"

"That's right."

Paul Walsh had learned what he had come to find out.

"BENJAMIN Fletcher, returning your call," Anna announced on the intercom.

Jeff MacKingsley drew a deep breath and picked up the receiver. "Hello, Ben," he said warmly. "How are you?"

"Nice to hear from you, Jeff, but I'm sure you're not interested in the state of my health."

"Of course I'm interested, but you're right, that's not the reason I called. I need your help."

"I'm not feeling very helpful, Jeff. That viper you call a detective, Walsh, has been intimidating my new client."

"Yes, I realize that, and I'm sorry. But listen to me. Do you know that your new client, Celia Nolan, is actually Liza Barton?"

Jeff heard the sharp intake of breath at the other end of the phone. "I have absolute proof," he said. "Fingerprints."

"You better not have fingerprints from the juvenile case."

"Ben, for now, never mind where I got them. I need to talk to Celia. I won't ask her one word about the homicides last week. Do you remember the name Zach Willet?"

"Sure. What about him?"

"Zach was shot in his car sometime last evening. Celia must have had an appointment to meet him. Her fingerprints are on Zach's car door and on his doorbell. I don't for one single minute think that she had anything to do with Zach's death, but I need to know why she was meeting him. Will you let her talk to me? I'm worried there may be lives at risk—including hers."

"I'll talk to her, then make a decision. Of course, I must be present, and at any point if I say, 'Stop,' you stop. I'll get back to you later, Jeff. And I'll tell you another thing. With all those people you've got working for you, have someone protect her. Make sure nothing happens to that pretty lady."

JACK had won the bet. I agreed that my eyes still looked tired but insisted that it was because I had a headache. Instead of paying him one hundred trillion dollars, I took him to lunch and bought him an ice-cream cone for dessert. I kept on my dark glasses and told Jack the light hurt my eyes because of the headache. Did he believe me? I doubt it. He's a smart and perceptive kid.

We arrived home to find two messages on the phone. As always, I was afraid it was one of the Lizzie Borden messages, but both were from Benjamin Fletcher, with instructions to call him immediately.

They're going to arrest me, I thought. They have my fingerprints. I misdialed twice before I finally reached him.

"It's Celia Nolan, Mr. Fletcher," I said.

"First thing, a client has to trust her attorney, Liza."

Liza. With the exception of Dr. Moran in my early days of treatment and the time Martin's mind was wandering, I have not been called Liza since I was ten years old. The matter-of-fact way in which Fletcher said my name helped to reduce the shock that he knew who I was.

"I wasn't sure whether or not to tell you yesterday," I said. "I'm still not sure if I can trust you. How did you know it was me?"

"Jeff MacKingsley told me about an hour ago."

"Jeff MacKingsley told you!"

"He wants to talk to you, Liza. But first I must be absolutely certain that it's in your best interest. Don't worry, I'll be there with you, but I am very concerned. He tells me that you left your fingerprints where a dead body was found."

"Does that mean I'm going to be arrested?" I could barely make my lips form the words.

"Not if I can help it. This is all very unusual, but the prosecutor tells me he believes you had nothing to do with it."

I closed my eyes as relief flooded every inch of my body. Then I told Benjamin Fletcher about Zach Willet. I told him about my suspicion that my father's death had not been an accident, that yesterday I had promised Zach one million one hundred thousand dollars if he would tell the police what really happened, and that Zach kept the evidence of Ted Cartwright's guilt.

"You're going to be giving MacKingsley some powerful stuff, Liza. But how did your fingerprints get on that car and doorbell?"

I told him all about my appointment to see Zach.

"Does anyone else know you were there?"

"No. But I did call my investment adviser yesterday and ask him to be ready to wire the money I promised Zach. He can verify that."

"All right, Liza," Benjamin Fletcher said. "What time is good for you to go to the prosecutor's office?"

"I'll need to get my babysitter. Four o'clock would be all right."

"Four o'clock it is," Fletcher said.

I hung up the phone, and from somewhere behind me, Jack asked, "Mommy, are you going to be arrested?"

MOST of the investigators in the prosecutor's office had been pulled off their own units to concentrate on the Mendham homicides. At three o'clock the group analyzing the phone records were ready to report their findings to Jeff.

"In the last two months Ted Cartwright has been in touch with Zach Willet six times," Liz Reilly, a new investigator, announced. "The last time was yesterday afternoon at three oh six."

"Cartwright and Henry Paley have been talking to each other a lot," Nan Newman, one of the veteran investigators, reported, "but there was no contact on Henry's phone with Charley Hatch."

"Paley's a lowlife," Jeff said, "and he hasn't accounted for his whereabouts when Hatch was shot. I've asked him to come in with his lawyer at five o'clock, and Ted Cartwright is coming at six.

"We know Robin Carpenter is a liar," he continued. "She lied about the date in Patsy's with her brother. His E-ZPass shows that he drove into New York at six forty that night, which is exactly what his ex-wife told Angelo.

"There are no calls from Carpenter to Hatch since last Friday. I believe that she was using a prepaid phone with no subscriber name to contact him. She must have told him to get one, too, because the woman whose lawn he was cutting saw him holding two phones. I also think that when he answered that call, he made an appointment to meet someone at the break in the hedge. Of course, we can't be sure that it was Robin who made that last call."

The investigators were listening quietly, following Jeff's reasoning, hoping for an opportunity to make a significant contribution. Then Mort Shelley opened the door to Jeff's office. They exchanged glances, and Shelley answered Jeff's unspoken question. "He's where he said he'd be. We've got a tag on him."

"Make sure you don't lose him," Jeff said quietly.

THIS was the courthouse in which the trial had taken place. As I walked through the corridors, I remembered those terrible days. I remembered the inscrutable gaze of the judge. I remembered being afraid of my lawyer. I remembered listening to the witnesses who testified that I meant to kill my mother. I remembered how I tried to sit up straight because my mother was always after me not to slouch. I was tall for my age, even then.

Benjamin Fletcher was waiting for me inside the main door of the prosecutor's office. He took my hand and held it. "It would seem I owe a little ten-year-old girl an apology," he said. "I got that child off, but I admit I bought Cartwright's version of what happened."

"I know you did," I said. "But you did get me off."

"When we get this behind us, I'm going to see that everyone understands what you have been through."

I could feel my eyes brighten, and I guess Fletcher noticed. "No charge," he added, "and it rattles my soul to utter those words."

I laughed, which was what he wanted. I suddenly felt confident that this hulking septuagenarian would take care of me.

Jeff MacKingsley's corner office was large and pleasant. I had always instinctively liked this man, even when I resented him showing up on my doorstep. Now he got up from his desk and came around it to greet us. I had done the best makeup job I could, trying to disguise my swollen eyes, but I don't think I fooled him.

With Benjamin Fletcher sitting beside me, I told Jeff everything I knew about Zach. And I told him that it was only in these last two weeks that I had remembered my mother's last words: *You admitted it when you were drunk. You killed my husband. You told me Zach saw you.*

Detective Ortiz and a stenographer were in the room, but I ignored them. Jeff let me talk almost without interruption. I guess I was answering all the questions he had planned to ask me. When I described going to Zach's house, he did prod me for details.

When I was finished, I said, "Mr. MacKingsley, I want you to ask me any questions you may have about Georgette Grove and Charley Hatch—"

"Wait a minute," Benjamin Fletcher interrupted. "We agreed we were not going to discuss those cases."

"We have to. It's going to get out that I'm Liza Barton." I looked at Jeff. "Does the media know yet?"

"In fact, it was a person in the media, Dru Perry, who disclosed it to us," he admitted. "At some point you may want to talk with her. I think she'd be very sympathetic." Then he added, "Is your husband aware that you are Liza Barton?"

"No he is not," I said. "It was a terrible mistake, but I promised Jack's father, my first husband, that I would not reveal my past. Of course, I will tell Alex now."

For the next forty minutes I answered every question the prosecutor asked me about Georgette Grove and Charley Hatch. I even told him about the Little Lizzie phone calls. At ten of five Fletcher and I said good-bye and left the private office.

There was a woman with gray hair at Jeff's secretary's desk. She was obviously very angry. Her back was to me, and I heard her say, "I told Jeff about Celia Nolan because I thought it was my duty. My thanks is that I lose my exclusive. The *New York Post* is giving all of page three to the 'Return of Little Lizzie' story, and they're practically going to accuse her of committing all three murders."

Somehow I made it to my car. Somehow I said good-bye to Benjamin Fletcher. Somehow I got home, paid Sue, and thanked her.

Jack was listless. I think he was starting to get a cold. I sent out for a pizza, and before it came, I got him into pajamas and changed into my own pajamas and robe.

I decided I would go to bed after I tucked Jack in. All I wanted to do was to sleep and sleep and sleep. There were calls from Mr. Fletcher and Jeff MacKingsley. I did not answer them, and both left messages expressing concern at how upset I must be.

Of course I'm upset, I thought. Tomorrow I'll be starring in "The Return of Little Lizzie." From this day forward, I will never travel far enough or hide deep enough to escape.

When the pizza came, Jack and I had a couple of slices. Jack definitely was catching some kind of bug. I took him upstairs. "Mom, I want to sleep with you," he said fretfully.

That was fine with me. I locked up and set the alarm; then I called Alex's cell phone. He didn't answer, but he had said something about a dinner meeting. I left a message saying that I was going to bed early and to please call me at six a.m., Chicago time. I said I had to tell him something important.

I took a sleeping pill, got into bed, and with Jack cuddled in my arms, I fell fast asleep.

It was pitch-dark when I felt my head being raised and heard a shadowy voice whispering, "Liza, drink this."

I tried to close my lips, but a strong hand was forcing them open, and I was gulping a bitter liquid that I knew contained crushed sleeping pills. From a distance I heard Jack's wail as someone carried him away.

"DRU, that leak did not come from this office," Jeff snapped, finally out of patience. "You seem to forget that Clyde Earley, among others, knows that Celia Nolan is Liza Barton. Frankly, I think that whoever planned that vandalism was well aware of her identity. The *Post* is barking up the wrong tree. Hang around, and I may have some real news for you."

Dru's anger subsided. "You're playing straight with me?"

"I don't think I've ever not played straight with you," Jeff replied.

Henry Paley and his lawyer arrived at five o'clock. Henry read a statement into the record that had obviously been prepared by his attorney. In a wooden voice he admitted that he had been at the

Holland Road house several times more than he had indicated, but he insisted that it was only carelessness in keeping his daily reminder. He went on to acknowledge that about a year ago he had been offered one hundred thousand dollars from Ted Cartwright if he was able to persuade Georgette to sell the land on Route 24.

"There has been a question as to my whereabouts on or around the time of the demise of Charley Hatch," Henry read. "I left my office at one fifteen and went directly to the Mark Grannon Real Estate Agency. There I met Thomas Madison, Georgette Grove's cousin. Mr. Grannon had made an offer to buy our agency.

"As for the late Charley Hatch, I may have seen Mr. Hatch when I was showing properties. I do not remember ever exchanging a word with him.

"Referring to the most recent homicide, I never met the victim, Zach Willet."

Looking pleased with himself, Henry folded his statement neatly and looked at Jeff. "I trust that covers the situation."

"Maybe," Jeff said pleasantly. "But I do have one question: Don't you think that Georgette Grove, knowing of your cozy relationship with Ted Cartwright, would have lived out her life holding on to the Route 24 property rather than sell it commercially?"

"I object to that question," Paley's lawyer said heatedly.

"You were in the vicinity when Georgette was shot, Mr. Paley, and her death made it possible for you to get a better deal than Cartwright was offering. That will be all for today. Thank you for coming in to make your statement, Mr. Paley."

THE heavy framed repository of Zach Willet's twenty-fifth anniversary memorabilia had been placed on a desk in a vacant office down the hall from Jeff MacKingsley. Investigator Liz Reilly had been instructed to review every card and picture and note.

Liz had a feeling that this hopelessly cluttered collage would be a perfect place to secret a picture or any small object that might otherwise be easily discovered in a drawer or file.

The tape on the pictures and cards easily separated from the corkboard that Zach had inserted for backing. Liz got a kick out of reading the first several notes of congratulation: "Here's to another 25, Zach"; "Ride 'em, cowboy"; "Happy trails to you."

She removed them one by one, until only the caricature itself remained in the frame. It had been drawn in crayon on heavy cardboard and was tacked to the corkboard. When she removed it, she turned the caricature over; taped to the back was a sealed 5-by-8 envelope. Liz decided to have a witness when she opened it.

She went down the hall to the prosecutor's office. "Mr. Mac-Kingsley, this was taped behind that caricature of Zach Willet."

Jeff looked from the envelope to Liz and back to the envelope. He got a letter opener from his drawer, slit the tape, and shook the envelope. Two metal objects clanked onto his desk. He pulled out a half-dozen photographs and a handwritten letter containing Zach's graphic yet oddly dignified description of how he had watched Will Barton die.

Jeff turned to Liz. "This is enormously important and just might be the break we need. Good work."

Liz left Jeff's office delighted with the prosecutor's reaction.

As Jeff stood alone, he was interrupted again as investigator Nan Newman rushed into his office. "Boss, you're not going to believe this. Rap Corrigan, the kid who found Zach Willet's body, came in to meet with me and give a statement. While he was there, Ted Cartwright came into the outer office with his attorney. Rap did a double take and practically pulled me down the hall to talk to me.

"Jeff, Rap swears that Ted Cartwright, minus a dopey-looking blond wig, is one of the two so-called moving men he let into Zach Willet's apartment yesterday."

TED Cartwright was dressed in an impeccably tailored dark blue suit, a light blue shirt, and a red-and-blue tie. With his crown of white hair and imposing carriage, he was every inch the powerful executive as he strode ahead of his lawyer into Jeff's office.

Jeff calmly observed the arrival. He did not offer to shake the hand of either man, but indicated the chairs that were pulled close to the desk. Detectives Angelo Ortiz and Paul Walsh were seated to the side of the prosecutor.

Cartwright's attorney introduced himself. "I am Louis Buch, and I wish to state for the record that my client has appeared here today voluntarily, to assist in your investigation of Mr. Willet's death."

His face impassive, Jeff MacKingsley looked at Ted. "How long have you known Zach Willet, Mr. Cartwright?"

"Oh, I think about twenty years," Ted answered.

"Think again, Mr. Cartwright. Isn't it over thirty years?"

"Twenty, thirty." Cartwright shrugged. "A very long time."

"Would you say you were friends?"

Ted hesitated. "It depends. I liked Zach. I love horses, and I admired his skill at handling them. On the other hand, it wouldn't occur to me to really socialize with him in any way."

"Then you don't count having a drink with him at the bar at Sammy's as socializing with him?"

"Of course, if I bumped into him at a bar, I would have a drink with him, Mr. MacKingsley."

"I see. When was the last time you spoke with him?"

"I called him yesterday afternoon, around three o'clock."

"And what was the reason for the call?"

"We had a good laugh over the joke he pulled on me."

"What was that joke, Mr. Cartwright?"

"Zach told my sales rep in Madison that I was giving him a town house. We had a bet on the Yankees–Red Sox game, and he had kidded me that if the Red Sox won by more than ten runs, I would have to give him a town house."

"When was the last time you saw Zach?"

"Yesterday, around noon, at the Washington Valley stables."

"I understand you had a quarrel with him."

"I blew off a little steam. Because my rep took him seriously, we almost lost a sale. I simply wanted to tell Zach that his joke went too far. But I called and apologized at three o'clock."

"That's very odd," Jeff said, "because a witness heard Zach tell you that he didn't need the money the town house was worth because he had a better offer. Do you remember him saying that?"

"That wasn't the conversation we had," Ted said mildly. "You're mistaken, Mr. MacKingsley, as is your witness."

"I don't think so. Mr. Cartwright, did you ever promise Henry Paley one hundred thousand dollars if he could persuade Georgette Grove to sell property on Route 24?"

"I had a business arrangement with Henry Paley."

"Georgette was pretty much in your way, wasn't she?"

"Georgette had her way of doing things. I have mine."

"Where were you on September fourth at about ten a.m.?"

"I was out for an early morning ride on my horse."

"Weren't you on a trail that connects directly to the private trail behind the Holland Road house where Georgette died?"

"I do not ride on private trails."

"Mr. Cartwright, did you know Will Barton?"

"Yes, I did. He was the first husband of my late wife."

"You were separated from your wife at her time of death?"

"The evening of her death Audrey had called me to discuss a reconciliation. We were very much in love. Her daughter, Liza, hated me because she didn't want anyone to replace her father."

"Why did you and your wife separate, Mr. Cartwright?"

"The strain of Liza's antagonism became too much for Audrey. We only planned the separation to be temporary, until she could get psychological help for her troubled daughter."

"You didn't separate because, when you were drunk one night, you confessed you had killed her first husband?"

"Don't answer that, Ted," Louis Buch ordered.

"It's all right, Lou. I'll answer their questions."

"Mr. Cartwright," Jeff said, "Audrey Barton was terrified of you. Her mistake was that she didn't go to the police. But you were afraid that she would go one day. There was always some question about the gunshot heard at the time Will Barton's horse went over the cliff."

"This is ridiculous," Cartwright snapped.

"No, it's not. Zach Willet witnessed what you did to Will Barton. We found interesting evidence in Zach's apartment—a statement he had written, plus a picture he took. He described what you did to Barton. He retrieved a bullet and its casing, and kept them all these years. Let me read his statement to you."

Jeff picked up Zach Willet's letter and read it.

"That is fiction and inadmissible in court," Louis Buch snapped.

"Zach's murder isn't fiction," Jeff said. "He was bleeding you for twenty-seven years and finally got so cocksure when he realized you killed Georgette Grove that he decided to be taken care of on a higher scale."

"I did not kill Georgette or Zach Willet," Cartwright said.

"Were you in Zach Willet's apartment yesterday?"

"No, I was not."

Jeff looked past him. "Angelo, will you ask Rap to come in?"

As they waited, Jeff said, "Mr. Cartwright, as you can see, I have the evidence you were searching for in Zach's apartment—the bullet and casing from the gun that you fired and the pictures that show where and when it happened. Later you donated that gun to the collection of firearms at a museum, didn't you? I am subpoenaing it so that we can compare the bullet and casing." Jeff looked up. "Oh, here's Zach's landlady's son."

At Angelo's prodding, Rap came forward to the desk.

"Do you recognize anyone in this room, Rap?" Jeff asked.

"I recognize you, Mr. MacKingsley, and I recognize Detective Ortiz. And this guy." He pointed at Ted. "Yesterday he came to our house dressed like a moving man. He had another guy with him. I gave him Zach's key."

"Are you positive?"

"I'm positive. He had a wig on, but I'd know that face anywhere."

"Thank you, Rap."

Jeff waited to speak until Rap left the room. "Robin Carpenter is your girlfriend," he told Cartwright. "You gave her the money to bribe her half brother, Charley Hatch, to vandalize the house known, thanks to you, as Little Lizzie's Place. You shot Georgette Grove. Hatch became a threat, and you, or Robin, took him out."

"That's not true," Cartwright shouted, jumping to his feet.

Louis Buch stood up, stunned and totally furious.

Jeff glared at Cartwright. "We know that you went to Audrey Barton's home to kill her that night. We know that you caused Will Barton's death. We know that you killed Zach Willet." He stood up. "Mr. Cartwright, you are under arrest for the burglary of Zach Willet's apartment. Mr. Buch, we are finishing our investigation, and we anticipate that Mr. Cartwright will be formally charged with these murders in the next several days."

Jeff paused, then turned to Detective Ortiz. "Please read Mr. Cartwright his rights."

I AM being carried downstairs. I can't open my eyes. "Jack." I try to call his name but can only whisper it. My lips feel rubbery. I have to wake up. Jack needs me.

"It's all right, Liza. I'm taking you to Jack."

Alex is talking to me. Alex, my husband. He is home, not in Chicago. I have to tell him tomorrow I'm really Liza Barton.

But he called me Liza.

There were sleeping pills in that glass. Maybe I'm dreaming.

Jack. He's crying. "Mommy. Mommy. Mommy."

"Jack. Jack." I try to scream but can only mouth his name.

There is cold air on my face. Alex is carrying me. Where is he taking me? Where is Jack?

My eyes won't open. I hear a door opening—the garage door. Alex is laying me down. I know where I am. My car, the backseat of my car. "Jack . . ."

"You want him? You can have him." It's a woman's voice, harsh.

"Mommmmmmy!" Jack's arms are around my neck. His head is buried against my heart.

"Get outside, Robin. I'm starting the engine." Alex's voice.

I hear the garage door close. Jack and I are alone.

I'm so tired. I can't help it. I am falling asleep.

AT 10:30 P.M., still in his office, Jeff waited for Mort Shelley. He had already been notified that a search warrant had uncovered the blond wig, the movers' uniforms, and Zach's boxes at Ted Cartwright's house. More important, a nine-millimeter pistol had been found in his safe.

We'll have Cartwright cold on this one, Jeff thought. The satisfaction Jeff would normally feel from the possibility of closing a case such as this one was outweighed by his concern for Celia Nolan. Or Liza Barton, he corrected himself. I'm going to have to be the one to tell her that her husband was setting her up to be accused of murdering Georgette Grove, he thought, and it's all about the money she inherited from his cousin, Laurence Foster.

There was a light tap at the door, and Shelley came in. "Beats me how this guy has managed to stay out of prison."

"What have you got, Mort?"

"Alex Nolan is a phony," Mort said. "He is a lawyer, and he is affiliated with a law firm that specializes in wills and trusts, but he has only a handful of clients. He's had several ethics violations filed against him and has been suspended twice."

Shelley consulted the thick file he was carrying. "He never made an honest dollar in his life. His money came from a bequest he received four years ago from a seventy-seven-year-old widow he was romancing. Nolan got three million dollars out of that scam."

"That's pretty good," Jeff said. "Most people would settle for it."

"Alex Nolan wants real money, the kind that means private planes and yachts and mansions."

"Celia—I mean Liza—doesn't have that kind of money."

"Her son does. Laurence Foster took good care of her, but the two thirds of his estate that he left to Jack contain Foster's share of patents for research he financed. There are three companies that are about to go public, and that will mean tens of millions of dollars."

"And Nolan knew this?"

"It was public knowledge that Foster was an investor in start-up companies. Wills are on file where they were probated. Nolan didn't need to be a genius."

Shelley picked another page out of the file. "We tracked down Foster's private nurses from the last time he was in the hospital.

One of them admitted that she took big tips from Nolan to let him in when Foster was dying and visitors were limited to immediate family. Nolan was probably hoping to get himself written into the will, but Foster's mind was beginning to wander, so maybe it was Foster himself who told Nolan about Celia's past."

Jeff's mouth tightened as he listened.

"Nolan is all smoke and mirrors," Mort continued. "He didn't own that apartment in SoHo. The furniture wasn't his. None of it was. He was using the three million bucks to convince Liza that he was a prominent attorney.

"I spoke to Celia's investment advisor. He told me that the way Foster set up his will, if Jack dies before he reaches twenty-one, everything he has goes to Celia. After her marriage to Nolan, Celia made him Jack's guardian as well as the trustee of his estate."

"I knew when Nolan sat in this office yesterday and referred to the picture Liza found in the barn as the one of the Barton family on the beach that he must be the one who put it there," Jeff said. "Last week I was in the kitchen when Liza gave it to me. Nolan came in as I was putting it in a plastic bag. He didn't ask to look at it then, but yesterday, despite all the Barton pictures that have been in the newspapers, he knew exactly which one it was."

"Robin has been his girlfriend for at least three years," Shelley said. "I took a picture of Nolan I got in the bar association directory to Patsy's. One of the waiters started three years ago, and he remembers seeing them when he was new on the job."

"I wonder if the plan to get Liza back into her old home was hatched after Robin went to work at the Grove Agency," Jeff mused. "Buy the house as a gift. Move her into it. Vandalize it to rattle her. Expose her as Little Lizzie. Count on a psychological breakdown so he could get control of the estate. But then something went wrong. That last evening in the office, Georgette must have found something that linked Robin to Alex. Henry told us that Georgette had gone through both their desks. She made a call to Robin at ten o'clock Tuesday night. Unless Robin comes clean, we'll probably never know the reason for it."

"My guess is that Robin was the one waiting for Georgette in the house on Holland Road," Mort volunteered. "She and Alex may have decided to try to point the finger at Celia by leaving her picture in Georgette's bag. And Robin might have taken something out of the bag that Georgette had found in her desk. Then, when Charley Hatch's jeans and sneakers and carvings were confiscated, he became too much of a danger. So their plot to get control of Jack's money caused them to commit two homicides."

"This may not be the first time Nolan has been involved in a homicide," Jeff told Shelley. "He was a suspect in the death of a wealthy young woman he had dated in college. She had dropped him for someone else, and he apparently went crazy and stalked her for over a year. I only learned that this afternoon."

Jeff's expression became grave. "First thing tomorrow I'm going to tell Liza what we know. After that, I'll order protection for her and Jack. If Nolan weren't in Chicago, I'd have a guard on them now. He and his girlfriend have to be getting very nervous."

The phone rang. Anna turned on the intercom. "Jeff, there's a Detective Ryan on the phone from Chicago. He says Alex Nolan slipped out of a dinner meeting more than three hours ago and hasn't showed up at the Ritz-Carlton."

Jeff and Mort jumped up. *"Three hours!"* Jeff exclaimed. "He could have flown back here by now!"

I HEARD the car's engine running. The fumes were making me drowsier, but I knew I had to fight it. Now that he was with me, Jack was falling asleep again. I tried to move him. I had to turn off the engine. If we stayed here, we were going to die. But my limbs wouldn't function. What was it that Alex had forced me to drink?

I was slumped against the cushion, half lying, half sitting. The sound of the engine was deafening. Something must be wedged against the gas pedal. Soon we would be unconscious. Soon my little boy would die.

"Jack, Jack." My voice was a broken whisper, but it went directly into his ear. "Jack, Mommy is sick. Help me."

Turning his head restlessly, he settled again under my neck.

"Jack, Jack, wake up. Wake up."

I was starting to fall asleep again. I bit my lip so hard that I could taste blood. "Jack, help Mommy," I pleaded.

He lifted his head. I sensed he was looking at me.

"Jack, climb . . . into front seat. Take car key . . . out."

He was moving. He sat up and slid off my lap. "It's dark, Mommy," he said.

"Climb in . . . front seat," I whispered. "Climb . . ." I could feel myself sinking slowly, words disappearing from my mind.

Jack's foot grazed my face. He was climbing over the seat.

"The key, Jack . . ."

From far off I heard him say, "I can't get it out."

"Turn it, Jack. Turn it . . . then . . . pull . . . it . . . out."

Suddenly there was silence, total silence in the garage. Followed by Jack's sleepy but proud cry, "Mommy, I did it."

I knew the fumes could still kill us. We had to get out. Jack would never be able to open the garage door by himself.

"Mommy, are you sick?"

The garage door opener, I thought—it's clipped onto the visor. I often let Jack be the one to press it. "Jack, open . . . garage door," I begged. "You know how."

I think I slipped away for a minute. The rumbling sound of the rising door woke me up for a moment, and it was with a vast sense of deliverance that I finally lost consciousness.

I woke up in an ambulance. The first face I saw was Jeffrey Mac-Kingsley's. The first words he said were the ones I wanted to hear. "Don't worry, Jack is fine." The second words seemed filled with promise. "Liza, I told you everything was going to be all right."

Epilogue

WE HAVE lived in the house for two years now. After much thought I decided to stay there. For me it was no longer the house in which I had killed my mother, but the home in which I had tried to save her life. I have used my skills as an interior designer to complete my father's vision for it. It is truly beautiful, and each day we build happy memories to add to my early childhood ones.

Ted Cartwright accepted a plea bargain. He got thirty years for murdering Zach Willet, fifteen years for killing my father, and twelve years for causing the death of my mother, the sentences to be served concurrently. Part of his agreement was that he would confess to intending to kill my mother.

He had lived in the house, and he knew that there was one basement window that for some inexplicable reason had never been wired into the security system. That was the way he got in.

He admitted that he had planned to strangle my mother as she slept, and if I had awakened while he was there, he would have killed me, too.

Knowing that the impending divorce would make him a suspect in her death, he had placed a call from our basement phone to his home and waited an hour before starting upstairs. He had planned to tell the police that my mother had asked him to come to our house the next day to discuss a reconciliation.

But that planned explanation had to be changed when I awoke and the confrontation and shooting occurred. Instead, on the witness stand at my trial, he testified that my mother had called and pleaded with him to come to the house while I was asleep.

Once in the house, Ted got the new code out of my mother's address book and disarmed the security system. He unlocked the kitchen door to make it seem that my mother's carelessness had allowed an intruder to sneak in. At my trial his story was that my mother had disarmed it and unlocked the door because she was expecting him.

Ted also indicated that the other "moving man" was Sonny Ingers, a construction worker on his town-house project. His identification of Ingers was corroborated by Rap Corrigan's description.

Henry Paley emerged from the investigation without any criminal charges. None of the evidence indicated that he knew about or was involved in any plan to harm anyone.

However, Robin Carpenter and Alex Nolan are both serving life sentences for the murders of Georgette Grove and Charley Hatch and for the attempted murders of Jack and me. Robin admitted that she had shot both Georgette and her half brother, Charley. She had taken from Georgette's shoulder bag the picture of her and Alex that Georgette had found in her desk.

So many people stopped by our house after Jack and I were nearly killed. They brought food and flowers and friendship. Some told me how their grandmothers and mine were schoolmates. I love it here. My roots are here. I've opened an interior design shop in Mendham, but I limit my clients. Life is busy. Jack is in the first grade and plays on every team he can find.

In the weeks and months following Alex's arrest, my relief over Ted's confession was overshadowed by my sadness at Alex's betrayal. It was Jeff who helped me to understand that the Alex I thought I knew had never existed.

I'm not exactly sure of the moment when I realized I was falling in love with Jeff. I think he knew before I did that we were meant to be together.

That's another reason why I am so busy. My husband, Jeffrey MacKingsley, is getting ready to run for governor.

A Conversation with

Mary Higgins Clark

SELECT EDITIONS: How did you get started writing?

MARY HIGGINS CLARK: I wrote my first poem when I was six or seven years old. I was always writing skits and making my brothers perform in them. We charged two cents to have people watch them in my garage.

SE: What did you do before you began writing professionally?

MHC: I went to secretarial school, then I worked in advertising. At age eighteen, I was secretary to the creative director and sitting in on meetings—why this ad campaign worked, why this one was a failure. Then, when I would have been a senior in college, I was a Pan Am hostess, flying all over the world. When I got married—I had only flown a year—I said I've got to learn how to be a professional writer.

SE: You have said that you

Vital Stats

EDUCATION: B.A. in philosophy, Fordham University, 1979
FIRST PUBLISHED STORY: "Stowaway," sold for $100 in 1956
FIRST PUBLISHED BOOK: *Aspire to the Heavens* (1969), a historical novel about George Washington
WEBSITE: www.maryhigginsclark.com

had eleven stories rejected before you got one accepted.

MHC: No, I was rejected forty times, but I had eleven in the mail at the time the first one was taken! I would get one back and retype the first and last pages, because editors always seem to leave their coffee spills. Then I started to get "not right for us, but try again" scrawled on the bottom of a rejection slip.

SE: When *Where Are the Chil-*dren? was published in 1974, were you surprised at its success?

MHC: I always knew I'd make it as a writer. It may sound crazy, but I always knew. There was no question in my mind.

SE: You are at least partly responsible for creating the "woman-in-peril" genre in contemporary fiction. How did that evolve?

MHC: Well, even though I use multiple viewpoints, my protagonist is a woman because a woman knows a woman best. Ruth Rendell said you should be able to put a book in a time capsule and when somebody reads it in one hundred years, they should not be able to tell who wrote it, a man or woman. But my view is that a woman knows a woman best. Therefore, the one whose actions are most significant to me have to be a woman's.

SE: It's a wonderful testament to you that you were able to raise five children almost single-handedly, put them through school, and have a career yourself.

MHC: A lot of women do it, and they don't have the blessings I had. A lot of women are working two and three jobs. I had the advantage of being able to get into a job that paid fairly decently. An awful lot of people

Damsels in Distress

The **WOMAN-IN-PERIL** genre of mystery stories—a.k.a. female in jeopardy or "fem-jep"—has a long history. Characters like Mary Higgins Clark's heroine Liza Barton have antecedents as old as medieval tales of chivalry, in which a woman waits for a knight in shining armor to rescue her from a wicked tormentor.

Tarzan's Jane, Dracula's Mina, and Dudley Do-Right's Nell are all archetypical women in peril. Famous films featuring women in peril include *Wait Until Dark* (starring Audrey Hepburn), *Gaslight* (starring Ingrid Bergman), and *Rosemary's Baby* (starring Mia Farrow).

"Lizzie Borden Took an Axe . . ."

Liza Barton, the heroine of *No Place Like Home,* is taunted with comparisons to Lizzie Borden, the infamous Massachusetts spinster who was accused but later acquitted of murdering both her parents on August 4, 1892. Lizzie, then thirty-two years old, was allegedly driven by a desire to inherit her father's considerable estate, the bulk of which he intended for his wife, who was actually Lizzie's stepmother.

Lizzie Borden is fixed in the American imagination for a number of reasons. Despite overwhelming circumstantial evidence that Lizzie committed these murders, it remains—at least technically—an unsolved crime. In fact, several books put forth the theory that Lizzie didn't do it, accusing variously the Bordens' maid, Lizzie's illegitimate half-brother, and Lizzie's older sister, Emma, who was a staunch supporter of Lizzie's at the trial but shunned her for the last twenty years of her life.

The case that has fascinated true-crime fans for over a century has inspired dramas, novels, poems, and even a ballet and an opera—and now Mary Higgins Clark.

have a much harder row to hoe.

SE: If you believe you can do it, that makes all the difference.

MHC: If you believe and have faith in yourself and you're willing to put out the effort, you can do anything you want to do. I would get up at five o'clock in the morning to write. A lot of people get up at five to jog or to exercise. I did something I wanted to do very much, and it was the only time I could do it.

SE: Your father died when you were young, and your first husband died when your five children were also very young. How did these tragedies shape you?

MHC: From the time I was ten, I was aware of the fragility of life. Things that are said, something going wrong, or the car breaking down—I've never let these things get to me because I know what's important.

SE: Have these tragedies made you think differently about the importance of family?

MHC: My family is tops to me. I think the most important thing in anyone's life is to be able to count heads at the end of the day. ∎

Random acts of violence

can sometimes be

the most calculated

crimes of all.

JONATHAN KELLERMAN

A Novel

--CHAPTER 1--

MAY brought azure skies and California optimism to Hollywood. Petra Connor worked nights and slept through the blue. She had her own reason to be cheerful: solving two whodunit murders.

The first was a dead body at a wedding. The Ito–Park wedding, main ballroom of the Roosevelt Hotel—Japanese-American bride, Korean-American groom, a couple of law students. Her father, a Glendale-born surgeon; his, an immigrant appliance dealer, barely able to speak English. Petra wondered about culture clash.

The body was one of the bride's cousins, a thirty-two-year-old CPA named Baldwin Yoshimura, found midway through the reception in an unlocked stall of the hotel men's room, his neck twisted so hard he looked like something out of *The Exorcist.* It took strong hands to do that, the coroner pronounced.

Petra, working with no partner once again, talked to every friend and relative and finally unearthed the fact that Baldwin Yoshimura had been a serious lothario who'd made no distinction between married and unmarried conquests. As she continued to probe, she encountered nervous glances on the bride's side. Finally, a third cousin named Wendy Sakura blurted out the truth: Baldwin had been fooling with his brother Darwin's wife.

Darwin was a martial arts instructor who worked at a studio in

Woodland Hills. Petra dropped in at the dojo, watched him put an advanced judo class through its paces. Stocky little guy, shaved head, pleasant demeanor. When the class was over, he approached Petra, arms extended for cuffing, saying, "I did it. Arrest me."

Back at the station, he refused a lawyer, couldn't wait to spill.

"What about your wife?" said Petra.

"What about her?"

"You didn't hurt her."

"She's a woman," said Darwin Yoshimura. "She's weak. Baldwin should've known better."

The second whodunit started off as bloodstains in Los Feliz and ended up with a d.b. out in Angeles Crest National Forest. This victim was a grocer named Bedros Kashigian. The blood was found in the parking lot behind his market on Edgemont. Kashigian and his five-year-old Cadillac were missing. Two days later, forest rangers found the Caddy pulled to the side of the road in the forest, Kashigian's body slumped behind the wheel. Dried blood had streamed out of his left ear, but there were no obvious wounds.

As far as Petra could tell, the grocer was a solid citizen, married, three kids, nice house, no outstanding debts. But a solid week of investigating Kashigian's activities gave rise to the fact that he'd been involved in a brawl two days before his disappearance.

Barroom melee at a place on Alvarado. Latino clientele, but Kashigian had a thing for one of the Salvadoran waitresses and went there frequently. The fracas got going when two drunks started pounding each other. Kashigian got caught in the middle and ended up being punched in the head. Only once, according to the bartender. An errant fist, and Kashigian had left the bar on his feet.

Kashigian's widow, dealing with her loss as well as the new insight that Bedros had been cheating on her, said hubby had complained of a headache. Couple of aspirins, he'd seemed fine.

Petra phoned the coroner, an unconscionably cheerful guy named Rosenberg, and asked if a single, bare-knuckle blow to the head could be fatal two days after the fact. Rosenberg said he doubted it.

A scan of Kashigian's insurance records showed hefty whole life and first-to-die policies as well as medical claims paid five years ago when the grocer had been involved in a nine-car pileup that had shattered his skull and caused intracranial bleeding. Brought into the ER unconscious, Kashigian had been wheeled into surgery where a half dollar–size piece of skull had been sawed off so his brain could be cleaned up. That section, labeled a "roundel" by Rosenberg, had been reattached using sutures and screws.

After hearing about the accident, Rosenberg had changed his mind. "The roundel was anchored by scar tissue," he told Petra. "And the darn thing grew back thinner than the rest of the skull. Unfortunately for your guy, that's exactly where he took the punch. The rest of his head could have withstood the impact, but the thin spot couldn't. It shattered, drove bone slivers into his brain, caused a slow bleed, and finally *boom*."

"Tell me this, Dr. R., could he have driven to the forest out of confusion?"

"Let me think. With shards of bone slicing into his gray matter, a slow bleed—yeah, he could've been hazy, disoriented."

Which didn't explain why Angeles Crest, specifically.

She asked Captain Schoelkopf if she should pursue homicide charges against the guy who'd landed the punch.

"Who is he?"

"Don't know yet."

"A bar fight." Schoelkopf flashed her the are-you-retarded? look. "Write it up as an accidental death."

Lacking the will—or the desire—to argue, she complied, then went to inform the widow, who told her Angeles Crest was where she and Bedros used to go to make out when they were teenagers.

"At least he left me some good insurance," said the woman.

WITHIN days after closing both files, the loneliness set in. Petra had made the mistake of getting intimate with a partner, and now she was working and living solo. The object of her affections was a taciturn detective named Eric Stahl with a military background in army special services and a history that had unfurled slowly.

The first time Petra had seen his black suit, pale skin, and flat, dark eyes, she'd thought, *undertaker*. She'd disliked him instinctively, and the feeling appeared mutual. Somehow things had changed. They'd started working together on the Cold Heart homicides, coordinating with Milo Sturgis in West L.A. to put away a psychopath who got off on dispatching creative types. Closing that one hadn't come easy. Eric had nearly died of stab wounds. Sitting, waiting, in the ER waiting room, Petra had met his parents, learned why he didn't talk or emote or act remotely human.

He'd once had a family—wife and two kids—but had lost everything. Heather, Danny, and Dawn. Taken from him cruelly. He'd resigned his military commission, spent a year doped up on antidepressants, then applied to the LAPD, where connections got him a Detective I appointment, Hollywood Division, where Schoelkopf had foisted him on Petra.

Whatever Schoelkopf knew, he'd kept to himself. Uninformed, Petra tried to get along, but faced with a partner with all the warmth of ceramic tile, she soon gave up. The two of them ended up splitting chores, minimizing the time they spent together.

Then came a night full of terror. Even now, Petra wondered if Eric had been trying to commit Suicide by Perp.

She had not been the only woman in his life, but when Eric woke up, it was her hand holding his, her eyes locking with his bruised, brown irises. During the months of recuperation, Petra cooked for Eric. Growing up with five brothers and a widowed father in Arizona, she'd learned to be handy around the kitchen. During the brief time her marriage lasted, she'd played at gourmet. Now a divorcée, she rarely bothered to switch on the oven. But healing Eric with home-cooked goodies had seemed terribly urgent.

In the end, Petra and Eric went from awkwardness to reluctant self-disclosure to friendship to closeness. When they finally made love, she found him the best lover she'd ever encountered.

They split up as partners and continued as lovers, living apart— Eric in his rented bungalow in Studio City, Petra in her flat on

Detroit, near Museum Row. Then September 11 hit, and Eric's Special Forces background made the department look at him in a new way. Transferred out of Homicide to the newly formed Homeland Security Squad, he was sent overseas for antiterrorist training. This month it was Israel, learning about suicide bombers and profiling and things he couldn't tell her about.

He called when he could, e-mailed her sporadically but couldn't receive electronic messages. She'd last heard from him a week ago. Jerusalem was a beautiful city, the Israelis were tough and tactless and reasonably competent; he planned to be back in two weeks.

Working solo suited her just fine, but she knew it was only a matter of time before some new transfer was foisted on her.

After closing Yoshimura and Kashigian, she took a couple of days off, figuring on a little downtime.

Instead, she got a bloodbath and Isaac Gomez.

IT HAPPENED the day she started painting again. Forcing herself to get up by ten and using the daylight to copy a Georgia O'Keeffe she'd always loved. A gray, vertical New York city scene from O'Keeffe's early days. Pure genius—no way could she hope to capture it—but the struggle would be good. It had been months since she'd lifted a brush, and starting out was rough. But by two p.m. she was in the groove. At six she sat down to appraise her work and fell asleep on the living-room couch.

A call from the station woke her up at one fifteen a.m.

"Multiple one eighty-sevens at the Paradiso Club, Sunset near Western, all hands on deck," said the dispatcher. "It's probably on TV already."

Petra flicked on the tube as she headed for the shower. A bunch of kids shot outside the Paradiso. Some sort of hip-hop concert, an altercation in the parking lot, gun barrel poking out of a car window. Four bodies.

By the time Petra got there, the area had been cordoned off and the victims were covered with coroner's tarp: a quartet of bundles lying at random angles under a blue-black Hollywood sky. The corner of one of the tarps had blown loose, revealing a sneakered foot. Pink sneaker, smallish.

High-intensity lights turned the parking lot glossy. What looked to be over a hundred kids had been divided into groups, guarded by uniformed officers. Five groups, all potential witnesses. The Paradiso, a movie theater turned concert venue, could seat over a thousand. These kids were the chosen few.

Petra spotted detectives Abrams, Montoya, Dilbeck, and Haas. Now that she was here, five D's for five groups.

MacDonald Dilbeck was a DIII with thirty years' experience, and he'd be the boss on this one. She headed over to him.

Mac was a sixty-one-year-old ex-marine with silver Brylcreemed hair and a gray sharkskin suit just as glossy. A five-eight fireplug, Mac wore a faux ruby high school ring and an LAPD tie bar. He lived in Simi Valley, and his civilian ride was an old Caddy. On weekends he rode horses. Married for forty years. Petra judged him smarter than most doctors and lawyers she'd met.

He said, "Sorry for screwing up your vacation."

"Looks like we need all the help we can get."

"It was a massacre. Four children."

He drew her away from the bodies. "The concert ended at eleven thirty, but kids hung around in the parking lot. Cars were leaving, but one reversed direction and backed up to the crowd. Slowly, so no one noticed. Then an arm stuck out and started shooting. Security guard was too far away to see it, but he heard a dozen shots. Four hits, all fatal, looks like a nine millimeter."

Petra glanced at the nearest group of kids. "They don't look hard-core. What kind of concert was it?"

"Your basic lightweight hip-hop, some Latin stuff. From what we're hearing, it was a well-behaved crowd. These are the kids unlucky enough to be sticking around when the black-and-whites arrived. All we've got out of them is a relatively consistent description of the shooter's car. Small, black or dark blue or dark gray, most likely a Honda or a Toyota. Not a single digit of license plate. When the shooting started, everyone dropped or ducked or ran."

"But all these kids hung around."

"Uniforms arrived within two minutes, code three," said Dilbeck. "Didn't let anyone leave."

"Who called it in?"

"At least eight people. The official informant's a bouncer." He frowned. "The vics are two boys and two girls."

"How old?"

"We I.D.'d three: fifteen, fifteen, and seventeen. The fourth, one of the girls, had no paper on her. It stinks, doesn't it? Maybe I *should* fold my tent." He'd been talking retirement for as long as Petra had known him.

"I'd like a look at the bodies before they get taken away."

"Look, then have a go at that nearest group."

Petra learned what she could about the victims. Paul Montalvo, two weeks from his sixteenth birthday. Chubby, round-faced. Smooth olive skin where it wasn't distorted by a gunshot under his right eye. Wanda Duarte, seventeen. Gorgeous, pale, with long black hair, rings on eight of her fingers, five ear pierces. Three chest shots. Kennerly Dalkin, fifteen, looked closer to twelve. Fair-skinned, freckled, shaved head. Black leather jacket, and skull pendant hanging from a leather thong around a neck that had been pierced by a bullet. In his wallet was a card proclaiming him to be a member of the honor society at Birmingham High.

The unidentified girl was probably Hispanic. Short, busty, with shoulder-length curly hair dyed rust at the tips. Tight white top, tight black jeans. Pink sneakers—the shoes Petra had spied—not much larger than a size five.

Another head shot, just in front of her right ear. Four others in her torso. The pockets of her jeans had been turned inside out. Petra inspected her cheap Leatherette purse. Chewing gum, tissues, twenty bucks cash, two packets of condoms.

Petra kneeled by the girl's side. Then she got up to do her job.

EIGHTEEN know-nothings.

She addressed them as a group, tried coming on gently, stressing the importance of cooperation to prevent something like this from happening again. Her reward was eighteen blank stares.

She had them form a line, took down names and addresses and phone numbers, acted casual as she checked out their nonverbal behavior. Two nervous girls stood out, a serious handwringer and a nonstop foot tapper. She held them back, let the others go.

Bonnie Ramirez and Sandra Leon, both sixteen. They dressed similarly—tight tops, low riders, and high-heeled boots—but didn't know each other. Bonnie was still wringing her hands as Petra reiterated the importance of being open and honest.

"I *am* honest," she said. Fluent English.

"What about the car, Bonnie?"

"I told you, I didn't see it. I really gotta go."

"What's the rush, Bonnie?"

"George's only babysitting till one, and it's way after that."

"You've got a kid?"

"Two years old," said Bonnie with a mixture of pride and amazement. "Rocky."

"Got a picture?"

Bonnie reached for her bag, then stopped. "What do you care? George said if I don't get home on time, he'll just leave, and Rocky sometimes gets up in the night. I don't want him to be all scared."

"Who's George?"

"The father," said the girl. "Rocky's a George, too. Jorge junior. I call him Rocky to make him different from George 'cause I don't like how George acts."

"How does George act?"

"He doesn't give me nothing."

SANDRA Leon had stopped tapping her foot, switched to hugging herself tightly. Dark skin clashed with a huge mass of platinum blond hair. Deep red lipstick. She wore cheap, fake-o gold jewelry. A parody of sexy—sixteen going on thirty.

Before Petra could ask, she said, "I don't know nothing."

Allowing her eyes to drift to the victims, to pink sneakers, Petra said, "Wonder where she got those shoes."

Sandra Leon looked everywhere but at Petra. "Why would I know?" Biting her lip.

"You okay?" said Petra.

The girl forced herself to meet Petra's gaze. Her eyes were dull. "Why wouldn't I be? Can I go now?"

"You're sure there's nothing you want to tell me?"

Sudden hostility. "I don't have to talk to you."

"Says who?"

"The law."

"You have experience with the law?" said Petra.

"My brother's in jail."

"Where?"

"Lompoc."

"Your brother's your legal expert? Look where he is."

Sandra shrugged. The platinum hair shifted. A wig.

Petra took a closer look. Noticed something else about the girl's eyes. Dull because they were yellow around the edges. "You okay?"

"I will be when you let me go." Sandra Leon righted her hairpiece and smiled. "Leukemia. They gave me chemo at Western Pediatrics. I used to have real nice hair. They say it'll grow back, but maybe they're lying." Tears filled her eyes. "Can I go now?"

"Sure."

- - C H A P T E R   2 - -

OVER the next week, five detectives worked the Paradiso shootings, interviewing family members of the dead teens, recontacting potential witnesses. None of the victims had gang affiliations; all were praised as good kids. The girl in the pink sneakers remained unidentified. One interesting fact from the coroner: The girl had undergone an abortion within the last few months.

Petra asked Mac Dilbeck if she could go to the media, and he said sure. Three stations ran sketchy renderings of the girl's face on the evening news. A few calls came in, nothing serious.

Petra worked the shoes, but they were just Kmart specials, made in Macao, shipped to the States in huge lots for over a year.

She tried to recontact Sandra Leon because Sandra had given off an uneasy vibe, though maybe it was just tension about being sick. The phone rang, but no one answered.

Ten days after the mass murder, the team still hadn't developed any leads, and at the next sit-down meeting, Mac Dilbeck informed them they'd been cut from five D's to three: He'd remain as the principal, and Luc Montoya and Petra would do backup.

After the meeting, Petra said to him, "The unidentified girl—I'm wondering if she's the key. No one's reported her missing. Maybe someone wanted her really gone."

Mac smoothed his glossy hair. "You want to try to chase her down some more?"

"I can try."

"Yeah, it's a good idea." He frowned. "I got a big fat 'what if' floating around in here—as in, what if there was no motive, just a bunch of bad guys out to kill some people?"

"Wouldn't that be lovely," said Petra.

Two days of working the anonymous girl proved maddening. Petra was at her desk eating a hot dog when the sound of a throat clearing made her look up.

Isaac Gomez. Again.

He stood off to the side, wearing his usual blue button-down shirt, pressed khakis, and penny loafers. Black hair parted and plastered down like a choir boy's. Smooth, brown face all freshly scrubbed. He held a stack of old murder books to his chest and said, "I hope I'm not bothering you, Detective Connor."

Of course, he was. And of course, she smiled up at him.

Every time she saw Isaac, Petra thought of a Diego Rivera kid grown up—the hair straight as brush bristle; the nutmeg skin; the huge, liquid, almond eyes; the clear hints of Indian blood in the elevated cheekbones and finely boned nose. Isaac was five ten, maybe one-fifty, with square shoulders, bony wrists, and a deliberate but awkward way of moving. Chronologically, he was twenty-two and a year away from his Ph.D. Lord only knew how old he was intellectually. But when conversation veered away from facts and figures, he could end up mired in aw-shucks adolescence.

"What's up, Isaac? What are you doing here at this hour?"

She expected a smile—the embarrassed smile she seemed to elicit from him. No smile this evening. He looked tense.

Eight fourteen p.m. The detectives room was nearly empty. She'd been playing with the computer, logging on to missing kids databases, still trying to trace the girl in the pink shoes.

"I got involved . . . started with one thing and ended with another." Isaac hefted the pile of blue notebooks.

"Why don't you pull up a chair," said Petra.

"I'm sorry if this is disruptive, Detective Connor. I know you're working Paradiso, and under normal circumstances I wouldn't intrude." Flicker of smile. "I guess that's not true. I've intruded quite a bit, haven't I?"

"Not at all," Petra lied. The truth was, babysitting Brain Boy could be a butt-aching disruption when things got busy.

Isaac sat. "I was working on my multiple regression analysis—plugging in new variables . . ." He shook his head, as if emptying it of extraneous information. "You don't need to hear all that. The essential point is, I was searching for additional ways to organize my data and, serendipitously, I came across something I thought you should see." He stopped. Took a breath. "It's going to sound . . . On the surface, it may look like nothing, some kind of coincidence, but I've done statistical tests, each one covering the mathematical weaknesses of the others, and it's obvious that it's not just a quirk."

Petra sat there.

"It's totally weird," he went on, "but I'm sure it's real."

He began to open murder books. He started off talking softly and ended up shooting out words, like an automatic weapon.

Assault-brain.

Petra listened. Brilliant or not, the kid was an amateur; this had to be nonsense.

IRMA Gomez had been working for the Lattimores for nine years before she said anything about the problem with Isaac.

Doctors Seth and Marilyn Lattimore lived in a nineteen-room Tudor on Hudson Avenue in Hancock Park. Both Lattimores were surgeons in their sixties—he a thoracic man, she an ophthalmologist. Both were no-nonsense perfectionists, but pleasant and generous when not weighed down by professional concerns. They cared deeply for one another, had raised three children, all presently in various stages of medical training.

Six days a week, Irma Gomez had taken the bus from her three-room apartment in the Union District and showed up at eight a.m. at the Lattimore mansion. She was a quiet woman, made quieter by her failure to learn English better during the eleven years she'd lived in the United States. She and her husband, Isaiah, had three kids, and by the time Irma began working for the Lattimores, Little Isaiah was four, Isaac two, and baby Joel a rambunctious infant.

Midway through the ninth year of Irma's employment, Dr. Marilyn Lattimore came down with an uncharacteristic cold and was home for two days. It was in the breakfast room that the conversation took place. Dr. Marilyn sat sipping tea and dabbing at her red, drippy nose. Irma was in the adjoining kitchen.

"Do you believe this, Irma? A week of surgeries and I come down with this arrogant little virus."

Dr. Marilyn was a pretty woman, small, with honey-colored hair. She walked two miles every morning at six a.m., followed by half an hour on an elliptical machine.

Irma said, "You strong. You get better soon."

"I certainly hope so. Would you be a dear and get me some of the fig preserve for my toast?"

Irma fetched the jar and brought it over.

"Thank you, dear."

"Something else, Dr. M.?"

"No, thank you, dear. . . . Are *you* all right, Irma?"

Irma forced a smile. "I fine, Dr. M.," she said and started to head back to the kitchen.

"Turn around and look me in the eye and tell me that. Please, Irma."

"I— Is nothing."

"Irma."

"I worry about Isaac."

"Isaac? Is he all right?"

"Yes, he very good. He eleven, now. Very smart." Irma broke down in tears.

"He's smart, and you're crying?" said Dr. Marilyn. "Am I missing something?"

They had tea and fig jam on thin toast, and Irma told Dr. Marilyn all of it. How Isaac kept coming home from school crying with frustration and boredom. How he'd finished all of his sixth-grade work in two months, taken it upon himself to "borrow" seventh- and eighth- and even some ninth-grade books and had sped through them. Finally, he was caught reading a prealgebra workbook and was sent to the principal's office for "unauthorized study and irregular behavior."

Irma tried to handle it on her own. The principal had nothing but disdain for Irma's simple clothes and thick accent; her firm suggestion was that Isaac concentrate on conforming to "class standards." When Irma tried to point out that the boy was well ahead of class standards, the principal cut her off and informed her that Isaac was just going to have to be content repeating everything.

"That's outrageous," said Dr. Marilyn. "A child that bright, Irma, there's no limit. . . . Give me that principal's number, and I'll have a little chat with her."

Irma looked down at the floor. Silence.

"What's the number, dear?" said Dr. Marilyn.

"I don' understand," said Irma finally. "I don' understand where Isaac come from. I not smart, Isaiah not smart, the other two . . ."

"You're smart enough, dear. Do you realize what a *gift* you've been given? What someone like Isaac could *do?*" Dr. Marilyn stood. "I'm going to call that fool of a principal. One way or another, we'll get to the bottom of this mess."

But Dr. Marilyn fared no better than Irma.

She then conferred with Dr. Seth, and the two of them took it upon themselves to confer with Melvyn Pogue, Ed.D., headmaster of the Burton Academy, where young John, Bradley, and Elizabeth Lattimore had earned nearly straight A's.

The timing was perfect. Burton had come under fire from some of its progressive alumni for being lily white and elitist.

"This boy," said Dr. Pogue, "sounds perfect."

"He's extremely clever," said Dr. Seth. "But perfection's a bit overreaching. We don't want to pressure the lad."

"Yes, yes, of course, Dr. Lattimore." In Pogue's top desk drawer was a freshly signed Lattimore check—full tuition for an entire year, with money left over for gymnasium refurbishment.

Isaac arrived at the Burton campus, just a brief walk from the Lattimore mansion, freshly barbered and wearing his best church clothes. A school psychologist ran him through a battery of tests and pronounced him "off the scale." A week later, he'd transferred to Burton as a seventh grader.

His brothers, happy and recalcitrant in public school, thought the whole deal was weird—the Burton uniform, with its blue jacket and striped tie, taking the bus to work with Mama, hanging with Anglos all day. When they asked Isaac about it, he said, "It's okay."

In reality, it was better than okay. It was fabulous. For the first time in his life, his mind was being allowed to go where it wanted. Despite the fact that most of the other Burton students regarded him as a little dark-skinned curiosity and he was often left alone.

He *loved* being alone. He read—chewed up books. He stayed in school well past dismissal time waiting for Irma to come by to pick him up, and the two of them would then embark on the long bus journey back to the Union District.

Isaac accustomed himself to a double life: Burton's beaux arts buildings and emerald playing fields by day, by night the burp of gunfire and screams and static-scratchy salsa outside the window of the closet-size bedroom he shared with his brothers.

After junior high, his four years of high school were compressed to two. He graduated at age fifteen with full honors and was accepted as a "special circumstances" student at the University of Southern California.

It was in college that he decided to become a doctor, and he earned a 4.0 as a bio major with a minor in math. USC wanted to hold on to him, and by the time he graduated summa cum laude, Phi Beta Kappa, at barely nineteen, he'd been accepted to the university's Keck School of Medicine.

His parents celebrated, but Isaac wasn't sure. Deep down he knew he wasn't mature enough for the responsibility of tending to other human beings. He requested and received a deferral, needing a break—something less structured. For Isaac that meant a Ph.D. in epidemiology and biostatistics. By age twenty-one, he'd fulfilled all his course requirements, earned a master's degree, and began work on his doctoral dissertation: "Discriminating and Predictive Patterns of Solved and Unsolved Homicides in Los Angeles Between 1991 and 2001."

Though care had been taken by the university to shield its boy wonder from publicity, news of Isaac's triumphs reached the desk of city councilman Gilbert Reyes, who promptly issued a press release in which he took credit for everything the young man had accomplished.

Upon the strong advice of his faculty adviser, Isaac attended a luncheon where he sat next to Reyes and contradicted nothing the councilman said. The experience left him vaguely unsettled, but when the time came to request access to LAPD files for his research, Isaac knew whom to call. Within two days, he had an authorized long-term visitor's badge, a jerry-built "internship," and guaranteed access to inactive homicide files. His desk would be at Hollywood Division, because Gilbert Reyes was a serious buddy of Deputy Chief Randy Diaz, the new Hollywood Division overboss.

Isaac showed up at Hollywood bright and early on an April Monday and met with an unpleasant police captain named Schoelkopf.

Schoelkopf regarded Isaac as if he were a suspect, didn't even pretend to pay attention as Isaac rattled off his hypotheses, nor did he listen as Isaac offered profound thanks for the desk.

"Yeah, fine," said the captain. "Ask for Connor. She'll take real good care of you."

It was nothing Petra would ever have noticed, even if it had stared her in the face. Isaac's neatly typed sheet lay flat on her desk. As he sat in the metal chair by her desk, she read the heading again: "June 28 Homicides: An Embedded Pattern?" Below the title was a list of six homicides, all on June 28, on or near midnight.

Six in six years. Her initial reaction was *big deal.* L.A.'s annual homicide rate settled in at around two hundred fifty. Meaning some days there was nastiness, others nothing at all. When you considered summer heat, June 28 would very likely be one of the high-ticket dates.

She said all that to Isaac. He shot out his answer so quickly she knew he'd been expecting the objection: "It's not just the quantity, Detective Connor. It's the quality. By quality I mean the inherent properties of the crimes, the . . ." He trailed off.

"Go on," said Petra. "Just keep it simple. I was an art major."

He colored. "Sorry, I tend to get—"

"Hey," she said, "just kidding. I asked you to tell me about your statistical tests and you did." At breakneck speed.

"The tests," he said, "aren't any big deal; they just examine phenomena mathematically. As in the likelihood of something happening by chance. I compared June twenty-eighth with every other day of the year. You're right about homicides clustering, but no other date presents this pattern. Even summer effects tend to manifest on weekends or holidays. These six cases fall on various days of the week. In fact, only one—the first murder—took place on a weekend."

"What else?"

"Okay . . . another way to look at it is to examine inherent base probabilities—" He stopped and blushed. "There I go again. Let's take it issue by issue. Start with weapon of choice. Firearms are the clear favorite of L.A. murderers. I've looked at twenty years' worth of one eighty-sevens, and seventy-three percent have been carried out with handguns, rifles, or shotguns. Knives and other sharp objects are next, at around fifteen percent. That means those two modalities account for nearly ninety percent of all local murders. The FBI's national figures are similar. So the fact that neither a gun nor a knife was used on any of the June twenty-eighth cases is notable. As is the nature of the fatal injury. In every data bank I've checked, blunt-force homicides never rise above the level of five percent. They're a rare occurrence, Detective Connor. I'm sure you know that better than I."

"Isaac, I just closed two cases. A bare-fist blow to the head and a broken neck via martial arts."

He frowned. "Have you seen many others?"

Petra thought. She shook her head. "Not for a while."

"If we get even more specific, cranial bludgeoning by unknown weapon accounts for no more than three percent of L.A. homicides. But it makes up one *hundred* percent of these cases. When you add the other similarities—identical calendar day, same approximate time, probable stranger homicides, and look at the probability of a chance cluster, you're moving way past coincidence."

Petra said, "That it?"

"Actually, there is a bit more. LAPD homicide detectives solve between two thirds and three quarters of their cases, yet all of *these* cases remain unsolved."

"That's because they're stranger homicides. You've been here long enough to see the kind of stuff we clear quickly: Some moron holding the smoking gun when the uniforms get there."

"I think you're selling yourself short, Detective Connor," he said sincerely. "Even stranger homicides get solved. But not one of these.

All that supports my thesis: These are highly irregular events."
She slid the list out from under his hand, took a closer look.

June 28 Homicides: An Embedded Pattern?

1. 1997: 12:12 a.m. Marta Doebbler, 29, Sherman Oaks, married white female. Out with friends at Pantages Theater in H'wood, went to ladies' room, never returned. Found in own car, backseat, depressed skull fracture.
2. 1998: 12:06 a.m. Geraldo Luis Solis, 63, widowed Hispanic male. Found in his house, breakfast room, Wilsh. Div., food taken but no money, depressed skull fracture.
3. 1999: 12:45 a.m. Coral Laurine Langdon, 52, single white female, walked her dog in H'wood Hills, found by patrol car, six blocks from home. Depressed skull fracture. Dog ("Brandy," 10 y.o. cockapoo) stomped to death.
4. 2000: 12:56 a.m. Darren Ares Hochenbrenner, 19, single black male, navy ensign, stationed in Port Hueneme, on shore leave H'wood, found in alley, Fourth Street, Cent. Div., pockets emptied. Depressed skull fracture.
5. 2001: 12:01 a.m. Jewell Blank, 14, single white female, runaway, found in Griffith Park. Depressed skull fracture.
6. 2002: 12:28 a.m. Curtis Marc Hoffey, 20, single white male, known gay hustler, found in alley, Highland near Sunset. Depressed skull fracture.

Petra looked up. "There doesn't seem to be any pattern victim-wise."

"I know," said Isaac, "but still . . ." He looked crushed.

"You've raised some interesting points." She pointed to the list. "But these people are all over the place in terms of sex, age, social class. We've got urban and semirural dumpsites. If this is some kind of serial thing, there'd most likely be a sexual angle, and I can't see what a sixty-three-year-old man and a fourteen-year-old girl would have in common as sexual targets."

"Why," he broke in, "does there have to be a sexual angle?"

"That's the way it tends to shake out."

"The FBI profile. Yes, yes, I know about all of that. I'm sure that typically there's some truth to that. But reality depends on which prism you're using. The FBI interviewed imprisoned killers and compiled data banks. But data are only as good as the sample, and who says killers who get caught are similar to those who don't?"

"What motive are you proposing?" said Petra.

Long pause. "I don't know."

Neither of them spoke. Isaac slumped. "Okay, thanks for your time." He scooped up the list and stashed it in the shiny brown briefcase he carried around. Petra had heard the comments behind Isaac's back. *Brainiac. Petra's little day-care project.*

Now she found herself feeling protective of the kid but annoyed. The last thing she needed was some theory that got her dredging up six years of cold cases. Not with four victims down at the Paradiso, one of them a girl she couldn't even identify. On the other hand, Isaac was smarter than she was. Dismissing him out of hand could turn out to be one of those *big* mistakes.

Isaac got to his feet. "Sorry for wasting your time. Is there something I can do for you on your main case?"

"My main case?"

"The Paradiso. I've heard it's been tough going."

"Have you?" she said. Hearing the chill in her voice, she coerced her lips to form a smile. Stratospheric I.Q. or not, he was a kid. An overly enthusiastic, pain-in-the-butt politically *connected* kid. "It's been a tough one," she agreed. "All those kids mowed down, no one willing to talk. What could you do for me?"

"I don't know," he said. "Maybe look at the data." Now he was blushing again.

"I'd appreciate it," she said. Not meaning a word, but keeping the damn smile on high beam.

Nearly nine p.m. The kid was working late, too. And not getting paid. She said, "How about some dinner—a burger, whatever."

"Thanks, but I need to get home. My mother made dinner, and it's a big deal to her if we don't all show up."

"Okay," she said. "Maybe another time." The genius still lived with his folks—the Union District, she recalled.

"Make me a copy of that list," she said.

Biiiiig smile. "Will do. Have a nice evening, Detective Connor."

"You, too." *Professor Gomez.*

A COPY of the list was on Petra's desk the following afternoon. There was a yellow Post-it in the upper right-hand corner: *"Detective C: Thanks. I. G."* She put it aside and spent the next two days talking to Missing Persons cops throughout California, faxing morgue shots of the girl in the pink shoes, getting a few callbacks but no leads. She thought about expanding to neighboring states.

Phoning her way through Arizona and Nevada took another full day. She then moved on to New Mexico, without success.

Another shift full of nothing made her grouchy. A touch of romance wouldn't have hurt, but it had been a week since Eric's last call. She wasn't even sure where he was.

Time to pack it in, go home, take a long, hot bath. She'd snarf whatever was in the fridge and hopefully have the energy to take a stab at her O'Keeffe project.

Just as she locked up her desk, her cell phone squawked from inside her purse. She fumbled past her gun, tissues, and makeup and caught it on the third ring.

"Hi," said a voice she'd once thought flat, mechanical, freakishly unemotional.

She said, "Hi. Where'd they send you now?"

"I sent myself. I'm down in the parking lot."

Her heart leaped. "The parking lot? Here? I'm coming down."

Eric stood next to Petra's Accord, half-concealed in the shadows. He had on a black nylon windbreaker, half-zipped over a white T-shirt, pipestem black jeans. Those black, crepe-soled shoes he liked for stakeouts. He looked even thinner than usual. Dark hair cropped even shorter—back to the military cut. A middle-sized, skinny guy with the pallor of a seminary student. No attempt to posture, but still the James Dean thing amped big-time, filling Petra's head.

How could she ever have thought him anything but sexy?

Petra hurried to him, and they embraced. He buried his face in her hair, held her tight—the pressure of a needy child.

She said, "You okay?"

"Now I am."

"Why didn't you come upstairs?"

"Technically, I'm not here."

She took his face in her hands, kissed his eyelids, then held him at arm's length. "Where are you supposed to be?"

"Jerusalem."

"What, you went AWOL?"

"The Israelis took a break because they've got business to take care of in Jenin. A chance came up to hitch a ride on a plane."

"How long can you stay?"

"I need to leave tomorrow p.m."

"One night," said Petra.

"Is that okay?"

"Of course." She kissed his nose. "You have a car?"

He shook his head. "Took a taxi."

They got into the Accord. Petra started the car and noticed the dark smudges under his eyes. "How long have you been in transit?"

"Twenty-three hours."

"Some hitch."

They went to an old-fashioned chianti-bottles-dangling-from-the ceiling taverna, ordered veal marsala and spaghetti with clams and slices of spumoni for dessert. No wine. Eric never drank.

Later, in bed in Petra's apartment, they were snuggled under the covers, and Eric began rubbing the twin soft spots just inside her shoulder blades. The places she'd told him always got sore.

"Oh, man," she said. "I'm not sure I'm gonna let you out of here tomorrow."

"You tie me up," he said. "It would be an excuse."

"Don't tempt me."

ERIC, THE MOST TACITURN OF men, sometimes mumbled in his sleep. But what woke Petra in the middle of the night was her own, internal voice—some kind of warning. She turned, stared at his face, and saw calm. The second time she awoke it was just after noon, and Eric was up and showering. By twelve thirty Petra was cooking eggs. They ate and read the paper—Lord, wasn't this domestic?

At one thirty, Eric kissed her and headed for the door.

"I'll drive you," she said.

"I called a cab."

He'd arrived with no luggage and was leaving the same way, wearing fresh duds selected from the clothing he'd left in her guest closet. Zipping halfway across the world with nothing but a wallet. Here and back. To see her.

She said, "Cancel the taxi. I'm taking you."

SHE didn't arrive at the Hollywood station until six twenty-five p.m. No messages from Mac Dilbeck or anyone else on the Paradiso case. What to do now?

A voice from across the room said, "Detective Connor."

Isaac Gomez, wearing an olive suit, yellow shirt, green-and-red rep tie, toted his briefcase toward her desk.

"Very spiffy," she said. "Heavy-duty meeting?"

The predictable blush darkened his neck. "A date," he blurted. "I had to go on a lunch date."

"*Had to?* You make it sound like homework."

Isaac sighed. "In a sense it was. I was assigned by my mother. She thinks I need to get out more."

"You disagree."

"I'm social enough, Detective Connor. My mother's notion of maximal personal success is that I meet a girl who elevates me socially. It's complicated, and I'm sure you're not interested."

He bit his lip. Poor kid was under real pressure.

"Hey," she said, "you're smart in all kinds of ways. You'll do what's best for yourself."

Petra pointed to the chair by her desk. He sat heavily.

"Lousy date, huh?"

"I'm that obvious?" He grinned, then said, "Anyway . . . about those June twenty-eighth cases. I neglected to mention that four of six took place here, in Hollywood Division."

"Isaac, I promise to take a look, but right now I'm tied up."

"The Paradiso shootings."

"Exactly."

"Has that girl been identified?"

"Not yet."

"Okay. Sorry for—"

"She had an abortion within the last month or two. That say anything to you?"

"The obvious thing," he said, "is a possible source of conflict. With the father. In certain situations, an unwanted pregnancy would be a pretty robust motive for homicide."

"She terminated the pregnancy, Isaac."

"But maybe she kept that fact to herself."

Petra considered that. Why not? "It's an angle. Thanks. Now all I have to do is figure out who she is."

She flashed him a smile and turned back to the mess on her desk.

"Detective Connor . . . Would it be feasible for me to ride with you? To observe what you do firsthand?"

"It's boring, Isaac. Lots of routine, lots of dead ends."

"That's okay," he said. "The longer I'm here, the more I realize how ignorant I am. I'm writing a dissertation about crime, and I don't know the first thing about it."

A trickle of sweat made its way down his left hairline. How long had he been building up the courage to ask her?

"Okay," she said. "Tomorrow morning, when I recontact some of the witnesses on the Paradiso case, you can come along. But only on one condition."

"What's that?"

"Start calling me Petra. If you don't, I'll start calling you Dr. Gomez."

HE'D DOZED OFF AND DREAMED, when the bus came to a quick stop. Jolted awake, Isaac looked up in time to see the driver throw out a homeless man who'd failed to produce the fare.

Angry words shot through the bus's wheezing door as the wretchedly filthy evictee stood in the gutter and howled vengeance. Isaac watched the man, bent over in shame, turned tiny by the bus's departure. The driver cursed and put on speed.

The cusp of violence, he thought. So much of the crime Isaac had studied began that way. Not the June 28 murders, though. They were something different, he was sure of it.

Now to convince Detective Connor.

Petra. Thinking of her by name was unsettling; it reminded him that she was a woman. He sat lower in his seat, wanting to sink out of view. Not that any of his co-riders were the least bit interested in him. Some were regulars and surely recognized him, but no one spoke. The Somnolent Express. Before being wakened, his dreams had been pleasant. Something featuring Detective Connor—Petra. Had he been in it? He wasn't sure.

She had. Lithe and graceful, that efficient helmet of black hair. The crisp features. Ivory skin. She wasn't anywhere close to the contemporary female ideal—blond, busty, bubbly. She was the antithesis of all that, and Isaac respected her doubly for being herself, not giving in to crass social pressures.

A serious person. There seemed to be very little that amused her.

She always dressed in black. Her eyes were dark brown. Searching eyes—*working* eyes—not vehicles for flirtation.

The overall impression was a young Morticia Addams, and Isaac had heard other detectives refer to her as Morticia. But also as Barbie. That he didn't get. Petra was no Barbie.

Just the opposite. Focused, intense.

Still . . . she was a beautiful woman.

PETRA stayed at her desk until well after midnight. After Isaac left, she talked to some Hollywood gang cops. They'd heard nothing about the Paradiso killings being turf related. Then she attempted to recontact all eighteen kids she'd interviewed in the parking lot. Twelve were home, but the teens reiterated complete ignorance. Among the six she didn't reach were her two nervous ones, Bonnie Ramirez and Sandra Leon. No answer at either number, no answering machines.

Once she got her purse from her locker, the thought of going home to an empty apartment repelled her. Filling herself a cup of detective-room coffee, she bought some insomnia. She brought the coffee back to her desk and sat there alone. She went through old messages, then filled out a long-overdue pension form.

What remained was Isaac's June 28 summary.

She separated the Hollywood cases from the others, copied down the vics' names, and logged on to the station's stat file. Just as Isaac claimed, all four remained open. Of the four primary detectives assigned to the case, she recognized two. Neil Wahlgren had been assigned the most recent murder: Curtis Hoffey, the twenty-year-old male hustler. Jewell Blank, the runaway teen bludgeoned in Griffith Park, had been given to Max Stokes.

Neil had since transferred to a Valley division, wanting to cut down on drive time. And Max Stokes had retired a year ago.

Meaning both cases could have gotten short shrift.

The cases were certain to have been transferred, but the computer didn't list the newly assigned detectives.

On to the next one. Coral Langdon, the woman who'd died with her dog up in the Hollywood Hills. That one had been handled by Shirley Lenois. Seeing her name made Petra's eyes ache. When Petra had started at Hollywood, Shirley had been the only other female homicide detective. A short, stocky, fifty-two-year-old woman with a corona of yellow-gray hair, Shirley looked more like a substitute teacher than a detective. She had five kids and treated Petra like the sixth. Last December, Shirley had died in a skiing accident.

Petra moved on to the fourth Hollywood murder. First of the six chronologically in Isaac's alleged series. Marta Doebbler, the woman who'd gone to the theater with her friends. Six years ago, well before Petra's time. Two detectives she'd never heard of, a DIII named

Conrad Ballou and DII named Enrique Martinez, handled the case. Maybe Ballou and Martinez had done their best, anyway.

Sometimes that didn't matter.

- - CHAPTER 3 - -

WHEN Petra showed up at ten the following morning, Isaac was at his corner desk poring over documents, pretending not to notice her arrival. She felt queasy, in no mood for babysitting. By ten twenty she'd swallowed two cups of coffee and was ready to pretend to be human. She waved Isaac toward the door, and he followed her, carrying his briefcase over. Dark blue slacks, navy shirt, a navy tie. Dressing for ride-along.

They exited the building together but didn't talk. Petra left her Accord in its spot and took the unmarked she'd signed out.

She steered out onto the street.

"What we're going to do today," she said, "is recontact two witnesses. Both are sixteen-year-old girls; both seemed nervous when I interviewed them the first time. One might have a reason to be nervous that has nothing to do with the case. She's got leukemia."

Isaac said, "That would do it."

"You okay? You seem a bit quiet."

"I don't have anything to say." A beat. "As opposed to most of the time."

She said, "Smart people have a right to talk, Isaac. It's the dummies who get on my nerves."

A smile. But it faded quickly. "I'm here to observe and to learn. I appreciate your taking the time."

"No prob." She headed down Hollywood Boulevard to Western, then over to Los Feliz. "The first girl is named Bonnie Anne Ramirez. She lives on East One twenty-seventh. You know the area?"

"Not well. It's mostly Mexican there."

And he was Salvadoran.

Petra said, "Bonnie's sixteen, but she's got a two-year-old."

No comment for half a block; then he said, "She was nervous?"

"A defiant nervousness. Which could just mean she doesn't like the police. She has no record, but in a neighborhood like that, you could get away with stuff without having your name on a file."

BONNIE Ramirez lived with her mother, three older brothers, and little Rocky in a tiny yellow clapboard bungalow that sat behind rusting chain-link fencing. She wasn't home, and her mother was caring for Rocky. The toddler slept in a crib set up in the nine-by-nine living room. The house smelled of good food and Pine Sol.

Anna Ramirez was a short, broad woman with hair dyed red, puffy cheeks, and flabby arms. She invited them to sit and brought out cans of soda and a bowl of pretzels.

Petra said, "Any idea when Bonnie's returning?"

Anna Ramirez shook her head. "You just missed her. She comes and goes. She was out last night, slept till ten, left."

"Out late?"

"Always."

"Do you know why we're here?"

"That shooting in Hollywood. Bonnie told me about it."

"What'd she say?"

"That it happened in the parking lot. She heard shots but didn't see anything. She said she talked to a lady cop. That was you?"

Petra nodded and said, "One of the kids who was shot was a girl we still haven't been able to identify."

"That's sad."

"I was wondering if Bonnie knew her," said Petra.

"You didn't ask Bonnie if she knew her?"

"I did, and she said no. I'm just following up."

Anna Ramirez frowned. "You don't believe her."

"It's not that—"

"It's okay. Sometimes I don't believe her. Her brothers all finished school. Two of them are in junior college, but Bonnie never liked school. Down deep, she's a good girl. . . ."

Petra nodded. "Anyway, ma'am, when she gets home, if you'd be so kind as to give me a call."

THE address Sandra Leon had given wasn't far from the Ramirez home, but when they got there, Petra knew she'd been had. The numbers matched a boarded-up bodega on a run-down stretch of abandoned homes backed by weed-choked alleys. Graffiti everywhere. Angry young men with shaved heads staring, sneering.

Petra got out of there fast. She drove to Soto Avenue, not far from the county morgue, and into the lot of a busy-looking gas station where she bought coffee for herself and a Coke for Isaac. As they drank, she got the number for Western Pediatrics Hospital, asked for Oncology, and waited a long time to be connected.

The secretary on the other end said, "That's confidential," when Petra asked for Sandra Leon's address.

Petra lied. "I have reason to believe that Ms. Leon is in danger because of a multiple murder that she witnessed."

Long pause. "You need to speak to her physician. That would be Dr. Katzman. I'll put you through."

What Petra got on the other end of the line was a soft male voice on tape. "This is Dr. Bob Katzman. I'll be traveling for the next two weeks, but I will be picking up messages."

Petra hung up and reconnected to the secretary. "Dr. Katzman's gone for two weeks. All I need is Sandra Leon's address."

"You're with the police?"

I am the police, honey. "Detective Connor." Petra spelled it. "Hollywood Division. Here's my badge number—"

"No, that's okay, I'll give you Medical Records."

Five minutes later Petra had the address Sandra Leon had listed on her intake form. The girl had signed herself into care.

"Who pays her bills?"

"CCS—Children's Cancer Service, a county fund," said the clerk. The other address Sandra had used was on Gower, north of

Hollywood. Minutes from the station. Petra got back on the free-way. "See what I mean," she told Isaac. "Tedious."

"I think it's interesting," he said.

"What is?"

"The process. How you go about putting it all together."

Petra didn't believe she'd put anything together.

They went to Gower Street. Unit eleven of a twenty-unit apart-ment complex the color of honeydew melon.

"Okay," said Petra, getting out of the car. "Let's see what our lit-tle fibber has to say for herself."

When she scanned the mailboxes, unit eleven was registered to "Hawkins, A." No "Leon" on any of the slots. The front door was unlocked. They climbed the stairs and walked to the rear of the hallway to number eleven. Petra rang the bell, and a very tall black man answered the door. Rapidograph pen in one hand, ink stains on his fingertips. What Petra could see of the apartment was spare and well kept. A drafting table was pushed up against a window.

"Yes?" said the man, twirling the pen.

"Afternoon, sir," said Petra, flashing the badge. "I'm looking for Sandra Leon. She listed this apartment as her address."

"Maybe she lived here once upon a time, but not for at least a year, because that's how long I've been here."

"Is there an in-house landlord or manager?"

"I wish. These luxury accommodations are shepherded by Fran-chise Realty, headquartered in the golden city of Downey. I can give you the number, know it by heart."

Back in the car, Petra called the company. No Leons had rented any apartments in the building during the seven years Franchise had managed the place. She hung up, told Isaac. "Sandra lied twice. And that makes me *real* interested in her."

She got back on the phone and left a detailed message for Dr. Bob Katzman.

Isaac said, "Now what?"

"Now we return to the station and I try to locate little Ms. Leon. When I hit a wall, I'll take a closer look at those files of yours."

"I've been looking into June twenty-eighth to see if there's some sort of historical significance. The best criminal link I've come up with is that John Dillinger was born on that day. That could be inspirational to a sociopath. But Dillinger was a bank robber, a grandstander, very dramatic. From what I can tell, this killer's just the opposite."

This killer. Pattern. The kid was convinced of one dark hand behind all six cases. Ah, impetuous youth.

IT WAS the wound pattern that snagged her. Six p.m. As predicted, she'd hit the wall on Leon. She phoned a nearby Mr. Pizza and called out for a small deep-dish with everything on it. Across the room, Isaac remained at his corner desk punching his laptop, jotting down notes. When the pizza came, she went over and offered him a slice. He said no thanks, tailed her back to her desk.

Petra selected a slice.

Isaac said, "Have a good evening," and left the station.

She poured more coffee, picked up one of the files, and began to read. Six autopsy reports written by six separate coroners. The language was nearly identical. Compression injuries of the occipital skull. Hit from behind. In every report, the weapon was described as heavy and tubular, approximately 77 centimeters in diameter in three murders, 75 in one, 78 in two. Which was close enough, given varying bone densities in people of different ages and sexes.

Two pathologists had been willing to speculate that the bludgeon was metal or hard plastic, because no imbedded wood fragments had been found. What *had* been found was lots of blood and bone frags. To Petra the weapon sounded like a length of pipe. Seventy-seven centimeters matched three inches on her old-fashioned ruler. Nice, hefty chunk of pipe. Deep-compression injuries.

Someone—if there was a someone—liked braining people.

She started with the detective she knew still on the job. Neil Wahlgren, the D on the Curtis Hoffey case. All she'd heard was he'd transferred somewhere in the Valley. It took a while, but she located his extension at Van Nuys Auto Theft. He was away from his desk, but the Van Nuys desk officer gave her his cell, and she reached him.

"Hey," Wahlgren said. He had a hearty voice that sounded genuinely warm. Petra recalled him vaguely as a big, ruddy Nord with a bulbous nose.

"I've been looking at some cold cases and came across one of yours. Curtis Hoffey."

Right away Wahlgren said, "Male pross, hit over the head."

"That's the one."

"Messy."

"Messy in terms of crime scene or detection?"

"Both. Couldn't make an inch of progress," said Neil. "Which is no surprise, I guess, a vic like that. Twenty years old, and from what I could gather, he'd been on the streets since twelve. Poor kid probably serviced the wrong john, but there was no talk on the street and no prior similars."

"I might have one—emphasize *might*. Someone was combing through old files and came up with half a dozen head bashes that match in terms of wound pattern and weapon guestimology."

Neil said, "That so? Well, I didn't hear anything about that at the time." Defensiveness had crept into his voice.

Petra said, "No way you could. It's probably nothing. So who caught the case after you left?"

"Don't know. Schoelkopf said he'd handle the transfer. He still there? Still being a total ass?"

"Still here. If he did transfer the case, there's no record."

"No surprise," said Neil. "Even at the time, he didn't want me spending too much time on it, said we needed to pay attention to gang murders."

"So Curtis had no family?" she said, using the vic's name.

"No one claimed the body. He got bashed up pretty good. If I never see another one like it, I'll be none the worse off."

JEWELL Blank, the fourteen-year-old girl murdered in Griffith Park, had relatives, but according to Detective Max Stokes's notes, they hadn't been helpful. Petra found no record that Jewell Blank's case had been transferred to another detective.

Max Stokes appeared to have worked the case hard, getting help, as it turned out, from Shirley Lenois. The two veteran detectives had scoured the streets, interviewed scores of other runaways, checked the shelters and the churches and the agencies.

Jewell had squatted, on and off, in some of Hollywood's last remaining abandoned buildings and was known to her street-kid peers as "stuck up," an assertive panhandler, an adroit shoplifter. Multidrug user. Not heroin, though. Needles scared Jewell. Petra returned to the autopsy report. No needle tracks. The tox screen revealed significant levels of cannabis, alcohol, and pseudoephedrine, probably from an OTC decongestant. According to the other kids, Jewell frequented the park when she got in a bad mood.

No, she'd never spoken of meeting anyone there.

She'd been found fully clothed with no evidence of rape.

A premortem snapshot had been stapled to the file; it looked to be a school photo of a kid around nine. Jewell Blank had been dark-haired, wan, freckled, reluctant to smile.

Was there any point in talking to Max? She looked around the room: three detectives hunched over piles of paperwork. That young, good-looking one, Eddie Baker; Ryan Miller, another stud; and Barney Fleischer, gaunt, bald, ancient, nearing retirement.

Petra walked over to Barney's desk. He was filling out a requisition form for office supplies. Demiglasses perched on his beaklike nose. His handwriting was almost calligraphic.

She asked him if he knew where Max Stokes was.

"Corvallis, Washington," he said, continuing to write. "He's got a daughter up there—Karen. She's a doctor, never got married, so you can probably find her under Stokes."

Petra called Corvallis and got office and home numbers for Karen Stokes, M.D. Max answered the phone.

"Petra Connor," he said. "To what do I owe the pleasure?"

Picturing Max's ruddy, mustachioed face, she told him about reviewing the file.

"You're thinking of reworking it?" he said.

"Don't know yet, Max. Depends on what I learn."

"I hope you decide yes. Maybe you can do better than me."

"You and Shirley, that's a lot of detective ability. Seems to me you guys did all you could."

"I thought we did. Poor little girl. Everyone said she was aggressive, had a temper, but looking at her . . . such a tiny little thing. It was brutal."

The autopsy report stared up at Petra. Jewell's stats: five one, ninety-four pounds. "Occipital injuries."

Max Stokes was saying, ". . . with the parents—actually, just one parent, the mother. Plus that boyfriend of hers. My gut pegged him as the bad guy. Your typical trash boyfriend scenario, maybe gets a little too close to the daughter, you know? I'd bet the boyfriend abused her; that would be a good reason for running away. I never asked him directly, just hinted around, and he got squirrelly. Plus, he had a felony record. Bad checks, attempted welfare fraud. But the guy had an alibi during the time of the murder."

"What about the mother?"

"Borderline retarded, if you ask me. She did seem to care a little, but every time she started to cry, the boyfriend nudged her and she shut up. His big concern was who was going to pay for the burial."

"One more thing, Max. I don't see any transfer."

"I wanted to transfer it to Shirley, and she wanted to take it. Actually, it was she who came to me, wanting to partner. Because she'd caught another case, couple of years before, that probably wasn't the same guy, but there were some similarities."

"Really?" said Petra.

"Yeah," said Max. "Another head bashing, but not a kid—some woman, up in the Hollywood Hills. That one, a dog got killed. What was the name . . ."

The name was Coral Langdon. Petra said, "Shirley thought the cases might be tied in?"

"At first she did, but in the end, she didn't. Too many differences, Jewell being a poor runaway and the other one being a financially comfortable divorcée with a nice house. On that one Shirley had worked the ex-husband as the main suspect. The divorce hadn't been friendly. Plus, neighbors said he'd always hated the dog. He claimed an alibi—at home watching the tube, no one else in the apartment. But she never found anything to contradict him."

"How come Shirley didn't get Jewell Blank's case?"

"I assumed she did," said Max.

"If she did, there's no record of it."

"That's kind of funny," said Max. "You remember Shirley. Tenacious. Real tragedy what happened to her."

She thanked Max, hung up, and turned to Coral Langdon's file.

The murdered woman's ex was an insurance salesman named Harvey Langdon. Insurance tipped you off to the best of motives, but Harvey had sold property casualty, not term life. Coral had worked as an executive secretary to an aerospace honcho, made a fine living on her own. The dog had been a bone of contention in the Langdon marriage. Harvey had expressed dismay at his ex-wife's demise but had smirked when hearing about the cockapoo.

The modus and the crime scenes—two females bludgeoned in wooded areas of Hollywood—had caused Detective Lenois to make a connection between Langdon and Jewell Blank. Had she been unimpressed by the June 28 angle?

Most likely she hadn't noticed. As a detective, Shirley would have zeroed in on crime-scene details.

The head bashing. Like Isaac said, it was rare.

Petra studied the photocopied driver's license attached to the file. Coral Langdon had been an attractive woman. Five seven, one-thirty. Slender. Probably strong, too. According to Shirley's notes, Coral had worked out at a gym, studied kickboxing.

Meaning whoever had brained her was in good shape. And stealthy enough to get her from behind.

Jewell Blank would've been a whole lot easier. No doubt, Shirley had wondered about that, decided it wasn't a match.

But *six* cases on the same date—that was different.

Like Isaac said, statistically significant. *Like Isaac said.*

Petra figured that phrase would be adhering to her brain for a while. She went back and studied the first two murders in detail. Marta Doebbler, the twenty nine-year-old housewife who'd gone to see a play at the Pantages, left for the ladies' room and didn't return; and Geraldo Solis, the Wilshire Division case. Elderly man found sitting at his breakfast-room table, brains leaking onto a plate of sausage and eggs. Now there was a charming detail.

A notation on Marta Doebbler gave her pause: Doebbler had been called out of the theater by a cell phone, and the detectives had traced the call to a pay phone around the corner from the theater. Had someone lured her out? The fact that she'd complied, coupled with her body being dumped in her own car, indicated that it was someone she knew. The detectives had interviewed the husband, an engineer named Kurt Doebbler, and remarked that he seemed "overly calm." Doebbler had an alibi—home with his and Marta's nine-year-old daughter, Katya.

She reread the Solis file. No sign of breaking and entering. Someone the old man had known as well?

She jotted down the names of the detectives on both cases. Conrad Ballou and Enrique Martinez on Doebbler, another unfamiliar name on Solis, DII Jacob Hustaad, Wilshire Division.

Barney Fleischer was still at his desk.

She approached him again, said, "Sorry, but I was wondering if you knew any of these guys."

"Got a cold-case assignment?"

"Self-imposed assignment," said Petra. "The kid, Gomez, thought I should look at a few old files."

"The genius," said Barney. "Nice kid. I like him."

"He talks to you?"

"From time to time. He likes to hear about the old days." Barney smiled. "And who better than a geezer like me?"

He peered at the list again. "Connie Ballou's a real old-timer. He left around five years ago." Barney frowned. "He had a bit of a drinking problem. We all knew about it; we all covered. One night he tanked up and crashed an unmarked into a building. That was kind of hard to cover for."

"How was he as a detective? When he was sober."

Barney shrugged. "That wasn't too often. But I heard he used to be okay in the early days."

"What about his partner, Martinez?"

"Enrique had no big problems, but was no great talent. I think he went over to Central Division as a deskman, but who knows how long he lasted there."

"He's living in Florida now."

"Makes sense," said Barney. "He's Cuban."

A lush and a no-talent. There was a good chance Marta Doebbler's murder hadn't been worked to the max. Nor, as far as Petra could tell, had the case been transferred. She asked Barney about that. Right away, he said, "Schoelkopf."

"He doesn't transfer cases?"

"He doesn't like to, if they've gone cold. What with all the manpower problems and the gang issues. You wouldn't know about that because you tend to solve your cases." Barney removed his reading glasses. His eyes were wide, clear, blue. "I know you don't like him, Petra, but I can't say as I'd do it any different. Cases go cold for a reason."

"Who says I don't like him?"

Barney grinned, and Petra returned the favor.

He looked at the list again, said, "Jack Hustaad's dead. Suicide. Jack was a four-pack-a-day smoker, got lung cancer, started chemotherapy, decided he didn't like it, and ate some painkillers."

"Thanks, Barney."

"I assume," said the old detective, "that you want your research kept private."

"That would be good," said Petra.

"No problem," said Barney. "I don't like him either."

--CHAPTER 4--

THE next day Mac called a noon meeting on the Paradiso shooting. He and Petra and Luc Montoya ate sandwiches in a small conference room and compared notes. Montoya was forty, bald, muscular, with a movie-star face. He wore a cream-colored sports coat, beige linen slacks, white shirt, pale blue tie. He didn't say much.

Mac had on the usual gray sharkskin and unreadable face.

He and Luc had dived into the witness pile, come up empty, and no local gang rumors were flying.

Petra told them about Sandra Leon's lies.

Mac said, "So we have no idea where this kid lives."

Petra shook her head.

Mac said, "That doctor of hers, think he might know?"

"I've got a call in."

After the meeting, Petra called Dr. Robert Katzman's office again and got transferred to the department administrator, a woman named Kim Pagionides.

"Sandra Leon," said Pagionides, as if she knew the girl. As if she disapproved of the girl.

Petra said, "You've seen her recently?"

"Oh, no." Small, nervous laugh. "No, I don't think so. I'll have Dr. Katzman get in touch when he gets back."

"I need to speak to him now. Where, exactly, is he?"

"Traveling. He's delivering papers at four scientific meetings. Important papers. We're talking about saving lives."

"And I'm talking about destroyed lives."

Kim Pagionides said, "Let me check his calendar."

A few moments later: "He's in Baltimore, at Johns Hopkins. Here's his cell phone."

"Thank you."

Petra tried Katzman's cell number and left another message. It was one forty-three p.m., and Isaac hadn't come in yet, and that was just fine with Petra. Less distraction. She called the LAPD pension office and asked for current stats on retired detectives Conrad Ballou and Enrique Martinez.

Martinez was living in Pensacola, Florida, but Ballou was relatively local. Out in Palmdale, a one-hour freeway drive.

With nothing more to do on the Paradiso case and feeling lonely and itchy, a one-hour drive didn't sound half bad.

She decided to take her own car. As she headed for her Accord, someone called her name. She turned, saw Isaac jogging toward her wearing a white shirt, khakis, and sneakers, briefcase slapping against his thigh. "Hey," she said. "What's up?"

"I got held up at school. I was hoping I could ride with you."

"It's fine," she said. "Actually, I'm heading out to talk to someone on one of your June twenty-eighth cases."

His eyes widened. "So you do see the validity of the—"

"I think you've put together something interesting. And seeing as I've got nothing else to do, why not check it out?"

As they headed toward the 5 on-ramp in the Accord, she said, "There's one thing we need to keep clear. This isn't an official investigation. It's important to be discreet."

"Sure. Of course."

"Especially Captain Schoelkopf," said Petra. "He doesn't like me. Going off on a tangent when I've got a big-time active case could complicate my situation further. Also, it looks as if he had specific feelings about the June murders. In every case, the investigating detective left for one reason or another. Some retired, some moved to other divisions, some died. By itself, that's not unusual. What is a bit unusual is that none of the files were transferred to new detectives. That's because Schoelkopf doesn't like transferring cold cases. So on the infinitesimal chance that we actually learn something about these murders, it's not going to reflect well on him."

A long silence filled the car before Isaac said, "I've complicated things."

"That's okay," said Petra. "Truth is, these victims deserve more than they got."

A few moments later: "Why doesn't he like you?"

"Because he's got poor taste."

Isaac smiled. "Yes, he does," he said.

SHE hooked onto the 210, then shifted to the 114, driving northeast through the beginnings of Antelope Valley. They passed through Burbank and Glendale and Pasadena along the way, and the rocky outcroppings and green belt that were Angeles Crest National Forest—the site of Bedros Kashigian's final moments and every psychopath's favorite dump spot.

As the drive stretched on, Petra told Isaac about being impressed by the wound patterns.

He said, "Similar dimensions. *That* I didn't notice."

And none of the detectives had noticed June 28. "You'd have to be looking for it."

He said, "That call from the phone booth is interesting. The possibility that it might be someone Mrs. Doebbler knew. What if Mr. Solis knew him as well? Someone familiar to all the victims."

"I thought of that," she said. "But it's a leap. If our killer was acquainted with all six victims, he had a pretty wide social network. We're talking runaways, male hustlers, executive secretaries, retirees, and that navy ensign."

Isaac stared out at the desert. Finally, he said, "Solis had breakfast food on his plate, but the murder occurred around midnight."

"People eat at odd hours, Isaac."

The car got hot. It was ten degrees warmer out here in the desert. A warm June to begin with.

June. Today was the fourth. If there was anything to this craziness, someone else would die in twenty-four days. She said, "So have you come up with any other notable June twenty-eighth occurrences in the historical archives?"

"Nothing profound." He spoke quietly. *Intimidated?*

"Tell me anything you've found," she said.

Isaac half turned toward her. "Basically, I've been logging into various almanacs; I printed some lists. But nothing jumps out. I looked at birthdays, and the farthest back I got was June twenty-eighth, 1367, which is when Sigismund, the emperor of Hungary and Bohemia, was born."

"Was he a bad guy?"

"Your basic autocratic king. Then there's Pope Paul the Fourth, the artist Rubens, a few actors. That's how I came up with John Dillinger. When I looked at June twenty-eighth as a date of death, I found a few more. But none of them appear connected to this type of thing."

"This type of thing?" said Petra.

"A serial killer."

The term set her teeth on edge. Too TV. Too damn hard to solve. "Which bad guys died that day?"

"Pieter van Dort, a Dutch smuggler. They hanged him on June twenty-eighth, 1748. Thomas Hickey, a Colonial soldier convicted of treason, was hanged in 1776. There's not much more until 1971, when Joseph Columbo, a New York mafioso, was gunned down."

"Anything of a more wacko criminal nature? A Ted Bundy?"

"No, nothing like that, sorry," he said.

June 4.

She drove faster.

They were well past Angeles Crest now, zipping past canyon after canyon at eighty-five miles an hour. A short time later, she exited at the first Palmdale exit and drove toward the address on Conrad Ballou's retirement forms, around three miles east.

Knowing about Ballou's alkie-burnout history, she figured him to be living in a depressing pensioner's SRO or worse. But Ballou's place was a medium-sized Spanish house in a pretty development. The streets were wide, clean, and quiet, and the houses had rear yards that looked out to a desert panorama.

She pulled to the curb. Ballou's place was done up beautifully with creeping dwarf junipers, mondo grass, lush Sago palms, and little cross-cut tubes of bamboo lining the pebbled walkway. A length of bamboo dipping toward a stone pot served as a fountain.

A Japanophile?

It didn't look like an alkie's place. Japanese letters were etched into the teak panels of the front door, above a weathered brass knocker shaped like a fish. Petra used the knocker. The man who opened the door was short, bandy-legged, lean but for a protruding belly that hung over his belt buckle, a carp-koi belt buckle.

Sixty-five to seventy, with a shaved, sunburned head and a drooping white mustache. He wore a denim work shirt, jeans, red suspenders, and lace-up boots. A handkerchief flapped from his rear pocket. He looked Petra and Isaac over. Clear eyes, pale blue, no booze blear. "Detective Ballou?"

Now the eyes were twin specks of granite. "Been a long time since anyone called me that."

Petra showed him her I.D and introduced Isaac.

He shook his head. "I'm out of all that. Breed and sell fish and don't think about the past." He started to step back into the house.

Petra said, "Marta Doebbler. Ever think about her?"

Conrad Ballou moved his jaw around. "Can't say that I do. Can't say that I give a damn about any of that."

"It hasn't been that long, sir. Six years. I'm looking into some cold cases, including Doebbler. If I could pick your brain . . ."

"Nothing to pick," said Ballou, rubbing his bald head. "According to the shrinks the department sent me to." He looked ready to spit. "I could've saved them the trouble. I wasn't nuts; I was a drunk. Thank God I didn't kill anybody." He shook his head. "They should've tossed my can out long before they did. Damn department."

"So you miss police work," said Petra.

Ballou glared at her. Smiled. Laughed.

"You like fish?"

"To eat?"

"To look at. C'mon in. And bring the intern with you."

Ballou led them through the house and out rear double doors to the backyard. Every inch of the quarter-acre space had been converted to fish ponds, rectangular cement tanks, a dozen of them, arranged in a grid with a walkway between them.

When Ballou approached the first pond, the surface broke and hundreds of little golden and pinkish fishy faces popped up.

Isaac was already three ponds ahead, bending low and examining the fish that had risen to greet him. He said, "Mr. Ballou, do you use domestic stock or are these from Niigata?"

Ballou stared at the kid. "You know koi."

"I've admired them. My mother's employers have a pond."

"Admire them, huh?" said Ballou. "Then get into it yourself."

"It's beyond my budget. And I live in an apartment."

"Hmm," said Ballou, "then get yourself a good job, work your tail off, and buy a house. Reward yourself with a Japanese garden and a pond full of *nishikigoi.* Come back and I'll give you a free *karasu*—that's the black one. Symbol of good luck."

Petra said, "I could use some luck. On Marta Doebbler."

Ballou said, "Here we were talking about pleasant things. . . . You drink tea?"

Back in his kitchen, he poured steaming green liquid into three stoneware cups. They sat at the kitchen table.

"Don't think I'm some fanatic. Asian culture soothes me. When I got out of rehab, a koi dealer—a nice old man in Gardena—hired me to mop up his place. I mopped for two years, kept my mouth shut, started asking questions by the third year, learned a bit. He died and put me in his will. Left me some of his breeding stock. That motivated me to buy this place, set up a little weekend business. It's real peaceful. I don't think about my other job with fondness."

Petra sipped the hot, aromatic tea.

"Marta Doebbler's a good example," said Ballou. "Ugly scene. When I think of the things I got used to working Homicide . . ." He gazed absently through the window. Then back at Petra. "What I remember," he said, "was that the husband was interesting."

Petra said, "Interesting as in prime suspect?"

The old guy nodded. "There was no evidence tying him to it. But I liked him for it." He picked up his tea. "His reaction to his wife's death was off. Stone-faced, not a tear. When I did the notification call, he just stood there staring. Then he says, 'I guess you'd better come in.' "

"Guy's an engineer," said Petra.

"So what?"

"Engineers, physicists, mathematicians. Sometimes they don't react emotionally the way the rest of us do."

Ballou said, "Well, Doebbler was a kind of rocket scientist, I guess. Worked over at Pacific Dynamics, electronics stuff."

"Anything besides his demeanor make you suspect him?"

"She was called out of the theater. It had to be someone familiar with her schedule. Who else would know where she was? And who else could've gotten her to leave the theater without telling her friends where she was going."

"The husband claiming an emergency," said Petra. "Maybe about the daughter."

"That would've brought her out," Ballou agreed. "The kid was Doebbler's alibi. Marta was having a girl's night out. I talked to the three friends she went with. When I pressed them, I could tell they didn't like Kurt. One even said she thought he'd done it."

That hadn't been in the murder book.

Petra said, "How'd he and Marta meet?"

"Germany. She was a brain, too, studying astronomy. He was a foreign-exchange student. After they got married, she dropped out and became a full-time mom."

"That could be frustrating."

"Sure, that's what I thought," said Ballou. "Maybe she tried to reduce her frustration the old-fashioned way. But if she was having an affair, I never found evidence of it."

Petra said, "Did you talk to the daughter?"

"Poor little thing, didn't want to pressure her." Ballou tugged at his mustache. "She sure reacted, crying all over the place. You'd think Doebbler would've tried to comfort her. All he did was offer her juice. I would've loved to make him for it. How come you're reopening it?"

"It may be related to some others."

"Others you suspect Doebbler did?"

"Others with some similar forensics. Five other brainings," said Petra. "Yearly intervals. All on June twenty-eighth."

Ballou gawked. "You're putting me on. Before Marta?"

"All *after* Marta. From what we can tell, she was the first. If it's a series."

"If? All on the same day? That sounds pretty convincing."

"But the victims are all over the place in terms of sex, age, and race." She gave him a few details.

"See what you mean. Still . . . So how'd you discover this?"

"Mr. Gomez, here, found them."

"By accident," said Isaac.

"I don't believe in accidents." He clapped Isaac on the shoulder. "You're definitely going to deserve a pond one day—a big one."

As THEY drove away, Isaac said, "Someone Marta knew. And home with his daughter isn't much of an alibi."

"Not much," Petra agreed. "With the girl sleeping, he could've phoned Marta with some ruse, lured her, done the deed, and come back." She retraced the drive through the outskirts of Palmdale and got back onto the 114. "One thing intrigues me, though: Marta was the only victim whose dead body was then moved by the killer. So maybe that does synch with someone who knew her."

Isaac said, "A man killing his wife and then going on to kill strangers is pretty unusual, right?"

"Can't say that I've ever heard of it."

Petra exited the 210 at Brand Boulevard in Glendale, drove to a quiet street, and pulled over. She'd brought copies of Ballou's notes and rifled through them until she found Doebbler's work and home numbers. It was just after five, meaning he could be either place.

The home was on Rosita Avenue in Tarzana, clear across the Valley to the west. At least an hour's drive. She ran a DMV check. Doebbler was listed as still there. Two cars registered in his name. A two-year-old Infiniti coupe and a three-year-old Toyota wagon.

She asked Isaac, "What's your schedule like? I can drop you off just as easily as go on."

"Go on where?"

"To Kurt Doebbler's house."

"Let's do it," he said, excitement in his voice. Then: "Could I borrow your phone, please? I'll let my mother know I won't be home for dinner."

KURT Doebbler's house was a pale gray two story traditional set in a low spot on the street. Doebbler's Infiniti, a champagne-colored coupe, was in view, sparkling clean. Parked in front of it was the gray Toyota wagon, with one flat tire and a veneer of dust.

The man who answered the door was nice-looking—tall, late thirties, with a broad-shouldered, angular build and a thick mess of wavy dark hair, graying at the temples. He had a prominent chin and nose, a generous mouth. He wore a baggy plaid shirt, sleeves rolled to the elbows, faded jeans, and white running shoes. A dinner plate dangled from one hand. In his other was a dish towel.

From inside the house, Petra smelled broiled meat. Dinner was over. She could use a steak. "Mr. Doebbler?"

"Yes." Friendly brown eyes, slouching posture.

Nothing weird so far. Let's see how he reacts when she shows him the badge.

Doebbler said, "Is there some kind of trouble in the neighborhood?"

"I'm a homicide detective from Hollywood Division, sir. I'm looking into your wife's murder."

"My wife?" The smile finally melted down. "I'm sorry. It's my brother Kurt you want. I'm Thad Doebbler."

"You live here, too?"

"No. I live in San Francisco, had to be down here on business. Kurt insisted I not stay at a hotel. You're reopening Marta's case?"

"Marta's case never closed, sir."

"Oh . . . well, let me get Kurt for you. He's up with Katya, helping her with her homework. Come on in."

Petra and Isaac followed him through a small, empty entry foyer into a modest living room.

"One second," Thad Doebbler said. He loped to the kitchen and returned minus the plate and the towel.

To the left was a right-angled oak staircase. Human speech filtered down from the second floor. Thad Doebbler walked to the bottom of the stairs and stopped. "I don't want to meddle, Detective, but my brother . . . he's been doing pretty well the past few years. Has something new come up?"

"Nothing dramatic. We're just doing our best to clear cases."

"Got it. Make yourselves comfortable. I'll tell Kurt you're here."

Petra and Isaac sat at opposite ends of a seven-foot sofa. Cattycorner to the couch were two of the starkest black leather chairs Petra had ever seen—tight black skin on chromium frames.

The man who came down the stairs was even taller than Thad Doebbler—six four was Petra's estimate. Thinner, too. The same thick, wavy hair as his younger brother but completely gray. Thick eyeglasses in silver frames. Similar features to Thad, but on Kurt Doebbler they didn't add up to handsome. He wore a white polo shirt, brown slacks, black shoes. He stood looking at them.

Petra said, "Mr. Doebbler?"

"You know that already."

"Do you have time to talk, sir?"

"About Marta."

"Yes, sir."

Doebbler said, "What about, specifically?"

He took one of the black armchairs, sat all tight and hunched up, long legs drawn up close. Bony knees.

She said, "This is going to sound like a stupid question, but is there anything you've thought of concerning Marta that you didn't tell the original detective six years ago?"

"Conrad Ballou," said Doebbler. "I called Ballou often. Sometimes he even called me back."

"Was there anything—"

"He was a drunk," said Doebbler. "The night he came to tell me, he reeked. I should've complained. Is he still working as a detective?"

"No, sir. He's retired. Did you feel better about Detective Martinez?"

"The only one I ever talked to was Ballou. And not very often." Doebbler's lips shifted to a very unpleasant smile.

Petra said, "I know this is tough, Mr. Doebbler—"

"Not tough. Futile."

Petra said, "The day your wife disappeared, you were here."

"Yes. Homework," said Doebbler.

"With your daughter?"

"She was sleeping. *My* homework. I take work home."

"You work with computers."

"I develop aerospace software."

"What kind of software?"

"Aircraft guidance systems, integrated spacecraft landing systems." Doebbler's tone said she couldn't hope to understand.

Isaac said, "Circular wave guides? Storage rings?"

Doebbler turned toward the kid. "Aerospace physicists and engineers design storage rings. I write the instructions that enable them to be used in a human-to-machine context."

One knee bounced. His mouth was set tight.

Petra said, "It would help if I had a feel for what Marta was like."

"She liked soft rock and bright colors. She liked the stars."

"Astronomy."

"That, and she regarded the stars as aesthetic objects," said Doebbler. "She wanted the world to be pretty. She was smart, but that was stupid." He stared at her and said, "Why are you here?"

"We're looking into some of our open cases, trying to see if we can resolve them."

"Open," said Doebbler. "That's a euphemism for failure. To you, Marta's a statistic."

"No, sir. She's . . . was a person. That's why I'd like to know more about her."

Doebbler seemed to consider that. He shook his head. "It's been a long time. I can't see her face anymore."

"That night," said Petra, "what was her mood?"

"Her mood? She was in a fine mood."

"She gave no indication of anything but seeing a play."

"That's what she told me," said Doebbler. His knee pumped faster. The hands grasping them were white-knuckled.

That question had gotten to him.

"June twenty-eighth," she said.

"What about it?"

"Does the date have any significance—"

"It's the date my wife was murdered. What is this, some kind of game?" Doebbler sprang up, made it to the stairs in three long strides. "I have to help my daughter. See yourselves out."

He disappeared. Isaac began to get up, but when he saw Petra remain in place, he plopped back down. Finally she got up and paced around Doebbler's living room, taking in as many details as she could before footsteps sounded on the stairs, and she motioned Isaac to the front door.

Her hand was on the knob when Thad Doebbler said, "Sorry. Kurt's been under stress."

"New stress?" said Petra, turning to face him.

"Work. It's a high-pressure job. Really, there's nothing more he can tell you about Marta."

Petra turned the knob and stepped outside.

Thad called after them: "I'm sure he'll want to know if you learn anything."

Even outside, walking to the car, the broiled-meat smell hung in her nostrils. She craved dinner. "Do I drop you back off or should we hit a coffee shop for some grub?" she said to Isaac.

He said, "I'm not really hungry, but I'll tag along."

Not hungry? Then she remembered: This one rode the bus, wore the same three shirts over and over. Eating out was probably a once-in-a-while McDonald's jaunt. She upgraded to a steak-and-seafood place near the Encino-Tarzana border. The dining room beyond the busy bar was cozy and dark, set up with red booths. The waitress who came to serve them was a strawberry blonde, young and cute and buxom, and Petra saw her give Isaac the once-over.

When Isaac slid as far from Petra in the booth as was possible and Petra ordered for him, the way you do with a child, the waitress smiled. After that, she flirted shamelessly with the kid.

He seemed oblivious, smiling politely and thanking Strawberry Shortcake profusely for every smidge of service.

Petra was ravenous and attacked her surf and turf.

"So what do you think of Mr. Doebbler?"

"Hostile and asocial. I can see why Ballou called him strange."

"Anything else about him set you off?"

He thought. "He certainly wasn't cooperative."

"No, he wasn't," she said. "But that could've been our popping in unannounced. After all those years of no progress, I wouldn't expect him to be a big police groupie."

A drunk and a no-show. LAPD at its finest. She wondered what Isaac thought about that. She went on, "What intrigues me about all that is Mr. Kurt Doebbler never complaining to their superiors."

Isaac put down his knife and fork. "He wouldn't, if he wanted the case to stay unsolved."

Petra nodded.

They ate some more. He said, "That comment about not remembering what his wife looked like? Sometimes borderline personalities have a problem maintaining mental images of those close to them. Flat affect, also. Except when they feel they've been betrayed. When that happens, they can get emotional."

"Betrayed as in the wife having an affair," she said. "That was just Ballou's offhand comment. Let's remember that there's no evidence linking him to the crime, and he does have an alibi, of sorts."

Isaac said, "So what's next?"

"Haven't figured that out. Assuming I want to work the case. Any of them." She shot him a fierce smile. "Look what you got me into."

Another classic Isaac blush. "Sorry if I've complicated—"

"You have," said Petra. "But you did the right thing."

ISAAC KNEW HE'D MADE A mistake. He'd had Petra drop him off at Pico and Union. Near the bus stop where he usually got off, four blocks from his building. Not wanting her to see the liquor stores and abandoned buildings that lined the route. The four-story stucco slabs, like the one his family lived in, marred by the acne of graffiti.

So he walked. A quick right turn at the late-night liquor store favored by old winos, then down dark side streets, past alleys, the usual sprinkle of lolling street people and addicts. Mostly he ignored them and they returned the favor. He'd been doing it for years, never had a problem. Tonight he had a problem.

He was unaware of them till they started laughing. A hoarse, high-pitched hooting behind him. When had they started following him? Had he been that spaced out?

More laughter behind him. Closer. Glancing over his shoulder, he saw them clearly as they passed under a street lamp. Three of them. Chattering, pointing, and bumping into one another maybe twenty feet from his back. Laughing some more. Mexican-accented Spanish interspersed with rude English.

Two more blocks till home. He turned.

They stayed with him. He walked faster.

All these years, despite the rotten neighborhood, he'd never had to deal with this before. Generally, he was home by eight. But tonight it was well after ten.

"Hey, you! Why you move you ass so fast?"

He began to jog and heard them whooping and running after him. He was drenched by a sudden, clammy sweat. Something hit him from behind, low in his back. Hard boot to the kidneys. Pain shot through him; he buckled yet managed to stay on his feet. Someone was yanking at his briefcase. The case flew out of his hand. Papers scattered. The computer, heavy, remained inside.

A fist—hard, sharp knuckles—grazed his cheek. He teetered, regained his balance, and faced them.

Younger than he'd thought. Fourteen, fifteen. Small, ghetto-stunted kids, two skinny, one a bit chunky. They were surrounding him, a trio of malignant dwarfs shuffling and cursing. The smallest flicked his wrist and flashed something metallic.

Oh, God, a gun? No, a knife.

The heavy one said, "Gimme the mawney. You wanna get *cut?*"

The little one with the blade danced closer, and Isaac saw the weapon clearly. Pocketknife, a cheap thing with a two-inch foldout blade. Jumpy little sociopaths. Not a good situation. He drew out his LAPD authorized visitor's badge and said, "Police. You walked right into a stakeout."

A nanosecond of silence. A hoarse *"Huh?"*

"Police!" he repeated, louder. Reaching into another pocket, he drew out his pen case because it was dark and around the right size. He pressed it to his mouth, said, "This is Officer Gomez calling for backup. I've got three juvenile two-eleven suspects. Probable narcotics violation as well. I'll hold them here."

Skinny looked at his knife. Deliberating. The second one, the one who hadn't spoken or done anything, took off and ran.

And then there were two.

Skinny had edged back but made no move to leave. Isaac walked toward him and ordered, "Drop that nail file, junior, and get down on the ground before I shoot your ass. *Do it!*" Chunky turned heel and ran. Skinny threw the knife at Isaac. The blade whizzed by his face, just short of his left eye, and the kid bolted.

Isaac stood there in the silence, waiting until he was sure they were gone before he began breathing normally. He went to retrieve his briefcase. Stuffed the papers back in. Then he sprinted the block to his building, ran around to the side, stomach churning. He vomited until the bile burned his throat.

When all his dinner was gone, he headed to his building.

Tomorrow, before he took the bus to the Hollywood station, he'd visit Jaramillo. Once upon a time, before the Burton Academy, before all the strange, wondrous, terrifying turns his life had taken, he and Jaramillo had been friends.

--CHAPTER 5--

KURT Doebbler's weirdness stuck in Petra's head, and after a few more days of nothing on Paradiso, she found herself thinking about him. It was just after noon; no sign of Isaac. No word from Eric. And the mellow-voiced Dr. Robert Katzman hadn't called her back.

Why *hadn't* Doebbler complained about Ballou? The more she thought about how shoddily the case had been worked, the less confident she felt about the integrity of the original file. Time to take a closer look at the other June murders.

In the Solis murder book, she found an interesting notation by Detective Jack Hustaad: According to Solis's daughter, the old man had been expecting a cable repairman the day he'd been bludgeoned. No sign Hustaad had followed up. Petra phoned Wilshire Division and learned that, unlike the Hollywood cases, Solis had been transferred after Hustaad's suicide. But not until two years after the murder. Solis had been passed to a DI named Scott Weber.

Weber was still at Wilshire, and Petra reached him at his desk.

He said, "I never got anywhere on it."

She told him about a possible cold-case similarity, talked about the wound pattern on Marta Doebbler, made no mention of the other murders or June 28.

"Don't see a match," he said. "People get hit on the head."

Not that often fatally. According to my expert.

"True," she said.

"What do you figure for the weapon on yours?"

"Some kind of pipe."

"Same here," said Weber. "Any physical evidence on it?"

"Not so far. There was a note about a cable repairman—"

"There was a cable call on yours?" said Weber.

"No. I was just wondering if that led anywhere."

"You're wondering if I followed up on it." Weber laughed, but the sound wasn't friendly. "I did. Even though it was two years later. Solis's cable company had no record of any visit. I talked to the daughter; turns out she maybe remembered something about the old man maybe saying something. Turns out no one saw any cable truck near the house. Okay?"

"Okay," said Petra. "Sorry if I—"

"I couldn't get anywhere on it," said Weber. "It's in the icebox."

No cable appointment. Did that mean a phony call had led Geraldo Solis to expect a visitor? If so, that could be a match to the phone-booth call that had lured Marta Doebbler from the theater.

Geraldo Solis's daughter's address and phone number were duly listed in the murder book. Maria Solis Murphy, age thirty-nine, Covina. A DMV check put her current residence in the city. Right here in Hollywood, Russell Street off Los Feliz.

Her work number matched an extension for Food Services at Kaiser Permanente Hospital. She was on shift, came to the phone, arranged to meet Petra in front of the hospital in twenty minutes. By the time Petra arrived, she was there.

Hard-body type, pretty, with very short dark hair tipped blond, wearing a pale blue dress, white socks, and tennies. Three filament hoops in one ear, a diamond chip and a gold stud in the other. Kind of punk for a woman of nearly forty—a woman with a gold wedding band on her ring finger—but Maria Murphy had an unlined face and an aerobic bounce in her step. Her badge said M. MURPHY, MS, REGISTERED DIETICIAN. She said, "Detective?" in a husky voice.

"Ms. Murphy."

"If you don't mind, I could use a little stretch. Been kind of cooped up." They walked west on Sunset, past the hospital.

Murphy said, "I'm very grateful you're reopening my dad's case."

"It's not exactly like that, Ms. Murphy. I'm a Hollywood detective, and I picked up a case that could bear some similarities to your father's. We're talking small details, ma'am."

"I discovered Dad's body. I'll never forget it."

That fact had been in the file. Geraldo Solis had been found slumped over his food at one a.m. Petra asked Murphy why she'd dropped in so late.

"I didn't drop in. I lived there. On and off. I was married at the time, and my husband and I were having problems. I stayed with Dad from time to time."

Petra glanced at Murphy's gold band.

Murphy smiled. "That's from my partner. Her name is Bella. I changed the rules midstream. Dave, my husband, was a good guy."

"He get mad?"

Murphy turned sharply toward Petra. "Don't even think that. Dave and Dad got along great. You want to know the truth, Dave and Dad had more in common with each other than with me."

"Other family?" said Petra.

"Two brothers, two sisters. Mom's been gone for a while. When she was alive, I suppressed myself. Not wanting to hurt her. After I came out, they all ganged up on me."

"You didn't want to hurt your mother, but your father . . ."

"You get to a point," said Murphy. "And Dad and I were never close. He was always working, always too busy. He did what he had to do; we just weren't close. Even after I started living with him, we had very little to say to each other."

"How long did you live with him?"

"A month or so. I kept most of my stuff at my house, would bring a few changes to Dad's. The story I gave him was I was working a double shift and didn't want to drive home tired. Dad's place was closer to the hospital."

"When did you tell your father the truth?" said Petra.

"I didn't. My sibs did. A few days before the murder."

"What about Dave?"

"Dave already knew. He wasn't angry; he was sad. Depressed. Don't even go there. Really."

Petra decided she'd be talking to Dave Murphy sooner rather than later. "So is there anything about your father's murder that you've thought about since the first detectives spoke to you?"

"I only talked to one detective," said Murphy. "Big, heavyset kind of Scandinavian guy."

"Detective Hustaad."

"Yes, that's him. He seemed nice. Had a real bad cough. Later, he called me to tell me he had cancer."

"The case was transferred to Detective Weber. He never talked to you?"

"Someone did call me," said Murphy. "He said he was taking over Dad's case, but I never heard from him again."

"Did Detective Weber ask you anything?"

"He asked about Dad expecting the cable guy. It was the only thing I did tell Hustaad that I thought might be relevant."

Petra kept walking, waited for more.

"I can accept facts, even if they're tough. If Dad had been killed by a burglar, the only way they'd solve it was if the same criminal did it again, right?" She turned to Petra. "Is your case a burglar, someone pretending to be a cable guy?"

"Everything's preliminary, ma'am."

"What was weird to me, if it was a burglar," said Murphy, "was that the only thing taken was food. A fresh head of lettuce, some whole wheat bread, and two cartons of lemon yogurt. But Detective Hustaad said they do that—eat food, mark their territory. He figured the guy got scared before he had time to steal anything."

"You're pretty specific about which food was taken."

"Because it was my food. I bought it the day before. Dad made fun of the way I ate. Called it rabbit chow."

Pain in her eyes said there'd been more than dietary conflict between father and daughter. Petra asked, "Is there anyone who'd want to get back at you through your father?"

"No," said Murphy. "No one. Since the divorce, everything's been smooth. Dave and I are friendly; we talk all the time."

"Any kids?"

Murphy shook her head.

Petra said, "Tell me about the cable call and why you think it could've been phony."

"That day in the morning, when I left for work, Dad told me the cable company was sending someone out to work on the set."

"At what time?"

"Late afternoon, early evening—you know how they are. Dad sometimes napped at that hour, wanted me to wake him by seven."

"Were you having transmission problems?"

"No, that's the thing," said Murphy. "Supposedly it was something to do with the neighborhood lines."

"He wanted you to wake him," said Petra. "So you were home by late afternoon?"

"No. I called at three, told Dad I'd be home late. He asked me to call again."

"At seven."

"Yes."

"Did you?"

"I did, and he was up. I'd left work early. It had been a tough afternoon, shuttling back between Dave and Bella. When I hung up with Dad, I was in my car. I took off and went to see Bella. We had dinner, went to a club, did some drinking. She wanted me to come home with her, but I wasn't ready for that, so she drove back to her place and I drove to Dad's. Walked into the house and smelled food—cooked food, bacon and eggs. Which was strange. Dad never ate late. If he ate heavy food too late, he had indigestion."

Maria Murphy stopped walking. Her eyes were wet. "This is harder than I thought."

"Sorry for bringing it all back."

"I haven't thought about Dad for a while."

They resumed walking. Petra said, "Someone had cooked."

"Breakfast food," said Murphy. "Which was also weird. Dad was a very disciplined person—ex-marine, very regimented. You ate breakfast food in the morning, sandwiches at lunch, a main meal at supper." She burst into tears.

"Ma-am—"

"His brains," Murphy blurted. "They were on the *plate*. . . . Can we please turn around now? I need to get back to work."

"Just one more question. The date of your father's murder, June twenty-eighth. Did that have any significance to you or anyone in your family?"

"June twenty-eighth," said Murphy weakly. "The only thing significant about that is Dad was murdered." She sagged. "It's coming up, isn't it? The anniversary. I think I'll go to the cemetery. I don't go very often. I really should go more."

INTERESTING woman. Going through major life stress at the time of her father's murder. Not getting sympathy from the old man, quite the opposite. Pulled in all directions, having to return to the old man's house. A father with whom she'd never been close.

It had to have been a tense situation.

Murphy was a strong woman. More than enough strength to bring a stout piece of pipe down on an aged skull.

Murphy's food was taken—healthy stuff the old man ridiculed. Maybe the old man had humiliated her one time too many.

Some melodrama.

And no evidence. Also, if Maria Murphy had murdered her old man, what did that say about Marta Doebbler and the other June 28 killings? She'd follow up on Solis, talk to Murphy's ex-husband. But something told her it would be a waste of time. If Isaac was right, this was something quite different from family passion gone bad. A woman lured from the theater. A hustler pulverized in an alley. A little girl brutalized in the park. A sailor on leave . . .

Eggs and brains on the plate.

This was calculated, manipulative.

Twisted.

WHEN she got back to the detectives room, the place was bustling with phone talk and keyboard clacks. Isaac was at his corner desk writing something in longhand, one hand cradling the side of his head. He gave her a quick wave with his free hand and returned to his work.

Petra poured coffee and flipped through her message stack.

Nothing but department memos. Six new e-mails on her computer: four department announcements, something she figured for spam, and Mac Dilbeck informing her that Homicide Special would most likely take over the Paradiso case by Tuesday if nothing broke.

She opened the message she thought was spam.

Dear Petra,

This is rerouted for security purposes, can't be answered. Everything's okay. Hope the same there. Miss you.

L, Eric.

She smiled, saved the message, logged off, and began looking for David Murphy. An easy trace. The five-year-old Covina address narrowed it right down to David Colvin Murphy, now forty-two. He'd moved to Mar Vista. She found his number. A woman answered.

"David Murphy, please."

"He's at work. Who's this?"

Petra recited her title. "It's about an old case. Are you familiar with Geraldo Solis, ma'am?"

"Dave's ex–father-in-law. He was . . . I'm Dave's wife."

"Where does your husband work, Mrs. Murphy?"

"HealthRite Pharmacy. He's a pharmacist."

"Which branch, ma'am?"

"Santa Monica. Wilshire, near Twenty-fifth."

Petra thanked her and hung up; then she called the HealthRite Pharmacy, Santa Monica branch.

David Murphy had a pleasant phone voice. Not surprised by her call. The wife had prepared him. He said, "Gerry was a good guy. I can't think of anyone who'd want to hurt him."

Petra said, "Well, someone sure did."

"Terrible," said Murphy. "So . . . what can I do for you?"

"Is there anything you remember about the day Mr. Solis was murdered, sir? Maybe something that didn't come up during the initial investigation?"

"Sorry, no," said Murphy. "It was a terrible day. Maria and I were in the midst of breaking up; she was driving back and forth between our home . . . between me and her . . . and Bella Kandinsky. She's her partner now. I'm sure Maria was feeling like the rope in a tug-of-war. I was pretty stunned."

"Stunned?"

"My marriage, suddenly over. Over another woman." Murphy laughed. "That was a long time ago. We've all moved on."

"At that time, Maria was living at her father's house."

"On and off," said Murphy.

"You ever go over to Mr. Solis's house?"

"I used to be there all the time. Gerry and I got along. That made it kind of rough on Maria. Gerry took my side. He was pretty conservative. Maria's choice was hard for him to swallow."

"That must've caused conflict between them."

"Sure."

"Heavy-duty conflict?"

Murphy laughed again. "You can't be serious. No, no, that's totally out of the ballpark. Don't even go there."

Same phrase Maria had used. "I was just asking," said Petra.

Murphy said, "Maria's a terrific person. She and Gerry had your typical parent-child things. No way could she have hurt him."

She defends him; he defends her.

"Mr. Murphy, in the file there's a note about a cable-repair appointment. Did Maria mention that to you?"

"No, but Gerry did. The guy was right there when I called."

"You called Mr. Solis."

"Sure. I wanted to find out where Maria was. She left our house pretty upset, and I assumed she went home. I wanted to smooth things out. Gerry answered, and he was grumpy because the cable guy had come late."

"What time was this?"

"Wow," said Murphy. "This was—what—five years ago? I remember it was dark already. And I'd been working late—I'd say eight, nine. Maybe even nine thirty. Gerry said something about the guy saying he'd show up by six, then calling to push it to seven, then still not making it on time. He was pretty annoyed."

Meaning Geraldo Solis, already annoyed by delays, could've had a serious chip on that evening.

She said, "Did Mr. Solis have a bad temper?"

"More like . . . a curmudgeon," said Murphy. "He was a very disciplined guy, ex-marine, expected the world to work on a tight schedule. When things didn't go that way, it bugged him."

"Like a late appointment." *Or a lesbian daughter.*

"The cable guy?" said Murphy. "Whoa. . . . But the police said Gerry was killed around midnight."

A cable guy who shows up after dark. Whose company had no record of any scheduled service appointment.

She said, "Did he tell you the reason for the appointment?"

"That's another thing that bothered Gerry. He hadn't complained about anything. It was the company saying they needed to come by. My God . . . you really think—"

"Mr. Murphy, did you tell any of this to the detective?"

"Hustaad? He never asked, and I never really thought about it. He wanted to know how I got along with Gerry. How Maria got along. He also asked where I was around midnight. Normally I'd be asleep, but that night I was pretty upset and went out with a buddy from work. We went out drinking, and I cried in my beer, so to speak."

"Can you remember anything else Mr. Solis said about the cable appointment?"

"Not really."

"And he definitely told you the man was in the house."

"Yes. . . . But maybe I assumed. He was talking softly, so I assumed someone was there. It's nothing I could swear to."

Petra thanked him.

He said, "Sure. Good luck. Gerry really was a good guy."

Petra took a bathroom break, risked more coffee, and returned to the June 28 files to review the other non-Hollywood case.

The sailor, Darren Hochenbrenner. On shore leave. According to two other sailors, they'd started out in Hollywood, but Darren had parted ways when they'd gone to a movie.

The body had been found downtown, on Fourth Street, pockets

emptied. Far from the other victims, the only black victim, and a probable strong-arm street robbery. She rechecked the wound dimensions. Perfect match to Marta Doebbler.

The listed detective was a DII named Ralph Seacrest. He was still working at Central. He sounded tired.

"That one," he said. "Yeah. Kid started off in your neighborhood, ended up in mine. First time in the city."

"He was stationed in Port Hueneme."

"That's not the city. Why're you asking about him?"

Petra spun him the usual yarn.

Seacrest said, "Another head bashing? Your vic get robbed?"

"No."

"Mine got robbed. This was a kid, got lost, found himself in a real bad neighborhood. Also, he was stoned."

"On what?"

"Mari-joo-ana, some booze. Don't hold me to that—it's been a while—but that's what I remember."

Petra hung up, checked Hochenbrenner's tox screen, found a blood alcohol level of .02 percent. At Hochenbrenner's body weight, that probably meant one beer. She wondered how hard Seacrest had worked the case.

A shadow fell across the file, and she looked up, expecting to see Isaac. But the kid was gone. He'd left without saying a word.

A civilian receptionist from downstairs, a blond cheerleader type named Kirsten Krebs, newly hired, hostile from the get-go, handed her a message slip.

Dr. Robert Katzman had returned her call. Half an hour ago.

Krebs was on her way toward the stairs. Petra said, "Why didn't you put him through?"

Krebs stopped. Turned. Glared. Clamped her hands to her hips. She wore a tight powder-blue stretch top, tight black cotton pants. Push-up bra. Long blond hair. "Your line was *busy*." Whiny. She sniffed and turned on her heel.

Petra called Dr. Katzman. Got his mellow voice on the recorded message and left a message of her own. Not so mellow.

THE JOKE: RICHARD JARAMILLO was fat, so they called him Flaco—"Slim" in Spanish. That was back in fourth grade. Then Jaramillo grew up and got skinny and the nickname fit.

Little else about Jaramillo had worked out so neatly.

Isaac had known him back in public school—a jumpy, scared fat kid who sat at the back of the classroom and never learned how to read. The teacher, faced with fifty kids, half of whom didn't speak English, assigned Isaac to tutor Flaco.

Flaco hated everything about school, so Isaac figured some kind of reward might work. Since Flaco was fat, he tried food. Mama was overjoyed when he asked her to pack extra sugar tamales in his lunch bag. Finally Isaac was starting to *eat*.

Isaac offered Flaco tamales, and Flaco learned to read at the first-grade level. Flaco never got far beyond that.

Then Flaco Jaramillo's father went to prison on a manslaughter conviction and the boy stopped showing up at school, period.

Five years later, the boys ran into each other.

It was a half day at Burton. Isaac had spent the afternoon at the Museum of Science and Industry, alone, and was returning home from the bus when he saw two black-and-white police cars parked at the corner, lights flashing. Up on the sidewalk, a few feet away, a small, thin boy in a baggy T-shirt, sagging pants, and expensive running shoes was being rousted.

Four muscular officers had him in the position: legs spread, arms up, palms pressed against the brick wall. Isaac kept his distance but stopped to watch. The police spun the boy around, got in his face, and yelled. The boy remained impassive.

Then Isaac recognized him. The baby fat was gone, but the features were the same. Isaac stepped even farther back, expecting the police to arrest Flaco. But they didn't; they just wagged warning fingers and shoved the boy around. Then, as if summoned by a silent alarm, all four got in their cars and sped away.

Flaco stepped into the street. Noticed Isaac. As Isaac turned to leave, he shouted, "What you lookin' at?"

His voice had changed, too. Small boy with a deep baritone.

Isaac started walking.

"Yo! You hear me?"

Isaac stopped. The skinny boy was advancing on him. Face dark and scrunched and intent. All that pent-up anger and humiliation ready to blow. Ready to take it out on someone.

Isaac said, "It's me, Flaco. Isaac Gomez."

Flaco's eyes became razor cuts. His skinny face was rodentine with the same oversized nose, weak chin, and bat ears that Isaac remembered. The ears looked even bigger, exhibited mercilessly by a shaved head. Flaco was short but broad-shouldered. He had tattoos on his knuckles and the left side of his neck. The one on the neck was a nasty-looking snake, mouth open, fangs bared. The number 187 was atop his right hand—the police code for homicide.

"Gomez. My teacher. Man." Flaco shook his head.

"So how you been?" said Isaac.

"I been cool." Flaco smiled. Rotten teeth. The herbal reek of marijuana permeated his clothing. That had kept the police on him. But Flaco had dumped his dope in time.

"So what's with you? Why you dressed like that?" said Flaco.

"Private school."

Flaco looked him over some more. Grinned. "You screwed up as a teacher, man. I don't know nothin'."

Isaac shrugged. "I was nine. I thought you were pretty smart."

Flaco's grin faltered. "Shows what you know."

He flexed the hand with the 187 tattoo. Reached out. Slapped Isaac on the back. Held his hand out for a soul shake.

Isaac said, "Good to see you, man. I'll be shoving off."

As Isaac turned, Flaco said, "You tried to teach me, I remember that. You gave me some tamales . . . thought I was smart, huh?"

"I did."

Flaco bared his bad teeth. "Shows what you know. Hey, man, check *this* out: How 'bout we like . . . talk, man. Like find out what's been happening all these years?"

Isaac thought about it, not for too long. "Sure," he said.

They ran into each other once or twice a year. Sometimes Flaco had no time for Isaac; other times he seemed to crave company. When they were seventeen, Flaco had Isaac decipher some probation papers because his reading had remained at the first-grade level. The papers said Flaco had stolen cigarettes from a vending machine and been sentenced to a year's probation.

The following year, Flaco showed Isaac his guns. A big black automatic weighing down a pocket of his saggy khakis; a smaller chrome-plated six-shot thing taped to his ankle. Flaco went on about the guns, what they could do, what a bargain he'd gotten on the purchase. Isaac listened.

ISAAC got off the downtown bus and found his way to the bar on Fifth near Los Angeles Street. Cantina Nueva was where Flaco hung out during the day. This afternoon the bar was overheated and dim and mostly empty. Flaco slumped in the booth, wearing a black denim jacket over a black T-shirt, empty beer and shot glasses in front of him. He'd grown his hair out, but in a weird style. Shaved on top, with two black stripes running along the side. Sleepily, he looked up as Isaac approached.

Quick soul shake. "Bro."

"Hey." Isaac slid across from him. He'd bought a tube of cover-up makeup, done his best to hide the bruise.

"Whussup?" Flaco's voice slurred.

"I need a gun," said Isaac.

"Say what?"

Isaac repeated it. "For protection. The neighborhood."

"Someone mess with you? Tell me who. I kill their ass."

"No, I'm cool," said Isaac. "But you know how it is. Things get better; then they get worse. Right now it's worse."

"A gun," he said. "It's like a—you know—a responsibility."

"I can handle it."

"Bang bang," said Flaco. "No, I don't think so, man."

Isaac started to get up. Flaco clamped a hand over his wrist. "Have a drink, bro."

"No, thanks."

"You turnin' me down?"

Isaac swung around in the booth, faced Flaco full-on. "The way I see it, you're doing the turning down."

Flaco's smile dropped.

"One drink," said Isaac. "Then I'm going."

Flaco teetered to the bar, returned with two beer-and-shots. As the two of them drank, he drew a white plastic shopping bag out of his black denim jacket and lowered it beneath the table.

"Happy birthday, man."

Isaac glanced down. He took the bag from Flaco. Heavy. At the bottom was something swaddled in toilet paper. Keeping his hands low, he unwrapped it. A shiny little thing. Squat, square-barreled, perfectly malevolent.

--CHAPTER 6--

BY FOUR thirty-four p.m. on Friday, June 14, Petra had left two additional messages with Dr. Robert Katzman, the last unmistakably cross.

Then she regretted her tone. Even if she finally reached the oncologist, big deal. He'd treated Sandra Leon for leukemia—what else could he tell her? She went downstairs from the detectives room, found Kirsten Krebs idling by the watercooler, told her to put Katzman through immediately if he called back.

Krebs stared at the floor and said, "Yeah, fine."

Petra returned to her desk feeling aimless. Just two weeks until June 28. No sign of Isaac for a few days. Had the kid lost his youthful enthusiasm about the nefarious plot?

She turned to the file copies, reviewed the two she knew the best—Doebbler and Solis—for new insights, and failed to come up with any. It stayed that way until she reviewed the coroner's report on Coral Langdon, the dog walker, and found something she'd missed. Stuck in the middle of a small-print hair-and-fiber list stapled under some lab results. Two types of canine hair had been found on Langdon's clothing.

The presence of cockapoo hair was self-explanatory. Little Brandy had been bludgeoned along with her mistress.

But along with the champagne-colored curls was a smaller but substantial number of straight, coarse hairs. Canine. No DNA had been analyzed to determine the breed.

There were plenty of reasonable explanations, including maybe Coral Langdon had owned two dogs. Except according to the file, she hadn't. Perhaps little Brandy had hung with a canine buddy.

Or Coral Langdon, walking alone at night in the Hollywood Hills in the company of a pint-size pooch that provided zero protection, had encountered another dog walker and stopped to swap dog chat. Dogs could be a great ruse for bad guys.

Petra thought about how Langdon might've gone down. A guy with a dog shows up on the quiet hillside road. Coral and Dog Guy stop to talk. Coral and Brandy turn to go.

Boom. Bashed from behind. Like all the others.

She was pondering this when Kirsten Krebs stomped up to her desk and straight-armed a message slip right in her face.

"He hung up?" said Petra.

"It's not the one you *said* to put *through,*" said Krebs.

Petra snatched the slip. Eric had phoned three minutes ago. No return number. The message on the slip, in Krebs's cramped writing: "Don't believe everything you see on the news."

"Whatever that means," said Krebs.

Petra said, "You told him I wasn't here?"

"He wasn't the one you *said,*" Krebs insisted.

"Damn." Petra reread the message. "Fine. Bye."

Petra headed for the locker room, where the latest cast-off TV sat. She switched it on, flipped channels until she found a local broadcast. Regional news, nothing remotely related to the Middle East. Her heart pounded. She hurried back to the detectives room. Barney Fleischer was at his desk.

She said, "Does anyone around here get CNN?"

"The closest place would be Shannons."

Irish pub, up Wilcox, a brief walk.

Petra racewalked to Shannons, sat at the bar, ordered a Coke. The flat screen was a fifty-two-inch plasma set tuned to MSNBC. She endured financial news; then, when the anchorwoman's voice rose in pitch, Petra's ears opened. "American military personnel may have been at least partly responsible for reducing the death toll from a suicide bombing in Tel Aviv . . ."

The details of the report included a beachside café on a restaurant-packed avenue that paralleled the Mediterranean. Israelis, a couple of German tourists, some foreign workers from Thailand. Unnamed American "security officers."

Terrorist with a bomb vest under his raincoat approaches from across the street. His black raincoat on a hot day would've tipped off anyone with the slightest powers of observation. It had. He'd been wrestled to the ground before having a chance to yank the detonator cord on his plastique-and-ball-bearing-and-nail-stuffed vest.

Moments later, Terrorist Number Two saunters over and pulls his plug. Taking two Israelis with him.

And: "Scores are reported injured . . ."

But for someone's sharp eyes, it could've been worse.

Eric had to be in good enough shape to call.

Petra tossed the bartender a ten and left the bar.

BACK at the station, she entered the detectives room and nearly collided with Kirsten Krebs. "*There* you are. He's on hold."

Petra ran to her desk and picked up. "Connor."

"The irate detective," said a mellow voice. Dr. Bob.

"Sorry about that, Dr. Katzman. It's been a tough week. Thanks for returning. As I mentioned, Sandra Leon was a witness to a murder, and we're having trouble tracking her down."

"Unfortunately, I can't help you with that," said Katzman. "She's no longer my patient. And I could never track her down, either."

"Where's she getting her chemotherapy?"

"Hopefully nowhere, Detective. Sandra doesn't have leukemia. Though she wanted us to think she did."

"She lied about being sick?"

"Lying," said Katzman, "appears to be one of her primary skills. I guess I misspoke when I said she was no *longer* my patient. She never was under my care in the first place. That's why I have no problem talking to you."

"Talk away, Doctor."

"She showed up last year with a letter from a physician in Oakland saying she'd been diagnosed with AML—acute myelogenous leukemia—was in remission, and needed to be followed. The letter also stated that she was an emancipated minor living with some cousins and would require financial assistance. Our social worker sent her to all the right agencies and booked her for an appointment with me. Sandra kept her appointments with the agencies but was a no-show at Oncology Clinic."

"What kind of agencies are we talking about?"

"There are several county and state programs set up for kids with cancer. They offer medication, transportation and housing vouchers, wigs when patients lose their hair. Copayment for treatment."

"Ah," said Petra.

"You bet," said Katzman. "And once a child's registered, the family also gets hooked into the general welfare system. Which gets you access to food stamps, et cetera."

"Did you ever see her?"

"Months after talking to the social worker. The first time she didn't show, we phoned the number she listed, but it was disconnected. That concerned me, but I figured she'd moved. Or changed her mind and went to another doc. Then some of her forms came in for me to sign off on, and I sent the social worker out on a home visit. The address Sandra gave us turned out to be a mail drop."

"Where?"

"I wouldn't know," said Katzman. "Maybe Loretta Brainerd, the social worker, would. So Sandra witnessed a murder?"

"Murders," said Petra. "The Paradiso shootings."

"I heard about that," said Katzman.

"You finally saw her," said Petra. "How'd you find her?"

"I had CCS—Children's Cancer Services—send her a letter to the effect that she'd lose her benefits if she didn't show up for her checkup. She was there the next day. In tears, all apologetic. She's a pretty good actress. Most important, I wanted to check her out medically, because I didn't like what I saw. Her complexion was yellow, especially the eyes. Jaundice can be a sign of relapse—infiltration of the disease into the liver. I ordered a full-panel blood workup. I ordered the tests back stat, scheduled her for a five p.m. recheck that day. She said she was hungry, so I gave her some money to get a hamburger in the cafeteria. She and her cousin."

"Her cousin?"

"Another girl, around the same age. The two of them showed up with a man, some guy in his forties. He dropped them off at the clinic and left, but the cousin stayed. The blood workup came back negative for leukemia but positive for hepatitis A—viral hepatitis. Which isn't as bad as hep C, but it should be followed. I was ready to admit her for observation, but she didn't show for the recheck. Big surprise. That's when I phoned the doctor from Oakland. He'd never heard of her. She must've forged the letter."

"Is she in danger from the hepatitis?"

"Hep A is generally self-limiting. That's doctor talk for 'goes away on its own.' "

"The cousin," said Petra. "What do you remember about her?"

"Quiet girl. Sandra was more outgoing, nice-looking kid, despite the jaundice. The cousin just sat there."

"Shorter than Sandra? Chubby? Curly reddish hair?"

Silence. "That sounds familiar."

"Did she happen to wear pink sneakers?"

"Yes," said Katzman. "Bright pink. I remember that."

"What can you tell me about the adult male?"

"All I remember is his dropping them off in the waiting room and leaving. All I really saw was his back."

"Thanks, Doctor."

"There is one thing," said Katzman. "Sandra gave her age as fif-teen, but my guess is she's older. Closer to eighteen or nineteen. I can't back that up scientifically. But there was a certain . . . confi-dence." He laughed. "About her confidence game."

SHE called Brainerd. The social worker barely remembered San-dra Leon. After hanging up, Petra thought back to the parking-lot interview. The girl had just witnessed the violent death of her "cousin" but had displayed no shock, no grief. On the contrary, she'd been dry-eyed. Impatient. The only thing that had sparked anxiety in the girl's eyes had been initial eye contact with Petra. Cool about the homicide but nervous about the cops.

An adult male had accompanied both girls. Sandra had mentioned a convict brother, a car thief. Petra flipped through her notepad, found her hastily scrawled shorthand: "Bro. GTA. Lompoc."

She called the state prison, spoke to an assistant warden, learned that two Leons resided within the walls: Robert Leroy, age sixty-three, fraud and grand theft; and Rudolfo Sabino, age forty-five, manslaughter and mayhem. The warden was kind enough to check both inmates' visitors lists. No one had been to see Rudolfo Leon for over three years. The older man, Robert Leroy Leon, had a bevy of visitors but no Sandra, no one close in age and appearance.

Another lie? Sandra Leon had progressed, officially, from witness to Person of Interest. Petra paged Mac Dilbeck and told him about the scam.

He said, "She knew the vic but wasn't upset. So maybe she knew it was going to happen."

"That's what I'm thinking."

"Good work, Petra. Nothing else on this adult male?"

"Not yet. I'm wondering about something else. Leon quoted me her rights, and I asked her if she had experience with the law. She told me a story about a brother locked up at Lompoc. Turns out to be another load of bull, but why would she volunteer the informa-tion when it would tie her in with a criminal?"

"Maybe your question threw her off," said Mac. "So she blurted out a half-truth, covered with a phony detail."

"A relative in the system," said Petra, "but not a brother. Maybe even a brother but not at Lompoc. That cancer scam was sophisticated. This girl's had experience; I wonder if she's part of a criminal enterprise—a family thing. Maybe the murder's related to some scam, and the girl in the pink shoes was the intended victim. Sandra wasn't freaked out because she knew."

"Okay," said Dilbeck, "time to check the entire system, state and federal pens, even county jails."

Petra then ran the name Leon through NCIC and the rest of the data banks and came up with way too many hits. She focused on Bay Area Leons, which narrowed the search to twelve. Two inmates—John B., twenty-five, and Charles C., twenty-four—fit the brother age range. Both were from Oakland, and when she pulled up their stats, she knew she'd earned her share of the taxpayers' money. John's middle name was Barrymore, and Charles's was Chaplin. Katzman's take on Sandra: *She's a pretty good actress.*

Then she learned that the men were brothers and allowed herself a grin. John Barrymore Leon was serving a five-year sentence at Norco for mail fraud, and Charlie Chaplin Leon had earned himself two years at Chino for theft.

The wardens at Norco were unavailable, and the guard supervisor was new. But his counterpart at Chino turned out to be a font of information. The Leons were members of an Oakland-based crime group called The Players, and several of their cousins had done penitentiary time. His estimate of their membership was fifty to sixty, most related by blood. The majority were Hispanic, but there were plenty of whites and blacks and at least two Asians.

Petra said, "Diversity in the workplace."

The Chino guard laughed.

"They use violence?" she asked him.

"Not that I've heard. They concentrate on scams. They like to think of themselves as actors because the boss tried to be one."

The boss was a failed actor with a history of property crimes.

Robert Leroy Leon, sixty-three, aka The Director. Currently resid-ing at Lompoc. Lots of visitors but no Sandra.

Mac had been dead-on: The girl had blurted out a partial truth. Logging on to Google, she plugged in "The Players" and came up with 1,640,000 hits. It was nearly seven p.m., and she was suddenly tired. She was staring at the screen, wondering where to go next, when Isaac's voice drew her away from all those zeros.

"Hi," he said.

Her eyes shot to the bruise on his cheek.

"Hey," she said. "I hope the other guy came out of it worse."

Isaac blushed. "No big deal," he said too casually. "The hallway was dark when I got home, and I bumped into the wall."

"Oh," said Petra.

"I was wondering if there was anything I could do for you."

It was seven thirty-two on Friday night. "Working late?"

"I had obligations on campus all day, figured I'd come by here, see if you needed me."

One million six hundred forty thousand hits.

Petra smiled. "As a matter of fact . . ."

She gave him the info on Sandra Leon and The Players and watched him hurry over to his laptop. Thrilled to be busy.

She was worn-out and hungry.

She returned to Shannons and ordered a Bud and a corned-beef sandwich. New bartender on shift, a woman, and she didn't squawk when Petra asked her to put on Fox News.

Petra chewed on her sandwich, drank her beer, ordered another, then shot her eyes to the TV when she heard "Tel Aviv."

The death toll had risen to three. The number of wounded was now twenty-six. Eric had phoned her, she thought, so he had to be okay. She made it home and painted like a demon until just after midnight. Then she switched off the lights and stumbled to bed. At four fifteen a.m. she was jolted awake by the phone.

"It's me," he said.

"Oh," she said stupidly, clearing her head. "How *are* you?"

"Fine."

"You're not hurt?"

"Tiny piece of shrapnel in the calf."

"Oh, God, Eric—"

"I was lucky," he said. "Couple of small punctures. No bone or tendon damage, just muscle. It feels like I worked out too hard."

"Where are you calling from?"

"The hospital."

"Which one? Where?"

Silence.

"Damn you," said Petra.

"Tel Aviv," he said. "I can't talk long."

Petra said, "You're the one who spotted the first one, right?"

"It was pretty obvious, Petra. Ninety degrees outside, he's wearing an overcoat and looking like he's about to throw up."

"So you're the hero."

"Bad word."

"Tough," she said. "I want you to be my hero."

He didn't respond.

"Sorry," she said. "I'm just . . . I was *worried*."

"I can be *your* hero," he said. "It's the other people who bug me."

ISAAC was waiting for Petra when she arrived Monday morning around ten thirty. She walked past him and continued to the ladies' room, needing to compose herself, frazzled despite the weekend.

Determined to put the bombing—and work—out of her mind, over the weekend she'd sustained herself with catch-up chores and manic bouts of painting. Now she stood at the mirror, primping her hair. *Thirty years old and my face is starting to sag.*

Eleven days until June 28, and she was no further along than when Isaac had presented her with his little gift.

The kid was out there, looking eager. She put on a businesslike expression and returned to the detectives room.

Isaac stayed at his desk until she beckoned him over.

"What's up?" she asked.

"As far as I can tell, law enforcement doesn't know much about

The Players. Currently, there are five alleged members in prison. Alleged, because all five deny membership in any group."

Petra took out her notepad.

Isaac said, "I've got it all saved, can print it out for you."

She put the pad away. "Who's in prison?"

"The two you found—John and Charles—are grandsons of Robert Leon. A nonrelative named Anson Cruft was convicted of possession of false identification papers, and a woman named Susan Bianca, who is locked up for pandering. She's a younger sister of Robert Leon's second wife, Katherine Leon. Robert's kind of interesting. Forty years ago he got a few parts on soap operas, here in Hollywood. But after that, nothing. Somewhere along the line, he turned to crime. He's Guatemalan but has lived here most of his life. His first wife was Mexican, the daughter of a Nuestra Familia gangster. She died of cancer." He shrugged. "That's all I know."

She turned to her own computer, pulled up Robert Leon's file on NCIC. The most recent mug shot showed a lean, silver-haired guy with a long, seamed face. Thick wavy hair combed straight back, jet-black mustache. Sixty-three, but he looked younger.

She asked, "Did you come across any sibs for the brothers?"

"Not specifically," said Isaac, "but I did find a story that said Robert Leon had lots of kids."

"Okay, thanks," she said. "This is great. You've given me something to work with."

"On June twenty-eighth I haven't come up with anything new. Maybe I made something out of nothing."

"You didn't," said Petra. "It's definitely something. Let me run with what you've given me on Leon and his gang; then let's get together later—say four or five—and brainstorm the June twenty-eighth stuff."

His smile was as big as the ocean.

Petra phoned Lompoc a second time and got the details on Robert Leon's visitors. Three names interested her. An eighteen-year-old female named Marcella Douquette with a Venice address, and two guys in their forties who'd listed residences here in Hollywood: Albert Martin Leon, forty-five, and Lyle Mario Leon, forty-one. She tried all three phone numbers. Disconnected.

Back to NCIC. Albert and Lyle had both done time for nonviolent crimes. Mug shots showed a clear resemblance to Robert Leon. Albert was no looker. He was a bad-check artist. Lyle Leon's hair was clipped at the sides, bushy and squared off on top. An earring and a bristly soul patch said this guy thought himself quite the hipster. He'd been busted for peddling worthless cleaning solutions to old folk. Small-time hustler trying to look like the Big Dude?

There was no mention of the relationship between either man and Robert Leon.

Albert and Lyle Leon's addresses were bogus. Neither con was on parole, and neither had registered any motor vehicles, so there was no way to trace them. No criminal record for Marcella Douquette.

It was time to do some legwork. Petra drove to Venice. The Brooks Avenue house was one of three clapboard single units on a dirt lot in definite gang territory. Teeny little shacky thing sitting on a raised foundation, the surrounding lot cordoned by chain link and full of litter. The shack was a total dive but only a quick hop to the beach. Venice Beach, where deviance was the norm and scamsters worked the tourists every Sunday. Perfect for The Players.

Petra got out of the car, let her fingers settle atop the spot on her hip where her gun rested. A platter of soupy gray fog pressed down on the ocean. She took in Marcella Douquette's alleged residence from a distance. The chain-link fence was locked and bolted but low, barely at waist level. Petra approached the property, got a toe-hold in a chain-link diamond, and was over.

No doorbell, no answer to her assertive knocks. She was about to walk around behind the shack when the door to the neighboring unit opened and a man stepped out, squinting.

Hispanic, mid-twenties, bare-chested, wispy crew cut. Wispy mustache to match. Like that old actor . . . Cantinflas.

He wore baggy blue swim trunks and nothing else. His soft, hairless chest—all of him—was the color of mocha ice cream. Burgeoning potbelly. No tattoos or scars that she could see. No macho swagger, either. Just a sleepy-looking flabby guy getting up at one twenty p.m.

She gave him a businesslike nod. "You live here, sir?"

"Just for the summer."

"When did you start living here?"

The guy stared at her. She flashed the badge.

"I started May one," he said.

"Why May?" said Petra.

"That's when school was over. Cal State Northridge. What's up?"

Petra evaded the question. "What're you studying?"

"Photojournalism. I live in the Valley, figured Venice would be a good place to get shots for my portfolio." He frowned. "What's going on? Are there problems? 'Cause I didn't realize how sketchy the neighborhood was, but now I see where it's at."

"Bad neighbors?"

"The whole neighbor*hood*. I'll probably leave end of the month."

Petra said, "I'm trying to track down a young woman named Marcella Douquette."

"She the one next door?"

"There's a girl living next door?"

"Used to be. Haven't seen her for a while."

"How long's a while?"

He scratched his chin. "Maybe a couple of weeks ago."

Right around the time of the Paradiso shootings.

Petra said, "Could I have your name please, sir?"

"Ovid Arnaz."

"Mr. Arnaz, I've got a photo here. Not the kind of thing you'd take. From the Coroner's Office. You up for looking at it?"

"I've been to the coroner's," said Ovid Arnaz. "For a class. We met with crime photographers."

Petra showed him the least disturbing postmortem of the girl in the pink sneakers. Arnaz regarded it without a trace of emotion. "Yup," he said. "That's her."

Petra phoned Pacific Division, explained the situation, and within five minutes three patrol cars had sped to the scene. The tech van took another twenty minutes to arrive, during which Petra talked more to Ovid Arnaz. He turned out to be a first-rate source. Photographer's memory, keen eye for details. He remembered Marcella Douquette's pink shoes—she always wore them—and described her face and body to a T. More important, he reported that she'd lived with two other people. Another girl, pretty, blond, who had to be Sandra. And an older guy with a weird, bushy haircut.

Lyle "the Dude" Leon.

Petra showed Arnaz Lyle's mug shot.

"That's him. Dressed like a pirate."

"What do you mean?"

"Silk shirts with big sleeves. Like pirates used to wear."

He was less helpful when it came to describing behavior or emotion. No, he'd never seen any conflict among the three of them. They went their way; he went his. "During the day, I'm mostly out shooting film. When I go out at night, it's in the Valley, 'cause that's where my friends live. Sometimes I spend the night there."

"With your friends."

Arnaz looked away briefly. "Yeah, or my folks."

Petra said, "Makes total sense. Long as you're out there, avoid the drive back."

"Yeah," said Ovid Arnaz. "And I know my equipment's safe."

MAC Dilbeck looked at the photo of Marcella Douquette. "Our victim," he said.

Petra said, "Maybe our main victim. She's got no record, but was living with a member of a known criminal enterprise. Could be the other kids just happened to be in the parking lot at the wrong time."

The two of them were having coffee at Musso and Frank in one of the stiff-backed booths. Petra was having apple pie, and Mac had chosen rhubarb with vanilla ice cream. Luc Montoya was off the Paradiso case with another assignment.

It was five p.m. and Mac had been on for a day and a half, but his gray sharkskin suit was immaculate and his white shirt looked freshly pressed. Petra had left a message for Isaac at USC, canceling their p.m. meeting.

Eleven days till June 28, but this was more important.

"So you're thinking this Lyle character's the one."

"He and Sandra Leon lived with Marcella in Venice. The Players have no rep for violence, but maybe internally it's different. Maybe Robert Leon rules with an iron fist from his cell in Lompoc. Sandra never visited him, but Marcella did last year."

"You're thinking she offended the boss."

"The coroner said she'd had a recent abortion. Maybe that broke some kind of rule."

"Getting pregnant or having the abortion?"

"Could be either," said Petra. "Maybe the father was an outsider. Or Lyle. He was living with both girls in a very small house— anything could've happened."

"What about Sandra?"

"Sandra's sick. Hepatitis A. That could've prevented her from conceiving, or Lyle knew about it and stayed away. Or he was the one who gave it to her."

Mac ate a small triangle of pie. "Kind of ironic, her trying to fake out like she had cancer and she's sick with something else."

"Maybe the group knew all along she was sick and has been taking advantage of it to pull off medical scams."

Mac put his fork down. "It's progress, but I'm not sure it's good enough to keep the downtown boys at bay."

"We hand them the I.D. and the probable cause, and they chase it down?"

"You know how it works, Petra."

"Fine," said Petra.

"It isn't, but"—Mac folded his napkin into a rectangle—"I'll do my best to see you get credit for developing the lead."

"Don't worry about it," she said.

"Sorry," he said. "Wish there was a choice."

"I understand," she said.

But she was thinking: *Maybe there is a choice.*

THE GUN DIDN'T WEIGH THAT much, but Isaac felt the difference in his briefcase. He'd swaddled the twenty-two in a cheap blue bandanna stuffed in the bottom of the case, under his laptop.

Getting the gun into the station was no problem. On most days, eyeball scrutiny of incoming traffic sufficed. Isaac's political connection had gotten him a clip-on LAPD badge and a 999 key that unlocked the rear door on the south side of the building. He rarely needed to use the key. The station was old, with an inefficient cooling system, and the door was generally left open for circulation.

He climbed the stairs, filled with pleasant expectations of his meeting with Petra.

Four male detectives were there, but she wasn't.

An hour later he finally accepted the fact she wasn't going to show. Packing up, he descended to the ground floor, made his way to the rear door. Closed now. He opened it on the overly lit expanse of asphalt. All those black-and-whites and unmarked sedans. Warm night. He wondered why she'd stood him up. She'd seemed to be taking June 28 seriously.

It's not a stand-up, stupid. She's a detective. Something came up.

He'd go home, arrive in time for dinner, make Mama happy. Tomorrow he'd head straight to campus. Hide away at his corner table in Doheny Library's third subbasement. He'd sit. Think. Needing to produce. Needing something to show Petra.

--CHAPTER 7--

TUESDAY afternoon. When Captain Schoelkopf called Petra in, she was ready. Knowing full well what she'd done and ready to take the heat. The approved way to get what she wanted would've been to notify the shift lieutenant, receive his permission to talk to the captain, obtain *his* permission to contact the department's public affairs office, make a phone request to the P.A. desk jockeys, follow up with a tedious written application that gave away too many facts of the case, and then wait for approval.

Her way had been to call up four TV field correspondents she knew. All four were interested, and she faxed the cleanest photo she had of Marcella Douquette, along with Lyle Leon's mug shot. Spicing up the package with intimations of mysterious "crime cabals" and pleas not to "say too much."

All four local news broadcasts aired the photos at eleven p.m., repeated it on today's morning broadcast.

At two p.m. Schoelkopf ordered her into his office.

She expected hell but got only lackluster purgatory. Schoelkopf, leaning back in his Naugahyde desk chair, tossed out all the appropriately hostile utterances. But not with his usual vitriol. He seemed distracted. When he paused, she actually said, "Are you okay, sir?"

He sprang forward, glared. "Why wouldn't I be?"

"You look a little . . . fatigued."

"Never felt better. Stop trying to change the subject. The facts are you screwed up by not going through channels and wasted everyone's time and quite probably messed up a case."

"I admit I was a little hasty, sir, but in terms of wasted—"

"HOMSPEC's taking it off your hands."

"First I've heard about that," she lied. "Is—"

He cut her off with a wave.

Then Petra noticed that the framed photo of him and his third wife was gone from his desk. Problems at home?

"Don't screw up again, or there'll be repercussions." Schoelkopf adjusted himself in his chair. "So what did all your media hype accomplish?"

"Nothing yet, sir, but the calls are still—"

To Petra's astonishment, Schoelkopf nodded, said, "Who knows, maybe something'll actually happen because of your screwup."

By four p.m., she'd fielded thirty-five messages resulting from the broadcasts, all duds.

Feeling low, she was about to call the day to a close when her phone rang and Eric's voice said, "I'm at Kennedy, scheduled for an eight o'clock to L.A. If it's on time, I should be in by eleven."

"Are you all right?"

"Yes."

"You're okay to travel? With your leg?"

"I considered leaving the leg but decided to take it along."

"Funny," she said. "I'll pick you up. What airline?"

"American."

She hung up with her heart pounding, filed what needed to be filed, shut down her computer, collected her stuff, and left the detectives room. She took the stairs down to the rear exit and nearly bumped into Isaac in the stairwell. The kid didn't drive. Why was he entering through the parking lot?

"I hoped I'd catch you," he said. "You were working pretty late last night."

Last night? Their meeting. Oh, crap. He didn't get the message.

"I'm sorry. Something just came up."

"On the Paradiso shootings?"

"Yup. And I've got to leave now." The decent thing would be to go back upstairs and schmooze with him. She was just too tired.

"Sure," he said. "Whenever you have time. I've got someone, a librarian at the university library, checking out historical references."

"What kind of references?"

"Old crime stories. Anything related to June twenty-eighth."

"You think someone's studying history and reliving it?"

"It's all I could come up with," he said. "I didn't tell her why, just asked her to focus on the date. She has access to the rare-book section. If something bypassed the Internet, she'd be the one to find it."

Petra said, "I appreciate the time you're putting in on this."

"It'll probably end up being futile."

"Now you're starting to sound like me," she said.

His smile was weak. "Anyway, have a nice evening."

She hurried to her car.

IT WAS one twenty a.m. on Wednesday, June 19. The flight's arrival had been delayed for two hours, and the baggage-claim area stank of uncertainty. Petra spent the time sitting and rereading a copy of *People* magazine. When the LANDED sign for Eric's flight was finally flashing, Petra stationed herself near the swinging doors that bottomed the arrival ramp. She peered through the glass.

Eric was among the last passengers to appear, and she spotted him well before he got to the doors. Dark blue sweatshirt, faded jeans, sneakers, his little olive-green Swiss mountain climber's backpack slung over one shoulder. Light wood cane in his left hand.

A limp.

When he saw her, he straightened and waved the cane as if it were superfluous. He came through the doors; she rushed him, hugged him. The cane bumped against her leg.

He said, "One suitcase." They walked toward the carousel, stood there, silent, as bags bumped through the chute. She got between him and the revolving luggage, kissed him hard.

On the ride home, he said, "Thanks for picking me up."

He touched her knee, withdrew.

"How's your leg? Really."

"It's okay. Really."

"Your place?" she said. Thinking she really didn't want to drive to Studio City.

"We could go to your place."

When they arrived, he pronounced himself "rancid" and took a shower. When he slipped off his sweatshirt, she saw white flesh and bones. A bandage on his shoulder.

"A fragment nicked me. It's nothing." He stepped out of his jeans. His left calf was encased in thick bandages.

She said, "You can get it wet?"

"There's inflammation but no infection. In a couple of days I'll find a doctor and have the dressings changed."

He headed for the bathroom, and Petra followed at a distance, then stood in the door as he hobbled into the shower, got a hard spray going.

To heck with this.

Petra stripped down and joined him.

ERIC GOT OUT OF BED, WENT TO the kitchen, came back with two glasses of water, handed her one.

"As far as the department knows, I'm on my way to Morocco."

"When will you tell the department?"

"Don't know if I need to."

She stared at him.

He said, "I've been thinking about leaving for a while. Except for you, I'm not happy. For a long time I figured I never would be happy, but now I'm thinking there's a chance."

"There's more than a chance," she said.

"My quitting," he said. "You wouldn't mind?"

"Why would I mind? Who better than me to know what you mean about the job? Any idea what you want to do?"

"Don't know," he said. "Maybe private work, basic P.I. stuff. I've had enough of politics. Think I'm crazy?"

"Of course not," she said.

"If I made a living at it, I could buy a house."

"That would be cool," she said.

"The Valley's probably all I could afford," he said. "But maybe I could find a place with good natural light. I could set up a room for you to paint."

"I'd love that."

"You've got major talent. Have I ever told you that?"

He hadn't.

He nuzzled between her jaw and her collarbone. Her nightstand clock said three eighteen a.m. She'd feel dead tomorrow.

WHEN the phone rang, she bolted up and was surprised to find Eric in her bed. Oh, yeah, the airport. . . .

The damn thing continued to blare. Eric's eyes opened, and he propped himself on his elbows. Wide awake—his training. Petra was still woozy. Five fifteen a.m. She snatched up the receiver. *"What!"*

"Oh, man, I woke you, sorry. It's Gil, Petra."

Gilberto Morales, one of the night detectives, a guy she liked. She didn't like him now.

He said, "Normally I wouldn't even bug you, but the desk guy was all hyped up. He came up here expecting to find you—you're still on nights, right?"

"The Paradiso thing's been carrying me over to days and nights." She was up now. "What's the desk guy have his shorts all bunched about?"

"The Paradiso thing," said Gil.

When he told her the specifics, she thanked him.

Lyle Mario Leon—scamster of old people, last-known roommate of Marcella Douquette and Sandra Leon, and the prime suspect for multiple murder—had phoned her three times. *Needing* to talk to her. Refusing to tell the desk officer why but insisting it was crucial.

Finally, during his five-o'clock call, Leon mentioned Paradiso, and Mr. Desk intercommed Petra's extension, got no answer, went looking for her in the detectives room. Told Gil to try her at home.

Eric said, "What's up?"

Too tired to answer, she stared at the cell number Leon had left. Probably a nontraceable rental. She punched the phone, got a recorded message: "This is A-One auction services. Our offices are closed now, but . . ."

Real urgent. She waited until it was finished and said, "This is Detective Connor—"

"Good, it's you," a man's voice broke in. "Thanks for calling."

Tensing with distrust, Petra said, "Who is this?"

"Lyle Leon. You ran my picture all over TV, so now we need to meet, Detective. You nearly killed me."

"You sound pretty alive to me, sir."

"I'm not kidding," said Leon. "You don't understand."

"Educate me."

"I know who killed Marcella. Killed everyone."

He wouldn't give details, insisted on a face-to-face. She told him to meet her at the station in an hour.

"No way. Too public. I can't take the chance. Now that they know who I am, I'm a target. I'm scared, not ashamed to admit it. I've done some things in my life, but this . . . It's a whole new game.

I'll meet you somewhere off the beaten path. How about a park?"

"I just waltz into some dark park at this hour because you claim to be someone with information."

"I've got more than information, Detective. I've got all the answers." Long pause. "Detective, I can solve your case, but we have to do this my way. How about Rancho Park."

"Not possible, sir."

"Okay," said Leon. "You make a suggestion. Bring other detectives with you; I don't care about that. I just don't want to be seen at the Wilcox station. For all I know, they're watching the place."

"Who's they, sir? Your fellow Players?"

Laughter. "I wish. Them I could deal with."

"Who, then?"

"This is my final offer: There's a Jaguar–Land Rover dealer in Encino, on Ventura. Nearby is a falafel joint. It's closed right now, but they keep their benches out. The car lot keeps its lights on, so some of the benches are illuminated. I'll wait on a dark one. When I see you approach, I'll step out with my arms up so you can make sure this isn't an ambush."

"Sounds pretty theatrical," said Petra.

"Life is theater, Detective. Say in an hour?"

Petra knew the exact spot; she'd eaten there. Sidewalk café. The similarities to Tel Aviv were creepy. But this was too good to lose. She'd figure out a way. She said, "An hour it is."

ERIC said, "Sure it could be an ambush."

"I call for uniform backup at this hour," said Petra, "everything goes crazy."

"Maybe it needs to." He'd watched her get dressed, hadn't commented until she asked him what he thought about the call. Now he got out of bed, limped to the chair, and reached for his clothes.

"What are you doing?"

"Backing you up."

"It's not necessary," she said. "Mac Dilbeck's the primary. I'll call, let him decide."

"You're the one the guy's expecting."

"That's because my name was attached to the news story."

Eric finished dressing. "Where's your extra gun?"

She said, "I really am calling Mac."

"Mac's a good man." He headed for her closet. He found her spare nine millimeter on an upper shelf, nestled in its hard-shell case, between two black sweaters. Found the black nylon holster she favored, adjusted the strap and set himself up.

Petra said, "You really don't need to do this."

"Yeah, but it's fun."

She dialed Mac's number.

VENTURA Boulevard at five forty-three a.m. was a dark and ghostly stretch buzzed by intermittent traffic.

Mac Dilbeck arrived in his old Cadillac DeVille, parked two blocks west, as arranged. He wore a navy sweatshirt, black slacks, dark shoes. First time Petra had seen him without a suit and tie. Luc Montoya arrived in an unmarked company car. Off the case, but this morning he was on it. Tense but smiling. Eric's presence elicited raised eyebrows from the two of them but no comment.

If this was a serious ambush, it could go beyond ugly. But Petra, having cruised by the falafel stand twice from the north side of the boulevard, was feeling relaxed. Neither she nor Eric had spotted anyone at or near the little kiosk.

Mac reviewed strategy. Petra would cross Ventura, approaching the stand from the north, her gun out but keeping it close to her body so as not to attract attention. Once at the building, she'd press herself up against the white stucco walls before announcing herself. Anyone behind the stand would have to slip around, show himself at least partially. The three other detectives, approaching simultaneously from east and west, would be ready for trouble.

The big question mark, as she saw it, was a drive-by from Ventura. Eric knew that, and she could tell it bothered him. He kept quiet. She felt better knowing he'd be scoping out the boulevard.

"You okay?" Mac asked her.

"Let's do it."

She walked briskly toward the kiosk. Before she got there, a man stepped out from behind the building, arms in the air, fingers wiggling. Spreading his legs, he leaned against an outdoor table.

Mac and Montoya swarmed him. Eric did the initial pat down.

The guy said, "It's so nice to be appreciated."

After the guy was cuffed, Eric patted him down again.

Same long, craggy face as the mug shot. She said, "It's him."

Lyle Leon wore a maroon Jacquard silk shirt tucked into baggy cinch-waisted black nylon cargo pants and lace-up boots with healthy heels. Like pirates used to wear . . .

The eraser-head coif had been mowed to a conservative bristle.

Leon smiled at her. "Can we talk now?"

The five of them piled into Mac's Caddy and drove around the corner to a residential side street. Lyle Leon sat sandwiched in back, between her and Luc. Trying to smile. Definitely scared.

Motivation. She liked that. "Tell us your story, Mr. Leon."

"Marcella was my niece. Sandra's my third cousin. I was supposed to take care of both of them, but it got out of control."

"Where are their parents?" said Petra.

"Marcella's father died years ago, and her mother left."

"What is Sandra's story?"

"Sandra's father's in jail in Utah, and her mother's got mental problems. What's the difference? The problem was Venice. We went there last summer, then again this year. The deal was we'd be working Ocean Front walk a couple of hours a day, have the rest of the day to enjoy the beach. The girls loved it."

"Working how?"

"Selling merchandise. Sunglasses, hats, tourist stuff."

Petra pictured fake gold chains that disintegrated into dust, sunglasses that melted in the summer heat. She said, "The girls loved Venice, but it turned out to be a problem."

"Marcella met a person." A beat later: "She got pregnant."

"And had an abortion," said Petra.

"You know about that."

"The autopsy showed it."

"The abortion was what started the problem. Supposedly. That's not what he said the first time around. Just the opposite; he was furious she hadn't taken precautions. I had to pay him off; he seemed fine with that. Then he showed up this summer wanting to know where the baby is. I told him there was no baby, and he went nuts."

"Who are we talking about?"

"Omar Selden. A seriously bad person. Gang member, though you wouldn't know to look at him. Half white, half Mexican, something like that. You'll have him in your records; he did some time for robbery. But never for what he really did."

"Which was?"

"Killing people," said Leon. "Lots of them, according to what he told Marcella. Even if half true, he's a monster."

"Who'd this Selden kill?"

"He claimed to be the head hit man for his gang—VVO. Said he'd also done freelance work in prison." VVO was Venice Vatos Oakwood, a tight band of low-grade psychopaths. "Once I paid him off," Lyle said, "I thought we were free of him. So I figured it was okay to return to Venice—the girls had really enjoyed the summer. Then stupid Marcella spots Selden on the walkway. I turn my head for a second, and she's winking at him. And he's winking back. Soon they're off on the sand, talking. Couple of nights later, he drops by."

Leon shook his head. "You saw Marcella. Dumpy, those stupid shoes. Sandra's a hard-body; put her in a thong bikini, she'd turn heads. So who does Selden develop a thing for? Marcella. And Marcella falls for it."

Teenagers, thought Petra. Even scam artists couldn't control them.

Then she flashed on Leon's leering description of Sandra and wondered where his head was at. She said, "Sandra has hepatitis."

Leon was silent.

"You knew, Mr. Leon. You showed up with her at the clinic. Did you ever get her any serious medical help?"

"It's self-limiting. It goes away by itself. I took good care of those girls. For ten years, on and off, they lived with me and ate well and learned to read, and I never touched them. Not once."

And the blue ribbon for fatherhood goes to . . .

She said, "So Selden and Marcella reignited their affair."

"It wasn't an affair," said Leon. "The first summer she snuck away to be with him. Idiot doesn't use a condom, and he's amazed when she gets knocked up. One thing he made painfully clear: He wasn't going to be a father. He threatened me until I paid him off and promised to finance the abortion. Thousand bucks, out of my pocket. A year later Marcella winks at him, and he's back. The week before the murder, I'm alone in the house 'cause I let the girls go to a concert. I dropped them off at ten, was supposed to pick them up at two a.m. By eleven I'm back in Venice, mellowing out. At eleven thirty, the door explodes and Selden is standing over me. He kicked the door in and is saying, 'Where's my son?' Idiot assumed it was a son. I told him there was no baby. I'd done exactly what he wanted. He says, 'No way, man, I never said that.' I try to reason with him."

Leon sucked in his breath. His cheek twitched. "First I think he's listening; then suddenly he *swells* up. All red in the face, screaming that I'm a murderer. That's when I realize he's nuts. Last summer he was freaking out because she was pregnant. Now he's screaming for his kid. Suddenly he's got a gun out and he's talking in this insane whisper about how he's going to blow my tongue out for lying. Finally I manage to talk him down."

"What deal did you make with him?" said Petra.

Leon didn't answer.

Mac said, "You did something you're ashamed of."

"The deal was," Leon said, "that I'd let him have another go at Marcella so he could knock her up again."

No one spoke. The Caddy felt hot and close.

He said, "I never intended to follow through. We made an appointment for the following night, and the idiot left looking happy. The moment I was sure he was really gone, I packed all our stuff out of there, picked up the girls, and left."

"Where'd you go?" said Petra.

"We have places," said Leon.

"Give us an address, Mr. Leon, or face a hindering-an-investigation charge."

Leon twisted to face her. "I call *you*, and I'm hindering?"

Petra got in his face. "Give us an address *now!*"

"Okay, okay. . . . I took them to a place in Hollywood." He recited an address on North McCadden. "If you go there, it'll be vacant. I'm scared as hell living out of my car." He touched her wrist. "Listen to me." She glared, and he pulled back. "Selden won't let go of this. You saw what he did to Marcella. To those other kids. On top of that, I don't know where Sandy is. The day after Marcella was killed, she disappeared. I'm thinking somehow she got spotted by Selden."

"Selden's everywhere?"

"He's like a mad dog on scent. The thing that scares me is I don't know how much Marcella told him. About where we stay."

"Maybe Sandra figured it was smarter not to stick around."

"No," said Leon. "She didn't take anything with her. Not her clothes or her frog—she's got a stuffed frog she sleeps with every night. I got it for her when she was little, told her it came from her mother. No way would she leave without it."

"She have any money?"

"I always let her keep some in her purse. But not much. A hundred bucks, a hundred fifty."

Enough for a bus ticket.

Leon said, "I'm scared she left for a short while, got abducted."

"Left for what?"

Leon hesitated. "Sandra had gotten into stuff."

"Drug stuff?"

He nodded. Downcast, every bit the failed parent. Then Petra remembered: The Players saw themselves as performers.

Petra said, "So you're figuring she went somewhere to score dope, got spotted by Selden."

"Had to be."

"Unless you killed Marcella. Sandra, too."

"Why," he said quietly, "would I do that?"

"Maybe there's more to your relationship with the girls than you've told us."

"Ask anyone," he said. "Anyone who knows."

"Should I ask Robert Leon?"

"Robert will talk, but he won't tell you anything."

"What does Robert think about Marcella's murder?"

"He's not happy. No one is. I'm going to have to leave."

"The Players."

"I messed up too severely to be allowed to stay. That's why I'm living out of my car. I can't stay in any of their properties anymore."

Mac said, "Cut to the chase. Where can we find Selden?"

"Marcella told me he lived in the Valley. Panorama City. Went back and forth between there and Venice. If your gang people don't have their heads up their asses, they'll have files on him."

The Valley-to-Venice route. Something Leon had said early on tweaked something in Petra's consciousness.

"Selden doesn't look like a gang member. How so?"

"No tattoos, and he's a fat boy—soft. He told Marcella he went to college for a year, some government-funded gang-rehab thing. Maybe he did. When you first meet him, he comes across not stupid."

"He into photography?" said Petra.

"That's him. Carries around a camera, claims to be taking pictures. That's how he hooked up with Marcella. Told her she was beautiful, wanted her to model."

They took Leon back to the station, put him in a holding cell and found the mug books.

One look confirmed it. Omar Arthur Selden aka Omar Ancho aka Oliver Arturo Rudolph. Longtime VVO member.

Petra had an aka that wasn't in the files. Ovid Arnaz.

"IT WOULD help," said Klara Distenfield, "if you could be a bit more specific about what you're after and why."

It was Thursday afternoon. Isaac, smiling up at her from his worktable in a remote corner of Doheny Library's subbasement, said, "Sorry, that's all I can say."

"Boy," said Klara. "Talk about high intrigue. Official police business, huh?" She was a senior research librarian, forty-one years old, bright and sophisticated, with a soft, heavy bosom, long red hair that she barretted at the sides, and a peach-blush complexion. Klara had a soft spot for graduate students. Isaac's reputation had preceded him, and the divorced mother of two gifted kids had made sure to be available when he had reference questions.

Isaac had fantasized wildly about her on and off since the first time they met. He said, "Nothing exciting."

"Do they treat you well over there?"

"Very well."

"Still," she said, "it must be quite a contrast to here."

Klara leaned against the table. Her breasts swung, luxuriant.

Older women. He just loved the way they . . . What was *wrong* with him? What was wrong was that he was a sexual retardate. A damned virgin.

"Well, that's all I've managed to come up with so far," Klara said. She aimed her gold-green eyes at the computer printout she'd laid on his work surface. Hundreds of historical events tied in with June 28. Nothing he hadn't seen already.

"I really appreciate the time, Klara."

"My pleasure." She shifted even closer, and his nose filled with the sweet scent of soap and water. "You really do look *tired*. Especially there." She indicated the skin beneath his eyes. A fingertip grazed his right cheek, and electric current sizzled along his thighs.

"I'm at the top of my game," he told her. "Energy-wise."

"Well, that's good."

Suddenly she leaned down. Presented her mouth to him.

Like stepping off a precipice, he moved in.

Now she was in his lap, arms curling around him. His hands found her back, her breasts. He reached under her dress. She wasn't stopping him.

--CHAPTER 8--

No TGIF end-of-week joy for Petra. It was Friday afternoon, June 21. She sat at her desk, wondering why Isaac hadn't shown up today or yesterday.

She walked over and asked Barney Fleischer if he'd seen the kid.

"Wednesday," he said. "He was here until around eight."

"All by himself?"

"I was here," said Barney. "Have you heard about Schoelkopf?"

"No, what?"

"Split from his wife, the third one." The old man smiled.

"It's L.A.," said Petra.

She sat back down, exhausted from the meeting.

With Omar Selden I.D.'d as the prime suspect for Paradiso, the logical step would've been to run an immediate search for the mass killer. Instead, Petra had been ordered to specify how she'd come up with Lyle Leon as a witness. Then: Sit tight until notified further by the Homicide Special Squad. The call came on Thursday. Big-time meeting tomorrow, Friday, at two p.m.

They'd adjourned an hour ago, at three. She and Mac Dilbeck and three golden downtown boys. The three HS detectives had turned out to be relaxed types, nothing but praise for the way Hollywood had come up with Selden. The confab ended up being Petra and Mac fact-sharing, and the hotshots reciting everything they knew about VVO and other Westside/Valley gangs. At two fifty-eight the head Downtown guy announced the plan, obviously preordained: The new San Fernando Valley Gang Unit would search for Omar Selden because, even if Selden was the shooter, he'd been accompanied by other gang members, and the takedown required specialists.

Don't call us; we'll call you.

Petra raised the issue of the missing Sandra Leon. The head Downtown guy said, "Wouldn't you say she's probably dead? We bring Selden in alive, maybe we'll find out the details."

Now she sat at her desk thinking about the June brainings, because there was nothing left to think about on Paradiso. The kill date was seven days away. Lord help the next victim.

Unless Isaac was wrong. But how could he be? The wound stats were nearly identical. Retrieving the June 28 files, she looked over the cases yet again, straining to come up with a unifying factor.

Half an hour later, it was killer 6, detective 0.

Her best weapon, she realized, was the Big Brain. But where was he? All that youthful exuberance, the way Isaac had latched on to her like a puppy. Why keep his distance now? Because she'd put him off? Or was it something to do with that facial bruise? No way did she buy his story about walking into a wall. Was Isaac in trouble?

She placed the six files back in a drawer and shifted her thoughts to Eric. She hadn't seen him since Wednesday morning when he'd slipped away—limped away—from the station as Lyle Leon was being booked. Drawing Petra into the stairwell, kissing her briefly, then hurrying off.

One call since then. The message slip had greeted her when she arrived this morning: "I'll be in touch soon. E."

Off doing his thing, whatever that was. Did that mean a prolonged retreat into one of those long, dark silences of his?

She phoned the Biostatistics Department at USC, was told Isaac was rarely in, but she could leave a message.

To heck with it, she needed a walk to bleed off nervous energy.

She collected her purse and left the station. Out in the parking lot, she saw two guys loitering by her car. A pair of suits she didn't recognize. Dark suits, badges on their breast pockets. They were waiting for her. She walked straight up to them. Two mustachioed guys, one fair-skinned, one swarthy. Blue tie, blue tie.

The light one said, "Detective Connor? Lew Rodman, the gang squad." All business, no smile. His partner's mustache was a black pencil line so thin it could've been grease pencil.

Gang guys wanting to talk to her directly about Selden instead of going through Metro? She *had* come up with the I.D. Nice to be appreciated. She smiled. "Good to meet you guys. So what's the plan on Omar?"

Rodman and Grease Pencil exchanged glances.

Pencil said, "Who's Omar?"

Nothing appreciative in their eyes. She said, "What's this about?"

Rodman said, "Can we talk somewhere private?"

"If you tell me what it's about."

Rodman looked at Pencil. The dark-skinned man said, "It's about an intern you supervise named Isaac Gomez."

"Isaac? Is he okay?"

"That," said Pencil, "is what we're trying to find out."

THEIR bronze Crown Victoria was parked at the far end of the lot. The car was stifling. Petra got in the back, and Rodman and Pencil—identified now as Detective II Bobby Lucido—sat in front and cracked their windows. Lucido looked over the seat. "So what can you tell us about Gomez?"

"Nothing," said Petra, "until you tell me why you want to know."

Lucido smiled at her. "Here's the situation: Gomez has been spotted consorting with a known drug dealer and all-around bad guy."

The facial bruise. The kid really was in trouble.

Petra said, "Who's the alleged bad guy?"

Lucido turned away from her, and Petra heard paper shuffling. Something passed over the seat: an eight-by-eleven, black-and-white glossy of Isaac and a skinny guy sitting together. Really skinny guy, the sunken cheeks and droopy eyes of a junkie. The two of them huddled in a restaurant booth. The junkie wore black clothes and had an aggressively bizarre haircut. Isaac looked like Isaac: neat, clean, button-down shirt. But different around the eyes. More intense than she'd ever seen him. Angry?

Petra said, "Who's the skinny one?"

"Flaco Jaramillo," said Lucido. "Known dope dealer, and there's talk he kills for money, though he never got called up for that."

Petra studied the photo some more. "Where was it taken, Detective Lucido?"

"Call me Bobby. This is Lew. The place we got the photo is on Fifth near L.A. Cantina Nueva. Dealers, border *coyotes,* freelance scum, your basic bottom-feeding dive."

"You have an undercover guy there?"

"Let's just say we're in a position to take pictures," said Lew Rodman. "And Flaco's the subject of lots of them. So when your boy showed up looking all preppy, he got noticed."

Petra said, "Obviously he knows Jaramillo, but that's a long way from being a k.a."

"They associate; they're known associates," said Rodman. "We're *not* getting Ph.D.'s, but we do know how to add."

"Any evidence Gomez is engaged in criminal activity?"

Bobby Lucido said, "He talked to Flaco; Flaco got up and went behind the bar, sat back down. A few minutes later, Gomez left with a briefcase."

"He always carries a briefcase."

"Bet he does," said Lucido.

Petra's gut churned. "So what do you want from me?"

"Nothing yet. Just keep an eye open for anything sketchy. The situation changes, we'll let you know."

"All of a sudden I'm working for you?"

Lucido said, "You're working for the department. Same as us. You got a problem with any of this, feel free to complain."

A short time later, Petra watched the Crown Victoria drive out of the parking lot. Isaac was into something *really* bad. She changed her mind about walking, decided to get her stuff, play hooky. As she reached the station's back door, someone called her name. She turned. And there he was, Mr. Double Life, waving with the hand that wasn't gripping his briefcase. He trotted up to her. The bruise was paler but still swollen and covered with pancake makeup.

"Hey," she said. "Been a while."

"Sorry. I've been burning the midnight oil."

Bet you have. "Dissertation stuff?"

"Mostly. Some June twenty-eighth research. Nothing to show on that, unfortunately. The librarian's still looking." He frowned.

Petra showed him her watch. Tiny black numerals in the calendar window declared 21.

"I know," he said. "I heard one of the Leons faces was on TV. So is Leon the shooter?"

She shook her head, unsure how much to tell him.

Engine noise made her look over his shoulder. A black SUV had entered the lot, and it nosed aggressively into the first empty slot. At the wheel was one of the Downtown hotshots. Confident as a movie cop. His buddy rode shotgun, same demeanor. Reflective sunglasses on both of them. The motor gunned, then turned off. Petra said, "Let's talk later," and held the door open for Isaac.

As she entered the building, Hotshot I approached and said to Petra, "Hi. Ready for the meeting?"

"What meeting?"

"In five. We called. Fifteen minutes ago."

While she'd been sitting in Rodman and Lucido's car. Short notice, like she was their hand servant.

She said, "What's up?"

Hotshot II said, "Let's meet and find out."

ISAAC set up his computer at his corner desk. He plugged in, pretended to have something to do.

Pretended nothing had happened with Klara.

But it had, and now he'd fouled things up personally and professionally. Taking advantage of a vulnerable woman, which by itself was sleazy. The bigger issue was mixing business with . . . pleasure and the risk of a screwup on the June 28 investigation.

He tried to rationalize it away by telling himself that Klara had taken advantage of him, the impressionable student.

But it had been great.

Afterward, she looked about to cry, so he kissed her.

"God, I'm still tingling," she said. Then the tears came. "I'm so sorry, Isaac. What do you need with a fat, hysterical old woman?"

That led to his reassuring her, caressing her.

They left the library together and walked to a coffee shop on Figueroa, across the street from the campus's eastern border.

At the restaurant, she led him to a booth and ordered mint tea and a green salad. Isaac asked for a Coke.

She touched the tips of his fingers. "You're a beautiful boy, Isaac Gomez. One day you'll be famous. I hope you think of me kindly when you are."

He laughed.

Klara said, "I'm not being funny."

The following day, he returned to the library, determined to meet Klara's eyes forthrightly. We're all adults here.

She wasn't at her desk.

"Sick," said Mary Zoltan, the assistant.

"Nothing serious, I hope."

"When she called in this morning, she sounded pretty bad."

"A cold?" said Isaac.

"No, more like . . ." Mary stared at him, and Isaac felt his face catch fire. "Whatever," said Mary. "Is there something I can help you with?"

"No, thanks."

She smirked.

THE second meeting was worse for Petra. Five minutes after it started, a Valley Gang Unit rep arrived, a huge man with a shaved bullet head, ice eyes, and all the charm of a virus. He kept inspecting his nails as Hotshot I gave more speeches about gang behavior.

The search for Omar Selden and associates was now an official task force. Schoelkopf had decided to sit in. Not that the captain said much. For the most part, he looked sleepy and small, and Petra, knowing about his third wife, felt sorry for him. She started nodding off as Honcho droned on. Finally the guy slapped his notepad shut and motioned for his buddy to collapse the easel.

"So," he said, "we're all on the same page."

Petra looked at the big gang sergeant and said, "One thing you might want to check out: Our boy Omar took college courses in photography. He listed a phony address in NoHo, so maybe he's got some kind of connection there."

"It was a *phony* address," Schoelkopf cut in. "That was the point of lying, Detective Connor. To throw you off."

Which was utter nonsense. Criminals lacked imagination, made stupid mistakes all the time. No one backed her up.

The gang guy stood to his full six four: "Never seen any gangs in NoHo, except when there's a street fair. No street fairs till next month." He left the room.

When Petra returned to the detectives room, Isaac was waiting for her. Now she did need to walk, and she told him so. They left the station and headed south on Wilcox. Isaac was smart enough not to talk as she stomped her way toward Santa Monica. Eventually, she cooled down. "So," she said. "June twenty-eighth. The date has to mean something—a birthday, an anniversary, something personal to the bad guy. I checked DMV stats on all the principals. None of the vics were born that day. So maybe our boy *is* a history freak." She waited for Isaac to comment. He didn't. "What keeps coming to me," she went on, "is an extremely seductive killer. Someone subtle about the way he sets things up. Marta Doebbler being called out of the theater; Solis possibly being conned by a phony cable appointment. Maybe he was also canny enough to use a dog as a lure."

She told him about the two kinds of canine hair found on Coral Langdon, recounted her dog-walker scenario.

"A choreographer," he said.

"That's a good way to put it. So what do you think?"

"You're right about the subtlety."

"Until he blitz-attacks the victims from behind and bashes their brains out. That's anything but subtle, Isaac. To me that says (a) cowardice, and (b) he's got lots of rage beneath the surface that he's able to control in everyday life. He functions well until he's triggered. We know the date is one trigger, but there has to be something about the victims."

They walked for a while before she said, "You okay?"

He startled. "Sure. Everything you're saying makes sense. I wish I had something to add, but I don't."

A half block later, he said, "One thing does occur to me. There's a discrepancy between Marta Doebbler and the others. If the killer was able to disguise himself as a cable repairman to get into Mr. Solis's place, Mr. Solis obviously didn't know him. If the dog theory's true, the same could go for Coral Langdon: She met a man walking his dog in her neighborhood, chatted, turned to go, and got bludgeoned. But he still could've been a relative stranger. That *can't* be true of Marta Doebbler. She wouldn't have left the theater in the middle of the show unless she knew who had called her. Plus, a stranger wouldn't have known Marta was *going* to the theater."

"Someone she trusted," said Petra. "Back to the husband. There's another discrepancy between Marta and the others. She was killed on the street but then placed in her car. You could look at that as her being treated with a bit more respect. Which would also fit with a killer who knew her well."

He grimaced. "I should've thought of that."

"That's why it's good to brainstorm," said Petra. They reached Santa Monica Boulevard. Traffic, noise, pedestrians.

Petra said, "Here's yet another distinction for Doebbler: She was the first. Detective Ballou told me he thought Kurt Doebbler's reaction was off, and then after I met Kurt, it got me thinking: What if the bad guy never set out to commit a string of murders? What if he killed Marta for a personal reason and found out he *liked* it? Got himself a hobby. Which brings us back to Kurt."

"A once-a-year hobby," said Isaac.

"An anniversary," she said. "What if June twenty-eighth is significant to Kurt because he happened to kill Marta on that day? So he relives it."

He stared at her. "That's brilliant." Return of the youthful exuberance. "Maybe," he said, "we should find out who knew she was at the theater. She went with friends, right?"

They returned to the station, and Petra pulled the Doebbler file. Marta had gone out with three friends. Melanie Jaeger and Sarah

Casagrande had been contacted. The third, Emily Pastern, had been out of town. According to Ballou's notes, neither Jaeger nor Casagrande knew for certain who'd called Marta out of the theater.

> Witness Casagrande reports that Victim Doebbler appeared agitated by telephonic interruption and that Vic Doebbler reacted quickly, "jumped out of her seat and just left."
>
> Vic's husband, Kurt Doebbler, denies calling Vic at any time that night, denies owning cellular phone. Pacific Bell confirmed said denials.

Ballou's next notation identified the origin of the call as the pay phone around the corner from the theater. Isaac, reading over Petra's shoulder, said, "Doebbler could've driven from the Valley to Hollywood, called Marta from the phone booth, and waited by her car."

Petra said, "I wonder if Doebbler has ever owned a dog."

She called Valley SPCA. No dog registrations at the Doebbler household. But plenty of people didn't register their pets.

Next, she phoned the numbers Ballou had listed for Marta's friends, Melanie Jaeger and Sarah Casagrande. Both were now owned by new parties. DMV records showed no listings for Jaeger anywhere in California, but a Sarah Rebecca Casagrande was listed on J Street in Sacramento. Petra got her number and phoned it.

The receptionist at a family medicine clinic answered. *Dr.* Casagrande was with a patient.

"What kind of doctor is she?"

"Psychologist. Actually, she's a psych assistant. Dr. Casagrande is a new Ph.D."

"This is Detective Connor, Los Angeles Police. Would you please have her call me?" Petra recited her number.

"The police?"

"Nothing to worry about," said Petra. "An old case."

Next, she tried Emily Pastern.

A machine picked up on the fifth ring, and a perky female voice said, "This is Emily and Gary. We're not in now, but . . ."

Petra sat through the message because the background noise had captured her attention: a dog barking.

By five thirty Friday, neither Dr. Sarah Casagrande nor Emily Pastern had returned her calls. She tried again with no success.

Everyone gone for the weekend.

Suddenly all the energy generated by her brainstorm with Isaac was gone. She walked over to his desk. He stopped typing, cleared his screen. She said, "Want some dinner?"

"Thanks, but I can't." He looked down at the linoleum. "Promised my mother I'd spend some time at home. She cooks these enormous meals and gets deeply hurt if no one's around to eat them. My father does his bit, but she wants all of us. My younger brother tends to stay out late, and sometimes my older brother eats on the job, comes home, and goes straight to sleep." He frowned.

"You okay?" said Petra.

"Tired."

"You're too young for that."

"Sometimes," he said, "I don't feel very young."

Petra watched him tramp off, lugging the laptop and his briefcase. Something was definitely weighing him down. That junkie putting on some kind of pressure? Maybe she'd disobey the Downtown gang guys and confront the kid. No, that would be a *really* bad idea. Her head hurt. Time for dinner. Another solitary night. Maybe Eric would call sometime during the weekend.

As she cleared her desk, he phoned, as if she'd conjured him.

"Free?"

"Just about. What's up?"

"Doing things," he said. "I'd like to tell you about them."

They met just after six at a Thai café on Melrose near Gardner.

They got seated immediately, served quickly, ate their papaya salads and *panang* curry with silent enthusiasm.

"So," said Petra, "what you been doing?"

Eric put down his fork. "Looking seriously into private work. The licensing requirements don't seem too tough."

"Don't imagine they would be." He'd done military special-op work, spent a tour as an M.P. detective before signing on with LAPD. All that had taught him endless patience for surveillance. Perfect for private work. "So you're definitely doing it?"

"Don't know." He rolled the fork's handle. Petra's warning system went on full alert. "Something else on your mind?"

He said, "Are you upset? At me. For quitting."

She laughed. "No way. Maybe I'll join you."

He said, "Paradiso?"

"That and other stuff. Then she was pouring it out: shunted aside on Paradiso, Schoelkopf dissing her in front of the others, zero progress on the June 28 killings, with the target date a week away.

"Any ideas?" she said.

"As far as Selden, you're right about the photography angle."

"You'd pursue it?"

"If it were my case."

"Well," she said, "go and tell the geniuses in charge."

"Geniuses are rarely in charge." An uneasy expression slithered onto his face.

"What?" she said. "You're holding back, Eric."

He rolled the fork some more, and she braced herself for yet another put off. He said, "If I go out on my own, it'll mean less money. Until I build up a clientele. I haven't been with LAPD long enough to get a city pension; all I have is my military pension."

"That's decent money."

"It pays the bills, but I couldn't buy a house." He returned to his food, chewed slowly, the way he always did.

She said, "A house would be nice, but it's not necessary."

"Your place is small. So's mine. I thought . . . if the two of us . . ." His shoulders rose and fell.

Petra's chest grew warm. She touched his wrist.

"You want to move in together?"

"No," he said. "Not the right time."

"Why not?" she said.

"Don't know," he said, looking about twelve years old.

She thought about the magnitude of his loss. What it took for him to express himself emotionally even at this level. Heard herself saying, "I don't know, either."

THE kitchen was hot and fragrant. His mother washed dishes, pivoted to accept Isaac's cheek peck. "No more work?"

"It's the weekend, Ma."

"You're not too busy to eat with us?"

"I smelled your food from miles away."

"This? It's not fancy, just tamales and soup."

"Sounds pretty fancy to me. Where's Dad?"

"On the way home. The Toyota acted up again. Montalvo *claims* some kind of filter." She scurried to the refrigerator, poured him a glass of lemonade.

"Joel's not coming home," said his mother. "A night class."

Isaac figured Joel was lying. He drained the glass of lemonade, headed for the room he shared with his brothers.

"Isaiah's sleeping, so go in quiet."

She stopped, turned. "It's nice you're here, my doctor." Returning to the stove. "For a change."

He removed his shoes and opened the bedroom door carefully, but Isaiah sat up in the top bunk.

"Man . . ." Rubbing his forehead. "It's you."

"Sorry," said Isaac. "Go back to sleep."

Isaiah sank down on two elbows. "You got a call. Some *lay-dee.*"

"Detective Connor?"

"Wasn't no detective." Isaiah grinned.

"Who?" said Isaac. Knowing. Dreading.

Isaiah's eyebrows bounced. "Someone named *Klara.*"

He'd never given her his home number. Now it starts.

He forced his voice calm. "What'd she want?"

"To *talk* to you, bro." Isaiah snickered. "I stuck her number under your pillow. Eight one eight—you messin' with a *Valley* girl?"

Isaac retrieved the scrap of paper.

"Thanks for taking the message," said Isaac.

CHAPTER 9

FRIDAY night, after dinner, Petra and Eric had driven to the Jazz Bakery in Venice. By eleven, Petra was bushed. The two of them returned to her place and fell asleep in each other's arms.

Saturday morning they awoke feeling fresh.

By early afternoon, they were checking out the NoHo galleries for some connection to Omar Selden.

The square mile encompassing Lankershim Boulevard just south of Magnolia had been a breeding ground for board-ups and petty crime for years. Transformed by creative types into an arts district, the area was an amalgam of pretty and seedy.

At two p.m. NoHo was peaceful and gray, livened in spots by the colorful signage of clubs and cafés and exhibitions. Foot traffic was moderate. They took Petra's car, parked on a side street, and went hunting. Eight galleries featured photography, and five were closed.

Flash Image, a half-width storefront next to a defunct theater academy, was all black-and-white camera work. Very good lighting and hand-lettered partitions showed a real attempt to spruce up what had obviously been a dump.

This month's exhibit was "i-mage: local artists do l.a."

An alphabetical list of half a dozen photographers was posted on the front partition. First on the list: Ovid Arnaz.

The multiple murderer was good with a camera. His contribution to the show: half a dozen street scenes, unframed and mounted on board. Buildings and sidewalks and sky and bare trees, no people.

Good use of structure, Omar. Decent composition.

The photos were dated six months ago and signed OA. The posted prices ranged from a hundred fifty to three hundred dollars.

Petra's black hair was tucked under a white-blond wig she'd used for undercover jobs back in her auto-theft days. Her duds were a long-sleeved black jersey top under a black denim jacket, tight black jeans, loafers, and big-framed Ray-Bans.

Eric wore mirrored ski shades, black jeans, a black V-neck, and soft shoes and had put on his black nylon baseball jacket with the custom gun pocket. His limp had subsided a bit, but his gait was still a bit off. No need for the cane, he insisted.

The pink-haired girl who worked at the gallery had smiled at him more than once from behind the scratched metal desk. Petra hooked her arm around his as they both stared at the same photo: the parking lot of the Paradiso—flat stretch of blacktop, devoid of cars, bounded by posts and chains. Different light. Longer shadows than the others.

Dated a week before the murder. The title: *Club*.

Take it home for only two hundred bucks.

Pink Hair came up to them. "Ovid is acute, isn't he?"

"Perfect aim," said Petra. "Where's he from?"

"Ovid? Right here in the Valley."

"How'd you find him?"

"He was part of a student class at Northridge," said Pink. "But he's the only one we took on. Way better than anyone else."

Eric leaned in closer to the photo, studied the details.

Pink Hair said, "Are you guys interested?"

Eric said, "Hmm." He wandered over to the next print. Full-on shot of a theater on Broadway, downtown. One of the old ornate dowagers. Its marquee now read JEWELRY! GOLD! WHOLESALE!

Petra eyed the Paradiso photo. "I really like this one."

Eric shrugged.

"These just have generic initials. We'd want it signed to us personally," Petra said. "After we *meet* the artist. We do that with everything we collect." She favored the girl with a cool smile. "Art's more than buying and selling. It's about chemistry."

"I guess I could ask Ovid. About signing it to you. Especially if you buy two."

"We begin any collection with a single piece," said Petra. "Take our time to see how we live with it. After that . . ."

She looked Pink up and down.

Pink said, "Well, sure. So which one—"

Petra said, "I assume you've got some stretch on the price. We always get twenty percent courtesy. On this, we were thinking more like twenty-five."

"I'm not the gallery owner," said Pink. "Twenty-five off would be . . . I mean, the owner's my boyfriend. I'm sure he won't mind. You guys look like serious collectors. It'll be okay."

Eric swiveled. Turned robot eyes on her. Petra thought the girl would swoon. "One fifty," he said.

"Sure, great."

Petra said, "When can we meet the artist?"

"Um, that's the thing. I don't know . . . Let me try to arrange it. If you leave a deposit—"

"We'll leave you fifty," said Eric.

Pink took the money. "Great. I'll take your number and let you know. I'm Xenia."

"Vera," said Petra as she scrawled her cell number. "This is Al."

"Vera and Al, great," said Pink Hair. "You won't regret it."

Back on Lankershim, strolling north along with the Saturday throng, Eric said, "Al and Vera."

" 'Cause we're silky smooth."

He smiled.

Petra said, "You're very good."

"At what?"

"Acting."

"Then I can get a job as a waiter, provide us some income."

Suddenly he veered out of the pedestrian stream. Placed his hands on her shoulders. "Sometimes I feel like I'm running on empty," he said. "You make me feel . . . fuller."

He pressed his cheek to hers, touched the back of her neck softly. She said, "You're good for me, too."

They stood there as people moved past them. Clanking sunglasses. Then weapons as their gun pockets brushed. The percussion made them break the embrace.

Petra smoothed down her jacket. "If Pinkie actually phones for a meet with Omar, I'll have to notify the task force. Which will cause all kinds of complications."

Eric said, "The task force should be grateful."

"And I should be rich and famous." She frowned. "I get them their suspect, hand them everything, and they're futzing around. The rationale is they've got to proceed cautiously in order to get Selden's associates. But if we had Omar in custody, we'd have a better chance of doing that."

"True."

"Sandra's probably dead, right?"

He said, "That's where I'd put my money."

From inside her purse, her cell phone squawked.

"Vera? This is Xenia, from the gallery. Guess what? I managed to find Ovid, and he's real close by. He can be there in a half hour to meet you and sign your print."

"Great," said Petra, her mind racing.

TRYING not to look panicked, Petra scanned Lankershim, found a Mexican café across the boulevard that had a clear diagonal view of the gallery's entrance. They lucked out by scoring a window booth.

Rummaging through her purse, she found the head Downtown hotshot's number and tried to reach him. Machine only at his desk number; no answer on his cell. She waited out the tape, recited clearly and slowly, hoped her fear didn't seep into the message. All three hotshots were checked out for the weekend. The big, aloof gang sergeant was gone, too.

She phoned Mac Dilbeck's house, and his wife, Louise, said, "Aw, honey, he took the grandkids to Disneyland."

"Not important," said Petra. "We'll talk tomorrow."

What next? Informing Schoelkopf was proper procedure but out of the question. He'd kill the whole deal, discipline her for insubordination, and Omar would get away.

That left her and Eric. He sat across from her, looking calm.

Serene, even. Any way you cut it, she was in trouble. Might as well catch a bad guy. They planned it this way: Omar Selden had never met Eric, so Eric would be the inside guy, returning to the gallery alone, pretending to browse. Petra would remain across the street in the café, her eyes fixed on Flash Image's front door. As soon as she spotted Selden, she'd connect with Eric's cell, ring twice, hang up.

After that, it would all be improvisation.

Twenty minutes after Xenia's call, Eric drained his coffee cup and walked out. Petra watched him ease his way across Lankershim. Gliding. Petra closed her eyes and took a deep breath.

She opened her eyes to see Omar Selden's stocky frame approaching the gallery from the south end of the boulevard. Twenty yards away. With a girl. Her frame was blocked by Omar's.

Petra autodialed Eric, beeped twice. Kept her eye on Omar. He appeared casual, not a care in the world.

She squinted, kept her eyes on both of them. Then Omar stepped ahead, and she got a partial look at his companion. Petite, long blond hair, nice figure. A black halter top with a shoelace back exposing smooth bronze skin. Tight jeans showcased slim but curvy hips. The girl turned, laughing at something Omar had said.

Sandra Leon.

Petra got the check, tossed money on the table, stuck her hand in her gun pocket, and left the café.

As she entered the gallery, Omar Selden was bent over the metal desk signing *Club*. Flanked by a stoic Eric and a grinning Xenia.

No sign of Sandra. Probably in the ladies' room. Good. Maybe this could go smoothly. Petra walked toward them. Omar looked up.

Eric said, "I decided to buy both of them."

Omar smiled. Barely glanced at Petra. No sign of recognition.

"Okay," he said. "Signed." Trying to be casual but pleased at the celebrity.

Petra was a few feet away when a voice behind her said, "Hey!"

Sandra Leon. Stepping out from behind one of the partitions. She was now staring right into Petra's face.

"Cops, Omar! They're cops!" Sandra screamed.

Selden dropped his pen, looked up, stupefied for less than a second. Then a foxy gleam brightened his eyes, and he reached under the baggy brown T-shirt.

Petra had her gun out. Sandra was pounding her back, still screaming. She shoved the girl hard with one hand, concentrated on keeping her Glock steady.

Omar got his hand out of his shirt. Aimed a black matte gun—a Glock, too, plastic, one of those fool-the-metal detector deals. Pointed straight at Petra's face.

Eric had moved directly behind Omar. Expressionless.

Eric's arm jumped ever so slightly. *Pop pop pop.*

Omar stiffened. His face scrunched with pain and surprise, and his mouth made a little stunned O. Then blood began seeping out of his nose and his ears as he toppled over.

Xenia stood against the wall.

Sandra Leon had rebounded from the shove and was up on her feet, flailing at Petra. Long sharp nails, jet-black, caught in Petra's jacket sleeve. When she tried to head-butt Petra, Petra slapped the girl hard across the face. The blow stunned her, gave Petra time to spin her around and kick her behind the knees. She pushed the girl down on the floor and got her cuffs out.

"Bitch murderer!" Sandra was screaming.

Xenia said, "I'm calling the police."

A SLEW of black-and-whites arrived with sirens blaring. Then crime-scene techs, the coroners. In charge was a Valley captain. He started off treating Petra and Eric like criminals but eventually eased up. Last to show up was the officer-involved shooting team— two Internal Affairs detectives with all the emotional resonance of statuary. They questioned Eric and Petra separately, Eric first.

Petra watched from ten feet away, knew the story he was telling, the one they'd prepared. It had been *his* idea to go looking for Selden; he'd had to overcome Petra's reluctance. Once the meet had been set up, she'd made multiple attempts to call for backup, finally decided there was no choice but to go ahead.

The fact that Eric had done all the shooting backed that up.

Clear and present danger, protecting a sister officer.

In the best of circumstances, he'd be suspended with pay for as long as it took to sort out the paperwork. If the media got hold of it, it could get ugly.

Petra had tried to talk him out of being the scapegoat.

He said, "That's the way I'm telling it. Back me up." Gave her arm a short, hard squeeze and left to face the turmoil. She stood by as the shooting investigators double-teamed him. Watched as they came up against his stoicism and started passing glances between them. She knew what they were thinking. *This is weird.*

Cops, even hardened vets, usually reacted to blowing out the back of someone's head with a modicum of emotion. For all the feeling he was displaying, Eric might've just filed his nails.

At three forty p.m., with the scene still cordoned and active, the head Downtown hotshot showed up, wearing a freshly pressed suit and tie. Meaning he'd been playing golf or whatever, had finally been reached, rushed home to dress for the occasion. Before he stepped into the mess, he looked around and saw the media vans outside the yellow tape. He frowned, spotted Petra, came toward her.

She told him the story. He said, "Messy," then left to confer with the techies.

Now two uniforms escorted Sandra to a cruiser and put her in the back. The black-and-white rolled away.

PETRA arrived at work on Monday, June 24, to find Kirsten Krebs's little butt perched on a corner of her desk. Right atop Petra's blotter. Krebs arched her back. One of her fingers twirled her blond hair. When she saw Petra, she smirked. Nicotine teeth. "Captain Schoelkopf wants you."

"When?"

"Now."

Petra sat down at her desk. "Comfortable, Kirsten?"

Krebs got off the desk and left, pissed off. Then she flashed a knowing smile. Like she was in on some private joke.

Were she and Schoelkopf . . . Could it be?

Schoelkopf's third marriage kaput—because of a woman even younger than the latest wife?

SCHOELKOPF sat back in his tufted leatheroid desk throne. The two side chairs usually positioned for visitors had been shoved into the corner. "You screwed up," he said without preamble.

"What can I say, sir?"

"You can say 'I. Screwed. Up.' "

"Is this confession time, sir?"

Schoelkopf bared his teeth. "Confession's good for the soul, Connor. If you had one, you'd understand."

Petra's hands clenched. *Keep your mouth shut, girl.*

Schoelkopf gave an airy wave, as if her control didn't impress him. "You contravened direct orders and messed up a well-thought-out task-force agenda."

"Sorry," she said.

"Don't think you're going to get any credit for Paradiso. Or publicity. TV interviews, all that. You and I both know that's what floats your boat."

"Getting on TV?"

"Any kind of attention. You're an attention junkie, Connor. You learned it from Bishop. You and him, Ken and Barbie. Big fashion show, huh?"

Stu Bishop had been her first Homicide partner—a brilliant, photogenic DIII widely rumored to be in line for a deputy chief promotion. He'd retired to take care of a wife with cancer and a slew of kids. Bringing him up now felt like sacrilege. Petra's face burned.

"First you sneak to the media with that picture of Leon. Then you ignore task-force instructions and sneak in your own little grandstand play. You're *toast,* get it? Suspended. Without pay, if it's up to me. Leave your gun and badge with Sergeant Montoya."

She said, "This isn't fair, sir."

"Yadda yadda. Go."

As she turned to leave, she noticed the date numerals on his desk clock: 24. Four days until June 28, and she was being cut off. From her files, her phone, access to data banks. From Isaac.

Fine, she'd adapt. Call the phone company and have her calls forwarded to her home number. Take what she needed from her desk and work from home.

When she returned to her desk, the top was cleared—even the blotter Krebs had sat on was gone. She tried a drawer. Locked. Her key didn't fit. Brand-new lock. "What the—"

Barney Fleischer said, "Schoelkopf had a locksmith in while you were in his office."

The old guy stood up, looked around, came over. "Meet me downstairs, near the back door. Couple of minutes."

He returned to his desk. Petra left the detectives room, descended the stairs to the ground floor. Less than a minute later, Barney came into view, wearing an oversized tweedy sports coat and draping a longer garment over one arm. A raincoat, a wrinkled gray thing that he usually stashed in his locker.

He eyed the top of the stairwell, descended all the way. Unfurling the raincoat, he produced half a dozen blue folders.

Doebbler, Solis, Langdon, Hochenbrenner . . . all six.

"Thought you might need this."

Petra took the files. "You're a saint."

"So they tell me," he said.

BACK home, she set up a workstation on her dinette table. Eric had left her a note on the kitchen counter:

P,
    Appts. at Parker until ???
        Love, E.

Love. . . . That started all kinds of gears grinding.

Time to concentrate on something she could control. She started with the phone company, put in the forwarding request. The operator started off friendly, came back a few seconds later with a whole different attitude.

"The number you're forwarding from is a police extension. We can't do that."

"I'm an LAPD detective," said Petra, rattling off her badge number. "Is there anyone else I can talk to?"

"Here's my supervisor."

A steely voiced, older-sounding woman came on. Same message, no give. Maybe the Fates were telling her something. Even so, she'd work June 28. To do otherwise would drive her crazy.

She got herself a can of Coke, sipped and flipped through her notes of the calls she'd put in Friday: Marta Doebbler's friends. Dr. Sarah Casagrande in Sacramento, Emily Pastern in the Valley. Emily, with the barking dog.

This time when she called, Pastern answered. No noise in the background. Still perky, until Petra told her what it was all about.

"Marta? It's been . . . years."

"Six years, ma'am. We're taking a fresh look at the case."

"I see. . . . What was your name again?"

Petra repeated it. Cited her credentials again, as well. Committing yet another breach of regulations.

Impersonating an active officer of the law.

Emily Pastern said, "So what do you want from me now?"

"Just to talk about the case," said Petra. "If we could just meet for a few minutes—at your convenience."

"How about in an hour?"

"That would be perfect," said Petra. "Name the place."

"Let's make it at Rita's—it's a little coffee place. Ventura Boulevard, south side, two blocks west of Reseda. They've got an outdoor patio. I'll be there."

PETRA made it to the Valley with time to spare, drove around a bit, pulled up in front of Rita's Coffees and Sweets right on time. The place was a pair of cute tile-roofed bungalows combined into one establishment. The outdoor patio was off to the right of the coffee house, surrounded by low wooden fencing with a latched gate. One woman sat there, visible from her bosom up. Pretty strawberry blonde, hair pinned loosely, mid- to late thirties, wearing a gauzy sleeveless smock the color of daybreak.

"Ms. Pastern?"

Pastern nodded, gave a small wave. So far, so good.

As Petra opened the gate, she saw that Pastern had chosen the table farthest from the restaurant. Her pale blue top was worn over fashionable jeans and white clogs. Lying at her feet was the reason why she wanted the patio: the biggest hunk of canine flesh Petra had ever seen. Head shaped like that of a hippo, resting on the flagstone floor. She stopped as the dog glanced up, drooled, and checked Petra out with tiny red-rimmed eyes. Intelligent eyes.

Emily Pastern bent in her chair and whispered something to the dog. The beast's eyes closed. "It's okay," said Pastern.

Giving wide berth to the behemoth, Petra settled in a chair, held out a hand. "Petra Connor."

"Emily." Pastern's fingers were long, cool, limp.

"Thanks for agreeing to meet with me, Emily."

"Sure." A waiter came over, and Petra ordered coffee.

An oversized mug of "daily blend" came, and the waiter took a few seconds balancing it on the table. Bit of a challenge; the top was fashioned of hand-laid mosaic tiles. Blue and yellow and green shards arranged in graceful florets and grouted carefully. Petra ran her fingers over the contours. Nice work, but impractical.

"Like it?" said Pastern. "The tiles. My work."

"Really? It's lovely."

"I don't do much art anymore," said Pastern. "Three kids; my husband's an orthodontist."

Petra said, "Busy."

"You bet. Would you tell me this, Detective: How come no one talked to me six years ago? My friends—the other women who were at the theater—were interviewed."

Because the D who worked the case was an alkie burnout.

Petra said, "Ms. Jaeger and Dr. Casagrande?"

Pastern's penciled brows arched. "Sarah's a doctor?"

"She's a psychologist in Sacramento."

"Isn't *that* something," said Pastern. "She always talked about becoming a therapist."

"How long's she been there?"

"She and her husband moved up there not long after Marta was killed. Alan's a lobbyist at the capital. How's Sarah doing?"

"Haven't spoken to her yet. Haven't been able to reach Melanie Jaeger, either."

"Mel's in France," said Pastern. "Got divorced and moved there a couple of years ago. Guess I'm the only one still in the Valley. So why wasn't I talked to?"

"From what I could tell, the detective couldn't reach you."

"He called when I was out and left his number," said Pastern. "I called him back."

Petra shrugged.

"Six years," said Pastern. "Is there some reason it's been reopened?"

"No dramatic evidence. We're just trying to be thorough."

"Do you have any theories who killed Marta?"

"Not yet. How about you?" said Petra.

"Sure do. I always thought it was Kurt. I'm not saying I *know* he did it. Marta and Kurt's marriage had always seemed off."

"In what way?"

"Remote. Platonic, even. Everything cools down eventually, but with Marta and Kurt you just felt there'd never been any heat in the first place. Not that Marta ever said anything. She was German, had that European reserve."

"Remote," said Petra, remembering Kurt Doebbler's flat affect. Two cool people. One had ended up beaten to a pulp.

"He still lives there, you know. In the same house. Seven blocks from mine. Have you met him?"

Petra nodded.

"So you know. I can't prove he did it; I just feel it. We all did—Sarah and Mel and I. Not just because Kurt's strange. Because of the way it happened. That night in the theater, when Marta's phone rang, she bolted up so quickly she nearly tripped over my legs.

Then she hurried out as if her life depended on it." Pastern smiled queasily. "That came out wrong."

Petra said, "Did she flip the phone open and read the sender's number?"

Pastern thought. "No. She just switched it off and got up and ran out. We were pretty taken aback. Generally, Marta was superpolite. Sarah wanted to go out and check immediately, but Melanie told her it might be a private family affair. Marta *was* a private person. So we shut up and waited until intermission."

"How long was that?"

"Maybe ten minutes," said Pastern. "I remember not being able to concentrate on the show. Then I figured she didn't want to cause any more disruption by coming back for such a short interval, was probably waiting for us in the lobby. The moment the curtain dropped, we hurried out to find her, but she wasn't there. We immediately called her cell, but no one answered. We decided to split up to look for her in the theater."

She frowned. "I got the job of checking the ladies' room. Marta wasn't there. Wasn't anywhere. The consensus was that she'd been called out on a personal matter, probably by Kurt. Maybe something to do with Katya; it had to be serious for her not to even tell us. Maybe she needed to keep her line clear, so we decided not to try to call her again and went back in, saw the rest of the show. After the show, the three of us walked to my car—I'd driven. Everyone except Marta; she came in her own car."

"Why?"

"She had an appointment in the city. She arrived when we did, parked right near my car. When we looked, her car was gone. That made sense to us—given what we figured."

"Where was the lot?"

"Right across the street from the theater."

Marta's vehicle had been found around the corner from the theater and two blocks down. Ballou had made no mention of it being moved from the parking lot.

Petra said, "What kind of appointment did Marta have?"

"She didn't say." Pastern shifted. Looked down at her tile-work. "Marta went into the city a lot. My initial take was that the Valley bored her. She grew up in Hamburg, which is supposed to be a pretty sophisticated city. Back in Germany, she'd been some sort of mathematician or engineer. That's where she met Kurt. He's a rocket designer or something like that—he was doing something for the government at one of the military bases. They got married there, had Katya in Germany, moved to the States soon after."

"Your initial take was boredom," said Petra. "Any other reason for her to come into the city frequently?"

"I don't want to say when I don't know."

"Did the Doebblers own a dog?"

"Never," said Pastern. "Kurt wouldn't allow it."

Petra said, "Could we talk more about Marta's errands in the city?"

"Okay. I might as well tell you, because you've taken the trouble after all these years and you do seem like someone who cares. I'm pretty sure Marta was having an affair."

"With who?"

"I don't know, Detective. But she gave off all the signs. Dressing better, walking bouncier—sexier. A glow. A fire."

Petra said, "Happier than usual."

"More than happier. *Alive.* Rushing here, rushing there. Which wasn't like Marta at all. It was true what I said about her being bored. But her way of coping had been stay-at-home stuff. Being a PTA mom, collecting—glass figurines, little Japanese teapots. Then all that stopped and she started driving into the city regularly."

"You're making a good case, Emily."

"Maybe Kurt found out. Maybe that's why he did it. It sure wasn't for any romantic reasons of his own. He's never remarried, and if he's been hooked up with another woman, I haven't heard."

"Would you have heard?" said Petra.

"Oh, yeah," said Pastern. "Our kids go to the same school."

Petra asked her if there was anything else she wanted to say, and when Pastern shook her head, she thanked her, fished a ten out of her purse, and stood.

Pastern reached for her own purse. "No, it's on me."

"Against regulations," said Petra, smiling.

"Okay, then, nice to meet you. Hope you get him."

PETRA drove east on Ventura Boulevard to Laurel Canyon, took that winding, leafy route back to the city. She zipped past what was left of the old Houdini estate. Some magic would be nice right now. Something to help her figure out if Emily Pastern's suspicions were right: Marta's infidelity, Kurt a revenge murderer. If so, Kurt had planned meticulously, lured his wife out of the theater, maybe using Katya as the bait. Kurt was a cold fish. You humiliate me; I kill you? No reason it *couldn't* have happened that way. He does Marta. Decides he likes it. Decides to commemorate the date.

Nice little profile she was developing. The only problem was, lots of stuff didn't fit. Like the dog hairs on Coral Langdon, when Kurt hated animals. And what of the phony cable visit to Geraldo Solis's house? How did Doebbler synch with that? If he'd wanted to commemorate his wife's murder, why not choose a victim similar to Marta? She ran through the rest of the victim list. Langdon, Hochenbrenner, the young black sailor. Jewell Blank and Curtis Hoffey, two street kids. What was the damned *pattern*?

As she reached Fairfax and Sixth, her phone beeped. Mac Dilbeck's mobile. "Just heard, Petra. Sorry," he said.

"Thanks, Mac."

"I should be thanking you," he said. "For clearing the case. Saving us the paperwork and the city a trial. Some types deserve killing, and he fit the bill. What's Eric's situation?"

"Meetings at Parker."

"When the dust clears, he'll be okay. I'm also calling to fill you in on Sandra Leon. The gods from Olympus allowed me to sit in on her interview. She wouldn't talk to them no matter what they did, so finally they left to *confer*." He snorted. "So while they're gone,

I do the grandfatherly bit, and guess what? She starts to open up."

"Oh, yeah," said Petra, smiling.

"Oh, yeah, indeed," said Mac. "I made sure the tape was running. By the time they got back with a plan, she's talking, and at least they're smart enough to keep their mouths shut. Sandra's story is she and cousin Marcella didn't get along too well. That s.o.b. Lyle Leon was messing with both of them for years, and they ended up competing for his attention. When Marcella got involved with Selden, Sandra figured that was wrong; she was the pretty one."

"Sounds like a motive for murder to me."

"You should've heard the kid, Petra. Cold. She was the one who told Omar that Marcella had aborted his baby. Told him Marcella had joked about it, called the baby garbage."

"Lord," said Petra. "She set Marcella up."

"She did more. She told Omar they would be at the Paradiso, pinpointed where and when Marcella would be coming out."

"Omar photographed the parking lot a full week before the concert. The whole thing was well planned."

"Oh, boy," he said.

"That's why Sandra was so cool after the shooting. She stuck around to gloat. That is one sick kid. What's she being charged with?"

"D.A.'s not sure yet. I'm pushing for a full one eighty-seven, but the only evidence is what Sandra said on tape, so maybe they'll plea it down to something juvie. She thinks she'll get away scot-free because she's seventeen. For all I know, she will. Some slick private attorney showed up this afternoon. I'm sure he's being paid by The Players."

"What about Lyle? He's open to a pedophilia charge."

"Lyle rabbited right after we let him out of the holding cell. Which would've posed some problems if Omar had gone to trial. For that, I thank you again."

"You're welcome," said Petra.

"Don't let them grind you down, kid. You're a solid girl."

SHRINKS KEPT FORTY-FIVE-MINUTE hours, so at four forty-five Petra tried the clinic where Dr. Sarah Casagrande worked, was transferred to voice mail, and left a forceful message. No return. She repeated the process at five forty-five. This time a woman's voice broke in.

"This is Sarah." Soft, hesitant. "I was just about to call you."

"Thanks," said Petra. "As I said in my message, Doctor, this is about Marta Doebbler."

"All these years. Has something changed? The detective I spoke to led me to believe the case was unlikely to be solved."

"Did he?"

"Yes. He said there was no evidence. He had suspicions, but nothing more."

"Suspicions of who?"

"Kurt. I felt the same way. All three of us did."

"Why did you suspect Kurt?"

"He made me uneasy."

"You're a psychologist. Care to diagnose?"

"I hate to do that. Long-distance analysis isn't worth much."

"Off the record, Doctor."

"Off the record, if I had to bet, I'd say Kurt displays schizoid tendencies. That doesn't mean he's crazy. It refers to an asocial personality. Flat emotion, a lack of connection to other people."

"Can that lead to murder?"

"Most asocial types aren't violent. But when they do act out—when schizoid tendencies are combined with aggressive impulses—it can be pretty horrendous."

Meticulous planning followed by stunning violence. . . .

"The Unabomber comes to mind," said Casagrande. "A loner who hated people. I'm not saying Kurt's like the Unabomber. That was serial murder. We're talking about someone killing his wife."

If you only knew. "If Kurt did murder Marta, what do you think his motive was?"

"I'd have to say jealousy. It's possible—and this is speculation—that Marta was seeing someone."

"So I've been told. By Emily Pastern."

"Emily," said Casagrande. "Yes, it was Emily who raised the possibility in the first place, but I'd been thinking the same thing. We all had, because of changes in Marta's behavior. She seemed happier. There was more . . . physicality to her."

"How long before she was murdered did she start to change?"

"I'd say . . . months. Four, five months. I suppose there could've been other reasons for it."

"Such as?"

"Trying to breathe new passion into her marriage. But I never saw any change in the way Marta and Kurt related."

"Which was?"

"Platonic."

The exact same word Emily Pastern had used. Petra pressed Casagrande more on the affair, got nothing but a polite denial of details. Running Casagrande through the events at the theater produced an account consistent with Pastern's. "Thanks, Doctor."

"I hope you succeed in getting him," said Casagrande. "If it is him. Have you considered his job?"

"Missile designer," said Petra. "Guidance systems."

"Think about that," said Casagrande. "He figures out ways to destroy things."

--CHAPTER 10--

ISAAC'S eyes had blurred twenty minutes ago, but he waited to take a break until he'd finished the *Herald Examiner* files.

His self-assigned task of today: going back to as many L.A. newspapers as he could find in the L.A. public library and reading every June 28 issue.

He whittled down the homicides to those that weren't bar killings or family disputes or related to robberies. But nothing matched the modus or the flavor of the six cases.

Three days to go until June 28, and after nearly seven hours of tedious, eye-straining work, he'd come up with nothing. He hadn't heard from Petra since Friday, had shown up at the station Monday morning, ready to brainstorm again. She wasn't there, and her desk was clear. Three other detectives were in the room. Fleischer, Montoya, and a detective from Central Division at the bulletin board.

"Any idea where Detective Connor is?" he'd said to no one in particular.

Fleischer waved him over. "She's not coming in. Suspended."

"Suspended? For God's sake, why?"

"Shoot-out, North Hollywood, Saturday."

"What happened?"

"Petra and another detective were staking a suspect. There was a confrontation, and the bad guy didn't respond appropriately."

"Dead?" said Isaac.

"Extremely."

"The suspect on the Paradiso case?"

"That's the one."

"For that she got suspended?"

"Rules were broken. It's a procedural thing."

"I don't have her home number. It's important that I get in touch with her."

"She have your number?"

"Yes."

"Then I don't see any problem, son."

She hadn't called, and now it was Tuesday.

Suddenly his neck kinked painfully, and he got up from his computer terminal in the history and genealogy catalog room. Over the past few days, he'd ignored half a dozen phone messages from Klara. Had stayed away from campus and made the public library his workstation.

The decision to break communication had been rationalized as kindness: Given Klara's fragile emotional state, wouldn't contact do her more harm than good? Thinking about it now, he couldn't believe what he'd done.

PETRA HAD SPENT A GOOD deal of Monday trying to locate Melanie Jaeger, the fourth member of Marta Doebbler's theater party, now living somewhere in the South of France.

She recontacted Emily Pastern and got her to specify "somewhere near Nice, I think." Using the Internet, Petra pulled up maps and phoned every listed hotel and pension in that region.

Being cut off from official data banks, the ability to use the reverse directory, and any clout with the airlines reminded her that she was just another civilian. It was a slow, painful process. Finally she struck gold at a place called La Mer, where a concierge who spoke beautiful English put her through to Madame Jaeger's room.

After all that, Jaeger had nothing new to tell her. She, too, was certain Kurt Doebbler had brained Marta.

By eleven p.m. Petra still hadn't heard from Eric. Popping a couple of Benadryl, she sank into ten hours of drugged-out sleep and awoke Tuesday, ready to work.

Back to the computer. Experienced private eyes had their own methods, could sometimes tread where cops couldn't. Her ignorance of all that bugged her. Eric was a fast learner. Soon he'd be in touch with all that good stuff. If he really made the move.

He called at noon. "Where are you?" she asked.

"Downtown. They're being . . . thorough."

"I'm really sorry, Eric."

"For what?"

"Your having to go through this because of—"

"No sweat. Got to go." Then, in a softer voice: "Honey."

KURT Doebbler's name did come up on the Pacific Dynamics home page. One of many names on a roster of the company's "Senior Staff." Kurt was listed as senior engineer and technical designer on something called Project Advent. No details on what that was. The website bio did note that Doebbler had "interfaced" with the 40th Engineering Battalion at Baumholden Army Base in Germany. Having spent his high school years as an army brat near Hamburg and speaking fluent German, "Kurt was a natural for the assignment."

That seemed odd. American army engineers would speak English. Was Kurt into hush-hush stuff?

She read on: B.S. from Cal Tech, M.S. from USC—Isaac's alma mater. Speaking of which, she hadn't talked to Isaac since Friday. With nothing to show, there was no sense bothering the kid. She kept reading. According to the bio, Kurt Doebbler was well regarded as a systems designer who'd worked at Pacific Dynamics for fifteen years. Meaning soon after grad school.

The German connection got her going in a whole new direction, and she spent the afternoon making international calls until she reached the right person at the Hamburg Police Department. Chief Inspector Klaus Bandorffer.

Adding yet another potential infraction to her departmental jacket, she told him the June 28 cases were being actively and officially investigated and that she was the lead detective.

"A serial killer, Detective—is it Connor?"

"Yes, sir."

"So you believe you have a suspect who may have lived in Hamburg?"

"It's possible."

"Hmm. During what time period?"

Kurt Doebbler was forty. "High school years" meant twenty-two to twenty-five years ago. She gave Bandorffer those parameters and the details of the head bashing.

"Your suspect's family name is Doebbler, Christian name Curtis?"

"Just Kurt. With a K."

Click click click. "I find nothing under that name in my current files, but I will check retrospectively. It may take a day or so."

Petra gave him her home number and her cell and thanked him profusely. She then tried every cable outfit in L.A., Orange, Ventura, San Diego, and Santa Barbara counties. No record of Kurt Doebbler ever working as an employee.

Still, Doebbler was all she had. Worse came to worst, she could stake out his house June 28. Hope for a miracle and prepare herself for disappointment.

Maybe it *was* time to try Isaac. He'd probably been by the station yesterday and learned about her suspension. She knew that hearing about her plight would upset him. Some babysitter she'd turned out to be. It was six-fifteen p.m., and all the university departments were closed. She phoned the Gomez residence, and Isaac picked up, sounding sleepy.

"Isaac, it's—"

A loud, flapping yawn drowned her out. Then: "This is Klara, right? Listen, my brother's—"

"This is Detective Petra Connor. You're Isaac's brother?"

Silence. "Hey, sorry, I was sleeping. Yeah, I'm his brother."

"Sorry for waking you. Is Isaac there?" The guy's vocal tones were a lot like Isaac's.

"He ain't here."

"Please tell him I called. Go back to sleep, Isaac's brother."

"Isaiah. . . . Yeah, I will."

At eight p.m. she went out. If she was forced to live like a civilian, she might as well reap the benefits. She ended up at a little kosher fish restaurant on Beverly, with fresh, tasty, cheap food and a counter pickup policy that avoided chitchat with the waitstaff. Lots of people and noise. Good. She ordered grilled baby salmon with a baked potato and slaw and snagged the last vacant table.

By nine forty-five she was back at her place. Eric's Jeep was parked on Detroit, and when she opened her door, he got up from the living-room couch and hugged her. He had on a tan suit, blue shirt, yellow tie.

"It wasn't necessary to dress for me, big boy."

He smiled and removed the jacket. "You eat yet?"

"Just finished. You were figuring on going out?"

"Out or in, doesn't matter." He moved to the kitchen, opened the fridge. "I'll forage."

"French toast," she said. "I do that real well."

She cracked eggs and sliced bread. He poured milk and said, "You haven't heard about Schoelkopf."

"What about him?"

"It was on the news."

"I haven't watched TV in two days. What's going on?"

"Dead," said Eric. "Three hours ago, His wife killed him."

"My God. Which wife?"

"The current one. How many did he have?"

"She was number three. What, she left him and then decided to kill him?"

"From what I hear," said Eric, "he left *her*."

No one from the station had thought to call her.

"What happened?"

"Schoelkopf moved out of the house a few weeks ago, rented an apartment. He was up there with his girlfriend, some civilian clerk. They headed out for lunch, went down in the sub parking lot to get his car. The wife stepped out and started shooting. Schoelkopf caught three in the arm and one right here." He tapped the center of his brow. "The girlfriend got shot, too. Then the wife turned the gun on herself."

"Is the girlfriend named Kirsten Krebs?"

Eric nodded. "You knew about it?"

"I guessed. Where's the wife?"

"Not expected to live. Krebs is in bad shape, too."

"I couldn't stand him, and Lord knows he despised me—why I'll never know—but this . . ."

"He hated women," said Eric.

"Schoelkopf dead. What will it mean for us in terms of our suspensions?"

"Before it happened, I was led to believe they weren't going to be too hard on either of us. It'll probably delay our dispositions."

"No matter to you. You're leaving."

"Maybe. I'm still thinking."

"Big decision, makes sense."

"We could still get a house," he said. "With both of us working, we could probably get a decent place sooner rather than later."

"Sure," she said. Surprised by the coolness in her voice.

"Is there a problem?"

"I'm a little overwhelmed right now. Dangling. And all because I helped get rid of a really bad guy. Plus, there's the June twenty-eighth stuff. Three days to go, and I've got squat."

"What about that husband—Doebbler?"

"Everyone's sure he killed his wife, but there's no evidence. He fits in some ways but not in others." She elaborated. He listened. Petra saw the eggs and bread and milk still sitting on the counter. Scooping butter into a pan, she turned on the gas, soaked the bread in the milk and egg mixture, and when the butter was bubbling, dropped in two slices.

Eric said, "You could surveil Doebbler on the twenty-eighth. He moves, he's your guy."

ISAAC almost left home on Wednesday morning without taking the paper bag. Plagued by restlessness all night, he'd slept until eight forty. His parents and his brothers were gone, and he admitted that the resultant silence was wonderful.

He put on fresh khakis and a short-sleeved yellow shirt.

Last night he'd allowed himself fantasies of living at the beach. Rich doctor, beautiful wife, brilliant kids, set up in one of those big houses on the Palisades. One day he'd be Dr. Gomez. Meanwhile, he'd gotten himself into a fix with Klara.

She kept calling. How long could that go on?

He'd have to deal with it. But today . . . the beach.

He went into the kitchen, put his briefcase on the counter, and poured a glass of milk. Changed his mind. He'd return to the public library. Problems were solvable; there had to be an answer.

He gulped the milk and headed for the door. Saw the bag on the tiny mail table to the right of the door. Brown paper, neatly folded—his mother's trademark. His name printed in red crayon. The exact same way she'd printed his lunches when he was at Burton. It had been a while since Mama had packed him a lunch. Maybe he'd ditch it, get himself a fried sausage from a street vendor near the library.

No way; the guilt would overwhelm him. He stuffed the bag into his briefcase, left the apartment, and hurried down the stairs.

As he hit the street, he changed his mind again. Two days of library work had produced nothing. What could he hope to find? He walked to Pico, caught the number 7 bus, and rode all the way to Overland when the aroma of his mother's food, seeping through the brown paper, got his gastric juices going, and he looked inside.

Atop the foil-wrapped morsels was a scrap of paper folded over. He fished it out, read "Bro." Isaiah's writing. He unfolded the note: "The lady cop called last night." Just that, no number.

He got up from his seat. Exited at the next stop.

THE station's rear door was locked. Since he'd been coming here, that had only happened twice. He found his 999 key. It didn't come close to fitting. Change of locks? Then he noticed the closed-circuit camera above the door. It made him feel like a suspect, and he turned his back. New security measures because of some terrorism alert?

He saw an old silver Cadillac drive into the lot and park. Detective Dilbeck.

Isaac approached the car, and Dilbeck rolled down his window.

"Morning, Mr. Gomez."

"The door's locked, and my key doesn't work."

"Mine neither," said Dilbeck. "Everyone comes in through the front until things calm down. Captain Schoelkopf was murdered yesterday."

"Oh, no."

"For the time being, they're being extra careful. Not that what happened to the captain applies to anyone else. He cheated on his wife. Hell has no fury and all that. You haven't annoyed any feisty females lately, have you, Mr. Gomez?"

Isaac smiled. His stomach churned.

Dilbeck got out of his car and began walking toward the lot's entrance. Isaac stayed in place.

"No work today, Mr. Gomez?"

Isaac half heard him, thinking, *Heightened security means a metal detector. The gun* ... "Actually, I'm on my way to school, just dropped by to get Detective Connor's number. She phoned me last night, but my brother neglected to write down her number."

"You know what happened to her?"

"Yes, sir. It's kind of important that I talk to her."

"We're sticklers for privacy around here. How about I call Detective Connor and tell her you stopped by. Give me a number where you can be reached."

Isaac gave him the BioStatistics office number. Now he *had* to return to campus.

He reached USC forty minutes later, took an indirect route to BioStat that circumvented Doheny, and headed straight for his mailbox. It had been days since he'd checked, and the box was stuffed. Five messages from Klara, all in the same curvy handwriting. Three were dated yesterday. Exclamation points. Sandwiched between those was a single slip listing Petra's name and a number to call.

A hand landed on his upper back. He wheeled and faced Klara Distenfield. She smiled and said, "Finally."

He ushered her into a nearby photocopy room.

"What an elusive fellow."

"Klara, I'm sorry—"

"You should be." No rancor in her voice. That made him *really* anxious. Her gold-green eyes narrowed. "Do you know how many times I've tried to reach you?"

"I've been out. Family issues." The prospect of constructing another lie exhausted him. "Nothing grave," he said. "It just took time."

"So you're okay?"

"I'm fine. What about you?"

"Me?" She laughed. "I'm great. Why?"

"I thought you were upset."

"I was a little . . . thrown. But then we had coffee, remember? And I was fine. Didn't I seem fine?"

"The next day," he said, "you weren't at work. Mary Zoltan said you were sick. She implied it was more than a cold."

"Mary's an idiot. I wasn't the least bit sick, I missed two days because my *daughter* was ill."

"Klara, what happened—"

"Was great. Don't see it any other way." She squeezed him, released him. Winked.

"Klara—"

"Don't worry, that's not an invitation for Episode Two. Because right now there are more important things to discuss. And that's why I've been trying to reach you for days. I finally came up with something on those June murders."

"What?"

"I do think I may have solved your mystery, Isaac."

THEY walked back to Doheny, blending with student traffic. Once they were inside, instead of descending to the subbasement, they climbed two floors.

The Rare Book Room was a series of locked chambers and brief, hushed corridors. Klara had all the right keys. She led him to a room marked READING. Inside was a medium-sized conference table, a photocopy machine, and a small desk sided by an armchair.

"That's for the student monitor," she explained. "Someone sits and watches when you read the really rare material. I told her to take an early lunch."

"I spent some time here," said Isaac. "Researching Lewis Carroll for an English class. Pencils, no pens, linen gloves when necessary."

He pulled up to the table. She settled next to him, unclasped her purse. And out came a booklet wrapped in a zip-sealed plastic bag. It had a brown cover and was printed in rough black lettering.

"It wasn't even cataloged in the main collection. It was in one of the appendices." Out of her purse also came a pair of soft white gloves. She rotated the booklet so the title faced Isaac.

He gloved up. Read:

THE SINS OF THE MAD ARTIST
AN ACCOUNT OF THE HORRIBLE DEEDS
of
OTTO RETZAK
Recounted by
T. W. JOSEPH TELLER, ESQ.
Former Superintendent of the Missouri State
Penitentiary
And Published by Him in St. Louis
A.D. MCMX

The brown cover was cardboard, brittle. Isaac lifted it gingerly, flipped open the booklet, and began reading. After covering a single paragraph, he turned to Klara. "You're brilliant."

She beamed. "So I've been told."

Otto Retzak was the son of Bavarian immigrant farmers who'd come to America in 1888 and ended up on a scratchy patch of rock-strewn land in the southern Illinois region known as Little Egypt. The sixth of nine children and the youngest son, Otto had been born on American soil on June 28, 1897—one hundred years to the day before Marta Doebbler's murder.

Isaac's hands started to shake.

Retzak was eight when his drunkard father abandoned the family. Considered extremely bright but uneducable due to "a frightfully overactive and heated temperament," Otto displayed a precocious ability to "wield charcoal stubs in a way that created faithful images." Otto's drunkard mother routinely beat him. The elder siblings sexually abused the boy. At age nine, the illiterate Otto burgled a neighboring farm of twenty-nine cents hidden in a flour jar and a "plump laying hen." The money was traded to another farm boy for a rusty clasp knife. The bird was found, its head yanked off manually. When confronted, Otto admitted his guilt "with no sense of childish shame." Beaten by his mother with special severity, he was turned over to the neighbors, who added their own lash work to his tender back and worked him as a barn hand for a month.

The day after returning home, Otto stabbed his younger sister in the face without provocation. As Superintendent Teller recounted: "A cold eye, even a sly smile, he did present to all those in attendance as the girl shrieked and bled."

The local sheriff was called in, and Otto was locked in a cell with adult miscreants. Two months later the boy, bruised and limping, was brought before an itinerant magistrate who sentenced him to five years in a state reform school. There, Otto claimed to have learned that "mankind is not glorious nor good nor fashioned in God's image. Rather it is a dung-heap of stink and sin and hypocrisy. The hatred that was to drive me for the entirety of my accursed life took hold and was fed in that dark place."

Bound over for two extra years because of disciplinary problems, sixteen-year-old Otto, now strapping and hard-muscled, was released. During his stay in the reformatory, the boy had been befriended by the wife of one of the guards, a woman named Bessie Arbogast. Impressed by Otto's drawings, she brought him paper and charcoal sticks, and it was to her house that he headed on his initial day of freedom.

What commenced was described in Retzak's alleged words, though the flowery language made Isaac wonder if Teller had taken substantial literary liberties: "In the chamber of her common little snuggery, I used a wooden hairbrush to bash her worm of a husband energetically about the head, then had my way with her."

William Arbogast survived the beating as a cripple. His wife's trauma rendered her "virtually mute."

Retzak escaped on foot and avoided capture. Traveling the country by hopping freight trains, he survived by eating pilfered produce and meals donated by kindhearted housewives. Often, he repaid them by doing odd jobs before moving on. Sometimes he left them drawings that were "universally appreciated."

"Interestingly," Teller went on, "during this period, Retzak did not choose to inflict similar punishments upon these altruistic women as he had upon Mrs. Arbogast. When I inquired as to the cause of this discrepancy, Retzak seemed genuinely puzzled: 'I do not know why I do what I do. Sometimes I have the urge and other times I don't. I do not regret the lack of restraint in my soul. I have been anointed by Satan.' "

Teller concluded, "One can only hope that exposure to the twisted workings of this monster's soul as put forth by this humble tract will benefit mankind. That is, in fact, the purpose of The Author."

At the age of eighteen, Retzak made his way to San Francisco, where he was hired as a deckhand aboard the steamer *Grand Tripoli,* bound for the Orient. The ship made a stop in Honolulu, where Retzak took shore leave and abandoned his post. "Soon," Teller recorded, "he was living in common law with a prostitute, a fallen Alsatian girl named Ilette Flam, and for a period of nearly one year, sustained himself with her ill-gotten earnings."

On Retzak's nineteenth birthday, Ilette threw a party for him at a waterfront dive. During that celebration, she made an offhand remark that annoyed Retzak, and when the two of them returned to their flat, an argument ensued.

Waiting until Ilette had fallen into a drugged stupor—"because she'd earned me a fair bit of money and she wasn't all bad"—Retzak put her to bed, turned her on her stomach, picked up an iron pry bar, and bashed the back of her head.

"The skull cracked like an egg," he said. "The sight of it thrilled me as nothing had thrilled me before. Suddenly I was awash in calm and sat gazing at my handiwork with rapture. It was a new feeling, and I quite liked it. I drew her."

It was, Retzak concluded, "a fine birthday present."

Isaac's throat had gone dry. June 28 had been a double anniversary for Otto Retzak. Commemoration of his birth, and the date of his first murder. His first victim, a common-law wife.

The L.A. killer had begun in 1997. Commemorating the centenary of Retzak's birth: his first victim, a wife.

Marta's friends were sure Kurt Doebbler had killed her. Sometimes things were just as they seemed. Isaac turned the page.

Upon finishing the drawing of Ilette Flam's mangled corpse, Retzak packed a duffel, walked to Honolulu Harbor, and got himself a job on an oil tanker bound for Venezuela.

"All the way there," declared Retzak, "the memory of what I'd done to the sow burned in my brain like a sacrament. It was on shore in Caracas, months later, that I allowed myself the next delicious indulgence. The proprietor of a beer-house, a foul-mouthed old Mestizo, got on my wrong side, and I decided he'd be the one. Waiting until he'd retired upstairs to his personal lodgings, I snapped the latch on the rear door of his establishment and surprised myself to find him awake and eating a late supper of pork and rice. I picked up a frypan. A lovely cast-iron implement it was. Within seconds, gray gelatin had leaked into that Hispanical dinner. No different did it look from the sow's, and I sketched the scene."

Retzak jumped ship and hid out in South America for several months. Eventually making his way back to the States, he tramped across the country stealing and doing odd jobs.

Murdering five more human beings.

The third victim was a matron walking her dog in an affluent suburb of St. Louis: "I'd watched this one for days, and I admired her form and her walk. I stole an old yellow cur from a front-yard in her neighborhood. That night, I stationed myself outside the sow's house and she emerged, as always, at nine p.m. with her fluffy little annoyance. I followed her at a distance until she entered a dark section of her street, then hurried after her, carrying my borrowed mongrel. When I was sufficiently close, I set the dog down, walked past her. Within moments we were chatting. After an exchange of polite utterances, she turned to leave and down came the ax handle I'd secreted in my coat."

Isaac hesitated before turning the page, knowing what would follow. Number four: A black sailor stalked, accosted, and bludgeoned in a Chicago back alley. Five: "An insolent prostitute, skinny as a young girl but syphilitic and insolent," brutalized in a New Orleans park. Six: "An abominable Nancy Boy living in the same hotel as myself in San Francisco."

Perfect matches all. But Retzak hadn't stopped at six. After hitchhiking from San Francisco to Los Angeles, the itinerant killer set up an easel near the central railway station. He tried to earn a living drawing caricatures of tourists. When his artist's career failed to materialize, Retzak resumed his pattern of thievery and transitory labor. His wanderings took him to Elysian Park, where "a sanitorium for tubercular war orphans and other sick children had existed for decades. Retzak attracted the attention of the staff by sitting on a bench near the children's rest area and drawing. They began regarding him as a "friendly, wholesome young man."

"It was then," he revealed, "that my eyes settled upon the smiley, chanting starchy-white nurses who attended to the little gaspers. My favorite was one sow, in particular, an Italian type, of fine form and dark eyes. She maintained a careful distance, seemed to harbor a disdain for Fine Art. I was determined to teach her a hard lesson."

"I need to know everyone who checked this out," said Isaac.

Klara didn't answer.

"Please," said Isaac. "It's essential."

"Finish reading."

When he did, she made him a copy of the booklet, then led him out of the reading room to her desk at the reference counter. One middle-aged woman spooled microfilm, her back to the desk. No sign of Mary or the other librarians.

Klara said, "Walk away. Over there." Pointing to a stack of periodicals. Isaac obeyed, pulled out a copy of *The New Republic,* and pretended to read as Klara sat down at her computer.

ISAAC sat at the dinette table of Petra's apartment as she leafed through the photocopy of the booklet.

"A nurse," Petra said.

"Maria Giacometti," said Isaac. "Her murder was different from the others. A lot more violent."

"Escalation is typical," she said. "What turns them on in the beginning stops working, so they get nastier." She turned the page, said, "Oh, my."

AT SEVEN, SHE'D GONE OUT FOR dinner with Eric. Then he drove up to Camarillo to visit his parents, said he'd be back in the morning. When she returned home just before nine, a message from Barney Fleischer was on her machine. Isaac Gomez had been by the station, had seemed anxious to talk to her.

She called the Gomez home. Isaac picked up, and when he learned it was her, he began talking at warp speed. "Thank God! I've been trying to get you all day! I've got the *answer*, Petra. To June twenty-eighth, the pattern, the motivation. Who and why, everything. Who his next victim will be."

"Who's *he?*"

Silence, then: "Doebbler!" Breathing hard, almost panting.

She picked Isaac up in front of his building at nine-forty. When he got in, she said, "Start at the beginning." As he chattered, she drove back to her place.

PETRA finished the booklet. "Where's the list?"

Isaac pulled a folded slip of paper from his briefcase, a computer printout from Klara's workstation—a list of everyone who'd requested a peek at the booklet. Short list.

September 4, 1978: Professor A. R. Ritchey, Pitzer College
May 15, 1997: K. Doebbler, using an alumnus library card

Kurt Doebbler had imbibed these horrors one month and thirteen days before murdering his wife. Isaac said, "My guess would be he already knew about Retzak and wanted to refresh his memory."

"Where else could Doebbler have gotten hold of something this obscure?"

"It's esoteric, but not really that obscure. Once I had Retzak's name as a key word, I went back on the Internet. He's been discussed in a few true-crime chat rooms, and the booklet is in the holdings of at least twenty campus libraries. Also, soon after it was first published, it was translated into French, Italian, and German. Doebbler lived in Germany as an adolescent."

"Makes sense," she said. "He could've stumbled across it, gotten stimulated, decided to take a second look." She got up and paced her small living room.

She said, "Okay, let's lay it out: Marta cheated on Kurt. He found out. He stewed, started to obsess, remembered the Retzak book from his impressionable teen years. Or, he was a true-crime buff; lots of serials are. Any clues from those chat rooms?"

"I skimmed them searching for some indication Doebbler was chatting. If he was, I didn't catch it."

"Damn," she said. "Okay, back on track. . . . Retzak's first murder stuck in his head: a common-law wife who ticked the guy off. Suddenly Doebbler finds himself to be a ticked-off husband, and Retzak's adventures take on a whole new meaning. He was reliving history, assuming the persona of a big-time monster." She shook her head. "Doebbler wanted to be Otto the Second. It's beyond twisted, but it makes sense."

"Victims with no apparent link gave him confidence," said Isaac. "Why would he even imagine getting caught?"

Petra smiled. "He wasn't figuring on you."

"I was lucky." Blushing. Cute. She wished she could find him a genius girlfriend.

Seven innocent people. She sat back down and reread the booklet. Despite Superintendent Teller's delicacy in dancing around the details, Maria Giacometti's murder was stomach churning. Retzak had been found sitting not far from the Elysian Park sanitorium, with the young woman's entrails around his neck. Peaceful expression on his face. "Sounds like he lost it," said Petra.

"Thank God," said Isaac. "Can you imagine the next one?"

"Seven for Mr. Retzak. Six, so far, for Mr. Doebbler," she said. "And we're going to make sure it stays that way."

She fixed coffee and gave the booklet's final chapter yet another scan. Retzak had gone to the gallows. Proclaiming his hatred for God, humanity, and "all that you brainless sheep deem sacred."

Petra said, "I wonder how many Italian-American pediatric nurses are out there."

"If Doebbler's a stickler, we should be looking for an Italian-

American pediatric nurse who takes care of respiratory patients."

"We're going to be surveilling Doebbler starting tomorrow morning. He's not going to get close to number seven."

"Just tell me what you want me to do."

Uh-oh. She said, "By 'we,' I meant police officers. I can't afford to involve you in this, Isaac."

His face fell. "Oh. Sure, I can see that."

"You're absolutely the hero of this story—without you nothing would've happened. But having civilians along on high-risk operations is a big-time no-no. I'm in enough trouble, can't afford more."

It would have to be her and Eric. Eric would be a major asset. He was great on surveillance, had the patience, the low resting heart rate. But a two-person surveillance was bare-bones.

She glanced over at Isaac. Crestfallen and trying to hide it. Could she risk it? No way. Especially not with Gang Control surveilling *him.* Maybe she should break *that* wide open.

She said, "So how's Flaco Jaramillo?"

Isaac turned white. Several moments passed. "Why do you ask?"

"You tell me, Isaac."

"Tell you what?"

"Your connection to Flaco Jaramillo. Detective Bobby Lucido. He and his partner spoke to me a few days ago."

Isaac's eyes flashed with anger. "You didn't think to tell me?"

"I didn't even consider it, my friend. Because I didn't know what you were up to. Still don't. They've got pictures, Isaac. Of you and a low-life dope dealer slash possible triggerman schmoozing it up in a low-life bar." She folded her arms across her chest.

He tried to force relaxation. His body cooperated, but his eyes were way too jumpy. Just like a suspect. The kid had broken the case, and now she was breaking him. Did life have to be this hard?

He said, "There's nothing ominous going on. Flaco and I go back. We grew up together. I tutored him in grade school. We run into each other from time to time. I know he's been in trouble, but I've never been involved in any of that. A few days ago he called me up and asked me to help him out with a family matter. His mother's sick. Cancer. She's illegal, can't qualify for Medi-Cal. He was under the impression I was already in medical school, figured I could help her get free medical care. I went to see him because he used to stick up for me when we were kids. I explained that I wasn't in the system. Couldn't do a thing. That's it."

"Is it?"

"Yes, dammit."

"You're not a dope courier?"

His eyes got wide. "Are you insane? I promise. I've never had anything to do with dope. *Never.* Petra, can you imagine what would happen to my med school career if I got caught doing something like that?" He frowned. "What a mess."

"If nothing happened, there won't be a problem."

"How can I prove a negative?" he said.

"Take a polygraph, if it comes to that. Once this case is resolved, I'll do what I can to run interference for you. So it's important for *your* sake that I don't lose any more department brownie points. Is there anything else you haven't told me?"

"No. Your suspension—that didn't have anything to do with me, did it?"

"No. That I did all by my little lonesome." She got up. "I'll drive you home."

They left her apartment, stepped out into the warm June air. Twenty-five hours until the killing hour.

--CHAPTER 11--

PLEXI-TECH, Inc., a massive, white, windowless hatbox of a building, set in an industrial park two miles north of the freeway, was ringed by an open, asphalt lot. The space was half filled with cars. Lots of empty slots. The first few rows provided a nice, clear diagonal view of the smaller structure across the street.

A sand-colored brick building. Black block lettering above the mirrored front door: PACIFIC DYNAMICS.

Doebbler's workplace was less welcoming than its looming neighbor. Wrought-iron fencing surrounded the property. A slot-key parking arm bisected the entry. A driveway snaked down to the left.

Petra was wondering about rear entry to the building when Doebbler's tall, angular form appeared at the top of the drive, walking slowly. Dunkin' Donuts bag in one hand, steel attaché case in the other. She watched as Doebbler strode over to Pacific Dynamics' front door and walked in.

That was at nine thirty a.m. It was now five hours later, Thursday, June 27, and nothing had happened. Petra and Eric remained at opposite ends of the Plexi-Tech lot, drinking coffee. Communication was via cell-phone speed dials.

She'd phoned Eric at his folks' home last night, just before midnight, after dropping Isaac at home.

The next day the two of them met up at six forty-five a.m. at a taco stand on Reseda Boulevard one mile north of Ventura. A five-minute drive to Doebbler's house on Rosita.

Eric, a stranger to the quarry, was the obvious choice as the up close. He headed north in his Jeep, found the pale gray house, continued up the street, and U-turned into a tree-shaded watch spot. Petra was stationed just south of Ventura.

At eight fifteen, Eric called in. "Doebbler and the daughter are getting into the Infiniti. . . . He's driving east. He should be passing you soon. I'll have a quick look around the back of the house and catch up with you."

Minutes later, Doebbler's champagne-colored sedan cruised through a green light at Ventura. Petra let two more cars pass before she pulled out and followed. Doebbler bypassed the freeway, finally pulling into a line of cars facing West Valley Comprehensive Preparatory Academy. No sign of Eric. Just as she started to punch in the speed code, she spotted a black Jeep in her rearview. He passed her without acknowledgment and then faded from view.

The Infiniti made it to the gate, and Katya Doebbler, tall for her age, her straight, dark hair pulled into a ponytail, got out and walked through the school's gates.

Sad-looking kid. Soon she'd be a lot sadder.

Doebbler pulled into the street and sailed by her, oblivious. Sitting tall, staring straight ahead, bespectacled, sharp-jawed. Both hands on the wheel. Law-abiding citizen.

Back on Reseda. Eric regained the number one position, and when Doebbler made his westward turn, the Jeep was three cars behind him. Half a mile short of his work address, Doebbler pulled into a Dunkin' Donuts, got out and ordered, emerged with a bag.

FIVE hours, eighteen minutes of boredom. In all that time, there had been just two interruptions.

At ten forty, Eric crossed the street to Pacific Dynamics, walked under the parking arm, and was gone for ten minutes. When he popped back up at Petra's window, he said, "Loading dock, bolted from the outside; doesn't appear to be in active use. If he drives out, he'll have to come back the way he went in."

"What about on foot?"

"Fifteen-and-a-half-foot block wall at the back. On the other side's some kind of warehouse. Unless he's a rock climber, there's no alternative exit. He leaves, we see him."

At eleven fifty, Petra left for a much needed bathroom break. Right after she'd settled back in her car, people began exiting Pacific Dynamics in small, chatty groups. Lunchtime. No sign of the quarry.

By three twenty p.m., Doebbler still hadn't appeared.

At three fifty-three, her phone squawked.

What could Eric have to say? She pressed TALK. "What's up?"

A cheerful voice said, "Detective Connor?" Teutonic accent.

"Chief Inspector Bandorffer." From Germany.

"Yes. I thought this might be a good hour to reach you. I came across something intriguing in our records. An assault. It occurred on June twenty-eighth and the details are provocative."

"What year?" asked Petra.

"Nineteen seventy-nine. A young woman named Gudrun Wiegeland, a cake icer at one of our finest bakeries, was attacked while walking home shortly before midnight. Two blocks from her destination, someone hooked an arm around her neck, pulled her down onto the street, turned her over onto her stomach, and began kicking at her ribs. Then she experienced crushing pain at the back of her head. The attacker remained behind her, so unfortunately, she never saw him. She was unconscious for two days, woke up, and had nothing of value to tell the police. Fraulein Wiegeland had a reputation as a wild girl, and our men suspected a former lover. But the crime was never solved. I have confirmed that your Mr. Doebbler and his family were living at the army base during that time."

"How many blows were delivered to the head?" asked Petra.

"One," said Bandorffer.

"Our boy bashes his victims repeatedly," said Petra.

"Perhaps he panicked. Being young and inexperienced. If it was your boy."

Twenty-four years ago, Kurt Doebbler had been eighteen.

Petra thought: Isaac had nailed it again.

She said, "Thank you, Inspector."

"HE'S here." Eric's whisper barely filtered through the phone. "Doing what?" said Petra.

"Reading a magazine and doing hand exercises."

"Hand exercises?"

"With a spring grip. While he reads."

"Getting in shape for his big night. Any weapon in sight?"

"No."

"What about Katya?"

"Not here."

"She's probably upstairs. He look tense?"

"Not really."

Petra clicked off. She was fifteen yards from Doebbler's front door, facing west. The Jeep was a ways up, just out of view, aimed east. No matter which direction Doebbler took, someone would pick him up.

Ten plus hours of nothing.

At four thirty p.m. Doebbler had left work along with a slew of other employees. After picking up a pizza, he drove to Katya's school, made it just before five. West Valley Comprehensive Prep looked closed, but Doebbler's bell ring brought a sullen Katya to the gate, accompanied by a female teacher-type who let the girl out.

The Infiniti headed straight home, arrived at five twenty-six.

Since then, no sign of him or the girl, and both of Doebbler's cars remained in the driveway. At nine, Petra and Eric agreed that someone should have a look from the backyard, just to make sure the quarry hadn't managed to sneak out on foot. Someone was Eric.

Petra's watch read nine twenty-eight. He'd been back there eight minutes, still hadn't emerged. Her phone vibrated. "Where are you?"

"Back in the car."

"I was looking for you. How the hell do you *do* that?"

"I just walked."

"Mr. Invisible. Anything new?"

"No."

A minimum of two and half hours to kill-time and Doebbler was sitting in his easy chair. Had he planned so well that there was no need to leave any earlier? Preselecting the prey. A nurse. Someone who took care of children.

Petra had already confirmed that no hospital remained in Elysian Park. When it came to kids, the first thing you thought of was Western Pediatrics Medical Center, back in Hollywood. Not that far from the park. At this hour, Western Peds was at least a half-hour freeway ride from Tarzana, so Doebbler was really cutting it close.

Five minutes passed. Ten, fifteen, still no movement from the gray house. A trip to Hollywood seemed increasingly unlikely, so she was wrong about Western Peds. Doebbler had probably aimed closer to home. Somewhere right here in the Valley.

FROM the upper bunk came the sound of Isaiah's snoring, loud and intrusive as a leaf blower. The eldest Gomez brother had come home late and exhausted. On the other side of the cell-like space, Joel slept on his air mattress, eyes closed, chest rising and falling slowly, a smile on his almost pretty face.

Isaac had eaten lightly and fallen asleep quickly. In the midst of a nightmare, he woke drenched with sweat and disoriented. Now he was wide-awake. Reaching out for the wooden crate that served as his nightstand, he got hold of his watch: eleven oh two.

Less than an hour to showdown. Soon it would be over.

He closed his eyes, and the facts loomed larger. Discrepancies impossible to ignore. Sliding out of the bunk, he found his briefcase, left the bedroom, and went into the kitchen, hoping his parents in the neighboring room wouldn't hear him. His mother, in particular, had the sleep rhythms of a Chihuahua.

Switching on the dim light under the stove, he sat and thought. Pulling his laptop out of the case and plugging it in—shifting the rag-wrapped gun in the process—he rummaged some more and finally came up with his seldom-used modem. Connecting the box to the corner phone jack behind the table, he booted up and hoped for the best. The modem buzzed and hummed and beeped, kept chirping its little modem song. Interminable!

"What's that?" called his mother.

"The thing that connects to the Internet, Ma."

The connection was finally completed, and he logged on to his university server. Scanning his bookmarks, he found the chat-room text he'd saved. Five minutes later, his heart was pounding so hard, it felt as if it would rip through his rib cage.

CrimeGirl: The way i see it OttoR was = to Manson or anyone.
BulldogD: U shouldn't glarify him he was just anther semi organize serial
CrimeGirl: It's not glorifying (spell-boy!!) It's telling it like it is.
P-Kasso: You're both missing the point.
Mephisto: Hey look! There's always some guy with a point.
CrimeGirl: Speak, P.
P-Kasso: Retzak stands above the others because of his artistic

integrity. His motivation is far more elevated than manson, bundy, anyone of that ilk. For him it was all about art.

BulldogD: Pee-Kasso. What U're one of those artsty fartsies, too, that's why U see it that way???

P-Kasso: I've been known to wield a brush.

BulldogD: How about a stout cudgel?

Mephisto: No answer now?

CrimeGirl: Guess he left.

P-Kasso: I'm still here. But now I'm leaving. You people are brainless.

P-Kasso: a self-styled artist. Retzak's biggest fan.

Isaac rescrolled the chat, read it again. Felt his fingers go cold. Then he logged off, unplugged the modem, hurried to the wall phone, and punched in Petra's cell. It connected to her landline. Her machine; he talked to it. Would she call home for messages?

The clock on the stove said eleven eleven.

P-Kasso. Rushing back to his room, he looked for his shoes. Shoes in hand, he ran back to the kitchen. The sole operating Gomez vehicle was the intermittently operant Toyota Corolla that Papa chanced driving to work. Keys dangled from a plastic frog screwed to the wall next to the fridge. The car was just back from the shop. Isaac slipped the ignition key off his father's key ring, began sneaking across the kitchen, feeling like a burglar, before he stopped.

Minor omission.

He corrected that. Left.

"YOU'RE sure?" said Petra. Eric had just returned from another look behind the house.

"He was watching TV. At eleven sharp, he got up, turned off the light, went upstairs."

Less than an hour to go.

"What do you think?"

"Tough call," he said.

"This doesn't feel right, Eric. Even if the kill-spot's some close-by clinic, he's cutting it too close. He's compulsive. If nothing happens within ten . . . fifteen minutes, I'm marching up to the front and ringing the bell."

THE Toyota stalled again. Third time in a mile. Isaac shifted into neutral, coasted into the right lane as cars sped around him. He tried to revive the ignition. A sputter, a nanosecond of panic, and the puny engine was chugging again. Barely.

He snail-crawled north on Vermont, struggling to keep the gas flow even, working at minimizing unnecessary stops and starts. It was a half-moon night, with pebbled lunar light filtering through neon and smog and humidity.

P-Kasso. Even if something was going to happen tonight, he'd almost certainly embarked on a fool's mission.

Heading for a destination based on theory and the cold, flat religion that was logic. It was the single best deduction, given the facts. But chances were he was wrong. Dreadfully, tragically wrong.

He made it to Fourth, Beverly . . .

He passed Melrose. Just another couple of miles. He'd park at a safe distance, proceed on foot. Check out the layout and find some kind of vantage point. The object of his guess was Western Pediatrics Hospital. The one place you could count on a slew of nurses who took care of children.

The car made a retching noise. Isaac's body lurched backward as the vehicle accelerated spontaneously. Two seconds later, the Toyota gave up.

On foot now, he jogged the half mile to Sunset, staying in the darkness, close to buildings. He reached his destination by eleven forty-three and slowed his pace as he ambled toward the big, blocky buildings of the hospital complex. Most of the structures were dark. He remained in the shadows as women, mostly young, in pastel uniforms, streamed out of several doors. Twenty or so nurses. End-of-the-day shift. If through some miracle he was right, the bastard would be watching. But from *where*?

Isaac watched the nurses arrive at a sign that said STAFF PARKING.

Arrows pointed both ways, and the group split into two. Most of the women headed west, a few east. Two lots.

He thought it out. If Doebbler were here, he'd want things as quiet as possible. East. He followed five female shapes down a surprisingly dim street. Half a block north sat a two-level parking structure.

The nurses walked right past the cement tiers, and Isaac saw the chained entrance. A sign hung from the mesh gate: EARTHQUAKE RETROFITTING, DUE FOR COMPLETION AUGUST 2003.

The nurses kept going. Twenty more feet, thirty, fifty. Nearly to the end of the block. Another sign, too distant to read, but Isaac made out cars in dirt. He sped up.

TEMPORARY STAFF PARKING. High-intensity lights bleached the rear right-hand corner of the outdoor lot. The left fixture was out, and half the space was a belt of black. Poor maintenance—or a predator's move? He crossed the street and slipped between two apartment buildings. He stepped back a foot, made sure he had a long but clear view of the dirt lot. For all he knew, Doebbler was watching.

Eleven fifty-four.

AT ELEVEN forty-six, Petra said, "I'm going to the front."

"Want me to stay back here?" said Eric.

"Yeah."

Removing her gun from her purse, she got out of her car, crossed to Doebbler's front door. Hand on the Glock, ready for anything.

She rang the bell. Nothing. A repeat ring elicited silence, too. She rang a third time. Nothing. She called Eric. "No response here."

"Same . . . Scratch that. He's coming down the stairs, switching on the landing light. Bathrobe and pajamas. Looks like you woke him."

"Weapon?"

"Not that I see. Okay, he's headed to the front. I'm coming around."

Kurt Doebbler's voice behind the door: "Who is it?"

"Police. Detective Connor." Petra had backed a few feet away. Behind her, concealed by bushes, Eric waited.

"Could you please open up, sir? Police business."

The door swung open, and Doebbler stared down at her, long arms crossed over a white terry bathrobe.

"Sir," she said, "may I come in?"

"You," he said with more contempt in that single word than Petra had believed possible. He blocked the doorway.

Petra said, "In for the evening, sir?"

He frowned. "In for the evening? As opposed to . . . ?"

"Going out."

"Why would I be going out?"

"Well," she said, "in a few minutes it'll be June twenty-eighth."

Doebbler went white. "You're sick."

"May I come in, sir?"

"For a little *social* visit?" said Doebbler. He managed a smile, detached, all mouth, no eyes.

She smiled back at Doebbler.

He slammed the door in her face.

ISAAC watched the digital numerals of his watch click into place. Twelve oh seven. All the day-shift nurses, gone.

He stayed in place, not knowing what else to do. Kept staring at the dirt lot. Three cars on the illuminated side, two, maybe three, parked in darkness; it was hard to tell. Why so few?

No big puzzle: The staff obviously preferred the western lot. Probably better lighting.

Twelve oh eight. He'd give it another five minutes; then he'd return to where he'd left his father's Toyota parked along Vermont.

At twelve nineteen, feeling like the idiot he was, he slipped out from his hiding spot and began walking south. Voices from Sunset made him stop. Female voices. Three women—small, young-sounding women—passed the parking structure and entered the dirt lot.

Isaac hurried back to his spot, watched them.

White uniforms, dark hair pulled into ponytails. They chattered gaily. Ten feet into the lot, one nurse veered into the light, the other two crossed into the darkened area.

No danger there. Doebbler wouldn't go for a pair.

The lit-up nurse started up her minivan and drove away. A set of headlights went on in the dark side, and a little sports car sped out.

Leaving one nurse. He waited for more headlights.

Darkness. Silence.

The futile whine of an engine refusing to turn over.

A car door opened. Shut. Then: a scream.

Reaching into his pocket, Isaac ran. The gun caught in the generous fleece of his sweatpants and refused to pull free.

He picked up his pace, shouted, "Stop!"

He ripped frantically at his pocket. The gun was hopelessly tangled. He reached the lot, sprinted across black dirt, unable to see anything, homing in on the site of the scream.

Then he saw: A man—a very tall man, wearing a long white coat, a doctor's coat—standing over a tiny, prone woman.

She lay on her stomach. One of the man's feet pressed down in the center of her back. Pinning her like a butterfly on a board.

She struggled in the dirt. Cried out again.

The man reached into his coat, drew out something the size and girth of a baseball bat. Not wood . . . translucent.

A thick rod of clear plastic. Slick, dense.

Isaac raced toward the tall man. Out of his mouth came a strange voice, hoarse, bellowing. "Stop or I'll shoot your ass!"

The man in the white coat maintained his foothold on the tiny woman. Isaac could see her terrified face now. Young. Latina.

He was three feet away, still struggling with the gun.

The tall man must've pressed down harder on the girl's cheek, because her features were now compressed. She choked, coughed.

The man faced him, translucent truncheon held diagonally across his chest. Very tall, broad-shouldered, powerful. Plaid shirt and jeans and sneakers under the white coat. Those shoes would leave marks in the dirt, but Thad Doebbler was a careful man, an artist; he would be sure to clean them up when he was through. Handsome man. Undeterred by Isaac's goofy presence.

Isaac said, "P-Kasso."

The cudgel caught filmy moonlight and gleamed.

Isaac's battle with his pocket continued. Suppressing panic, he analyzed. Felt around. Some metal piece on the gun was snagged on fleece threads, the key was to free it with a circular movement.

Thad Doebbler, his foot still on the girl's back, stepped forward with his free leg. The motion brought him within two feet of Isaac's head. Striking distance. He lifted the weapon, and Isaac danced back, while yanking his pants upward. Tight around the crotch.

Thad Doebbler laughed.

The little dark girl moaned in pain.

Thad Doebbler closed another few inches of the space between him and Isaac.

Isaac said, "Let her go or I'll shoot you. I mean it."

Thad Doebbler regarded him with amusement. "With what?"

Isaac yanked the gun free. Stepped within the downward arc of Thad Doebbler's murderous arm. Dodged the crushing blow by inches and managed to aim upward. For the handsome face.

He pressed the trigger. Shut his eyes and kept pressing.

--CHAPTER 12--

A HISTORIAN, Thad. A renaissance man, of sorts. Website designer, graphic artist, alternative comix illustrator, computer animator.

Sculptor in Lucite and polymer resins and space-age plastics. Petra was forced to admit that his work showed talent. She was investigating his residence in Oakland. It was Monday, July 1.

Last year he'd exhibited across the bay in San Francisco, at a Post Street gallery. Two to three grand per piece, and three had sold.

P-Kasso. Him and Omar. Her year for artists.

Bundles of spare Lucite rods in various sizes were stacked neatly in Doebbler's garage.

The largest conformed to the June 28 skull compressions.

When she'd met him at his brother's, he'd claimed his home base as San Francisco. But his digs were in the Upper Rockridge district of Oakland, a cute little mock Tudor on a hill, landscaped prettily.

Attached to the garage out back was a four-hundred-square-foot windowless cinder-block add-on secured by a bolted steel door. Thad Doebbler's track-lit studio. Thad Doebbler's museum.

Twenty-four years of dark side.

The guy had kept every Playbill, airline ticket, and receipt cataloged compulsively. Within moments, Petra was able to verify his quarterly flights to L.A. But Petra already knew that Uncle Thad stayed with older brother Kurt and niece Katya. Bunking down in a spare bedroom next to Katya's, where he kept a few pairs of pants, three shirts, a leather jacket, and a black Italian sports coat. Nothing of obvious forensic value, until the techies managed to scrape tiny little stains from two of the shirts and a jeans leg that had somehow managed to survive laundering and pressing.

Three of the stains were too degraded for DNA analysis. One was a perfect match to Marta Doebbler, another fit Coral Langdon's genetic makeup, a third matched that of Darren Hochenbrenner.

Petra had made it to the June 28 scene after hearing about it on her scanner, just after the debacle at Kurt Doebbler's house.

When she got there, Isaac was being treated like a suspect by two Hollywood D's who didn't know him well enough. He'd dropped Councilman Gilbert Reyes's name and that of Deputy Chief Randy Diaz. Finally someone called Diaz, who drove up in a Corvette. Just in time for Petra to grab him and brief him.

"The kid solved it, sir." She spat out details.

Diaz said, "Impressive. Think he'll share credit with the department?"

"I don't think credit matters to him," said Petra. "He's a good kid, a great kid. I vouch for him absolutely."

Isaac using an illegal gun to kill Thad could be a problem, they agreed.

Diaz said, "It can be dealt with." Long, searching look of Petra's face. "So can *your* issues, Detective. If everyone's discreet. There are going to be some changes in your division. I'd like them to be smooth."

"What changes?"

Diaz put a finger over his lips. Walked over to Isaac.

THE following night, Petra flew to Oakland, and Sunday morning, accompanied by an Oakland D named Arvin Ludd, she began the first of two solid days in the cinder-block trove. The best stuff was to be found in a double-wide black filing cabinet, in a folder marked TRAVEL. He'd filled three notebooks with detailed accounts of murderous fantasies initiated at age twelve. The melding of sex and violence and power, solidified by a chance encounter with a copy of the Teller booklet, found in a Hamburg antiques store.

"Retzak is me, and I am him. I don't know why people like us are what we are. We just are. I like it."

After that: a lifetime of converting fantasy to reality.

Thad described his failure to murder the German cake icer, Gudrun Wiegeland, as "an understandable lapse, given my youth and inexperience." At the time of the Wiegeland bludgeoning, he'd been a sixteen-year-old army brat.

It took another eight years for him to try another murder.

After a two-year stint in the army, Thad moved to Pittsburgh and enrolled in Carnegie-Mellon as an art-and-design major. Soon after graduation, he waylaid an eighteen-year-old coed named Randi Corey as she enjoyed a late-night campus jog. June 28, 1987. The spring semester had ended, but Corey had remained for the summer to practice with a gymnastics coach.

Thad Doebbler had stayed in town to murder her. The girl incurred three crushing blows to the back of her skull and, according to a newspaper clipping Thad had mounted in Volume 1 of his chronicles, was "likely to remain in a persistent vegetative state."

Still in training.

Sandwiched into the book were the drawings. Horrible because the bastard really *could* draw. End of Volume 1.

She flipped the next book open. After almost murdering Randi

Corey, Thad had adhered to the June 28 pattern. But not with yearly regularity. The crimes had depended upon his travel schedule.

June 28, 1989: A computer seminar in Los Gatos, California. Thad had flown in from Philadelphia, where he'd been temping as a bank teller while seeking employment in the computer animation biz. Shortly after midnight, Barbara Bohannon, secretary to an Intel executive, was brained in the subterranean parking lot of her hotel.

June 28, 1991: In Philly, another computer conference. At one-fifteen a.m., the body of Melvyn Lassiter, a room-service waiter at the Inn at Penn, was found on a street in West Philadelphia. Crushed skull, missing wallet.

June 28, 1992: Denver, Colorado. Animation conference. Ethel Ferguson, fifty-six, a breeder of standard poodles, was found bludgeoned in a wooded area near her home.

June 28, 1995: Oceanside, California, Matthias Delano Brown, seaman, USN, brained near the docks.

Then: sister-in-law Marta.

Lover Marta.

Thad recounted the affair in prurient detail. During the three-month adultery, he traveled to L.A. twelve times, telling his brother that he'd gotten an illustration job at a Beverly Hills ad agency.

A near disaster was averted when Kurt returned home shortly after leaving to get a trade journal he'd left near his recliner. After that, Marta insisted they tryst at motels in Hollywood.

The "downtown errands" she'd lied about to her friends.

When Marta announced to Thad that she loved him, was ready to leave Kurt and Katya, he decided to kill her. He thought it out, waited until her theater night. He phoned her cell from a nearby booth, telling her he was just around the corner, had planned a surprise: meeting her at her car after the show. He'd booked a room at the Hollywood Roosevelt Hotel. But now he wasn't feeling well. Chest pains, probably nothing, but he was going to drive over to the Hollywood Presbyterian emergency room just to make sure.

She freaked and insisted on taking him. Met him at her car.

Before she knew it, he was sitting behind the wheel. Driving away. Looking fine. "Thought you were sick," she said.

He laughed, told her they were through.

She began sobbing, wanted to know why.

He parked on a dark side street. Took her in his arms, kissed her. Shoved her away roughly and got out.

She went after him. He shoved her to the ground and smashed the back of her skull with the Lucite club he'd concealed in his coat.

"This jaunt solidified my goals," he wrote. "This was the closest I'd come to ecstasy. And to honoring the memory of that sage, O.R. Something worth appreciating. Worth celebrating yearly."

Petra read the rest of it quickly, turned to the back, and found the postmortem sketches of Marta Doebbler and the others.

That evening, in her room at the Jack London Inn, she took a very long, very hot bath, watched Court TV, and managed to keep a room-service cheeseburger down.

Her cell phone rattled on the nightstand. She picked up the phone, studied the readout, hoped it was Eric. They had a dinner date tomorrow back in L.A. Big splurge. Intimations—as much as Eric was capable of intimating—of serious talk, career plans.

The phone read out a 213 number. Not Eric, but someone she didn't mind talking to. "Hi," she said.

"Hi," said Isaac. "Hope I'm not bothering you."

"Not at all. What's up?"

"I just thought I'd tell you I was by the station today, and there's a new captain. Someone named Stuart Bishop. He made a point of coming up to me, said he knows you. He seems friendly."

"Stu? You're kidding."

"Is there a problem?"

"No," said Petra. "He's terrific. Used to be my partner until he left the department."

"Oh. I guess he's back."

There'll be changes in your division.

"How're *you* doing, hero? When's the ceremony?"

"Friday, next week. I hope they cancel it."

"Hey," she said, "enjoy the moment. You and Councilman Reyes, adoring citizens, the press. You deserve it."

"I'm no hero, Petra. I was lucky."

"You were smart. Heather Salcido was lucky."

Cute little Heather from Brea, California. Dark-haired, big-eyed, petite, and twenty-three. Cheerleader-pretty despite all those cheek abrasions. A newly graduated R.N., she'd worked Pediatric Pulmonary for less than a year. Still lived at home. Traditional family: dad a retired sheriff, mom a housewife. From the way the girl had gazed at Isaac from her hospital bed, from the way he'd looked at her, the kid's relationship to the world of law enforcement might take on a whole new twist.

"No," he said. "It was luck, that's all."

"Then you're a lucky guy," she said. "And I thank you."

"I should thank you. For teaching me so much."

"My pleasure, Dr. Gomez."

"One more thing . . ."

"The gun," she said. "It's been logged into evidence as a legally registered firearm. Registered to you last January; you even merited a concealed-weapon permit. Because of your law-enforcement activities and living in a high-crime area."

"Thanks," he said.

"Sure," she said. "Now go have some fun."

ISAAC cut into his hangar steak. Big as a baseball mitt. Soft as a doughnut.

"Like it?" said Heather. She'd made unbelievable headway with her T-bone and sirloin tip combo.

"It's great," he told her, meaning it.

"I love this place," she said. "Partly because of the food, but also because of all these memories I have. Back when my dad was with the sheriff's department and he had to be in court late, he'd take us here. Rather than battle the traffic back to Brea, Mom and my brother, Gary, and I would meet him, and we'd have a huge meal."

She patted her mouth with a corner of snow-white napkin. Pretty mouth. Bow-shaped. The scratches on her smooth, olive cheek were healing nicely.

"My family doesn't eat out."

Heather said, "A lot of families don't. Actually, we don't very often. That makes it more special, don't you think?"

He smiled. She smiled back, and they both ate. Drank wine. Red wine—a six-year-old California cabernet way past his budget. He'd faked out choosing from the five-page wine list. Pretending to contemplate, he'd finally jabbed randomly and hoped for the best.

Heather took one sip and said, "Oh, man, this is fantastic. You know your wine."

He'd visited her twice in the hospital, but this was their first date. Spur-of-the-moment thing after the ceremony on the front steps of city hall.

The ceremony had turned out to be Councilman Gilbert Reyes, a couple of flunkies, the media, Isaac, and his family. His parents beamed and his brothers squirmed as he accepted the official commendation and then made a cursory speech. He hated every minute of it. Longed for the solitude of the library, his laptop and books, and the opera of deduction. He got through the ordeal, shaking hands and smiling and waiting for an opportunity to escape. Then Heather came up to him. Councilman Gilbert Reyes spotted her and had her pose for stills, sandwiched between himself and Isaac.

Later, Isaac found out she'd wanted to be present for the whole thing but had arrived late because of traffic. "I heard your speech, though," she assured him. "And the ceremony was on KFWB. Daddy always listens to news and talk radio— Oh, here he is."

A big square truck of a man stepped out from behind the departing media hounds. White hair and mustache, outdoor skin, iron grip. Then a small, slender, vivacious woman, young-looking for her age, whom Heather resembled. Heather would age well.

Nancy and Robert Salcido thanked him, then turned to converse in Spanish with Irma and Isaiah Gomez, Sr.

Somehow Isaac and Heather drifted away from the crowd. Somehow she got him talking about himself. "A Ph.D. and an M.D.," she said. "That's ambitious—that's unbelievable! Don't tell anyone, but I've been thinking of med school, too."

"You should go for it," he said.

"Well," she said, "thanks for the vote of confidence. I don't know. Maybe I will. Well, it was nice seeing you again."

"It doesn't have to end."

She gave a puzzled look that made his heart sink. Then a smile.

"As in lunch," he said. "As in now."

"Now? Okay. I'll tell my parents. They were figuring to go out as a family, but I like your idea better."

AT A loss for a restaurant, phony cool guy that he was, he was grateful when she came up with Leonard's. Despite the fact that it would empty his wallet. What the heck. Live dangerously.

Now he watched Heather slice pink meat off the bone, chew, swallow. Everything she did was adorable.

She said, "What? You got really quiet, Isaac."

"I'm just enjoying myself," he said. "The peace and quiet."

"Of course," she said, reaching over and placing a hand atop his. He felt his skin go hot.

She said, "Life's so funny, you know? You plan and scheme and then, out of nowhere, something happens."

"I know," he said. "I'm so sorry you had to go through that."

"Oh, no," she said, squeezing his fingers. Smiling. "I wasn't talking about *that*."

The Creative Process of
Jonathan Kellerman

"WRITERS are basically psychological vacuum cleaners. The good ones know what choice tidbits to pick out of the bag."

This is how best-selling novelist Jonathan Kellerman answers the irresistible question, "Where do you get your ideas?" With typical self-deprecating humor and sharp self-analysis, Kellerman, who is also a clinical psychologist, is clearly at ease when discussing the creative process. Of *Twisted*, his latest blockbuster suspense tale, he says, "The story sprang from my rather warped imagination, not from a real case. For me, a novel takes months, even years, to materialize. It's the product of thought fragments, dreams and daydreams, conversations, and other bits of mental flotsam that one picks up over time."

Kellerman is one of the world's most popular authors (his books

Vital Stats

BORN: New York City, 1949
RESIDENCE: Beverly Hills, CA
FAMILY: Wife, novelist Faye Kellerman; four children
EDUCATION: B.A. in psychology, UCLA, 1971; Ph.D. in psychology, University of Southern California, 1974
HOBBY: Collects vintage guitars
WEBSITE:
www.jonathankellerman.com

have been translated into two dozen languages). He is also one of the most prolific. Since 1985, when he published his first novel, *When the Bough Breaks,* introducing the phenomenally successful mystery series featuring psychologist Alex Delaware, he has averaged a book a year. He is the author of numerous essays, short stories, and scientific articles, two children's books, and three volumes of psychology, including *Savage Spawn: Reflections on Violent Children* (1999), a treatise on child psychopaths. He has also teamed up with his wife, Faye, creator of the Peter Decker/Rina Lazarus books, to launch a new series. Their first collaboration, *Double Homicide* (2004), was an instant bestseller.

Lately Kellerman has been more productive than ever. This latest surge in creativity, including *Twisted, Double Homicide,* and a new Alex Delaware novel, *Rage* (2005), was the result of a marathon writing stint that took place as two of his children were getting married just twenty-eight days apart. "As anyone who's done a wedding knows," says Kellerman, "the role of the father of the bride/groom is to write checks and have no opinion. So I was doubly mandated to have no opinion. I escaped the process by hiding in my office and typing away. Faye's the hero. She did the wedding work and still managed to get some writing done."

As for assuring the quality of his high output, Kellerman admits he's a perfectionist by nature, a trait that has won him numerous literary kudos, starting with an Edgar award from the Mystery Writers of America for *When the Bough Breaks.* He is also a very disciplined writer who diligently

Great Minds

Isaac Gomez, *Twisted*'s crime-fighting grad student, is many things—socially awkward, reckless, impressionable . . . and an off-the-charts genius.

To qualify as a genius, you have to have an IQ of at least 140 (average IQs fall between 90 and 110). Geniuses are rare, constituting the top one percent of the population in brain power.

The word "genius" is Latin and originally referred to a guardian spirit. When you think about it, that's a perfect description of Jonathan Kellerman's Einstein intern of the LAPD.

Follow That Squad Car!

Petra Connor is a hardworking cop. Unlike amateur sleuths such as Miss Marple or Lord Peter Wimsey, when she's hot on the trail of a killer for the LAPD, she is also on the job—a job with well-established, sometimes boringly methodical procedures. Mystery fans who enjoy the thrill and immediacy of crime-solving the way the police really do it love this category of fiction called the **POLICE PROCEDURAL**. Of noble lineage, the procedural dates all the way back to Wilkie Collins's classic, *The Moonstone* (1868), which featured Sergeant Cuff of Scotland Yard, with his magnifying glass and probing questions. Today, squad cars, crime-scene tape, oddball coroners, and chilling forensic clues are standard issue in this brand of true-to-life cop fiction. If you liked *Twisted,* try solving crimes with Ed McBain and Michael Connelly. We think their procedurals are, well, arresting.

works at his craft at least five days a week, whether or not he feels "inspired" to do so. In a recent online interview with Bookreporter.com he explains, "My perfectionist personality and compulsive nature don't allow me to send a manuscript in until I'm relatively happy with it. I say relatively because I'm rewriting constantly, and there are always changes one can make. But at some point one needs to put the book aside and move on."

Another quality assurance factor is that this author writes only about what he knows, and knows well. If Los Angeles and its notorious surroundings come alive in his books, it's because he lives there, loves the city, and knows it intimately. Even when writing about foreign venues, such as Jerusalem, his home in the late 1960s and the setting for *The Butcher's Theater* (1988), Kellerman has to have direct experience of a place to replicate its atmosphere and the idiosyncrasies of the people who live there.

And speaking of real people, if his lovably flawed heroes and eerie villains seem ultrareal even though they are purely fictional, it's because Dr. Kellerman is an expert in how the human mind works—especially when it's twisted. ∎

Being a
criminal defense attorney
would be a great gig—
if it weren't for the clients.

FALSE
TESTIMONY

A Crime Novel

ROSE CONNORS

Award-Winning Author of *Maximum Security*

Massachusetts Rules of Professional Conduct

Rule 3.3—Candor Toward the Tribunal

(e) In a criminal case, if defense counsel . . . knows that the client
has testified falsely, the lawyer shall call upon the client to rectify
the false testimony and, if the client refuses or is unable to do so,
the lawyer shall not reveal the false testimony to the tribunal.

ONE

Monday, December 13

A PERSON of interest. That's what local authorities dubbed Charles
Kendrick, the senior United States senator from the Commonwealth of Massachusetts. He wasn't a target of the investigation,
they told him. He was merely an individual believed to have information relevant to the search.

And he did. Twenty-five-year-old Michelle Forrester was a member of his D.C. staff. He hired her more than three years ago, just
after she graduated from the University of Virginia with dual degrees in government science and drama. An ambitious and disarm-
ingly attractive young woman with obvious political aspirations
of her own, she quickly became Senator Kendrick's preferred
spokesperson. For the past year—while rumors ran rampant about
his planned bid for the Democratic nomination—Michelle Forrester fielded questions at his frequent public appearances. She en-
abled the senator to say his piece at each event and then make a
dignified—perhaps even presidential—exit.

This past Thursday, Michelle handled the members of the media after the senator addressed a standing-room-only crowd at Cape Cod Community College in Hyannis. The evening news featured a poised and charming Michelle entertaining endless inquiries from local reporters, joking and laughing with them easily and often. She extended Senator Kendrick's sincere thanks to all of them, for their attendance and their attention, before she left the auditorium.

And then Michelle Forrester vanished.

She was due at her parents' home in Stamford, Connecticut, the next day to help prepare for a cocktail party to be held that evening in honor of her father's sixtieth birthday. She didn't show up—not for the preparations and not for the party. She was expected back at work in D.C. first thing this morning. She didn't show there either. At that point the search began in earnest.

Postpone it. That's what I advised when Senator Kendrick called my office at ten a.m. He'd stayed on the Cape after Thursday's speech, intending to work by phone and fax through the holidays from his vacation home in North Chatham. The Barnstable County district attorney's office called his D.C. number first thing this morning, and his executive secretary phoned him right away with the message. It was from Geraldine Schilling—the district attorney herself—wanting to set up a time when she might ask him a few questions. Today, if at all possible.

Senator Kendrick made it clear to me from the outset that he wasn't seeking formal representation. He simply wanted to know if one of the lawyers in our office would be available by telephone in case he needed a word of advice during his interview.

Twenty-four hours, I told him. *Of course you'll cooperate with the investigation, and of course you'll do it promptly; time is paramount in these matters. But you shouldn't speak to the DA without an attorney at your side.* He was quick to inform me that he *is* an attorney— Harvard-trained, he added—whereupon I recited my personal version of the old adage: Never mind the fool; the lawyer who represents himself has a certifiable moron for a client.

Answer questions tomorrow, I urged. *We'll go to the district attorney together in the morning. That way, if her questioning takes a direction it shouldn't, I'll be the one to hit the brakes. You'll remain
the willing witness, reluctantly accepting advice from your overly
protective attorney.*

Senator Kendrick's laughter took me by surprise. I wasn't trying
to be funny. After a good chuckle, he thanked me for my time. And
before I could answer, I was listening to a dial tone.

"GOOD of you to join us, Martha." Geraldine Schilling is the
only person on the planet who calls me Martha. And she knows
damned well I'm not here to join anybody. Charles Kendrick called
me a second time—ten minutes ago, at one-thirty—because he's
worried. And he should be.

"Party's over, Geraldine. No more questions."

"Attorney Nickerson can be a bit rude." Geraldine directs her
observation exclusively to Senator Kendrick as though I'm not in
the room. "I should have trained her better," she adds.

Geraldine "trained" me for a solid decade, when I was an assistant DA and she was the first assistant. If she'd done the job as she
intended, I'd still be a prosecutor, not a member of the defense bar.
I lift her black winter coat from the back of an upholstered wing
chair in the corner and hold it out, letting it dangle from two fingers. "Adios," I tell her. "You're done here."

She accepts the coat but doesn't put it on. Instead, she takes a
pack of Virginia Slims from its inside pocket. She tamps a cigarette
from the pack, shakes her long blond bangs at me, then turns to the
senator and arches her eyebrows. She seems to think he might over-
ride my decision.

"You're done," I repeat. "Senator Kendrick spoke with you voluntarily this morning, but he's not doing that anymore. He called
his attorney. That's me. And I've asked you to leave."

"Marty, is that really necessary?" Senator Kendrick is seated on
his living room couch, a deep-maroon, soft leather sectional. Behind him, through the floor-to-ceiling windows, is a heart-stopping

view of the Atlantic. His long legs are crossed—in perfectly creased blue jeans—and his starched, white dress shirt is open at the collar.

"Take a look outside," I tell him, pointing to a pair of windows that face the driveway. "Then you tell me if it's necessary."

He stands, sighing, and crosses the antique Oriental carpet to the polished hardwood at the perimeter of the vast room. I eye his chiseled profile as he parts the curtains and leans on the sill. He's silent for a moment as he gets a gander of the scene that greeted me when I arrived. "Standard procedure?" he asks at last.

"Not even close," I tell him.

Four vehicles occupy the crushed-shell driveway. The shiny Buick is Geraldine's; she gets a new one every two years without fail, always dark blue. The ancient Thunderbird is mine. The enormous gray Humvee, I can only presume, is the senator's. And the patrol car belongs to the town of Chatham. Two uniforms stand in front of it, leaning against its hood and talking.

The Kendrick estate sits on a point, a narrow spit of land that juts out into the Atlantic. It has a solitary neighbor, a small bungalow, to the north. Otherwise, the Kendricks enjoy exclusive use of this strip, the front and sides of their spacious house bordered by nothing but open ocean. The cops are in the driveway for a reason, not passing through on their way to someplace else.

"The one closest to us is the chief," I tell the senator. "Ten bucks says he'll shoot the lock off your front door if your friend the DA here presses the right button on her pager."

Senator Kendrick pulls the curtains back together and turns to face Geraldine. She dons her coat as she stares back at him. "Senator," she snaps, her tone altogether different than it was just moments ago. He stiffens beside me. "We've barely begun to check out your story," she says, "and already, parts of it don't fly."

He takes a step toward me, but I don't look at him. "That can't be," he says.

"Shut up, Senator." The utter shock of my command renders him compliant. I keep my eyes fixed on our district attorney. She carries little more than a hundred pounds on her five-foot-two-inch frame, but there's not a tougher DA in the Commonwealth.

I take my cell phone from my jacket pocket and flip it open as I walk toward the kitchen—and Geraldine. "At this point," I tell her, "you're nothing more than a common trespasser."

She laughs.

"And *I've* got the chief on speed dial too."

She laughs again, but she moves toward the kitchen door. She pauses, digs out a lighter from her coat pocket, and ignites the tip of the cigarette now pressed between her well-glossed lips. She opens the inner door, sucks in a long drag as she reaches for the outer one, and then blows a steady stream of smoke over her shoulder, her smoldering green eyes moving from mine to the senator's. "Mark my words," she says to both of us. "I'll be back."

"How's Chuck?" Harry stares at the snowy road ahead as he asks, a small smile tugging at the corners of his lips. He apparently finds it amusing that the Commonwealth's senior senator is proving to be a less-than-model client.

"*Chuck* is the same as he was this morning," I tell him. "Difficult." I flip the heater in Harry's old Jeep up another couple of notches and shift in the passenger seat to face him.

"Makes sense," he says. "The guy's usually the one calling the shots; he isn't used to taking orders."

"I'm not issuing orders, Harry. I'm offering advice."

He smiles at me and then swallows a mouthful of coffee. "And you're just the drill sergeant for the job." He laughs.

Now there's a sentiment every fortysomething woman hopes to hear from the man in her life.

It's three o'clock, and we're pulling into the Barnstable County Complex, headed up the hill to the house of correction. We'll spend the next couple of hours with Derrick Holliston, a twenty-two-year-old creep who's accused of murdering a popular parish priest last Christmas Eve. Harry is Holliston's court-appointed defender and—according to Harry—neither of them is happy about it.

Harry and I will spend the rest of the afternoon walking Holliston through his direct testimony. Tomorrow, we'll prepare him for cross. His first-degree-murder trial starts Wednesday morning. And unless Harry can convince him otherwise, Holliston intends to take the stand. He plans to tell the judge and jury that he acted in self-defense; that fifty-seven-year-old Father Frank McMahon made aggressive sexual advances toward him on the evening in question; that when Holliston resisted, the older man became violent. If Harry's instincts are on target—and I've never known them to be otherwise—Holliston's story is just that. Fiction.

Harry pulls into a snow-clogged spot and parks near the steps leading up to the foreboding house of correction. He leaves the engine running, though, and shifts in his seat to lean against the driver's side door. "The guy's a liar," he says.

"You don't know that, Harry. You think he's lying, but you don't know it." Harry and I have had this discussion a hundred times over the course of the past year.

"Trust me," he says. "I know."

"No, you don't. There were two people in St. Veronica's Chapel when it happened. One of them is dead. Holliston is the only living person who was there. No one can prove he's lying."

Harry shakes his head. He's struggling with the ugly issue that confronts every criminal-defense lawyer sooner or later: what to do when you believe—but can't prove—your client's story is fabricated. If he could prove it—before Holliston testifies—he could move for permission to withdraw from the case completely. As it stands, with nothing but his gut telling him his client's a liar, he's stuck. And once Holliston testifies, Harry will be stuck for good. At that point, even if he were to discover slam-dunk evidence of perjury, he'd be obligated to keep it to himself. The Massachusetts Canons of Professional Ethics say so.

"I can prove Holliston's lying," he says, still staring uphill. "Give me fifteen minutes alone with him—in a dark alley."

"Listen to yourself, Harry. If you ever got wind of a cop saying something like that, you'd call him a miscreant. You'd raise the courthouse roof to suppress his testimony. And then you'd go after his badge."

Harry nods, conceding all points. "Let's get this over with."

We emerge into the late-day mist and both lock our doors before slamming them shut. The stone steps are covered with snow, and I opt to climb the hill beside the steps instead, where my boots can find a little more traction. Harry trudges up the hill, too, on the opposite side of the stairs. "So what did you tell old Chuck?" he asks, glancing sideways at me. "What are his marching orders?"

"I didn't give him marching orders, Harry."

"Oh, right. Advice," he says, feigning the utmost seriousness. "You gave him lawyerly advice. What was it?"

At six feet, 210, Harry has a good half foot and ninety pounds on me. But I'd like to clock him upside the head anyway. "Simple," I say. "I told our senior senator to keep his mouth shut."

Harry laughs out loud, sending a cloud of white vapor into the cold air ahead of us. "Simple? Are you serious, Marty? The guy's been a politician his entire adult life. You think it's going to be simple for him to keep his mouth shut?"

I walk ahead of Harry as the guard at the front booth presses a button that opens the prison's enormous double doors. "It better be," I answer over my shoulder. "The guy's front and center in a high-profile missing-person case. And the young woman's been gone four days now. He damn well better keep his mouth shut."

The front desk is manned by two guards who would look ominous even without their shiny weapons. We hand over our Massachusetts bar cards to be checked against the list of warden-approved appointments and empty our pockets of keys, paper clips, and coins. Harry pulls Derrick Holliston's thick file from the battered schoolbag he carries in lieu of a briefcase. The file goes in with us; the bag stays here.

Once each of us is stripped to a single layer of clothes, we're directed—one at a time—through the metal detector beside the desk. A third guard meets us on the other side of it, his expression wary.

We wait with the vigilant guard while the two at the front desk rummage through Holliston's file. Minutes pass before they turn it over to the cautious one, who directs us toward the dingy corridor behind him with a toss of his crew-cut head.

Harry and I lead the way, our escort three paces behind with the file tucked under one arm. "Stop right there," he orders after we pass the first door on our left. He keeps his focus on us as he opens the door and steps aside. He hands the file to Harry when we approach, and Harry enters the meeting room first.

Our client is already here. Derrick Holliston is seated at a small, banged-up card table. Harry drops the heavy file onto the table and roots through his jacket pockets until he comes up with his glasses. "This is Marty Nickerson," he says to Holliston as he puts them on. "She'll sit second-chair at trial."

Harry and I frequently second-chair for each other. In a trial, an extra set of eyes and ears can be critical. The second-chair also takes a witness or two in most cases, giving lead counsel a much-needed breather. We've decided I'll handle Tommy Fitzpatrick in this one. He's Chatham's chief of police. And I was an ADA long enough to establish a pretty good rapport with him.

Holliston stares at me for a moment, then turns his attention back to Harry. "Good," he says. "You need help."

Harry lets the remark pass. He sits and starts unpacking the file without a word. I claim the only remaining seat.

"First of all," Harry says, opening a manila folder in the middle of the table, "let's go over the Commonwealth's offer again."

"Let's not," Holliston says, mimicking Harry's cadence. "Let's tell the Commonwealth to stick its lousy offer where the sun don't shine. I told you—I ain't doin' time. Not for this one."

Harry leans back on two legs of his chair. "You are if you're convicted," he says evenly. "You're doing endless time."

"Well, now, that's where you come in, ain't it? You got a job to do, remember? You're the guy whose job is to get me off."

On the surface, Harry appears entirely unaffected by his client's comments. But I know better. He'd like to deck this smart-ass.

"I'm also the guy who's supposed to advise you," he says. "And I'm advising you to seriously consider pleading out."

"Yeah? Well, you can stick your advice right up there with the offer." Holliston stands and presses his back against the wall. He's a wiry man, five-ten or so, with a sketchy mustache and greasy brown hair that hangs below his collar. "I told you a hundred times," he says, jutting his chin out at Harry. "No deal. What're you, deaf?"

Holliston reaches up to the low, suspended ceiling and dislodges one fiberglass square. He peers into the opening, presumably expecting to find the treasure he stashed up there the last time he was here.

"Did you lose something?" Harry asks.

Holliston glares at him like an impudent child. "No, I dint *lose* nothing," he says. He goes back to examining the gap he created. "I was an electrician in a prior life," he says. "I like wires."

Harry laughs. "I'm surprised you had a job in your prior life," he says. "That's more than you can say this time around."

Holliston glares at him again.

"What's the offer?" I ask them both.

"Murder two," Harry says. "Eligible for parole in fifteen."

"You can't *not* consider it," I tell Holliston. "You're looking at life if you get bagged for murder one. This deal gets you out in your late thirties—still young enough to build a decent future."

Holliston snorts and spreads his arms wide. "What's with you people?" he asks. "First I get this guy"—he tosses his head toward Harry—"wantin' to sell me down the river. And now you come in here tellin' me I don't need to have a life till fifteen years from now. What the hell kind of sorry lawyers are you?"

"Advising you is part of our job," Harry tries again.

"You already done that part," Holliston fires back. "I ain't takin' your advice. Get to the other part of your job. Tellin' me how to tell them people what happened that night."

Harry drums his fingers on the table. He's resigned. Holliston claims he acted only as necessary to preserve his own life. If the jury believes him, he'll walk away a free man. And like it or not, we have a duty to try to make that happen.

Harry leans back on his chair, staring at Holliston. He cups his hands behind his head and takes a deep breath. "Go ahead," he says at last. "Tell us your tale."

TWO

MY SON is a freshman at Boston College. He finished first-semester finals on Friday, and he's home now for winter break. I'm surprised to see his pickup in the driveway of our Windmill Lane cottage, though, when Harry and I pull up at six o'clock. I thought Luke would be out with his buddies by now.

Harry and I hang our damp coats on hooks inside the kitchen door before we wander into the living room. The woodstove is crackling, and the TV is on, but no one's watching. Luke hustles down the stairs, and Danny Boy, our twelve-year-old Irish setter, saunters behind, his tail wagging instantly at the sight of his buddy Harry. "Mom," Luke says as his six-foot-three frame stoops in front of the mirror above the couch, "I'm really glad you're here."

This sentiment can mean only one thing: my son is broke.

"Could you float me some cash?" he asks, running one hand through the thin black locks he inherited from me. "I'll pay you back when I'm working."

"And when will that be?" I know the answer. No time soon.

"Summer," he says. "I'll pay you back in the summer."

I find a twenty in my jacket pocket and hand it to him.

He winces.

"What?" I ask. "You need more?"

"Maybe another?" he says, his voice pleading. "I have a date," he says, "and I want to take her someplace decent."

Harry pulls his tattered wallet from his back pants pocket and presses a second twenty into Luke's palm. "I'll contribute," Harry says. "Young love is one of my favorite causes."

"Hey, thanks," he says, punching Harry on the arm.

Harry flops down in the middle of the couch and props his feet on the coffee table. Danny Boy hops up and sits beside him, then curls into a big ball and rests his graying head on Harry's lap. "Who is she?" Harry laughs. "Who's the lucky lass?"

"You won't believe it," Luke says, grabbing his parka from the closet. "She's the senator's daughter. And she's great."

I freeze. "Which senator?"

"Kendrick," he answers, zipping his coat. "Abby Kendrick. I just met her a few days ago."

"How'd *that* happen?" Senator Kendrick and his wife have only one child. And everyone knows she's following her father's footsteps through the hallowed halls of Harvard.

Luke shrugs. "Her roommate is dating a guy in my dorm," he says. "And they finished with finals an entire week before we did. They came over to visit the night they finished, and a bunch of us went out for Thai to celebrate. Abby and I ended up sitting next to each other, and we got to talking. She's staying in town with her folks through the holidays. So I asked if she'd like to grab a bite sometime, and she said sure." He turns to Harry. "Can you believe it? She said sure."

Harry kicks his shoes off and loosens his tie. "Life is good," he tells Danny Boy, "whenever she says *sure.*"

"Hey, look at that," Luke says. "There she is."

Luke's staring at the TV. And there she is.

Senator Kendrick is on-screen, flanked by his wife and daughter. A talking head in the upper right corner tells us the senator held a press conference outside his Chatham home at four o'clock today. He repeated the detailed descriptions of Michelle Forrester, her electric-blue BMW roadster, and the clothes she was wearing when she was last seen four days ago. He pleaded for anyone with information about her to come forward. He also gave out a newly established 800 number for his D.C. office.

So much for my "keep your mouth shut" admonition. Harry's right. My newest client isn't very good at following directions.

Luke walks closer to the TV screen and points at the senator's daughter. "Is she great," he says, "or what?"

My son is right. Abby Kendrick is tall and lean—athletic-looking— with dark red hair, an alabaster complexion, and finely carved features like her father's. She's stunning.

Harry gets up from the couch and pulls two more twenties from his wallet. "Take her someplace better than decent," he says, handing the bills to Luke. "And tell her to order the lobster."

A GROWN woman who voluntarily refers to herself as "Honey" is suspect in my book. The senator's wife has a perfectly serviceable given name—Nell—but she prefers her nectar nickname instead. At her husband's public appearances she insists that the members of the media address her by her self-imposed moniker. And now, in her state-of-the-art, sun-drenched kitchen, she demands the same of me. "Please, dear," she says each time I speak to her, "call me Honey."

This is the first time I've met Mrs. Kendrick, and I'm not surprised to find her ill at ease, uncomfortable in her own skin. That's exactly how she always seems on television.

The all-white kitchen is on the landward side of the house. A wrought-iron table and six matching, cushioned chairs are situated in an alcove a few feet from glass sliders. The senator and I are settled across from each other, coffee mugs in hand.

Honey is lean like her husband and daughter but not as tall as either of them, with a winter tan and short, salon-assisted amber hair. In tailored dark slacks, a powder blue cashmere sweater, and pumps, she looks like she thinks I came here this morning to take photos. She flutters around the room, opening and closing drawers and cupboards; stacking and restacking magazines on the counter; offering us coffee cake, fruit, and yogurt.

"Not for me," I tell her a third time. Her husband says no again too. "Honey," the senator says quietly, "please join us. Marty doesn't have all day."

He's right about that. I'm supposed to meet Harry at the house of correction at ten—an hour from now—and it's a forty-minute drive from here.

Mrs. Kendrick nods at her husband's request and wipes her hands on a terry-cloth towel. She doesn't sit, though. She leans against one slider and turns her attention to me.

"You need to be quiet," I tell them both.

"What?" the senator says.

"About Michelle Forrester," I add. "You need to zip it, publicly and privately. No more press conferences. No more media events of any kind. No more conversation about her, unless it's with me."

The senator looks into his coffee mug for a moment. When his eyes meet mine again, they're angry.

"You're being unreasonable," he says. "That woman worked for me for the past three and a half years, and she's vanished without a trace. You expect me to stand by and say nothing?"

"That's right. Until we get a handle on what's happened here, that's exactly what I expect."

He looks into his mug again, silent for now. I turn to his wife. She shifts away from me. Her gaze settles on the bungalow next door. "And I expect it from both of you," I tell her.

She doesn't react at first. "Me?" she says at last. "What in the world do I have to do with it?"

"Plenty. At this point, anyone who ever crossed paths with Michelle Forrester has something to do with it."

Honey looks over at her husband and gives him a tight, decidedly unsweetened smile. "Well," she says, "Michelle and I certainly crossed *paths.*"

I intend to find out what she means by that, but quick footsteps in the next room make me hold my tongue. Abby Kendrick breezes into the kitchen in gray sweats and white sneakers, her long, lustrous hair in a loose ponytail. She pours a glass of orange juice from the ceramic pitcher on the counter before she looks up at any of us. Her pale, gray-blue eyes match her father's; they widen as she takes her first sip. "Oh," she says, "sorry. I didn't know we had company."

"Abby"—her father lifts his coffee mug toward me—"this is Ms. Nickerson."

She gives me a little wave from across the room.

"Call me Marty," I say, hoping I don't sound too much like Honey.

She nods, studying me as she takes another swallow. Her expression says she's certain she knows me from somewhere but can't quite put her finger on it.

I know how she recognizes me, of course, and I wonder if Abby needs her gorgeous gray-blues examined. Aside from our nine-inch height difference, Luke and I are dead ringers for each other. We share the same black hair, fair skin, and dark blue eyes. She realizes before I say anything, though. "You're Luke Ellis's mom, aren't you?" she says. "I had dinner with him last night."

"So I heard. He managed to squeeze me in for five minutes before he dashed out to pick you up."

She raises one eyebrow. "You're a lawyer, aren't you?"

I nod again, amazed. My son must have mentioned his mother.

She sets her glass on the counter, looks from one parent to the other, then frowns. "Why are the two of you talking to a lawyer?"

Her mother walks toward her—and away from our discussion—before the question ends. "It doesn't concern you, Abigail."

Abby stares at her father. He hesitates for a moment, watching his wife's back, then meets his daughter's gaze. "We're discussing the Forrester matter," he says.

"What about it?" This time the question is directed at me, but the senator answers first. "We're talking about the investigation," he says. "That's all."

Abby folds her arms and smirks. "Investigation? Please. No need for an investigation. I know exactly what happened." She stares angrily at her father. "And so do you."

"Abigail," her mother snaps, "this isn't the time."

"Too much nose candy." Abby fires her words at me, ignoring her mother. "Too much white stuff up the nose."

Silence. For a moment, no one in the room seems to breathe.

Finally, the senator takes a deep breath and turns to me. "Michelle had a problem," he says, "a couple of years back. But she was past that. She'd put it behind her."

"Oh, right," Abby laughs, but it's not a happy one. She takes her juice from the counter and heads out of the kitchen. "Sure she did," she calls over her shoulder. "And she gave up *men* too. The word on the street is she was headed straight for the convent."

Honey scowls at her husband and follows her daughter toward the living room. She pauses, though, in the doorway, and turns back to me. "I'll be happy to abide by your instructions," she says. "As far as I'm concerned, the name Michelle Forrester need never be mentioned again."

Senator Kendrick plants his elbows on the table and buries his face in his hands as his wife leaves the kitchen. I set down my coffee mug, check my watch, and wait. I had two appointments scheduled for this morning. This was supposed to be the easy one.

DERRICK Holliston has had a change of heart, it seems. I'm only about twenty minutes late for our jailhouse meeting, but apparently he and Harry have already covered a lot of ground. "Maybe I won't, then," he says as the young guard with the crew cut pulls the meeting room door shut behind me. "Maybe I won't."

"Won't what?" I already know the answer, I think—his tone tells me more than his words—but I want to be sure.

"Testify," Holliston says as I join him and Harry at the rickety table. "Maybe I'll just keep my mouth shut."

I'm a little concerned about what led to this switch. I'm no fan of Holliston's, but like it or not, he *is* our client. If he wants to take the witness stand, it's not our job to talk him out of it. "Fill me in," I say as I turn toward Harry.

"We were just going over the police report," Harry says, tossing his pen on top of a dog-eared copy of it. "It's in there. The whole *story*." His emphasis on the last word says it all.

"So?" I ask. I'm pretty sure I know where this is going, though.

"So Tommy Fitzpatrick will say it for us," Harry answers. "The chief questioned Holliston personally, as soon as he was picked up, and recorded his version of events. My bet is Fitzpatrick will be the Commonwealth's first witness. He prepared the primary report, and he'll testify to its content. All of it."

Holliston not only waived his right to remain silent on the morning of his arrest, but he spilled his guts to anyone who'd listen. While that's generally not a good idea, it just might work to his advantage now. His story has been memorialized in painstaking detail by Tommy Fitzpatrick, Chatham's chief of police.

"So the jurors will hear what happened," Holliston explains, "but they don't hear nothin' about my priors."

His priors aren't pretty. If the prosecutor were to line them up side by side, in chronological order, the jury would see the perfect evolution of a sociopath, each crime more violent than its predecessor. The jury won't see anything of the sort, though, because the prosecutor can't do that—Holliston committed all but one of his crimes when he was under eighteen.

"Most of your priors won't come in anyhow," I remind him. "Your juvenile record is sealed."

"Yeah, but I got that assault." He sighs. "That'll come in. And it don't make me look good." He shakes his head slowly.

Holliston has one conviction on his adult tab. If he takes the stand in this trial, that conviction will come in. It's a given. And it's a problem.

Four years ago, the manager of one of Chatham's premier restaurants was assaulted and robbed. Bobby "the Butcher" Frazier, longtime caretaker of Kristen's Pub, was closing the place that February night. As he stood on the snowy brick walkway inserting his key to flip the back door's deadlock, a young white male wearing a ski mask emerged from the darkness and demanded the night-deposit sack Bobby had stashed under one arm.

The Butcher told the masked man to take a hike. A fistfight ensued and Bobby was stabbed during the course of it, the knife penetrating just below his right shoulder. Down but not out, he grabbed his attacker's hand—along with the knife inside it—and continued to fight. Eventually, though, the masked man kicked Bobby to the ground and fled with the cash.

The Butcher was lucky; his injuries weren't all that serious. He was treated at Cape Cod Hospital that night and released the next day. Because of his assailant's mask, he was unable to give the police a description beyond approximate height and weight. The Chatham cops suspected Derrick Holliston from the start—he'd been released from a juvenile detention facility just a few days earlier, on his eighteenth birthday—but they had precious little in the way of evidence to back up their suspicions. Until they got the results from the Commonwealth's crime lab.

DNA evidence pegged him. Holliston must have sustained a substantial cut during his struggle with the Butcher. Blood evidence tied him to the scene, to the victim, and eventually, to the empty cash sack retrieved from a Dumpster a block from the pub. On top of all that, the unemployed Holliston had more than two grand in cash when he was arrested at the Monomoy Moorings Motel.

The judge sentenced Holliston to five-to-seven, and with time off for good behavior, he served just over four. He'd been out little more than a month when Father McMahon was murdered.

"Yeah," Holliston says, pointing at Harry, "for once you're right. We'll let Fitzpatrick do it. I kinda like the idea of the police chief tellin' them what happened."

Harry closes his eyes, shakes his head.

Holliston half laughs. "So it's settled. I ain't takin' the stand."

Harry starts repacking his schoolbag. "Well," he says, "then we'll see you in the morning. If you're not taking the stand, there's no need to prepare you for cross."

Holliston smiles at Harry. "Right again," he says.

Harry ignores him, bangs on the door for the guard.

Holliston's still smiling as he leaves. "Go ahead," he says over his shoulder. "Take the rest of the day off. Both of you."

TAKING the rest of the day off isn't an option for either of us. Harry went straight back to the office to spend the rest of the day preparing for trial. I took the Mid-Cape Highway in the opposite direction, destination Stamford, Connecticut. For reasons I can't articulate, I want to meet the Forresters. Maybe I want to get some sense of Michelle through her family, to glean some idea of where she might have gone if the worst hasn't happened.

Michelle's mother was hesitant when I called from the road. After a few minutes of conversation, though, she relented. She muffled her phone, consulted with her husband in hushed tones, and then agreed they'd meet with me at their home this afternoon.

Traffic is light, and I find myself pulling into the Forresters' gravel driveway a little past three, less than four hours after leaving Barnstable. I park next to a blue Jaguar, shiny beneath a thin coat of fresh snow. I'm not the only visitor, it seems. I grab my briefcase and walk back toward the Forresters' front entrance.

Their colonial is large, with cream-colored clapboards and hunter green shutters. Dormant rosebushes ramble along the sides of the house and into the spacious backyard. An in-ground pool is sealed for the season, dead leaves scattered across its blue vinyl cover.

The front door is already open when I reach the steps leading to the porch. "Attorney Nickerson?" A woman in jeans and a black turtleneck hurries outside, not stopping for a coat.

"Marty," I tell her, extending my hand. She's about thirty, obviously not Michelle Forrester's mother. The sister, I realize after a moment.

"Meredith Forrester," she says as she shakes my hand. "Michelle's sister."

Her shoulder-length hair is jet black like Michelle's. Her complexion is flawless, and her pale blue eyes don't quite match; one's a little lighter than the other. "My mother called me at work after she spoke with you," she says. "She asked me to come over; both my parents wanted me to be here for your visit. I hope you don't mind."

"Not a bit," I assure her.

"I want to mention something to you," she says, folding her arms at her waist, "before we go inside."

"Meredith, you'll catch your death of pneumonia!" It's Michelle—thirty-five years from now. She's in the doorway, frantically waving at both of us, telling us to come in from the cold.

"This is my mother," Meredith says as we enter. "Catherine."

I shake Catherine's hand, then look back at her elder daughter. I want her to hold on to that *before we go inside* thought she wanted to mention. She nods at me; she will. She takes my parka when we enter the foyer and motions for me to follow her mother, who's already into the next room. "Warren," Catherine says, "Mrs. Nickerson is here. The lawyer who called earlier."

Warren is on his feet when I enter the living room, in front of a brown leather recliner, his cardigan unbuttoned and his pipe unlit. He turns my way, and I realize he's the source of Meredith's slightly mismatched eyes. His handshake is firm, his lined face exhausted.

"Call me Marty," I tell him.

"Marty it is," he says. His words are flat, without inflection. He points at a small sofa. "Please," he says, "have a seat."

"Can I get you anything?" Catherine asks. "A cup of tea?"

I shake my head as I settle on one end of the sofa, next to the crackling fire. "Thank you, but no," I tell her. "I'll only stay a few minutes; I won't take too much of your time."

Meredith crosses the room and sits beside me while her mother claims the chair next to Warren's, a smaller version of his.

"Catherine tried to explain," Warren says, "but I'm still not clear. What is your role in this . . . situation?"

"I represent Senator Kendrick," I tell him.

"Why?" he says.

Fair question. "Because the authorities have been talking with him. And anyone being interrogated in a serious investigation is well advised to be represented by counsel."

He nods, but the furrows in his forehead deepen. "We watched the senator's press conference yesterday," he says. "We appreciate everything he's doing. Tell him that for us, will you?"

A guilt spasm seizes my stomach. Just a few hours ago, I put the kibosh on any future press conferences; I don't mention that, though. "I will," I assure the weary Warren Forrester.

"That number," Catherine says, "that eight-hundred number

Senator Kendrick gave out, I think that's going to help; I think it will make a real difference. Someone is bound to call in."

She nods emphatically at each of us, dry-eyed. She means what she just said. Hope is a relentless emotion.

"Is it possible," I ask, "that Michelle felt overwhelmed by the pressures of her job and decided to escape for a while?"

No doubt they've been asked this question a hundred times. But I have to ask it too.

"No," Warren says. "That's not possible." Catherine shakes her head. Meredith does too.

"What about college friends?" I ask. "Might she have gone to stay with an old UVA buddy?"

All three shake their heads now. "My parents are sick with worry," Meredith says quietly. "Michelle would never do that to them. Never."

I change the subject. "Is there a boyfriend?"

Catherine shakes her head yet again and actually smiles a little. "Boys," she says. "Michelle always has plenty of boys around."

Warren nods, leans back in his chair, and closes his eyes.

"Most days the phone rarely rings," Catherine says. "But when Michelle's home, it doesn't stop."

"But no one in particular?" I ask. "No one steady?"

"No," Catherine says. "Not that we know of."

I stand, take two business cards from my jacket pocket, and hand one to Meredith, the other to her mother. "I won't keep you any longer. But please call if you think of anything—anything at all—we might have overlooked. Senator Kendrick will do everything he can to help."

Meredith gets to her feet as I say my good-byes to her parents. "I'll see you out," she says as she walks ahead of me.

Meredith is quiet as she hands me my parka and then dons her heavy black overcoat. We exit into the late-afternoon cold, and she pauses on the porch. "There is something else," she says. "I don't think it matters, really, but since you're the senator's attorney, I guess it's okay to mention it to you. Maybe you already know."

I stop one step below her and shrug, hoping to give the impression that I probably *do* already know. But I'm pretty sure I don't.

"My sister is in love with Charles Kendrick," she says, fingering her top button. "And I believe he loves her too."

This news isn't exactly a shock. Honey's performance this morning gave me a pretty good push in that direction.

"They had an affair," Meredith continues. "They started seeing each other—secretly—after she'd worked for him a couple of years. He ended it four months ago, when his wife found out."

I nod.

"Michelle was devastated," she says.

I nod again, thinking I need to have yet another heart-to-heart with my not-so-candid client.

"I know it sounds tawdry," Meredith says as she starts down the steps, "but it wasn't. I only saw them together a few times, but there was no denying they had genuine feelings for each other."

I study Meredith for a moment, wondering if she's angry with the senator for hurting her little sister. If she is, it doesn't show.

"Meredith." I stand in the middle of the snowy driveway. "I'd like to know if you've mentioned this to anyone else."

She looks down at her boots. "The district attorney."

"Geraldine."

She nods. "Honestly, I wasn't trying to cause trouble for him—politically or personally. But I couldn't *not* mention it. What if it turned out to matter somehow and I had kept quiet?"

She's not crying, but her eyes are filled to the brim. "You did the right thing," I tell her.

She shakes my hand, then heads back to the house.

It's barely four o'clock when I pull out of the Forresters' driveway. I toy with the idea of calling Senator Kendrick from the car to ask what other secrets he's keeping. I decide against that call, though. Some conversations should be had face-to-face.

THREE

Wednesday, December 15

JUDGE Richard Gould was elevated from the district court bench to superior court just over a year ago. It was a well-deserved promotion. A highly intelligent, serious man, he runs an efficient, on-schedule courtroom. Even so, any lawyer who's ever practiced before him knows that the rights of litigants—particularly those of criminal defendants—are his foremost concern. Derrick Holliston is lucky to have ended up on Judge Gould's docket.

The judge isn't here yet. Neither is Harry. Geraldine Schilling is, though, already set up at the prosecutors' table with her young assistant, Clarence Wexler. They're reviewing exhibits, leaning toward each other from time to time to whisper.

Two court officers bustle about behind us, seating sixty potential jurors in the old courtroom's small but stately gallery. From them, Geraldine and Harry will select fourteen, twelve of whom will decide Derrick Holliston's fate.

The side door opens, and a prison guard enters, heavy holster low on his hips. Our client follows and a second guard brings up the rear. The accused is free of hardware, wearing black slacks, a gray suit coat, and a white dress shirt, neatly pressed. I'm taken aback.

All criminal defendants are permitted to "clean up" for trial—get a haircut, a shave, a set of decent street clothes—but this particular defendant cleans up exceptionally well. His once-greasy brown hair has been recently introduced to shampoo. It's trimmed short and parted precisely. The sketchy mustache is gone. His near-constant sneer has been erased. He looks like the guy next door—if the guy next door happens to be an Eagle Scout.

A low murmur emanates from the crowded gallery as Holliston

approaches the defense table. He settles into the seat next to mine. "Get rid of the cat-licks," he says matter-of-factly.

It takes a moment for me to get it. "We don't know their religions," I tell him. "The jury questionnaire doesn't ask that."

He snorts and the familiar sneer resurfaces. "What?" he says, his voice low. "You don't know one when you see one?"

"I guess not."

He shakes his head at my incompetence. "That lady there"—he twists in his chair toward the benches behind us—"on the end, front row. She look like a cat-lick to you?"

"She looks Italian," I answer.

He faces front and plants both hands on the table, resting his case. "You ever knowed a guinea what *ain't* a cat-lick?"

I lean back against the worn leather of the high-backed chair and close my eyes. Some conversations aren't worth finishing.

Harry arrives and hoists his bulging schoolbag onto the defense table. "What's up?" he asks.

"We were discussing the finer points of jury selection," I tell him.

He glances sideways at me as he unpacks, then blinks twice when he takes in our client's new persona.

"So what's the plan here?" Holliston says from my other side. "You people got a plan or you just wingin' it?"

Harry laughs and tosses the pleadings file, a blank legal pad, and a few pens onto the table. He says nothing.

"Judge Gould likes to complete jury selection the first morning," I tell our client. "It'll be a late lunch break, though."

Holliston purses his lips; he seems not to approve of late lunches.

"After that," I continue, "the prosecuting attorney will deliver her opening statement. If there's time, Harry will deliver his before we wrap up for the day."

"And if there ain't time?"

I shrug. "Then he'll do it tomorrow morning. Either way, he'll open. Don't worry."

"Oh, I'm worried," Holliston says, staring up at Harry.

Harry doesn't let on that he hears. He walks away from us, delivers a short stack of documents to Geraldine, another to the court-room clerk. Judge Gould emerges from chambers as Harry returns to our table. Billy "Big Red" O'Reilly tells us to rise.

Judge Gould has already welcomed the sixty citizens seated in the gallery. He gestures to those of us seated at the tables. All four lawyers stand and face the back of the courtroom. After a signal from me, Holliston does too.

"Ladies and Gentlemen," the judge says, "before we get started, I'd like all of you to look at the lawyers and the defendant involved in this case. If you even think you might know any of them—no matter how remotely—please raise your hand."

Two go up.

"You, sir." The judge points to an elderly gentleman in the front row. "Which of them do you know?"

The older man stands, points his hat at Geraldine. "The district attorney," he says. "She's a neighbor."

"Thank you for telling us. You're dismissed with the sincere grat-itude of the court." The judge nods to the two officers standing against the back wall, and one hustles down the center aisle to usher the disqualified juror out of the courtroom.

The elderly gentleman looks surprised at first, then nods and du-tifully follows the uniform toward the back doors.

"And you, ma'am?" Judge Gould directs his question to a middle-aged woman six rows back. She points to Geraldine too. "I don't *really* know her," she says. "I've seen her on the news."

"You may be seated," Judge Gould says. He looks out at the whole panel. "We're not concerned at the moment about anything you might have seen or heard through the media. We want to know about personal contact, if any."

The woman sits down.

"Ladies and Gentlemen," the judge says, "I'm going to read a brief description of the case we're about to try. When I finish, I will ask each of you to consider whether anything you've heard will make it particularly difficult for you to be fair and impartial. I cau-tion you that nothing I say constitutes evidence. What I am about to read is merely a summary of the positions taken by each side."

It's far more than that. Every word a judge utters during a murder trial is taken to heart by jurors. They have a difficult job, to say the least; they look for guidance wherever they can.

"Last Christmas Eve," the judge reads, adjusting his dark-framed glasses, "Francis Patrick McMahon, a Roman Catholic priest assigned to St. Veronica's Parish in Chatham, was found dead on the floor of the chapel's sacristy. The collection money from the Christmas Vigil Mass was gone. The medical examiner determined that the deceased had suffered multiple puncture wounds, one of which proved fatal. The Commonwealth accuses the defendant of inflicting those wounds. It charges him with first-degree murder, committed with extreme atrocity or cruelty."

Judge Gould pauses for a sip of water.

"The accused, Derrick John Holliston, does not deny inflicting the fatal wound," the judge continues. "But he does dispute the allegation that his actions constitute murder. He maintains that his conduct was entirely lawful, that the deceased was the assailant. More specifically, the defendant maintains that the deceased became sexually aggressive and when he—the defendant—resisted, the deceased became violent. The defendant contends that he acted only as necessary to preserve his own life."

Judge Gould pauses again. "The Commonwealth disputes the defendant's self-defense claim. And the cash from the Christmas Vigil Mass collection has not been recovered."

The judge removes his glasses, sets them on the bench, and leans on his forearms. "I ask each of you to take a moment now," he says to the assembly, "and reflect. This will not be an easy case for anyone involved. The evidence from both sides will be graphic. It will be difficult to see and hear. But I ask each of you to alert us now if you believe you will have trouble being fair and impartial, listening to all of the testimony with an open mind."

We attorneys swivel our chairs so we can see the jurors seated behind us. For a moment, the silence remains undisturbed. But then a man in the center of the room gets to his feet and steps into the aisle. He looks to be about fifty, wearing blue jeans, a flannel shirt, and work boots. "I might have a problem with that," he says.

Two women follow his lead. The first moves into the aisle across from him. She's about my age, in a tailored, navy blue pantsuit and heels. "I may also," she says. The second woman is probably seventy. She stands, her silver hair stiff above the collar of a charcoal gray coatdress. She nods at the judge but says nothing, a silent *ditto*.

"Thank you," Judge Gould says to all of them. "Thank you for your candor. Now I ask the three of you to come forward."

Judge Gould questions each of the three individually in his chambers, with the lawyers present. After a prolonged discussion, he dismisses one of the potential jurors and passes the other two on to the next phase of jury selection.

DOTTIE Bearse has been Judge Gould's courtroom clerk since his district court days. When he made the move to superior court, he arranged for her to transfer as well. I've never heard the judge ask her for anything; she's always two steps ahead of him.

Dottie now stands behind her desk, holding what looks like a small fishbowl. She draws consecutive slips of paper from it, reading a name from each, and one by one, fourteen potential jurors file into the box. Harry takes three blank sheets of legal-size paper from his file and hands two of them to me. Holliston looks hostile when I pass one to him with a pen. "It gets hard to keep them all straight after a while," I explain to him. "You might want to jot down their names and seat numbers."

I turn away and face Dottie, who's delivering copies of the jurors' questionnaires to both tables. I divide my sheet into fourteen squares, each with a seat number, and fill in their names, ages, and occupations as the judge asks them all the boilerplate questions: Does anyone work for law enforcement or have a relative or close friend who does? Has anyone been the victim of a violent crime?

A couple of jurors are excused on the basis of their answers, and Dottie pulls two more slips from her fishbowl. Robert Eastman and Alex Doane, both in their midfifties and wearing suits, fill the vacant seats. Yes, they heard the questions asked of the others. No, neither of them has anything significant to report.

Judge Gould moves on to the legal standards jurors are expected to honor the presumption of innocence, the burden of proof, the unanimous verdict. He asks if any of them will have difficulty accepting those parameters. Not a single hand goes up this time. Every last one of them plans to play by the rules.

The judge keeps Geraldine and Harry on a short leash as they ask their follow-up questions. In the end, neither of them has a valid challenge for cause as far as I can see, but Geraldine announces she does. "Number eight, Your Honor, for cause."

Juror number eight is a twenty-seven-year-old lobsterman from Hyannis. He told us that his view of the Catholic Church in general is grim, the result of too many years spent in repressive parochial schools. He also said that view wouldn't affect his judgment in this case one whit. Geraldine doesn't have a leg to stand on here.

Judge Gould apparently thinks likewise. He smiles at her. "Not going to happen, Ms. Schilling."

She shakes her head and exercises the first of her three peremptory challenges. The lobsterman takes his leave, and his replacement answers all the preliminary questions. It's our turn now. "Mr. Madigan?" the judge says.

Harry leans forward on the table and arches his eyebrows at Holliston. It's routine to solicit opinions from criminal defendants during voir dire. Holliston takes the pen I gave him earlier, reaches over to my diagram of the jury box, and draws a big X through the Margaret Murphy square. She's a fourth-grade teacher, an ex-nun.

"Are you sure?" Harry asks.

Holliston draws another X on top of the first one.

Harry excuses Margaret Murphy, and she looks a little bit hurt as she leaves the box. Dottie pulls another slip from the fishbowl, and we repeat the litany with Ms. Murphy's replacement. Geraldine exercises her second peremptory, dismissing a middle-aged woman from Wellfleet who confessed to a lifelong belief that Catholicism, with all its martyrs and miracles, is nothing more than myth. A tall black man replaces her, a native of Haiti, according to his questionnaire.

Holliston stiffens at once. He grabs my diagram and draws an X through the newest candidate's box even before he sits down.

He pushes my diagram, with its new *X,* across the table toward Harry. Harry sighs and closes his eyes, but says nothing. He's not obligated to follow Holliston's instructions, of course. But most criminal defense lawyers honor their clients' wishes when it comes to jury selection.

Judge Gould walks through the preliminaries with the tall Haitian, and then Harry dismisses him. Just like that. Without a single follow-up question. The dismissed juror doesn't react at all, but the judge does. He sees what's going on here, and he's appalled, but there's not a damned thing he can do about it.

The ball is back in Geraldine's court. She stands but doesn't say anything, looking down at her own hand-drawn diagram of the jury box.

"Number two," she says at last. "The Commonwealth respectfully excuses juror number two."

I'm surprised. Juror number two is a sixty-year-old carpenter who told us he views the Catholic Church's insistence that its priests remain celibate as "abnormal." Otherwise, though, he has no feelings about the Church one way or the other. If I were in Geraldine's shoes—and I was for many years—I'd keep him. I wouldn't run the risk of ending up with someone more opinionated in his place.

The carpenter exits and Dottie pulls yet another slip from the dwindling supply in her glass bowl and seats the newest juror.

The judge runs through the preliminaries with the new juror and turns his attention to Harry.

"Mr. Madigan, anything further?"

Holliston takes his pen and reaches over to my diagram again. He draws an X through the number-one box and another through number seven—opposite ends of the front row—Anthony Laurino and Maria Marzetti. Maria is the woman Holliston identified as a *cat-lick* as soon as he arrived this morning.

"We don't get two more," I tell him. "We get one. Three total."

He looks at me, and his eyebrows fuse.

"Hold on," Harry tells both of us. "We've got a decent panel right now. Why take a chance on making it worse?"

Holliston takes his pen and darkens the X over juror number one. Anthony Laurino must go. I've no idea what rationale is at work here. But I do know our exercise of peremptories bears a frightening resemblance to ethnic cleansing.

Even so, Harry seems prepared to let our client call the shots. He shakes his head and leans close to me. "Are we forgetting anyone?" he whispers. "I'd hate like hell to leave a left-handed Latvian in the room." He stands and perfunctorily bounces Anthony Laurino.

Dottie draws another slip from the few left in her bowl, and the final juror is seated with little fuss.

FOR attorneys in the midst of trials, lunch breaks have little to do with food. Unless, of course, the attorney is Harry Madigan. We're at the Piccadilly Deli, waiting for his mega–meatball sub with extra mozzarella and a gallon of Tabasco. Harry downs a quart of chocolate milk. I sip my coffee and call the office.

The Kydd answers on the third ring. "Marty," he says as soon as he hears my voice, "this is nuts. We need a secretary."

He's right; we do. The three of us have been operating without administrative help for two years now. It's getting old.

"Well, why didn't you say so sooner, Kydd? I'll hire one today."

Harry opened our South Chatham office a couple of years ago, after spending two decades as a public defender. I joined him within weeks, having resigned from a ten-year stint with the district attorney's office six months earlier. We recruited Kevin Kydd right out from under Geraldine's nose.

"I'm not joking," he says. "I've spent the entire day talking to walk-ins and fielding phone calls. I'm getting zero done here."

I know how frustrated he is; I've been there. "Hang in there," I tell him. "We're hoping to bring an administrative person on board in the new year."

A deli worker delivers Harry's sub to our table, and Harry grabs a second quart of chocolate milk from the cooler. He takes an enormous bite of his foot-long feast while I jot down a list of the phone calls we've missed so far today.

"And the senator," the Kydd says. "He called just before you did."

"What did the good senator want?"

"He needs to see you. He's coming in this afternoon. Says it's important that he see you today."

"Did he say why?"

"Nope. Once he found out when you'd be back here, he seemed anxious to get off the phone. Wish they all felt that way," the Kydd adds. "Every other joker who calls this joint wants to tell me his life's story."

"Have you had lunch?"

Like Harry, the Kydd tends to get pretty cranky when he misses a meal. "Lunch?" he bellows. "I haven't had time to pour a second cup of coffee. How the hell would I have gotten lunch?"

"Order in," I tell him. "And put it on the tab. We'll see you in a few hours."

He's still complaining when I snap my cell phone shut.

Harry swallows the last of his sandwich, then dumps his trash in the bin. I stand to put on my coat, but his expression stops me.

"What?" I ask.

"We can't leave yet," he says.

He carries his empty tray to the counter, exchanges a few words with the clerk, and then hurries back to our table.

"Is there a reason?" I ask.

He leans down to whisper. "They have apple pie," he says. "And it's warm."

FOUR

"AN ICE pick," Geraldine says. She's seated at her table, next to Clarence Wexler, motionless. She was in that spot when the rest of us left for the break at two, and she was there when we got back an hour later. This isn't normal. Geraldine Schilling rarely sits; her metabolism doesn't allow it. Everyone involved in this case seems unusually troubled by it. Everyone except Derrick Holliston, that is.

The courtroom isn't filled to capacity, but it's close. Even so, there's not a sound in the room as we all wait for her to continue. "Our medical examiner will tell you that Father Francis Patrick McMahon was stabbed to death with an ice pick."

She wheels her chair back, away from the table, and stands. "Stabbed," she repeats. "Eight times."

Fourteen pairs of eyes remain fixed on her as she takes slow, deliberate steps toward the jury box. No one blinks.

"Three times in the left shoulder." She holds up one finger, then a second, then a third. "Twice in the right." She adds her little finger, then her thumb, and falls silent again.

Juror Maria Marzetti closes her eyes. Juror Cora Rowlands does too, then bites her lower lip. No one else moves.

"Twice in the upper abdomen," Geraldine says at last. She uses both hands now to continue the count. "And once . . ."

She leans on the rail of the jury box.

". . . directly into the aorta."

Most of them react. A few shake their heads; others cover their mouths. All but two look away from Geraldine as they absorb the information she's giving them.

"Dr. Ramsey will tell you that Father Francis Patrick McMahon bled to death in minutes. He was dead less than an hour when his body was discovered by his pastor."

Calvin Ramsey has been Barnstable County's medical examiner for a year and a half. His report nails Holliston—to the corpse, to the scene, and to the weapon—six ways from Sunday.

"Dr. Ramsey will also tell you that blood samples taken from the crime scene came from two sources."

Geraldine walks slowly across the room to our table. It's time to point.

"Most of it came from the deceased," she says. "But some, trace amounts, came from this man."

Holliston looks directly at her index finger as if he's staring down the barrel of a shotgun. And he is.

"He admits it," she says. "He admits stabbing the priest to death. But he wants you to say it's okay."

Harry shifts in his seat. She's inching toward improper territory; he's preparing to pounce.

"This man," she says, still pointing, "wants you to say Father Francis Patrick McMahon deserved it."

Harry explodes as he jumps to his feet. The gavel pounds the desk three times before he finishes the word *objection*.

The judge is on his feet too. "Attorney Schilling, you know better." He's not shouting, exactly, but he's close.

"Move for an instruction, Your Honor." Harry's shaking his head at the inadequacy of the remedy even as he asks for it. The damage is done. The words can't be unspoken.

"The jury will disregard the prosecutor's last comment," Judge Gould tells the panel, "in its entirety."

The judge sits again, his attention back to Geraldine. "One more remark like that, Counsel, and your opening statement is over."

"My apologies to the court, Your Honor."

Baloney. Her apologies are offered strictly to mollify the jury. "Move on," says Judge Gould, frowning at her.

"After Dr. Ramsey testifies," she says, "you'll hear from Chatham's chief of police, Thomas Fitzpatrick. He'll tell you it took a full week to assemble the forensic evidence necessary to file charges. Chief Fitzpatrick will tell you this defendant told his tall tale immediately—as soon as the police stormed his apartment. The chief will also tell you this defendant told no one about the alleged sexual assault until that time. Think about that."

She pauses so they can.

"Think about the fact that this defendant"—she points at Holliston yet again, from across the room—"claims he was sexually assaulted by Father McMahon, claims a physical altercation ensued, an altercation so serious he had no choice but to stab the older man in self-defense. Eight times, remember."

Every juror nods. They remember.

"And then he told no one. For a week." She turns to stare at Holliston. He gazes straight ahead. "He told no one until he was charged with murder. He told no one until he needed an excuse."

Harry gets to his feet.

Judge Gould holds up both hands, palms out; an objection isn't necessary. "Counsel," he says, "move on."

She looks up at him and smiles, but she doesn't answer. She turns to the panel instead. "And finally," she says, "you'll hear from Monsignor Dominic Davis, the pastor of St. Veronica's Parish."

Harry drops back into his chair.

Geraldine leans on the rail of the jury box. "Monsignor Davis will tell you that the defendant's claims are false. He'll tell you Father McMahon never assaulted anyone, sexually or otherwise, in his fifty-seven years of life. The pastor will tell you the deceased was a man of God, a man of principle, a man of peace."

She walks toward us. "Now I can't tell you," she says, "whether or not you will hear from this defendant. He's under no obligation to testify." She stops in front of our table, then does a U-turn and walks toward the jurors again. "But I can tell you this: You will hear his version of the events that transpired in St. Veronica's sacristy last Christmas Eve. You will hear it even if he doesn't take the witness stand—because it's what he told the police officers when he was arrested. His story is part of their report."

Geraldine Schilling is good at what she does.

"So, bear in mind, as you listen to the recitation of events as described by the defendant, that it's nothing more than that. His story. His belated attempt to justify a senseless, vicious murder."

With that, she nods up at the judge, fires a final glare in Holliston's direction, and reclaims her seat next to Clarence.

Judge Gould checks the pendulum clock hanging on the wall behind the jury box. "Ladies and Gentlemen," he says, "we'll hear from the defense now. After that, we'll adjourn for the day."

Harry stands, buttons his suit coat, and takes a halfhearted stab at straightening his tie. Holliston gets to his feet as well. I reach up and take hold of his jacket sleeve to tell him to stay put.

Holliston shakes my hand away and steps out from behind the table. Harry looks over at him, then down at me, and I shrug. I don't know what our client's up to. And then—in a millisecond—I do.

"Siddown, Madigan," he says as he struts toward the jury box. "You're fired."

GERALDINE paces around Judge Gould's chambers like a woman possessed. She stops short, faces the judge, and plants her hands on her narrow hips. "He can't do this," she says, exhaling so hard her blond bangs billow.

She knows better. He can. Derrick Holliston is entitled to represent himself if he so chooses. It's a constitutional guarantee. It's also a judicial headache. And a prosecutorial nightmare.

The newly pro se defendant helped himself to a seat as soon as we filed in here. Two guards keep watch on either side of him, standing just inches from his chair. Clarence, Harry, and I are lined up against the side wall. Even Judge Gould is on his feet, leaning against the bookcase behind his desk. "Mr. Holliston," he says, his tone grave, "I urge you to reconsider."

Holliston snorts. "That's what I did," he says. "I reconsidered. I want the job done right. So I'm gonna do it myself."

"Taking this step will dramatically increase the likelihood of conviction," the judge tells him. "And if you are convicted of first-degree murder, you'll spend the rest of your earthly days behind bars. I'm sure your lawyers have explained that to you."

Holliston wags a finger at Judge Gould. "My *used-to-be* lawyers explained that to me. And I don't like the idea of spending the rest of my *earthly days* behind bars. That's why I'm my lawyer now."

The judge sighs and turns to Harry.

Harry shrugs and looks up at the ceiling. "He's a big boy. He's made his decision. Let him live with it."

Not exactly what the judge was hoping to hear.

"Mr. Holliston, you don't have a clue." Geraldine pivots in her spike heels to face him. "Don't think we're going to handle you with kid gloves. You'll be held to the same standards every *real* lawyer is held to in that courtroom."

Holliston yawns. He's unimpressed.

Judge Gould pulls his chair out from the desk and sits. "Look," he says to Holliston, "we can't stop you. If you're determined to represent yourself, you have an absolute right to do it."

Our ex-client almost smiles. At last, an acknowledgment of his vast power. "That's right," he says, looking pleased that the judge finally figured it out. "So let's get on with it."

The judge checks his watch. "Not so fast. It's late," he says. "I'm going to dismiss the jurors for the day. If you're still sure of your decision in the morning, sir, you may deliver your opening statement then."

Holliston looks like he wants to argue, but Judge Gould doesn't give him a chance. "Mr. Madigan, Ms. Nickerson," he says as he stands, "I want you in the courtroom throughout trial."

The judge continues talking as he heads for the door. "I want you waiting in the wings," he says, "ready to jump back on board if the defendant changes his mind."

He reaches for the doorknob, then stops. "And Mr. Holliston," he says, turning to face him.

Holliston stares back at him, signature sneer in place.

"I sincerely hope you will."

HARRY and I pull into our newly plowed office driveway at five. Charles Kendrick is already here. The senator's enormous gray

Humvee is parked next to my tired Thunderbird. Harry cuts the Jeep's engine and jumps out, eager to play GI Joe with our senior senator's tank.

He strolls around in the falling snow, peering through the Hummer's windows and whistling. "Damn," he says, running his gloved hand along the hood. "I could *live* in this thing."

"No, you couldn't," I correct him as I head for the old farmhouse. "The rent would kill you."

The Kydd is seated behind the antique pine table in the front office, just hanging up the telephone. He points to the ceiling with his coffee mug as soon as I close the door and then scrawls on a yellow legal pad: *nervous breakdown in progress.* Senator Kendrick is upstairs in my office, and apparently he's not doing well. I head for the wrought-iron spiral staircase. Harry hasn't come inside yet. He's still hovering around the Hummer, mentally moving in.

Senator Kendrick is standing, gazing out the double-hung rear windows, taking in the view behind our farmhouse-turned-office-building. He wheels around when I reach the top step and shoves both hands deep into his pants pockets. "Marty," he says, his tone suggesting he's been waiting all day, "you're here."

I gesture toward the couch against the far wall and he takes a seat on one end of it. I slide my briefcase onto the desk and join him. He leans forward when I sit, elbows on his knees, head lowered.

"What's wrong?" I ask. "What's happened?"

"There are things I haven't told you," he continues. "And I should."

"And you just realized this today?" I'm pretty sure I know what he's decided to tell me, of course, but I don't let on.

"Yes," he says. "I'm sorry. I should have leveled with you."

He pauses again. And again I wait.

"About Michelle Forrester." His eyes meet mine for the first time today, then dart to my empty desk chair.

"We had an affair," he says quietly, reexamining the rug.

I nod and wait for him to continue.

"It went on for about a year. And then my wife found out."

"How?"

He shakes his head and sighs. "She and Abby went to San Francisco to spend a week with my in-laws. Michelle stayed with me in Boston for part of that time."

"In Boston?"

"I keep an apartment there," he says. "I'm in the city a lot for political events and fund-raisers. Sometimes I'm just too damned tired to drive home afterward."

That makes sense. But taking Michelle Forrester there sure as hell didn't. I raise my eyebrows at him.

"I know," he says. "It was stupid. But remember, we couldn't go to a hotel. Or even a restaurant."

He's right, of course. They would have been on the front page of every rag in the nation if they had.

"In any event," he says, "Honey had a tiff with her mother, cut the visit short by a couple of days. She and Abby flew into Logan late one night and decided to stay at the apartment." He looks up at me and shakes his head. "It was ugly," he mutters.

"How long ago?"

He leans back against the couch, stretches his long legs, and faces me. "Four months. Just before Abby went back to school."

"What happened?" I ask.

He half laughs. "What didn't happen? Tears. Threats. Tantrums. And not just Honey. Abby too."

"But your wife didn't leave you."

"No," he says. "I begged her not to. I swore I'd end it with Michelle. And I did. That day."

"Okay." I stand and cross the room, then take the chair behind my desk. "This is going to come out. Law enforcement will analyze every detail of Michelle Forrester's existence with a fine-tooth comb before this is over. Sooner or later, they'll get to you."

It's his turn to stand now. He walks toward the two upholstered wing chairs facing my desk and leans on the back of one. "Sooner," he says. "They'll get to me sooner, not later."

"There's more."

He nods. "We were together Thursday night," he says. "The night before she disappeared."

Sometimes I think no client can say anything to surprise me anymore. Other times, I know better.

"It wasn't planned," he continues. "She stopped by the Old Harbor Road house after she finished at Four Cs."

"Four Cs" is local parlance for Cape Cod Community College—the last place Michelle Forrester was seen.

"Hold it." I raise my hands to stop him. "She was in Hyannis. She was due in Connecticut the next morning. Are you telling me she drove a half hour in the wrong direction for an impromptu visit?"

He nods again, a faint smile on his face. "That's exactly what I'm telling you. She knew I'd be at the house alone. She showed up at about seven. She was quite pleased with the way the press conference had gone. Michelle wanted to talk about it."

He shrugs, as if the rest was inevitable.

"What time did she leave?"

"Before six," he says, "the next morning."

"In the dark."

"That's right." He meets my gaze now. "We have a neighbor—in the bungalow behind our place. She's a year-rounder."

Let's hope she's a blind year-rounder.

"Michelle and I had spent time at the Chatham house before," he says. "She always parked in the garage, left before daybreak, kept her headlights off until she reached the main road."

Senator Kendrick straightens, walks around the chair he's been leaning on, and drops into it. "I'm sorry," he repeats. "I know I should have told you sooner."

His eyes meet mine when I look up, and the emotion in them is genuine. He's beyond worried; he's terrified. "I just didn't think anything bad had happened to her," he says. "But now I'm afraid I was wrong."

THE neighbor isn't blind, as it turns out. She's deaf. Helene Wilson greets me at her kitchen door with a broad smile, a notepad, and a pen. When I start to explain my uninvited appearance on her doorstep, she shakes her head at me. "I'm deaf," she says, handing the pen and paper to me. "You'll have to use this."

I write my name, then a short message explaining my role as her neighbor's attorney. She invites me inside at once, and the clarity of her speech takes me by surprise.

"My deafness," she says, as if reading my mind, "is relatively new. Until a few years ago, my hearing was perfect."

What happened? I write on the notepad.

She takes my parka and hangs it on a hook to the side of the door. "I'm what's known as a late-deafened adult," she says. "There are more of us around than most people realize."

This is news to me. Again, she seems to read my mind.

"The Association of Late-Deafened Adults has fifteen chapters throughout the United States. All the members are like me: folks born into the hearing world, enjoying the pleasures sound brings to life—music, laughter, rainfall—and then it all starts to fade. Then—poof!—one day sound is gone. Completely."

She delivers her history without a shred of self-pity. A fiftysomething, blue-eyed blonde who's probably five feet on her tiptoes, she's got *hot ticket* written all over her. She leads the way through a galley kitchen and into a softly lit living room.

The living room is richly decorated in a colorful Southwestern motif, warmed by a crackling fire. A pair of eyeglasses sits on top of an open hardback book on the coffee table. "Can I get you anything?" Helene gestures toward a wet bar at the other end of the room.

I shake my head. It's late; I want to get home. *I won't stay long,* I write on the notepad. *Thanks for seeing me.*

The sofa is upholstered in a soft, taupe corduroy. Helene joins me on it, her eyes curious. "What can I do for you?" she says.

I hesitate for a moment. *I'm looking into the disappearance of Michelle Forrester,* I write at last.

Her bright expression darkens as she reads. "A terrible thing," she says, shaking her head. "Her people must be worried sick."

I nod.

"If I can help," she adds, "I certainly will."

Time to face the music. *When was the last time you saw her?* I scrawl.

"Michelle was here last Thursday night," she says at last. "Next door."

There it is. *Did you see her arrive?* I write.

"Not exactly," she says.

I arch my eyebrows.

"She got here around seven," Helene continues. "I remember because I'd just finished watching the news, and Michelle had been on it." Helene points toward a corner cupboard that houses a modest TV. "Closed captioning," she adds, smiling.

She's two steps ahead of me. *Not exactly,* I write. *You didn't exactly see her arrive. What do you mean?*

She shrugs. "It was dark," she says, "so I didn't see Michelle pull in. But her car passed in front of my house." She points over her shoulder, out the window behind us.

I'm still for a moment, and Helene seems to sense my questions. "Michelle's car has been here before," she says, "many times. She always keeps her headlights off, but I know when she comes and goes. She drives a sporty, foreign number. I know the feel of it. The senator pulled in at around five-thirty that afternoon. Michelle arrived just after seven."

My pen is paralyzed. It won't take much longer for the Chatham cops to unearth this information. Once they do, they'll take it straight to Geraldine.

"She left early the next morning," Helene adds. "And I saw her little hot rod that time. She left a bit later than she normally does. It was starting to get light already."

A wave of relief washes over me. My client faces an outraged wife and a political scandal. But this last piece of information should ultimately shield him from our district attorney, at least. I pull a business card from my wallet and hand it to her. *If you think of anything else,* I write.

She puts a hand on my forearm to stop me. "I'll call you," she finishes for me. "And I mean it," she says, tucking my card into her pocket. "I will. I'm not the least bit afraid to get involved."

I don't doubt that for a minute. Something tells me Helene Wil son isn't afraid of much.

FIVE

Thursday, December 16

BIG RED hustles out the side door as soon as Judge Gould's eyes give him the go-ahead. Derrick Holliston has made up his mind. He'll represent himself. He's every bit as determined this morning as he was in chambers yesterday.

"Mr. Holliston," the judge says as the door clicks shut behind the bailiff, "you're absolutely certain about this?"

At least Holliston has the good sense to stand as he replies. "Hell, yeah," he says. Geraldine groans.

My bet is that's the first of many groans we'll hear from Geraldine Schilling during the next couple of days. No prosecutor wants to take on a pro se defendant; it's a lose-lose proposition. If she hammers on Holliston for every mistake he makes, the jurors will think she's a bully. If she doesn't, he'll muddy the record—and the jurors' minds—with all sorts of information that doesn't belong there.

Harry and I pack up and move to the bar, where the half-dozen chairs reserved for attorneys are empty. They're the only seats in the house that are. Every row in the gallery is packed.

Holliston stands, wheels the two chairs Harry and I had been using away from the defense table, and parks them against the wall. He centers his own chair and settles into it. He's sculpting a scene for the jurors, one with a message: The world is against him. And he's all alone.

"Crazy like a fox," Harry whispers.

Big Red returns, the jurors single file behind him. Most look surprised as they take in the sea of spectators. I twist in my chair to absorb the scene with them, and I spot dozens of familiar faces. The front benches are peppered with press. The whole room is sprinkled with Chatham residents. And dead center in the front row sits Bobby "the Butcher" Frazier.

The Butcher's straight black hair is slicked back, and the top half of his white dress shirt is unbuttoned, the collar spread wide. He wears no undershirt, despite the December cold. And there's a reason, I realize after a moment. A few inches of his scar are visible, below the right shoulder, bisected by a solitary gold chain. My eyes move to his, and he meets them with a steady gaze. The Butcher would like to be a part of this trial. He'd like to be Exhibit A.

Judge Gould bids the jurors good morning, and they all return the greeting. Most look more relaxed today than they did yesterday, their surroundings not quite so foreign now.

"Ladies and Gentlemen," Judge Gould says, leaning forward on the bench, "there's been a change in plans. The defendant has chosen to represent himself," the judge continues, "and he's entitled to do so. You're to draw no inference from his decision, entertain no speculation about it."

All of them look at Holliston now, then at us. No doubt they're wondering why Harry and I are still in the courtroom.

"At this time, Ladies and Gentlemen"—Judge Gould takes his glasses off and leans back in his tall, leather chair—"the defendant will deliver his opening statement."

Holliston stands and runs both hands down the front of his suit coat, then starts toward the jury box. I can't see his face from where we're sitting, but the jurors' expressions tell me he's making eye contact with them, one by one, as he crosses the room. He stops a couple of feet from the box and clasps his hands behind his back. "I was lookin' for work," he says.

"Here we go." Geraldine's up and headed for the bench.

The judge pounds his gavel. "Mr. Holliston," he says, beckoning with one hand, "approach."

The room grows noisy while the three of them huddle at the side of the bench farthest from the jury. No doubt the judge is instructing Derrick Holliston on the ABCs of opening statements; teaching him that the word *I* doesn't belong in the room right now; informing him that the only way he gets to tell the jurors he was looking for work is by taking the witness stand. They've already heard that particular tidbit, though. It can't be taken back.

Harry clears his throat and leans close to me. "This little development is going to wreak havoc with the game plan," he says.

He's right, of course. The game plan calls for two days of witness testimony, less if the defendant doesn't testify. At that point, the jurors will be sequestered until they return their verdict. Though no one can predict how long deliberations will take in any case, Judge Gould fully anticipated sending them all home in plenty of time for Christmas. That's open to question now.

"What do you think?" I ask Harry. "New Year's Eve?"

He shakes his head, his hazel eyes on Holliston's back. "Nope. I'm thinking little pink hearts."

The judge wraps up his instructions and directs the defendant back toward the jury box.

Geraldine shakes her blond bangs as she returns to her table and takes her seat next to Clarence. She's disgusted.

Harry pulls a yellow legal pad from his schoolbag and draws three hearts on it, an elaborate arrow piercing each one.

"It's like the boss lady said," Holliston tells the panel, pointing back at Geraldine. "You'll hear it from the cop."

Geraldine turns and looks at Harry and me, then rolls her green eyes to the ceiling.

"Not just any cop," Holliston continues. "The top dawg. He'll tell you what went down that night. He'll tell you all about it."

Geraldine stands, anticipating the pretend lawyer's next transgression. Judge Gould fires a silent warning at her. Holliston hasn't crossed the line this time. Not yet, anyhow.

"He'll tell you that priest hit on me."

So much for not crossing the line.

"He'll tell them no such thing!" Geraldine's chair topples backward. She's halfway to the bench, both hands in the air.

The gavel descends.

Harry draws a line through his artwork. "Faith and begorra," he says. His brogue is atrocious. "We'd best push our finish date back a wee bit." He replaces each heart with a shamrock.

"Move for an instruction, Your Honor." Geraldine is livid. She'll get her instruction, but Judge Gould waves Holliston over for another sidebar tutorial first.

The judge stands, moves to the far side of his bench again, and delivers another lecture. He points his index finger at Holliston's chest repeatedly as he reiterates the ground rules. Holliston is entirely unruffled; he seems to think his opening statement is proceeding quite smoothly.

"Ladies and Gentlemen," Judge Gould intones, "you will disregard Mr. Holliston's last comment."

They nod in unison.

"Mr. Holliston"—the judge sighs—"you may proceed."

Holliston moves closer to the box. "Okay, now," he says, "like I was sayin', the top cop is gonna tell you what I told him. He's gonna tell you five things."

He raises his hand and holds up one finger, à la Geraldine. "First," he says, "that priest hit on me. And I mean big-time."

"Mr. Holliston," the judge warns.

"So I say to him, I say, you know, I ain't that way." Holliston holds up his other hand and flutters it.

Geraldine drops her head back against her chair and stares at the ceiling.

"Mr. Holliston," Judge Gould repeats, his tone menacing now.

"But the priest don't like that," Holliston says. "He ain't takin' no for an answer. He starts gettin' rough, *real* rough."

Judge Gould looks skyward, praying for patience.

Holliston stares at his solitary raised finger as if he'd forgotten it was there. "Okay," Holliston says, adding two more, "so that's three. He hits on me; I say no way; he goes wacko. So then I defend myself. I mean, what guy in his right mind ain't gonna defend himself against *that,* right?"

I can think of dozens of adjectives to describe Derrick Holliston. *Right-minded* isn't one of them.

Geraldine flings both arms in the air.

"Mr. Holliston," the judge says yet again.

Holliston doesn't even turn around for the judge's latest admonition. "Okay," he says to the jurors, "the cop is gonna tell you I *told* him I was defendin' myself. And he's gonna tell you I grabbed for somethin' to fight the guy off with. Turns out it was some kinda pick, a long, pointy thing."

"Your Honor." Geraldine's up again.

"What?" Holliston asks her. "I told the cop that. He had his tape recorder goin'. Plus he wrote it down. I watched him."

Judge Gould bangs his gavel. "You'll direct your comments to the court, sir. No one else."

Holliston looks up at the bench and shrugs.

The judge takes a deep breath and exhales slowly. "Move on, sir," he says.

"So listen to that cop," Holliston tells them. "You don't need to listen to nobody else, as far as I'm concerned. Nobody else got anything to say that matters."

I expect Geraldine to jump up again—Holliston's way out of line—but she doesn't. Instead, she leans back in her chair and crosses her lean legs. She's relaxed. I'm confused.

"Uh-oh," Harry says, and my confusion evaporates. He's right. Geraldine is happy with these particular inappropriate comments. We'll probably hear them again—next time from her.

"I FIGURE this guy can take it from here," Holliston says, jerking his neatly groomed head back toward Harry.

We're in chambers, once again listening to the defendant dictate the procedural details of his murder trial. He's reversed his position, decided he wants representation after all. He announced his change of heart as soon as Geraldine called her first witness. Judge Gould immediately declared a recess, excused the jurors, and ordered the attorneys—even the faux attorney—into chambers.

The judge isn't happy. "Mr. Holliston," he says, "this isn't a game."

"You got that right." Once again, Derrick Holliston is the only person in the room who's seated. He's slouched in one of the two chairs facing the judge's desk, a slight smile on his face.

Geraldine's been pacing since we came in here, but she stops short in front of Holliston now and glares down at him, her green eyes aglow. "You're not going to take the stand, are you?"

Harry's between the two of them before I realize he's moved from his spot against the wall beside me. "Whoa, sister," he says, his open palm almost touching Holliston's face. "You don't get that information now."

Massachusetts attorneys adhere to an archaic tradition of referring to each other as "Brother Counsel" or "Sister Counsel." Even so, Harry makes Geraldine crazy when he calls her plain old "sister." He also makes her crazy when he's right. And he's right now. She doesn't get that information yet. A criminal defendant can decide to testify—or not—at any time before the defense rests.

She wheels around to face the judge, her eyes on fire now. "Do you see what's going on here?"

He does. We all do. Holliston has *already* testified. He told the jurors his story without taking the stand—without submitting to an oath, without facing cross-examination, and without risking the admission of his prior attack on the Butcher. Harry was right. Crazy like a fox.

Judge Gould nods at Geraldine and tosses his glasses on the desk. "Mr. Holliston," he says, "how many times do you intend to change your mind on this issue during the course of trial?"

Holliston takes a few moments to mull it over. "Prob'ly not again," he says. He looks over at Harry and sneers. "The rest of this shouldn't be that hard, so I think he'll be okay from here."

The judge looks at Harry. "You're ready, Mr. Madigan?"

Harry nods.

Judge Gould sighs and looks around the room at all of us as he retrieves his glasses and heads for the door. "All right, then," he says. "Let's get on with it."

The judge exits chambers first, and Big Red calls the courtroom to its collective feet. Holliston and his escorts follow, Geraldine and Clarence close behind. Geraldine pauses and turns back to Harry, frowning. "I hope I don't live long enough to have to say these words again," she tells him, "but I'm damn glad you're back on board."

SIX

CALVIN Ramsey is all business; he always is. His direct testimony went by the book. Ivy League educational background, stellar employment history, and impressive professional affiliations filled the first twenty minutes or so. Details of his current responsibilities as Barnstable County's medical examiner took the next fifteen. Testimony specific to this case filled a solid hour.

The doctor's direct testimony included the introduction of five black-and-white photographs, all taken during the autopsy he performed almost a year ago, on the day after Christmas. Each shows a puncture wound, or a combination of puncture wounds, on Francis Patrick McMahon's body. Most of the jurors looked disturbed as the graphic images circulated among them.

Under Geraldine's careful questioning, Dr. Ramsey tied Derrick Holliston to the dead man in no uncertain terms. Prints, hair follicles—even fibers from Holliston's jacket and jeans—all combine to leave little doubt as to who paid an unexpected visit to St. Veronica's sacristy last Christmas Eve.

The medical examiner's direct ended with the crux of the matter: The deceased sustained eight puncture wounds in all. Five would have been non-life-threatening, had they been treated in time. The abdominal wounds—even if medically attended promptly—may or may not have proved fatal. It remains an open question. The aortal puncture, of course, is anything but. It cinched the priest's fate instantly. "The entry wound is tiny," Calvin Ramsey told the attentive jurors, "but that one was fatal. Father McMahon expired within minutes of this puncture being inflicted."

Now it's Harry's turn. He scoops all five photographs from the jury box railing and returns them to Geraldine's table, facedown, before he speaks. "Dr. Ramsey," he says as he walks toward the witness box, "you're aware, are you not, sir, that Mr. Holliston admits stabbing the deceased?"

"Yes."

"Yet you went to great lengths here today to prove it."

Dr. Ramsey actually smiles at Harry. "I answer the questions, Mr. Madigan. I don't choose them."

Touché. Harry's not surprised by the doctor's response; he knew it was coming. But he's got precious little to work with in this case. He needs to raise every issue he can so he'll have some material he can weave into a credible closing argument. "Were any of the deceased's wounds inflicted from behind?" he says at last.

The witness tilts his head to one side. "From behind? No, certainly not. The puncture wounds are all on the front of the body."

Harry nods repeatedly, as if this fact is particularly meaningful. "Mr. Holliston and the deceased were face-to-face, then," he says, "when the altercation occurred. Is that correct, Doctor?"

"I would assume so," the witness answers. He loosens his tie, looking uncomfortable. Maybe it's the word *altercation*.

Harry walks back toward our table, his eyes on the floor. At this point, he has enough to argue in closing that the Commonwealth's theory of the case doesn't make any sense, that a face-to-face confrontation is far more consistent with Holliston's version of events. He turns back to face the witness when he reaches our table. "Thank you, Dr. Ramsey," he says. "Nothing further."

Judge Gould tells the doctor he's free to go. Geraldine's on her feet, in front of the bench, looking anxious to call her next witness.

Judge Gould looks down at our eager district attorney and then checks the pendulum clock. It's one-fifteen. He announces the midday break almost apologetically; he knows Geraldine would rather steamroll ahead. She returns to her table, shaking her head.

The judge instructs the jurors not to discuss the case until they begin formal deliberations. He tells the lawyers to be back and ready to roll no later than two-thirty. When he stands, we all follow suit and watch as he disappears into chambers.

Big Red leads the jurors out the side door. As soon as it shuts behind them, one of the prison guards slaps the hardware on Holliston and points him toward lockup. Holliston looks over his shoulder and sneers at us as he leaves. "You heard the man," he says to Harry. "Make sure you get back here on time. Two-thirty sharp."

Harry doesn't even look in Holliston's direction. We grab our coats and head for the side exit without a word. It's Piccadilly Deli time again, but Harry promised we'd make it quick today. Chatham's chief of police is Geraldine's next witness. He's mine to cross. And—Holliston's high hopes notwithstanding—my gut says the chief will be our biggest problem.

THE Kydd isn't answering the phones—not the office line and not his cell. I'm listening to the Kydd's personal recording, telling me in Southern-speak to wait for the beep before leaving my message on his cell phone. I obey, ask him to call me as soon as he can, and then give up and join Harry at our usual table near the front windows.

"Where the hell is he?" I don't expect Harry to know; I'm just thinking out loud.

"Maybe he's doing what we're doing," Harry suggests after he swallows. He toasts me with his chocolate milk. "Lunch."

I shake my head; that explanation doesn't fit. Much as he hates his "secretarial duties," as he calls them, the Kydd takes his office obligations seriously. If he's not there, something important has called him away. My stomach churns as my brain replays yesterday's confession from Senator Kendrick. *They'll get to me sooner, not later. . . . I just didn't think anything bad had happened to her. But now I'm afraid I was wrong.*

"Besides," Harry continues, finishing off the first half of his foot-long sub, "the Kydd's about had it with telephones. And who the hell can blame him?"

"I don't think so," I tell him. "I don't think the Kydd would leave the office and shut down his cell just because he's sick of taking calls. Something's up."

Harry shrugs. "If so, the Kydd will handle it. And if he can't, he'll call. He's got a good head on his shoulders."

That's true. Still, I find the Kydd's absence unsettling.

"You're worried about Chuck, aren't you?" Harry asks. I filled him in on Charles Kendrick's most recent revelations on the way to the courthouse this morning.

"You bet I am," I answer. "*Chuck* needs serious damage control. Even the best-case scenario leaves him in a world of hurt."

We're quiet while Harry polishes off the second half of his mid-day meal, and I'm relieved when the last of it disappears. I'm anxious to get back. I want to collect my thoughts before I face Chatham's chief of police, a credible witness if ever there was one.

I drain my coffee cup and reach for my coat, but the look on Harry's face stops me short. His hazel eyes focus on something over my shoulder. He nods emphatically.

"Pecan," he explains. He has no choice; he's powerless in the face of the mighty pecan.

I check my watch and head to the coffee station for another half cup, telling myself to chill. We have plenty of time, really; it's two-ten, and the deli is just a stone's throw from the courthouse. My cell phone sings as I reach for the pot.

I pour quickly, then pull the phone from my jacket pocket and breathe a sigh of relief when the incoming number lights up. "Kydd," I answer, "you had us worried."

"Marty," he says, "where are you?"

I laugh as I head back to the table with my refill. "Funny, I was about to ask you the same question. At the Piccadilly. Where else would we be in the middle of a trial day? And where the hell are you? I've been trying to reach you for almost an hour."

"Listen," he says. "I need to make this quick. The reception here is iffy. I'm too close to the water."

"Where the hell are you?" I repeat. "It's fifteen degrees outside, for God's sake. Hell of a day to take a stroll on the beach."

"I'm not *strolling,*" he says. "Trust me on that." He takes a deep breath, and I wait. "I came here to meet a team from the ME's office," he says. "Smithy Stewart gave me a heads-up."

I set my cup down and then freeze beside our table, unable to sit. Smithy Stewart has been Chatham's harbormaster for decades. He doesn't ordinarily deal with the folks from the ME's office.

"I called as soon as I could," the Kydd says. "They just left."

Not only am I able to sit now, but I need to. "With a corpse," I say as I drop into the chair across from Harry.

"That's right," the Kydd says. "Smithy spotted it during routine patrol this morning. In Pleasant Bay, floating toward shore with the incoming tide."

"Kydd," I ask for the third time, "where the hell are you?"

"Smithy brought the body to the nearest town landing," he says. "We all met him here. At Cow Yard."

Cow Yard. Off Old Harbor Road. A quarter mile from the Kendrick estate.

I force myself to breathe. "And?" I ask the Kydd. I'm pretty sure I know what's coming, though.

The Kydd takes a deep breath. "Caucasian female," he says. "Between twenty and thirty. Shoulder-length hair. Black."

I press against the high-backed chair and close my eyes, my mind unwillingly traveling to the Forresters' wraparound porch in Stamford. I try hard not to imagine the knock on the front door that will rouse first Catherine, and then Warren, from their well-worn family-room chairs. I try even harder not to picture their faces as they struggle to comprehend the hushed words delivered by some unlucky Connecticut cop.

The line is suddenly clear. "Marty," the Kydd says.

"I'm here," I tell him.

"Smithy recognized her from the news," he says. "It's Michelle."

TOMMY Fitzpatrick is a cop's cop. Tall and broad-shouldered, with a full head of strawberry blond hair going pale as he ages, he's a commanding presence in any room. The courtroom is no exception. He's in full dress blues, entirely at ease in the witness box, his hat resting on the railing, his written report in his lap. He speaks directly to the jurors as he answers Geraldine's questions, as if he's known each member all his life. He's been Chatham's chief for one decade, he tells them, on the force just shy of three. He'll mark his thirtieth anniversary in June, and he'll retire at the end of that month.

Geraldine half-sits on the edge of her table, digging a spike heel into its leg, while the chief chats comfortably with the jurors. She's trying to be patient, doing her best not to rush the preliminaries. She wants these jurors to like Tommy Fitzpatrick, after all, to trust him. He's a critical prosecution witness.

The chief pauses for a sip of water, and Geraldine bolts from her table as if fired from a cannon. She carries two small stacks of eight-by-ten glossies to the witness box and sets them on the railing. Harry pulls our copies—a half dozen in all—from his schoolbag. They're shots taken by the crime-scene photographer in St. Veronica's sacristy last Christmas Eve. Unlike the autopsy photos introduced this morning, these are in vivid color.

Harry spreads our copies across the table so we can follow along as Geraldine recites the necessary litany for each. "Were you present when this photograph was taken?" she asks the chief. "Does it accurately depict St. Veronica's sacristy as it appeared on the night in question?"

The chief delivers the requisite number of affirmatives for each glossy, and Geraldine moves the court for permission to "publish" the first. She wants to give it to the jurors, tell them to pass it around. Judge Gould nods his assent, and Geraldine hands the first glossy to Juror Gregory Harmon. He doesn't flinch when he takes it, but Cora Rowlands does. She looks sideways over his shoulder, erect in her chair, both hands pressed to her mouth.

Cora Rowlands's eyes fill immediately. I feel a twinge of sympathy for her. At times, our system demands extraordinary efforts from ordinary citizens. This is one of them.

Geraldine takes a glossy from the second stack—a duplicate of the one being circulated in the jury box—hands it to the chief, and asks him to identify it.

"This is the sacristy as we found it," he says, "when we first arrived on the scene, before anything was touched."

Harry pulls our copy to the edge of the table. Francis Patrick McMahon is sprawled on the gray slate floor, his black cassock twisted and soaked in a sea of blood. His head is pointed toward a corner of the room, and his eyes are open. His face, though uncut, bears half a dozen maroon blood blotches.

Geraldine asks Tommy Fitzpatrick to walk the jurors through each of the remaining photos, and she publishes each one to the panel as he does. The next four are close-ups of Father McMahon's wounds, most notably the fatal puncture to the aorta.

Harry pulls each of our copies forward on the table as the chief explains it, making a neat stack near the edge. We study each one as the chief testifies, then scan the members of the panel for their reactions. Holliston folds his arms and turns away from us, looking like he doesn't want to stick around for much more of this.

The last shot, number six, is different from the others. It's a photograph of an empty wicker basket, sitting on the sacristy's tidy counter.

"And finally," Geraldine says to the chief, "would you explain to the jurors the significance of this shot."

He nods and takes another sip of water. "We went back for that one," he says, "after we interviewed the pastor."

"Why was that?" Geraldine says.

"The pastor was the first person on the scene," he says. "After he called us, he noticed the basket. He told us it shouldn't have been empty; it should have held the Christmas Vigil collection."

"Has it ever been recovered?" she asks.

"Not yet," he says. "So far we haven't found anything that was taken that night."

Something about that answer bothers me. I'm on my feet before my brain knows why. "Hold it," I say.

"Hold it?" Judge Gould echoes, and I can't blame him. That's not my usual mode of objecting—or anyone else's, for that matter.

My pulse is racing, but my mind is way ahead now. "Move to voir dire the witness, Your Honor."

"What?" Geraldine pivots to face me, plants her hands on her hips. "My Sister Counsel can't voir dire this witness. She can wait her turn, ask whatever burning questions she has on cross."

"These questions need to be asked now," I say, "while we're discussing these photographs."

"Ms. Nickerson," the judge says, "this is highly unusual."

A flurry of activity makes me turn. Geraldine is back at her table, exchanging hurried whispers with Clarence, rummaging through her file, confirming my hunch.

"I know it's unusual, Judge." I turn back to face him, but he's not looking at me. He's watching the pair of panicked prosecutors instead. A quick scan of the room tells me everyone else is too.

"Your Honor," Geraldine says, "it seems my office may be guilty of a minor oversight. Perhaps we should take a short recess so we can rectify the matter."

"No recess," I say. "Move to voir dire the witness. The motion's pending."

The judge is quiet for a moment, his eyes moving from me back to Geraldine. "I'll allow it," he says at last.

I pounce before the district attorney can argue further. "'So far we haven't found anything that was taken that night.' That was your answer to the prior question, was it not, Chief?"

He looks surprised, but not worried. He doesn't know what the hell's going on here, but he'll answer the questions put to him. "Yes," he says. "That was my answer."

"Tell us specifically, Chief, what it is you haven't found."

He shrugs. "Like I said, we haven't found anything. Everything that was taken from the church that night is still missing."

"What else was taken from St. Veronica's Chapel that night?"

He opens his written report and skims through it. "A monstrance," he says, tapping the page.

"Tell the jurors what a monstrance *is,* will you, Chief?" He'll be broadening my vocabulary as well, but I try not to let on.

"It's a solid-gold stand," he says, "used to hold the host when it's exposed on the altar for any length of time. The host is inserted into a small window at the top, so it can be viewed by the visiting faithful but not touched. Until fairly recently, only an ordained priest was permitted to touch the host."

"And you're certain it was taken from the chapel the night Francis McMahon was killed?"

"The pastor is," the chief says. "Monsignor Davis said the monstrance was to be on display from the end of the Vigil Mass until midnight."

I check in with Harry, and he gives me the go-ahead nod; we're on the same page. I wait, though, until the room falls silent. I want to say it quietly, calmly. "We move for a mistrial, Your Honor, on the grounds of prosecutorial misconduct."

The place erupts.

Judge Gould bangs his gavel repeatedly, then signals Big Red to get the jurors out of here. He jumps up and descends from the bench as they file through the side door, his steps heavy. "Counsel," he says, heading for chambers, "inside. Now."

We follow the judge into chambers, Geraldine and Clarence behind us. Geraldine's on the defensive even before her sidekick shuts the door. "It was an oversight," she says, "nothing more than that."

Harry actually laughs. "I hope our district attorney won't take offense," he says to the judge, "but we see it differently."

Judge Gould eases into the chair at his desk. "Ms. Schilling," he says, "this is not a matter the court takes lightly."

I slip into a seat in front of the desk, and Geraldine perches on the chair next to mine. She's silent, a rare phenomenon.

"Assuming the best," the judge continues, "that it was an honest mistake, your office's failure to disclose the missing monstrance to the defense is a problem. A real one."

"We kept it quiet initially," Geraldine says, "as an investigative tool. Frankly, by the time we were preparing for trial, I'd forgotten all about it."

The judge shakes his head, looking like he's about to tell her that good intentions don't make a whit of difference, but Clarence pipes up first. "It's my fault," he says. "I dropped the ball."

He's visibly distraught. He's also correct. It's his job to worry about the details—especially the technical ones—while Geraldine focuses on the big picture. He's a decent sort, Clarence, but as Harry's fond of saying, he's about two oysters shy of a bushel.

Geraldine shuts Clarence down with one raised hand. "Okay," she says to the judge. "My error. But what difference does it make? It's not as if Holliston ever claimed he *didn't* kill the priest. The missing monstrance doesn't change anything."

She's right. It doesn't. But as every criminal-defense lawyer learns in the first week or so of practice, a prosecutorial error—even one that has no real bearing on the substance of the proceedings—is a rare gift.

"You're wrong," Harry says to her. "It changes a lot. It's one more item that *wasn't* in Derrick Holliston's possession when he was picked up, one more item that *wasn't* found in his apartment when he was taken into custody. It's one more piece of evidence that tends to prove his version of events."

He's good, Harry Madigan. If I didn't know better, I'd think he believes what he's saying.

Geraldine throws her hands in the air. "Go ahead," she says. "Take your mistrial. I'll refile before the day is out."

She's calling our bluff, of course. We don't really want a new trial, and she knows it. We'll never get another opportunity like this one.

"We'll settle for an instruction," Harry says. This is a break few criminal defendants get. The judge will tell the jurors that the district attorney's office misbehaved, failed to play by the rules. And from that moment on, our case will be about the DA's misconduct, not Holliston's.

"All right, then," the judge says as he stands, "let's get on with it. I'm sorry," he says to Geraldine from the doorway, "but you'll have to bring your pastor in tomorrow."

She nods, then follows him out of the room without a word. Clarence slinks out behind her. Harry and I follow.

Holliston's angry eyes bore into us as we approach the defense table. "I dint take no monster," he says. "I hope you told them people that."

Neither of us answers. Instead, we focus on Judge Gould, who's already settled on the bench. "Ladies and Gentlemen," he says to the panel, "it has come to the court's attention that certain material evidence known to the district attorney's office has not heretofore been disclosed to the defense."

The jurors' gazes move from the judge to Geraldine.

"In the Commonwealth of Massachusetts," Judge Gould continues, "the prosecuting attorney bears a burden of full disclosure. In other words, it is incumbent upon the prosecutor to disclose all material facts to the defendant and his lawyers prior to trial. In the case before us, the prosecutor failed to do so."

Again, the jurors turn their attention to Geraldine.

"In particular," the judge says, "the district attorney's office failed to inform the defense that an item of value, a solid-gold monstrance, was taken from St. Veronica's Chapel on the night of Father McMahon's death."

Holliston bolts upright. He looks indignant.

"The prosecution's failure to disclose is particularly troubling when the evidence is exculpatory, as it is here. Like the collection proceeds, the monstrance has never been recovered. It was not in the defendant's possession at the time of his arrest."

The jurors' eyes move to our table now.

"Our supreme judicial court has recently held that judges should begin instructing juries in criminal trials to be 'skeptical' when either police officers or prosecutors fail to abide by the rules. Mr.

Holliston is entitled to every reasonable inference you may draw from the missing monstrance. He's also entitled to every reasonable inference you may draw from the district attorney's failure to disclose that fact."

Harry snaps a chewed-up pencil in two. "How many times in the past twenty-three years have I wished Geraldine Schilling would screw up?" he says. "Why the hell did she do it now?"

THE T-intersection outside our 1840 farmhouse-turned-law-office is the gateway to Chatham. The antique cape next to our building houses the Chatham chamber of commerce, where volunteers and merchants welcome weekly renters and day-trippers throughout the summer, recommending breakfast joints, fish markets, and seal-watch cruises; handing out menus, maps, and brochures.

During the season, traffic is perpetually heavy here, both two-lane roads constantly clogged with carloads of tourists headed for beaches, shops, and restaurants. After Labor Day, the stream of visiting vehicles thins, the whole area growing markedly quieter overnight. By this time of year it's normally downright desolate. Not today, though.

Today the chamber of commerce parking lot is full. Cars and trucks that couldn't find space in that lot are strewn along both sides of our road, though no parking is allowed on either. Chatham cops are all over the place, slipping orange cardboard citations under icy windshield wipers and directing traffic impatiently while a solitary tow truck tries to make its way through the quagmire.

Our narrow driveway is filled to capacity, the Kydd's pickup and my Thunderbird hemmed in by cars I've never seen before. Harry pulls in next to Senator Kendrick's Hummer. "Oh, good," he says as he cuts the engine. "Company."

We climb out of the Jeep. Harry's name is called out more than once—and mine too—but I can't decipher much else. Two TV vans idle in the chamber of commerce driveway, their lights and cameras pointed in our direction. It's after six; it should be pitch-black out here now. But, thanks to the TV crews, it's not.

As we enter, the front office is empty, and the sounds of the TV tell us the Kydd and Charles Kendrick are in the conference room. They barely look up when we enter. They're in side-by-side wing chairs, their eyes glued to the evening news. Michelle Forrester is the top story. The four of us watch in silence as two coast guardsmen lift a draped stretcher from Smithy's patrol boat and carry it to the county van waiting at Cow Yard.

Geraldine Schilling appears on the screen, looking like she just emerged from a two-week stint at a Beverly Hills spa. The autopsy is ongoing, she tells the horde assembled outside the superior courthouse. She expects to have the medical examiner's report first thing tomorrow morning. She'll issue an update then. The anchorwoman pauses for a station break. The Kydd hits the mute button.

Harry rests a hand on the senator's shoulder, then drops into the chair beside him. "How're you holding up?" he asks.

Charles Kendrick shakes his head slowly, his eyes still glued to the glow of the television screen. He doesn't answer.

I unbutton my suit jacket and half-sit on the edge of the conference room table. We're going to be here for a while, it seems.

"Geraldine called," the Kydd says. "She wants Senator Kendrick to come in tomorrow. She said she'd see him at his convenience— before the Holliston trial resumes in the morning, at lunch, or at the end of the day. She's hoping he'll do this voluntarily."

"She is not," Harry says. "She knows better."

"But shouldn't I? Shouldn't I at least *try* to help?" The senator directs his query to Harry, but Harry turns to me.

"No," I say. "You shouldn't."

"But—"

"Everything is changed now." I hold up both hands to cut him off. "Michelle is dead. You can't help her. No one can. All you can do by talking now is hurt yourself."

The senator's eyes move from mine to Harry's to the Kydd's. No doubt he's hoping one of them will contradict me. No luck. He turns back to me, resigned. "All right," he says. "You tell me what to do. And I'll do it."

This is a first.

Charles Kendrick's gaze returns to the TV screen. Coverage of the Michelle Forrester story has resumed.

"I loved her," he says to no one in particular.

And I believe him.

IT'S almost nine by the time Harry and I pull up to my Windmill Lane cottage. A candy-apple Mustang is parked behind Luke's pickup in our newly shoveled driveway. Harry whistles and strolls around it as soon as we get out of the Jeep, and then he points out the Harvard bumper sticker. "Looks like your son has a visitor," he says, shaking his head. "Damn, that guy's doing something right."

"What does that mean?"

He shrugs. "You saw his heartthrob," he says. "And she drives *this* to boot."

I stare at him.

"This isn't one of the new ones," he tells me, examining the car again. "This baby is restored—vintage."

I'm feeling a bit vintage myself at the moment.

He chuckles. "That Luke," he says, "I've got to hand it to him. He's doing something right."

"So you mentioned."

Harry looks up all of a sudden, his eyes wide. "Of course," he says in a professorial tone, "I prefer a more *mature* woman myself."

"You're not helping your cause." I head for the back stairs.

"Preferably with a not-so-high-maintenance car," he says.

"Give it up, Harry."

"With extremely high mileage," he calls after me.

"*Not* helping."

"And a low-to-the-ground chassis."

We're laughing uncontrollably by the time we spill through the kitchen door. I slice a loaf of French bread and take a wheel of Camembert and a bag of green grapes from the refrigerator. Not until we go into the living room do I realize it's dimly lit. My son has taken a stab at ambiance. A first, as far as I know.

A floor lamp in the far corner is on its lowest setting, and two tapered candles flicker on the coffee table. The only other light in the room is the glow behind the glass doors of the woodstove. Abby Kendrick is seated on the couch, flanked by Luke and Danny Boy, and it's tough to tell which of them is more smitten.

Luke flips on the light by the couch as soon as we join them. No need for ambiance now. "Harry," he says, "this is Abby Kendrick."

Harry shakes her hand. "Hello, Abby," he says. "We were just admiring your Mustang. It's a beauty."

I arch my eyebrows at him. He must be using the royal *we*.

"And you know my mom," Luke says to Abby.

"Yeah." She smiles at me. "We met the other day."

"You two are in early," I say as I sink into one of the overstuffed chairs facing the couch.

"Yeah," Luke says, "we were thinking about watching a movie, but there's not much on." He picks up the remote and hits the power button, as if he needs to prove it.

"You have trouble finding parts for that thing?" Harry asks Abby.

She shakes her head. "My dad knows a guy," she says, "who services it for us. He never seems to have trouble finding parts."

Abby looks like she has more to say, but her eyes dart to the TV behind me, and she stops talking. Harry and I both turn to see what's caught her eye. A banner at the top says BODY OF SENATE AIDE FOUND IN CAPE COD WATERS.

"On Cape Cod today," a Boston anchorwoman says, "the body of Michelle Forrester, the senate aide who's been missing since Thursday, was found in the shallows of Pleasant Bay."

The color drains from Abby's face. "Did you know?" she asks me.

I nod. "We heard about it this afternoon."

"Does my father know?"

"Yes," I say. "He just left our office."

"How is he?"

"He's upset," I tell her honestly.

"I'm sorry," she says to Luke, "but I should go. My dad must be a mess."

She's right about that.

"Okay," Luke says. "Sure. I'll walk you out."

Harry and I are quiet as they put on their coats and head for the door. "That'll be interesting," Harry says as it shuts behind them.

"What will?"

"The dynamic in the Kendrick household tonight," he says. "You saw Chuck in the conference room. He's not going to be able to hide his pain, not even from his wife." He runs his hands through his tangled hair. "What in God's name does it feel like to watch your spouse grieve his dead lover?"

I shake my head at him. I hope I never know.

The kitchen door slams and Luke appears in the living room doorway a few seconds later. He looks serious, worried even, but his eyes are bright, his cheeks flushed. And something tells me it's not just the winter wind that accounts for his high coloring. He points toward the road out front, toward the fading sound of Abby Kendrick's candy-apple coupe. "Is she great," he says eagerly, looking from Harry to me, "or what?"

SEVEN

Friday, December 17

MONSIGNOR Dominic Davis is in full Roman Catholic regalia—Geraldine's brainchild, no doubt. I'm not a member of the flock, but I've met enough priests in my day to know they don't *always* sport ankle-length robes and pastel accessories. The monsignor's skullcap and waistband are a pinkish purple, and a matching sash on his right side flows to the hem of his black linen cassock.

Geraldine ignores me. She stands beside Monsignor Davis and beams at him as he raises his right hand, places his left on the Holy

Bible, and takes the oath. "Your Eminence," she says as he sits, "please state your full name and occupation for the record."

Harry turns to me, his hazel eyes as wide as they get, as the priest introduces himself to the jurors. "Your *what?*" he whispers.

"Don't look at me," I tell him.

"And how long have you served as the pastor at St. Veronica's Parish?" Geraldine asks.

"Eight years," the witness says.

"Thank you, Your Eminence." Geraldine glows again. "Now, in the course of your service at St. Veronica's, did you come to know the Reverend Francis Patrick McMahon?"

"I did," he answers.

"Tell us about your getting to know each other, if you will, Your Eminence."

Harry turns to me and rolls his eyes back in his head. "I'm going to object like hell," he says, "as soon as she kisses his ring."

"Frank—Father McMahon—was already stationed at St. Veronica's when I was named pastor," Monsignor Davis says. He looks toward our table for the first time, his gaze settling on Derrick Holliston. The priest's dark brown eyes convey not a shred of reproach, but Holliston twists in his chair and stares at the side wall anyway.

"So am I correct in presuming that you and Father McMahon got to know each other fairly well during the years you served together?"

"We did," he says, turning his attention back to the jury.

"Tell us about him," she says.

Harry's on his feet, headed for the bench. "Your Honor," he says, "I hate to interrupt my Sister Counsel. But I have to ask the court to set some parameters here."

Judge Gould nods. Technically, this witness shouldn't be on the stand more than five minutes; he has precious little to say that's relevant. Since we've put the self-defense claim into play, he's entitled to opine that Father McMahon wasn't a violent man, that he had no propensity toward assault, sexual or otherwise. Beyond that, the dead priest's character is of no import.

Geraldine isn't happy with Harry's request, though. She'd like to keep the priest in the witness box all day. If the jurors like him, if they conclude he's a decent, moral man, they're likely to presume the same of his late colleague.

"Counselor," the judge says to her, "narrow your question, please."

She will, but not before she throws her hands in the air and shakes her blond head at the jurors.

Harry backs up to our table, watching her performance.

Geraldine turns and smiles at him. "Where is Father McMahon buried?" she asks, still looking at Harry.

"Behind the church," the witness answers. "There's a small cemetery back there, a dozen or so ancient graves clustered around a statue of Saint Veronica. Frank used to go out there in all sorts of weather to say his Divine Office."

Geraldine's eyebrows arch before she turns back to her witness. "Divine Office?"

"Canonical prayers," Monsignor Davis explains to the jurors, "prayers we priests recite every day. Frank liked to say his out behind the church. He seemed to find peace there, amid the centuries-old graves and the image of our parish's patron."

"Ah, Saint Veronica." Geraldine's somber expression suggests the witness just raised a critical point. "Tell us about her."

"Ms. Schilling," the judge says, "I think we're going pretty far afield here. Let's get back to the matter at hand, shall we?"

"Yes, Your Honor. Your Eminence, tell us what you remember about last Christmas Eve."

"Well," the Monsignor says, "Frank and I always took turns celebrating the Christmas Vigil Mass. Last year was his turn." For the first time since he took the stand, he looks sad.

"Whichever one of us wasn't celebrating the Vigil always came over to help out with Communion," he says. "I helped Frank last year, and then went back across the street to the rectory." He shakes his head again. "Not a day goes by that I don't regret it. Things might have turned out differently if I'd stayed."

He's right, of course. Things almost certainly would have turned out differently if he'd stayed. If Holliston's telling the truth, the presence of a third party would have nixed any amorous advances, real or imagined. If Holliston's lying, the two-to-one ratio might have scared him off.

"But you went back to the chapel again later, is that right?" Geraldine turns away from the witness and walks slowly toward us, staring at Holliston.

"I did," Monsignor Davis says. "We'd finished with Holy Communion just before eight. Frank would've given the final blessing a few minutes after that. When he wasn't back at the rectory by nine, I went across the street to see what was keeping him."

Geraldine pauses, clasps her hands behind her back, and takes a deep breath. "Tell us, Your Eminence, what you found when you returned to the chapel that night."

Harry's up. "Absolutely not," he says.

Judge Gould nods; he knows what Harry's about to say. And he agrees. Geraldine has a half-dozen graphic crime-scene photographs in evidence. She doesn't get a verbal description as well.

"It's cumulative," Harry continues. "It's out of the question."

"That's nonsense," Geraldine counters. "The monsignor's entitled to tell us what he found when he went back to the church."

"No, he's not." Harry's directly in front of the judge. "Not after she introduced multiple photographs of the scene. At this point, the prejudicial impact of this testimony far outweighs its probative value. It's nothing but repetitive."

Judge Gould nods. "Sustained," he says. "Monsignor Davis, please disregard the district attorney's last question."

"Whatever you say," the witness answers.

"Ms. Schilling," the judge adds, "move on."

She plasters a resigned expression on her face. "Your Eminence," she says, "are you aware that the defendant in this case has raised a self-defense claim?"

"I am," he says. Geraldine's continuing her slow journey toward us, staring at Derrick Holliston's profile.

"You're aware, are you not, Your Eminence, that the defendant claims Father McMahon made inappropriate sexual contact with him, that Father Francis Patrick McMahon became violent when his advances were rejected, so violent, in fact, that this defendant had no choice but to fight for his own life?"

The monsignor is quiet for a moment. "I am," he says to the jurors. "I'm aware of those claims, all of them."

Geraldine stops smack in front of Holliston and turns to face the witness again. She doesn't say a word until the room falls silent. "Now I ask you, Your Eminence," she says quietly, "based upon your knowledge of Father Francis Patrick McMahon, based upon the totality of your experience with him, are this defendant's claims credible?"

Monsignor Davis doesn't answer right away. He seems to search for words. "They're not," he says at last. "They're simply not."

Geraldine doesn't move. Finally, she looks at Harry. "Your witness," she says.

Harry stands and smooths his suit coat, then walks toward the witness box. "No disrespect intended here," he says, "but I'm going to have trouble with this 'Your Emperor' thing."

"Your Honor!" Geraldine's on her feet, but Harry keeps going.

"Any reason I can't just call you Monsignor?"

Most of the jurors laugh now. Even Judge Gould struggles to suppress a smile.

"None at all," the priest says. "Monsignor will do nicely."

Geraldine shakes her head and drops back into her chair.

"Monsignor Davis," he says, "the collection money disappeared last Christmas Eve, didn't it?"

"It did."

"Any estimate on how much money vanished?"

The monsignor shrugs. "Most years the vigil collection brings in more than a thousand dollars."

"Anything else disappear that night?"

Monsignor Davis nods. "The monstrance," he says. "The holy monstrance was taken from the altar."

"Yesterday afternoon, Monsignor, we heard testimony from Chatham's Chief Fitzpatrick."

The witness nods again.

"He told us you discovered Father McMahon's body in the sacristy, called the police, and *then* noticed the empty collection basket. Do you agree with that sequence of events?"

"I do," the priest says. "That's exactly how it happened."

"When did you notice the monstrance was missing?"

"Right away," Monsignor Davis says. "As soon as I entered the church, I saw that the altar was empty. I thought Frank had taken the monstrance to the sacristy to polish it up a bit."

"When you called the police, did you mention the monstrance?"

"No." The Monsignor shakes his head. "I don't remember what I said, to tell you the truth, but I'm certain I spoke of nothing but Frank."

"When did you mention it?"

"That night. I met with the chief and another officer after the medical examiner's people took Frank's body away. I tried to explain the significance of the consecrated host, the urgency with which our parishioners would want it recovered."

"Did you meet with the chief or other Chatham officers after that night?"

"Oh yes," the witness answers. "Three, four times, maybe."

"What about our district attorney?" Harry asks. "How many times would you say you've met with her?"

"Five or six," the monsignor says.

"Did you mention the monstrance at each of those meetings?"

"I'm sure I did," the priest says. "It's been a constant concern."

"Would it be fair to say, Monsignor Davis, that during your multiple meetings with the Chatham police and with our district attorney, you expressed more urgency over the disappearance of the monstrance than you did over the missing money?"

"Just a minute." Geraldine heads for the bench. "This witness isn't a forensic expert," she says. "His 'sense of urgency' about a particular piece of evidence doesn't amount to a hill of beans."

398 | *Rose Connors*

Harry laughs. "I missed the hill-of-beans class in law school," he says, "but I do believe my Sister Counsel is telling us this witness's opinion on the matter is irrelevant."

Judge Gould looks as if he's prepared to rule, but Harry keeps talking. He turns to the jurors. "That would be the same Sister Counsel who withheld the fact of that theft from the defense for an entire year." He points back toward our table. "Maybe our district attorney would like to object to this man's having a trial at all. Maybe it would be more convenient for her if we just lock him up now, ask questions later."

"Mr. Madigan!" Judge Gould bangs his gavel hard. "You've made your point," he says. "You may proceed." He turns to Geraldine. "Ms. Schilling, your objection is overruled."

She storms back to her table, and Holliston jabs my arm with his elbow. He actually looks pleased when I turn to face him—a first. "Now we're gettin' somewhere," he says.

I'm weary of him.

"Monsignor Davis," Harry continues, his voice raised as if he's still arguing, "can you answer the question, sir?"

The monsignor looks flustered. "What was it?" he asks.

Most of the jurors chuckle.

"Damned if I know," Harry says.

The entire panel laughs now. Geraldine is furious.

Harry points to the court reporter, an attractive, thirtysomething brunette who's new to her courthouse job. She stops tapping and reaches for the narrow strip of encoded paper that snakes from the front of her machine. She clears her throat. " 'Would it be fair to say, Monsignor Davis,' " she recites in a monotone, " 'that during your multiple meetings with the Chatham police, and during your multiple meetings with our district attorney, you expressed more urgency over the disappearance of the monstrance than you did over the missing money?' "

The monsignor nods emphatically. "Absolutely," he says. "We hated to lose so much money, especially at that time of year. But the theft of the monstrance was far worse."

"Tell us why," Harry says.

The monsignor pauses now. "The consecrated host," he says at last, "is the body of Our Lord Jesus Christ."

Juror Maria Marzetti bows her head at the mention of the Lord's name. Another juror makes the sign of the cross; when she raises her hand to her forehead, I realize she's cradling rosary beads. Holliston notices, too, and turns to stare at the wall again.

"You must understand," the witness says. "The consecrated host is not a *symbol* of Christ's body, it *is* his body."

"We'll take your word on that," Harry says. "But what about the other two?"

"Other two?"

"Aren't there three of them?" Harry asks. "A trio?"

The monsignor breaks into a smile. "You're referring to the Trinity," he says to Harry. "The Holy Trinity."

"Bingo," Harry says.

Geraldine jumps to her feet. "For God's sake, let's not go down that path," she says. "We'll stipulate to the doctrine of the Trinity. Father, Son, and Holy Ghost."

"*Spirit,*" Monsignor Davis says to our district attorney. "We call the third member of the Trinity the Holy Spirit."

Harry turns and gives Geraldine a smile, this one accompanied by a wink. "Been a while, heh, Counselor?"

"Mr. Madigan!" Judge Gould bangs his gavel again.

Harry nods up at the judge, then turns back to the witness. "The man in charge wants me to wrap it up here," he says to Monsignor Davis. "So let's talk turkey."

The monsignor laughs a little. "Okay," he says. "Let's."

"Father McMahon was already dead when you entered the church last Christmas Eve, wasn't he?"

"Yes," the priest says, "he was."

"And you didn't see what happened to him, did you?"

Monsignor Davis hesitates.

"You saw the aftermath of what happened," Harry adds quickly, "but you didn't see the altercation itself."

This clarification seems to assuage the witness's concerns. "That's correct," he says. "I didn't."

"So what you've offered us here today, Monsignor Davis, is your opinion, isn't it? You've testified to your *opinion* about what Father McMahon may or may not have done that night."

Again the priest hesitates, and again Harry jumps in quickly to clarify. "In other words, your testimony isn't based on anything you perceived through your physical senses, is that correct?"

"That is correct," he says after a moment. "But bear in mind that my vocation—my life's work—isn't based on anything I perceive through my earthly senses either."

Harry should have seen that answer coming, but he didn't. And there's no way in hell he wants to end the cross-examination on that note. "In any case," he says, "you're not here today under subpoena, are you?"

"No, I'm not."

"And, Monsignor, your voluntary appearance here today is explainable—at least in part—by the fact that Francis Patrick McMahon was your good friend, isn't that true?"

"In part," the witness says. "Yes, I agree with that."

"Is it fair to say that by showing up here today voluntarily you hoped to honor your good friend's memory, to seek some semblance of justice for his untimely death?"

Monsignor Davis is quiet. "I suppose that is true," he says at last. "Certainly the part about honoring Frank's memory." He pauses and tilts his head to one side. "But perhaps a man can't do that answering lawyer questions."

Now it's Harry's turn to be quiet. "Perhaps not," he says after a moment. He walks toward our table, but then stops. "About the weapon," he says. "Where did it come from?"

"It was in the sacristy," the priest says. "The chapel is an old building; we're constantly making minor repairs, it seems. We keep a wooden box—a crate, I guess you'd call it—on one side of the counter. It's full of hammers, pliers, screwdrivers—all sorts of tools. The ice pick was among them."

"Thank you. And one last thing, Monsignor." Harry's still standing in the middle of the room. "I want to offer you my sincere condolences on the loss of your good friend."

Some defense lawyers routinely offer condolences at the beginnings of cross-examinations, hoping some prosecution witnesses will let down their guards. Harry doesn't. He's offered his sympathy to this witness—at the end of cross—because he means it.

Monsignor Davis seems to sense as much. He swallows a lump in his throat. "I go out there—to the small cemetery—to pray for Frank every morning," he says to Harry. "And when I finish, I pray for Mr. Holliston."

Harry's surprise is genuine. He looks from Monsignor Davis to Holliston, and then back to the priest again. "Thanks," he says as he sits.

The monsignor nods.

Holliston leans forward, not looking the least bit pleased anymore. His face is scrunched into a maze of hatred and disbelief. "Thanks?" he says too loudly. *"Thanks?"* He points at the witness box. "That guy calls me a liar and you say *thanks?* Whose side are you on?"

Harry stares back at our client but says nothing. And there's a reason for that, of course. He doesn't know whose side he's on.

CRIMINAL-DEFENSE lawyers lose. It's what we do. We lose when we know we should. We lose when we think we shouldn't. And we lose when we're damned certain we should carry the day.

It's odd, then, to watch Harry worry about winning. He's been tense in his chair beside me throughout our fifteen-minute break, his hands clutching the armrests, his eyes closed. He doesn't open them when the guards usher Derrick Holliston back to our table, but he does when Big Red comes through the side door with the jurors. Harry's quick to change his posture now, too, sitting up straighter, adopting a serious, confident demeanor.

"Mr. Madigan," Judge Gould says when the last juror is seated, "you may proceed now, sir."

"Reasonable doubt," Harry says as he stands. "When all is said and done, this case boils down to one issue: reasonable doubt."

He unbuttons his suit coat and shoves his hands into his pockets as he leaves our table. "Judge Gould will instruct you that the Commonwealth bears the burden of proving every element of the crime charged beyond a reasonable doubt."

He stops in front of Geraldine's table and glances at her, then resumes his trip toward the jury box. "The judge will also tell you that proof beyond a reasonable doubt is proof that leaves you *firmly convinced* of the defendant's guilt. You should convict Mr. Holliston of murder only if you are *firmly convinced* that he did *not* act in self-defense."

Harry turns and looks at Geraldine again. "And you can't be," he adds. "Not on the evidence produced in this courtroom."

Harry shifts his attention to the jury again. "There are a few things we know for sure," he continues. He leans on the railing of the jury box. "We know Mr. Holliston admitted his role in Father McMahon's death from the outset. We know he told the chief of police about the unwelcome sexual advances and about the ensuing struggle on the morning of his arrest. And we know he stuck to his guns during every subsequent interview."

A few of the jurors have pens in their hands, notepads on their laps. No one's writing anything, though. They're motionless.

"And that's not all we know," he says, his voice growing louder. "We know the district attorney's office concealed evidence." His voice is booming now. "Critical evidence."

Geraldine looks up and meets Harry's accusing eyes.

"Why did they do that?" Harry turns back to the jurors. "Why did they conceal a material fact from the defense?"

The spectators stir and Harry waits. "I'll give you one reason," he says when the silence is complete. "They did it because the missing monstrance blows yet another hole in this sorry excuse for a case, another hole in a case that already looks like Swiss cheese."

He walks slowly across the room and points at Geraldine. "Our district attorney would have you believe Mr. Holliston entered St.

Veronica's Chapel last Christmas Eve intending to commit a felony. She'd have you believe he killed Father McMahon in the course of committing that felony. But there's a problem with our district attorney's theory," he says quietly. "She has no evidence to support it."

Geraldine exhales as Harry leaves her table and walks toward ours. "Not one shred of evidence ties this man to *anything* that was taken from the chapel that night. Now," Harry continues, "let's talk about the evidence we *do* have." He points at the empty witness box. "The Commonwealth called three men to this stand, credible individuals one and all. And every one of them gave you crucial information—critical facts—that support Mr. Holliston's version of the events that transpired last Christmas Eve."

Harry pauses in front of our table, picks up a pen, and points it at the panel. "First we heard from Calvin Ramsey," he says, "our medical examiner. Our district attorney failed to elicit one fact during his direct examination that contradicted what Mr. Holliston has told law enforcement from the beginning. Not one."

Harry begins a slow stroll back toward the panel. "Dr. Ramsey delivered a critical fact during cross, though. He told you the medical evidence supports only one conclusion: Mr. Holliston and the deceased were face-to-face throughout the altercation. Face-to-face combat isn't consistent with a robbery—certainly not a planned robbery—no matter how you slice it.

"Next we heard from Chief Thomas Fitzpatrick," he says, "a stand-up guy if ever there was one. Such a stand-up guy, in fact, that he outed our district attorney."

"Your *Honor!*" Geraldine Schilling has probably never heard herself described as outed before.

Judge Gould shakes his head at her, says nothing. Nondisclosure doesn't go over well in his courtroom, unintentional or not.

"And finally," Harry says, "this morning we heard from Monsignor Davis. We heard about all sorts of things during his direct examination, didn't we? None of it had a damned thing to do with this case, but it was interesting, nonetheless."

He leans on the jury box railing. "The monsignor did have two things to tell us that matter, but our district attorney didn't raise either one. Only during cross-examination did the witness get to address two issues that actually bear on this case. They're important. Keep them in mind."

A couple of the note-takers shift in their seats, pens poised.

"First," Harry says, "let's talk about the weapon, the ice pick. Monsignor Davis told you it belongs to the parish. It was in a wooden crate on the sacristy counter. It's *not* something Derrick Holliston brought with him that night. So our district attorney would have you believe Mr. Holliston went to St. Veronica's Chapel intending to rob the collection money, prepared to kill anyone who tried to stop him, but he didn't bother to bring a weapon along. He simply assumed there'd be one on hand."

Harry faces the panel, his hands in his pants pockets again. "Common sense, Ladies and Gentlemen," he says. "The district attorney's theories don't hold water."

He starts walking back toward the prosecutors' table, and I'm pretty sure everyone in the courtroom knows what's coming. Geraldine does, anyway. She folds her arms across her chest and squares her shoulders. "Now," Harry says quietly, staring at her, "let's talk about the monstrance."

He doesn't, though. He doesn't talk about anything for what seems like a full minute. He finishes his trip to the prosecutors' table and stands facing them, his profile to the jury.

"Monsignor Davis told us he met with Chatham police officers three or four times," Harry says at last. "And he met with our district attorney five or six times. And at every meeting—*every* meeting—he brought up the topic of the missing monstrance, stressed its significance to him and his parish."

Harry leans toward Geraldine, palms down on her table. "Yet our district attorney chose *not* to mention that significant topic to us," he says, his voice barely more than a whisper.

No one else in the courtroom makes a sound. Harry waits until the silence is physically uncomfortable. "Our district attorney charged Mr. Holliston with first-degree murder," he says at last, "a charge that carries a mandatory life sentence. And for a solid year after she issued that charge, she hid a critical fact—an exculpatory critical fact—from the accused and his attorneys."

Another hefty silence.

"Bear in mind," Harry says as he stands up straight and faces the jurors again, "our district attorney didn't rectify the situation voluntarily. She got *caught.*"

All fourteen jurors look at Geraldine now. She doesn't look back at them, doesn't react to Harry's words at all.

"This is Derrick John Holliston's trial," Harry says as he walks toward our table, "no one else's. But the system governing this trial belongs to all of us. *We* are responsible for our system. *We* are accountable for its integrity." Harry turns and fires another pointed stare at Geraldine. "*We* are blameworthy for its lack thereof."

She sighs and shakes her head at him, but she doesn't speak.

Harry turns back to the panel. "You saw the crime-scene photographs, Ladies and Gentlemen. You don't need me to tell you that *wasn't* the scene of a robbery. It was the scene of a sexual assault. It was the scene of panic, of outrage."

With that, Harry walks behind our table and drops into his chair. The courtroom is soundless. Not one juror moves a muscle.

Even Holliston seems pleased with Harry's closing argument. "About time," he says as soon as Harry reclaims his seat.

Harry doesn't even look at him. He leans on his elbows, hands clasped, and stares straight ahead.

"You did a good job," I whisper. "You were effective."

He takes his glasses off and throws them on top of a legal pad before he looks at me. "That's great," he says, shielding his mouth from the jury with his hand. "Wrong. But effective."

"OUTRAGE," Geraldine says as she stands. "I find it surprising, baffling even, that the defense would speak of outrage."

She sorts through the stack of glossies on her table, the exhibits introduced during Tommy Fitzpatrick's testimony, and selects one. She covers the distance to the jury box slowly, in silence, then holds the photograph up in front of the panel. "We, as a civilized society, are the ones who should be outraged."

The jurors split evenly. Half revisit the scene of the dead priest sprawled on the slate floor of the sacristy, his blood-soaked cassock twisted, his shattered glasses nearby. Half don't. One squeezes her eyes shut tight.

"That man," Geraldine continues, still displaying the glossy as she turns to point at our table, "did this. He admits it. But he wants you to say he's not responsible for what he did. Why? Because he wants you to buy into his cockamamie self-defense claim. He wants you to believe that this fifty-seven-year-old man attacked him, that the attack was so threatening, so brutal, he had no choice but to do *this* to protect himself."

She barrels toward us. Geraldine Schilling has raised steamrolling in spike heels to a performance art. "This man," she says, pointing at Holliston, "wants you to believe he had to stab Father McMahon eight times to protect himself."

Geraldine raises a fist in the air and slams it downward, stopping just inches from Holliston's shoulder. "One," she says. Again, she raises her fist and thrusts it down at him. "Two."

She continues the count, each imaginary stab more forceful than the last. Holliston doesn't even flinch.

The blanket of silence that covers this courtroom is complete. Geraldine turns away from Holliston and delivers the final blow toward the jurors. "Eight!" she bellows.

No one moves. Not a single juror. Not Holliston. Not Geraldine. "How many puncture wounds did it take before Father McMahon staggered backward?" she says at last.

She walks back toward the jury box. "Did Father McMahon reel after the second puncture? After the third? Did he fall after the fourth?" She stops in front of the jury box and slaps her open palms on its railing. A few of the jurors jump. "Did it take *eight?*"

She turns and glares at Holliston, then faces the panel again. "I think not," she whispers. "That man is a murderer. And like the vast majority of murderers, he's also a liar."

The jurors are attentive, focused. Their faces reveal nothing.

"His defense is a fabrication. An entire week elapsed between Father McMahon's murder and this defendant's arrest," Geraldine continues, "and he told no one of this brutal attack he claims to have suffered at the priest's hands."

She half laughs. "This defendant is trying to sell you a bill of goods, Ladies and Gentlemen. Don't let him. One man—and one man only—was attacked in St. Veronica's sacristy last Christmas Eve." She holds up the glossy again. "This one."

Even fewer members of the panel choose to look at the grisly crime scene this time. These jurors have about had it.

"Mr. Madigan spoke with you at great length about reasonable doubt," Geraldine says. "On the subject of reasonable doubt, I tell you only one thing: the operative word is *reasonable*."

A few jurors nod at her. A few others jot quick reminders in their notepads.

"Mr. Madigan also spoke with you at length about the monstrance," she says. "On the matter of my failure to disclose the missing monstrance to the defense, I tell you two things. First, it was a mistake—my mistake. And second, it doesn't have anything to do with the defendant's guilt or innocence."

Geraldine folds her arms, pressing the glossy to her side. "The defendant would have you believe that a man with no history of violence, a Catholic priest who led a life of prayer, a life of service to others, suddenly—at the age of fifty-seven—revealed his never-before-seen diabolical side. And he did it on one of the holiest nights of the year."

She half laughs again. "That, Ladies and Gentlemen, is the theory of this case that doesn't hold water."

She paces the length of the jury box, her arms still folded. "Common sense, Ladies and Gentlemen. This case isn't about unwanted sexual advances. And it certainly isn't about self-defense."

They stare at her, rapt, all fourteen of them.

"We all know what happened here," she says. She raises her favorite glossy again, says nothing.

Three-quarters of the jurors avert their eyes this time around. Geraldine waits, her silence suggesting she'll stand there for the rest of the month if that's what it takes to get them to view the bloody scene one last time. And one by one, they do.

"This is what happened," our district attorney says at last. "A holy place. A holy man. An unholy crime."

EIGHT

"RELAX," Harry says as he drops into the chair across from mine. "It's Friday. Maybe he went out for a beer."

I stare across the table at him, drumming my fingers on the red Formica. "When was the last time you saw him go out for a beer at two in the afternoon?"

The Kydd isn't answering the phones again. And we've already learned what that means: nothing good.

"Well, then maybe he's doing a little Christmas shopping. 'Tis the season, you know."

I frown. Even he doesn't believe the Kydd is shopping. We're back at the Piccadilly, where today's special is a fried clam roll, with fries and slaw on the side. Harry ordered two. He needs to keep his strength up, he said, while the jury deliberates.

"I just wish he'd return my messages, tell us what the hell is going on."

"Don't worry," Harry says, squeezing open the spout of his second chocolate milk. "Bad news keeps, remember?"

He's right. That's precisely why I'm on edge.

"Oh, look," he says, sounding delighted, "it's the God Squad." He waves toward the door, as if he's hailing a cab, so I turn to find out who's here. It's Geraldine, with Monsignor Davis in tow.

"Over here," Harry calls, still waving at them. "Join us, Your Émigré. And by all means, bring your friend."

Oddly enough, he does. They cross the room and stand beside our table. The monsignor smiles at us. Geraldine doesn't.

"What keeps you in our midst, Padre?" Harry sticks a thumb out at Geraldine. "You're not trying to save her wretched soul, are you?"

Monsignor Davis laughs, then grows serious. "The Kendricks are part-time parishioners," he says. "I thought I might be of some assistance to them, offer some spiritual support."

My stomach knots. "The Kendricks? What about them? Why do they need support, spiritual or otherwise?"

The monsignor looks suddenly worried. He doesn't answer; he turns to Geraldine instead, giving her the floor. She has news, apparently, and before she says a word, I know exactly what it is. "Charles Kendrick is in custody," she tells me. "I thought you'd want to know. He's in lockup now. Your associate is with him."

So much for the Kydd's shopping spree.

"Arraignment is scheduled for five," she says.

"Five? All the players are here now. What are we waiting for?" Not that I'm in any big hurry. Harry was right. Bad news keeps.

"To accommodate the Forresters," she says. "They asked that we give them enough time to make the drive from Stamford."

Of course they did. Warren, Catherine, and Meredith want to hear Geraldine's evidence against the senator firsthand. They want to ask the question all murder victims' families ask, the one that's never adequately answered: *Why?*

Geraldine turns and heads for the door, her mission apparently accomplished. Monsignor Davis starts to follow, but he pauses and rests a hand on my shoulder. "I'll say a prayer," he says.

"Thanks," I tell him.

With that, he leaves, and for a split second I wish I were Catholic, a notion I've never stumbled upon before. Faith might help. I wish mine weren't so riddled with doubt.

WE'RE in lockup. We've been here for the better part of three hours now: Charles Kendrick, the Kydd, and I. Our client's mantra hasn't wavered. "I don't have any idea," he tells us again and again. "I don't know anything about it. I swear."

"Our district attorney has been wrong in the past," I tell him, "but she's never been sloppy. She had you hauled in here; that means she's got evidence. If you know what the evidence is—or even what it might be—it would behoove you to give us a heads-up. I'm tired of running this race a lap behind Geraldine Schilling."

"I don't," he says, looking from me to the Kydd. "I swear to God I don't know what evidence she could have. I would never lift a hand to Michelle. I had nothing to do with her death."

Maybe politicians are particularly persuasive by nature. Or maybe I'm going soft in my middle age. Whatever the reason, I believe him.

A series of knocks quiets us, and then the door opens. "It's time," a uniformed guard says as he and his partner crowd into the small room.

Charles Kendrick and his escorts enter the main courtroom of the district courthouse first, the Kydd and I bringing up the rear. The noise in the enormous room escalates as soon as the first trio clears the doorway, before I can even see inside. I'm startled by the volume.

Half the year-round residents of North Chatham are here. The Kendricks' deaf neighbor, Helene Wilson, is among them. Her gaze moves from the senator to me, and she shakes her head. Her eyes are worried.

Members of the press corps jockey for the front spots in the side aisles. Most of the reporters call out urgent questions as we approach our table. They're wired. The senator's arrest isn't just a scoop; it's a scandal.

Honey Kendrick is already here, seated in the front row, directly behind our table. Abby sits on one side of her, holding her mother's hand. Monsignor Davis is on the other, seated sideways and talking quietly with both of them. Mother and daughter are in tears; the monsignor is doing his best to console them.

Only two chairs are pulled up to the defense table. The Kydd points to the empty seats at the bar, telling me he'll sit back there.

"Not on your life," I tell him. "Find another chair and sit right here." He retrieves another chair from against the side wall without argument. No sooner does he sit than the room falls abruptly silent.

The sudden quiet prompts those of us seated up front to shift in our chairs. The explanation stares back at us. The Forresters—Mom, Dad, and big sister—are just inside the back doors, looking straight ahead at our table, at the senator, at the man they've been told murdered Michelle. Even at this distance, their expressions shut us down. They're stricken. In pain. And it's physical.

The chambers door opens, and the bailiff tells us to rise. I'm surprised when the judge emerges—pleasantly so. All arraignments are held in district court and most are presided over by district court judges. The chief judge apparently made a special request on behalf of our senior senator, though. Leon Long is here for this one, and he ordinarily presides in superior court.

Judge Long is the only black judge ever to sit in Barnstable County. And no matter which bench he's on, he's a welcome sight to members of the defense bar. In his courtroom, the presumption of innocence is real, and the prosecution's burden is steep. He bangs his gavel before he sits, but it's not necessary. The Forrester family has already called this room to order.

The courtroom clerk stands, recites the docket number, and then announces, "The *Commonwealth of Massachusetts versus Charles Johnson Kendrick.*"

Geraldine is up instantly. "Your Honor," she says, "Mr. Kendrick is charged with the first-degree murder of Michelle Andrea Forrester, a murder committed with extreme atrocity or cruelty."

Judge Long looks at me and shakes his head, ever so slightly. The signal is almost imperceptible, but it's there. And I've tried enough cases before him to know what he's telling me. He doesn't want to hear the senator's plea yet. He wants the district attorney to put her cards on the table first.

"Ms. Schilling," he says, "let's hear the facts."

Most Barnstable County judges will take a simple plea from the defendant—guilty or not—before they call for a recitation of the facts. Not Leon Long. In his courtroom, the defendant need not say a word until the government demonstrates it's got something real against him.

Geraldine seems ready to do just that. "As you are undoubtedly aware, Your Honor, Ms. Forrester went missing last Thursday, eight days ago. She was last seen at Cape Cod Community College, wrapping up a press conference for her employer." Geraldine stops and points at the senator.

"Charles Kendrick was one of the first witnesses we interviewed. I spoke with him personally, Monday morning and again Monday afternoon. On both occasions, he claimed he had no contact with the deceased after the Four Cs press conference."

Geraldine looks over at us and almost smiles before she continues. "The deceased's automobile, a BMW roadster, was found on Tuesday, parked deep in the woods near the intersection of Old Queen Anne and Training Field roads in Chatham."

I turn to check in with the Kydd, then with the senator. They're as surprised as I am. This is the first any of us has heard of Michelle's car being found.

"That's right," Geraldine says. "We withheld that fact from the public, pending the results of forensic testing."

Geraldine returns to her table, and Clarence hands her three documents. She delivers one copy to us, passes another up to the judge, and holds on to the third. "Hair follicles and skin fragments," she says. "Multiple samples. *All* match those of the deceased."

The judge studies his copy of the report, then peers over the rims of his half-glasses. "That's to be expected," he says to Geraldine. "It was her car."

"True," she says. "That *is* to be expected." She turns and walks slowly toward us, her eyes holding the senator's. "But not in the trunk."

A single sob fills the room, then ends abruptly. Catherine Forrester sits in the front row behind the prosecutors' table, both hands pressed over her mouth. Her eyes are squeezed shut, and two rivers course down her cheeks. She's flanked by Warren and Meredith, both fighting losing battles with their own floodgates.

Geraldine waits, longer than necessary, still staring at the senator. "Counselor," Judge Long says quietly, "continue."

"Blood," she says, looking up at him. "We also found a solitary— but sizable—patch of blood on the upholstery in the trunk. It, too, matches that of the deceased."

The judge nods. Geraldine goes back to her table, retrieves an evidence bag, and hands it up to him. "And this," she says. "A rope, approximately eighteen inches in length."

Judge Long scrutinizes the bag, then looks back at Geraldine. "Ordinary clothesline," he says.

"Exactly," she agrees as she walks toward us again. "What we *didn't* find," she says, "is the spare. The BMW roadster's spare tire is ordinarily stored in the trunk. Michelle Forrester's was missing." She slaps a hand on our table, and the senator jumps a little beside me. "Until this morning," she says, glaring at him.

Senator Kendrick stares back at her, then at me, and shakes his head. He doesn't know what she's talking about.

"As we all know," she says, turning away from him and facing the bench again, "Chatham's harbormaster found Ms. Forrester's body yesterday, floating in the shallows of Pleasant Bay."

Catherine breaks down again. Geraldine pauses, allowing the mother's sobs to take center stage.

"Our medical examiner performed the autopsy yesterday," she says at last. She retrieves another set of documents from Clarence and delivers copies to us and to the judge. "This is his report."

I check the signature line, then pass it over to the Kydd.

"Cause of death," she says, holding up her copy of the autopsy report, "cerebral hemorrhage."

Catherine's sobs had softened, but they escalate again. Geraldine turns to look at her. "Induced by blunt trauma to the cranium," she says quietly, "a single heavy blow to the skull. She was dead before her body was dumped into the ocean."

All three Forresters are audibly crying now. Everyone else in the room is silent. The senator is rigid beside me.

"My office secured a search warrant this morning," Geraldine continues as she marches toward us, "for the Kendrick property on Old Harbor Road." She pounds our table, her fist landing squarely in front of our paralyzed client. "We found Michelle Forrester's spare. In this man's garage."

A surge of commentary erupts in the gallery. The judge pounds his gavel, hard. Geraldine is on the move; she's got more.

"We also found a coil of clothesline hanging on a nail," she says, pointing at the evidence bag on the bench. "That clothesline."

Judge Long looks down at the rope but doesn't react.

"We found blood on the garage floor," she says. "Traces, but enough. It's a match."

Geraldine returns to her table. Clarence kneels beside it, retrieves a long, narrow, plastic-wrapped package, and hands it to her. It's almost as long as she is.

"And finally," she says, "we found this."

She lays it on the bench. "A shovel," she says. "The shovel that was used to murder Michelle Andrea Forrester."

The onlookers grow noisy again, but Judge Long doesn't bother to hush them. Instead, he goes back to the lab report, and the Kydd pushes a page from our copy across the table to me. He's highlighted the portion that details the evidence found on the underside of the shovel's heavy metal base: hair, blood, skin fragments. All Michelle's, along with a small slice of her scalp.

I lean toward my client, hoping he'll have something to say, some theory about what the hell happened here. He doesn't, though. He's turned completely around in his chair, his eyes locked with Honey's. She's staring back at him, dry-eyed, open-mouthed. She looks horrified. So does he.

Judge Long sets the lab report on the bench. He's quiet for a moment—as is everyone else in the room now—staring down at the damning report. When he turns his attention our way, his somber expression says it all. Geraldine Schilling has done her job;

she's assembled a case against the senator, a real one. "Counsel," the judge says to me, "how does your client plead?"

"Guilty." The voice is loud, and it takes a second for me to realize it came from the seat next to mine. The senator is on his feet in a flash. I grab his arm. "Shut up," I tell him. "Now."

He shakes my hand away. "I'm ready for sentencing," he says to the startled judge. "I'm guilty."

The room goes nuts. Judge Long bangs his gavel a half dozen times. "Senator Kendrick," he says, "you're represented by counsel, sir. Your attorney will enter your plea. Please be seated."

The senator moves out from behind our table. "My attorney doesn't know anything about it," he says. "I lied to her."

The noise in the gallery goes up another decibel.

"Look," he says to Judge Long, "Michelle Forrester and I had an affair."

Pandemonium erupts behind us.

"I broke it off," the senator continues, "four months ago. But last Thursday . . ." He turns to Honey and grimaces. "I lapsed."

"Senator Kendrick," Judge Long says, almost shouting to be heard above the ruckus, "I strongly advise you to sit down now."

It's pretty clear the senator isn't going to take the judge's advice. "Michelle and I spent last Thursday night together," he says. "It was a terrible mistake."

"Senator!" The judge is on his feet now. He bangs his gavel once more, hard. "Please, sir, be seated."

Not a chance. "Michelle read more into that night than I intended," the senator says. "She thought we'd reestablished our prior relationship. She thought we'd go forward as a couple. Michelle wanted more from me than I was free to give."

Honey buries her face in her hands, sobbing. Abby wraps her arms around her mother; then she breaks down too.

"When I explained that to her," the senator continues, "she got angry. She threatened to go to my wife. And then . . ."

He pauses for a breath, and I realize that he's trembling.

"And then I lost my temper." He shrugs, exactly the way he did in my office when he described Michelle's impromptu visit to Old Harbor Road. *The rest was inevitable,* he's telling us.

I don't buy it.

"Your Honor," I shout above the ruckus, "we ask the court to enter a *not* guilty plea at this time."

"That's out of the question." Geraldine is shouting now too. "The man already entered a plea. He can't change it now."

Judge Long bangs his gavel repeatedly until the crowd quiets. "You forget, Ms. Schilling, that this man's plea is not entered until I accept it." His words are quiet, measured. "And I don't." He looks from Geraldine to me to the senator. "I don't accept *any* plea at this time."

He packs up his file and stands. "We'll reconvene on Monday morning," the judge says as he leaves the bench, "first thing. The defendant will enter his plea at that time."

Geraldine shakes her head; she's frustrated.

Judge Long pauses and turns to the defense table. "Senator Kendrick," the judge says, "I suspect your lawyer plans to spend some time with you this weekend."

I sure as hell do. They both look at me, and I nod.

Judge Long turns his attention back to the still-trembling senator. "I strongly suggest you listen to her, sir. Take her advice." He takes another quick glance at me, then heads for chambers.

The room erupts again as soon as the judge exits.

"What the hell was that?" I bark at my client.

"It was a confession," he says.

"It was not. It was an act. You were lying."

He shakes his head, his eyes angry. "You don't know what you're talking about," he says. "I was owning up to my crime."

"You were owning up to someone *else's* crime."

He takes a deep breath before he answers. "That's ridiculous," he says, his voice even. "But I understand. You're a criminal-defense attorney. You're not used to people coming clean."

"What I'm not *used to,*" I tell him, "is standing by while my client pleads guilty to a crime he didn't commit."

He looks into the distance, grits his teeth, and says nothing.

"Listen to me," I tell him, "we're talking about first-degree murder here, life behind bars. Life. Whatever it is you're hiding can't be worse."

His gaze returns to me. "You don't know that," he says.

And he's right. I don't.

HARRY doesn't pull into our office driveway when we reach it; he cruises on by. "What?" I ask. "The day hasn't been long enough? We're taking a joy ride now?"

"Just a short one," he says.

He's out of his mind. It's seven-thirty. He hung around the superior courthouse until six, when the Holliston jurors retired to their hotel for the evening, then he crossed the parking lot and caught the final moments of chaos in the district court. It was pushing seven by the time we extricated ourselves from the reporters and made our way to his Jeep.

"Are stores open?" Harry asks now.

He really isn't of this planet. "It's eight days before Christmas," I tell him. "Of course they are."

"How about flower stores?" he asks.

I stare at him. My feet hurt, my head aches, and my stomach's growling. I want to sit someplace warm and quiet and eat dinner, not go shopping—for flowers or anything else.

He narrows his eyes. "Thought I'd pick up a little something for my special someone," he says.

That's a bald-faced lie. He knows me well enough to know that at this point in the workweek, I'd rather have a back rub than a bouquet of roses.

"Well, she's out of luck," I tell him. "I don't think you'll find any florists open at this hour." I lean over and kiss his cheek. "But I bet she'd settle for a filet mignon and a good Cabernet."

"You read my mind," he says. "How about Pete's?"

Pete's is a celebrated steak house on Main Street in Chatham. The entire menu is top-notch, but it's the baked stuffed potatoes that bring Harry to his knees. "Sounds good," I tell him. "There's just one problem."

"What's that?"

"You've already passed it."

"I know," he says. "We'll come back. I want to make a couple of stops first." He pulls into the parking lot of the Chatham Village Market and stops in front of the Christmas trees.

"I need a wreath," he says. He hops out and heads for the small shanty that serves as a temporary shop. I watch while he chats with the tree merchant, a burly man in denim overalls and a striped stocking cap. In no time at all, Harry's headed back, his purchase complete. He hands me a fragrant circle of pine.

It's understated, lovely. "Where are you going to hang it?" I ask as Harry puts the Jeep back in gear.

"I'm not," he says. He turns right out of the driveway, heading eastbound again.

"Pete's is the other way," I remind him.

"One more stop," he says, covering my hand with his. "Promise."

We ride in silence for a short while. Harry takes a left on Old Harbor Road, then a right on Highland Avenue. I'm downright stunned. "We're going to church?" I ask. "The *Catholic* church?"

He shakes his head as he parks on the street. "Hell, no," he says. "The steeple would implode if we did."

Harry takes the wreath from my lap and gets out of the Jeep, so I follow. A few dozen cars are already parked in the church's large lot, and more are pulling in. A lighted sign near the front steps explains. The children's Christmas pageant begins at eight, fifteen minutes from now. The organist has already begun, though. "O Come, All Ye Faithful" wafts through the air. Harry sings along as we walk around the side of the church.

He stops when we reach the back of the church. I realize we're in a small cemetery, the one Monsignor Davis described on the witness stand. Now I understand Harry's need for a wreath. There are about a dozen graves back here, situated randomly around a stone image of a woman clutching her heart.

We locate Father McMahon's burial site easily. Harry sets the wreath at its base, and the two of us stand in silence, staring at the grave of a man neither one of us ever met. His simple stone is inscribed with a passage from scripture:

> *Come to Me, all you who labor and are burdened,*
> *and I will give you rest. Take My yoke upon*
> *you and learn from Me, for I am gentle and lowly*
> *in heart, and you will find rest for your souls.*
> *For My yoke is easy and My burden is light.*
> *Matthew 11:28–30.*

"It's a damned shame," Harry says. "Derrick Holliston murdered a good man. And then I murdered his memory."

"You were doing your job," I tell him.

Harry shakes his head. "My words maligned a man who didn't deserve it. I'm responsible for them."

"You don't know what happened here a year ago."

"Yes, I do," he says quietly

Here we go again. "You don't, Harry. You have your suspicions, but you don't *know* anything about it. Maybe it went down just as Holliston said."

He arches his eyebrows at me but says nothing.

"Christmas visitors!"

Monsignor Davis opens his arms, welcoming us, as he approaches. "As the Magi visited the Christ child in the manger, so you've come to visit our Father McMahon."

"Damn," Harry says, shaking the priest's hand. "We forgot the frankincense. And the shops are plum out of myrrh."

The monsignor laughs. "Not to worry," he says. "Frank would be glad just for your visit."

"Don't be so sure about that," Harry says. "If I were Frank, I wouldn't offer me an eggnog."

Monsignor Davis looks curious but apparently decides not to inquire further. "Any word from the jury?" he asks instead.

"Nada," Harry tells him. "They've quit for the night."

The monsignor checks his watch, then heads for the back door. "The pageant's about to begin," he says. "Are you coming?"

Harry starts to laugh, then catches himself. "Maybe some other time," he says. "The camels are hungry."

The monsignor waves and then turns away from us, laughing as the heavy door slams shut behind him.

Harry drapes his arm around my shoulders as we head back toward Old Harbor Road. "Who're you calling a camel?" I ask.

He lowers his head, his expression hangdog. "I knew *that* was a mistake." He smiles apologetically.

Harry makes a U-turn, heading for Pete's, and in the dim glow of the streetlights, he looks a little bit sad.

"Remember," I tell him, "even if you're right about Holliston, you don't have a monopoly on lying clients. I've got one on my hands too."

"So you said." He reaches over and cups my cheek in his palm. "What makes you so sure?" he asks.

"I don't know," I tell him. "But I am. Charles Kendrick is lying. He's taking the rap for a murder he didn't commit."

"You don't know that," Harry says. "You can't."

He's right, of course. I can't.

But I do.

NINE

Saturday, December 18

SATURDAY mornings in our office tend to be busy, particularly for the Kydd. He handles most of the misdemeanors that come our way, and Friday nights seem to foster misdemeanor mania. Minor drug busts, barroom brawls, and petty thefts fill our front office.

Harry and I pour mugs of coffee, then head upstairs to my office. Neither of us expects to get much work done today, but we need to be here, ready to race to the courthouse, in case the Holliston jury reaches a decision. Generally speaking, jurors don't like weekend duty. A quick determination of Derrick Holliston's fate wouldn't surprise either of us.

Harry sets his mug on the coffee table and flops on the couch. I take a seat at my desk, figuring I'll sort through the week's phone messages and mail. The intercom buzzes before I get started, though. "Marty," says the Kydd, "there's someone here to see you. Her name's Helene Wilson."

"Send her up," I tell him.

She appears at the top of the spiral staircase in a red cable-knit sweater and blue jeans. "I'm sorry to show up unannounced," she says. "I was planning to call on Monday, but I was driving by and saw all the cars parked outside, and I thought maybe you were here, even though it's Saturday."

She's worked up, speaking quickly, her cheeks flushed. I rummage around on my desk to find a legal pad and pen, then write: *It's fine. I'm glad to see you.*

Harry's on his feet, and I make the introductions, hers out loud, his on paper. They both sit, side by side, on the couch, and I grab a chair from in front of my desk and face them, my eyes on Helene.

"I saw Senator Kendrick's arraignment," she says. "I was there, in the courthouse, yesterday."

Of course she was. I noticed her before we got started.

"Is he sticking to it?" she asks at last. "Is the senator still claiming he killed the young woman?"

I nod again, though if Charles Kendrick had changed his mind during the last twelve hours, I'd probably be the last to know.

She shakes her head. Again her eyes are worried, her expression distressed. "Something is terribly wrong," she says.

I lean forward, closer to her. Harry eyes her carefully too. *Why do you say that?* I scribble.

"Because Michelle Forrester was alive and well when she left the senator's home on Friday morning," she says. "I saw her leave. It was her car. I *saw* it."

Harry reaches for the pen and paper. He looks bothered, even skeptical. *The BMW roadster is a popular car,* he writes. *Maybe a different roadster happened down your lane that morning.*

She shakes her head. "No," she insists, "it wasn't. They showed *her* BMW roadster on the news last night. And they reported for the first time that it has a silk rose attached to the antenna, a yellow one. *That* was the car I saw, fake flower and all."

Harry and I are quiet as we absorb this information. The intercom buzzes yet again and it takes me a moment to react. It squawks three times before I answer. "What is it?" I ask, still staring at Helene.

"Big Red called," the Kydd says. "The jury's done. You guys have a verdict."

WEEKEND verdicts tend to slip beneath the public's radar screen—at least until the following Monday. Most journalists and courtroom aficionados are at home with their families on weekends. So I expected the parking lot to be relatively empty when Harry and I pulled into the county complex in his Jeep on this snowy Saturday. I was wrong.

Like the lot, the main courtroom in the superior courthouse is packed. Big Red is the only bailiff on duty and he's got his hands full. The benches and aisles are already full, so he props open the rear double doors. The overflow crowd can watch from the hallway.

Geraldine and Clarence are seated at their table, their demeanors decidedly different than they were forty-eight hours ago. Even if the jurors agree with Geraldine that her office's failure to disclose the disappearance of the monstrance doesn't amount to a hill of beans, the appeal will be a nightmare. Geraldine looks stressed. Clarence looks much worse.

The side door opens, and two guards usher Derrick Holliston to our table. He seems completely composed. He pauses when he reaches the table, staring at something behind me, and I turn to find out what's caught his attention. It's Bobby the Butcher—and Monsignor Davis—side by side in the front row.

"Sit down," I tell Holliston.

He does, but he takes his time about it, sneering at the two before he complies. When I check on them again, their eyes say it all. The monsignor would like to save Holliston's soul. The Butcher would like to wring his neck.

Harry plants his elbows on the table, his head in his hands. He looks far more worried than Holliston does. His isn't the usual defense attorney's concern, though. The jurors in this case have four potential verdicts, as is true in most first-degree-murder trials. And Harry's not sure which one of them worries him most.

In all murder cases, the judge is obligated to instruct the jury on every lesser-included offense that might be supported by the evidence. Case law is clear that an instruction is required where *any view* of the evidence would support the lesser-included result. As a practical matter, this means most murder juries are asked to choose from among first-degree, second-degree, and manslaughter charges. The fourth option, of course, is an outright acquittal.

Geraldine argued yesterday that a manslaughter instruction shouldn't be given in this case. Giving an instruction on it would do nothing more than invite a compromise verdict. And *not* giving the instruction would actually *benefit* the defendant, she claimed. If the jurors fail to find the required elements of second-degree murder, they'll have no choice but to acquit.

Our district attorney's argument was a loser. Voluntary manslaughter is defined as an unlawful killing with intent to kill, but without malice. The statute specifically provides that a killing is done "without malice" if it results from an excessive use of force during self-defense or if it occurs in the heat of passion caused by reasonable provocation. Technically, at least, the jury could be justified in finding either of those scenarios in Holliston's case.

Big Red calls us to our feet as the chambers door opens, and Judge Gould strides quickly to the bench. "Bring them in," he says as he sits, and the bailiff heads for the side door.

He returns in seconds, the jurors filing into the courtroom behind him in complete silence. Most of them avert their eyes as they take their seats in the box. I scan the panel quickly, searching for the telltale white paper, and it takes only a few seconds for me to spot it. Juror Gregory Harmon clutches the form in his right hand. It's the verdict slip.

Judge Gould bids the jurors good morning as they take their seats, and they all return the sentiment. He nods to our table, and Harry and I get to our feet. Holliston takes his time joining us.

The judge pauses to allow Dottie Bearse to recite the docket number, and then he turns back to the panel. "Ladies and Gentlemen," he says, "have you reached a verdict?"

Gregory Harmon stands. "We have, Your Honor." There's not a sound in the room.

Big Red hustles to the jury box, retrieves the verdict slip from Gregory Harmon, and ferries it across the courtroom to the bench. Judge Gould reads in silence, his expression neutral.

The judge passes the form back to Big Red, then turns to Dottie again. "Mr. Foreman," she says, "in the matter of *The Commonwealth of Massachusetts versus Derrick John Holliston,* on the charge of murder in the first degree, murder committed with extreme atrocity or cruelty, what say you?"

Holliston drums his fingers on the table. He's impatient; it seems he's got other matters to attend to. I step on his foot, hard.

Big Red returns the verdict slip to Gregory Harmon, and the foreman opens it to read. "On the charge of murder in the first degree," he intones, "we find the defendant, Derrick John Holliston, not guilty."

The courtroom erupts. More than a few of the spectators shout angry criticisms at the jurors. An even greater number actually boo. The Barnstable County Superior Courthouse sounds like Fenway Park during a Derek Jeter at bat.

Judge Gould bangs his gavel repeatedly, but it has little effect. Holliston turns around, a small smile spreading across his lips. I turn, too, to take in the scene. Most of the spectators are on their feet, and more than a few of the shouters have their fists in the air. Big Red hurries down the aisle, pulling the worst offenders from the benches, steering them toward the back doors.

The judge is on his feet now, too, his gavel working like a jackhammer. "We'll sit here all day," he shouts, "and we'll eject every last one of you, if that's what it takes to restore order."

Holliston lets out a little laugh beside me; he's enjoying this.

Monsignor Davis isn't. He and the Butcher may be the only two people in the room who are still in their seats. The monsignor's eyes are closed, his head bowed and his lips moving rapidly. The Butcher's eyes are closed, too—they're squeezed shut, in fact—and his fists are clenched. Whatever modicum of confidence he may have had left in our judicial system after his own ordeal with Derrick Holliston has just gone up in smoke.

Big Red has managed to part the lobby crowd, creating a path by which his worst offenders can exit. The noise level drops a notch once they're gone, but the judge keeps hammering. "Quiet," he shouts. And this time, for some reason, he gets it.

"Another outburst like that," he says, catching his breath as he sits, "and we will empty the gallery." He waits, letting his words sink in. "Ms. Bearse," he says at last, "you may proceed."

Generally speaking, the courtroom is not a place for the weak-kneed. Even Dottie Bearse, who's spent her entire adult life working in this arena, looks shaken. "Mister Foreman," she says, "in the matter of *The Commonwealth of Massachusetts versus Derrick John Holliston,* on the charge of murder in the second degree, murder committed with malice, but without deliberate premeditation or extreme atrocity and cruelty, what say you?"

Gregory Harmon swallows hard as he opens the verdict slip to read again.

"On the charge of murder in the second degree," Gregory Harmon recites, "we find the defendant, Derrick John Holliston . . ." The foreman pauses, and, much to my surprise, he looks up, directly at Holliston. "*Not* guilty."

Maybe it's due to the effectiveness of Judge Gould's threats. Or maybe the spectators used up their outrage when the murder-one verdict was announced. Whatever the reason, the courtroom at this moment is still, silent.

The judge has his gavel in hand, but he doesn't need it. "Ms. Bearse," he says, "you may proceed."

"Mr. Foreman," Dottie says, "in the matter of *The Commonwealth of Massachusetts versus Derrick John Holliston,* on the charge of voluntary manslaughter, a killing with intent but without malice, done either through an excessive use of force in self-defense or in the heat of passion caused by reasonable provocation, what say you?"

Gregory Harmon is still looking directly at Holliston. "On the charge of voluntary manslaughter," he says quietly, "we find the defendant, Derrick John Holliston . . ."

He drops his hands to his sides. His eyes are still fixed on our client. And his gaze is steady.

"Guilty."

Holliston's up. The guards lunge for him at once, but they're not fast enough. His chair topples backward to the floor. Our table flips over in the other direction. And then all hell breaks loose. The crowd is in an uproar.

"This is bogus!" Holliston screams. The guards tackle him, and within seconds, they have him out flat on the carpet, cuffed and shackled. He's still screaming, struggling against the thick arms that restrain him. "You people don't get it!" he screams. "That priest attacked me! This ain't nothin' but bogus!"

Again, Derrick Holliston's legal analysis is lacking. The verdict *isn't* bogus. In many ways, it's entirely consistent with *his* version of events. The crime-scene photographs have *excessive force* written all over them.

Holliston staggers when the guards yank him to his feet. "Defective assistance of counsel," he shouts at Judge Gould. "That's what we got here. Defective assistance of counsel."

"Ineffective," Harry tells him. "It's *ineffective* assistance of counsel."

"There, you see?" Holliston says to the judge. "He admits it."

"Call for the colloquy, Your Honor," Harry says.

The colloquy is a ritual employed for the recording of verdicts in criminal cases in the Commonwealth. It occurs after the foreperson announces the verdict in open court, and the clerk marks it on the indictment form. Though not required by any published rule or statute, well-established case law mandates the use of the colloquy in all criminal cases. In a vehicular-homicide case that Harry and I tried together last year, a juror suffered a heart attack and died after the verdict was returned but before the colloquy was conducted. On appeal, Harry argued that the affirmation of the other eleven jurors was insufficient to sustain the guilty verdict. He won, the appellate court agreeing with his claim that a valid verdict can be rendered only by the final concurrence of twelve jurors.

We're in no shape to begin the colloquy at the moment, of course. Our table is still on its side, files and papers strewn across the carpeted floor. But Harry wants to call for the process quickly, before Holliston gets himself ejected from the courtroom.

Judge Gould turns to our client. "Mr. Holliston," he says, "I am loathe to prevent any criminal defendant from witnessing every moment of his trial."

One of the guards moves Holliston out of the way as if he's a dog on a lead, while the other helps Big Red right the table. Harry joins them in picking up the mess.

"But mark my words," the judge continues, "I will have you removed from this courtroom if you cause any further disruption."

The guard points Holliston to his now-upright chair, and he shuffles toward it, his face red, his eyes furious.

Judge Gould takes a deep breath and looks out into the gallery. "Ms. Bearse," he says, "you may begin."

Dottie stands, looking even more unnerved than she did after the first melee. "Mr. Foreman," she says, "and members of the jury, harken to your verdicts. On your oath, you do say that on the indictment for voluntary manslaughter, Derrick John Holliston is guilty, so say you, Mr. Foreman?"

Gregory Harmon has been on his feet this entire time. "Yes," he says. "I do."

Dottie looks to the other members of the panel. "So say you all?"

Eleven heads nod. "Yes," they say in unison.

Harry's up. "Call for a poll," he says.

Harry calls for a jury poll after every guilty verdict, regardless of how clear the jurors' answers are during the colloquy. In essence, the poll asks the same questions the colloquy does, but it puts the matter to each juror individually. Even a slight hesitation can fuel a flurry of posttrial motions and appellate arguments.

"Mr. Harmon," Dottie begins, "is this your verdict?"

"It is," he answers.

"And is it the unanimous verdict of this jury?"

"Yes," he says as he sits.

"Mrs. Rowlands," Dottie continues, "is this your verdict?"

"Yes," she says. "That's my verdict."

"And is it the unanimous verdict of this jury?"

"It most certainly is," Cora Rowlands replies.

Dottie continues through the front row of the jury box, putting the same pair of questions to each juror, getting the same pair of responses in return.

Geraldine leaves her chair and walks toward our table while Dottie Bearse continues the poll. She walks behind Harry's chair, keeping her distance from Holliston, and leans over the bar. "I'm sorry," she says to Monsignor Davis.

"Don't be," he tells her. "It's enough. Mr. Holliston will have plenty of time to reflect upon his wrongdoing. Maybe he'll even ask the good Lord for forgiveness. Father McMahon wouldn't have wanted anything more."

Holliston snorts beside me, and I elbow him. "Maybe not," Geraldine says to the monsignor, "but I sure as hell did."

I'm sure she did. But overall, I believe Geraldine Schilling is relieved. Holliston isn't going to walk after all.

Dottie wraps up the poll, eliciting twenty-four affirmatives in all, none uncertain in any way. Judge Gould thanks her when she finishes and then turns to the panel. "Ladies and Gentlemen," he says, "I extend the county's sincere thanks to each and every one of you. You have served well."

"My ass," Holliston says. I should stomp on his foot again, but I don't bother.

"Now before you go," the judge continues, "I warn you that the attorneys in this case—at least some of them—will try to speak with you before you leave the courthouse. They'll undoubtedly want to know what evidence you found persuasive, what issues were key to your decision. You're free to converse with them if you so choose, but you're under no obligation to do so. As of this moment, you're free to go. And you take with you the sincere thanks of this court."

With that, Big Red leads his charges back to the jury room to retrieve coats, hats, and other personal belongings. I head for the back doors, Clarence Wexler just a few steps behind me. Harry will stay here, in the courtroom, to make posttrial motions, and Geraldine will stay to oppose them. While that's going on, I'll try to corner as many jurors as I can. So will Clarence.

Gregory Harmon and Cora Rowlands are the first to appear in the hallway, Robert Eastman and Alex Doane right behind them. I approach them, and they stop as a group. "Excessive force?" I ask. "Is that what you hung your hat on?"

Gregory Harmon nods as the other three turn to him. "Pretty much," he says. He seems uncomfortable, though.

Clarence snags the next group that emerges from the jury room, and he ushers the three of them to the other side of the corridor. If they're going to tell him his screwup with the monstrance was significant, he doesn't want me within earshot.

"Does that mean you believe Mr. Holliston's version of events?" I ask my foursome. "Do you believe Father McMahon attacked him first?"

They exchange knowing glances, but no one answers. "Not exactly," Harmon says at last.

"What then?"

"Excessive force is what we hung our hat on," he says. "It's not really what we believe."

I'm confused. Their expressions tell me it shows.

"We don't believe Father McMahon attacked that young man,"

Cora Rowlands says. "We don't even think the priest made advances. We just couldn't say, beyond a reasonable doubt, that he *didn't*."

"But if you couldn't say *that* beyond a reasonable doubt," I ask, "didn't you feel you should acquit?" That's sure as hell what the judge told them to do. He specifically instructed them that they should acquit Mr. Holliston unless the Commonwealth proved, beyond a reasonable doubt, that he did not act in self-defense.

They all shake their heads. "No way," Alex Doane says. "After what he did to Father McMahon, to another human being? No way were we putting him back on the street."

The jury room door opens again, and Maria Marzetti joins us. Alex Doane and Robert Eastman part to make room for her, and then Eastman points toward the courtroom. "There's a lot of anger in that young man," he says.

He's right about that, of course. But the last time I checked, harboring anger wasn't a punishable offense on the Commonwealth's penal code.

"Let me make sure I have this straight," I tell them. "You couldn't find beyond a reasonable doubt that Holliston *didn't* act in self-defense, but you convicted him of manslaughter anyway?"

They all look at one another before nodding at me. "That's what we did," Gregory Harmon says, "and we justified it with the excessive-force provision. But the bottom line is that guy needs to go to jail. No way he should be walking the streets."

With that, four of them leave. Maria Marzetti hangs back, though. "Listen," she says when she finally looks up at me, "I'm not proud of the route we took, but I believe justice was served."

I shake my head at her. "Were the judge's instructions unclear?"

"Not at all," she says. "As far as they went, they were perfectly clear. But we didn't feel they went far enough. We didn't feel they really covered this situation."

I lean against the wall, wondering why we bother to give jury instructions in the first place.

"Sometimes you have to trust your gut," Maria adds. "And in the end, that's what the twelve of us did." She gives me a small smile, an almost apologetic one, and then heads down the hallway.

I take my time heading back to the courtroom, the juror's words hot on my brain. *Sometimes you have to trust your gut.* I agree with her. It's on that basis alone that I'm going to deliver a stern lecture to Senator Kendrick when we're through here. Maybe his overnight in the house of correction has instilled some sense in him; maybe now I'll be able to persuade him to enter a not-guilty plea on Monday morning.

Harry and I discussed Senator Kendrick's case at length during dinner last night. Harry pointed out that the senator seemed to know something terrible had happened to Michelle Forrester on Wednesday—when he showed up in my office to confess to having been with her the night before she disappeared—even though her body wasn't discovered until the next day. "Charles Kendrick almost certainly knows more than he's saying," I told Harry. "That's been a given with him from the get-go. But he didn't kill Michelle. I'm certain of that."

The courtroom is all but empty when I return. The benches are cleared, and Derrick Holliston has been carted away. Judge Gould is still on the bench, though, with Geraldine and Harry engaged in some last-minute haggling before him. I head toward our table, intending to sit, but a sudden realization stops me. Senator Kendrick *did* know something terrible had happened to Michelle on Wednesday. He knows a hell of a lot more than he's saying. And now I know too.

"Excuse me, Your Honor." I change direction and head for the bench instead.

Judge Gould and Harry both look surprised. Geraldine looks annoyed. She was midsentence when I interrupted.

"I'm sorry," I tell them all. "But I need your car keys, Harry."

He looks at me as if I've lost my mind. We're forty miles from Chatham; he doesn't like the idea of walking home in the snow.

"I'll come back for you, Harry. But give me the keys. Now. I have to go this instant."

TEN

"YOU caught them again," I say quietly. "It was bad enough the first time, at the apartment in Boston, but this was more than you could bear. After his pleading. After his promises. After you took him back."

Honey Kendrick is a better actress than I would have guessed. If I didn't know better, I'd think she was really in the dark, clueless about what I'm saying. We're at the scene of the crime—her dormered, three-car garage—in the bay closest to the house. She was in here when I pulled up in Harry's Jeep, standing perfectly still, staring at the vacant spot where Michelle Forrester's car would have been.

"You arrived last Thursday night," I continue, "not Friday. You got here the night of your husband's press conference at Four Cs. Maybe you thought you'd surprise him."

She stares at me, her eyes wide.

"But he's not the one who got the surprise, is he? Maybe you parked here, in the garage, and recognized her car. Or maybe you stopped in the driveway, went inside, and heard them. Either way, you caught them again."

Honey stares at the floor, says nothing.

"So you waited." I point to a wooden staircase leading to the second story. "Those dormers, they accommodate a spare bedroom, don't they?"

She nods and tears up all at once.

"You waited there, probably, until morning."

She bites her bottom lip, and her tears spill over.

"You didn't plan it. You'd never plan such a thing."

She shakes her head.

"But when you saw her the next morning—young, full of promise, and radiant after a night with *your* husband—something snapped. You wanted her to ache as much as you did."

The door at the top of the staircase opens. Abby emerges, walks down a couple of steps, and stands still, staring at us. She's obviously been listening; her face is ashen. I won't stop, though.

"So you reached for something—anything—you could use to make her hurt. It turned out to be the shovel. And in a split second, without any forethought, you swung. Once."

"With a strength you never knew you had."

The words are calm, steady. And they're coming from Abby.

I'm uncertain for a moment, unsure what to make of her comment. And then—in a heartbeat—I'm not. Honey Kendrick *doesn't* know the details. Abby does.

Her mother is a step ahead of me. "Abigail," she says, her voice trembling, "be quiet this instant."

Abby doesn't seem to hear. "And then," she says, "even though you've never seen a dead person before, you know you're looking at one."

She walks toward us, down the stairs, her cheeks tear-streaked. "And then you panic—like you've never panicked before. You can't move at first, you're paralyzed, and then you can't *stop* moving. You have to get rid of her somehow. Her and her car. And her stupid car is so small she won't fit in the trunk."

She stops at the bottom of the steps, looks at her mother, then at me. "So you take out the spare," she says.

She's on autopilot. Her mother can't change the course.

"And somehow you get her into the trunk, but it still won't shut. So you find a piece of clothesline, and you tie it."

"Abigail, please," Honey says, "stop." Her words are flat, though. Even she knows it's too late. Abigail can't stop.

"And then you dump her into Pleasant Bay because she's already dead, and there's nothing you can do about it."

Honey backs up to the wall, slumps against it.

"And then you leave the stupid car in the woods. And you know somebody's going to find that, but you don't know what else to do."

Abby pauses to breathe. She isn't pale anymore; she's flushed from the base of her neck up, red blotches on both cheeks.

"And then your father gets arrested for it," she says. "And at first you think that's not so bad, because he *didn't* do it, so he'll get off."

If only it were that simple.

"But then he pleads guilty, and you don't know what's going on. Until he stares at your mom that way. And then you do."

She looks me square in the eyes and waits.

"He thinks *she* did it," she says at last, pointing at her mother. "Just what you thought. And he's going to take the blame for her, go to jail for her, give up everything for her. *That's* how much he loves her. More than he ever loved that *girl*." She points at the empty parking spot, as if Michelle is still here.

And she is. For the Kendricks, all three of them, Michelle Forrester will always be here.

ELEVEN

A Week Later

HARRY'S second-floor apartment is empty, the fireplace cold. I'm surprised at first, but after a moment I realize I shouldn't be. I have a pretty good hunch where he's gone on this Christmas morning. I back the Thunderbird out of the office driveway and head toward St. Veronica's in the steadily falling snow.

When Luke was little, he couldn't bolt out of his bed fast enough on Christmas mornings. He'd burst into my bedroom well before dawn, Danny Boy hot on his heels. They'd both tug at my blankets until I opened my reluctant eyes. Those days are long gone, of course. Luke and Danny Boy were sound asleep—both snoring—when I left our cottage twenty minutes ago. Sleeping in is a luxury Luke will enjoy only for another couple of weeks. Classes resume in early January.

Abby Kendrick's won't, though. She may return to Harvard someday—her father has vowed she will—but it won't be anytime soon. Geraldine Schilling offered her a better-than-decent plea bargain—a reduction to involuntary manslaughter, a dismissal of the obstruction-of-justice charges, and a recommendation to the court for leniency in sentencing—all in exchange for a full written confession, and all with the blessings of the Forrester family. Abby took it.

She was arraigned and sentenced in a solitary proceeding on Wednesday morning, just forty-eight hours after all charges against her father were dismissed. Judge Leon Long took Geraldine's leniency recommendation to heart. He gave Abby six-to-eight years, a decidedly light term under current statutory guidelines. With good behavior, she'll be out in five.

Our system worked for Abby Kendrick—not a claim every criminal defendant can make. It worked in part because our district attorney recognized a critical fact: Abby's crime—though undeniably heinous—was born of passion. It also worked because her case ended up on the docket of Leon Long, a man who carries a hefty dose of compassion into the courtroom every day of his working life.

Honey headed to San Francisco, to stay with her parents for a while, as soon as the sheriff's patrol car left the Barnstable County Complex with her only child in the caged backseat. She told her husband to expect the process server on his doorstep—with her petition for divorce in hand—within the week. Charles Kendrick says he won't contest it. He doesn't plan to fight for his long-held seat in the U.S. Senate either.

It wasn't until Honey pulled out of the county complex on Wednesday that I noticed Luke's truck idling in the driveway, a few spaces behind where her car had been parked, a half dozen spots from where the sheriff's patrol car had been. There were tears on his cheeks when I started walking toward him, but he was quick to brush them away before rolling down his window. "She'll be okay," he said. "Abby's strong. She'll get through this."

At that moment, my maternal pride hit an all-time high. I hope he'll always be as fiercely loyal to his friends as he is today. And as to Abby Kendrick, I also hope he's right.

Harry's Jeep is parked on the street, in front of the chapel's main entrance. I pull in behind it and cut the engine, then walk around the stone building to the small graveyard in back. He's sitting in the snow, leaning against a leafless tree. He's facing Father McMahon's headstone, the old schoolbag serving as an armrest. He looks up and musters a smile as I approach.

"How long have you been sitting here?" I ask.

He checks his watch. "Sixty seconds or so."

I laugh. "You're in a time warp, Harry. I just left your apartment. I'd have seen you if you were only a minute ahead of me."

"I haven't been to my apartment yet," he says.

Harry spent last evening at the cottage with me. We ate a late dinner in the living room, close to the woodstove, and then decorated a Charlie Brown tree. Luke got home at midnight and regaled us with tales of the fabulous young woman he'd just met—we have an endless supply in this town, it seems—before laughing out loud at our yuletide efforts. Harry left about an hour later, and I assumed he was going home to bed, as any normal person would.

I squat beside him, look closer at his face. His normally ruddy complexion is pale. "You haven't slept," I venture.

"I've been busy."

"Doing what?"

He thinks about it for a few seconds. "Breaking and entering. In the night."

I stare at him.

"What the hell are you talking about, Harry?"

"I paid a little visit to Derrick Holliston's bachelor pad."

He can't be serious. "Holliston's been in the county jail for a year. Hasn't someone else rented that place by now?"

Harry shakes his head. "I worried about that too. I thought I'd have to knock on the door and introduce myself to the new tenant. Turns out it wasn't necessary. A slightly overserved neighbor of his was just stumbling home when I got there. He said that unit's been vacant since the cops carted Holliston out of it."

"How'd you get in?"

He takes his left hand from his coat pocket; it's bandaged. "Broke a window in the kitchen door," he says. "It was pretty easy."

I can't squat any longer—my middle-aged hips are complaining—so I kneel on the snow beside him. "Help me out here, Harry. Why in God's name did you break into Holliston's old apartment?"

He reaches into his schoolbag and pulls out a sack—a faded blue pillowcase. "Go ahead," he says, "have a gander."

Cash. The bottom third of the pillowcase is filled with cold, hard cash—bills of almost all denominations.

"The coins are on the bottom," Harry says, "mostly quarters. A year's worth of trips to the Laundromat."

"Let me guess." I tear my eyes from the mound of money and look back at him. "You're thinking this is last year's Christmas Eve collection."

"I'm not *thinking* anything," he says. "I know it is."

He reaches into his schoolbag again, pulls out a second pillowcase—a mate of the first—and hands it over.

I know without looking, but I peer inside anyway. And there it is: the monstrance. Tommy Fitzpatrick described it to a T. A solid-gold stand, about a foot tall, its gleaming surface intricately carved. And the small, off-white wafer—the host—is still inside the monstrance's circular window. I look up at Harry and then back to the pillowcase. "The cops would've turned Holliston's apartment inside out looking for this evidence," I tell him. "How did you find it?"

He taps his temple. "Kidneys," he says. "Holliston told us he was an electrician in a prior life, remember?"

I'm blank for a few seconds, but then I do. "If Holliston's apartment has a suspended ceiling, you wouldn't be the only one to notice. The cops would have dismantled it first thing."

"It doesn't," he says. "The ceiling's plastered. And it's intact. Or it was, anyhow, until I got there."

It occurs to me that Harry probably needs a good lawyer. Maybe

Bert Saunders is available. "What did you do to the ceiling?" I ask. I'm not sure I want to know, though.

"Took it down," he says.

"Took it *down?*"

"Just one corner," he adds. "The only spot that had been hollowed out."

I stare at him. Again.

"Holliston did a good job," he says. "I'll say that much for him. Maybe he was a plasterer in a prior life too."

I look down at the monstrance but don't say another word. The implications of this discovery are just beginning to hit me.

Approaching footsteps break the silence. It's Monsignor Davis. He's in formal robes—it's Christmas, after all—but they're mostly hidden by a heavy gray coat. "You're getting to be regulars around here," he says, smiling at us through the snowflakes.

"It's a temporary obsession," Harry tells him. "Don't go signing us up for catechism class."

Monsignor Davis laughs, shaking his head. "Paying a visit to Father McMahon?" he asks us.

Harry nods. "And to you, too, whether you like it or not." He holds out a pillowcase, the one full of money. "Here," he says, "this is yours. And I hope you'll believe me when I tell you I didn't have it until a couple of hours ago."

The monsignor looks into the sack, then at me, then at Harry. "Glory be to God," he whispers. "What *is* this?"

Neither of us answers. We wait.

His expression changes, the explanation dawning on him. "But there's no way to know," he says. "Is there?"

I hold out the second pillowcase, and Monsignor Davis drops the bag of money on the snow. He looks inside the second sack, then at us, then back inside. He takes hold of the ornate gold stand and drops the empty pillowcase on top of the cash. His eyes are damp when he looks up. "Glory be to God," he whispers again.

We stand in silence for a few minutes, the monsignor's eyes glued to the monstrance, the snow collecting on our hats and coats. "Justice," he says at last. "Another bit of justice for Father McMahon."

That's not true, of course. In the end, Derrick John Holliston is the only one who even came close to finding justice. He got exactly what the Constitution promises: He was judged by a jury of his peers, peers he pretty much hand-selected. Judge Gould sentenced him to twelve-to-fifteen on the voluntary manslaughter conviction. If he keeps his nose clean—and Holliston seems able to do that when he's on the inside—he'll be out in a decade. Francis Patrick McMahon didn't fare nearly as well.

"I'm sorry," Harry says, resting his bandaged hand on the monsignor's shoulder, "about everything."

Monsignor Davis takes in the bandage, then looks closely at Harry's face. "Why don't you come to Mass?" he says. "Both of you. The eight o'clock starts in just a few minutes. Share your burdens with the good Lord."

Harry holds up both hands, palms out, to stop him. "I'm sorry, Your Emerald," he says, "but it's been sort of a rough morning. Could we not do the God thing right now?"

The monsignor's laugh is hearty. He shakes Harry's hand, then mine. "All right," he says, "we'll do the God thing later."

Harry starts to protest, but the monsignor cuts him off. "Whether you like it or not." He retrieves both pillowcases and heads for the church's back door, the sack of money at his side, the monstrance pressed to his chest—no, to his heart.

"Hey, Padre," Harry calls after him.

Monsignor Davis stops on the bottom step and turns.

"Merry Christmas," Harry says.

The monsignor nods, then smiles and disappears inside.

Harry retrieves his considerably lightened schoolbag and drapes his arm around my shoulders as we head for the cars. "Come back to Windmill Lane," I tell him. "Luke probably isn't up yet, but I've got eggs and bacon. He'll follow his nose downstairs as soon as we start cooking. After we eat, we can open presents."

Harry's expression brightens at once. "Eggs and bacon?" he says as he climbs into his Jeep. "It really *is* Christmas."

LUKE'S ALREADY UP, AS IT turns out. I can tell by the thickness of the white smoke billowing from our brick chimney when I pull into the driveway. The woodstove was on a slow simmer when I left the cottage. It's cranking now.

His truck is parked next to my spot, buried under a foot of snow and blocked in by a silver Miata, its black retractable roof barely wet beneath a thin layer of the white stuff. It's a car that's normally garaged, apparently, and not one I recognize. Harry parks his Jeep behind my T-bird and eyes the Miata as he emerges. "Your son has a caller," he says as we head for the house, "and I'll bet the farm she's of the female persuasion."

He's right, of course. "Mom, Harry," Luke says when we come into the living room, "this is Chloe."

Chloe is the sweet young thing we heard about last night, and she appears to be on her way out. They're both on their feet, and she's zipping up her jacket. Luke didn't overstate his case; she's a knockout. Danny Boy is seated at her feet, panting up at her.

Luke looks happy; I didn't say anything embarrassing, I guess.

"Chloe," I say, "we're just about to make breakfast. Will you join us?"

"I would," she says, "but I promised my mom I'd be back to help with breakfast at home. We have a houseful. Thanks, though. I just came by to drop off a little present."

"Look," Luke says. "Chloe brought me this."

He holds up a pink box adorned with a brown ribbon, a combination near and dear to Chatham's locals and visitors alike. It's from the Candy Mansion, Chatham's source of all things sweet.

"Truffles," Luke says, and my mouth waters. The Candy Mansion's truffles are legendary. No doubt more than a few will disappear before we crack the first egg.

Luke and Danny Boy walk Chloe to the kitchen door. Luke's in sweats and socks, and Danny Boy has turned into a steadfast homebody in his old age, so neither of them is going any farther than that.

Harry manages to contain himself until the door slams shut, but then he lets out a loud whistle. He punches Luke on the arm—hard—when he rejoins us in the living room. "Nice work," Harry says. "And truffles to boot."

Luke shrugs and laughs, then looks down at his socks. He thinks he does nice work, too, it seems.

Danny Boy barks and lifts his front paw to Harry's shin.

"Okay," Harry says, shaking the outstretched paw, "you do nice work too."

Danny Boy barks again, a happy one, and we all laugh. My son. And Danny Boy. The chick magnets.

Luke walks to the front window, pushes the lace curtain aside, and stares out into the driveway until we hear an ignition turn over. "Is she great," he says, turning back to face Harry and me, "or what?"

Both Sides of the Aisle with
Rose Connors

Vital Stats

RESIDENCE: Chatham, MA
FAMILY: Husband David Farrell, admiralty attorney; two sons
EDUCATION: Mount St. Mary's College; Duke Law School
PROFESSION: Attorney
NUMBER OF MARTY NICKERSON BOOKS WRITTEN: 4
INSTRUMENTS PLAYED: Piano, guitar, violin
HOBBY: Clamming

IN HER nearly twenty years as a litigator, Rose Connors experienced the courtroom from both sides of the aisle, as both prosecutor and defense counsel. This has made her acutely aware of the kind of dilemmas that may be faced by her different characters, a sensitivity she uses to great effect in *False Testimony*.

Connors once commented that while as a prosecutor she was tasked with achieving justice *and* guaranteeing the defendant's rights, when she switched to the side of the accused, her task instantly became more straightforward. "A good defense lawyer," she said, "does everything she or he can to secure the client's acquittal and freedom." Period.

But she also knows that defense attorneys are human and have human consciences. And that's the basis of the ethical quandary at the heart of *False Testimony*. Harry Madigan and Marty Nickerson are required by the rules of professional conduct to put on a spirited defense for their client, even though they find his story hard to credit. The fact that Derrick Holliston has every incentive to fabricate a story that would shift blame onto the victim, Father Frank McMahon, only adds to the problem. They don't want to be party to destroying the cleric's good name.

But the rules are clear: Even if Harry knew for certain that Holliston was lying, he could not expose him; the most he could do is withdraw from the case. As it is, despite his suspicions, Harry's obligations to his probably prevaricating client remain. To some this may seem excessive, but Connors portrays it as part of the burden of justice our society shoulders in order to safeguard rights designed to protect us all.

Rose Connors has explored such interesting elements of our criminal justice system (while telling cracking good stories!) in four novels now. Her debut, *Absolute Certainty*, published in 2002, won the Mary Higgins Clark Award given by the Mystery Writers of America. Her next two novels, *Temporary Sanity* and *Maximum Security*,

Legal Thrills

If drama is conflict wedded to storytelling, then the *LEGAL THRILLER* could be drama's purest form. Literary criminal trials often unfold as a kind of duel between two conflicting narratives, stories told serially by prosecution and defense, each selecting favorable bits of evidence and contending for the hearts and minds of jurors and readers alike. The resolution will usually appeal to our innate sense of justice. Perry Mason creator Erle Stanley Gardner was an early practitioner of this literary form. John Grisham, Steve Martini, and Linda Fairstein—like Rose Connors, lawyers all—are some contemporary contributors to this ever popular mystery genre.

both appeared in Select Editions.

Connors received her law degree from Duke in 1984, and while she says she has recently "cut back somewhat" on the amount of time she puts into practicing law, she hasn't abandoned her profession. "I need my regular courtroom fix," she says.

Despite her busy schedule, she says she is hard at work on her fifth Marty Nickerson novel. ∎

Manhattan in 1943

is no place

for a girl gumshoe.

But the men are at war,

and murder still happens.

What's a gal to do

except find out whodunit?

THIS
DAME
FOR
HIRE

A Novel

SANDRA SCOPPETTONE

PROLOGUE

New York City—1943

AT TEN FIFTEEN in the p.m. I was walking along Bleecker Street near Thompson, going home after putting on the feedbag with my friend Jeanne Darnell. It was snowing big wet flakes. Snow never brought nasty cold with it, so I was warm enough in my blue cloth coat. I didn't own a fur anyway, not even muskrat. Since there'd been no tip-off on the weather, I wasn't wearing galoshes, and my feet were getting the full winter-weather treatment.

When it snowed in the city, it was always quiet, and I could almost con myself into thinking I heard the flakes land.

Then in the next second, I tripped over something on the sidewalk, flew through the air, and landed on my hands and knees. My coat and skirt hiked themselves up around my keister, and I was glad there was no one on the street at this embarrassing moment.

My knees were chilled, but the snow cushioned my fall, and I was sure the only thing hurt was my pride. There's nothing like a fall to make you feel stupid. Even alone on a Greenwich Village street.

I rose to my feet. What had I tripped over?

A few feet behind me I saw what looked like a pile of rags. Almost at once my heart did a tumble, and I knew that these weren't rags at all, but something alarming, something sinister.

I inched my way closer and saw what I'd suspected. This was a person. Was it someone else who'd fallen and got knocked out?

I bent down and right off took in that the white snow had a dark patch near the person's head. And I knew. Not because I was a detective, which I was, but because it was so clear.

This was blood, and the side of the victim's head was bashed in so that I couldn't see a profile, but the length of the hair and the clothing told me I was looking at a woman. A very dead woman.

1

I DIDN'T start out to be a private eye. I thought I was gonna be a secretary, get my boss his java in the morning, take letters, et cetera. Hell, I didn't get my degree in steno to put my life on the line. It was true I wanted an interesting job, but that I'd end up a PI myself . . . it never entered my mind.

Back in 1940 when I went for my interview, one look at Woody Mason and I thought for sure it was gonna be a bust.

There he was, brogans up on the wobbly wooden table he called his desk, his trilby pulled so low on his head it was a week before I knew he had straw-blond hair. A butt hung from his thin lips.

"I'm Faye Quick," I said.

"Good for you."

"Mr. Mason, I came for the job. You wanna good secretary or not?" That got his attention.

Mason slid his legs off the desk and eyeballed my gams. So what did I expect from a gumshoe?

"Are ya?" Mason asked.

"Am I what?"

"Quick."

To myself I thought, *Hardy, har, har,* but I didn't say it. I gave him a look instead.

"Sorry. Guess ya get that a lot."

"Yeah."

"Sometimes I open my big yap too much. So Miss Quick, you wanna work for me?"

"That's the general idea," I said, and thought maybe he was a little slow or something. But Woody Mason was anything but slow, I was to find out.

We went through some Q and A's, then he hired me on the spot. I was slaphappy getting a job my first day looking.

That was how it was then.

But in '41 the Japs hit Pearl Harbor, and by January of '42, Woody Mason was in the army and I was running A Detective Agency. The *A* didn't stand for anything. He named it that so it would be first in the phone book. By the time I took over, I knew almost as much as Woody, but in the beginning it was a scary idea.

"I'm not sure, boss."

"Ah, Quick, you can do it. I got confidence in ya. When I come back from this clambake, I wanna have a business to come home to. You gotta keep the home fires burning, like they say."

"Even still. I can't be a PI."

"Why not?"

I wanted to tell him I didn't know how, but he knew that was a lie. So I said, "I'm afraid."

"Hell you are, Quick. I never saw the likes of you when it comes to guts."

I had been on a few stakeouts with him and never showed any fear even when we got into close shaves.

"If you're thinkin' of some of those cases we did together, well, I had *you* with me, Mason."

"Ah, you coulda handled them alone. I know ya, Quick. I knew it from the first day I laid my headlights on ya. And now I gotta get my rump overseas and knock off some Nips. Ya gotta take over."

"What if I'm so lousy at this I lose the agency."

"Ya won't."

And so far I hadn't.

I'm not what you'd call a raving beauty, but some even call me pretty, and I agree I'll pass. Take today. I was wearing a short-sleeved cream-colored dress that was covered with bright blue intersecting circles, cinched below my bosom, and belted at the waist. My hair was black, the long sides ending in a fringe of manufactured curls, and every hair in my pompadour was in place. But I was getting sick of this style, and I'd been thinking of changing. Maybe I'd get it cut short, shock the pants off my pals. Rolling and pinning were getting to be a pain in the derriere.

My mouth was small but full; my nose had a little bump, but it was okay. So the point was that even though I *looked* like any twenty-six-year-old gal ankling round New York City in '43, there was one main difference between me and the rest of the broads. Show me another Jane who did my job, and I'd eat my hat.

Once or twice I had some numbskull who thought a dame couldn't handle his so-called important case, but most people didn't care that I was a girl, and they knew any self-respecting male private dick was fighting to keep us safe.

So I wasn't hurting for things to do when my secretary, Birdie, showed the Wests into my office. But I was surprised, even though it was no mystery why they'd come to me as I was the one who'd discovered their daughter's body and no one had been arrested so far. I lit a Camel and listened while they talked.

The man and woman who sat on the other side of my desk were in their late forties to early fifties and looked fifteen years older. Having yer child murdered will do that to you.

Porter West was a big man, but he slumped in his chair. His brown eyes were dull and defeated. His wife, Myrna, was a thin brunette with skin that looked like tracing paper and eyes too sad to look into.

"Will you take the case, Miss Quick?"

"Yeah, I'll take it," I said. "But starting this late after the murder will make it harder."

"Well, the police haven't done anything," Mrs. West said.

I knew the coppers had probably done plenty. Still, this was what people who were connected to unsolved murders believed. I didn't say this to Mrs. West. I nodded in a way I hoped would give her the idea that I was sympathetic, which I was.

"You have to understand that chances are slim that I'll find the killer. My fee is—"

"We don't care what the fee is," West said. He was a lawyer with an important firm, and the Wests were in clover.

"I have to tell ya anyway."

When that was settled, West gave me a picture of his dead daughter, a folder that included a history of Claudette West's short life, and all the newspaper clippings about the case. The murder, as I well knew, had taken place four months before.

"You don't have police reports or even the names of possible suspects?" I asked.

"There was only one. Her ex-boyfriend, Richard Cotten." Mrs. West wrinkled her small nose like she was smelling Limburger.

"He was never charged," West said.

"But he *was* a suspect?" I knew he was.

"For a time."

"I guess neither of ya liked him much."

"Liked him? Cotten is a despicable bastard," he said.

"Tell me why ya say that?"

"He didn't love her. He was only interested in her money."

I'd heard this before, but mostly from wives hiring me to follow husbands they think are stepping out on them.

Mrs. West said, "He was from a poor family and was raised by a working mother. She was never there, and Richard ran wild."

"Father?"

"Shot in a bar fight when Cotten was four," West said. "Richard is a very angry person."

"Did he hit your daughter?"

He said, "Oh, no. But he showed it in other ways. The way he talked to her. He always acted as if she was dumb. That's what we observed the three or four times we saw them together."

"Claudette would have told us if he'd hurt her," Myrna said.

I wasn't sure that was true.

"You said *ex*-boyfriend. How long before the murder had they split up?" I asked.

"Only a few weeks," West said.

"Did he go to NYU, too?" I already knew the answer from reading the papers.

"Yes. And he's still there. They were juniors when it happened. Being a suspect didn't change his life; it made him a kind of hero."

I also knew this, but I wanted to get the skinny from the father.

Anger flashed in West's eyes. "Some of the students got behind him, saying he was being picked on because he was poor."

"That he was a wonderful, kind boy," Mrs. West said.

"And there were no other suspects?"

"None that we knew about," said Mr. West.

That didn't mean there weren't any. I'd have to meet with a police dick named Marty Mitchum. He'd been Woody's connection, and Woody had passed him on to me. Or maybe it was me to him.

"So, you suspect Cotten because he said mean things to your daughter and Claudette dumped him? I'm not crossin' you, Mr. West. I'm just tryin' to get things in place."

"Yes. When she broke it off with him, he knew that the pot of gold was out of reach, and it made him furious."

This last was speculation, but I'd keep it in mind when I met with Cotten. "Is there anything else I should know?"

Almost invisibly West shook his head at Myrna like a warning.

"No," he said.

"Okay. That's all for now. I'll need your phone number."

I took the number down, and West handed me a check.

"You'll call us every day?"

"That's not how I usually operate," I said.

"That's how *I* expect you to operate."

"What I normally do is call the client if I have somethin' to tell."

"I don't care what you normally do. I want you to call us daily."

This was getting my goat, but I wanted this case. "Okay."

West put a hand on his wife and guided her toward the door. They went out and didn't look back.

Charming people, I thought. Then I brought to mind what they'd been through, who they'd lost, and I gave them some slack.

I thought about when West shook his head at his wife and knew it could've meant a simple no to my question, but I felt it meant something else. I didn't know what it was. But I knew I'd find out.

AFTER the Wests left, there was a tap on the pebbled glass in my door, and I told Birdie to come in. I never thought I'd have a secretary of my own when I was learning typing and shorthand.

"Were they who I think they are?"

"Yep."

"Jeez, Louise, they hire you?"

"They did."

Birdie Ritter was what you'd call a tomato. She was tall, five feet eight inches, unlike me, who measured just under five feet four. Her blonde hair fell to her shoulders and flipped up in a Bette Davis style that framed a heart-shaped face. Bee-stung lips were painted scarlet, and Birdie's big eyes were the color of Milk Duds. She wore a pink blouse, wide collar with pearls at her throat, and a gray skirt.

"Guess it makes sense," she said. "I'm goin' to lunch if it's okay by you. I'm meetin' Pete over at the Automat."

"Thought you weren't gonna see him anymore."

"Ah, Faye, he's better than nobody. Pickin's are slim these days."

I guess that was one way of looking at it.

"Have a slice of apple pie for me," I said. There's nothing I liked better than Horn and Hardart apple pie with a slice of cheddar.

"I'll do that," Birdie said, and gave me a jaunty salute.

After she left, I recalled the last boyfriend I'd had. It was a year ago. Private Don McCallister had a hooper-dooper southern accent, and he was a nice kid. Then he'd been sent overseas, and a letter came from Don's brother telling me Don had been killed.

I swore I wouldn't get stuck on anyone again until this war was over, and I hadn't. Sometimes I'd volunteer at the USO Canteen, dance with some of the boys, but that was as far as it went.

Enough of that.

I glanced at the blank paper in my Underwood, then began to make a list of names from the clippings in the folder the Wests had left. I found names of Claudette's friends and teachers, all of which I added. And, of course, Richard Cotten's name.

I pulled the paper from the roller and slipped it into my pocketbook. Time to do legwork. That was what this PI game was all about, hitting the sidewalk and gabbing with everyone ya could.

But first I dialed Marty Mitchum, my personal friend at the NYPD, to set up a drink date later on. Then I got my purse, grabbed my tan spring coat and my brown felt hat off the rack, and left the office.

The weather was getting nice, so I didn't button my coat as I walked out of my building and onto Forty-third Street. I loved living in New York City. There was always a feeling of life going on no matter what time of day or night. I ankled over to the subway at Broadway and Forty-second and descended. Once down there I dropped a nickel in the slot, went through the turnstile, and waited for my train. First on my docket was Richard Cotten.

Cotten's building was on West Eighty-eighth. I saw by the buzzer that he was on the fifth floor. I didn't bother to ring, preferring the surprise of my arrival at his door.

This was an older building, and the walls needed paint. Most walls needed paint these days, and they'd stay that way until the war was over. I made my way up four flights. Cotten lived in 5C. I knocked.

In moments he opened the door and gave me a fast once-over. "Who are you, and what do you want?"

The friendly type. I handed him my PI license. "I have a few questions."

"I have nothing to say." He started to shut the door, but my foot was in place. I hated this part because it always hurt.

"Ya got nothin' to say, ya can say no to my questions."

He stared at me. Finally he opened the door, and I went in. He knew why I was there but pretended not to.

Richard Cotten was taller than me by about five inches and had a full head of dark curly hair. He had cold blue eyes and a straight nose. He wore dungarees and a white shirt, sleeves rolled up.

"What kind of questions?"

"About Claudette West."

"Is this never going to end?"

"Not until the killer is found."

"I'm not the killer."

"I know you're not," I said. I didn't know this at all, but I needed to make nice with him. "I want to learn more about her so I can find the killer."

"Sit down."

We both sat. Me on a clumpy chair, him on a sagging, faded flowered sofa. The place was neat for a college student.

"How long did you date Claudette?"

"I didn't just date her. We were engaged."

This was news to me. "So how long?"

"Two years, four months, seven days."

I noted this display of caring. "She have other boyfriends?"

"I told you we were engaged."

"So why'd ya split? She break up with you?"

He waited a second. "Yeah. No. I mean, it was sort of mutual."

"I didn't have that impression."

"Impression? Who from, the Wests? Did they hire you?"

I ignored all his questions. "Did you like Claudette's parents?"

"Hated their guts. It was like I didn't exist when they were around. Neither of them ever said anything to me except hello and good-bye. I always knew why."

"Why?"

"Because I'm not of their class."

"Claudette was a rich girl, wasn't she?"

"I guess. Yes."

"How'd you feel about that?"

"It got in the way sometimes. I don't have an extra dime. So sometimes she'd pay. A lot of times."

"You didn't like that?"

"No. It was awkward. But she wanted to do stuff all the time and knew I couldn't afford to. So that way we didn't have to sit home."

"And you were gonna marry her?"

"I thought so until near the end. We started to get tired of each other, I guess. Thing was, I was sick of the money thing."

"And was she sick of it, too?"

"She never said."

"I heard that you didn't accept the breakup."

"Did the Wests tell you that?"

I ignored his question again and stood up. I hadn't expected to get a confession or anything much out of him. I'd wanted to see what he was like, and now I'd seen.

"Where are you going?"

"To see a man about a dog." My pop had said that to me when I was a kid, and when he didn't come home with the dog, I cried.

"That's all you want to know? That's it?"

"That's it," I said, and left.

On the street I made a few notes. I didn't particularly like Cotten, but I didn't despise him either. He was a zero. I suppose he could've killed his girlfriend in a fit of jealousy, but he didn't seem to me to have real passion. I wasn't persuaded that he was the killer.

LATER I went to Smitty's on Forty-sixth, the watering hole where I often met Marty Mitchum. Marty was sitting at the bar facing the door, the tail end of a cigar clenched between his choppers. He wore his hat perched on the back of his head, a thatch of straight brown hair hanging over his forehead like stubborn bangs.

He saw me, got up, and walked my way. "Faye, good to see ya." He pecked me on the cheek. "Let's get a table."

I followed him to the rear of the joint where we took our seats in a scrappy red leather booth. Mitchum's brown eyes were red-rimmed like he was tired or hung over. His navy blue suit jacket had seen better days, and his wide patterned tie was loose at the neck.

"So how's tricks? Ya hear from Woody?"

"Yeah. A letter came last week. He's in the thick of it, and ya could say he isn't exactly a happy boy."

"When you write back, tell him I said hello. I wish I was younger so I could give them Krauts and Nips a piece a my mind."

Marty was about forty, I guessed. "Be glad you didn't have to go. It's no picnic over there, says Woody."

"You wouldn't understand, Faye." The bags under his eyes seemed to get darker.

"Yeah, maybe." He was right. There was something about men that made them want to fight this war. Me? I was glad I was a girl so I didn't hafta go. But guys felt differently about it.

To break the silence I said, "I got a new case, thought ya might be able to gimme some dope on it."

"Ya know I will if I can." He looked relieved that I was changing the subject. "What's the deal?"

"Claudette West. Remember?"

"Sure thing. Wasn't on it myself, but I know guys who were. You been hired by who? The parents?"

I could tell Marty 'cause he was my friend. Any other law I'd keep my trap shut. "I need to know if there were any other suspects beside the boyfriend, Cotten. And I wouldn't mind anything else you might come up with."

"Ya want the autopsy?"

"Might as well."

"Sure thing." He slapped his forehead with a meaty hand. "Hey, I'm just rememberin', you found the body, didn't ya?"

"That's right."

"So, this is like a personal thing with you, right?"

"I didn't think so, but maybe it'll turn out that way. I usually don't have anything to do with dead bodies."

"I'll get on it first thing tomorrow. Good enough?"

"You betcha," I said.

MY FLOP IS A TWO-ROOM apartment on Grove and Bleecker Streets in Greenwich Village. This was another reason why the case had piqued my interest. I'm close to Seventh Avenue, and I'd found her body near Seventh.

We don't have a lot of murders in the Village since Prohibition was lifted, although we still have a rep for other nutty goings-on. The Village was a haven for bohemians of all types. And the notion of free love lingered like a fading fragrance.

I liked living down here 'cause of the attitudes most people had. No judgments. And you didn't have to wear your glad rags all the time. Most weekends, when I did my chores, I wore a sweater or blouse with my gray gabardine slacks. I figured if Katharine Hepburn could wear them, so could I. But I wouldn't dream of going uptown decked out that way.

When I got off the subway at Christopher and Seventh Avenue, I made my way along Bleecker till I came to Grove, where near the corner I climbed the stone steps to the big front door.

In the foyer I opened the second door and went to my apartment. My place had once been the parlor floor of a town house. I looked up at my high ceiling and admired my red velvet draperies on either side of the two huge windows that faced Grove. It was a big room with two sofas and three chairs. Bookcases stuffed from top to bottom lined one wall. And the right-hand front corner was empty. As soon as I had enough money saved, I was gonna buy a piano. I loved to tickle the ivories. And I wasn't a bad canary either. No June Christy, but I could do a good rendition of "As Time Goes By."

I sat there staring at the spot where my piano was gonna go. This West case was gonna be hell.

2

THE next morning I decided to skip the office and give my pal Anne Fontaine a jingle. I had a feeling she might be helpful on this case. She said she'd meet me downtown at a used-book store on Fourth Avenue called The Bookman.

As I left my apartment, my neighbor across the hall, Dolores, was sweeping the floor in front of her door. Even though we had a janitor, Dolores did this every day. She was about seventy-five, and she wore a blond wig, making her look wacky. Well, that's what she was. Wacky but nice. We exchanged greetings.

I took the subway to Fourth. Inside The Bookman, the smell was pure mold. But that was jake with me 'cause most of the books on the shelves weren't moldy. I'd been browsing about fifteen minutes when I saw Anne walking toward me. As eye-catching as ever, she wore a long colorful garment, which she'd draped so that it hung on her frame perfectly, like Dorothy Lamour, though you couldn't call it a sarong. A cream crepe jacket cloaked her shoulders. She had her own sense of style, too. She marched to a different drummer.

"Faye," she said.

We kissed each other's cheek.

"How are ya, Anne?"

"Fine," she said.

I didn't believe her. She was never fine. There were the usual dark circles beneath her brilliant blue eyes. And although she wore her blond hair neat and short in its wavy way and her makeup was perfectly applied, I could tell. Being psychic took a lot out of her. It had always been like that.

Just walking around and seeing or knowing things didn't weaken her too much, but when she was doing her clairvoyant stuff for someone, it was different. Anne would sometimes get sick to her stomach or get dizzy or both. But she felt since she had this gift it was her duty to help people.

Anne came from an upper-class family who lived on a gated block in the swankiest part of Newark, New Jersey. Her parents had wanted her to be a college professor or a doctor, even though it would be hard for a girl to do that. Anne'd gone to Vassar, but after she graduated, she felt she could do more good in the world if she plugged away at her clairvoyant knack. And she had a trust from her grandmother, so she didn't have to worry about do re mi.

She moved to New York and got her own place. She didn't advertise or anything, but word got around, and soon she was finding lost things and sometimes lost people, and, although it made her sick, it also made her happy.

Anyway, I'd become aware of her psychic abilities the first day she spoke to me in the hall of Newark High. We were both sophomores. She stopped me and said, "How's Paul?"

Paul was a boy I was smitten with, but I hadn't told anyone and had never gone out with him.

"How d'ya know?" I said.

"It's written on your forehead in green."

I slapped a hand over where she said it was.

She laughed. "Don't worry. I'm the only one who can see it."

"What are ya, some freak or somethin'?" I asked. Subtle as always. And kind, too.

"Yes," she said, and walked away.

Two days later I saw her sitting under a tree, eating an apple.

I stood over her. "I'm sorry I said what I did."

"That's okay."

"You're used to it, huh?"

She stared at me, then patted the ground next to her.

I sat.

"Are you a psychic, too?" she asked.

"No. Is that what you are? A psychic?"

"I guess. It's been happening all my life. I know things. I see things, like the name on your forehead. I don't usually say anything. I don't know why I did with you."

"'Cause you knew I was special?"

"Are you?"

I shrugged.

And that was the beginning. We became best friends.

Now I said, "Wanna go have some coffee?"

"Sure, there's a diner over on Third."

At Third Avenue we crossed under the El. Earl's Diner was in the middle of the block. We took a booth near the back, opened our menus, and took a gander. I knew right away I'd have bread pudding.

"I'm not hungry," Anne said.

She was never hungry. She ordered tea. Personally I didn't know how she could drink that swill.

"So what's up?" she asked.

"You remember that murdered student, Claudette West? Her parents came to see me yesterday."

"To hire you?"

I nodded. "Father was a pain in the derriere. He kept harping on the ex-boyfriend, said he was the only suspect. Joker by the name of Richard Cotten."

"Nothing about Brian Wayne?"

"No. Who's he?"

"He was her literature professor." Anne sipped her tea. "In some article there was a brief mention of people in Claudette's life. He was listed. When I read his name, I started to feel dizzy and queasy, the way I do."

Had I missed Wayne's name in the clippings? Or did West leave out that report 'cause he was so fixed on Cotten? I took out my notebook and wrote down Wayne's name and what he taught.

"Anything or anybody else interest ya?"

She closed her eyes. "No. Not now."

The waitress threw my bread pudding in front of me. Bread pudding wasn't the ordinary dish that some people thought it was.

There are all kinds of variations, but this beauty in front of me looked like the real McCoy. I slipped my spoon into the confection. It had the feel. And when I put it in my mouth, it had the taste.

"Good?"

"Perfect."

Anne smiled 'cause she was familiar with my sweet tooth.

"I'm glad," she said. And I knew she was.

I said, "Anne, will you work with me on this case? It's so cold I might need help." I hated to ask her 'cause I knew she'd go through hell if she helped. I also knew she always wanted to do good things.

"Of course I will, Faye."

"I don't know exactly what I want ya to do yet."

"That's all right. Get me something Claudette used or wore."

"I will. I don't want to ask the Wests right away because . . ."

"They'll think you're a crackpot," Anne said.

"I . . . I guess they would."

"Don't feel bad. If I didn't know that by now, I'd be in trouble."

True. She had no illusions about how anything to do with her being psychic affected most people.

"I feel like a crumb bum askin' ya. It takes so much out of ya. But you're willin' to help, anyway?"

"What's a psychic for?"

WHEN I got back to the office, I heard the phone ring, and Birdie shouted, "Faye, it's Marty Mitchum." Who needed an intercom when Birdie had a voice like Betty Hutton?

I picked up.

Marty said, "I got some dope, Faye."

"Shoot."

"Funny the Wests didn't tell ya what was in the autopsy report. Claudette West was three months pregnant."

The image of the Wests in my office came back to me. Especially the way he almost imperceptibly shook his head at his wife when I asked if there was anything else I should know.

"Marty, ya sure the Wests knew about this?"

"Oh, they knew, all right. That guy, Mr. West, leaned on an assistant to the coroner to tell him the whole thing. I wish we had a way to know who the father was."

"Yeah. That might give us our killer. Well, there isn't a way. Did ya find out anything else?"

"There was this other monkey they liked for a few secs."

"Brian Wayne?"

"Yeah, how'd ya know?"

"The papers."

"Oh. So ya know he was her teacher then? Ya gonna have a sit-down with him?"

"Soon as I can. You got anything else?"

"I get anything else, I'll phone ya."

"Right. And thanks, Marty."

Claudette West pregnant. And the parents knowing and not telling me. These were significant things. I supposed that Cotten was the father, but ya never knew. Maybe there was a mystery man. Did the Wests know who the father was? That would have to wait till later. Right now I wanted to talk to Brian Wayne.

NEW York University's buildings were on the north side of Washington Square Park in Greenwich Village. At the bottom of Fifth Avenue was the so-called entrance to the park, where the Washington Arch stood. It was a copy of Paris's Arc de Triomphe.

Sometimes on Sundays I'd go to the park with the *New York Times* and sit on the grass or a bench and peruse the paper. I wouldna minded taking a load off right then so I could watch the citizens making their way to and fro, but I had work to do.

At an information desk right inside the main building, I learned the floor and room number where I could find Dr. Brian Wayne.

When I got to Room 504, I put my ear against the wooden door and listened. There was muffled sound, but I couldn't make it out. So I knocked. The sounds from inside stopped. I knocked again.

"Yes, who is it?" a male voice I took to be Wayne's.

I told him who I was. "I'd like to talk to you."

"I'm with a student now."

"I'll wait," I said.

"Well . . . well, all right. We'll just be a moment."

"That's okay. I got all day." I wanted to be accommodating so he'd be more willing to answer some questions.

I couldn't help hearing some strange sounds from inside, like they were rushing around or something. I wanted to believe it was the gathering of books and papers.

Not too much time passed before the door was unlocked (that it was locked struck me as strange) and the good doctor and his student stood in front of the closed door.

She was a babe in the woods and had what they called a pert little nose. Her hair was blond, and her lips were cherry-colored. She wore a red-and-white-checked dress. In her arms she balanced a large black notebook with two other books stacked on top. Her pretty face had a rosy hue, and she never once looked at me.

"Thanks for your help, Dr. Wayne."

"You're welcome, Miss Bergman."

With that, Miss Bergman quickly made her way down the hall.

Brian Wayne watched her go. The guy was a walking cliché of a professor. He had dark hair, graying at the temples, a handsome craggy face, and he wore a white shirt, green-and-white four-in-hand, a brown gabardine jacket, tan trousers, and brown oxfords.

He turned back and gave a smarmy smile that I knew he thought dripped with charm. It didn't do the trick for me.

"She sorta looks like Claudette West, don't ya think?" I said.

He didn't blink. "Now that you mention it, I suppose she does in a negligible way. If it's Miss West you want to talk to me about, I've told the police all that I know, which isn't much."

"Can we go into your office?"

He seemed uncomfortable for the first time.

"Let's go to the cafeteria. I need a cup of coffee." He turned and locked the door.

I got the idea Dr. Wayne didn't want me to see the inside of his office, but I didn't know why. Too messy?

"It's only one flight down," he said. "Let's take the stairs."

He opened the door to the stairs and motioned me through. I couldn't help feeling a little uneasy about taking this lonely route. There was something about Wayne that gave me the willies.

But nothing happened, and soon we were entering the cafeteria, which was loaded with people. We found a table near a wall.

"What would you like, Miss Quick?"

"You're havin' java, I'll have the same."

"Fine. I'll be right back."

I lit up and looked around the place, which was jumping with students. There were a few older types, and I guessed they were teachers exempt from the war.

Wayne came back with two coffees and sat down.

"Now," he said, "what exactly can I do for you?"

"What were ya doin' upstairs with the cutie who looks like Claudette West. Why were ya locked in with her?"

"You make it sound prurient, Miss Quick."

I knew he thought I wouldn't know what the word meant, so I played along. Always better to let them think they're smarter than you are. "You talkin' lecherous?" I didn't smile.

His mouth twitched. "You make it sound that way. We weren't locked in in the way you're implying. I always lock my door when I'm with a student so no one can barge in with stupid questions."

"Ya do that with Claudette West?"

He took a belt of his java and set it back in the saucer. "I just told you I do that with all my students."

"So ya locked yourself in with Claudette."

"You're a very irritating girl," he said.

"So I've been told. Could ya answer the question?"

"Yes. Of course I did. Why would I treat her any differently from other students?"

"You tell me." I blew a plume of smoke past his head.

"There's nothing to tell. I *didn't* treat her differently."

"So, ya have affairs with *all* your female students?"

He started to get up, and I put a hand on his arm. "Sorry," I said.

"That was uncalled for."

"You're right. Tell me about your relationship with Claudette."

"My *professional* relationship was professor and student."

"Dr. Wayne, I've been led to believe it was somethin' more."

"Then you've been led astray."

"So why don't you level with me and tell me about Claudette."

"There's nothing to tell. I was her professor in comparative literature. She chose to do a paper on Henry James. I was her adviser."

"So she'd see ya outside of class?"

"In my office, yes."

"Ya never saw her anywhere else?" I noticed that he was chewing the inside of his right cheek.

"No."

"Tell me about her."

He looked at me blankly. "What do you mean?"

The question seemed easy as pie to me, so I didn't know what his dilemma was.

"I want ya to tell me what she was like, what your impressions of Claudette were."

Wayne seemed to be twisting in the wind. "She was a nice girl. I thought very highly of her."

"Was she smart?"

"Yes. And diligent about her work."

"Did ya think she was a looker?"

He pursed his lips, annoyed by the question.

"She was attractive. Well groomed," he said.

"She confide in ya about personal things?"

"She spoke of her boyfriend, Richard Cotten."

"What'd she have to say about him?"

"She wanted to end the relationship. Said he was too possessive."

"Sounds like she spoke to ya about pretty intimate things."

"No. Not really. Only about Cotten."

"Did she tell ya she was pregnant?"

His head flipped back as if I'd slapped him. "No. She didn't."

"Be honest, Dr. Wayne. You ever pitch woo with Claudette?"

"Pitch woo?" he said, his nostrils flaring.

"Yeah. Make love."

"Never."

Since there was no way to prove a negative, I didn't pursue this.

"She ever mention any other guy?"

"No."

"Well, I guess that's all for now," I said, and stood up. "Thanks for talkin' to me."

Standing, he said, "You're welcome. Miss Quick? Are you certain Claudette was pregnant?"

"Yeah, that's what the autopsy showed."

"I see." He seemed a little down in the dumps.

"Well, I'll be seein' ya."

He nodded and sat again while I walked away.

I wasn't sure what it meant in the grander scheme of the case, but I knew for sure that he'd been sleeping with Claudette West.

3

I WAS pretty hot under the collar about the Wests not telling me about Claudette being pregnant. I wanted to know their reasons.

I caught an uptown subway. Out on Eighty-sixth Street I crossed Broadway to walk over to Central Park West. In minutes I found the Wests' swanky building, awning and doorman in place. I wasn't worried about getting in 'cause West would wanna see me. And then I realized he'd be at work. I'd been so fit to be tied about feeling I'd been hoodwinked by the Wests that I'd forgotten. Then I thought maybe it was okay after all. I might do better with the missus alone.

The doorman made me think of Ebenezer Scrooge.

"May I help you?" he asked.

"Yeah. I'm here to see Mrs. Porter West."

He picked up a black contraption and pushed a button.

"A Miss Faye Quick is here to see Madam. Yes, I'll wait."

I figured some maid was tellin' the missus. The doorman spoke into the blower again.

"All right, I'll send her up."

He directed me to the tenth floor, but not before he gave me the once-over and showed me a kisser that said I didn't pass muster.

This was one of those deals that had only two apartments to a floor. The door on the left side opened, and there stood a girl in a gray maid's outfit.

"Miss Quick?"

"That's me."

She stepped aside as I entered. We were in a foyer with a marble floor, a couple of mean-looking chairs, and some potted plants. I waited until she closed the door, then followed her as she led me to a large living room.

I suppose it was Louis somebody furniture, but I wasn't up to snuff on my antiques. All I knew was that it spelled plenty of lettuce. Everything was in its place except for Madam, who was nowhere in sight.

"Please take a seat, and Madam will be right in."

"Thanks."

I looked around trying to figure out which would be the most comfy seat, sorta a losing battle in this case. Before I could decide, Myrna West was entering with a man who was not Porter.

"Hello, Miss Quick. This is my brother, Cornell Walker."

We greeted each other. Walker was obviously a younger brother. He had brown hair and blue eyes like his sister's and was wearing a Marine uniform. Perfect features made him a looker if ya liked that type. He even had a cleft chin.

"I'm sorry to barge in on ya this way," I said.

"That's all right. I presume you have a good reason."

I didn't answer.

Myrna motioned to the stiffest-looking chair in the place. They both sat on the couch.

"Cornell is home on leave," the missus said.

This I could see. "And where's home, Captain Walker?" I knew my ranks.

"When on leave, I live here with my sister." He smiled crookedly. This wasn't that unusual an arrangement.

Myrna said, "Do you have some news for us, Miss Quick?"

"Call me Faye." I didn't know how much to say in front of the brother. I glanced his way purposely.

"You can say anything in front of Cornell."

"You're sure?"

"Of course."

"I was thinkin' your husband would be here, but then I realized he's probably at work."

"Yes."

"It's not so much that I have any news; it's more some questions."

"We told you everything we know."

"Did you?"

"Is that an accusation?"

"It's a question."

Cornell took Myrna's hand. "Don't get upset, Myrna. Miss Quick is making sure you haven't forgotten anything, isn't that right?"

"Ya could put it that way. Mrs. West, why didn't you tell me your daughter was pregnant?"

She sucked in her breath like I'd punched her. "How dare you suggest such a thing."

"I'm not suggesting. It's a fact. She was three months pregnant."

Angry color rose in Cornell's cheeks. "I presume you have something to back that up."

These people were always presuming. "Yeah, I do. It's in the autopsy report."

"That's a lie," Myrna said. I didn't expect that much fury from her. She was a lot different without Porter.

Cornell said, "Wait a minute, Myrna. Did you see the report?"

Her bosom was heaving as she tried to catch her breath. "Porter did. He said there was nothing I needed to know."

"Damn him," Cornell said.

"You don't like your brother-in-law, Captain Walker?"

"No, I *do* like him. I just don't like it when he treats Myrna like she's not part of the picture. If Claudette was pregnant, Myrna had a right to know. I'm sure he thought he was protecting her, but . . ."

"Porter's always been that way," she said.

"And it's time he stopped," Walker said.

"Mrs. West, when you were at my office, I asked ya if there was anything else, and your husband gave ya a tiny shake of his head, as if there *was* somethin'. Somethin' he didn't want me to know."

"I don't remember that."

"I think ya do. And if ya want my help finding your daughter's killer, ya gotta come clean with me, completely honest."

"Do you know who was the father of Claudette's child?" she asked.

Just like I hadn't said anything about being honest. "No, I don't."

"Myrna, is there something you're keeping from Miss Quick?"

"Porter will kill me," she said.

"I won't tell him if you don't. Seems like since he didn't tell you an important thing, ya have some leverage here."

"She's right," Cornell said.

"You're absolutely sure that Claudette was pregnant?"

"The coroner is absolutely sure, Mrs. West."

After a few moments she said, "Porter hates Richard Cotten, you know that."

I nodded.

"No matter what the evidence said, he wanted the killer to be Cotten. But . . . there was this other boy. Claudette had just begun to see him. Only two weeks before she was killed. He was the kind of boy Porter wanted for her, from a very prominent family. Porter said there was no point in dragging that family into this because he knew Alec couldn't have had anything to do with it."

"And how did he know that?"

"He said people with Alec's breeding didn't do things like that."

"Is that right?" I said. "Amazin' deduction."

"That's why Porter looked at me that way. He was afraid I might give you Alec's name."

"Will ya give it to me now?"

"He couldn't be the father of the child," she said.

I gave Cornell a pleading look.

He put his arm around her and squeezed gently. "Myrna, tell Miss Quick what she wants to know."

"Even if you don't tell Porter about where you got the boy's name, he'll know it was me."

"Ya mean nobody else knew who he was?"

"Well, yes, people did. They went out in public. And that's another reason Porter thinks Richard killed her. He thinks he saw them someplace together."

"Did Claudette say that happened?" Walker asked.

"No. Oh, you people don't know how angry Porter can get."

"How angry?" I asked. I felt a little alarmed. "He doesn't hit ya or anything like that?"

She sat up straight, "Of course not. What kind of people do you think we are?"

I thought I'd let that one pass. No time to explain it happened in the best of families.

"Myrna," Walker said. "You have to tell Miss Quick whatever you know."

There was a long silence while she thought it over.

"Are you going to tell the police?" she asked.

"That depends on what I find out."

"Oh, what's the difference? His name is Alec Rockefeller."

MYRNA told me that the Rockefeller kid lived on Park Avenue. Where else? Armed with his address I took a bus across Eighty-sixth Street through the park and another down Fifth to Sixtieth.

Myrna said Alec was in his twenties, good looking, courteous, and charming. He'd come to the funeral and had visited the Wests once a week for about a month, and then he stopped. She figured it was too painful for him. She also said he was a second cousin of a more famous Rockefeller but couldn't remember which one.

The building I was looking for had a doorman, of course. My life was getting to be nothing but these mugs. This one was wearing a green uniform with the usual generous gilt. I honestly didn't know how I was gonna get into a Rockefeller household, but I had to try.

"Good afternoon," I said.

This one touched the shiny black bill of his cap and nodded politely. "How may I help you, miss?"

"I'm not sure I have the right address, but I'm supposed to meet with an Alec Rockefeller."

"I'm afraid we don't have any Rockefellers in this building."

"No Alec Rockefeller?"

"No *any* Rockefeller. Believe me, I'd know."

"Of course, ya wouldn't be doin' your job if ya didn't, right?"

"That's precisely right. Good day, miss." He walked quickly to the door and opened it for an older woman in a dark fur coat.

"May I get you a cab, Mrs. Skeffington?"

"No, thank you, Chester. I'm going to walk. It's a lovely day."

"Yes, madam." She turned and started down Park.

Should I, or shouldn't I? I decided I would. When the light was in my favor, I scurried across the avenue and started downtown, the whole time with my eyes on Mrs. Skeffington.

At Fifty-seventh she crossed to my side and headed down the block. I followed. There were a lot of people on Fifty-seventh, so I didn't have to be too careful shadowing her. We crossed Madison, and about two yards in she went into a door. There was a sign on it that said: GEORGE BAILEY, FINE ART.

I waited a minute, and then I opened the door of the Bailey Gallery. Inside, the walls were hung with pictures the likes of which I'd never seen. Every one of them looked like a blank canvas. But the name of the show was above the paintings. WHITE ON WHITE.

There was a girl at a desk with sleek black hair who gave me the once-over, and Mrs. Skeffington seemed to be the only customer. Her back was to me as she stared at a picture that I could now see had white paint on the canvas. I didn't get it.

But I sauntered over to stand next to her, not too close. I was looking at the picture next to the one she was looking at.

From the corner of my eye I saw Mrs. S. look at me, so I turned to look at her. She smiled and was starting to turn away when I said, "Mrs. Skeffington, what a surprise." I put out my hand, which she took in the tips of her gloved fingers. "How are you?" I said.

I could see she was flummoxed, but she wasn't letting on. She was a fine-boned lady with eyes that had a sparkle.

She said, "I'm fine, and how are you?"

"Just fine, thanks. Mrs. Skeffington, I can see you aren't sure you remember me."

"Oh, no. Of course I do. I'm simply at a loss as to where we last saw one another."

"It was the Rockefeller party."

"Oh, of course. How silly of me. The Rockefeller party." She held out her arm and swept her black-gloved hand, as though it was a wand, toward the pictures. "Well, are you a devotee?"

"First time," I said.

"How did you hear about him?"

Good thing I read the social notes in the paper. "Brooke," I said.

"Really? I didn't know she knew about Ronald."

Trying to sound giddy, I said, "Back to the Rockefeller party. I don't know them very well, do you?"

"Very."

"Oh, good. I was curious about one of them."

She looked skeptical and curious at the same time but didn't say anything like a normal person would. She just waited.

I could feel sweat starting under my arms and on my back. "A young man, maybe twenty or so. He was so nice to me. You see I felt a little faint, and he took me outside to get some air. When we came back in, I lost track of him, and I so wanted to thank him. His name was Alec Rockefeller. Do you know him?"

"No, I don't. Alec you say?"

"Yes. Quite good-looking. Blond. Maybe six feet tall." I smiled. "I believe he is a cousin. Perhaps distant."

"Yes. I know the Rockefellers very well . . . all of them. And I've never heard anyone mention an Alec."

"But surely you met him at the party."

"Surely I didn't. Clearly he was making sport of you passing himself off as a Rockefeller."

"Oh, dear, oh, dear." I tried to look as though I might faint, but I didn't know how to fake that. I thought it was best to blow the joint. "I'm so upset, I must go."

"Yes, you look quite peaked."

I made for the door. As I was leaving, I called over my shoulder, "Say hello to Mr. Skeffington for me; he's such a lovely man."

Before I closed the door, I heard her reply.

"Yes, especially now that he's dead."

I ran down the stairs and out onto Fifty-seventh, where I took a right. Had to do it, didn't ya, Quick, I said to myself. Always that one final thing that gives the game away. Oh, well. What could she do to me anyway?

When I got to Fifth, I started downtown and didn't stop until I made my way home. My near catastrophe with Mrs. Skeffington made me feel a little shaky. Sometimes I didn't know where I got the nerve. Woody would've been proud of me.

Mrs. Skeffington was only one source, and I knew I'd have to check out others, but I had the nasty feeling that she was right.

There *was* no Alec Rockefeller. So *who* was this considerate, charming young man? And *where* was he? And *why* did he say he was a Rockefeller? And *how* in Hades was I going to find him? And most of all, did *he* kill Claudette West?

I thought about Claudette. She was shaping up to be a mystery in herself. Her mother didn't know she was pregnant, and there were all these men in her life. Brian Wayne, Richard Cotten, the so-called Rockefeller, and the father of her baby, who may or may not be another guy. Claudette kicked up her heels a lot, to say the least.

While I was turning the key in my apartment door, a newish neighbor from upstairs came down into the hallway, and I wasn't fast enough to escape. Not that there was anything really wrong with Jim Duryea, but I was not in the mood.

"How are you, Faye?"

"Just fine, Jim. You?"

"My mother's coming to visit."

"Oh, that's nice." He looked like he'd been beaten with a cat-o'-nine-tails. "Or is it?"

"She's a lovely woman."

"But?"

"I was wondering, Faye. Do you think you could meet her?"

This was coming from left field. Why would Jim Duryea want *me* to meet his mother? We'd never even been on a date. He was a man in his forties and not my type. And it wasn't only 'cause he combed his hair from the bottom of the right side over to the left to disguise his baldness. Although that didn't endear him to me.

I hardly knew what to say. "Are you havin' a party or somethin'?"

"No, it's not that. I just thought you'd like each other."

"Oh, I see." But I didn't.

He brightened up. "Then you'll do it?"

"When is she blowin' in?"

"Tomorrow. But I thought the night after that you could come to dinner."

I wanted to give an outright no, but he looked so pathetic that I sashayed around.

"You know my work, Jim, so I can't make real firm plans. Somethin' might come up, and I wouldn't want to disappoint ya."

"Could we say it's tentative then?"

"Sure."

He grinned like a baby getting his first taste of sugar.

"Oh, thank you. You don't know how much this means to me."

MY BEDROOM was big, with a fireplace I never used. Two huge windows faced the back of another building, so I'd hung long white curtains. Against the right wall was a mahogany highboy. And on the left was a matching chest of drawers with a mirror.

I sat in bed, my hair bobby-pinned and rolled, two pillows be-hind me. I had my radio tuned to a music station. And while Tex Beneke and The Modernairs sang "I've Got a Girl in Kalamazoo," I went over my notes.

I wasn't any closer to finding out who killed Claudette than I had been the day before. The first thing I had to do in the morning was to find out who this joker Alec Rockefeller really was. Gabbing with Claudette's pals might be my road in. I'd made a list of them I'd found in the newspaper clippings. And maybe it was time to use Anne. I wondered what Porter West would say if I asked for a piece of Claudette's clothing?

The Voice came on next singing "Night and Day." The year be-fore, I'd gone to the Paramount to hear Frankie sing. It was a night I'd never forget. All around me girls were screaming, but Frank Sinatra was singing just for me. That's the way he made me feel.

When Frank finished his song, I turned off the radio and picked up a book. I knew I was gonna be asleep in minutes. Maybe if I was lucky, I'd dream about Frankie taking me out on a date.

THE next day Birdie was pecking away when I got into the office. I gave her the list of Claudette's friends I'd jotted down.

"I need phone numbers and addresses on these, Bird."

"Sure thing," she said, and got back to the typewriter.

I hung up my hat and coat, went into my office, and sat down at my desk. I was flipping through the mail when I heard the phone ring. Then Birdie yelled my name.

"Yeah?"

"Pick up. It's an Alec Rockefeller."

I reached out to the phone like it was a snake. Then I asked my-self what the hell I was afraid of.

"Hello," I said.

"Faye Quick?"

"Yeah. Who's this?"

"Alec Rockefeller."

I didn't bother to tell him there was no such person 'cause I knew he knew this. "What can I do for ya, Mr. Rockefeller?"

"Isn't it more like what I can do for *you?*"

"Okay. I'll bite."

"I didn't kill Claudette West."

"Thanks for bein' so honest, Mr. Rockefeller. What makes ya think I'm gonna believe that?"

"Why shouldn't you believe it?"

I ignored the question. "I'd like to meet ya, Mr. Rockefeller."

"I bet you would."

I couldn't figure how he knew I was looking for him. I hadn't even begun.

"Mr. Rockefeller, ya want to tell me how ya knew to call me?"

"I have my sources."

"So do I. Why don't ya tell me yer real name?"

There was only the sound of static on the line.

"Alec?"

"Why are you calling me Alec if you don't think that's my name? Now listen, Miss Quick. I want you to stop looking for me. I've told you what you need to know. There's no point in going any further."

"Just 'cause ya tell me ya didn't kill Claudette proves nothin'. Why are ya so scared to meet me?"

There was a silence, and then he spoke like he was clenching his teeth. "I'm not scared, Miss Quick. I just choose not to."

I heard the click when he hung up like it was a clap of thunder. How did this guy even know I was on the case? The only people who'd mentioned him to me were the Wests and Myrna's brother.

So who was he? He didn't threaten me, but there was menace in his voice. If I didn't back off, I wondered if he'd come for me, punch my ticket? Most cons didn't get violent, but ya never knew. Somehow I had to find him before he got to me.

I decided to call Claudette's closest friend, June Landis. Her phone number was on the list Birdie had typed up for me. I dialed Landis and made an appointment with her for later that morning.

JUNE Landis was definitely whistle bait. Blond, tall and slinky, skin like marble, eyes so blue they looked salty, and a mouth that must've driven the guys wild. She was wearing a blue dress with buttons down the side and a collar that looked like a sailor suit.

The living room we sat in was snazzy but a long way from comfortable. What was it with these people who were in the bucks? Hadn't they ever heard of soft furniture?

A maid, with skin the color of Hershey's milk chocolate, served us coffee and little buns.

"Thank you, Hattie," June said. When the maid was gone, June allowed as how we could begin the consultation, as she called it.

I'd already thanked her for seeing me, so I didn't have to go through that again. I wanted one of those buns but didn't think a snatch and grab would go over big, so I waited for the Landis dame's cue.

"I'm told that you were a close friend of Claudette's," I said.

"Her *best* friend." She blinked back tears, then produced a lace handkerchief and held it tight.

I've noticed how these broads with bucks can always come up with a hanky even though there was no place they could stash it.

"She told ya secrets?"

June smiled. "Certainly."

"She tell ya about Alec Rockefeller?"

"She did." June leaned forward and picked up the glass plate with the buns. "Would you care for one, Miss Quick?"

"Oh, all right. Yes, thanks." I reached out in a casual way, trying to give the impression I could take 'em or leave 'em.

But while my hand was still hanging in the air, she withdrew the plate, picked up a bun with something that looked like giant sterling silver tweezers, and transferred it to a smaller china plate. She handed it, and a cloth napkin, to me.

"Thank you."

"Would you like sugar and cream?"

"I take it black."

When we were done with that rigamarole, I asked her if she knew Alec Rockefeller.

"I met him several times."

"What did ya think of him?"

I thought I saw a blush spreading across her creamy cheeks.

"In a word, he's a dreamboat."

I took a bite of my bun so I could chew over her description of Alec. The bun was a tasty little thing, but I had no idea what it was. I guess it was a rich people's bun.

"A dreamboat, hmmm? Did ya want him for yourself?"

She sat straighter in her chair, looking like she was gonna give me the business. "He was Claudette's boyfriend."

"That's true. So what did Claudette tell ya about Alec?"

"She said that even though she'd known him only a short time, she was sure she was in love with him. Oh, poor Claudette."

"Did she think that he was in love with her?"

"Yes. And she hoped Richard wouldn't find out about them. She was afraid of Richard. He has a terrible temper, and he was jealous of everyone. She couldn't even look at another boy when he was around."

"What would he do?"

"Oh, he'd drag her out of wherever they were. Sometimes he'd yell at her."

"Did ya ever see Richard hit her?"

"Oh, no. Nothing like that."

"Was she still afraid of him after they broke up?"

"Absolutely. She thought he might be angry that she had gotten involved again so soon."

"Let's get back to Alec. What else did Claudette say about him? I just wanna know how they spent time on their dates?"

"He took her to swell places like Twenty-one and the Latin Quarter, all the big nightclubs."

"Did she tell ya where he lived?"

A look passed across her face that I couldn't nail down.

"No. No, I don't think she ever did."

"Would ya say that they were serious about each other?"

"Well, she wouldn't have married him right away. She very much wanted to finish school."

"To be what?"

"Not to *be* anything. She just wanted a college education. Then she'd get married like everyone else. But not before."

"Did Alec know her plans?"

"Yes. He was disappointed. He wanted to marry her right away."

"Pretty fast operator, wouldn't ya say?"

"I guess so. But some boys are like that, don't you find?"

"Some," I said. I took another bite of my bun, and it was gone. June hadn't even touched hers.

"Would you like another bun, Faye?"

I wanted one like crazy. "No, thank you, June. Did Alec try to pressure Claudette?"

"A little, I think. But there's something you should know about Claudette. She fell in and out of love all the time."

"Even when she was with Richard?"

"Oh, yes. But she didn't do anything about it. She was prone to crushes."

"Was Alec a crush?"

"I think he was more than that."

"Have ya seen Alec lately?"

"Why would I see him?"

Her question told me that she had. When they ask a question back instead of a yes or no, they're usually lying.

"Why wouldn't ya?"

She shrugged.

"Did Mr. West tell ya I was workin' this case?"

"Well, yes. I guess he did."

"Did you mention my name to anyone?"

"I might have mentioned it to Peggy Ann Lanchester."

"So why'd ya mention me to her?"

"Oh, I don't know. We were just chatting on the telephone about this and that."

"Did ya tell Alec?"

"I told you I haven't seen Alec."

"Since when?"

"Maybe a week before Claudette . . . Claudette . . . you know."

A lotta people had a hard time using the word *murdered* or even *died*. So I supplied it for her.

"A week before she was murdered?"

"Yes."

"What if I told ya that Alec Rockefeller isn't his real name?"

"Why would you tell me that?"

"Because it isn't."

She jumped up from her chair and flounced around, lit a ciga-rette, and started pacing back and forth, puffing on her cigarette like she was Bette Davis.

"Why do you say that, Miss Quick?"

"There is no Alec Rockefeller. No Alec in that family."

"Then who is he?"

"I was hopin' you'd tell me. I'd like to meet the young man who calls himself Alec Rockefeller. Could you arrange that? Maybe ya have an address or phone number for him."

Suddenly she stopped pacing and stared right at me. "No. No, I don't." There was that odd look on her face again.

"Yer findin' it strange now, aren't ya? Strange that ya don't know where he lives or what his number is."

June dropped into her chair and wilted like a plant in the desert. "Why? Why would Alec lie about who he is?"

"How do ya get in touch with him, June?"

"He calls me," she said.

And there it was, the admission.

"So could we be honest about stuff now?"

She nodded.

"When'd ya talk to him last?"

"Yesterday."

"And did ya tell him about me?"

Sheepishly she said, "Yes, I did."

"Don't feel bad. How were ya supposed to know?"

"I feel like a fool."

I shoulda known she wasn't feeling bad about me. Dames like this were pretty swellheaded.

"When did he first get in touch with you?"

"About a month after Claudette . . . died."

"And ya went out with him?"

"Well, yes."

"Ya have a date with him comin' up?"

"No. He said he'd call."

"Your friend, Peggy Ann, do ya think she might know somethin' about Alec that you don't know?"

"No. Peggy Ann only knows what I've told her."

"Are ya sure?" I knew how con men operated. Should I tell her? I thought I should. "June, dollars to doughnuts, the man who calls himself Alec Rockefeller is most likely a con artist."

"A what?"

Was it possible she was hearing this term for the first time? It was pretty clear that the big blue marble she lived in was like night and day from the one where I knocked around. So I explained.

"Mr. Rockefeller might be seein' Peggy Ann, too," I said.

"But she'd tell me."

"Would she? It wouldn't be the first time two gals were seein' the same guy and one of them kept zipped about it."

"I can't believe all this. Do you think Alec, or whoever he is, killed Claudette?"

"I don't know. But I need to rule him out. I gotta meet him."

"And you want me to make a date with him for that purpose?"

"You catch on fast. Either you or Peggy Ann. That's why yer gonna call her now. I want ya to tell her everything I told you and ask her nicely if she's seein' him. Tell her ya won't be mad."

June went to the telephone and dialed. She said hello, and I could tell it was Peggy Ann. I listened while June talked turkey. It took a while, but finally she gave me a high sign. Then she thanked Peggy Ann and told her she'd call her back later. June looked like she'd been leveled and wasn't gonna get up for the count.

"She's meeting him at the Four Oaks for cocktails this evening at six."

I NEEDED an escort to get into the Four Oaks, so I called on Marty Mitchum. He picked me up at five-forty, and I filled him in on the Alec Rockefeller connection while we walked down Bleecker toward the restaurant.

"So yer thinkin' this bozo might've knocked off the West gal?"

"I don't know. But he was after her money for sure, and maybe when she shot down his marriage plans, he went bonkers."

"What good would it do him to put her on ice?"

"We gotta remember she was pregnant."

"Yeah, but ya said she was only seein' this guy for two weeks before she was rubbed out."

"That's what the Wests said."

At the door of the restaurant, Marty held it open for me, and I went in. The restaurant was a huge room with tables covered in enough white cloths and settings of sparkling silver to make me squint. The maître d' greeted us. At this hour all the tables were empty, and even the bar had only three customers. He escorted us to a table right next to the kitchen door.

Our waiter appeared. "May I get you a cocktail?"

"I'll have a manhattan," I said.

"I'll have a beer. Rheingold."

"Certainly, sir." He seemed to disappear like a ghost.

I glanced at my watch. It was six. They should be arriving any second.

As the waiter came back with our drinks, I saw them come in. June had described to me the pale pink jacket and the matching chapeau that Peggy Ann Lanchester was wearing.

Whoever he was, he was something all right. A long drink of water in a tweed suit, resting on wide shoulders, narrowing at the waist, looking like he'd been born in it. He wore a silver tie and a gray trilby, which he lifted, revealing blond hair. From where I was sitting, he looked every bit as good as he'd been advertised.

"They're here," I said to Marty, whose head was down. "Don't look yet. Talk to me like we're having fun."

I watched as the maître d', holding what's-his-name's hat, led the couple to a table in a private corner far from the kitchen. After the waiter took their order, the guy placed his hand over Peggy Ann's, which was conveniently lying on the table. She batted her blinkers at him, all misty and adoring. I hated dames who played that game. On the other hand, maybe Peggy Ann was demonstrating her thespian skills 'cause June had told her the truth about this monkey.

Once they had their drinks, I pushed back from our table in Siberia. "Wish me luck," I whispered.

"I'm right here, ya get in trouble."

After a deep breath, I walked straight to their table and sat down in the empty chair facing Alec, not giving him a chance to rise.

"I thought it was you," I said to him.

"Yes, it's me," he said, being a gentleman. I thought the statement was pretty funny under the circumstances.

"Aren't ya gonna introduce me?" I looked at Peggy Ann.

He was rattled. I could see doubts flickering in his deep brown eyes. I waited. He took a pull on his martini.

Peggy Ann asked, "What's wrong?"

"Nothing. I . . . I'm so sorry and terribly embarrassed, but I can't bring your name to mind. Although your voice is familiar."

"That's funny," I said, "'cause your name has slipped my mind, too, and yer voice is *very* familiar." I could see that he was beginning to get the picture. "I just know we met at some party."

"The Astors' perhaps?"

"Could be. Then again it might've been at the Rockefellers'."

A flush started creeping up his neck.

Peggy Ann laughed on cue. "Oh, tell her, Alec."

"I'm . . . I'm . . ."

"You silly," Peggy Ann said. "Alec is a Rockefeller."

"Really?"

He nodded.

I said, "Who are your parents, Alec?"

"I'm a distant cousin," he said. The rest of his martini disappeared. "What did you say your name was?" he asked softly.

I ignored his question. "It's the strangest thing. I thought I knew about *all* the family. But I've never heard anyone mention an Alec."

His eyes flashed anger, and I was sure he knew who I was. "I'm not certain I understand," he said.

"I think you do. What's your *real* name, bub?"

"I don't want to appear rude, but I think it's time for you to leave this table."

"And I think it's time for you to come clean."

"I'll have to call the waiter," he said. "I'm beginning to think we've never met before."

"You're right. We haven't. But we've talked on the phone. I'm that private eye you threatened, and you're an impostor."

"How dare you—"

"Take yer outrage somewhere else, and tell me yer name before I ask my cop friend over there to join us." I motioned toward Marty with a toss of my head.

"This is impossible," he said.

"Quit stallin'. I've got some questions about the death of Claudette West."

"I had nothing to do with that," he said.

"Maybe, maybe not."

"Peggy Ann, I think I should escort you to a taxi," he said.

"She stays. She knows yer a fraud, mister."

He looked trapped.

"So who are ya? Ya might as well tell me 'cause the cat's outta the bag with the Rockefeller thing."

"I haven't done anything illegal," he said.

"Impersonation isn't exactly kosher."

"I wasn't impersonating anyone. I just used another name."

"But for what purpose?"

He glanced from me to Peggy Ann and back to me. I couldn't remember when I'd last seen anyone look so much like a dead duck. I gave a signal to Marty.

"What's up, Faye?" he asked when he got to the table.

"Would ya walk Miss Lanchester to a cab?"

"My pleasure," he said.

Peggy Ann rose, glomming on Alec before she left. "I think you're one of the most contemptible people I've ever met."

He said nothing, but he didn't lift his head either.

Marty and Peggy Ann shoved off.

"So," I said, "who are ya?"

"Nobody."

"I know that, but what's your real moniker?"

"Leon Johnson."

"Where do ya hail from?"

"Ohio."

"But ya been in New York for a while, huh?"

"Yes."

"Do ya have an alibi for the time of Claudette West's murder?"

"Yes, I do. But I don't want to use it."

"Why not?"

Marty came back and joined us.

"This is Leon Johnson. Detective Mitchum."

"Hello," Leon said.

"Leon here was just tellin' me he has an alibi for the night in question, but he doesn't wanna use it."

"It involves a young lady, and I don't want to compromise her."

"Awww. Ain't that somethin'," Marty said. "A real gent."

"Listen, Leon, if you don't cough up your alibi, Detective Mitchum is gonna have to take ya in. You're a prime suspect."

"That's what I've been afraid of."

"But not afraid enough to drop your con. How come ya didn't skip town after Claudette was killed?"

"You're not going to believe any of this."

"Try us."

"While I was dating Claudette, I fell in love."

Marty mimed playing a violin.

"But not with Claudette. Even so, I had to go on with the plan, so I asked her to marry me. It was the night before she was killed."

"What did she say when ya asked her to be yer blushin' bride?"

"She said she couldn't because she was in love with someone else."

Another one? Or was it Brian Wayne? "She tell ya who it was?"

"No. She said she couldn't."

"Because he was already hitched?" I asked.

"She didn't give me a reason, and I didn't push it because, frankly, I was relieved."

"How long had ya really been seein' each other?"

"A few months."

"Why didn't she want her parents to know before those last two weeks when ya made it public?"

"I'm not sure, but now I think it must've been because of the man she was in love with."

"Did ya know she was pregnant?"

He looked like I'd thrown a glass a water in his face.

"No. No, I didn't know that."

"You the father?"

"Absolutely not."

"How can ya be so sure?" Marty asked. "Just between us guys, ya can't always be that sure."

As if I didn't know what he was talking about.

"We never . . . we never went that far. She wouldn't. She said she was saving herself for marriage. Boy, she had me fooled." He actually sounded like the injured party.

"Let's get back to yer alibi, Leon."

"Will you have to tell anyone else who I was with?"

"We'll have to check it out with her."

"Oh, God. This is awful. Her name is Gladys Wright."

"Who's that?" I asked.

"She's Claudette's favorite aunt. Myrna West's younger sister."

GLADYS Wright met me at the door in a silver satin dressing gown that had a split up the side showing a nicely turned ankle. Her almond-shaped eyes were azure. She wore her bleached blond hair in a chignon, and her makeup was dead on, not too much, not too little. Obviously, Gladys and Cornell had gotten the looks in the family. Her apartment was in the Village on Eleventh Street, a four-story walk-up, which took me by surprise. I expected to find anyone related to Myrna West in a swankier building.

"Miss Quick? Come in."

Her voice was throaty, like she'd been yelling all night. I followed her down a long hall to a large living room. The walls were painted white, and three large windows were partially covered by yellow checked curtains. The furniture was mismatched, as if she'd thrown it all together in a hurry.

"Sit down," she said, motioning to a comfortable-looking tan sofa. At last, a piece a normal furniture.

I sat. She took a blue chair across from me and lit a cigarette.

"You said you wanted to talk to me about Leon."

"Have ya always known him by that name?"

"No. My niece introduced him to me as Alec Rockefeller."

"When did ya find out he was Leon Johnson?"

"About a week after I'd first met him. He phoned to say he wanted to talk to me about something important. Naturally, I thought it had to do with Claudette, so I agreed."

"Ya didn't think ya needed to check with Claudette first?"

"I was planning to tell her after I met with him."

"And did ya?"

"No. I didn't."

"Why not?"

"Because Leon and I began an affair that night."

"Ya didn't feel you were betrayin' your niece?"

"I didn't think about it."

This was one cold cookie.

"So that night Leon confessed to you who he really was? Ya didn't think he was a con artist?"

"Oh, I knew he was."

This dame was drivin' me bananas.

"So how come ya got involved with a con?" I asked.

She laughed, low like a vamp. "I've been *married* to worse."

"Married. So that's why your name is Wright instead of Walker?"

"My third dismal failure. The marriage was annulled. But I kept his last name."

"Why?"

"Why not? Besides, everything was already monogrammed."

"So why didn't you go back to Walker, yer maiden name?"

"Hard to believe I was ever a maiden. Anyway, maybe I don't like being related to Cornell."

"Your own brother?"

"Half brother."

"So, what's wrong with Cornell?"

"Everything. Let's just say I find him incredibly boring."

"That's all ya want to say about him?"

"Miss Quick, a person can be stupid, arrogant, or cruel, but if he's boring, that's it for me. Thinking about him makes me want to have a drink. So what else would you like to know?"

"I guess I'm wonderin' why ya didn't let anyone know that Leon was a phony."

"If Leon got Claudette to marry him, we'd all be in the money."

That knocked me for a loop.

"Ya mean ya would've let him marry her for her money? Yer favorite niece?"

"When did I say she was my favorite niece?"

"I thought you were her favorite aunt."

"Two and two don't always make four. I won't deny being fond of Claudette, but fondness never trumps money. And, as you can see, I'm in need of some." She swept her arm from right to left, taking in the living room.

This was colder than a well-digger's behind, and I was caught flat-footed for a moment.

"Claudette refused Leon's marriage proposal. So what was the plan then?"

"June Landis."

"What were ya gonna do, go through the whole set until he snagged one of them?"

"Something like that."

This was too much for me. I'd been on plenty of cases that were down and dirty, but this was a winner.

"So Leon was with you when Claudette was murdered, is that right?"

"He was. Right in there." She pointed to a door, which I took to be the bedroom. "From seven in the evening, all night." She smiled.

"What time did he leave here?"

"About nine the next morning. Right after I got the call from Myrna about Claudette."

"Why should I believe ya about him bein' here? Yer a con, which means yer a liar."

She shrugged. "Don't believe me then."

But I did. She hadn't pulled any punches about anything else. Besides, there was no reason for Leon to kill Claudette unless she'd caught on to their scheme. I put that idea forward.

"Even if she had, Leon was here all night."

"So you say."

"That's the best I can do, Miss Quick."

It was time for me to scram.

I COULDN'T CROSS LEON OFF MY list 'cause there was still the possibility that Claudette had wised up and was gonna expose him.

It was time for me to get a piece of Claudette's clothing from the Wests. I was drinking coffee in my pj's, and my hair was still in pins and rolled up. I wondered if someday they'd have something like phoneavision? I'd hate that 'cause I'd never be able to make a call unless I was dolled up.

Myrna answered.

"I'd like to come up and see ya, Mrs. West. I want to ask a favor."

"All right. When do you wish to come?"

I looked at my clock. "In about an hour."

She agreed.

Hashing over my visit with Gladys the night before, I thought, *Who says Claudette West's killer has to be a man?* Dames didn't top my list of murder suspects, but that didn't mean there weren't any. What about Ruth Snyder or Lizzie Borden or Belle Gunness?

So maybe Gladys knocked off her niece. But why? 'Cause Claudette wouldn't marry Leon? That didn't wash. I was still searching for a motive while I finished my java and took my shower.

When I left my apartment, Jim Duryea was in the hallway. He tried to act casual, like he just happened to be there, but I knew different.

"Hello, Faye."

"Hi, Jim. I'm runnin' late as usual."

"I hope you won't be late tonight."

Uh-oh, I'd forgotten.

"I'm making sweetbreads with asparagus for an appetizer and braised rabbit for the entrée. For dessert a chocolate mousse—"

"Where'd ya get the rations for all that?"

His face flushed. "I've been saving them up for this occasion."

How Jim's destiny landed in my mitts was beyond me, but that's how he made me feel. "Jim, I'll do everything in my power to get to dinner on time."

PORTER, Myrna, and Cornell were all in the living room when I arrived. Kinda like finding a firing squad waiting for me.

"What news do you have?" Porter asked.

"Alec Rockefeller is a con man named Leon Johnson."

Pursing his mouth, Porter said, "I don't see how that's possible." I was dealing with a character who couldn't stand being wrong.

"Mr. West, it *is* possible. I've met with Johnson."

"He admitted pretending to be a Rockefeller?"

"Yeah, he did."

"Outrageous. Have you had him arrested?"

"On what charge? He didn't do anything criminal."

"What do you mean? He might have killed Claudette."

"But he didn't. He has an alibi."

"How do you know it's real?"

"It's been confirmed." The last thing I wanted to do was bring in Gladys Wright as the alibi witness.

"By whom?"

"I'm sorry, but right now that's privileged information."

Porter's face looked like it might explode. "I'm paying you, Miss Quick."

Cornell Walker said, "Porter, why don't we give Miss Quick a chance to explain things to us?"

"Us? Frankly, Cornell, I don't know why you're in this meeting."

"Claudette was my niece. You think I don't care who killed her?"

Porter ignored him. "We're back to Richard Cotten, aren't we?"

"Not necessarily," I said. "Another reason I came here was to ask you for a favor. I know this is gonna sound odd, and I'll understand if ya don't wanna go down this avenue, but I have to ask."

"Get to the point, please," West said, checking his watch.

"A colleague of mine uses a technique that's a little unusual, but I respect her, and it's worked before."

"What is she, a clairvoyant?" Cornell asked.

"Not exactly."

"Not *exactly?*" Porter said. "Are you thinking of suggesting a séance?"

"No." I could see how this was gonna go over. "My colleague is psychic and—"

Porter bounded up and started pacing. "Miss Quick, is this why you're here, to waste my time?"

"I'm curious, Porter," Myrna said.

He glared at her as if he hoped the look would clam her up.

"Go on," Cornell said. "What have we got to lose?"

I didn't find him so boring!

"My colleague works by touchin' clothin' of the deceased."

Myrna said, "Oh, I've heard about that."

I went on quickly. "If ya have a piece of clothin' that Claudette wore, I'd like to take it to my colleague."

"We have all her clothing," Myrna said. "We haven't been able to part with it yet. I'll go get something." She hurried from the room.

Porter said, "You're giving her false hope."

"There's a chance we'll get some help from this. As Captain Walker said, what've ya got to lose?"

The two men glared at each other.

"Captain Walker, is it just you two?"

"Two what?"

"Sorry. Brother and sister. Are there any others in your family?"

"Myrna's my half sister. Our father married twice. Myrna's mother died when she was small. Her father married my mother, who already had a daughter—Gladys, my other half sister and then together they had me."

"And where is Gladys now?"

"God knows," Porter said.

"Why do you say that, Mr. West?"

"She's a wild thing. Married three times before she was thirty."

Myrna came back in the room carrying something pink clutched against her breast.

"It's a sweater," she said.

"That's fine." I stood up, and she handed me the sweater. "Thank you. I'll call ya. I can see myself out."

At the door Cornell stopped me.

"Miss Quick. Please don't let my brother-in-law put you off."

"Oh, he doesn't. You don't like each other much, do ya?"

"I think that's safe to say." He smiled. Him I could go for, cleft chin and all.

"Any special reason ya don't like him?"

"I don't like the way he treats Myrna, for one thing."

"When we first met, ya said ya liked him."

"I didn't want to indicate my real feelings in front of Myrna."

"How did he treat Claudette?"

"That's complicated. He adored her, but she was more his possession than his daughter. He acted as if he owned her."

"But he didn't treat her like he treats his wife?"

"Oh, no."

"Would ya say he loved his daughter?"

"Yes. But when Porter loves someone, it's not pure. It's laced with a kind of quid pro quo. He gave her anything she wanted, and she gave him total loyalty."

"In what way?"

"I hate to say this, but she and Porter were lined up against Myrna. Claudette always took her father's side, and sometimes they'd make fun of Myrna."

"Nice," I said.

"I don't want to give you the wrong idea about Claudette, Miss Quick. She was a wonderful girl. And if she defied Porter, like she did with that Cotten boy, he'd get very nasty."

"Let me ask ya somethin', Captain Walker. Do you think Porter West was capable of killin' his own daughter?"

"I think Porter West is capable of anything."

ANNE Fontaine's apartment was a third-floor walk-up on the East Side overlooking Tompkins Square Park.

She opened the door as I hit the last step. I'd called ahead but hadn't said exactly when I'd be there. "How's tricks?" I said.

"Not a good way to greet a psychic," she said, smiling.

We went inside. The living room was always like night 'cause Anne didn't open the heavy curtains on the two windows. She had a bamboo sofa that was colorfully covered in a striped pattern, ditto for the two bamboo armchairs. All the walls had bookcases crammed with books she'd read.

I sat in one of the chairs. Anne sat across from me on the sofa.

"So," she said. "You brought me a piece of Claudette's clothing."

I hadn't told her this on the phone. I'd just said I wanted to see her. But it didn't bowl me over or anything, 'cause I was pretty used to this kinda thing from Anne.

"Yeah." I picked up the bag from my lap.

"Toss it."

She caught it with one hand. I watched as she reached into the bag and pulled out the pink sweater. She held it in her hands and closed her eyes.

I waited. It felt like hours were slipping by.

Finally, Anne said, "A man has touched this sweater. Did the father touch it when it was given to you?"

"No."

"Rough."

Her face got all screwed up like she was in pain. It was tough to keep my trap shut, but I knew the drill.

"Oh, God. No. Very rough."

She was swingin' her head back and forth.

"Stop it, stop it," she said.

Anne was moving around on the sofa, and then she jumped up. With one hand she swung at the air. "Don't. Don't do that. Oh, no. Oh, God." She crumpled to the floor, and her eyes opened.

I stayed still, asking only if she was okay.

She nodded and stood up very slowly, the sweater still in her hands as she went back to the sofa.

My patience, not my long suit, caved. "What happened, Anne?"

"There was a man," Anne said. "He was trying to hurt me. But I don't think he wanted to kill me."

"What did the man look like?"

"I don't know. His face was blurry. He was in the shadows."

"How'd ya know it was a man?"

"His hands. I could see them because they were pulling at me, then grabbing me hard. He hurt my arms. This man was strong." She shuddered. "And then it turned into what it always does lately."

"What?"

"There's a battlefield. No matter what images I start with, they devolve into a battlefield or a foxhole or something to do with war."

"Does it happen every time ya try to do somethin' like ya did today?"

"No. Not all the time."

"Are there certain visions that connect to war themes?"

"I don't know. I haven't thought about that."

"So what do ya make of the stuff ya saw before the war scenes?"

"That's pretty clear. Someone, some man, was trying to make Claudette do something she didn't want to do."

It could be her killer, or it could be Leon or Richard or Brian Wayne. Or some guy I didn't even know about yet. Maybe the one she said she was in love with.

"I got a sense. A feeling. Different feelings go with different images. Even though he hurt me . . . her . . . it wasn't pain he wanted to inflict. He wanted his will to overcome hers. That has a different feel to it. And then, of course, colors."

She'd told me before that different feelings had different colors that went with them.

"What color did ya see?"

"Red. A very deep red."

"And that means?"

"Domination."

As I KNOCKED on Jim Duryea's door, I gave my watch a look-see. It was seven-thirty on the dot. The door opened, and there he was in a red smoking jacket with lapels of black velvet. His trousers were gray gabardine.

"Welcome, Faye."

I'd brought a bottle of Chianti, and I held it out in front of me, speechless.

He took the bottle. "Thank you. Come in, come in."

When I stepped across the threshold, I felt like I was gonna suffocate. Every square inch, as far as I could see, was filled, decorated, covered. It was like being in a museum, except museums left space between items. There were figurines, tiny boxes, glass objects, pottery, china cups, and geegaws on every available surface.

The walls got the same treatment with mirrors, paintings, drawings, and other hanging objects I didn't wanna even guess at.

"You look lovely," he said.

I'd worn a dress I'd had for years, but it was in good shape. "Thanks."

"Come, meet Mother."

Mother, I could see, was seated in a throne-like chair near one of the large windows.

"Mother, this is Faye Quick. Faye, my mother."

"Howdayado, Mrs. Duryea." I held out my hand.

She took it and squeezed hard. Mrs. Duryea was a large woman with a big head and curls of gray hair. She was wearing a navy dress that must've come from the Thirties. It buttoned at the neck, had long sleeves and no particular style that I could put the squint on.

"Pleasure," she said. But her brown eyes said otherwise.

"Look, Mother, Faye brought us wine."

She flashed a fake smile.

I rattled my noggin for an excuse to get outta there, but nothing came to me.

"Sit down, Faye." He pointed to a red velvet sofa. "Would you like a sherry?"

Mother, I saw, had her glass on a table next to her chair.

"Sure," I said.

Jim went into the kitchen while Mother and I laid our glims on each other. I broke first. To one side of the room Jim had set up a table and chairs. I could see that each place had swanky silver.

"Jimmy's father went to the corner store for milk and never came back," she said.

What do you say to that? I nodded and smiled.

"You think it's funny? Nothing funny about it."

"No, I don't think it's funny. It's sad."

"Jimmy tells me you're a private investigator. Think you can find him?"

"Your husband?"

"Well, who else are we talking about?" She reached for her glass and drained it. "Jimmy, I need to be filled up again."

"Coming, Mother."

Mother held out her glass. Jim took it from her without a word and went back into the kitchen.

"So," she said. "You think you can find Mr. Duryea?"

"When did he disappear?"

"It was May twenty-seventh, nineteen aught one."

"Mrs. Duryea, that's forty-two years ago."

"That's correct. Good at math, aren't you?"

"Here you are, Mother." Jim handed her the sherry. "And one for you, Faye. I'll just go get mine."

He came back and sat on the opposite end of the sofa. I wondered if he knew just how much he clashed with it.

"So what are you two talking about, hmmm?" he asked.

I started to answer, but Mrs. Duryea cut me off with a firm "Nothing."

"I heard your voices. It must have been something."

My lips stayed zipped.

"We were just making pleasantries, Jimmy, that's all."

"Oh, I see."

Mrs. Duryea said, "How do you feel about Mr. Roosevelt, Faye?"

I wondered if this was a trick question and gave Jim a gander, but he was staring at Mother. I decided to tell the truth.

"I like the president very much," I said.

"Good. Think he'll win this war?"

"Yeah, I do."

"So glad Jimmy was too old to go."

"I'm sure ya are." I looked at Jim, who seemed uncomfortable. Maybe he thought I didn't know his age.

"Anybody getting hungry?" he asked.

"We're having cocktail hour, Jimmy."

"Yes, Mother."

"Now, Faye," she said. "I hope you're not going to hurt my Jimmy."

"Mother, please."

"That last one did."

I felt for him. I was sure he didn't wanna be talking about this. "Do *you* think the president will help us win the war?" I asked, trying to change the subject of Jim's love life or whatever it was.

"We're finished with that topic, Faye. Pay attention. Jimmy's a sensitive boy, and a girl like you has to take special care not to hurt his feelings. That last one did him in. What was her name, Jimmy?"

"Mother, I told you, she wasn't a girlfriend."

"I know you said she was a customer, but that didn't fool me."

I realized that I had no idea what Jim did for a living. So I asked.

"I have an antique shop."

"And that's where you met her, but she was more than a customer. Can't fool a mother, you know. Now what was her name?"

"Oh, Mother."

"Come on, tell me."

"Claudette," he said.

That gave me a turn to say the least. "Claudette?"

"Well, whatever her name was, she broke your heart."

"That's not true. Don't listen to her, Faye. She was a customer."

I had to get the skinny on this. "What was her last name, Jim?"

"West," he said. "I think she must have moved away because I haven't seen her in months."

How many Claudette Wests could there be? And was Jim ignorant of what had happened to her? How could he be? It was plastered all over the papers. I had to start easy.

"I'm afraid she stopped caring for you, Jimmy," Mother said.

"I'm sure Faye doesn't want to hear about this," Jim said.

"I'd be tickled pink to hear about Claudette," I said.

"There's not much to hear. She was quite young. Very refined. Anyway, she was a customer."

"What did she buy?"

"Jewelry. A bracelet, cuff links. Small things. No furniture."

"Cuff links?"

"Yes. She said they were for someone special."

"That should have been a signal right then," Mrs. Duryea said.

"Mother, please. They could've been for a family member." Did Porter or Wayne wear cuff links? Or Leon?

"One day I asked her to have lunch with me. It was that hour. And she did."

"Where'd you go?" I asked.

"To the Algonquin. It was a pleasant two hours, and that's all there was to it. I never saw her again, actually." He blushed and looked as though this was the first time he'd made that connection. "I'm going to put the finishing touches on dinner," he said.

I grabbed his arm. "Jim, don't ya know what happened to Claudette West? Don't ya read the newspapers?"

"As a matter of fact, I don't."

"He barely knows who Mr. Roosevelt is," Mrs. Duryea said.

"Jim, when did Claudette West stop coming to your store?"

He closed his eyes while he noodled the question around.

"As if he doesn't know the exact day and minute," Mrs. D. said.

His eyes flew open, and the look he turned on Mother was burned up. I hadn't seen this side of him before. He was way past simmer, but not a muscle moved. He coulda been set in concrete.

I wanted to break this up. "Jim, ya remember when ya took her to lunch?"

"It was in January. There was snow." He kept staring at Mother.

"I hate to be the one to tell ya this, but Claudette is dead, Jim. She was murdered."

"What?" Jim popped up as though the sofa spring beneath him had sprung.

"You do it, Jimmy?" Mother asked.

"Murdered." He brought his hands to his face, one on each cheek. "It's impossible," he said.

"It happened in January. Probably around the time ya last saw her. Would ya describe her to me so we can be sure?"

In a wistful voice he said, "She was beautiful. Her skin was so soft. Looked soft. Her eyes were a cinnamon brown. She was tall for a girl, maybe five seven, about a hundred pounds."

"I think it's the same one, Jim."

"Who would hurt her? Who did it?"

"We don't know yet."

"We?"

"I'm investigating this case."

"That's too much, Faye."

"Whaddaya mean?"

"How could we both be involved with Claudette?"

"Thought you weren't *involved* with the girl, Jimmy?"

"We live in the same building," he said, ignoring his mother. "It's all so strange."

"I have to admit it's a coincidence, which I basically don't believe in. Coincidences, that is." *Could he have done it?* I wondered. "But there's one big difference. You knew her before she died, and I got involved after she died."

"After she died," Jim said.

"So she didn't jilt you, after all, Jimmy."

A goofy smile creased his face. "No. No, she didn't."

It wasn't surprising that Jim was a queer duck; I'd already known that. And now that I'd gotten a load of Mother, let's just say my impression was confirmed. But it was as plain as his smoking jacket that all Jim's thoughts of Claudette had not been platonic.

"You cared for her, didn't ya, Jim?"

"She was very kind to me. And always so polite, refined, a lady. She was interested in the arts, opera, dance, you know. I'd planned to ask her to go with me to the opera the next time she came into the store. But I never saw her again. Now I never will."

I wasn't gonna ask him if he killed her 'cause what murderer was gonna say yes? But I was sure gonna follow up on this.

"I hope you'll excuse me, Faye. I don't think I can go on with our plans."

"That's copacetic, Jim."

I got up and started toward the door, Jim behind me.

"Please forgive me, Faye. I'm so shocked."

"I don't blame ya. If there's anything you can think of that might help me, you'll let me know, won't ya?"

"Of course," he said. "Thank you for being so understanding."

I nodded and took my leave. I wanted to get to my phone to call Marty. Maybe he could find out something about one James Duryea, antique dealer and liar.

AFTER I talked with Marty, I grabbed a jacket and my pocket-book and left my apartment. I headed toward Blondell's, which was an eatery I could afford. I was damn hungry and in seventh heaven I didn't have to eat a rabbit.

But that was the only thing I was glad about. This case was under my skin and getting more wacky all the time.

I lit a cig and waited for my meal. Why did Jim Duryea lie about Claudette West? It was no coincidence that we were both involved with her. He had to know I was on the case, and that was why he'd invited me to dinner. It had nothing to do with his mother.

The truth is, when I first laid eyes on Jim, I thought he might be a pansy; not that I cared, but that's why I was so bowled over when he invited me to dinner. Then I thought it was to impress his mother, make her think he liked girls. But now, finding out he wanted to date Claudette, I was all balled up.

Why did he want me to know that he knew her? And he did. He knew his mother would warn me not to hurt her son, mention his last love; that was part of their dance. And did he really not know Claudette was dead? I decided he *did* know, but that still didn't tell me why he wanted to let me in on their acquaintance.

I ate in a trance, paid my check, and went out into the night.

The streets were quiet as I walked home. Nightlife was at a minimum these days. And most windows had blackout shades, so the streets were pretty dark.

When I turned the corner of Fourth and Jones, I could hear footsteps behind me. I knew by the sound it was a man, and I didn't think much of it until I turned the corner and he was still with me.

I sped up, and so did he. I didn't wanna turn around, but it was either that or taking a chance a being decked or worse. I stopped. So did he. I swiveled around. There was nobody there that I could see. But it was pitch on the street.

"Who's there?" I didn't expect an answer. If you're shadowing somebody, ya aren't about to tell them. But I wanted to let whoever it was know I was onto him. Now what? I couldn't stand there all night. I wasn't far from home, so maybe I could run for it.

I turned on a dime and hit the grit as fast as I could. So did he. Right in the middle of my block I got it on the back of my head.

WHEN I came to, I saw a lotta faces looking down at me. I realized I was in my living room on one of my sofas.

"How do you feel?" A woman. "Oy vey. Some night."

No mistaking that voice. It was Dolores, my next-door neighbor. What was she doing in my apartment? What were all these people doing? And who were they?

I tried to sit up, but the pounding in my head made me dizzy, and I lay down again.

"Like death warmed over," Dolores said.

"I think we should get an ambulance." A man. "She could have a concussion for all we know."

That was Jerome Byington. I'd know his baritone anywhere. He lived on the fourth floor.

"No ambulance," I said.

"I don't think she needs stitches." Bruce Jory. Across the street.

"Are you a doctor, may I ask?" Dolores.

"I think we should all calm down." Ethel Kilbride. Across the hall from Byington.

I refused to ask what happened like I was in some detective pulp. I kept hoping somebody would say.

"A drink of water," I said.

"I'll get it."

"Are you in a lot of pain, dearie?" asked Ethel.

"It hurts some."

"Who would bang a nice girl like Faye on the head, is what I want to know?"

There it was. And then it came back to me. The footsteps, the running, the . . . nothing. I guessed that was when I got it.

"Well, we all know what line of work she's in," Jory said.

"So? Who says a detective has to get a bang on the noggin?" Dolores.

"Tell us what happened, my dear." Byington.

"I really don't know how it happened," I said.

"You were lying like a lox in the middle of the block. Clobbered by some gangster."

"I doubt it was a gangster, Dolores."

"What's all the nit-picking? The important thing here is to see if she needs a doctor."

Someone handed me a glass of water. I sat up slightly to drink it. "No doctor," I said. "I can tell I don't need one." I didn't want to get stuck in the emergency room all night. I remembered I was waiting to hear from Marty.

"You was some lucky girl, Faye."

"I know. I guess I coulda been killed."

"That, too. But I mean being found like that."

"Who found me?"

"I did," Jim Duryea said.

"*You* found me?"

"Yes. I'd taken a walk, and on my way back there you were,

right in the middle of the block. I tried to carry you here, but I couldn't manage, so I knocked on Jory's door. Fortunately, he's on the first floor. He came running, and we carried you home."

I wanted to say, "Isn't it more likely you hit me over the head?" but I didn't. "Thank you."

The phone rang, and I tried to get up, but Ethel Kilbride gently pushed me back.

"Would somebody answer that?" I said.

Jerome picked it up on the third ring.

"Is it Marty Mitchum?" I said.

Jerome asked the caller. "Right you are, Faye."

"Tell him to get over here pronto." I wasn't about to be left with Duryea playing nursie, and it could easily go that way.

Byington hung up. "He said he'll be right over."

Easing up to a sitting position set off the tom-toms in my head, but they weren't as loud as they'd been.

Dolores said, "You shouldn't sit up; you might exasperate it."

When I finally got myself up, I looked around. I didn't think I'd ever had this many people in my place at one time.

"Alevei," Dolores said with a wave of her hand.

From talking with her I knew this Yiddish expression meant something like "it should only happen to her."

"She should have a doctor."

"She doesn't want a doctor."

"Who cares. She doesn't know what's good for her."

"I say . . ."

It went on that way for what seemed like hours, and then the doorbell rang, and I knew I was saved. Jim Duryea, that jack-of-all-trades, played doorman letting Marty in.

I don't think I'd ever been so happy to see a man in my life. I *knew* I'd never been happier to see Marty.

"What the hell is goin' on here?" he said as he looked from one person to the next.

"It's okay, Marty," I said.

He came over to the sofa. "What happened, Faye?"

I started to explain, but the help from the chorus only got Marty confused.

"Hey, hold it. One person at a time. Who found Faye?"

Duryea said he had. He blabbed the same spiel he'd told before, word for word. I was glad Marty was getting a load of Jim so he'd know who I was talking about.

"Thanks. You've all been swell to Faye here, but she needs some quiet now."

Oh, thank you, Marty.

"Okay. Let's go," Dolores was like a sheepdog herding them all toward the door.

When they were gone, Marty said, "Lemme see that bump, kid."

He sat next to me on the sofa, and I bent my head so he could get a good look.

"Size of an egg," he said, and touched it. "That hurt?"

"A little."

"It didn't break the skin. Ya don't need stitches or nothin', but ya could have a concussion."

"Ya think so, Dr. Mitchum?"

"Ya know what ya have to do if ya have a concussion, don'tcha? Ya gotta rest."

"In bed?" I was scared he'd say yes.

"Maybe not, but at least here on the sofa. This was no tap, Faye. It could be dangerous ya go runnin' around."

"Marty, I'm working a case. I can't take time off."

"Ya have to take a day at least."

Enough of playing the patient. "Ya know the guy who told ya what happened to me?"

"What about him?"

"He's Duryea. Did ya have a chance to check him out?"

"Matter a fact, I did. He's got a yellow sheet long as my arm. But only two arrests stuck."

"Yer kiddin'. What for?" Now I was sure Duryea had been the one to knock the daylights outta me before coming to my rescue.

"Mostly fraud. Antiques."

"That's what he does now. He says he has an antique store."

"He does. Nothin' to stop the guy. He's done his time."

"He's been in the slammer?" That knocked me back on my heels.

"Twice. Once in his twenties and once about ten years ago."

"Listen, Marty, he knew Claudette West. He says she was a customer. His mother says he was in love with her. I'm beginnin' to think maybe he killed her."

"Why would he?"

"Maybe he was tryin' to pull his fake antique scam again with Claudette, and she found out. Maybe she led him on, then dropped him. Maybe she sweet-talked him, but he saw her with other guys."

"Ya think maybe he beaned ya?"

"It's lookin' more like that with each passin' minute."

"Don't ya think it's queer that this guy lives in your buildin'?"

Cops believed in coincidence less than I did. "Yeah, I do. But ya know, somethin' just occurred to me. He only moved in about a month ago. I wasn't on the case then, but as ya know, it was in all the rags that I found Claudette."

"Yer thinkin' maybe he tracked ya down and there just happened to be an empty apartment in this buildin'?"

"Why not?"

"Okay. Let's say that's true. Why is he interested in *you?* Especially since ya wasn't on the case yet?"

"I'm not sure."

"Ya know what, Faye? I think we should ask him."

"When?"

"Now. We'll have the jerk come down here. What number is his crib?"

I told him. "Ya sure this is a good idea, Marty?"

"Why not? If nothin' else, we get him rattled. And I don't think he'll come after you no more. You'll be okay?"

"Sure. Go."

When he was gone, I was sorry I hadn't told him to lock up and take my keys. But then he woulda known I was a scaredy-cat, and that wouldna been good for me and him working together.

I'd never been attacked before, and it sorta had me rattled. I didn't remember Woody warning me about that. He said a lotta stuff before he left, told me to watch my back, be careful, but not that I might get clobbered. Least I didn't think he did.

The thing was, whoever kayo'd me wasn't out to kill me, so what was the point? Was it a sign for me to take a powder from the case? The only person who'd care one way or another would be the killer. So he knew where I lived and had followed me home from Blondell's. I knew it was a man 'cause of those footsteps I heard.

Would the next time be more than a warning? Would he kill me as well? But even if he knocked me off, wouldn't the Wests hire somebody else? Well, nobody ever said murderers were smart.

The door opened, and I held my breath until I saw Marty. Jim Duryea was right behind him.

"Mr. Duryea has agreed to honor us with his company. Take a load off, Mr. Duryea." Marty pointed to my reading chair.

As Duryea sat, he said, "Please call me Jim."

Marty sat on the other sofa, putting Jim between us.

"Jimbo, we got a few questions, like I told ya upstairs. Our pal here got a little riled up at one point, didn't ya, Jimbo? I think he doesn't wanna talk about Claudette."

"No. I don't."

"Have ya told Jim about what we know, Marty?"

"Not yet."

"Know? What do you know?"

Marty took a pad outta his pocket, flipped it open, and pretended to study what was there.

"Let's see. We know about the first con that landed ya behind bars."

Jim looked like he'd eaten a bad piece of rabbit. And then he put his head in his hands. Marty and I looked at each other. We knew he'd spill the beans now.

Duryea mumbled something.

"Speak up, Jimbo. We can't hear ya."

He lifted his head. "My mother doesn't know about any of this. She thinks I was out of the country for those six months."

"Let's talk about tonight," Marty said. "Did you knock out Faye?"

"God, no. I like Faye."

I said, "How come you moved into this building? And don't tell me it was 'cause ya liked the apartment."

"I *did* like the apartment. But that wasn't the only reason."

"Faye was the other reason, wasn't she?"

"Yes."

"'Cause of Claudette?" I asked.

"Yes."

"I wasn't even on the case yet, Jim."

"But I knew about you. You found her."

"You kill Claudette, Jimbo?"

I couldn't believe Marty was asking him that.

"Kill her? I loved her."

"Let me run this by ya, Jimbo. Claudette found out some con you was cookin' up, and ya had to get her outta the way."

"No. I told you, I loved her. I've gone straight. No more cons."

"So why did ya want to be in this buildin' . . . 'cause of me?"

"I picked up the paper, and there was Claudette, front page, and the headline SOCIALITE MURDERED."

"You told me ya didn't know she was dead."

"I lied."

"Ya know, Jimbo, this still doesn't explain why ya moved in here to be close to Faye." We stared at him, waiting.

"I wanted to be close to Faye because she was one of the last people to see Claudette. It made me feel I'd hung on to some small piece of her."

"Well," Marty said, "that's what makes horse races."

LIKE they say, I was back to square one. Not entirely 'cause I still had Cotten, ex-boyfriend; Brian Wayne, English professor; Leon Johnson, aka Rockefeller; and Jim Duryea in my sights. They were pretty flimsy suspects, but they were all I had so far.

I was taking the day like I'd been told to. I'd called Birdie to tell her, but it was strictly on the q.t.

I had a slight headache, and every so often my vision was blurred up. Lying around never appealed to me, and my eyes kept me from reading. So I put on the radio for company and sorta listened to Don McNeil's *Breakfast Club.*

While I was lying there, I decided I had to work backward. What was Claudette doing on Bleecker that night? Was she *going* to meet someone or *coming* from seeing someone?

As for the father of Claudette's unborn child, there was no one I could rule out. Not even Johnson/Rockefeller, 'cause no matter what he said about no sex, it didn't have to be true. I hadn't asked Cotten about their sex life 'cause, I had to admit, it hadn't entered my noggin. How could I've been such a dumb bunny? Well, I was learning on the job, after all. At the time I saw Cotten, I didn't know Claudette was three months pregnant when she died.

This brought me back to Brian Wayne, the obvious next choice. Maybe he was the first choice. Even so, I had to ask Cotten first.

I started feeling excited, like I wasn't at a dead end after all. But I was sidelined, on the bench, having to rest.

I sat up and slowly swung my drumsticks over the edge of the sofa so I was sitting straight up, feet on the floor. I felt a little dizzy, but that passed. I stood, real gingerly. I took a few steps, then another few, and before I knew it, I was in my bathroom. I washed up as best as I could and then went into my bedroom. I picked out a nice polka-dot dress. No creep was gonna keep me down.

I dialed Cotten. He answered on the second ring. I told him who I was.

"I thought you were through with me."

"I have to ask ya a question, Richard. It may be embarrassin', but I need to know."

"What?"

"Did you know Claudette was pregnant when she died?"

There was a long silence on the other end.

"Richard?"

"Yes. I'm here."

"Did ya know?"

"No. I didn't."

"Was it yours? The baby?"

"No. I never slept with Claudette. She wouldn't."

"Got any idea who the father might be?"

Silence and breathing again. "Do you know how pregnant she was? I mean, how many months?"

"Three months. Why?"

"Oh."

"Oh?"

"Well, six months before she died, we stopped seeing each other for a short time. Two weeks."

"She seein' somebody else then?"

"I don't know. If she'd been six months pregnant, then it would've been during that time. She told me she had one date."

"Who with?"

"I think his name was Garfield."

"First name or last?"

"Last. I can't think of his first name."

"Ya gotta try, Richard."

"What difference does it make? It's the wrong time period."

"Do ya think she might've seen him again later?"

"You mean when we were back together?" He sounded like this would be impossible.

"Well, yeah."

"Claudette would never have cheated on me."

Why should I clue in this also-ran that she probably had a lotta boyfriends while she was supposed to be with him? "Can ya think of Garfield's first name, Richard? Could ya work on it today?"

"I'll try."

"Okay. I'll give ya my office number, and ya can leave it with my secretary 'cause I'll probably be out."

I gave him the number and hung up. Everything was getting real interesting again.

The bulb clicked on over my head while I was getting dressed that I should try to interview Brian Wayne's wife. I wasn't sure how I was gonna get her to talk to me, but I had to give it a shot.

MAUREEN Wayne lived on West Ninth Street between Sixth and Fifth. It was a small white building, set back from the street. A nicely trimmed hedge bordered a little plot of grass. There were three names on the bell roster. I knew I was taking a chance not calling ahead, but I pushed the bell for Wayne. In a minute the door opened, and I saw a pretty woman about my height. She wore a blue-and-white dress with puffed sleeves.

"Yes?" she said.

"Mrs. Wayne?"

"Yes."

"My name is Faye Quick, and I'd like to talk to you for a little bit." I was afraid to mention her husband before I got in. "This is a confidential matter."

She squeezed her dark brows together so they looked like one.

"You're one of Brian's sluts, aren't you?" She started to close the door, but I put my hand up against it and held it there.

"I'm not one of anybody's sluts," I said.

"Then what the hell do you want?"

I had no choice. "I wanna talk to ya about yer husband."

"I knew it. I have nothing to say. Brian no longer lives here—"

"Mrs. Wayne, I'm not a girlfriend of his. I'm a private investigator." I dug around in my purse and handed her my license. "Your husband is involved in a murder investigation."

It wasn't a total lie. *I* was investigating him.

"I thought that was all over. It was months ago, wasn't it?"

"True. But it's not over. I've been hired to look into it again. You don't have to cooperate with me, but I wish ya would."

"I don't see why I should, but come in." She opened the door, and I stepped into the vestibule. "I'm on the top floor," she said.

When we got to the third floor, she opened the door to a large room with a skylight letting the sun stream in. The furniture was big and floppy and a far cry from most of the stuff I'd seen on this case. I sat on the rose-flowered sofa. Maureen sat in a comfy-looking chair across from me.

"So what can I do for you?" she asked.

"As you know, Mr. Wayne was questioned in the Claudette West case. The case still hasn't been solved."

"And that's why you were hired? By the parents, I'd guess?"

I didn't say anything.

"Sorry."

"You seem quite angry at your husband."

"Wouldn't you be? He's been involved with one girl after another."

"Claudette West bein' one of 'em?"

"I don't see why not."

That was less than I'd hoped. "How long have ya been married?"

"Ten years."

"And how long has he been up to his . . . shenanigans?"

"An interesting way to put it. Brian, as far as I know now, has been cheating on me since the second month of our marriage."

I knew a lotta guys cheated, but Wayne seemed like he was a major leaguer.

"And these other gals, were they mostly his students?"

"I think so. The ones that came to me were."

"Came to you?"

"It's hard to believe, isn't it? But, yes, they did, some begging me to give him a divorce when Brian had told them I was the only reason he wouldn't marry them. Ridiculous. He no more wanted to marry any of them than pigs can fly. It was the last one who came here that made me kick him out."

"What was different about her?"

"She was pregnant . . . and it wasn't a ploy. I could see that she was. Of course there was no way to prove it was Brian's baby, but I knew she was telling the truth."

"How long ago was this?"

"A year ago."

I'd gotten my hopes up. "What did ya do?"

"I told her I'd never give him a divorce."

It was time to tell her about Claudette. "You probably don't know this 'cause it isn't common knowledge, but Claudette West was three months pregnant when she was murdered."

Her hand flew to her chest as though to keep her heart in place. "No . . . but you don't know if it was Brian's, do you?"

"Not for sure. But it's beginnin' to sound more likely with every word ya say."

"Wait a minute. You don't think Brian killed her because she was pregnant, do you?"

I shrugged.

"Listen, Miss Quick, Brian's a terrible man. An adulterer, a liar, a predator. But he's not a murderer."

"How can ya be so sure?"

"There are certain things you know about a man when you live with him all those years. And I *know* he wouldn't steal a life."

"Would ya say that Brian's not a violent man?"

"I would. He wouldn't hurt a fly."

If I had a nickel for all the times I'd heard that one. "And ya don't know if he was havin' an affair with Claudette. She never came to you?"

She stood up. "I think it's time for you to leave, Miss Quick. I knew nothing about this Claudette. But I'd swear on a stack of Bibles that Brian had nothing to do with her death. Now I'd like you to leave."

I stood up, gathered my coat and hat, and made my way to the door. Maureen Wayne was right behind me like a shadow. She reached in front of me to open the door.

I took my time going down the stairs. Out on the sidewalk I lit up even though I knew *nice* women didn't smoke on the street. My little skirmish with Maureen Wayne made me want to rebel.

It must be swell to be so sure of things. But I couldn't take Maureen Wayne's word for gospel. I didn't know her Brian the way she did, but I *did* know that even though he wouldn't hurt a fly, that didn't mean he couldn't kill a girl.

I WAS so close to NYU that I decided to visit Brian Wayne again.

As I waited outside his office, I could tell no one was inside, but I hoped he'd show up soon. Think of the devil. There he was, turning the corner toward me, and then he stopped.

"You again? I told you everything I know."

"Yeah, but that was before I talked to your wife."

He took a step backward. "You saw Maureen?"

"I did."

His face squirreled into a mask of hate. "My wife has serious problems."

"Far as I could tell, her most serious problem is you."

"Let's not stand out here." He unlocked his door.

Inside the small room it looked like trouble lived there. Books and papers were everywhere. A chaise longue and a desk took up most of the space. I wondered how many professors kept a chaise in their offices. It smelled of smoke and perfume. Many perfumes.

I picked up some papers from the straight-back chair on my side of the desk and held them in my lap.

"Sorry about the mess," he said.

"Before we go any further, where were ya last night?"

"I was playing poker with friends."

"Can ya prove that?"

"Of course."

"Good." I didn't really think Brian had attacked me, but I had to rule him out.

"Just what did Maureen tell you?"

"That you're a ladies' man. Even so, she didn't seem to know about Claudette West."

"I told you there was nothing to know." He shot his cuffs, and a ray from his lamp threw a glint in the air. Cuff links.

"Nice links," I said.

He looked at one of them as though he was surprised it was there. "Thanks."

"Who gave them to ya?"

He pursed his lips together. "I bought them myself."

"No ya didn't. Claudette give them to ya?"

"As a matter of fact, she didn't."

"Who did?"

"Another girl. Look, what does this have to do with anything? My cuff links."

"I happen to know Claudette bought some cuff links for a man."

"Not for me."

"Then who gave them to ya?"

"What kind of cad do you think I am? I'll never tell you her name."

"Very honorable. Don't make me laugh. Those cuff links could put ya in the hot seat." They couldn't, but he didn't know that.

He looked like he'd just swallowed a dose of cod-liver oil. "Her name is Joan DeHaven."

What a true-blue guy!

"Do you have to talk to her? Ask her about the cuff links?"

"Of course I do." I wasn't so sure about that.

"Oh, God." He slumped in his seat.

"Did ya think about what I told ya last time we spoke?"

"You mean about Claudette being pregnant? What about it?"

"How come she didn't tell ya, do ya think?"

"That's not something a nice girl would tell her professor."

"Can it, Brian. We both know you were sleepin' with her."

"I told you—"

"Yeah. You told me. Now I know different. The daddy couldn't be Cotten 'cause they never did it, and Leon—"

"Who?"

"Doesn't matter. Anyway, you're the only one left."

"All right. I had an affair with Claudette, but it was over a year ago. I had nothing to do with either her pregnancy or her death."

I was set back on my heels that he admitted the affair. And if he was telling the truth, then he couldn't have been the father.

"Any way ya can prove when ya broke it off with Claudette?"

"Of course not. But I'll tell you this." He sat up straighter. "Claudette still considered me a friend. And even though she didn't confide that she was pregnant, she did tell me she was in love. She couldn't say who it was."

"She ever mention the name Alec Rockefeller?"

"Yes, she did. But that wasn't who she was in love with. She said she was seeing Alec to keep her parents happy."

"Why would she tell you about this secret love?"

"Because she knew I cared about her. And I did."

"Yer tellin' me that Claudette was seein' someone she didn't want anyone to know about?"

"Yes. And she wasn't happy about it. She called it 'a stinking mess.' That was the way she put it."

"Did you ask her if the guy was married?"

"I didn't."

"She gave ya no clue as to who he might've been?"

"Nothing, except that her parents would have hit the ceiling because this was a worse choice than Richard Cotten."

7

I LAY on my sofa, Harry James in the background playing "I Had the Craziest Dream." The canary was Helen Forrest. It fit my mood to a T. Everything I'd been hearing seemed like a crazy dream.

I didn't seem to be moving forward on this case . . . more like I was running in place or going round in circles. Didn't I start the day right where I was now?

I knew there was a missing man in Claudette's life, and I couldn't find out who it was. Was it this Garfield character whose first name I didn't even know? And all Anne could say was that some man was violently trying to make Claudette do something she didn't want to do. That wasn't much help. I'd left the sweater with Anne in case she wanted to take another stab at it, but I wasn't counting on it.

Then there was me getting clobbered. I had no more idea who did that than I'd had the night before. It still didn't make sense to me. I guess I had to face that it was a warning to lay off.

The phone rang, and I got up slowly, walked across the room, and picked up. It was Birdie.

"Just let me sit down a sec, okay?"

"Sure. Ya feel that bad, Faye?"

"Nah. A little dizzy is all."

"Ya think ya should see a sawbones?"

"Nah. I'll be all right. What's cookin' there?"

"The boyfriend, that Richard Cotten guy, called because he remembered the first name of Garfield."

"Give."

"It's Warner."

"Don't tell me . . . he lives on Park Avenue, right?"

"Wrong. Hell's Kitchen. I looked him up in the phone book."

This Claudette had across-the-board taste. Hell's Kitchen was bad enough, but the next thing I'd hear she had a boyfriend on the Bowery.

"Gimme the address."

"Nine ninety-one West Forty-third. Are ya goin' there now? It ain't safe there, Faye."

"Yer thinkin' in the past, Bird." I cut the connection before she could say anything else.

Claudette dating somebody from Hell's Kitchen surprised me. Not that everybody who lived there was a crook or a rough guy. The place had cleaned up a lot since the Ninth Avenue El came down. I'd heard a lotta actors lived there 'cause it was cheap.

Maybe Garfield was an actor. Warner Garfield. It had an actor's ring to it. That was probably it. And it fit. An actor wouldn't be Porter West's cup a tea. For him an actor probably *would* be worse than Richard Cotten, student.

And maybe the baby Claudette was carrying belonged to Garfield. Let's say she succumbed to Garfield's charms, instead of resisting like she did with Richard. The time period he'd given me wouldn't have left her three months pregnant when she died. But she coulda picked up with Garfield again without Richard knowing or catching on. Maybe three months after her first breakup with him. Maybe keeping both guys on the string while dating Alec Rockefeller, too, even though that one was for show.

I knew sitting around my apartment would drive me batty while there were still threads to follow. Or even territory I could go over again. A second look can pay off sometimes, Woody had taught me.

Maybe Leon knew something about this Garfield guy. I checked my pocketbook. My trusty little pad was inside with Leon's number in it. But there was no answer when I tried it. On about the fifth ring the face of Gladys Wright swam into my think box. Maybe that's where he was. The lovebirds in their nest.

Gladys answered, and when I ID'd myself, her groan practically took my ear off.

"Is Leon there? I need to talk to him."

"Well, he's in the bath."

"Get him out."

"No."

"Ya want me to come over and do it myself?"

"Not particularly."

"Then get him out of his bath and on the phone."

"Oh, all right."

She slammed the phone down, assaulting my ear again, and I could hear her moving away, her heels tapping the floor.

"Hello?"

"Leon?"

"Yes, Miss Quick."

"I got a question for ya, Leon. Does the name Warner Garfield mean anything to ya?"

Silence.

"Are ya there?"

"I'm thinking."

"Either it does or it doesn't. Ya know the name Warner Garfield?"

"She mentioned it. Claudette."

"What did she say that he wanted?"

"She said he was after her for a date. That he was a queer duck, and he gave her the heebie-jeebies," Leon said.

"Ya let it go at that? Ya didn't give two figs about a girl who found this Garfield guy creepy? Ya didn't think she might be in danger?"

"It didn't sound dangerous to me. Claudette was very dramatic, you know. She was always in a squeeze about something. If it wasn't her father, then it was her ex. Or it could be she didn't have the right dress for some deb ball. She could make anything seem like life and death."

"And one of those times it was," I said. "Anything else about Garfield? She did go out with him, ya know. At least once."

"I had no idea. It didn't sound like that when she mentioned him. She gave me the impression that he *wanted* a date, but there was no way in hell he was going to get one."

"Did Claudette ever give ya a pair of cuff links?"

"No. She never gave me anything."

"Okay. Yer sure that's all ya know about Garfield?"

"I swear."

I hung up. There was a possibility that Warner Garfield was a danger to her, at least in Claudette's eyes. How could I know what was what until I got hold of him.

I didn't like carrying a gun, but it didn't seem like such a bad idea, considering where I was going and who I was planning to drop in on. Woody had given it to me right before he left. Marty had taken me to an empty lot in the Bronx and taught me how to use it. I turned out to be pretty good. But I never liked it. Still, I knew it was dumb not to take the thing with me this time just in case.

I laid the gun inside my pocketbook like it was a corpse in a casket. I grabbed my coat and left the apartment, toting a gat.

I TOOK the subway and got off at Forty-second and Seventh and walked west. I passed the many movie theaters, crossed Eighth Avenue, and started into the heart of Hell's Kitchen.

The neighborhood's grisly stuff was mostly in the past, although the area still had some active gangs. But I knew it wouldn't be smart to walk along these streets at night, even with an escort.

I found Garfield's tenement, but there were no names listed by the door, no bells. Beyond the front door was a small vestibule with mailboxes along one wall. Garfield's was near the left end. But it didn't tell me his apartment number or what floor he was on.

The inside door was unlocked, and I knew I had two choices. Either knock on every door or find the super, if there was one. I started knocking. First apartment no one answered, second someone did. He was big. Big head, big shoulders, big chest.

"Would ya know if a Warner Garfield lives here?"

"He's on the fourth. Number 402." He slammed the door shut.

"Thanks," I said.

I climbed the stairs, kicking papers and other garbage out of my way. When I reached 402, I knocked.

Nothing. I put my ear to the door and thought I could hear running water in the distance, like it might be coming from a faucet at the other end of the place. There was no other sound.

I knocked again four or five times, then turned the door handle. The place was unlocked. This surprised me. And it spooked me, too. I heard Woody's voice in my mind.

Take out the gun, Faye.

I knew it was the right thing to do even though it made me more scared. I opened my purse, lifted out the gun, and, like Marty showed me, held it out in front of me at arm's length.

Real quiet, I pushed open the door. The sound of running water was louder, coming from the other end of the place. This was a railroad apartment, with the rooms lined up one after another off a hall. The joint was dark except for a light at the end of the hallway.

I could keep sneaking down the hall, peering into rooms until I found someone or didn't, or I could announce myself with a holler. Of course, finding me with a pointed gun might not make the tenant too happy. Even so, I chose the yell.

"Hello. Anyone home?"

Nothing. Just the running water.

I inched in, until I came to a door on my right that was open.

Gun in front of me, I looked in. A bedroom with a mussed-up bed, a dresser, a chair with trousers and a shirt hanging over the back, an undershirt on the floor. But nobody was in there.

I could feel the droplets of sweat on my forehead turning to trickles starting down my face. I took some more baby steps, the gun sorta wavering in my wet grip like a divining rod.

"Anybody home?" My voice was more like a warble than a shout.

Nobody answered. I don't know what I woulda done at that point if somebody had.

Next I came to the kitchen. It had a range, sink, icebox, and a small table with two chairs. But no one sitting there.

As I moved down the hall, the sound of running water got louder until I was outside the door where it was coming from. The top half of the door had pebbled glass, and through it I could see the glow of a light inside.

The water sounded like it was turned on full force in a sink. I stood to one side of the door. Although I couldn't see through the glass, if anyone moved inside the room, I knew I'd see a shadow.

No dice. And the water kept running. After a deep breath I slowly turned the door's knob and inched the door inward.

The water was pounding against the sink like I'd thought, and the ceiling light was on. The bathtub curtain, streaked with mildew, was pulled closed. I knew I had to look behind it.

I felt like a horse's ass. What was so tough about tugging a stupid bath curtain? Everything. I had the terrible feeling I'd find something I didn't wanna find in that tub.

Okay, Quick, I told myself, you can do it. I reached out and pulled back the curtain, exposing the tub. And what was in it. I gasped.

He was dead. That was clear. He was in his drawers. His trousers, shirt, and undershirt were missing. He was stuffed into the tub so that his legs bent at the knees. One side of his head was smashed in and covered with blood. I couldn't get a look at his face, but it didn't matter. I was sure I didn't know this stiff, although I had to assume he was Warner Garfield 'cause he was lying in Garfield's tub.

When I looked more carefully, I saw two bullet holes in his chest.

I had to call the cops. I left the bathroom and walked still farther down the hall to the living room. On a table next to a broken-down sofa was a phone. I picked up the receiver and dialed zero.

"Operator."

"I wanna report a murder."

"Where are you located?"

"Nine ninety-one West Forty-third Street. Apartment 402."

"I'll connect you with the precinct in that area."

The desk sergeant took the details and told me to sit tight, the cops were on their way.

I needed a break from Garfield's digs, so I stood in the hall. I knew the guy in the tub hadn't been there long 'cause the smell woulda driven me out sooner.

You don't bleed after yer dead. Woody had told me that. So I figured Tub Man was kaput from the head injury by the time the killer pumped lead into him.

I hadn't looked around the place 'cause I didn't want to disturb anything or spread my fingerprints around. I knew they were on every door I touched, but that was about it.

I heard them coming like a herd of buffalo. It sounded like the whole police force as they ran up the stairs. But it was only four cops with drawn guns.

And they were all pointed at me.

"Hey," I said, holding my hands up.

"Who are you?"

"I called this in."

"Yeah? Where's the victim?"

"In the bathroom down the hall. In the tub."

"Drownin'?"

"No."

He eyed me suspiciously. "Webb, you stay with her for now."

The other two followed him.

"Name?" Webb asked.

"Faye Quick."

"Ya know the victim?"

"No."

"How'd ya happen to be in his bathroom?"

I knew this was just the first of many times I'd have to answer this and the first of many times I'd get the look or the laugh.

"I'm a private detective."

Webb laughed.

DETECTIVE Lake didn't laugh.

He was tall and thin and wore his trilby toward the back of his head. He had a long face with deep-set brown blinkers and a nice nose and mouth. I liked the way he looked.

I figured he was about thirty. He wore a gray suit, and a short chain dipped into the small pocket of his vest where he kept his watch. His hands were in his trouser pockets as he paced back and forth on the worn rug in Garfield's apartment.

"So you didn't know Garfield at all, is that right, Miss Quick?"

"That's right."

"Tell me again why you came here?"

"A case I'm workin' on. I wanted to question him."

We were interrupted then by a cop bringing in the guy from downstairs who'd told me which crib was Garfield's.

"What the hell, you do this?" He pointed at me.

Lake said, "Shuddup, bud. What's your name?"

"Jack Gorcey. Why?"

"You know Warner Garfield?"

"I seen him around. Why? What's goin' on?"

"Take him," Lake said to the cop holding Gorcey's arm. To me he said, "Excuse me, Miss Quick. I'll be right back."

I nodded and smiled like some schoolgirl. But that's what I felt like. Sort of all fluttery inside.

I was alone in the crummy living room. Detective Lake was taking Gorcey to identify the body. Suddenly I heard a noise from down the hall. It was definitely someone throwing up, and I didn't think it was Detective Lake or the cop.

When they came back to the living room, Gorcey looked like he'd aged about twenty-five years. He was pale and shaky.

"Sit down," the cop said.

Gorcey fell into a stained and shabby chair.

"When's the last time you saw Garfield?" Lake asked.

"Yesterday. Why?"

"Was he with anyone when you saw him yesterday?"

"Nah."

"Excuse me," I said.

Lake turned to me, a surprised look on his face. I guess he wasn't used to being interrupted when he was grilling someone.

"I'm sorry to butt in, but I'd like to show Mr. Gorcey a picture." He took a beat, then agreed.

I got Claudette's photo out of my purse and passed it to Gorcey.

"Do you know who that is? Ever seen her?" I asked.

"I seen her somewhere, but I ain't sure it was with Garfield."

Everyone had seen her at the time of the murder. This snap had been in all the papers, and that made it heavy sledding for me.

"Think," Lake said.

I coulda clicked my heels that he was helping me out.

"I'm thinkin'. Yeah. I coulda seen her with him. But not in a long time."

"What's a long time?" I asked.

"Maybe six months."

"What was she doin' with him?"

"How should I know? What am I, a mind reader?"

This made me think of Anne. I needed something that belonged to Garfield. But I couldn't explain this to Detective Lake.

"Mr. Gorcey, did he seem chummy with this girl?" I asked.

"She was holdin' his arm when they went down the street, that's what ya mean."

"That's just what I mean." I looked at Lake. "Just one more question." Back to Gorcey. "Do ya think she coulda been his girl?"

Gorcey dropped his head into his hands.

Lake said, "He doesn't know."

"Okay. Thanks, Detective."

"My pleasure, Miss Quick." He smiled, and he looked adorable.

"Okay. Did you see anyone you didn't know come in here between yesterday and today?"

"Only her." He pointed at me. "And I wouldna seen *her* she hadn't knocked on my door."

Right then my hand slipped between the sofa cushions and landed on something. Something that wasn't the sofa.

"How about the other tenants in the building? You know any of them?"

"I keep myself ta myself."

"Right. Okay, Mr. Gorcey, go back to your palace, and don't take any sudden trips."

I carefully pulled what was lodged between the cushions until I saw it was white crumpled cotton. Whatever it was was probably Garfield's. I slipped it into my pocketbook while nobody was looking.

Detective Lake handed out assignments. "You two question the other tenants. After the coroner and the fingerprint guys get done, you two toss this place. I'll be back soon."

Then he turned to me.

"Miss Quick, may I escort you out?"

How could a girl refuse? "Sure."

We walked down the three flights and out to the street.

"Well," I said, "thank you, Detective." I hoped my voice wasn't shaking like my insides were.

"Would you like to have a cup of coffee?" he asked.

Trying to sound easygoing, I said, "Why not?"

We walked in silence toward Eighth. When we reached the corner, he pointed across the avenue.

"That's not a bad coffee shop over there."

The sign spelled out KELLAWAY'S. I nodded.

As we crossed, I kept bumping him 'cause I was walking like I had a few too many. I hoped he didn't notice. When we got to the place, he opened the door for me and we went in.

It was your regular coffee and eggs joint, and we took a booth near the middle. The crowd was light this time of day.

A waitress with a rag of brown hair came to our table.

"So?"

"What would you like?" he asked.

"Just a cup of j . . . coffee."

"Same," he said.

"We got a nice blueberry pie," the waitress said.

"No thanks," I said.

He shook his head.

She looked at us like we were the scum of the earth for turning down the pie, then went to get our coffee.

Detective Lake smiled that smile. "I don't think she likes us."

"Not too much," I said.

"So, Miss Quick, tell me how you happened to become a private investigator?"

"It's sort of a long story."

"I have time."

The waitress put our coffee in front of us. I started my tale of how I became a gumshoe. Lake listened without interrupting, which was a first from any man I knew.

"That's very interesting," he said when I was done. "Can you discuss the case you're on now? I thought I recognized the girl in the picture you showed Gorcey."

"Then ya know what case it is."

"I suppose I do, but I thought it had reached a dead end."

"Somebody didn't think so."

"I won't ask who hired you."

I knew I woulda told him if he had. After all, he was a cop. A detective, no less.

"Sorry," I said.

"No, no. I understand and respect you for your professionalism."

"Thanks." I was such a phony I embarrassed myself. "What about you? What made ya become a cop . . . a policeman?"

He laughed, and the sound was deep, real genuine, and full of fun. "You can call me a cop, Miss Quick. That's what I am."

I smiled. "And you can call me Faye. That's *who* I am."

"I'm John, but most people call me Johnny."

We exchanged a look that lasted a few seconds, and my stomach did a roller coaster.

"I became a cop because my father was a cop and his father was a cop. Not an interesting story like you have."

"But ya like it, don't ya?"

"I do. Especially since I made Homicide. I don't usually mention that to girls, but I know you understand."

Girls. Plural. I wondered how many there were. "Yeah, I do. It's a lot more excitin' than catchin' burglars or breakin' up car rings, I imagine."

"How about you? Do you find murder cases more interesting?"

"I'll tell ya a secret. This is my first one."

"And Garfield was your first body?"

"No. I'm the one who stumbled over Claudette West lyin' on Bleecker Street."

A spark lit up his peepers. "Ah, that was you. That must have been quite a shock. Well, both of them must have been shocks."

"I was almost expectin' Garfield. At least once I got into the apartment. I could hear the water runnin', and nobody was answerin' my calls. I knew there was a good chance I'd find a body."

"I can see that. But the West discovery was a true surprise."

"That's fer sure."

He took out his gold pocket watch, and my heart sank a little.

"I should get back," he said.

"Me, too. Not back to Garfield's, but I got plenty a work to do."

He picked up the check and paid, and then we went outside.

"Well, Faye, I've enjoyed meeting you."

I thought I might die right then. He was gonna leave, and that was gonna be that.

"Yeah, me too. Thanks for the coffee." I held out my hand to shake.

He took it and kept it wrapped in his. "We should exchange phone numbers . . . since our cases overlap. One of us might come up with somethin'."

Struggling not to come apart at the seams, I said, "Yeah. That's a good idea." I reached into my pocketbook, bumping against the gun, and came up with a paper and pen.

He was already writing on a pad. When we were both done, we traded our numbers.

"When the boys finish tossing the apartment, they'll probably come up with something for you."

"Thanks."

He put out his hand, and I took it. I wondered if he'd forgotten that we'd already done this.

"It's been really nice, Faye."

"Yeah, it has."

He let go of my hand and touched the brim of his hat. "Good-bye for now."

"Good-bye."

He turned and crossed Eighth, and I turned away fast, in case he looked back. I walked down Eighth toward my subway.

Nah. I floated toward my subway.

ON THE way home I'd realized that during our yakety-yak Detective Lake and I had never once mentioned Warner Garfield. I didn't know anything more about the clown than when I'd gone to his door, except he was dead and a lousy housekeeper. Which made me think of what I'd lifted from Warner Garfield's sofa and stuffed in my pocketbook. I scooped it up and shook it out. An undershirt.

With dried blood on it.

It could've been Garfield's, but why would the killer stuff it in between the cushions like that? Also, I'd seen an undershirt lying on the floor in Garfield's bedroom. Maybe this one belonged to the killer. And the *blood* on it was Garfield's. That made more sense. But stuffed in the sofa? That made no sense. Whoever it belonged to, I knew I should've turned it over to the police. To Johnny. I could give him a call to say I had it. But what would he think of me holding out like that? I had another idea.

I went to the phone and dialed Anne. I filled her in, and we agreed to meet the next day. Then I called the West house.

A man answered, and I asked for Porter. When he asked who was calling and I'd told him, he said, "Oh, hello, Miss Quick. Cornell Walker here."

Myrna West's half brother. We made some chitchat, and then he got Porter. After our initial hellos, I said, "Did Claudette ever give ya a set of cuff links, Mr. West?"

"Claudette has given me many sets over the years."

"How about in the last year?"

"No. Not since she was in high school. Is there anything else?"

"Another name's come up. Did Claudette ever mention Warner Garfield?"

"Never."

"Could ya ask Mrs. West if she knows the name?"

"If I don't, she doesn't."

He had Myrna West on some tight leash.

"How about your brother-in-law? Could ya ask him? Maybe Claudette mentioned the name to him in passin'."

"Who is this person? What did he have to do with my daughter?"

"I'm not sure yet. That's why I'd like you to ask Mrs. West or Captain Walker."

"Is Garfield a suspect?"

"For the moment I haven't ruled him out." I didn't want to tell West yet that Garfield was dead. "So could ya ask Walker?"

"Hold on."

Softly, I started singing "That Old Black Magic" and almost got to the end before West came back on the line.

"Cornell never heard the name. Now tell me who Garfield is."

"Was," I said.

"Was? You mean he's dead?"

"Yes."

"Then what could he have to do with Claudette?"

"He's only been dead about twelve hours. Murdered. I found the body and called the police."

"Again? You found a body again?"

I ignored him. "I know Claudette knew him, but I don't know what their relationship was. That's what I'm tryin' to find out."

"This has gotten very complicated, hasn't it?"

"Murder is always complicated, Mr. West."

"What's your next move?"

Telling him that I was going to turn Anne loose on a bloody undershirt didn't seem like the right answer to give Porter.

"Pinnin' down Garfield's connection to Claudette." All true.

"Yes, of course."

"So you'll keep your ears open for anything about him?" Me and Porter. A real team.

"Certainly."

He told me to call him the next night, and we hung up.

After I put the receiver back in the cradle, I sat at the telephone table, unmoving. I *did* need to find out what the connection was between Garfield and Claudette, but I had no idea where to start. It was something Woody had warned me might happen. You're working on a case, moving along, and suddenly a wall comes up in front of ya, and there's no way over, around, or under it. When that happens, he'd told me to take a break. Go to a movie. Drop into your favorite restaurant. Knock back a few drinks. I wasn't going to do any of these things by myself. Not tonight. I dialed my office, and when Birdie answered, I asked, "What are ya doin' tonight, Bird?"

"Nothin'."

"How about we go to a USO dance?"

"Faye, I don't think ya should be jumpin' around after what happened to ya last night."

"Is that how you dance, Birdie? Ya jump around?"

"Don't get smart with me. You know what I mean."

"I feel fine, and I need some distraction from this case. It'll free up my mind. Woody told me so."

"Yeah?"

"Yeah. So whaddaya say, Bird? We meet up for a couple a cocktails at the Hotel Astor, then have a sandwich at Lindy's followed by a piece of cheesecake, then ankle over to the USO."

"You buyin'?"

"Who else?"

"What time ya wanna meet?"

WHILE we walked to the USO from Lindy's, Birdie said, "So, these soldiers and sailors, do they expect anything from ya, Faye?"

"Like what?"

"Ya know. After. Later."

"I suppose some might, but that depends on how ya act with them. Mostly these guys wanna talk. They're away from home, and they're homesick. They wanna talk to ya about their girlfriends or their hometown folks. Stuff like that."

"I get it."

"Good."

When we got there, a girl at a table right inside the door took our names and what we were volunteering for. Some girls played Ping-Pong or cards, were hostesses, or handed out doughnuts and coffee. And then there were others, like us, who wanted to dance.

We went into the large main room where the girl spinning the platters had on Bing Crosby singing "All or Nothing at All." Lots of couples were on the floor, but there were still plenty of boys standing around, waiting for the right girl or, as I'd discovered before, just too shy to ask.

"What now?" Birdie asked.

"Ya pick out a guy and ask him to dance. C'mon, I'll show ya." I spotted a couple a guys standing near the table with doughnuts on it, and I grabbed Birdie's hand and pulled her over with me.

"Hiya, soldier," I said to a red-haired, freckle-faced kid. "I'm Faye, and this is Birdie. Wanna cut a rug?"

His eyes lit up like I was a Kewpie doll he'd just won.

"Sure. I'm Lon. This is Rory Tracy."

"Hiya, soldier," Birdie said, following my lead.

Rory said, "I'm a Marine."

"But yer all soldiers, aren't ya?" she asked.

"No, Bird, not exactly. I'll explain later," I said.

"I'll explain now," Rory said, and asked Birdie to dance.

Bing was winding up as we moved away from the sidelines. The next number started right away, and it was a jitterbug.

"Can ya do it?" Lon asked.

"You bet," I said.

And we were off. That soldier knew his stuff. He swung me around, slid me through his outstretched legs and up again, spun me behind him, pulled me back, and generally wore me out.

When it was over, I told him I needed a break, and we sat down listening to Glenn Miller playing "Chattanooga Choo Choo."

Private Lon Calhoun was from Iowa and told me all about himself for the next half hour. I didn't have to pretend I was interested 'cause I was. I'd always liked to hear about other people's lives.

Later we danced again, many times, until I had to tell Birdie that we had to go. The boys offered to see us home, but we said we'd grab a checker instead.

I'd distracted myself, forgotten the case for a few hours, and where was I now? Feeling like something was just out of reach, something important that would help me with the case. My mental picture of that soldier and Marine, our dancing partners, nagged.

SITTING at my desk the next morning, everything seemed easy. I guessed my night on the town had done the trick. That made me think of Lon and Rory, and the nagging feeling came back for a flash, then disappeared.

The first thing I did was to call Claudette's friend June Landis. After the niceties were out of the way, I asked her if she'd ever heard Claudette mention Warner Garfield. She clammed up like I'd asked her for the combination to the family vault.

"June? Was she datin' him?"

"Hardly." June couldn't help herself. She sniggered. "She couldn't stand him. But he wouldn't stop pestering her for a date."

Leon had said the same thing.

"Do ya know how she met Garfield?"

"Through this acting group she was involved with. God, don't tell her parents she hung around with actors."

"What's the name of the actin' group?"

"I don't think I ever knew that. I know they were in Greenwich Village though."

Big help. "There are tons of actin' groups in the Village. Can ya tell me anything that might help me find them?"

"Gee, I don't think so. Wait, I remember a play they put on last year that she went to. It had an *M* in the title ... *Moonbeams and Mulberries*. That's what it was called."

The title alone probably made it a big hit.

"Well, thanks." I said, and hung up. I had to find that acting group. Maybe there was something in Garfield's papers that would help. I opened my pocketbook. The paper Detective Lake had given me had his precinct and his work phone number below his name, *Johnny Lake*. I dialed.

The desk sergeant took the call and put me through. I could feel myself blushing all over when I heard his voice.

"Miss Quick, good to hear from you."

"Faye, remember."

"Right. Faye."

I loved the way he said my name. "I need some help. I imagine when ya tossed Garfield's apartment, ya came away with a lot of paper, right?"

"Yes."

"I was wonderin' if any of those papers named an actin' company?"

"I don't know, but I can find out. Hold on a minute."

"Sure." My heart was thumping like a bass drum. I tried to remember if I'd ever felt like this, and all I could come up with was Spencer Nelson. Fourth grade. Pretty pathetic.

"Faye? My guy tells me there are three cartons full of papers. So far they haven't come across anything about an acting company. I told them to be on the lookout for it, though. When we've finished, I think I can arrange for you to have access."

I knew this could take forever.

"That's nice of you, John."

"Johnny."

"Johnny." I smiled. "Thanks." I didn't want to hang up, but I was clean outta Garfield questions.

"Now that I have you, I was wondering if you'd like to have dinner sometime. We can discuss the case."

"Well, yeah, sure. That'd be nice."

"Great. I'll call you."

"Swell."

We said good-bye.

I felt depressed. How come he didn't ask me right then for dinner? I knew I shouldn't be complaining. He brought up the subject of a date. At least I thought it was a date. But maybe not. He did say we'd discuss the case. Course that could be an excuse. Maybe he was too shy to ask me outright? I wished girls could ask men out. If I was a man and saw a girl I liked, I'd just ask. Oh, the hell with it.

Maybe if I went to some of the established theater companies and asked, someone might be able to point me . . . and then I thought of Claudette's things. I was sure the Wests hadn't thrown anything away. Claudette might've kept a playbill.

I decided not to let the Wests know I was coming.

CAPTAIN Cornell Walker was the only member of the West household at home. When we were settled in the living room, he asked the reason for my visit.

"I don't think you'll be able to help me, Captain. I need to know what plays Claudette saw in the last six months of her life."

"I can name some of them."

"How's that?"

He smiled, but his blue eyes didn't have a twinkle in them.

"I took her to a few."

"Was one of them *Moonbeams and Mulberries?*"

"No. That sounds dreadful."

"Yeah, it does." I figured that wasn't the only play this group ever did. "So what were the titles of the plays you took her to see?"

"Let's see. We saw *Blithe Spirit, The Eve of Saint Mark,* and—"

"Those are Broadway shows, aren't they? I was thinkin' more along the lines of small theater companies, downtown, maybe."

He looked like he was smelling a dead mouse. "No, that wouldn't interest me, and I'd never take my niece to something like that."

"What if I told ya she hung around with actors and actresses from one of those groups?"

"I'd wonder where you got such information."

I ignored this. "I was hopin' maybe I could look through some of Claudette's papers, keepsakes, a scrapbook if she had one, that might turn up a lead to the group. When will Mrs. West be home?"

"I don't know. Why repeat rumors to Myrna about Claudette associating with theater people? You'd only distress her."

"What've you got against theater people?"

"Nothing. We just have different . . . our worlds are poles apart, Miss Quick."

"Ya don't get murdered too often either, I bet."

"I beg your pardon?"

This bozo was turning out to be a stiff. Then I remembered what Gladys had said about him. Boring.

We heard the door open, then footsteps. "Cornell? Are you home?"

"In here, Myrna."

She came in with a twirl, although her suit skirt didn't budge. "How do you like it?"

Cornell looked embarrassed. So did Myrna when she realized I was there.

"Oh, Miss Quick. I didn't know . . . I wasn't expecting . . ."

"I like your suit, Mrs. West." It was royal blue, the jacket boxy with its padded shoulders.

"Thank you." She'd pulled herself together. "Well, I don't want to interrupt your little chat."

"We were finished, Mrs. West. It's you I need now."

She exchanged a look with Walker that I couldn't pin down. "What can I do for you?"

"You ever hear of a play called *Moonbeams and Mulberries?*"

"Awful title. But it seems familiar. Yes, I think Claudette went to see that play. She said she knew someone in it. Not well, of course."

I didn't want to get too excited. "A small actin' company put it on, I think."

"Yes. They were down in Greenwich Village. Near her school. Oh, I begged her not to go to that place. I knew it meant mingling with those ragtag people all the time. Why couldn't she go to Bennington or Radcliffe? None of this would have ever happened if she hadn't insisted. She never would have met that horrible boy."

She dropped into a chair, exhausted. It was more than I'd heard her say in all the times I'd seen her.

"I'm sorry. What was it you wanted to know?"

"The name of that actin' group, if you remember."

"How could I forget? HeartsinArts. All one word."

WHEN I left the West apartment, I made my way to Seventh Avenue, where I hopped a subway. I was in my own backyard in ten minutes and knew exactly where to start now that I had the name of the group. At the intersection of Seventh, Christopher, and West Fourth, there was a store named Village Cigars. I knew Nick Jaffe, the owner, 'cause that's where I bought my cigs downtown.

"Pack a Camels coming right up, little lady."

"Thanks. Nick, I need to know somethin'. I'm lookin' for an actin' group, the name of HeartsinArts. Ya know where they meet?"

"Sure I know. Nice kids. They're on Perry Street near Hudson."

"Thanks. Ya just made my life a lot easier. Take care of yourself."

In five minutes I was where Perry met Hudson. Being it was such a nice day, a few people were sitting on stoops. I picked out a gal, maybe in her forties, who looked friendly.

"Excuse me. Have you ever heard of an actin' group called HeartsinArts?"

She looked at me funny for a sec, then burst out laughing.

"Heard of it? Honey, you're looking at it. I run the group, such as it is." She stuck out her hand. "Dinah Dumont. Who are you?"

I shook her hand. "Faye Quick. Private investigator. You ever heard of Claudette West?"

"Familiar, but I can't place the name."

"How about Warner Garfield?"

Her face went dark. "That one. I kicked his behind right out of my class and my troupe."

"Why?"

"Look, you don't want to know about this stuff. Trust me."

"Whether I want to or not, I need to know it. Warner Garfield's been murdered."

"You're kidding me. Well, good riddance to bad rubbish."

I couldn't help being a little shocked by that reaction. "You don't care that he was murdered?"

"After all the ones *he* murdered?"

I felt a thump in my gut. "Whaddaya mean?"

"I mean Warner Garfield was a murderer, plain and simple," she said, and stood up. "I have to go teach a class in a few minutes."

As she started to turn away, I grabbed her arm. "Please. Explain."

"Garfield does abortions. Or did. Believe me, I didn't know that when he joined the troupe, or he never would have gotten through the door."

"An actor doin' abortions as a sideline?"

"And second rate at both. One of the girls told me . . . that's when I gave him the boot."

"How long ago was that?"

I watched her do a mental count.

"About four months ago. You trying to solve Garfield's murder?"

"No. I'm tryin' to find out how Garfield was connected to Claudette West."

"She have an abortion?"

"No." *But she probably was going to,* I thought.

"I have to go," said Dinah Dumont.

"Thanks. You've been very helpful."

She disappeared inside the building.

An abortionist. I wondered if I'd been standing in his operating room at any point. Had he killed a girl accidentally, and then somebody paid him back? This abortionist news made me think his murder had nothing to do with Claudette. On the other hand, maybe she'd been planning to have an abortion, and Garfield was the one who was gonna do it.

Walking away from the HeartsinArts building toward my street, I thought again that maybe Garfield did kill her. Motive: Passion?

Rejection? But if he did, who killed him and why? Maybe the two murders, like I'd thought, *weren't* connected. Claudette may have set up an abortion with Garfield, but somebody killed her before he could do it. Probably the father of her unborn child.

Did Garfield know who the father was? Or the murderer? I didn't think it would be beneath Garfield to blackmail someone. That someone probably killed him. And knocked me over the head as a warning. Whoever clocked me would have no problem putting my lights out permanently. Not a comfy thought.

I HOTFOOTED it home. The phone was ringing as I walked into my place. It was Birdie.

"Where ya been?"

"Workin'."

"I got a whole lotta calls for ya. Three from Detective Lake. He said it was real important."

My heart thwacked against my chest.

"He's not at his precinct. Here's the number ya can reach him."

I hung up in a hurry, but probably all he wanted was to give me some info about the case. I dialed the number.

"Joe's Chili Parlor," a woman's voice said.

"Is Detective Lake there?"

"Yup. Hey, Johnny." It felt like forever until he picked up.

"Hello."

"It's Faye."

"Faye. Thanks for getting back to me. How are you?"

"I'm fine. You?"

"Fine."

This didn't seem like a business call to me. Neither of us said anything for a few secs; then he said, "We found the name of the acting company. We also found out that Warner Garfield did some nasty stuff on the side."

Do I tell him I know this? I didn't want to sound too smart for my own good. I decided to play it out. "What kinda stuff?"

"He . . . he helped out ladies in trouble."

Was I supposed to act like I didn't know what that meant? Make him think I was a birdbrain? I couldn't. If that was the kinda girl he wanted, then he wasn't the guy for me.

"I heard that," I said.

Silence.

"Sounds like you've been doing all right without my help."

Oh, jeez. I couldn't make out the sound in his voice. Was he upset or proud of me? Hells bells. I had to be who I was and not worry about him every minute, no matter how the ladies' magazines said I should act with a man.

"I had some luck." This was true. "But what I don't know is his connection to Claudette West."

"I have that." His voice sounded sunnier.

"Can ya tell me?"

"Garfield had a little book with pages of dates and initials. The initials C. W. were there in early January, but they'd been crossed out. They appeared again the day after Claudette was murdered. Not crossed out. She probably got cold feet the first time. I know this doesn't prove anything, but I think on circumstantial grounds we can assume that she'd made arrangements to . . . see him."

That made me smile. Lake was being so careful not to offend me in any way. I guessed I shoulda appreciated it. But he'd have to know the true me sometime if we were gonna . . . gonna what?

"That's about it," he said.

"Well, that's a lot."

"Most of it you already knew." Down again.

"Not the important thing . . . the connection between the two."

"That's true." Up.

"Do you have any idea who knocked Garfield off?" I asked.

"Not yet. But we'll find out."

I knew this wasn't necessarily true. "Yeah. I bet ya will. I'm wonderin' if the same person who killed Claudette, killed Garfield."

"What would be the motive?"

"Another thing I gotta pin down."

"I think . . ." he said. "I think we should meet and talk this over."

"Okay." My pulse was racing.

"How about tonight? Dinner?"

"Let me check my calendar." Now that was just plain stupid. As if I wouldn't know what I was doing that night. Those magazines, which I only read at the beauty parlor, had infected my brain. I was never gonna read them again.

"Johnny? Tonight would be fine."

"Good. How's seven for you?"

"Fine. Where?"

"Where do you live, Faye?"

Did he want to pick me up at my place? For some reason that made me very nervous. You'd think I was a slob or something when I was really very neat.

I told him where I lived.

"Okay. I'll pick you up at quarter to seven. You think about where you'd like to go. See you later."

"Bye." But he'd already hung up.

The thought of him coming here gave me the jimjams. I looked around my living room. There was the empty space waiting for my piano. How could I explain that unless I told him the truth? So, I'd tell him the truth. All he could do is laugh. But right away I didn't think Johnny Lake would laugh at me 'cause I wanted to play and sing. It wasn't like I thought I was gonna perform in clubs and become a star. Lots of regular people had pianos.

So why was I so nervy? It'd been a long time since I'd had a real date, and I wanted this guy to like me. But if he didn't like me already, why'd he ask me out to dinner? He coulda talked about the case on the phone or asked to meet me for a cup of coffee. Dinner was different. Dinner was the real thing. Enough.

I sat on my sofa with a yellow pad and a fountain pen. I needed to figure out who knew both Claudette and Garfield and also who knew she was gonna have an abortion.

Claudette met Garfield at HeartsinArts, probably during the first breakup with Richard. When she split with him again, she went back to the acting group, and Garfield was still there. Then Dinah

Dumont chucked him out. And that woulda been a plus for Claudette to learn what else he did besides act badly, 'cause by then she knew she was gonna need him. Maybe one of the actors was the baby's father, and he set up the appointment with Garfield. That way, Garfield woulda known who the father was, known he probably killed Claudette, and he coulda been blackmailing him. But why would the father need to kill her if Claudette was gonna get rid of the baby?

It didn't add up. How about the other way around? The father hired Garfield to knock off Claudette 'cause he didn't know she was planning an abortion, and Garfield wasn't about to tell him. But was Garfield a killer? Performing abortions wasn't the same as killing an adult human being in cold blood? At least I didn't think so.

If that theory was gonna fill the bill, the father would have to have some loot. I didn't know any actors with extra greenbacks to throw around. And paying somebody to rub out your pregnant girl-friend wouldna come on the cheap. The idea of an actor being the dad was starting to look flimsy.

Why did Claudette say Garfield was trying to date her? Even if he was, she made him sound like a lounge lizard trying to wear her down. According to Cotten and June she thought of him as a pest. If he was gonna perform an abortion on her, why mention him at all? When she'd told Cotten she'd dated him, she didn't know she'd be needing his services down the line. Maybe she was just trying to make Cotten jealous.

The important thing was that Claudette had scheduled an abortion twice and her second appointment was the day after she was killed. Then months after her murder somebody knocked off Garfield. Once again I tumbled to the fact that there might not be any connection between the two murders. But it seemed a lead-pipe cinch there was.

The father of Claudette's unborn child was the number one suspect. And come to think of it, Anne's vision of a man forcing Claudette to do something against her will coulda been having the abortion. Maybe she'd decided against it a second time . . . three

months was risky enough, and papa settled on wiping out everything the night before. Two for one.

It felt like I was on to something. The father had set up a meeting in the Village, then crowned her on Bleecker Street because she
refused to go through with the abortion.

Brian Wayne still wasn't off my list. Neither was Jim Duryea. I
didn't think Duryea could've been the father, but he might've murdered her for rejecting him. Nah. Besides, why would he kill
Garfield? But I couldn't know for sure, so he stayed on my list.

Brian Wayne was my first choice as father and killer. I had to find
out if he knew Garfield. How? I needed to check his alibi for the
time of Garfield's murder. Before I did that, I needed to meet with
Anne to give her the undershirt from Garfield's apartment.

WHEN Anne opened her door, she said, "Who's Johnny Lake?"

"Ah, no. Is it written on my forehead?"

"In green. Come on in."

We sat down in the living room.

"So who's Johnny Lake?"

"Just a cop on a case."

"But you like him, don't you?"

"I'm havin' dinner with him tonight."

"Are you sure? I feel something blocking the date."

"Is he married?"

"No."

"Then why—"

"I'm not telling you anything else about your date. That would
ruin all the fun. So you have something for me?"

I reached in my pocketbook and pulled out the rolled-up bloody
undershirt and handed it to her.

She shook it open. "Oh, nice. You want me to tell you what type
of person this belongs to or if there's a trauma connected with it?"

"Both would be nice."

She ran her hands over the shirt, and soon she closed her eyes.

"It belongs to a violent man. He has blood on his hands."

And his shirt, I thought. This could be Garfield, but I didn't think so.

"I see an *M*."

"Any other letter?"

"No. Books. Lots of books. And a gun."

I knew there weren't any books in Garfield's place. I'd have to ask Johnny if he'd found a gun.

"The *M* is very strong. Flashing red."

"What else?"

"Oh, no," she said. "The damn battle scenes." Her eyes opened. "Although these were different. These felt connected to the shirt."

"You mean other times when this happens to ya, there's no link, no hook?"

"Yes. The pictures of war are separate. Let's just say it felt different this time. But that may not mean anything."

I wasn't so sure, even though I couldn't put it together.

"Tell me whose shirt this is?" Anne asked.

"I don't know. I found it in a guy's apartment. A dead guy. I don't know if it's his shirt or somebody else's."

"I'm sorry I couldn't help, Faye."

"But ya did. At least now I have an initial."

"That *M* could stand for anything."

"But maybe it's the initial of the killer."

"Could be. There's something else it could stand for though."

"What's that?"

"Murderer," she said.

I LEFT Anne's and started walking east. I had no idea where I was going until I hit Washington Square Park and landed on a bench facing the fountain.

What was that letter *M* Anne saw? She said it was flashing, so it must've been important. I was convinced it was an initial. Myrna? Maybe Myrna knew something she wasn't telling. Maybe she didn't even know she knew it. Maybe I could jar something loose if I gave her a complete report. But how was I gonna get to her?

The West apartment was out. I had to get Myrna to meet me somewhere. Would she be too afraid?

Gladys Wright! Myrna's stepsister. True, these two didn't seem to have much use for each other, but maybe in this case the relationship could be useful.

I called Gladys from a phone booth.

"Gladys, I need to talk to Myrna, and I need to talk to her alone. I figured if you called her and asked her to meet ya, she would."

"Wrong. Myrna doesn't want anything to do with me."

"If ya said it had somethin' to do with Claudette, she'd see ya."

"Hey, what is this?"

"A trick."

"You want me to trick my stepsister into seeing you?"

"Right. Will ya do it?"

"It's sort of amusing. All right, sure."

"Tell her to meet you in the park by the Garibaldi statue in an hour and not to tell anybody where she's goin'. I'm in a phone booth, so ya can call me back here."

I gave her the number. Five minutes later Gladys called back.

"She'll be there. You could've knocked me over with a feather. She was even nice to me. But when you turn up, I guess she'll hate me again."

"I'll try to smooth things over."

"Ah, who cares?"

She did, I thought. She hung up.

I went back to the park and sat in a place where Myrna wouldn't see me, but I'd spot her standing by the statue.

Behind me and across the street was the building where Brian Wayne taught and had his trysts with young girls. A terrible realization hit me. I *wanted* Wayne to be the killer. It didn't matter that he had an alibi. They can always be gotten around. No question, I hated this Casanova. But I couldn't let that cloud my thinking.

About five minutes to the hour Myrna West appeared at the right side of Garibaldi. I walked toward her. She saw me.

"Miss Quick?"

"Hello, Mrs. West."

"I'm meeting my sister. I'm surprised to see you . . ."

She got it then. Her expression was less angry than sad.

"I see," she said. "I'm *not* meeting my sister." She looked down and fiddled with her brown handbag. "Porter has told me I'm not to talk to you alone."

"That's why the sham, Mrs. West."

She pouted like a little girl but finally nodded.

"Will ya talk to me?"

"I might as well. I'm here now. But I'll get my head handed to me if Porter ever finds out."

"There's no way he's gonna find out unless you tell him."

I took her to the Reggio, a coffee place with the best espresso in the Village. She ordered an espresso, and I had my cappuccino.

I hit the ground running. "I'd like to tell ya everything I know so far about the case, Claudette, everything. And then I'd like to see if anything new rings a bell. Do ya understand?"

"Yes, I suppose."

"So as I'm tellin' ya this stuff, I want ya to interrupt me at any time yer reminded or hear of somethin' we haven't talked about before."

"All right." Her pinkie finger stuck out as she lifted her espresso.

I started to talk like I was tellin' a story, everything in order. She said nothing. But I kept going. And then she interrupted me.

"Warner Garfield?"

"Ya've heard his name?"

"You might as well know, Miss Quick, I always knew that Alec Rockefeller was a fraud. Claudette told her uncle, and he told me. Cornell said Claudette pretended to date him when she was seeing her real boyfriend, Warner Garfield."

My head was reeling. "Did he tell ya why Claudette was doin' that?"

"He said Warner Garfield was an actor, and she knew we wouldn't approve of him. Cornell and I decided it would be best if we didn't tell Porter. We agreed she'd probably get over this fellow, but if Porter knew, he'd make a fuss and force Claudette's hand."

"Meaning what?"

"She was so rebellious." A slight smile snuck onto her face. "When Porter carried on about Richard, I think it made Claudette stay with him longer than she would have."

I recalled that Captain Walker had denied knowing anything about Garfield. Under the circumstances, what else could he do?

"I can see yer reasonin'. So ya didn't tell Claudette ya knew either."

"No. Cornell wanted to remain her confidant."

"Yeah, sure."

"Was Mr. Garfield the father of Claudette's child?" Myrna asked.

"I don't know. But I doubt it. You see, Warner Garfield was—"

"Well, well, look who we have here," said a voice.

And when I looked up, I saw that it was Captain Cornell Walker.

"Cornell. What are you doing here?" Myrna asked.

"I might ask you the same." He pulled out a chair. "May I join you?"

I wanted to say no, but I thought that was Myrna's place. It was a stretch to think this was an accidental run-in.

"As you can see," Myrna said, "I'm having coffee with Miss Quick. Are you following me, Cornell?"

"Don't be foolish. I was walking by, and I saw you inside."

"But what are you doing down *here?*"

For these people, as I'd heard over and over, being in the Village was as likely as being on the moon.

"I often come to Greenwich Village, Myrna. I enjoy the atmosphere."

Myrna turned to me. "Cornell plans to be a painter when the war is over. He's very good."

He shrugged, trying to take the shine off her words.

A waitress came and took Cornell's order.

"So why'd ya follow her, Captain?"

"Miss Quick, if my brother says—"

"Mrs. West, I'm a detective, and it's my job to detect. That's what I'm doin'."

"It's all right, Myrna. Actually, I did follow you."

"Why?" She looked shocked.

"Because I promised Porter I would. He's worried about you. I must say I find it odd that you'd meet with Miss Quick by yourself. Shouldn't Porter be consulted when the case is involved?"

I said, "Sometimes a one-on-one works better. But since you're here, maybe ya can help us."

The waitress put an espresso in front of the captain.

"How can I help?" He took a sip of his coffee.

"Ya can tell us exactly what Claudette told ya about Warner Garfield."

He gave Myrna a swift, angry glance.

"Don't worry, I'm not gonna drop a dime on ya to Mr. West."

"I don't have much to tell. Claudette thought she was in love with Garfield. I decided it was best not to tell Porter since the fellow was an actor. I knew Myrna wouldn't prevent Claudette from seeing him."

"Did ya ever meet Garfield?"

"No. Claudette didn't want me to for some reason. I assumed she thought I'd find him wanting and never pushed her for an introduction. I never thought it would go so far."

"So far. Whaddaya mean?"

"Claudette was pregnant, so obviously it must've been Mr. Garfield's child, wouldn't you think?"

"Did you know she was pregnant before she died?"

He hesitated a moment. "Claudette told me everything."

"And you didn't tell me, Cornell?"

"Well, what would you have done if you'd known?"

Without a moment's thought she said, "I would've sent her abroad to have the child and then given it up for adoption."

"You wouldn't have wanted her to have an abortion?" Cornell whispered the last word.

"Of course not. I don't happen to believe in that."

"Did Claudette?" I asked him. "What was she plannin' on doin'?"

"She didn't know what she was going to do."

"Did she wanna have it?"

"No. I mean, she did, but she didn't know how to tell Myrna and Porter."

"Ya know, Captain, earlier ya said, 'Obviously it musta been Mr. Garfield's child.' Didn't ya know? Didn't Claudette tell ya who the father was?"

"No, she didn't."

"Didn't you ask?" Myrna said.

"I never questioned Claudette. She told me what she wanted me to know."

"And she didn't want ya to know who the father was?"

"Apparently not."

"Didn't ya wonder why?"

"I think she was afraid I might do something."

"Somethin' like what?"

"I don't know. Maybe she thought I'd confront the father. Do you think he did it?"

"Who?"

"Whoever the father was."

"Might be," I said. "Wouldn't be the first time a pregnant mother was murdered by a boyfriend. Ya brought up a good point, Captain. If we could find out who the father was of Claudette's baby, we'd probably find out who killed her."

Myrna said, "Well, Cornell's right. It must be this Garfield man."

"We'll never know."

"Why not?" she asked.

"Because he's dead."

Myrna's gloved hand flew to her mouth.

Walker said, "How do you know?"

"I found the body. But let's not get into that."

"You make it sound like he was murdered," Myrna said.

"He was."

"Wait," Walker said. "This doesn't make sense. Somebody kills Claudette months ago and now kills the father of the baby?"

"Then Mr. Garfield couldn't have killed Claudette, could he, Miss Quick?"

"He *could* have, Mrs. West. But I don't think he did." I weighed telling them more about Garfield and Claudette's scheduled appointment with him the day after she was murdered. But I had a feeling the less I told, the better it would be.

"Who killed Garfield?" Walker asked.

"Don't know yet. It just happened."

"It had to be someone who knew he and Claudette were connected, don't you think? Someone who knew he was the father of her child?"

"Anyone come to mind?"

"I think it takes us right back to Richard Cotten," he said.

"Does it? Ya think Claudette told him she was pregnant by another man when she wouldn't sleep with him?"

"How do you know she wouldn't sleep with him?" Myrna asked.

"He said so. And he was pretty upset about her bein' pregnant, which I told him. He didn't know before that."

"And you believe him?"

"Why shouldn't I believe him? He and Claudette split several weeks before she was murdered. It was a mutual agreement."

"That's not what she told me," Walker said.

"No? What did she tell you?"

He settled into his chair like he was about to tell us a long story.

"Claudette told me that she'd tried and tried to get Richard out of her life, especially when she'd fallen in love with Warner. But he wouldn't let her go."

"What's that mean, *wouldn't?* How could he stop her?"

"He threatened her. He said if she tried to leave, he'd kill her because he couldn't live without her."

"Wait a minute. How come ya didn't tell the police that at the time of the murder?" I asked.

"I wasn't here. I was in South Carolina. Parris Island."

"But you came home for the funeral, Cornell."

"That's true."

"So why didn't ya tell the cops then?"

"I did."

"But you never told us," Myrna said. Her voice had risen.

"I didn't want you to know then how much I knew. I thought the police would handle it. It's not my fault they could never get anything on that boy."

I made a mental note to check with Marty as to how much Walker told the cops.

Myrna turned to me. "It has to be Richard."

"The cops'll shake him down for an alibi on Garfield's murder."

"Oh, he'll have one. He's very smooth," Walker said. "So you found the body. Again. In a movie you'd be the first suspect." He smiled, making his perfect looks more so.

"Yeah. How about you, Captain? Ya have an alibi for Garfield's murder?"

He just stared at me.

"Let's see. I remember the first time I met ya, you said ya loved your niece. And you've just told us how she confided in you. It wouldn't be outta left field to think you'd wanna avenge yer niece's murder."

"Loving someone doesn't mean you'd kill for them, Miss Quick."

"Sometimes it does."

"Well, not this time."

"Can't take a joke, Captain?"

"I don't think this is a laughing matter."

"Really? *You* just joked about it, sayin' I might be a suspect in a movie. What's good for the goose is good for the gander, they say."

He gave me a glorious smile. "You're right. You have me there."

"By the way, Captain, did Claudette ever give ya cuff links?"

"Cuff links?"

"Cornell, she did. This past Christmas."

"Oh, that's right. She said they were for me when the war was over. Beautiful things, too."

"They were," Myrna said. "Jade."

After finishing his espresso, Cornell said, "Well, Myrna, I think it's time to go."

She looked at him like he was loony. "I didn't come with you, Cornell."

"I know, but you're going to leave with me. It's for the best."

It was pure and simple blackmail. "Go ahead, Mrs. West, I think we're finished here. Thank you for seein' me."

Myrna gave a slight nod and stood up.

"Good-bye, Miss Quick," Walker said.

As they got to the door, Myrna turned her head and gave me such a down-in-the-dumps look I almost went after her and hauled her back. But I knew there'd be no point. Then they were gone.

I sat sipping my cap and smoking a cig. So Walker believes Garfield was the father of Claudette's baby. Not 'cause she told him, but 'cause he thinks he's put the puzzle together. And that Richard's the killer. Even though Richard had no idea Claudette was sleeping with someone until after she died.

And I felt about Richard as I always had . . . no passion.

Why would Claudette tell her uncle that she was in love with Warner Garfield? He was an actor, and no one, including Walker, would approve of him. But she told others, like Richard and June, that she thought Garfield was a creep who wouldn't leave her alone. And why use Alec/Leon to cover seeing Garfield when she was probably using Garfield to cover her real lover?

So who was her sweetheart? Immediately I was back at Brian Wayne. He'd told me his affair with Claudette ended a year before she died. That didn't make it true. He could've been seeing her right up to the end. Or maybe he cut her off when she told him she was pregnant. But how did he hook up to Warner Garfield?

Wayne could've been afraid that Claudette might expose him, so he'd arranged for an abortion. Either he knew of Garfield from an unknown source or Claudette told Wayne herself. But if Wayne never laid eyes on Garfield, why would he kill him? Maybe he was afraid Claudette had given Garfield his name, and he wanted to clear the slate. That was possible.

Did he have an alibi for Garfield's murder? I really needed to have another talk with Dr. Wayne. The sooner the better.

BRIAN Wayne and I sat in a booth at Pete's Tavern on Eighteenth Street. We each had a glass of Pete's famous Original Ale in front of us. Wayne looked like hell. He had deep bags under his eyes, and the crags in his face were like cracks in a dried-up field.

"Ya look like ya haven't been sleepin' much, Brian."

When he glanced at me, I saw that his eyes were small and red-rimmed. I thought of a rat.

"I've been under a lot of pressure. Why did you want to see me again?"

"New developments. Another murder."

"Who?"

I told him about Warner Garfield.

"What's that got to do with me?"

"That's why I'm here, Brian. I'd like to know if it has anything to do with you."

"I never heard of Warner Garfield."

"You admitted to havin' an affair with Claudette."

"Over a year ago."

"Yeah, that's what ya said. But now I'm wonderin' if maybe ya picked up where ya left off, ya know what I mean?"

"I do, and I didn't."

"Ya said Claudette confided in you."

"Yes."

"She tell ya she was gonna have an abortion?"

"I told you before I had no idea that Claudette was pregnant. So how would I know she was going to have an abortion?"

"I know exactly what ya told me before, but this is now. I'm givin' ya a chance to set the record straight."

"I knew Claudette, I had an affair with her more than a year ago,

I didn't know she was pregnant or that she was going to have an abortion, and I've never heard the name Warner Garfield until today."

"Where were ya night before last?"

"I was with my wife, begging her to take me back." His humiliation and sense of shame showed.

"And is she gonna?"

"No."

Good for her. "You were there the whole night?"

"No. I left our . . . her house about ten o'clock and went to the San Remo to get drunk."

"Okay, ya went to the San Remo. Did ya meet anybody there?"

"I went there so I *wouldn't* meet anybody. San Remo is a working-class bar."

"Would anyone remember that you were there?"

"I don't know. The bartender might."

"So after gettin' plastered at the San Remo, where did ya go?"

"I went back to my room." He chewed at the inside of his cheek.

"Which is where?"

"Across the street from the San Remo on MacDougal."

"Anybody see ya there?"

"No. Of course not. It was about two in the morning."

"So you just went home and went to sleep?"

"I passed out. On the floor. Believe me, I'm not proud of it."

I figured he was telling the truth. Much as I wanted it to be true, I didn't have too much hope that he'd killed Garfield.

"And ya never heard the name Warner Garfield from Claudette?"

"Why wouldn't I tell you if I had?"

"Lots of reasons. Ya wanna hear my theory?"

"No."

He wasn't gonna get off that easy.

"You're the father of the now deceased child Claudette was carryin', and you wanted her to have an abortion by Garfield. She said she would, but then she changed her mind, so you whacked her.

Then Garfield, who knew you were the father, started blackmailin'
you, so ya whacked him, too."

"Can I go now?"

"Yeah, beat it."

YOU'D think I was a boozehound the way I was going from one
bar to another. I met Marty Mitchum at Smitty's around four
o'clock. He had a boilermaker, and I had a Coke.

"Tell me about Garfield?" I took out my notebook.

"Yeah. He's got a sheet. Small stuff."

"Abortion?"

"Nah."

"Anything on his whereabouts the night he was croaked?"

"Nobody seen him that night."

"Except for whoever knocked on his door, I guess."

"Yeah."

"How many guys who do abortions just open their doors to anybody, ya think?"

"I'll take a wild guess. None."

"That's what I'm thinkin'."

"So ya sayin' Garfield knew his killer?"

"Sounds like it to me," I said.

"So who was that?"

"That's what I wanna know. It could be almost anyone, Marty,
but I think it was somebody has a tie with Claudette."

"How'd ya get there?"

"She knew Garfield at HeartsinArts, an actin' company, and she
was scheduled for an abortion the day after she died. And ya know
how much I like coincidences."

"'Bout as much as I do. But if the man did abortions for a lotta
girls, they all had boyfriends, probably fathers, maybe brothers."

I doodled on my pad. "Yeah, I know. And there are a lotta guys
connected to Claudette. But not a one of them knew she was pregnant, accordin' to them. Except her uncle, and he didn't know who
the father was."

"So somebody's lyin' is yer thinkin'?"

"That's it. Claudette had to sleep with somebody to get pregnant."

"I'd say that's a good bet."

"So I'm thinkin' that the father of the baby went to Garfield's with Claudette to set up her appointment, and that's how Garfield knew him."

"And then what . . . so he went with her . . . so?"

"I think Garfield was blackmailin' him 'cause he knew the guy knocked off Claudette."

"Why would the guy kill Claudette if she was havin' an abortion?"

"That's where I get caught in a goat's nest."

"What are ya doodlin' there?" Marty reached for my pad.

I tried to stop him, but I wasn't fast enough.

"Who's Johnny?"

"Nobody."

"Ya can't fool me, Faye. C'mon, who's Johnny? Hey, what's wrong? Ya look like ya seen a ghost."

I was staring across at the pad. I'd been scribbling Lake's name, but I'd also been doodling *M*s, the initial Anne saw when she touched the undershirt.

"Excuse me, Marty, I gotta make a call."

"Ya leavin'?"

"I'll be back." I raced to a telephone booth.

I found a dime in my pocket, dropped it in, and dialed.

Anne answered on the second ring.

She said, "I'm so glad you called, Faye. I have something to tell you. I tried an item of clothing from someone else, and there were no battle scenes."

"Great but—"

"No, listen. Then I gave another go at the undershirt you left with me. Battle scenes."

"So?"

"I think they mean something. They're not random after all."

It probably did mean something, but all I could think of was my question. "Okay, Anne, I hear ya. But I gotta ask you a question.

You remember the *M* ya saw flashin'? Could it have been a *W?*"

She was silent for a second.

"Well, sure. Why not?"

"That's all I wanted to know. I'll call ya later."

When I'd looked across the table at my pad, the *M*s I'd doodled looked like *W*s. If *W* was an initial, this case had a lotta those. Starting with West.

I SAID good-bye to Marty and went to my office.

There were a dozen pink memo slips waiting for me. Not a one was important. There were none from Johnny, but why would he call me if we were gonna see each other that night?

I got out my yellow pad and started making my *W* list: Porter West; Myrna West; Brian Wayne; Cornell Walker; Gladys Wright.

It was a leap to believe Porter West would kill his own daughter. It's not unheard of, but the police woulda ruled him out first thing. And his motive? He didn't know Claudette was pregnant until the autopsy, and he didn't know Garfield existed. And why hire me?

Myrna West. I'd nixed her myself.

Brian Wayne. The most likely. But I still hadda check his alibi for the Garfield murder. This meant going to the San Remo bar and seeing his wife again.

His wife! Maureen Wayne. I'd forgotten to list her. Brian said his wife didn't know who the girls were, but that was just his thinking. Maybe Maureen knew Claudette was pregnant and thought, wrongly or rightly, that the baby was Brian's. What kind of alibi did she have? What did she know about Warner Garfield? And did she have a motive to kill him? I wanted her alibi for his rubout, too.

Cornell Walker. He had an alibi for Claudette's murder. But what about Garfield's? Claims he didn't know she was gonna have an abortion, but I only had his word for that. He might've been convinced that Garfield was the father of Claudette's child and thought Garfield killed her. A revenge murder. Where was he the night of Garfield's murder? When I'd asked him, we'd gone into our pitiful comedy routine, and he never did answer me.

Gladys Wright. Although she was a cold, calculating con, she never had a motive for killing her niece. The plan to get Claudette's money was ruined before her murder. And what about Garfield? Did Gladys even know the bum was alive ... when he was? Claudette could have told her favorite aunt his name but with which story? Garfield as creepy pest who wouldn't lay off or wonderful Warner, her latest conquest?

Either way, would Gladys have done anything about it? And why? Still, I needed to know where she was when Garfield got it.

So there it was, laid out on my yellow pad, my thoughts on each one. My first two choices were one or the other of the Waynes. If I could knock a hole in Brian's alibi or find out Maureen didn't have one, I might solve this thing.

I looked at my watch. Holy moley. It was quarter after five. Johnny was picking me up in an hour and a half. That didn't give me a lotta time to go home, get dolled up, and be ready when he arrived.

When I glanced back at the pad, all at once it struck me. I'd been so fixed on the murders being connected that I also thought they had to be done by the same person. But they didn't. I didn't have to connect the murders. I needed to concentrate on one or the other. I'd been hired to find out who killed Claudette West, so that's what I was gonna do. Keeping my number one job in mind, I examined everybody on the pad I'd listed, over and over, and it still turned out that I needed to see Maureen Wayne right away.

There was one rap on my door before Birdie looked in, wearing her hat and coat.

"Ya leavin' early, Bird?"

"Early? It's six o'clock. I stayed late to finish some work, ya ungrateful wretch."

"Omigod." I'd lost track of time again. "I got a date tonight."

"Oh, yeah?" Birdie raised her eyebrows twice like Groucho Marx. "Who ya got on the string?"

"Probably nobody now. I'll never make it home in time. I gotta try to call him. Bird, do me a favor?"

"What?"

"Try to find the home number of John Lake."

"Oh, the cop."

"Detective."

"Forgive me for livin'."

"Do it. Please."

She sighed and left my office. I dialed his precinct. He wasn't there, and nobody would tell me where he was. Then Birdie came back.

"So here's his number," she said, throwing a piece of paper on my desk. "Good night."

"Bird, don't. I'm sorry, okay?"

She looked at me. "I'm not your slave, ya know. I don't like to be talked to that way."

"I'm sorry, yer right. I'm a little overwhelmed right now. Forgiven?"

"Okay." She grinned. "So, the detective asked ya out. Ya like him?"

"I don't know him, but I think he's pretty nice."

"'Bout time ya found somebody ya like. Uh-oh, I'm keepin' ya from callin'."

"That's okay."

"Nah. Call him. I'm gonna skedaddle."

Before I could say anything more, she was gone.

I dialed John at home. I felt funny about calling there, but I didn't know what else to do. He answered.

"Hello, Johnny. It's Faye."

"Faye? Everything all right?"

"Not exactly." I had trouble getting out the words. "Listen, something's come up. Work. I gotta cancel our date for tonight."

"Oh? I'm sorry to hear that. Anything to do with Garfield?"

"No. It's the West murder . . . the case I've been workin' on."

"I understand. I've been in the same fix myself plenty of times."

"I hope . . . I hope we can do it some other time."

"Sure."

When I said good-bye, I felt like I'd never hear from him again. Oh, hells bells. I had to hold on to my concentration. First stop, Maureen Wayne.

IT WAS DARK BY THE TIME I got downtown. I walked over to Ninth Street, where Maureen Wayne lived. Our last meeting hadn't gone too well, and that was putting it mildly. I had to try.

I rang the bell, and she opened the door.

"What do you want?"

"I have to talk to you again. There's been another murder."

Her face showed shock. It looked genuine.

"Who was it?"

"A man named Warner Garfield. Please let me in."

"I don't know why I should, but all right."

She opened the door, and I followed her up to the living room.

"So who was this Garfield person?"

"He was an actor and an abortionist."

"Nice combination. What does he have to do with Brian?"

"When did ya see him last?"

"Two nights ago. Here."

"Why?"

"He wanted me to take him back. That's what he said anyway."

"What time did he leave here?"

"About ten."

It jibed with what Brian had told me. "How did he seem to you?"

"Well, what do you think? He wanted his family back, and he wasn't getting his way. That's what Brian always wants, *his* way."

"And when he doesn't have things go his way, what does he do?"

"Well, he doesn't kill people, if that's what you're getting at."

I was, but I didn't expect her to tell me that. "Course not."

"But you think he killed that man, don't you?"

"I don't know what to think. Did Brian call ya later?"

"I can't be sure. The phone rang about midnight, but no one spoke on the other end. I heard a lot of noise in the background, people talking, but nothing from the caller."

I was sure it was bar noise and that the caller was Brian. So far his alibi was checking out. At least until midnight.

"I'm gonna ask ya somethin' that'll make ya mad."

"As if you haven't already. What?"

"You remember me askin' about Claudette West?"

"Yes. You thought Brian might have killed her. I believe she was one of his paramours."

"Yeah. You ever meet her?"

"I told you I hadn't last time. No."

"Can ya tell me where you were on January twentieth?"

"You were right. You're making me mad. I have no idea what I was doing that night."

"Ya keep a date book or anything?"

She stared at me. "You have no real right to ask me these questions, do you?"

"Nope."

"At least you're honest." She got up, crossed to a mahogany secretary, opened it, and pulled out a burgundy-colored book.

"Here," she said, dropping it in my lap, "find the date yourself."

"Thanks." I opened it.

There it was, January 20: "7:00: dinner with Mother and Dad. 8:30: *Something for the Boys* (Ethel Merman)."

"I'm sorry. I had to know. I had to rule ya out."

"Please don't ever come here again."

"I don't think I will." I was convinced Maureen Wayne had nothing to do with the murders.

I HIT the bricks and made my way home. For my money neither of the Waynes had anything to do with Garfield's murder.

Maureen was in the clear on Claudette's murder, and Brian didn't look as good as I'd once thought. Most likely he and Claudette had the affair when he'd said they did. And I doubted that Brian Wayne ever looked back. A *new* conquest was the important thing for him.

By the time I got to my building, I was not a Little Mary Sunshine 'cause I was nowhere. It was only eight o'clock, and I wanted to be out having dinner with Johnny Lake. Instead I was gonna eat a bowl of oatmeal by myself.

I opened the big front door, and Dolores was, as usual, sweeping the hall outside her place.

"Pretty late for that, isn't it?"

"Good thing I was out here, bubee."

"How come?"

"Well, I wouldna seen yer boyfriend. What a cutie he is."

"Dolores, what're ya talkin' about? I don't have a boyfriend."

Johnny would never have shown up here after I broke the date. Would he?

"Don't kid a kidder, Faye."

It was useless to keep denying that I had a guy, so I took another tack. "Okay, what did he say to ya?"

"When I came out, he was fumbling with his keys in front of yer door."

Now I knew it wasn't Johnny, and I felt a little panicky. "Dolores, nobody has a key to my apartment but me. How do ya know this guy ya saw wasn't tryin' to break in?"

"Ya think I'm a nitwit? I asked him who he was lookin' for, and he told me Faye Quick. That's you, ain't it?" She cackled crazily.

"Did he say why he wanted me?"

"Course not, and I didn't ask. He's a beauty. Nice dark hair and eyes like an angel."

"What was he wearin'?"

She shrugged. "Wearing? A suit. A shirt. A tie. What else? I said I'd be glad to give a note to you."

I counted to ten. "Where is it?"

"In my pocket." She reached into a pocket on her blouse and held it out to me. "I gave him the paper."

"Whaddaya mean?"

She shrugged. "He wanted paper to write you a note, so I gave him paper. What's wrong with that?"

"Nothin'." I took the paper and unfolded it.

Dear Faye,

  Sorry I missed you. Maybe next time. Why am I saying maybe? Next time will definitely come.

The signature was scribbled. I couldn't make it out.

"So?" Dolores said.

"I don't know who this is from."

"So why'd ya give this fella keys to your apartment?"

"I didn't. That's what I've been tryin' to tell ya."

"Ya mean he was tryin' to break in?"

"I think so. Tell me again what he looked like."

"Nice lookin'. I'm sorry, Faye, if I done a dumb thing. I shoulda called the cops, huh?"

I put a hand on her sleeve. "How could ya know?"

"You think he'll come back? He could murder us in our beds."

"Calm down, Dolores. He's not comin' back." I didn't know that. But I wanted to make her feel better.

"I think I'll go in now," she said.

"Good idea." We each turned toward our doors. My hand was shakin' when I put my key in the lock. Then Dolores cried out.

"Faye. Maybe this'll help. He looked like Cary Grant."

"Oh, thanks, Dolores. Yeah, that'll help."

"Ya know who he is now?"

"No. But it gives me somethin' to go on. G'night, Dolores."

Inside my apartment, I felt scared. I wondered if my gate-crasher had wormed his way into my place somehow. I could see the kitchen and living room from right inside my door. That left the bathroom and bedroom. I couldn't move. I felt glued in place.

Hey, I had my gat! Yeah, but it was up in the bedroom closet.

I tiptoed over to one of the drawers in the kitchen and took out the carving knife. I made my way to the open door of the bedroom. One of the big windows at the rear was open halfway. I couldn't remember if that's the way I left it.

I couldn't just stand there with the knife in my hand. All I had to do was take one step forward. If anyone was in my bedroom, I'd see him right away. Unless he was in the closet.

I took the step. Nobody.

Now I had to deal with the closet. I reached out with my free hand, and it hovered over the glass doorknob. I raised my right arm and held the knife above me.

In one swift motion I turned the knob and pulled open the door. Nothing. Nobody.

I hadn't realized I'd been holding my breath until I let out what sounded like the sigh of a lion.

There was still the bathroom.

I could see the bathroom door. Closed, the way I always left it. I could hear my mother's voice telling me it wasn't proper to leave a bathroom door open. I took the same position I'd taken at the closet in the bedroom and turned the knob with my left hand.

Nothing. I dropped my knife hand to my side. I was bushed and slumped against the cool tiles on the wall. So Dracula wasn't in my crib. At least I felt safe again.

I put the knife on the kitchen table and started to fill the coffee-pot with water. It was then that Dolores's words hit me: *He looked like Cary Grant.*

I stood there, the pot in my hand, water running from the tap.

"What a knucklehead," I said out loud.

I turned off the water, grabbed the phone, and called Marty.

When Marty answered, I asked him if he'd do something for me. He said he'd take care of my request, then asked where to meet. I told him.

He said sure, he'd be there soon as he could. I knew he wouldn't let me down. After I hung up, I marched straight into the bedroom and headed for my gun.

10

HOW many times in the past week had I stood outside the Wests' building? Once again I hadn't made an appointment. I didn't want to give them advance notice.

The doorman rang their apartment and told whoever picked up I was there. Myrna met me at the door.

"You should have called, Miss Quick. Be careful what you say; Porter's got his dander up."

Poor, poor Porter, I thought, as I walked behind his wife on the way to the living room.

When I said hello, there was no response. He stared at me for a few secs. Then he said, "Once again you've arrived unannounced."

He took a deep drink from what looked like a mean martini. Cocktail hour. How nice. How genteel.

Porter pointed to a chair for me to sit, then took a spot on the sofa while Myrna perched on the edge of a straight-back chair.

"All right, what did you come here for? Surely, you haven't solved the case. I know that's too much to ask for."

I realized Porter sounded slightly soused.

He wasn't finished. "Actually, Miss Quick, you're fired."

I knew I had to stall until Marty got here. "Would ya mind tellin' me why?"

"I'd like to know that, too," Myrna said.

"Because for one thing you don't follow rules. Rules are the basis of our society. Without rules we'd be savages."

"Seems to me some people are savages even with rules."

"Those people break them, Miss Quick. I don't know anything about your background. It's possible you weren't brought up the way Claudette was."

I couldn't believe it, but he started crying in this weird gulping way. I didn't think I'd ever see that.

Myrna went over to him. "Oh, Porter, you're going to make yourself sick."

"I'm fine."

He patted her on the shoulder and picked up his drink.

"What were we talking about?" he asked.

"Ah, you mentioned Claudette and that she was brought up with rules." From what I'd learned of her, she didn't pay much attention to her father's rules or anyone else's.

"My little girl," he said.

Porter was more than slightly soused. He was getting good and drunk. And it seemed to bring out his sentimental side. I thought it might be a good time to throw some info his way.

"Mr. West, did you know a man named Warner Garfield?

"No."

"What if I told ya that Garfield was an abortionist."

"I'd say he was barbaric. I suppose you're going to tell me that he performed one on Claudette, aren't you? But you can't because she was pregnant when that bastard Cotten murdered her."

"That's true. He never performed an abortion on Claudette. But your daughter knew him. She told some people he was her boyfriend and others that he was hounding her. Do ya know why she'd do that, Mr. West?"

"She wouldn't know a person like that. I refuse to believe it."

"She met him at the HeartsinArts actin' company."

"Claudette didn't belong to any acting company."

Myrna gave me a warning look that I took to mean I shouldn't say she knew about the group or Garfield. I gave her a tiny nod.

"Mr. West, I don't think you knew your daughter as well as you think ya did."

I believed that Porter didn't know of Garfield. But I was stalling for time. I heard the front door slam. Footsteps down the hall and then the appearance of Cornell Walker.

"Miss Quick," he said. "I didn't know you'd be here."

"Why would ya?"

"I wouldn't." He smiled and cocked his head to one side. "So why *are* you here?" He walked to the liquor cabinet and poured some whiskey over ice. Then he sat down in a wingback, crossed his legs, and looked at me.

"I think I'd like to ask you a question, Captain."

"All right."

I opened my pocketbook and took out the piece of paper Dolores had given me. Then I handed it to him. "This yours?"

He gave it a glance. "Yes. I'm glad you got it. Sorry I missed you."

"Ya have a lousy signature."

"I do, don't I?"

Porter said, "What's going on?"

"I went to visit Miss Quick, but she wasn't home, so I left a note with a very nice woman who was cleaning the hall."

"What kind of a note?" Porter asked.

"The kind that says I was there," Walker said. "What's the—"

A buzzer sounded.

Myrna said, "That's from downstairs. The doorman. I wonder if we have another visitor." She scurried outta the room.

I hoped it was Marty 'cause I didn't like how things were going.

Myrna poked her head in. "Are you expecting a Marty Mitchum, Miss Quick?"

"I am."

"All right then." She disappeared.

Walker said, "Who's Marty Mitchum?"

"A cop friend of mine."

"Why is he coming here?" Porter asked.

"Remember when I first came in, ya asked me if I'd solved the case and then ya fired me before I could answer? Well, yeah, I've solved the case." I hoped like hell that was the truth.

Walker said, "How great, Miss Quick. Tell us."

"I will. But I have to speak to Detective Mitchum first."

Myrna came in with Marty and introduced him to Porter and Walker.

"Detective, ya got somethin' for me?" I asked.

"Yeah, I do."

"If you'll excuse us for a minute." Marty and I went into the hall.

"You were right," he told me.

"You're sure? Gimme a name."

"Corporal Edward Dunne."

"How'd ya do this over the phone?"

"I got my ways." He gave me a grin. "Threat of a court-martial is a great convincer."

"Swell. Okay, we're goin' back in there. Be ready for anything."

"I always am."

We went back in, and I sat in my chair. Marty sat on the other end of the sofa.

"What's this all about?" Porter asked.

I saw that he'd made himself another martini. "Captain Walker, ya wanna tell me why ya came to my apartment?"

"I wanted to see you. Is that so strange? You're a very attractive young lady."

"Ya make it a habit of trying to break into ladies' apartments?"

"I beg your pardon?"

"Dolores, the one who gave ya the paper, said she saw you tryin' to get into my place with a key." I wanted to throw him off balance before I got to the big stuff.

"Well, she's lying." He took a slug of his drink.

"Nah. Not Dolores. She said ya looked like Cary Grant."

"That's very flattering but not accurate."

"I think it's the cleft in your chin that made her think that. It's what made me know it was you, crummy signature or not. Does the name Edward Dunne mean anything to you?"

"Of course. He's assigned to me."

"A loyal guy, huh?"

"Yes, why?"

Sweat popped out along his brow. "So loyal that when the cops checked out your alibi for the night of Claudette's murder, Corporal Dunne said you'd been there all night, didn't he?"

"I had been."

"No, Captain Walker, you hadn't."

Marty said, "Corporal Dunne admitted to me half an hour ago that you weren't there that night."

"Well, then he's lying."

"Everybody's lyin'. Ya notice that, Detective?"

"Can't miss it."

"Why would Cornell lie about where he was?" Myrna asked.

"Because he killed your daughter, Mrs. West."

All three of them rose to their feet. Porter was a little wobbly, but the other two stood at attention.

"This is outrageous," Walker said.

"Why would Cornell kill my daughter? His niece?" Myrna said.

Porter said, "I think we've had enough of this. You'd both better leave now."

"Not yet. I think you all should sit down." Surprisingly, they did.

"Cornell," Myrna said, "tell them you didn't have anything to do with this. He was in South Carolina when it happened."

"No, Mrs. West. He wasn't. He was in New York with Claudette tryin' to convince her to go through with the abortion she had planned for the next day."

Walker laughed. "I think Porter's right. You should both leave. Myrna, buzz the doorman."

She didn't answer, and she didn't move.

"Then we'll have to call the police," Walker said.

"I *am* the police," Marty said.

Walker was starting to look desperate around the edges. I flashed on him in his uniform and realized that that's what had been nagging at me the night Birdie and I went to the USO. The uniforms were telling me something then, but I wasn't hearing.

Myrna said, "We called him in South Carolina the next day."

"What time was that?"

"I don't know. Everything was still so confusing and awful."

"It was late in the afternoon," Porter said. He seemed to be sobering up.

"Plenty of time for the captain to get back to Parris Island. What did ya tell Corporal Dunne when he learned your niece had been killed the night before?"

Marty said, "I can answer that one. Walker told Corporal Dunne he'd had a rendezvous with another captain's wife that night, so Dunne never put the two things together."

"This is getting more absurd every minute," Walker said.

"Is it? See, I know ya went to see Warner Garfield to arrange the abortion. When I heard the initials C. W. had been crossed out in Garfield's book two weeks before, I thought they stood for Claudette West and that she'd decided against it, then changed her mind, rescheduled for January twenty-first when the C. W. appeared again. But now I know the first set of initials stood for Cornell Walker, and Garfield had crossed them out because you'd been there, made the arrangement, and paid him."

"You don't know what you're talking about," Walker said.

"I think I do."

"Even if that's all true," Myrna said, "why does that make my brother a murderer?"

"I'm sorry to tell ya this, Myrna, Porter, 'cause this case is rotten enough, but Claudette's baby was Cornell's. Claudette was in love with him, and they'd been havin' an affair. Then she got pregnant."

Myrna was crying softly. Porter looked shell-shocked. Walker was trying to hold my gaze.

I went on. "Claudette had agreed to the abortion at first and then changed her mind. So Cornell had to get himself up here to try to convince her to have it. When she wouldn't agree, he killed her."

Walker laughed again.

"Why do you keep laughing, Cornell?"

"Sorry, Myrna. I'm laughing because she has it so wrong."

"Wrong?" I asked.

"Yes, wrong. It's true I made the arrangement and gave the money to Garfield, but—"

Myrna's gasp cut him off.

"I'll kill you," Porter said, trying to rise, but Marty held him back.

"Go on," I said.

"*I'm* the one who didn't want her to go through with the abortion. That's why I came up here. To convince her *not* to have it."

"Why?" I asked.

"Because I loved her and I wanted her to have our child. I'd agreed to the abortion in a weak moment. But her death was an accident, I swear it. We were walking along in the snow, arguing, and she kept on insisting she was going to have the abortion. I grabbed for her, and she slipped and went down, hitting her head on a cement step. She was dead. I didn't know what to do."

"Hittin' her head on a step couldna caused all that blood," I said.

"It didn't. That's right, but I had to make it look like she'd been murdered so I . . . I smashed her head against the step until there was enough blood to make it look like a real attack."

"Ya know what, Cornell? You're still lyin'. People don't bleed after they're dead."

His stare at me was cold. Those eyes glinting like ice chips.

"Ya might as well admit what really happened 'cause we know ya killed Garfield, too."

"Really? How did I do that?"

I couldn't tell him about the undershirt and what Anne experienced when she'd held it in her hands and how the battle scenes were 'cause Cornell was in the Marines.

"I'll leave that to the DA. I'll just say this. We know Garfield was blackmailin' ya 'cause he'd put two and two together."

"He was scum."

"I agree with that," I said. "So what really happened with you and Claudette."

"She was willful and disobedient. She insisted on going through with the abortion, so I smashed her against a building."

Myrna was cryin'. "It's unbearable."

"You're the scum, Cornell; that's who's scum," Porter said.

"I wasn't going to have my child ripped from her."

So he killed them both himself. It wasn't logical, but then murderers often aren't. Especially when there's passion involved.

I nodded at Marty, and he stood up and crossed the room.

"Stand up, Walker." He did, and Marty clapped the cuffs on him. "Let's go."

I wanted to comfort the Wests, but I didn't know how. There wasn't any comfort for something like this. They'd have to find their own way out of it. If they ever could.

IT TOOK me a little while to feel clean again. But I wasn't sure how long it would take to get rid of the sick feeling I always got when I thought of the West/Walker case.

The day after Walker was arrested, I got a call from Detective Johnny Lake.

"I hear you broke the case," he said.

"I guess so." I felt like a rat treading on his toes. But what was done was done. He could hate me for the rest of my life. I was sorry it hadn't worked out with him, but I knew I'd get over it.

"Why didn't you call me when you went to the West apartment?"

"It's not a very nice reason."

"That's okay."

"I didn't think of it."

He laughed.

"At least you're honest, Faye."

When he said my name, I felt tingles.

"I'm always honest," I said.

"Were you honest about why you broke our date?"

"Yeah, I was."

"Then maybe we can try it again sometime."

The "sometime" line, I thought.

"Sure," I said. I knew I'd never hear from him again.

"How about Wednesday?"

That hit me like a bombshell. "Ya mean the day after tomorrow?"

"This is Monday. So the day after tomorrow. Right."

I wanted to shout my yes, but I said it just as casual as I could.

"I'll pick you up at your apartment at seven, if that's all right?"

I didn't have any pressing engagements, so I said, "That's fine."

By five to seven on Wednesday he hadn't called to break the date. I was looking swell and feeling like a million bucks even though my insides were doing a tap dance. I took a last look in the mirror, and then the bell rang.

Hubba-hubba!

Getting to Know
Sandra Scoppettone

Vital Stats

BORN: Morristown, NJ, 1936
ASTROLOGICAL SIGN: Gemini
RESIDENCE: Southold, NY
BOOKS WRITTEN: About 20
PSEUDONYM: Jack Early
INTERESTS: The Yankees,
    computers, reading
FAVORITE MOVIES: *The Grifters,*
    The Godfather
FAVORITE MUSIC: '40s music
WEBSITE:
    www.sandrascoppettone.com

SANDRA Scoppettone has always been a writer, but she did not start out writing mystery novels.

The author grew up in suburban New Jersey and graduated from Columbia University in 1954. Initially she tried her hand at writing novels, but her first several attempts were never published. By 1960, she decided to turn to drama.

She wrote plays and television scripts throughout the 1960s, and many of her works were performed on network TV and off-Broadway. In the early 1970s, Scoppettone resumed her dream of writing fiction by using her experience directing teenagers in a summer theater as the basis of her first young adult (YA) novel, *Trying Hard to Hear You* (1974). Several more YA books followed, and Scoppettone became known for writing about sensitive topics for teens, such as alcoholism and substance abuse.

In the 1980s, Scoppettone decided to concentrate on adult detective novels. She says the transition from writing YA books to mysteries wasn't difficult, because she simply writes about what interests her.

Scoppettone is best known for her 1990s Lauren Laurano detective series, which she ended after five books because she was "getting tired of writing about the same people over and over. . . . I've always said that no one should write more than four in a series, and I believe that, even though I did a fifth. I don't know how Sue Grafton does it."

Of the various mystery genres, Scoppettone says her favorite is the private eye novel "because you can comment about the culture and society in a way you can't in other forms." *This Dame for Hire* is the first in a planned series about scrappy 1940s private eye Faye Quick.

Scoppettone gives her fans a glimpse into the ups and downs of a writer's life through her web journal, or blog. Visitors to her website can check in on the progress of her current project and how pleased—or displeased—she is with her work. ∎

The P.I.'s Have It

They usually work in seedy offices. They often wear ratty overcoats and beat-up hats and have a cigarette or cigar hanging from their lips. And like Faye Quick in *This Dame for Hire*, they are inevitably keen-eyed, resourceful, and smart. Sir Arthur Conan Doyle spawned one of mystery's most popular genres by creating Sherlock Holmes, fiction's first private eye. Other icons of the **PRIVATE EYE** mystery genre include Dashiell Hammett's Sam Spade, Raymond Chandler's Philip Marlowe, Sue Grafton's Kinsey Millhone, and Robert B. Parker's Spenser.

One of the hallmarks of private investigators, especially those of the hard-boiled variety, is their unique way with words. Below are some of our favorite terms.

Beanshooter—gun
Box job—a safecracking
Cabbage—money
Ice—diamonds
Meat wagon—ambulance
Mouthpiece—lawyer
Oyster fruit—pearls
Rattler—train
Schnozzle—nose
Snap a cap—shout
Ticket—private eye license
Wise head—smart person

ACKNOWLEDGMENTS

Page 161: Bernard Vidal. Pages 5, 162, 327, 443, and 575:
© Nova Development Corporation. Page 163: AP/Wide
World Photos. Page 325: © EXLEY-FOTO. Page 326: © 2005
iStock International Inc. Page 442: Carol Barry. Page 574:
© Linda Crawford.

The original editions of the books in this volume are published and copyrighted as follows:

NO PLACE LIKE HOME, published at $25.95 by Simon & Schuster, Inc.
© 2005 by Mary Higgins Clark

TWISTED, published at $26.95 by Ballantine Books, an imprint of The Random House
Publishing Group, a division of Random House, Inc.
© 2005 by Jonathan Kellerman

FALSE TESTIMONY, published at $24.00 by Scribner, an imprint of Simon & Schuster, Inc.
© 2005 by Rose Connors

THIS DAME FOR HIRE, published at $21.95 by Ballantine Books, an imprint of The
Random House Publishing Group, a division of Random House, Inc.
© 2005 by Sandra Scoppettone

The volumes in this series are issued every two to three months.
The typical volume contains four outstanding books in condensed form.
None of the selections in any volume has appeared in *Reader's Digest* itself.

Any reader may receive this service by writing
The Reader's Digest Association, Inc., Pleasantville, NY 10570
or by calling 1-800-481-1454.
In Canada write to:
The Reader's Digest Association (Canada) Ltd.,
1125 Stanley Street, Montreal, Quebec H3B 5H5
or call 1-800-465-0780.

Some of the titles in this volume are also available in a large-print format.
For information about Select Editions Large Type call 1-800-877-5293.

**Visit us on the Web at:
www.rd.com (in the U.S.)
www.readersdigest.ca (in Canada)**